GHOST OF THE SHADOWFORT

THE BLADEBORN SAGA: BOOK TWO

T. C. EDGE

COPYRIGHT

First edition: March 2021
Cover Design by Polar Engine

CONTENTS

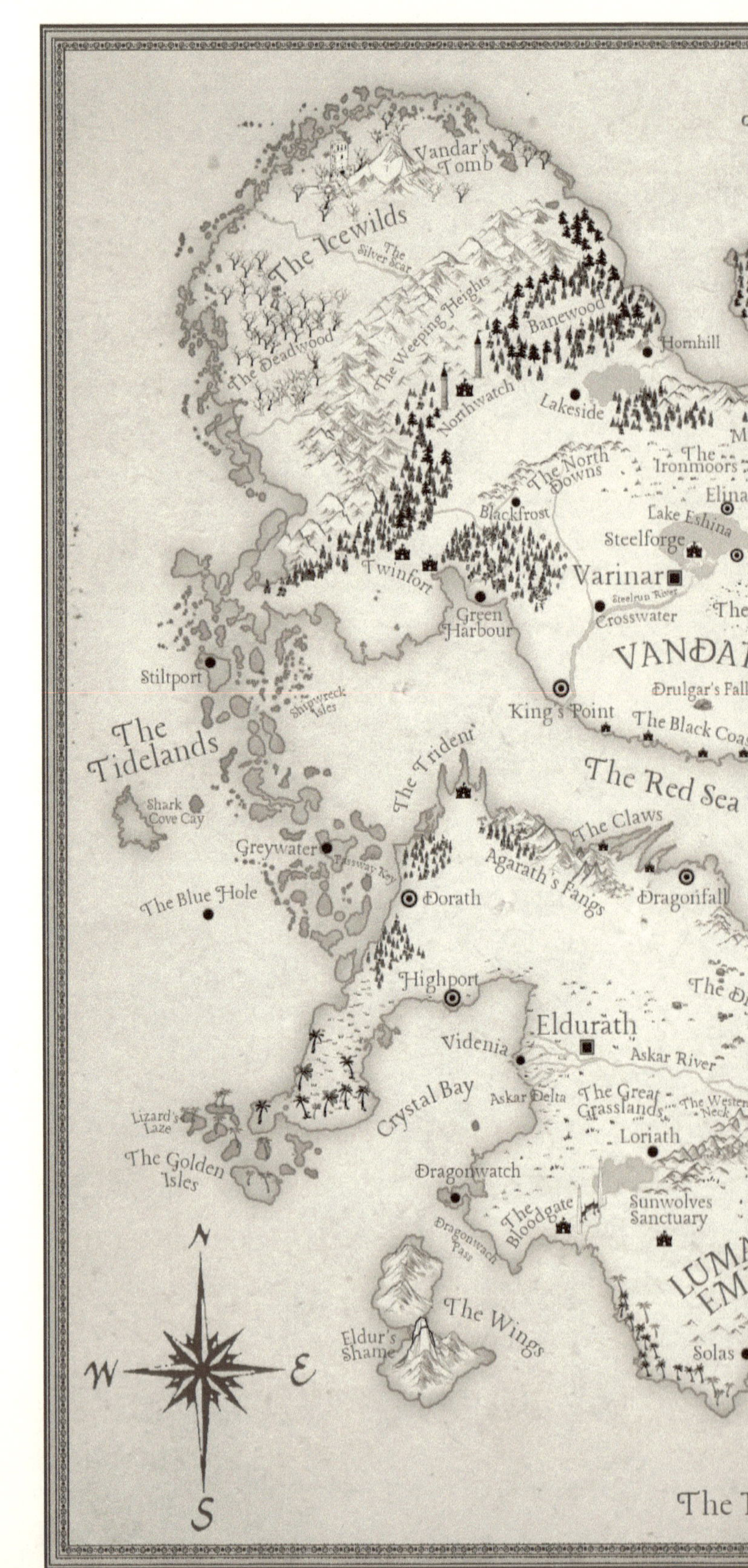

Vandar's Tomb
The Icewilds
The Silver Scar
The Deadwood
The Weeping Heights
Banewood
Hornhill
Northwatch
Lakeside
The North Downs
The Ironmoors
Elinar
Lake Eshina
Blackfrost
Steelforge
Varinar
Steelrun River
Crosswater
Twinfort
Green Harbour
Stiltport
Shipwreck Isles
King's Point
Drulgar's Fall
The Black Coast
The Tidelands
The Red Sea
The Trident
Shark Cove Cay
The Claws
Greywater
Agarath's Fangs
Dragonfall
The Blue Hole
Dorath
Highport
Eldurath
Videnia
Askar River
Crystal Bay
Askar Delta
The Great Grasslands
The Western Neck
Loriath
Lizard's Laze
The Golden Isles
Dragonwatch
The Bloodgate
Sunwolves Sanctuary
Dragonwatch Pass
The Wings
Eldur's Shame
Solas
N
W
E
S

100 miles
The Lonely Isle
The Tower of Rasalan
The Grey Keep
The Highplains
Holashan
Daarl
Azure Isles
Falana
Thalan
Vandar's Mercy
Blackhearth
Ethior
Twinbrook
TUKOR
The Three Peaks
Broadway
Rockfall
Steelport
Bleakrock
Stormhold
Snowmelt Mountains
The Forks
Northgate Castle
Oakshore
RASALAN
The Lowplains
Julia
Tish
Gustas
Windwake Islands
The Stormy Sea
Ilithor
The Stonehills
Harrowmoor
Shellcrest
Calmwater
The Crescent Coast
Tukoran Warcamp
Rasal Warcamp
The Links
Eastwatch
Tukor's Pass
Krarl
Whaler's Bay
Doublebay Harbour
Redwater Bay
Lakeheart
Bhoun
Galaphan's Grounding
The Four Sisters
Burning Rock
Celaph's Mire
Mudport
Eagle's Perch
Dragon's Bane
Bay of Mourning
Death's Passage
Moonbear Mountain
Bloodmarsh Isles
Blademelt
The Everwood
Cloaklake
Skyloft Fort
ARAMATIA
Matia
The Aramatian Plains
Kolash
Starcat Keep
Aram
The Islands of Tellesh
PISEK
The Pisek Desert
Coast of Plenty
Miren
The Twin Suns
Sutrek
SOLAPIA (Sunrise Isle)
Bay of Stars
Lumara's Teardrop
Arore
Islands of the Moon

PROLOGUE

Eldur hobbled toward the mouth of the rocky passage, clinging to a staff that shone out with a great white light. Beyond, a cavern opened out, so vast its walls were hidden from sight, its ceiling lost to the darkness above.

Screams echoed. Screeches in the void. To men they were of terror and flame and death, but to Eldur they were music, a song so familiar to him, so fond, so loved. A weary smile broke upon his once-ageless lips as he stepped out beyond the passage. There were so many, so many corridors and caverns and tunnels he'd travelled to get here, down so deep where none other dare go. Above, the air stirred, as great shadows moved above him, pulling at his cloak as they passed, screaming in delight at his coming.

"My friends," Eldur whispered, looking up as the dragons flew by. "My friends, I have missed you so."

He continued, drawing along his ancient, wearied frame, his staff tapping on uneven stone with each aching step. Everything inside him hurt. His body, wounded so gravely by Varin and his great golden blade. His mind, tortured by centuries of war and suffering and grief. They had built such a peace together, he and Varin and Ilith and the others, a peace following an age of war. *Did I break it?* he wondered. *Should I have done more?*

A gentle stirring moved through the cavern, a breeze, a breath, coming from the heart of the cave. Eldur looked up and saw him now, the mountain that was moving, its great, scaly summit lifting up and down as he filled and emptied his colossal lungs. He crept on, as the Lord of Dragons loomed, shackled down here in the depths by great unbreakable lengths of chain. Fetters that Eldur himself had set. "Drulgar," he whispered. "Drulgar, I have come."

The mountain shifted, and the air shook, and the dragons screeched and fled. Eldur dropped to his knees, and from the shadows of that hulking body, a massive head came forth. It swung out on a long thick neck and slumped heavily down onto the rock before him, shattering the stone. Eldur remained on his knees, as the dragon's great eye opened up in the gloom. It held a light of its own, striated in shades of gold and orange and red, cut through by a purply-black diamond-shaped pupil. He looked at Eldur for a long moment, considering him, and in that moment the demigod saw his pain. "I am sorry, Drulgar," he whispered, dipping his chin. "I am sorry, I had no choice."

A rumble moved through the cave, the loose rock on the floor rattling. Eldur stilled until it was over, but he knew Drulgar's sounds. He knew the dragon understood. And he could see the question in his eyes. "Varin," he said softly in answer. "Varin did this to me. He did it for the death of his children, Drulgar. For the son and the daughter you killed."

Drulgar settled, and from the corners of his mouth, fire spouted, hot and red, swirling up the sides of his black-scaled face. Eldur watched on, feeling the warmth move through him. He waited until he felt it was right, and then said, "Your son is dead, Drulgar. Karagar...Varin killed him."

The great dragon lifted his chin and untethered a deafening roar. The very blood in Eldur's body seemed to boil, the entire cavern, the entire mountain, the entire island trembling. Down came a rain of dust and grit and stone, and through the depths of the cave larger hunks of rock fell. "You will bring down the mountain, Drulgar," Eldur whispered calmly. "Settle, my friend. Settle."

The Lord of Dragons slumped back down with a shuddering

crash, as his roar echoed into the black. He turned that great eye on Eldur once more. *Why are you here?* it asked.

"I come to sleep," Eldur said in a tired voice. "To join you here in your slumber." He looked into that diamond slit, and answered the question he saw. "I do not know," he said. "Decades. Centuries. I will die when I must. But for now, I rest."

He stepped in and sat down, laying his back against Drulgar's hard scaly neck. He could feel the warmth, the slow deep thud of his heart. *It matches mine,* he thought, *as it always did when we flew.* His lips curled up into a wistful smile. Those days were gone now...*forever gone,* he knew. *Neither of us will soar again.*

He let out a sigh as he shifted and settled, his heart beating in sync with the mountain at his back. He could feel the weight of the age in his bones, more and more now since the gods had fallen. *How old I am?* He didn't even know. He had died seven times already, and been resurrected the same, Agarath raising him from the dead again and again, but now...now it was different. The gods had left centuries ago, and when his heart stopped for the eighth time, there would be no one to bring him back.

Does that make me a coward, coming here? he asked himself. *Should Varin not have killed me when he had the chance? Should I not have demanded it, rather than creep to these depths to fester in darkness, and in shame?*

He had no answers, and no choice now, but to sit and rest and wait. The others were still alive. Varin and Ilith and Thala and Lumo. They'd all come together after the War Eternal and made their pact. They'd built their cities, raised their lands and borders, prospered across decades of peace. *Until you changed that, Drulgar,* he thought. *Until you changed it all...*

Another mournful sigh rustled through his lips as he reached out and placed his staff on the dark stone floor, shining its pure white light out into the cave. *My tomb,* he thought, *my shame.* Behind him Drulgar's pulse was weakening, slowing in time with his own. He could feel his strength ebbing away, drawing him into a dreamless slumber. *How long?* he wondered again. *How long will it take me to die?* They still didn't know, none of them did. Decades of peace had been followed by a century of war, and still they lived on, on and on and on.

His eyes drew shut in a long slow blink, as the pull of sleep came stronger. *No...just a moment longer.* He could sense Drulgar fading, stilling. *The mountain goes dormant,* he thought, *and I'm to follow.* He laboured to keep his eyes open, looking into the cave, feeling the gentle eddies in the air as the dragons whipped and wheeled in silence. *Is this it? Truly it?* His heart thumped out a final beat. His eyes drew in a final glance. And then shutting, the orb on his staff went out. Plunging dragon and demigod into an endless dark, from which neither would ever wake.

1

Jonik

3,350 Years Later…

Jonik ran his hand down the side of Shade's black coat, whispering softly to calm the horse as the ship laboured against the lumbering waves.

The air was thick with damp and a heavy scent of manure pervaded the hold, a dozen other horses lined up in their stalls, stamping nervously. The space was cramped and unclean, dim and dank, and the rest of the ship was little different. In fact, Jonik rather preferred the smell here than in the stinking den he had to share with the crew. There were twenty of them, fishermen all, and the stench in their communal quarters was little short of unbearable at night. Many shared the rather foul malady of incessant and gratuitous flatulence; added to the stink of fish and body odour, it made for an eye-watering combination.

Jonik hadn't been sleeping well.

The world moved again, up and over a wave, sliding down the other side before levelling off. Jonik felt his gut lurch and gave Shade another reassuring stroke, though in truth it was for Jonik's benefit more than the stoic steed; the elegant Rasal thoroughbred had been uncomplaining for the duration of the five-day trip, where Jonik hadn't fared so well. It was his first time on the churning seas, and as methods of travel went, he considered it acutely disagreeable.

"I think I need some air," he muttered, giving Shade a final pat. Then he patted his own stomach - very gently, of course - and smiled queasily. "I wouldn't want to throw up down here in your fine quarters, Shade."

The horse flicked his glossy mane in amusement, and Jonik moved back up to the surface of the vessel, venturing toward the quarterdeck where the captain - a man named Gill Turner - stood at the helm, manning the wheel. He was a figure of broad proportions, with square shoulders, an ample gut, tangled flaxen beard, and eyes sharp as sabres. A strong wind was assaulting him and causing his tan leather coat to flap energetically against his back. That same wind was filling the bone-white sails, hauling the ship over the surging, white-crested waves at a notable clip.

Jonik strode up the steps to the quarterdeck to join him. A light rain was falling, and where they were headed, the skies were clogged with thunderclouds. The weather looked a great deal worse out there. He drew up near the captain, who was searching the southern horizon with the learned intensity of an experienced seaman. "You'll want to cling on, boy," the man growled, giving him a cursory glance. "This is gonna get worse before it gets better. Best not linger up here too long, else you want to be swept overboard."

Jonik didn't want that at all, though the idea of heading below decks was equally unappealing in this weather. He shielded his eyes from the spitting rain and looked out at the thickening black-grey skies. There were dark cloudbursts spread across the horizon, and the waves were growing increasingly grumpy, thrashing about as though the sea was in a strop.

"She's petulant today," he noted dourly. "We're not going to sink, are we?" A tremor of concern moved through him as he posed the question. He didn't much like the water; it was about as far removed as possible from the mountain-life he knew. After all he'd been through in Varinar, the idea of dying out here on the open sea filled him with a sense of bitter indignation. *It is not how I am meant to go. There are things I need to take care of first.*

"We might," Turner admitted candidly, grinding his lemony teeth as he squinted against the rain. "Any storm can pull down a ship if it's got the mind for it, lad. Let's hope this one's all bluster, no muster, hey?"

He offered a grin as Jonik moved to the bulwark, where he could better stabilise himself against the side of the ship. "How far to Greywater?" he called over the howling gale. "You said we'd be arriving this afternoon."

"Yeah? And when'd I say that?" the captain snickered.

"When we left Green Harbour. You said we'd reach Greywater within five days. That was five days ago."

Turner guffawed. "Well look at you, keeping track o' things. The sea don't play like that, boy! Five days can become ten...or forever if she has a mind to sink ya. Best we can hope for is that this storm blows us off course a bit. Winds, waves, currents, krakens. None of them play by your rules, lad."

Jonik sighed, idly observing the men as they rushed about on deck, pulling at ropes and rigging and tending to matters he didn't fully comprehend. There was an urgency to their work, but it hadn't yet devolved into panic.

"What's your rush, anyway?" the captain asked, as a sudden squall drenched the quarterdeck, soaking Jonik's black cloak. "You got somewhere you need to be?"

"Nothing you need to know about, Captain Turner," Jonik rasped. "No questions asked, remember? That was the deal we made."

A yellow grin spread itself across Turner's face. "True enough, and I'm a man o' my word. You gave me enough coin to fasten my lips, I'll grant you that. Just asking for curiosity's sake is all. You don't strike me as a man with a plan."

Good read, Jonik thought warily, though perhaps he wasn't as hard to decipher as he believed. He'd met Captain Turner in Green Harbour, a bustling port-town in the southwest of Vandar, about a week after butchering that demon and his men in Russet

Ridge, and had quickly identified the craggy-faced seaman as a man of loose morals. A generous purse was handed over - Jonik had, of course, looted the dozen or so men he'd killed for coin and other valuables - and that was that.

For the past five days, captain and crew had occasionally probed at his intentions and identity with the odd remark though never much more than that. They were fishermen, heading for the Tidelands to catch a bounty, and trade a few horses on the side; simple men who cared little for the grander machinations going on beyond their line of sight. Jonik had heard them speaking one quiet, star-strewn night about the death of Aleron Daecar, and the drama that had unfolded in Varinar over the past couple of months, but most of them seemed entirely disinterested in the lives of lords and kings. The Shadowknight - or *former* Shadowknight - was thankful for that. It was his firm intention to leave all that behind, and being reminded of what he'd done...of the horror he'd inflicted upon his own family...wasn't something he wanted to dwell on.

"Well, if you're looking for somewhere to stay in Greywater, I know a few good options," Turner continued. "And if you're looking for work...well, I can probably help you with that too."

"I'm no fisherman, Captain Turner."

The man laughed thunderously, a match for the storm. "Oh, I can tell that easy enough! No, you're a sellsword I figure, and an effective one too. How else would you have such a heavy purse on you, and ride such a fine steed as that Rasal below decks? And that blade you keep hidden away..."

Jonik pulled his cloak tighter, weighted with rain, black as death. He'd been careful to keep the Nightblade hidden at all times, but of course the black scabbard he kept it in had been exposed once or twice. Not that they knew what was fastened within it.

"Godsteel, is it?" Turner asked, arching a brow. "I take you as a Bladeborn, the way you carry yourself. For a man who's never been to sea, you balance far too well on deck, suspiciously so I'd say. Most greenhorns slide about as though they're walkin' on ice, but you...nah. You move like you were born on this ship. Gotta be the effect of that godsteel you're gripping beneath your cloak there. Heightens your senses and balance, so I hear." He peered at Jonik's hip. "Mind if I take a look?"

Jonik hesitated a moment. He had no intention of unveiling the Nightblade but carried a godsteel dagger too that would serve the same purpose. He reached in and took it from its sheath, brandishing it for Turner to see. The subtle mist from the dagger's edge breathed skyward, blending in with the spindrift and spitting rain.

"Now ain't that a thing," the captain whistled, pursing his lips as he admired the ten inch length of godly steel. "Not sure I've ever had a Bladeborn on this humble little boat o' mine." He briefly turned his eyes forward, spinning the wheel to starboard as they rode another wave. All over the seas were thrashing white and rough, and away in the distance, Jonik heard a rumble of thunder give out its bellowing call. "I got some Seaborn blood in me, you know," Turner added with a note of pride. "Long way back on my mother's side, but tis there all the same. Can hold my breath for fifteen minutes and dive a hundred metres deep, no trouble. It's why they call me Gill." He tapped his neck. "Like the fish, see." Then he laughed again, guiding the ship over another wave. "So should we go overboard, you stick close to me, boy. Godsteel ain't gonna save you out here, but I might. We're all at the mercy of the tempest now."

Already, the bubbling black clouds were looming closer and they were heading swiftly toward a dense patch of swirling rain and fog. From below, one of the crew came rushing up to the quarterdeck, boots pounding the sopping planks. His name was Braxton, though they called him 'Brown Mouth' for the frankly disgraceful state of his teeth. As far as Jonik could figure, he was Turner's second-in-command. "Cap'n, Grim Pete's got a bad feeling about this one," Brown Mouth said hurriedly. He was about the same age as the captain - somewhere in his late forties - with pockmarked, sun-burnt skin and a jaw that jutted out a fraction to the right as though it had been broken once and never properly set right. "He's bleating that we outta turn around.

Thinks we're gonna go down, he does...it's got the men all spooked."

"Since when does Pete have a good word to say about anything?" Turner responded. "We call him 'Grim' for a reason, Brown, but I'll not have that scrawny bastard stirring the crew into a panic. You get up there and tell him to clamp his jaw shut, else I'll throw him overboard myself. You got that?"

Brown nodded. "Loud n' clear Cap'n, but..." He paused at Turner's narrow glare. "Maybe he's right on this one. The storm looks mighty fierce out there. Might be better to turn west and head for the Agarathi coast, find shelter in some bay and drop anchor till the waters calm..."

Captain Turner shook his head. "We'd get broadsided if we turned against the waves, and capsize for certain. We got no choice now but to head into the heart o' it, and hope the gods are in a jolly mood. I'll not have us sucked down to *Daarl's Domain*, no way, no how. Now tell Grim to shut his rotten trap. I can hear his bloody mewling from here."

True enough, Grim Pete's panicked cawing was beginning to rip through the howling winds toward them. Jonik could see the gangly, gaunt-faced man up in the crow's nest, waving his arms wildly and calling for the crew to turn them around.

"Right, Cap'n. I'll go tell him." Brown shot off, and within moments he was bellowing up to Pete with a scolding for all the crew to hear.

Jonik watched on, feeling more than a little disquieted by the growing intensity of the storm, as the ship grew tiny amid the towering black swells. No matter that he held a Blade of Vandar, it wasn't going to help him out here. *It didn't for King Lorin, after all*, he thought. *He died at sea with the Nightblade in his grasp. Don't let the same thing happen to me...*

He held the blade in question for comfort, clinging to the hilt beneath his cloak, as another jagged finger of lightning scratched through the skies, briefly illuminating the gloom. For a moment...just a moment, he thought he saw the shape of land on the dark horizon. He shot a hopeful glance at Turner. "Did you see that, Captain?"

Turner nodded, sharp-eyed, missing nothing. "Aye. Land," he said calmly. "We're nearing the eastern isles of the Tidelands, but they're still some way off. We'll make it, lad, don't fret. I've seen worse weather than this, a dozen times before, and not once have I been bested."

Jonik found that rather hard to believe; he raised his eyes in doubt.

"A skeptic, hey?" Turner said, flicking a smile. "Didn't you hear what I said to you, boy? I'm Seaborn, deep in my bones, and we folk are one with the water. Forget Grim's yowling, he does it every time the wind whips up a bit. Tis his job to sniff out good fishing spots, and there're few better at that to be fair to the man, but when it comes to steering a ship through rough weather..." He prodded a finger at his chest. "That's *my* job, lad, and one I've been doing all my life. You just cling on tight and watch. I'll see us safe to harbour."

For the next hour, Jonik remained by the bulwark, clinging to the Nightblade to stabilise himself as he watched the sea unleash the full horror of her wrath. He was trained to be fearless, true, though even the former Shadowknight felt a strain in his chest that approached panic, as his heart thrashed hard and heavy between his ribs, and the waves swelled wild and wanton beneath the keel. They grew larger and larger still, until the peaks seemed tall as mountains, and the troughs as deep as the darkest rifts. The ship flew down the slopes and crashed back up through the watery bluffs, and standing immovable at the helm, Captain Turner roared his orders over the tumult, spinning the wheel to the left and right with the fevered intensity of a man fighting for his life.

Jonik watched in awe of the sheer brutality of it, yet in some ways it was all familiar. Those mountain-like waves were as the great peaks he knew at the Shadowfort. Those plunging troughs between them were as the deep ravines that stretched into depths unknown. And the storm...the storm he knew well enough, its song as sweet to him as the soft lullaby of a loving mother. He stood there, as the pin-like needles of rain cut at his cheeks, and the winds swirled and blared around him, and his mind went back to that dark, dangerous place...that place where he'd grown up, trained, been forged into a weapon with no purpose but to kill.

A part of him missed it. How could he not? The pain and suffering had become as kin to him...a part of him...a ritual of the only life he'd ever known. There was a comfort in the violence, dysfunctional though it was, and often he returned to it in his dreams. *Will I ever see it again?* he wondered. *Will I return to seek vengeance, for what they forced me to do?* He didn't know, not yet. All he could be sure of was that they would come after him now. It was the only thing in his life that was certain.

A bellow caught loud in the air, ripping Jonik from his thoughts as Turner called out for the men to brace. "Big wave to starboard! Grab ahold o' somethin'!"

Jonik's eyes sped to the right, where a huge swell was surging toward the prow of the ship. The crew rushed to fasten themselves where they could, grabbing at ropes and rigging and tucking themselves in tight against the walls. Jonik saw Brown Mouth speed for the foremast, tangling himself up in a net beneath the sails. With little for him to cling to up on the quarterdeck, Jonik quickly drew out his dagger, dropped to his knees, and slammed the tip of the godsteel blade through the planks at his feet. He gripped the hilt with both hands, wedging himself against the gunwale just as the wave crashed into him.

It hit.

It hit *hard*; much harder than he'd expected, and for a moment he was completely submerged, the entire ship swallowed by the sea with only the masts poking through the surface. His vision and hearing blurred, blunted by the water, and for a second he thought that was it. Over. That he'd die at sea like King Lorin, and take the Nightblade down to the depths to be lost all over again. But no. A few thudding heartbeats later, the waters surged off the decks, the ship bobbed back upright like a cork and his ears refilled with the howling song of the storm. Jonik looked up, wiping the salty seawater from his eyes, to find Turner still at the helm, hunkered down, clutching the wheel with his powerful grip. His eyes were forward, narrow, scanning. He called out over the roaring storm, "Numbers! Numbers, Brown! Count 'em!"

It took a mere second for a voice to call back. "Man overboard, Captain! Jakken's in the drink! Off to port!"

Then a second voice followed, tagging in right after the first. "Another, Cap. Polver's gone over! To port...forty yards!"

Men were pointing, rushing to the left side of the ship as their fellow crewmen were washed away. Jonik drew back to his feet and scanned that way, pulling his dagger from the wood as he stood up straight. Through the blaring storm he could hear their spluttering screams of terror as they were sucked into the maelstrom, their arms flailing wildly.

Brown Mouth came stampeding up the main deck, "We gotta do something, Cap!" he roared. "We can't let them die out there!"

Turner shook his head with the cold calmness of a man who knew there was no hope. Both men were being tugged away from the ship and going after them wasn't an option. "Nothin' we can do for them, Brax. You know it as well as I. They're in *Matmalia's* arms now. We can only hope she takes 'em safe to land."

Brown Mouth Braxton grimaced, looking forlornly out to sea, but was too experienced a seaman to argue otherwise. They were dead and he knew it. He whispered a quick prayer under his breath as several members of the crew checked for damage down on the main deck. One of them - a fresh-faced teen called Devin - came running over with a concerning report.

"There's a crack at the top of the mainmast, Captain," he called in a panicked voice. "The winds are pulling too hard at the sails. She might snap free if this goes on much longer."

"We'd best take down the topsail," Brown Mouth said to that. "Leave the fore topsail and jib for now."

They'd already taken down the more fragile sails to stern when the storm picked up, though there were still a couple flapping on the mainmast and at the front, a lateen sail was rigged up behind the foremast. Captain Turner considered it for a moment, then nodded, just once. "Take 'em down, Brown," he said. "We lose that mast and we're done for."

Brown Mouth nodded and wheeled away, as the crew flew into action, furling the large, square sail on the mainmast before it could do any further damage. The ship was starting to look bare, like a leaf-less forest in winter, though it seemed the only safe course of action. If the masts were pulled down they'd be at the mercy of the winds and the currents once the storm passed. Jonik turned again to observe the captain. Deep lines were starting to rut his forehead as he continued to scan the horizon, and that early confidence he'd portrayed was gone. The waves weren't growing any smaller, the winds weren't easing, and half of his orders to the crew were being swallowed by the bellowing thunder and howling gale. Above, the gloomy afternoon was quickly giving way to an oppressive, all consuming darkness, only punctuated by the occasional streak of lightning. Their situation was starting to feel increasingly desperate.

Jonik turned his eyes to port, gripping his dagger, trying to see through the void. The land he'd spotted earlier was much closer now, but Turner appeared to be guiding the boat *away* from it. He frowned. It was almost directly to their left, stretching some miles across the horizon, only a mile or so away. "You're not going to try to make land?" he called, confused. "We're close, Captain. Real close."

He wondered if the fisherman could even see it. Without his godsteel-enhanced vision, Jonik would struggle to spot it in these conditions, even when the lightning burst alight in the skies.

"I know we're close," Turner grunted . "But there's nowhere safe to land out there, and the last thing we need is to get dashed against them rocks."

Jonik frowned. As far as he saw it, getting shipwrecked on some rocks was a better option than being sunk out at sea. He turned again to the left, and stared, narrowing his focus. His eyes searched through the gloom, the fog, the rain, and caught sight of several rugged beaches that looked welcome enough for a beleaguered ship. "There are some beaches," he shouted out. "Direct to port." After five days at sea with these men, he was starting to pick up a bit of their lingo. "Can't we try to land there..."

"No!" said Turner immediately. "I just told you, it's too dangerous. We go near land and gods know what's lurkin' beneath the waves for us. You see beaches, you say? But can you see under the water too? These islands are surrounded by submerged rocks that'd be only too happy to rip our guts out. You don't know what you're talking about, boy. I can't afford to suffer any more damage to my ship. If I do, I'm done for. You hear me? Done for!"

Jonik bit his tongue and decided not to push the issue. Turner was an experienced captain and knew what he was doing, though something told Jonik the man was more interested in saving his ship than saving his crew. Many of the men were new to his command, having been picked up in Green Harbour, and fishermen and sailors were hardly in short supply. But his ship? If it suffered major damage then the repairs would likely cost a fortune, money that Turner clearly didn't have. *No, why else would he have been so eager to have me aboard?* Jonik thought. *He needs every coin he can get his hands on...*

The conditions continued to worsen. With the topsail taken down, the ship ceded more power to the elements, and on the main deck, the crew had little to do but fasten themselves where they could and try to hold out. Amid the clamouring winds, the petrified yowling of Grim Pete leaked into Jonik's ears, and he noted Captain Turner glancing up at the man with a murderous look in his eyes. More waves drenched them, drowning the decks again and again before draining off through gaps in the bulwark. A great deal of it was also surging below decks, the ship gulping it down eagerly as it drunkenly staggered across the sea. Jonik could sense the vessel growing worryingly heavy beneath his feet.

He marched up to Turner again and took a grip of the helm to steady himself. "We take on much more water and we'll sink," he said, narrowing his eyes. "We *have* to try to make land, Turner." He pointed to port. "There's another island out there, not far away. Rocks or not, I don't care. I'll not die on this ship on account of your money troubles."

Turner looked at him angrily. The tension was starting to tell. "And what do you know of my money troubles, boy? Or how much water we can take on till we sink? Taking on a bit o' drink right now will only serve us well. You'd know that if you'd spent more than a few days at sea. It'll add more ballast and help keep us stable. We're too light and that's a problem...all we've got are those horses down there, and a dozen ain't enough weight in weather like this..."

Horses. *Shade.* Jonik reached out and snatched at Turner's sodden collar, pulling him forward. "My horse isn't ballast, Turner," he growled menacingly, becoming *that* man again, that man trained to kill. "If he drowns down there, I'll have your head up here. Believe me, your fate will be the same as his."

Turner quivered a little under the close attentions of the former Shadowknight. Jonik had been a placid passenger throughout the trip until now, though this storm was enough to fray even his blunted nerves. "All right, young lad, I...I hear ya. I meant nothin' by it, just that a light ship's a vulnerable ship in weather like this. Those horses are helpin', that's all. I got no intention of seeing any of them to harm, believe me. They're valuable." He smiled uneasily. "And your Shade most of all."

Jonik nodded and drew back a little. "I'm going to check on him." He took a step away and then glanced back. "You get us out of this, Turner," he warned. "I've been through far too much to die on this rotting boat."

He turned again at that, striding quickly below decks, down two floors to the cargo hold where the horses were being kept. Arriving, he found it submerged in two feet of water. The hold had a bilge where the water could drain out, but it seemed to be filling more quickly than it could empty.

Jonik cursed as he turned his eyes around the dim-lit space. A single lantern swung on the wall at the far end, providing miserly illumination, but the others had been torn free by the rocking of the ship and put out in the frigid water. He stepped down and made quickly for Shade, who stood calm and quiet in his stall. The others, however, were panicking, whinnying wildly with each wave, with each new surge of seawater flowing down the steps.

"It'll be fine," Jonik said, speaking to Shade. He ran a hand down the horses's flank. "All of us. We're going to be fine. Tell them, boy. Keep them calm if you can."

Shade flicked his mane in understanding and made a few light whickering sounds for the benefit of the other steeds. It had little effect, though a couple of them seemed to relax. Jonik moved over to the more animated mounts in a bid to pacify them, speaking quietly, stroking their chins and sinewy necks. He had a way with horses, a fondness for them and other beasts that hardly extended to his fellow man. Men were too complicated. They were cruel and manipulative, greedy, gluttonous, and ever they strove for *more...*

A heavy jolt rumbled through the ship, and Jonik sensed a great rending of wood. He spun his eyes forward. It came from the prow, a juddering impact, as though the ship had hit something beneath the waves. *A rock?* Were they getting closer to land? He gave Shade a firming glance and darted back up the steps. The roar of the storm assaulted his senses once more as he turned up to the captain, still manning the helm. "What happened?" he called out. "Felt like we hit something?" He scanned, but saw no land nearby. The only islands remained some way off.

Turner looked similarly bewildered. "Don't know, ain't no rocks out here, the waters are too deep," he shouted from the quarterdeck. "Some flotsam or debris in the sea, maybe..."

It happened again. This time off to the starboard side, right near where Jonik was standing. He heard a heavy crack of splitting timber and the entire vessel trembled as though struck by something in motion. Jonik looked again at Turner and saw his eyes widen in alarm. The captain glanced over the edge and seemed to spot something. Then his voice tore loud and wild, spreading from stern to bow. "Kraken!" he roared. "KRAKEN!" The crew looked up in panic. "Daarl's sent a beast to take us! We've bested the storm too long, and she's had it! Weapons, men! Prepare to fight!"

The ship flew to chaos, as men untangled themselves from the rigging, rushing to compartments built into the boat, pulling them open, snatching lances and poles and rusted swords. Jonik sped back up the steps to the quarterdeck, as Brown Mouth followed. No sooner had the three gathered than the ship trembled again, rocked by another impact, this time to port.

Their eyes swung that way, as several of the crew rushed to look over the edge. Up in the crow's nest, Grim Pete had found some courage and was shrieking loudly, pointing, trying to judge where the beast might appear next. It was all happening so quickly. Already, men were flinging harpoons into the froth, surging back to fetch more, returning to the side of the ship to take aim.

Up by the wheel, Brown was yelling into the captain's ear. "Land, Cap'n! We gotta make for land! We'll not survive long against a beast that size! We ain't whalers! We can't defend ourselves like they can!"

It seemed Turner had little choice now. He scanned and quickly spun the wheel, turning the rudder, ordering for Braxton to man the sails. His second-in-command sped off on tremulous legs, as a further impact rattled underfoot, knocking the man off his feet. He fell heavily, tumbling down the steps onto the main deck, but scrambled straight back up and continued right on. Up in the crow's nest, Grim Pete was hollering and pointing, though his words were lost to the din. Jonik followed the flow of his finger instead, and that's when he saw it; a thick, slithery, serpentine arm snaking up the side of the ship. It drew up and over the edge of the wall, deep grey on top and lighter beneath, shimmering in the lamplight. Its underside was marked by a thousand suckers, *tasting* the ship's surface, *scenting* the men as it crept up onto the deck.

Others saw it, shouting in fright, throwing spears on instinct. Several lances struck and embedded themselves deep into the thick-muscled limb, which coiled like a serpent, withdrawing for just a moment, before lashing violently out. A man was hit, flying rearward, his back cracking against the mainmast. He fell limp, his spine shattered. A second sailor was quickly snared by the tentacle, coiling around him as he drew a knife and started stabbing wildly. The arm squeezed, constricting with boundless power, crushing the sailor's chest and collapsing his lungs. Jonik could see his eyes popping from his skull as the slithery arm drew swiftly back to the water, taking the sailor with it.

Other battles were unfolding elsewhere. Several more tentacles were rising out of the surf. Some slipped quietly up onto the deck, sliding between obstacles in ambush and dragging screaming men to their deaths. Others lifted vertically from the churning waters, prodding, thrusting, throwing men off their feet. The sailors were shouting, cursing, swinging swords, throwing spears. Grim Pete was shrieking wildly up above. Brown Mouth had been drawn into the action. Some men were climbing the rigging to escape the chaos, showing themselves to be cowards. Jonik watched, momentarily stunned by the sheer madness of the spectacle.

"Well! What the hell are you waiting for!" surged Turner's voice, ripping Jonik from his reverie. He turned, and found the grizzled captain staring at him. "You're Bladeborn, aren't ya! Help, man, for gods' sake, help!"

Jonik shook the final swirls of fog from his head, turning forward. He opened his cloak and reached for his blade. His dagger wouldn't do, not against such a foe as this. But he had a rather more potent weapon to hand.

He drew the Nightblade, dark as a dreamless sleep, its surface refusing to catch the light as he brandished it to his side. He looked upon the carnage and a strange smile rose on his pallid face. *Have you ever tasted kraken before? No? Then you're in for a treat.*

He sped across the quarterdeck and into the maelstrom, moving with inhuman speed. Down the starboard side of the vessel at the midship, a pair of muscular tentacles were searching for prey, creeping up behind two burly men as they swung swords at another invading arm. Jonik cut through one, then the other, leaving two severed limbs writhing on the deck, deep black blood pumping from the open flesh as the stumps shot back into the surf.

His smiled broadened, and the Nightblade seemed to ripple with glee. He caught sight of another limb, rising high out of the waves, as thick as a man's body. It turned to *look* at him, its tip curling around itself as though forming a fist, which came flying right at him half a heartbeat later. He sidestepped, swung, and enjoyed a shower of warm black blood for his trouble. The severed tentacle slammed heavily down onto the deck at his feet, as the rest of it recoiled and thrashed, disappearing back into the waves.

Jonik turned and looked out, and there he could see it, the vast shadow in the water. There were several different species of kraken, and many other sea monsters besides, but these giant, squid-like creatures were more deadly than most. He faced the fiend, and for a moment, thought he could see a great, bulging eye staring at him from the depths. He felt no fear, no panic, no dread. Only a sense of...*affinity* with the beast. *Because that is what I am,* he thought. *I am a monster...just like you.*

A call caught his attention. Further up the ship, several enormous tentacles were flailing savagely, sweeping men into the air, crushing them, tossing them into the black abyss. The ship lurched to the right as a pair of those great, fleshy arms placed their weight upon the vessel, angling it to starboard. Jonik glanced again into the ocean. The great shape beneath the waves was rising, nearing the surface, breaking through the waves, *climbing.* A huge, horrifying face appeared, a blubbery mass of bulging flesh, set with a giant, open maw. A half dozen layers of razor sharp teeth extended into the void beyond, as several smaller tentacles began picking men off the deck, tossing them inside the gaping hole. At the flanks of the monster's head, those massive eyes extended out, as large as giant, circular shields, deep orange with black pits for pupils. Staring. *Smiling.*

Across the deck, several more of the men were lost to their terror as the monster rose up, scrambling away up the rigging, hunting higher ground. Many others were already dead. Only a few brave souls continued to fight, swishing wildly with their swords and throwing their spears. Jonik noticed Brown Mouth dive beneath a swinging limb and rise up against the starboard bulwark, a harpoon in hand. He took aim and threw, the lance cutting meekly into the creature's gigantic head. Several other spears were thrown, but did no damage. If a half dozen lost limbs didn't faze the fiend, a few little pricks of steel weren't likely to.

Jonik ducked as another swinging arm came his way. A great wind flowed over him as the meat rushed passed, and he swung upward, cutting it in two. His eyes darted to the kraken's face, and in that great eye, he saw a flinch of pain. He narrowed his gaze, bared his teeth and knew what he had to do. This thing would take them down, sailor, steed, and ship all, dragging them to the darkness where Daarl, goddess of the depths, made her domain.

I cannot let that happen. I will not die on this gods-damn boat.

Jonik remembered his mantra, the verses taught to him by his order. To act, and not think. To do, and not question. He stepped up onto the bulwark, as the world fell to chaos around him, and the ship groaned under the monster's great bulk. *I hold a piece of Vandar's Heart in my hand. And by his will, I act.*

He leapt over the edge, holding the Nightblade aloft, and let his form fade into the darkness. The creature never saw him coming, and through the wild net of swinging limbs he fell, turning the tip of the Nightblade down, driving it deep into that huge, staring eye.

The kraken let out a bizarre, trumpeting bellow, as Jonik thrust the blade right up to the crossguard, and ripped it back out, bringing a spray of black blood and sinewy slime with it. The creature thrashed madly, and with a powerful surge Jonik pushed off with his legs, thrusting himself upward and over to the creature's opposite flank. He took aim again, holding the Nightblade point down, landing at the edge of the other bulging eyeball. It gave no resistance as he plunged the steel right up to the hilt, so deep he felt his fist press through the breach. He pulled back again, swinging easily through the organ. The eyeball split in two, gushing gore as that same echoing shock of noise erupted from the monster's maw.

On the deck, the tentacles were drawing back, wriggling and writhing like worms as they retreated. The water churned as a dozen limbs slapped down upon the monster's face, trying to crush the hidden menace. Jonik saw one coming and darted left, and the limb smashed hard against the kraken's blinded eye. It cried out in a strange, plaintive whine, as another limb swept past his feet. He leapt up, hurdling it, and began stabbing again, cutting at the top of the monster's head. More pitiful roars filled the air. More limbs thrashed to dislodge him. And still he cut, again and again, until the meaty floor at his feet was slick with black blood, a soggy mass of mushy pulp.

The beast suddenly shifted, withdrawing its bulk from the ship, and the vessel surged back to port, swaying on the water, free of the kraken's grip. Jonik turned his eyes up. The remaining crew were there, at the edge, cheering, throwing spears, as the bulbous mountain of slippery flesh made haste in its retreat. One such spear came close to him, cutting into the pulpy flesh between his feet. The creature rumbled in agony again as Jonik looked up through the flapping sea of limbs, searching for an opening. He crouched, dropping to his haunches, and then, seeing a gap, he flew.

With a powerful burst, he bounded for the boat as it swayed wildly on the waters. The blinded beast was in full flight, sinking away into the depths to lick its wounds, yet as Jonik rose high through the air, so a final whipping tentacle caught him.

It hit him hard in the flank, sending him careening across the ship and crashing heavily into the forecastle. The Nightblade came loose from his grasp, thudding dully onto the deck, and both man and blade took form. Men gasped as he reappeared, his body crumpling into a heap of back leather and fur. He tried to breathe, but the air was gone from him. He blinked, fighting to stay conscious. Failing.

The blackness closed in.

2

Saska

The lands down south of the great fort of Harrowmoor, deep in the foot of southwest Rasalan, were rank with the stink of death and ash.

They'd passed several villages just that day and all were stricken and black, looted of all treasure and half their residents besides. At each one, Marian had called out for survivors to hear whatever report they might give them. They crept from the mills and squat stone keeps and whatever other sturdy buildings remained unburned, crawling like ants from a hill. The reports were always the same. Soldiers had come and ransacked them, stealing treasure and food, horses and livestock, burning the buildings and scorching the fields.

And this place will be no different, Saska thought, as they came upon another village, bordered by great naked oaks and towering, lonely pines, the earth carpeted with needles and soggy brown leaves slick from the recent rains. The snows that had been tumbling down further to the north hadn't yet reached this far south, yet as autumn inked into winter it had grown cold and crisp regardless.

Saska felt a chill run up her spine that had nothing to do with the weather, as she looked upon the devastated village. Dead men lay all about the place, their chests full of shafts, great cleaving wounds cut into their flesh. Outside the village, a pile of corpses had been gathered and burned on a large communal pyre, a putrid smoke seething from the heap. Others were still being collected by the survivors, labouring beneath the bleak afternoon skies. There didn't seem many left. Only the old and young and women. The place had been stripped of its men, and Saska knew just how that felt.

"Who leads here?" Marian called out, turning her eyes over the listless villagers. Dressed in her flowing grey cloak and sitting atop Stormwind she looked almost too noble when set against such a place.

The villagers looked at her with vacant, empty eyes. It took a further prompting from Roark for one of them to stagger off and return a few moments later with a stout little man wearing the garb of a sea cleric. His dark blue robes were muddied and stained with blood and he looked like he hadn't slept in a week. He ambled over and sighed out his name. "Father Pennifor, my lady. I took charge after..." He exhaled again and left the rest unsaid, as Marian swiftly slipped off her mount to join him in the squelching dirt.

"My condolences, Father." She placed a tender, doeskin-gloved hand on his shoulder, towering over him. He was a small man with thinning hair, about as wide as he was tall. He looked broken, like so many others they'd come across. "When did they come?"

"Late last night," Pennifor told her with a weary croak. "We had a handful of soldiers here to guard us but they didn't last long. There must have been a hundred of them; we stood no chance. None at all." A dispirited breath emptied from his lungs. "The rest of us have been trying to burn the dead to stave off disease and such, but it's hard work with the few we've got left." He looked hopefully at Roark and the others. "Might you lend a hand, perchance, since you're here? Help ease the burden a little?"

Marian nodded slowly. "Of course, Father." She turned to Roark, who remained on his mount behind them, with Quilter, Braddin and Lark beside him. "As the cleric requests. Go help gather the dead, and do it gently. Lend a hand wherever else you're needed. Braddin, you're good with timber. Help them build the pyre."

The four men climbed from their saddles without complaint, hitched their horses, and bustled off to help. Lark's lute was bouncing against his back as he loped away. *He'll be singing a plaintive eulogy soon, no doubt,* Saska thought. The young mercenary had a song for all occasions, and recently, they'd been of a sorrowful ilk.

"Your men were all killed?" Marian asked the ageing pastor. "For resisting?"

Father Pennifor huffed. "You call holding up your arms and laying down your weapons resisting? They were killed for no reason, my lady, none at all. I'll accept armed men being cut through in a war, but those who'd already surrendered? These Tukorans are beasts make no mistake. We're hearing it all over; every village is suffering the same."

Marian offered a condoling nod. "We've seen many such places," she agreed. "Do you know of any villages that haven't yet been attacked in the region?"

The priest thought for a moment. "Off east, perhaps," he said. "Deeper into the Lowplains. The men rode off that way, so I'm guessing that's their next target. There are many places out there, ripe for their ungodly work."

"And the men who attacked you here. They were Greenbelts? Kastor men?"

The man shrugged, though his shoulders only had the energy to inch a fraction or so up and down. "I don't rightly know, my lady, but I suppose some wore green belts around their waists, if that's what you're asking. A couple were killed, if you want to take a look." He pointed to a pair of corpses, left to rot beside the stables. "All were garbed in brown Tukoran coats, and looked the same to me. I didn't think to ask of their lordly allegiance, though thinking about it, I saw a few bearing a bear paw print as their standard. That's the Kastor crest as I understand it."

"It is," Saska said, dismounted from Spot, her bouncy little steed, boots sinking into the mud. Like Marian, she was well wrapped in grey wool and fur to combat the cold, her hands gloved, a fine scarf encircling her neck. She stepped forward, drawing the old man's attention. "Were women taken?" she asked him, in a balanced voice. More and more, she took her cues from her mentor, adopting Marian's measured manner. "We've been told that the women are being lined up in the villages and tested for Varin blood. Did that happen here?"

The man's eyes darkened further, such as they could. "Aye," he said. "Our womenfolk were gathered and their commander went down the line with a dagger. I was barricaded in the chapel at the time over yonder, but I'm told it was godsteel. They're looking for Bladeborn you say?"

"Did they find any?" Marian questioned.

The priest looked up to her. "Here? Oh no." He sounded bemused. Then his expression changed, sinking into anger. "I wish we'd had a trained Bladeborn with us, by the gods I do. Might have made them think twice, given that commander of theirs something to think about. He was Bladeborn himself, must have been to carry that godsteel dagger, though didn't take part in the slaughter. No challenge for him I guess." He sighed again.

"A company of a hundred men would commonly be led by a Bladeborn," Marian said instructively. "A weak-blooded one, most likely, and little better than a regular man-at-arms, but a man with a trickle of Varin blood all the same. The best of them tend to get swept up into the Emerald Guards."

"Aye, same as happens here with our Suncoats, though not heard a peep from them lately. Suppose they're busy elsewhere, are they? I'd hope so, at least, though from what I've heard they're all gathered up at Harrowmoor, tucked in tight for winter."

"Yes. We have a strong contingent garrisoned at Harrowmoor under Lord Paramor's command. The Tukorans need to take the fortress if they're to safely continue their advance north. However, many others have been sent to try to slow Prince Rylian's assault on the coastal cities. Regrettably, we don't have the numbers to defend every town and village, Father, and you're unfortunately situated here. Lord Kastor has been given the responsibility of clearing these lands and he has permitted his men to pillage and plunder as they see fit. Prince Rylian's forces operate under tighter restrictions."

The priest made a disdainful noise, and waved his hand. "I'll believe that if ever I see it. You can't corral men in war, my lady; plundering is part of the deal. It's their reward for risking their lives and marching so far from home. They take their treasure and that makes it all worth it. Believe me, I know. These lands were full of feuding not so long ago and I saw it myself firsthand. If we can do it to our own countrymen, what hope do we have when fighting a foreign invasion?"

"The War of the Lowland Lords?" Marian asked.

"Aye, the very one, though I'd hardly call it a war. Just lords fighting lords for their lands and titles, and as ever, the smallfolk ended up suffering the worst of it. But no matter, so long as the highborn have their way." He huffed and shook his head. "I'd like to hope you're of a more noble sort, my lady, but in war even the noblest can turn wicked."

Marian looked over the bodies being carried for cremation. There was a single wheelbarrow left for the purpose; all the others looked to have been burned during the razing. "I'll not argue with you, Father," she said. "I know the corrupting effects of war well enough. That's the very reason we're here, though I'll not trouble you with our full purpose. Take some solace, if you can find it, in knowing that your day here is done. They'll not come back this way, and you can focus on rebuilding. Do you have sufficient stocks of food for winter?"

"Now that half of us are dead, aye, there's enough to go around should we ration it. Us old folk and women don't eat so much as the men, so I suppose that's one thing less to worry about." He looked to the steaming pile of corpses, shoulders slumping. "Those Greenbelts had a good root around but didn't get into our secret stores. So long as they don't come back, we'll get by."

"They won't." Marian said it as a promise, but had little to back it up. As far as they'd heard, there were many roving bands of Tukoran soldiers raiding across the south, striking out at will from the main warcamp in search of plunder. One group might have passed this way and taken the cake, but that didn't mean another wouldn't come by and look for crumbs. "Keep your food stocks hidden anyway," Marian added, "just in case anyone comes back this way. And be careful of bandits. They thrive during war and it's not just Tukorans we need to worry about."

"Deserters," grunted the old priest. "Won't be long before half the army's abandoned the cause if they haven't already. These are lawless lands and lawless times, that's true, but we've got nothing to give anymore, save a few sacks of grain and casks of cured meat. With some luck we'll be left alone."

Saska didn't mention that there were still plenty of women here too. In fact, they made up the majority of those who remained, and they'd make a prize as well for base men if there was no coin or treasure to loot.

A chill west wind blew through the village, causing the smoke to swirl and scatter off eastward. Saska pulled her coat tighter. It was mid-afternoon and yet already darkening, the days growing shorter as they grew colder, night speeding on fast. It had truncated their travels somewhat, receding their time spent on the road as they'd journeyed south from Northgate Castle on the northern banks of the Forks river. For three days they'd stayed there, enjoying the bear-like Lord Buckland's hospitality before heading south amid the falling snow to Harrowmoor, a fort to match Northgate in scale.

It was built high up on the moors, well protected by moats and great, thick walls, so wide they felt more like tunnels when passing through. At the heart a huge keep soared skyward on a bailey and the battlements were plenty, arranged with ballistas and catapults and other such engines of war. Saska had heard that the bolts the ballistas shot were often tipped with godsteel, and that the archers had arrows of the same. "They can pierce godsteel armour," Marian had told her, as she took her on a tour, and they looked out from the battlements over the sweeping plains. "People think a fully armoured Bladeborn knight is invulnerable, but that isn't true. We have defensive measures to give them pause. Sieging this fort will not be easy."

Her words gave Saska confidence, though still, it seemed only a matter of time before the Tukorans marched on Harrowmoor and brought their own siege weapons to bear. And then it would be onto Northgate, and then Thalan itself, by which time how many people would have died? Thousands of soldiers had already fallen between the warring armies, and this was only the beginning. How would things look in a month, or two? How many would be dead then?

Saska sighed, looking over the bones of the village. Only the chapel and rectory remained intact, and the mill, thick stone as it was, still sat by the river with its great wheel turning forlornly on the water, groaning as it did so. The stables were half burned to ash, the timber yard was gone. There was a tavern that had been set ablaze, still coughing smoke to the leaden skies, and half the single storey shacks and cabins these people called home had been pulled apart during the sacking.

I wonder if Del was part of it, came a sullen thought. It was the same thought she had every time she came across another plundered settlement, and every time she'd make sure to check the dead in fear she might see his face among them. She left Marian and the old cleric to their discussion and walked toward the two dead Greenbelts he'd pointed out, lying outside the burnt-out stables. That now familiar chill throbbed through her blood, but she didn't have to get too close to see that neither were her friend. They were grim-faced and much too old, and unless Del had shortened by a half foot, too squat to be the sweet boy she knew. She pushed at one with her foot, rolling him over, and saw a broken arrow embedded in his heart, piercing his leathers and mail through the bear print crest of Kastor. The other had been taken similarly; shot through the neck by a sleek ashwood shaft.

"Brave lad who killed them," croaked a voice. Saska turned to find the cleric approaching with Marian still at his side, hands held behind her back as she strode along next to the shuffling old man.

"Who was it?" Saska asked. She looked again at the two dead Greenbelts. It can only have been an ace archer who killed them, judging by the placement of those arrows.

"Just a boy," said the priest sadly. "Teen named Mattius not yet into his fourteenth year, voice barely broken. He was a hunter, and a good one too, as you can probably tell." He glanced past the village, across the narrow river toward a patch of woodland. "They made him suffer for it, though. Hung him up on a tree far side of the brook and filled him full of bolts, laughing as they took their turns." He grimaced, swallowing to hold back his tears. "Evil work, it was, pure evil. And that Bladeborn commander, he just stood by, grinning. He didn't pull a string, just watched. That's worse, if you ask me. He might have given him a quick death, but no...tortured him, a boy, just for defending his village."

Saska may have wept if she wasn't so angry, and in her heart, a red rage fought against a cold blue chill for space. She looked at Marian. "We should go," she said, without thinking. "They might not have gotten too far. Their tracks will be easy enough to follow after the rains."

Marian turned east. She looked like she yearned for justice too but was wise enough to temper such a thought. "We can't fight a hundred men, Saska. This commander and his soldiers will have their reckoning, but it cannot be by our hand." She looked at Saska for a moment to make sure she understood, then turned to the priest once again. "Might you be able to describe the man? I'll have word spread through the Suncoat ranks to take his head for young Mattius. And for the others he murdered here."

"Much obliged, my lady," cracked Pennifor's old voice. He frowned, as though trying to clear his thoughts, and wiped an eye. "He was young, erm, fresh faced, in his early twenties I thought. No beard. Dark hair, curly, down to his neck. Wore fine armour, though not godsteel I don't think. Maybe the breastplate was...and the helm, but not the rest it didn't look to me." He thought again, as Marian waited patiently for further details. "Had a scar on the side of his neck, right side as I recall. Looked like an old war wound to me, though what war a man of his age fought in, I don't rightly know."

"Could have been inflicted by a variety of means," said Marian. "A personal dispute. A sparring accident. A tournament wound." She placed a hand on his shoulder. "Thank you, that should be enough to go on. I suspect he's a knight of House Kastor, perhaps even a relation to his lord. Cruelty runs deep in their blood." She gave Saska a glance at that. "I'll put the word out. He'll not live long, Father Pennifor."

"My thanks to you, my lady." He laughed hollowly. "But I am in remiss; I've not yet asked your name."

"It's Marian of House Payne."

Pennifor smiled fondly. "Then Lord Tandrick Payne is your father?"

"My uncle," corrected Marian. "My father died when I was a child. I grew up in Lord Tandrick's halls."

"Fine halls, I'll wager, over there in the shadow of the Stormwall Hills. I hear he's mustered a force of some five thousand to help guard the coast. Good man. And fondly thought of around here. He helped bring an end to the fighting," Pennifor added, noting the questioning look on Saska's face, "with that war I spoke of, between the Lowland Lords. Might have become a proper war if he'd not intervened. Saved many lives, so we see it here." He dipped his head belatedly. "It's an honour to meet you, Lady Payne. Will you stay, for the night at least? There's room in the rectory, if you want it."

It didn't seem the worst idea, not with the light already dimming. As deadly as Marian was, if they were set upon at night by a strong force of Tukorans they'd struggle to see the dawn. Roark and the others were capable swordsmen but no Bladeborn and Saska was still getting used to her new skin. Marian considered it, taking her time as she liked to, until a further word from Pennifor sealed it. "We'd all feel a great deal safer tonight knowing you and your men are here," he coaxed. "Just one night, Lady Payne. I have some wine, if that helps. And cured boar, for your troubles."

Marian smiled. "Keep the boar," she said softly, "and the wine as well. We'll not strip you of the little you have left, Father. Shelter is all we ask for, and warmth from the cold. We need no more than that."

He took her hands, looking tearful. "Thank you, my lady, truly," he croaked. "Thank you for your kindness."

He spoke as though she'd saved the man's life, though in truth it was they who were getting the better of the bargain. After spending the last few nights in the cold, a roof over their heads would be welcome, and by the look of the rectory, they'd be plenty warm as well. Father Pennifor set off to make preparations for their stay, as Marian and Saska stepped to join the others. She waved them all over and they gathered around, breath fogging, sweat from their labour licking at their foreheads. They were hardy men, but lugging corpses wasn't anyone's idea of fun. None of them looked particularly happy.

"Thanks for doing this," Marian started, passing each a grateful glance. "Saska and I will lend a hand now, though it doesn't look like there are too many left. Lark, clear your throat. I think a doleful song or two might be in order when we burn the bodies - it might offer some comfort to the villagers, though I'll check with Father Pennifor first. We can sing something more cheery when we tuck in for the night."

"We're staying, then?" asked Braddin, his dented bronze shield ever on his back should they be set upon by enemy soldiers.

"Pennifor is preparing a place for us in the rectory," Marian confirmed. "Should be warm enough. We'll head off east at first light; the men who did this went that way. They were here looking for Bladeborn, we're told."

"And the rest," grunted Quilter, spitting to the side. "Stripped this place bare as a newborn by the looks of it."

"They find any?" asked Roark. "Bladeborn?"

Marian shook her head. "No, but they're looking, and that's all we need. Seems there are plenty of villages to the east that haven't been sacked yet. Roark, are you up for a ride?"

Roark came to attention, nodding. "What do you need?"

"Head east. Take Quilt with you. I want you to ride hard and fast and find somewhere that hasn't been attacked. Somewhere on the warpath that'll be hit in the next day or so."

"Right. To insert the princess?"

Saska felt an extra few beats scuttle through her chest. That was the plan, after all. To find a village, place her among the residents, and wait for her to be discovered as Bladeborn and taken to Kastor's warcamp. Then the real work would begin.

"So long as she's still willing, yes."

"I'm willing," said Saska defiantly.

The men smiled. "Part of me feels for him, that Cedrik Kastor," said flat-faced Quilter. "He ain't got a clue what's headin' his way."

"He must have, the enemies he's made," returned Braddin, who they sometimes called Sir Brad for his debatable ancestry. "I'll bet he sleeps with one eye open and a host of knights at his door. Slaying that man won't be easy."

"Thanks Brad," said Saska. "That makes me feel a lot better."

Lark nudged her in the arm in an affectionate way as he stood beside her, and there was a quietly reassuring look on his face. The other three saw Saska as a surrogate daughter or little sister of sorts, though Lark occasionally looked at her differently. He was sweet, to be fair to him, and handsome in his own dopy, doe-eyed way, and of course he had that voice. He'd often used it, Saska had heard, to snare the attentions of women, and had even sung a tune for her one night in the wilds, when he thought the others were sleeping and the wine had softened his mind. The cackling nearby put a swift end to it, though, and his cheeks had flushed beet red, clear enough to see even in the dark. He'd made no further overtures toward her since, and that was probably for the best.

"It's getting dark," Marian noted, in a voice that urged action. She looked at Roark and Quilter pointedly. "Best hit the saddles, and get riding. Don't take any chances if you run into a Tukoran patrol. Avoid them and the road where you can."

"Understood." Roark turned to Quilter, nodded, and then the two men strode off. A few moments later, they were riding out against the grey, vermillion-streaked skies, fading quickly into the pall of darkness as they galloped away east over the ranging moors.

The rest set back to their work, hauling bodies and building the pyre on which to burn them. Marian had been right - there were only a few left - but few was a few too many for Saska. It wasn't pleasant work.

It was fully dark by the time they were done and the air had grown bitterly cold. The villagers gathered, cloaked and mantled and mournful as they stood beside the basic timber pyre, hastily constructed from wood from the yard and whatever dry logs could be scrounged from the forest. It burned easily when put to the flame, and the brisk night air was shooed away as the flames reached high into the blackened night skies. Lark stood by with his lute, ready to pluck a string and croon, but first some words were shared by those who wanted to share them. There must have been a dozen mourners who spoke, telling of the men they'd lost. Their fathers, husbands, brothers, sons, those who'd fought valiantly to defend their loved ones, and those who'd stood by and been killed anyway.

Saska kept to the rear, not wanting to intrude, and in her heart a great weight pressed hard and cold as she listened to the stories. Braddin and Marian stood tall beside her, quietly observing the cremation, and beyond the voices of the mourners, a deep reverential silence took root.

When they were done, Lark was invited to sing. He stepped forward, and rather than swinging his lute from his back let his voice flow a cappella, singing more soulfully than ever before. It was the Mourning Prayer, a common eulogy in Rasalan, an ode to the lost and the new path they were to tread. A song, Saska knew, that would be sung throughout the lands.

Tonight. Tomorrow. For many more nights to come.

3

Amron

Keep Daecar felt empty.

More empty than it ever had.

It wasn't so long ago that it housed a thriving family, and hosts of loyal knights and courtiers besides. Now it felt a mausoleum, dark and cold and full of dread.

Amron Daecar, lord of his house, and former First Blade of Vandar, tried to push back the thought, hard though it was, as he sat at the head of the thick oakwood table set at the heart of the family feast hall. It was dim-lit and mournful, as it had been for weeks, and much of the food sat untouched.

So many empty seats, he thought, looking out, nursing a cup of water. He might have had some wine to brighten his thoughts, but knew himself rather too well for that. One would become two and two would become twenty, and however brightened his thoughts might become, they'd grow dark as death the day after. He'd promised himself he'd abstain from now on and had been obedient to his word thus far. But still...it was tempting. Any man who'd once struggled with the bottle knew all too well its lure.

And all too well its dangers, he thought, setting the latest spur of temptation aside.

He cut at his venison and hooked a piece into his mouth,

chewing lazily on the bloody meat. Down the table, Amara and Lillia were sat next to one another in spiritless, whispered conversation, and to Amron's left, old Artibus was busily scribbling on a scroll of parchment, occasionally turning his attention to his food or wine but mostly focusing on his work. Amron tried to get a look at what he was writing, but the scholar's penmanship was appalling and looked another language to his eyes. There were several diagrams and calculations that he was also having trouble understanding. "What's that you're working on, Artibus?" he asked him. "Another treatment?"

Artibus looked up, then nodded. The old family physician had been working hard with him over the past couple of weeks in a final, valiant effort to rehabilitate his left arm. They'd made some progress on his injured right thigh - his limp wasn't quite so pronounced or painful now - but that left arm remained belligerently unusable for all but simple tasks.

"Yes, though it's still theoretical at this point, Amron," Artibus said with a note of energy otherwise missing from the hall. "There's a new ointment that I've been working on with a couple of Rasal Seaborn mages at the university that may have some deep healing properties, but it's far too early to know how effective it might be."

Amron nodded in an absent sort of way, as Artibus dipped his quill pen into his inkhorn and continued scratching. Nothing they did had worked thus far and he didn't imagine this would be any different. That left shoulder of his had been so gravely cleaved that the nerve damage seemed irreversible. A deep healing ointment wouldn't correct that.

No, only a god can do that...

He looked down the table to his thirteen year old daughter, sitting quietly with Amara, prodding listlessly at her food. Amara was trying to brighten the child's mood, a noble effort that looked to be failing. Lillia had fallen deeper into her slump over the last two weeks, still grieving Aleron's heartbreaking loss, stricken by fear that her beloved Elyon would never return home. *How can I leave her too?* Amron thought wretchedly. *How can I even ask it of her? And at a time like this...*

That had been his plan, after all. To set out on a perilous journey to the holy mountain of Vandar's Tomb, seek deliverance...seek a miracle...from the spirit of a fallen god. It was a venture that carried substantial risk, and he had no true idea of what he'd find out there in that vast, frozen wilderness where so much menace of the ancient world still lurked. Yet still it drove him, that faint hope that the old miracles he'd heard tell of, and read of in the ancient scrolls, might turn out to be true. That Vandar might raise him from the dead as he had Varin so many times in the past. That even the spirt of a long-dead god might have that power...that power to return him to health, make him whole and one again.

He sighed. Down the table, Lillia continued to work a few diced carrots around her plate, poking at them with her two-pronged fork, her face slumped into her palm as she leaned heavily on her elbow. Amron had planned to talk to her about it, to only go if his daughter permitted it. He'd tried to bring it up once or twice, but each time the right words had eluded him. What to say to her? He'd have to tell her the truth of it, present the full danger of the quest. Tell her that the chances of him ever coming home were slim, that if he were to leave, he might never come back.

But how could he ask her to make such a decision? To weigh her father's fate in her palms, having just lost one brother, and watched another march off to war. What sort of father would do that to his child? What sort of man would put that on his daughter's shoulders?

He'd been foolish to ever think he could put her in such a position, and yet he couldn't bring himself to leave without her blessing. It left him here, enduring Artibus's experimental treatments, sitting idle as the world fell to war. Try as he might to just be Lord Daecar, he was struggling to adapt to this new place of his. Perhaps it was his own ego, but he felt as though he still had some part to play in the wars to come. He had been the north's foremost champion for twenty years, and now, just as the world threatened to fall to ruin, he had been thrown from his lofty perch.

His thoughts blew as such, a cold wind through his mind,

frigid like the winter that had begun to settle upon the city. It made it all the more urgent, this fateful quest of his. Delay further and the snows would thicken to the north, and the passes through the Weeping Heights would become impossible to traverse. If he didn't leave soon, he never would. *And perhaps that would be for the best.*

Artibus ended his latest bout of scribbling, and picked up his small cup of wine. He took a sip. "I hear our troops reached Eastwatch this afternoon," he noted, setting down his quill. "They're making good time, it seems."

"There is no time to lose, Artibus." Amron drew a sip of water to his lips, wishing it were something else. "They'll likely spend the night in camp there and move off at dawn. It will be another week or so before they link up with the Tukorans in Rasalan. It can't come quickly enough."

"You're singing a different tune, then," Artibus said, placing down his goblet, popping a grape into his mouth. "Ever you fought to keep us out of the war, yet now you speak of hastening the Rasal defeat. I find that curious, Amron."

"Things have changed," Amron said through a weighty sigh. "We have no choice now but to push for a quick victory, and the cessation of hostilities. A prolonged war will only redden the earth and rob us of good fighting men; Rasal, Tukoran, and Vandarian all. That is in no one's interests, Artibus. The north must be secured, and expediently so."

"You sound like my cousin," said Amara down the table, twisting the stem of her chalice between her long, painted fingers. "I had not expected you to take up Janilah's words so quickly, Brother."

"Don't start, Amara." Amron levelled her with a glare, sensing that quarrelsome tone to her voice. "I did not set us onto this path, and have no power to guide us off it either. But this path we are on, and if we're to march it, we might as well do it fast."

Amara drew on her wine. "Of course. I only meant to point out how well this is all going for my kingly cousin, watching from the safety of Ilithor. Everything that has happened recently has been rather...favourable to him, wouldn't you say?"

"It's been favourable to many," Amron pointed out. *And unfavourable to many others.*

"Yes indeed. And would you put my beloved husband among that number, I wonder? Your brother has seen his position improve of late, has he not?"

Amron delayed a moment in answer, wondering whether to engage with her or not. She liked little more than setting free her lance-like tongue, and he had to consider whether he had the energy to spar with it right now. "Some might say so, yes," he said eventually, though in a tired voice that brooked no interest in an argument. "He has won the Sword of Varinar, but lost a nephew dear to him. I'm unsure of how to weigh the balance of that, to be honest. Deep down, I do not believe that Vesryn would ever have knowingly had a part in Aleron's death."

"Unknowingly, then," said Amara, taking a sip of wine. "But let us be quite clear; Vesryn *won* nothing. He took the Sword of Varinar by default and leads the Knights of Varin by the same. Something is amiss here. I love my husband dearly, but have little doubt he is being used...and so I return to the man who benefits most from it all - Janilah. He is ruthless and powerful enough to have set all this to motion, and I don't think we've seen the last of it yet."

Amron nodded slowly, wearily. "Perhaps," he said, thoughtfully stroking his thick-stubbled cheek with his working right hand. "Though hearing such a thing from you is hardly a surprise, is it? Your dislike for Janilah is no secret, after all."

"And so that invalidates my point? I speak only of facts, cold and hard and irrefutable. Look at how things have taken shape these last months, Amron. I know it makes you uncomfortable, but my cousin cannot be counted beyond reproach, just because he frightens you."

"He doesn't frighten me," Amron said calmly, refusing to take the bait.

"Well perhaps he should. That man will lead us all to ruin, believe me. I've half a mind to return home to his halls and stick a knife in his throat myself."

Artibus raised an eye, sitting back in his chair. "An overreaction, surely?" he said. "With all due respect, Amara, this sounds like conjecture and convenience on your part. And much as you may deny it, your hostility toward Janilah does rather cloud your judgement..."

"Does it, Artibus?" Amara turned on him sharply. "I would say the opposite, and suggest that my intimate knowledge of my cousin should elevate my judgement of him, not befoul it. You may know him as a warrior and a king, but I know different. I grew up in his halls and witnessed firsthand what sort of man he is."

"And when was the last time you saw him?" challenged Artibus. "When was the last time you were in Ilithor? Have you even returned there since you came here to wed Vesryn? I'll confess, if there's been such an occasion, I do not know of it, and believe me, I don't miss much."

"No of course you don't. Wise old Artibus, the all-seeing eye." Amara smiled and Artibus gamely smiled back. The two enjoyed their verbal jousts and they were never especially scornful in tone. "But your point escapes me. You're saying that Janilah has changed during my time away from his halls? That he's somehow different to the man I knew growing up? Forgive me if I struggle to believe you, Artibus. So far as I hear, my cousin has only gotten worse."

"He's gotten older, Amara. Of course he's gotten worse."

Amara chuckled and raised her chalice in toast. "Oh, I can hardly argue with that. Each year I grow more bitter, after all, so I suppose I concede the point." She turned to Lillia, and began stroking her hair. "And poor little bear, having to put up with us miserable old goats all evening. Sorry if I'm being grumpy, sweetheart. Why don't you go practice with your new dagger? I'm sure young Jovyn's lurking about somewhere. He always seems happy to train with you in the yard."

Lillia's cherubic little face blossomed into a smile. She looked to Amron hopefully. "Can I, Father? Do you mind if I leave the table?"

Amron smiled at her. "Of course, darling. Just be careful, OK."

"I will." She grinned again, stood, and hurried away, wasting no further time in their tedious old company.

It had been Elyon's idea, to gift Lillia a godsteel dagger, and one Amron had agreed to after a short period of deliberation. In any normal circumstances, he'd have refused the request, but Elyon had persuaded him that Lillia would be better able to protect herself if she carried a secret godsteel blade, and could take advantage of the physical powers it bestowed upon her. Given the dangers they were facing, Amron had soon relented. There seemed plenty of sense in it, and by now he was fully onboard.

Her footsteps echoed through the corridors as she shot off to find Jovyn, who had more or less moved into the castle now, taking claim of a room down on the lower floors. That had been Elyon's idea too. He'd asked his squire to remain behind, rather than riding with him and the army, telling Amron that Jovyn's mother was unwell, and that the boy wasn't ready for war. It was a lie. The boy was ready, willing, and more than capable, and when Amron had enquired into the health of his mother, he'd drawn a blank face and proven that a lie too. His mother was just fine. No, this wasn't so much about Jovyn, as Lillia, Amron had come to realise. Elyon has asked the boy to stay on her account. To watch over her. To help train her to harness godsteel. And true enough, it was about the only thing that passed for pleasure for her now.

Amron smiled as it all ran through his head, watching his daughter scuttle off. "She'd have made a fine knight," he said wistfully. "Were she born a boy, she'd have been just as good as Aleron or Elyon, I'll wager."

"I suppose you wish that, do you?" asked Amara. "That she were born a boy?"

Amron's smile dissolved into a frown. "No, of course not. What sort of question is that?"

"A fair one, and one not intended as a slur, if that's what you're thinking. I've known enough Bladeborn knights to have learned that every one of them wishes for sons, Amron. A litter of clones to follow in their footsteps. It's perfectly natural. What else would you do with your ancestral swords?"

"Hang them on the wall," Amron grunted, turning to his left. There, Vallath's Ruin - or the Mercyblade as he preferred to call it - had been set, lit by a pair of lanterns set in sconces either side. Silvery blue mists softened the edges of the enormous blade, and in the firelight, its length glowed with a subtle red tint.

"Is it to stay there forever now?" Amara asked him quietly. "I'd say there's folly in that, judging by the way you look at it, Amron. It haunts you that you can no longer wield it. Why not put it somewhere out of sight? There's no sense in suffering needlessly, is there?"

Suffer, he thought. *It is not by the sight of the blade of my house that I suffer.*

"I may yet take it up again one day," he found himself saying, staring at it. In a way, it was more fond to him than the Sword of Varinar. Not as powerful, no, but he'd dealt greater justice with it, drawn more blood, made his name when holding that blade. By the time he took up the Sword of Varinar the war was all but done, and rarely had he drawn it in anger since. It had become little more than a ceremonial weapon to him. Only now that it was with Vesryn, would it get another taste of death.

"Well I'm happy to see that you haven't yet given up hope," Artibus said. He looked at Amron with tentative eyes. "I had gotten the impression that you were largely humouring me and my treatments."

"I appreciate your tireless work, Artibus," Amron turned to him with a grateful smile. "But..." He paused and drew a breath. Something in him felt like he needed to speak, to confide in them his plan. *I need to hear another voice on it,* he thought, coming to a decision. *A voice of reason to turn me from this course.* Both Artibus and Amara were sharp as scimitars and would put his foolish whimsy to bed.

He found Amara peering at him from down the table, the stem of her chalice clasped lightly in her fingers, twirling. "But?" She leaned forward a little. "Is something on your mind, Amron? You've been particularly lugubrious this evening, even for you. I can tell your thoughts are wandering, and not down a pleasant path, I'll venture." She glanced to the door, as though to make sure Lillia was gone. "Come, you can speak to us; is that not why we're here, to share comfort, and grief? You need not suffer alone, dear brother. What is it?"

Amron's will weakened at her tender words and he felt his sorrow climbing up his throat. He swallowed it back down, before drawing a long breath to steady himself. He'd wept his last the day Aleron had died and hadn't shed a tear since. It was not the Vandarian way to show such weakness in public. If he were to succumb to his grief, he'd do so alone. As he always had.

"I'm...thinking of leaving," he said, testing the waters with those words. Artibus immediately stiffened and sat up, but Amara just watched on, keen-eyed and curious. No one spoke until Amron continued. He looked at his old friend, sitting concernedly on his left. "I appreciate all you've done for me, Artibus, but truly, my arm is useless now. I'm not sure anything you can do will change that."

He raised it, laying it on the table. Pain shot through him, up his arm, through his shoulder, stabbing at his flesh, prickling his skin. He grimaced and gripped his cup, closing his fingers with effort, lifting it to his lips. It took all he had to take a sip without dropping the goblet, and when he set it back down, his hand was shaking violently. He looked at it, eyes wreathed in darkness, feeling...betrayed by the limb. "You see," he whispered. "Useless."

Artibus watched on sympathetically, though his sympathy had its limits. "It may yet work, Amron; don't give up hope. I have also considered further surgical work. If we might open the wound and get a better look at the damage, we may be able to..."

"Do you really believe that, Artibus? Answer me honestly. Will any of your therapies work?"

It was clear before the old man spoke that he didn't believe that at all. He was doing this for Amron's mental health, largely; to give him something to cling to, something to focus on after the death of his son. "They may give you some more mobility," he said after a time. "You'd be able to attend to simple tasks more comfortably, and without so much pain, and in time we may further reduce your limp as well..."

"I think you're missing the point, Artibus," cut in Amara. "He isn't asking to be able to hold a cup of wine without spilling it. He's asking if he'll ever be the man he was. If he might be able to fight, when the war reaches our door."

"If that is the question, then we all know the answer," Artibus said plainly. "I think we've known it all along."

Amron nodded silently. Their work together had only ever been about making him more comfortable. Full restoration of his strength was never in the running.

"Where will you go?" Amara asked. He looked at her. She sat openly, without judgement, and he appreciated that. She had every right to be dubious, after all, given his history of running from his grief.

"North," he said, whispering the word into the cavernous dining room. He paused, and felt stupid for even saying it. "Beyond the Weeping Heights...to Vandar's Tomb."

Artibus spluttered, spitting up his wine. "What...what sort of madness is this, Amron? You're hardly fit to climb the stairs of this castle, let alone those mountains. What on earth would you go there for?" His frown was so deep his eyes were all-but lost under his brow. "This is your grief talking, and nothing more. It is folly. And you know it."

Amron almost smiled. He'd expected such a reaction from the old man and had even hoped for it, in part.

"You'd go seeking salvation?" Amara asked, more evenly. "In the hope that Vandar may grant you a blessing?"

Hearing it from another pair of lips brought home how ridiculous it was. He dipped his eyes. "I know how it sounds..."

"It sounds bloody ludicrous," Artibus snorted. "No one has travelled to that mountain for hundreds of years, and there's a damn good reason for that. You'd die, Amron, you and every poor soul you convinced to go with you. And even should you make it, what then? You don't truly believe the accounts of miracles, do you? That is folklore, nothing but superstition bred among the commoners."

"Not so," countered Amara unexpectedly. "I have read accounts of prominent men who once ventured there, and spoke of the blessings they received. Sir Oswald Manfrey for one. It's a famous tale, Artibus. Everyone knows it."

It was indeed a well known fable, though like all such legends it had its detractors and by the looks of it, Artibus comprised part of that number. Oswald Manfrey had been a Bladeborn of middling skill, so the story went, beholden by a lifelong ambition to become a Knight of Varin, but lacking the required level of prowess to join their ranks. In response to this, he made the trek to Vandar's Tomb, it was said, descended into the depths of the mountain, and returned a figure of frightening power. He subsequently went on to conquer his ambition and more, mastering the forms, rising to the position of First Blade, and leading the Varin Knights in war. Most famous of all was his battle with Karlog the Knight Killer, and Bagazar the Brute. They were two of the most feared dragons of the time and Sir Oswald defeated them both, in single combat, at the very same time. It was a quite extraordinary story that Amron had always enjoyed, and one he looked forward to hearing firsthand when he eventually rose to sit nearby to Sir Oswald at the vaunted end of Varin's Table.

Artibus, however, made clear his skepticism with a grunt. "Oswald Manfrey was nothing but a late bloomer," he said, reaching out to refill his small goblet. "Some say his journey to Vandar's Tomb never even happened, or that he merely came to some epiphany whilst there, and realised what he could achieve if he truly committed to his training. That's hardly the same as healing a lame limb, is it? Personally, I've never been of the belief that Vandar's spirit lingers there, handing out miracles to whomever might stumble by."

"No one stumbles by, Artibus, don't be silly," tinkled Amara in retort. "It's said that finding one's way into the heart of that mountain is a near impossible challenge in itself. That those caverns and caves are filled with countless skeletons of men who got lost and never made it out. To reach that holy place requires extraordinary courage and sacrifice. Vandar only blesses the worthy, and the worthy..." She glanced at Amron. "...they are rare."

A gentle frown moved over Amron's eyes. He hadn't anticipated this level of understanding from Amara, and had prepared himself for a rather more withering response

"Well forgive me if I find it all rather too opaque," Artibus went on. "This concept of worthiness is entirely subjective, and as a scholar I'm more inclined to objectivity and fact. But even if it were true, and Amron might find himself miraculously healed by the will of a fallen god, he'd still have to get there first. I'd love to know how you think that's possible, Amara, with the sundry terrors that clot the way. Once that route was well protected, but for centuries now it's been left unattended and given over to the wilds." He blasted out a breath, gulped a mouthful of wine to refuel, then continued. "And that's to say nothing of the matter of navigating those caves and tunnels of yours. I'll not have Amron joining the *countless* skeletons there, as you put it. It would be a wholly unbecoming end for such a man as he."

"Oh, I agree entirely, Artibus. You think I want Amron to go marching off on such a foolish endeavour?" She laughed. "No no, of course not. You know how I like to play devil's advocate; that's all this is. A spirited discussion, no more."

Artibus looked at her closely, unsure. "Well I...I would hope that's the case. I feared you were going to quote me Galin Lukar next, to back up your point."

"Did you now? I hadn't actually thought of that, though since you mention it, King Galin *did* travel there too, I suppose."

Amron found himself smiling, against his better judgement, as he sat watching the two. Galin Lukar was Janilah's direct ancestor, - and thus distantly related to Amara as well - and had been the serving First Blade of Vandar when he abandoned the kingdom, gathered up his army in East Vandar, and marched on Tukor to conquer it for his house. It was said that a secret journey to Vandar's Tomb had precipitated that venture. To some, it was to seek the strength to triumph against the Tukoran army, and successfully siege the great city of Ilithor. To others, he did it to secure Vandar's blessing, and assuage his guilt at abandoning his own kingdom. Either way, like with Sir Oswald, the plan had borne considerable fruit.

"He *allegedly* travelled there," Artibus corrected, unwilling to be won over. "These stories get so warped over time that it's impossible to put any faith in them. And as I've already implied, reaching the mountain was immeasurably more simple then, when it was being mined for godsteel. Galin Lukar's journey there would have been three hundred years ago - if it ever actually happened - when mining operations were still ongoing. If I recall correctly, they ended soon after, and very few people have gone there since."

"True," nodded Amara, smiling easily. "Though I've read an account or two of others who braved the route, and came out declaring themselves blessed by a god. What must it be like, I wonder, to bask in such a profoundly powerful presence? I can see why people would be enticed by it, despite the dangers. There are worse reasons to risk one's life, Artibus."

"Yes, if you're at your wit's end or have nothing to live for, perhaps. That's why these stories breed so enthusiastically among the commoners. You work with the poor, Amara, and know how desperate many are down in the Lowers. They cling to hope wherever they can find it. But such notions have no place in this castle, nor in the mind of its lord." Artibus looked to Amron with a final word of appeal. "Please, do reconsider this, Amron. I know you're struggling, but suicide is not the answer, and let us be quite clear: that is all this is."

The old physician fell silent with those words, and Amara, for once, didn't fill the space. They both looked to Amron, who'd sat in quiet observation, listening to their debate. It had gone largely as expected. Other than Amara's faith in the fables, they both seemed to agree that the enterprise would be too risky.

"I thank you for your counsel," he said after a short period of reflection. "I will admit, this thought has been with me for some weeks, and has at times had me close to the saddle. There is but one thing that has held me back - Lillia. I'll not go without her blessing, and have come to see that even asking for it is unfair. I cannot expect her to make that decision." He looked at them in turn. "Thank you again. Your words are what I needed."

He stood at that, took up his crutch, and ambled his way out of the room. He didn't need the crutch, really, though it was less painful to walk with it under his arm. Down through the castle he went, navigating its echoing halls and corridors, so stripped now of the laughter and music and mirth they'd once held. Those who remained here - the courtiers and loyal attendants of the house - moved about the place so solemnly, and even they had become but a few. Some had gone to war. Others had been driven off by the ghosts that now haunted these halls. Others still had decided to swear allegiance to rival houses, as though sensing already that House Daecar was approaching ruin.

Is that what this is? Is this the slow death of my house? Am I to preside over its fall? Amron's thoughts cluttered miserably as he walked down through the keep. For years he'd been the de facto ruler of Vandar, peerless as a warrior and politically revered besides. Now both were gone, and across his hereditary lands in the northwest of the kingdom, even some of his vassals were beginning to lose faith in him.

It might just be that I'll travel there anyway, he thought, *at least for a time.* The Daecar lands spread across a large swathe of Vandar around the North Downs, centred at the castle-town of Blackfrost, the ancestral seat of House Daecar. Usually, he'd travel there regularly and attend to the knightly houses and lords who lived upon his lands, governing the many towns and estates in the region. It was an important part of his obligations as Lord of House Daecar, and one he'd been neglecting of late. If he were to stop the rot, and keep the wolves from the door, he'd need to make an appearance. *My people need reassuring,* he thought. *They need to know that this house will survive these troubles, and come through them as strong as ever...*

He continued on in thought, until eventually the sound of laboured breaths, of huffing and puffing, caught in his ears. He shambled quietly down a corridor, not wanting to interrupt, and entered onto the terraces overlooking the training yard of Keep Daecar. Down below, Lillia and young Jovyn were sparring, the boy taking her through a few drills taught to him by Elyon. Amron kept to the shadows, standing beside a pillar beneath the shaded canopy above. The yard was open, lit by the soft caress of moonlight, the skies crisp and clear above. Around it, set upon the walls, lanterns warmed with firelight, casting shadows through which the two youngsters danced.

A soft smile gripped at Amron's lips as he watched his daughter train. She was good. So good he felt more pride than sorrow at that moment, and yet within that pride was a sadness that he'd never let her train before. No, it wasn't the custom here, but what harm was there in a noble girl learning to defend herself? Lady Melany had, after all, a discovery that Amron and Elyon had made the very night Aleron died. If she could, why not Lillia? She'd never be a knight, or march to war, but surely she'd be better served with a few inches of godsteel tucked away among her clothes?

"Do you think she might try to go with you?" came a voice to his side. He startled at the suddenness of it and turned to find Amara drawing from the shadow of the corridor. Her eyes were on Lillia, speeding around the yard, kicking up dust in her wake as she blazed a trail across the sands. "Is that why you're afraid to tell her? You believe she'll follow you on your quest?"

Amron turned back to look at his daughter. "She might," he admitted quietly. "But I'd never let her, nor see her come to harm. I want to protect her, Amara, but how can I, as I am?" His brow crinkled regretfully. "She doesn't look at me like she used to," he said, a pain in his voice. "I see it, more each day I do. She used to gaze at me like I was a hero, like I was Varin himself reborn. I know it sounds foolish, but I...I miss that. And that look in her eyes...it's the way the world sees me now. Just a cripple in need of their pity. I don't know how to be that person. I thought I did, but I don't."

Her arms moved around him, and before he knew it, she was taking his great body into a tight embrace. "She loves you, Amron," she said into his ear, up on her toes to reach his towering height. "She loves you more than she ever has before. I promise you, she does."

You promise, he thought. *You promise and you lie.* But still he smiled wanly to those words in thanks as he drew back from her, then said, "I'm thinking of travelling to Blackfrost. Our people need reassuring. I was wondering..." He cleared the lump from his throat. “I was wondering whether you and Lillia would like to come too?"

Her lips were in an immediate smile. "I can think of little I'd like more, and I'm sure Lillia would say the same. Though..." She looked to the yard. "Best bring young Jovyn along too. It's a long enough journey without distraction and we both know how she gets. She'll need someone with whom she can let off some steam. Jovyn will do nicely. He can keep her company on the road."

Amron narrowed his eyes on the boy. "And what company does he intend, I wonder?" he said, with the cynicism of a protective father. "I suppose you've seen how he looks at her?"

"Every boy his age looks at her like that, and many others besides. He's fourteen, Amron, and Lillia is a rare beauty. What do you expect?"

"I know just what to expect. I was fourteen myself once, after all. And that's what concerns me."

"Well it shouldn't. Not with him. And are you sure you were ever fourteen? I had the impression you were sculpted from stone and brought to life as the full-grown man you are.” She grinned, then looked back to the yard. “Don’t worry about the boy. He adores Elyon and is scared stiff of you. He'd never dream of putting a hand on her, if that's what you're suggesting."

Amron turned to look at the two of them again. "You were saying?"

At that very moment, Jovyn just happened to have his hands on Lillia's sword arm, instructing her on the right posture for a particular type of thrust. Amara laughed, though quietly enough so the two didn't hear them. "An ill-timed comment on my part," she said. ”So, when do you plan on leaving? I'd counsel a quick getaway personally, with winter fast approaching."

"Well I don't see that there's much keeping us here right now." Amron hid the bitterness from his voice, though inside it burned hot as coals. "I'm sure Lord Taynar has the governance of this city in hand, and can do without me for a few weeks."

"Let's be honest, Amron, he can do without you *forever*. As soon as you're gone, he'll throw his hands to the skies and rejoice, I'm certain of it. And so will I truth be told." She sighed nostalgically. "I've not visited Blackfrost in some years now, though can't be sure with all the wine I've drunk tonight. It will be nice to see the North Downs again regardless. I miss those rolling heights, especially when coated white for winter."

"Well then I suppose it's settled. We can leave on the morrow, if you can manage your affairs in time?" He was referring mostly to her work with the poor, though that could easily be handed off to others while she was gone. She nodded her agreement, and a rarely chipper smile moved onto Amron's lips. "Good, then I'll have word sent to Lord Taynar," he said, adding a note of humour to his voice, "so he can make arrangements for the party."

Amara frowned, apparently not getting his meaning.

"You know…because I'm leaving?" He vented a tired sigh. "It was meant to be a joke. Or have I lost my humour too, along with the use of my left arm?"

Amara patted him sympathetically on that very limb. "Amron, sweet brother, you never had any humour to lose."

She grinned in a gloriously playful way, coiled her arm around his, and led him away back into the castle, to leave the youngsters to train in peace.

4

Elyon

Elyon Daecar perched on the lip of a broad stone windowsill in the fortress of Eastwatch, enjoying the cooling effects of the wintry breeze at his back.

The chamber to which he'd been summoned was warm to the point of stifling, with three separate hearths burning bright and an unnecessary number of candles melting eagerly around the room. It was, of course, by King Ellis Reynar's order. The man didn't only dislike the cold, he had an aversion to it that bordered on lunacy.

All cloaks had been discarded, hung on hooks near the large arched door, where an attendant stood in diligent preparedness to hand them back out when the meeting was done. These meetings had become a daily occurrence over the past two weeks on the road, taken in the great castles and forts and lordly estates littered along the route from Varinar. Their purpose was always the same - to discuss the most recent news about the war, and whatever gains and advances the Tukorans had made. Despite the exciting nature of the topic, they were generally quite banal affairs under the officiation of King Ellis, who had no skill whatsoever as a war leader.

We'll be rid of him soon, Elyon thought, looking at the king as he settled into his seat at the head of the rich ebony table, wrapped in luxuriant cerulean robes. In the morning, the king was to part ways with the host and venture northwest to Ilithor to treat with King Janilah, taking Sir Nathaniel Oloran, the new Commander of the Greycloaks, and several others with him. Elyon raised a little grin at the thought. *I doubt Janilah will be so eager to tend to his quirks,* he mused. *And Ilithor gets bitterly cold during winter, or so I hear.*

The shuffling continued as the small assembly arranged themselves around the table, positioned at the heart of the warmly furnished room. It was a parlour, really, set up high within the upper reaches of Eastwatch Castle, fit with a generous collection of unholstered armchairs and trestle tables and thick red rugs on the grey stone floor. Knowing Ellis's preference for furnace-like temperatures, Elyon had made swiftly for the single window, where the high setting allowed for a pleasant breeze to ease its way through the opening. It also provided a fine view over the fortress and surrounding grounds, and ranging lands beyond. Though night was coming swiftly upon them now, the faint shadow of the great, monolithic statues of Tukor's Pass could just about be seen, soaring into the cloud-cloaked skies away on the eastern horizon.

The meeting began. As ever, King Ellis opened proceedings with an interest in hearing the latest reports. Elyon yawned. So did several others. Still, Vesryn, as newly appointed First Blade, set into a dutiful summary of what he'd discovered from the crows.

"Prince Rylian's siege of Shellcrest has been completed and he's taken full possession of the city," he began. "Overtures have been made further down the coast, though skirmishes are few and far between at this point. The Rasals continue to retreat from the fighting when they know they have little hope of victory, and are amassing in their cities and forts to take advantage of their defences." Vesryn shuffled through a few scrolls, laid out before him. "Several hundred more men were lost yesterday, including a small host of Emerald Guards. It seems most of them fell during the fighting in Shellcrest, though reports of poisonings appear to have grown more common too."

A few bitter groans went out. Everyone knew that the Rasalanians loved their tricks and potions and poisons were among them. It wasn't a pleasant way to go, not for a fighting man who expected to fall by blade or bow.

"Are the tasters not doing their jobs?" queried his uncle Rikkard, as he sat languidly back in his chair, stretching after a long day's ride. "Surely they have them, to make sure the food and wine is safe?"

Vesryn continued to look over the scrolls. "It seems there was a particular breakout at a feast, once Shellcrest was taken," he explained. "A hundred men were lost, it says, on account of a few contaminated barrels of ale. A parting gift from the Rasals before they fled..."

"Poison is the weapon of women and the weak," Sir Dalton Taynar interrupted in a clipped, spiteful voice. "We'd best grow wise to this tactic, and soon, Vesryn. I echo Sir Rikkard's query - why are the tasters not doing their jobs? It's the only one they have, and it isn't exactly difficult."

Not difficult, but certainly risky, Elyon thought. He could hardly imagine a more unpleasant role than acting taster to some lofty lord or knight, wondering whether the next bite of bread or sip of wine would have them doubled over, spewing blood.

Vesryn gave Sir Dalton a wary look. There was a tension between the two, one that had been present, and growing, throughout the trip. The reason was really rather simple. Sir Dalton resented Vesryn for claiming the post of First Blade by default, and commonly questioned him in a bid to undermine his authority. Sir Brontus Oloran occasionally did the same, though was of a more pleasant disposition than the Taynar heir. It was no surprise that they were the two most vocal. The two of them had been the losing semi finalists in the Song of the First Blade, after all, and both felt they had the better claim to be leading the Varin Knights than Vesryn.

"You'll have to pose that question to Prince Rylian when we reach Rasalan, Sir Dalton," Vesryn said after a short pause. "There is no answer in these scrolls, though by all means, read through them yourself if you wish." He gestured to push them down the table, but Sir Dalton didn't react. "I presume the men broke into the barrels without thinking and duly lost their lives for the trouble," Vesryn went on. "Men can be too hasty after a victory, and think the danger is done. That isn't always so. And they paid the price for that oversight."

"Well I hope your men won't be so foolish, Lord Kanabar," came the king's nasally voice. He snickered and looked to the large figure of Wallis Kanabar, Lord of the Riverlands, who'd been tasked with assembling the army here at Eastwatch. "We can ill afford to lose good fighting men to poison, can we? What a waste. And to shed a hundred in one go?" He clicked his tongue. "It doesn't bear thinking about."

"No indeed," rumbled Lord Kanabar's deep bass voice. He was father to Sir Borrus and much like his son in size and character, a burly old man with a deep red beard and bald head who'd lived war all his life. "But let me put your concerns to rest, Your Majesty. The men of East Vandar are the best fighting men in all the kingdom, hardier than those northerners up near the Weeping Heights, and a damn sight more gritty than the men of the Ironmoors. Iron may be the moors, but not the men who dwell upon them." He laughed to himself, and sped an eye toward Sir Dalton, a man of the Ironmoors himself. "Just look at you, Sir Dalton, miserable and grim and skinny as a harpoon." He patted his belly, and Elyon smiled. Borrus had clearly taken that particular habit from his gregarious father. "We breed them bigger over here. Feed a man well and he'll fight that little bit harder, I always say. And lest we forget, we protect two borders down this way, both north and south…and south is worse. For hundreds of years we've kept watch over Death's Passage and held the swarthy Agarathi hordes at bay. Rest assured, young king, the men I've mustered are not to be unmanned by some Rasal trickery. They'll fight well and fight true. It's just a shame you won't be there to see it."

Ellis made a little awkward chuckle. He was no fighter, and had no skill with the blade, quite unlike his father and grandfather before him. "I'm sure you'll send me ample report, Lord Kanabar, as I treat with King Janilah in Ilithor," he said eventually, a little blush warming his cheeks. "I leave the army in your capable hands." He smiled uncomfortably, pulling at the lanky tuft of hair he'd been growing on his chin. "So what of the siege of Harrowmoor?" he asked, shifting into a pose that he probably considered regal. He began drumming his fingers on the wooden table. "Any further news on whether Prince Rylian intends to assault the fortress soon? Or are they waiting for us to arrive to share in the slaughter?"

"I believe that is the current plan," said Vesryn, sitting on the king's right flank. Beside him, leaning against the rough-carved wooden table, was the gleaming Sword of Varinar. His struggles to master it had continued on the journey thus far, though he was gradually getting a better handle on its power. "If we're allied to the Tukorans, we'll be expected to pay our share of blood. Sieging Harrowmoor will not be simple, and Northgate even less so, lest the rivers freeze solid enough for us to cross, and that hasn't happened in a hundred years." He shook his head. "Prince Rylian won't march on Harrowmoor until we've joined them, of that I'm sure."

"I agree," said Sir Killian Oloran, in that soft, spidery voice of his. "It makes no sense for the Tukorans to waste men in the siege when we're so near." He sat upright in his chair, closest to the nearest hearth, though didn't seem so troubled by the heat as the rest. "I presume Lord Kastor will have cleared the lands south of Harrowmoor by the time we arrive? Any further news in that regard?"

Vesryn shuffled back through the rolls of parchment, searching for the latest from Kastor's camp. The two Tukoran armies had been taking on different roles over the last fortnight, with Rylian driving the assault of Shellcrest and the coastal fortifications, and Kastor tasked with clearing the southern Lowplains in preparation for the siege of Harrowmoor.

"Several more towns have been razed in the area, as well as a host of smaller settlements," Vesryn said, scanning the notes. "A few dozen losses have been reported by the Tukorans. Not many, all regular soldiers. It suggests that these towns are largely undefended. Not surprising, with the Rasals running for their forts."

"Then why are they being attacked?" Elyon found himself asking. The eyes of the room moved to the window where he perched. "If these settlements pose no threat, then is it really necessary to burn down people's homes and kill their men?"

Vesryn drew a breath. "Unpalatable as it may be, Elyon, these towns and settlements must be cleared of threats to ease our northern advance," he said. "I'm assured by Lord Kastor that the commoners are not being killed without cause, and that only those who elect to fight back are being slain."

"If you pick up a sword in anger then that makes you a threat," added Sir Dalton. "Whether trained or not, Bladeborn or not, you cannot expect to be handled with care if you swing a sword or loose a shaft from a bow on an enemy. That's war, Sir Elyon. Once you live through one or two you become desensitised to the injustices of it. A man who bears arms against you needs to be put down. It is no more complicated than that."

"One or two, Sir Dalton?" asked Vesryn. "I recall you were but a teen when we fought the War of the Continents. Pray tell what other war you've fought in."

"It was a figure of speech, my lord. And though not quite a war, I've fought to defend my father's lands across the Ironmoors from bandits quite often, so you know."

"Bandits?" Vesryn held his smile. "Well now, forgive me. I had no idea you'd warred against such formidable foes."

Sir Dalton's expression remained resolutely unmoved. "At least I've drawn my sword these last two decades, Vesryn. That's more than one can say about you."

"If drawing a blade against bandits is the benchmark, then I meet it every night when I cut at my steak," came the First Blade's swift retort. "Bandits pose no threat to men like us. If anything, I'd say that a piece of bloody meat is more perilous; I might choke on it, after all." His smile broke out. "I risk more when I eat my dinner than you do drawing steel on poor and broken men."

"So sympathy, is it? For bandits?" Sir Dalton shook his head in rebuke. "They are not poor and broken men but vagabonds and thieves and a whole lot worse. And there are occasionally Bladeborn among them too, bastards and deserters and the like. A challenge? No, of course not, but a damn sight more deadly than you and your hunk of beef."

"Yes…if you say so, Sir Dalton," dismissed Vesryn. He waved his hand and turned away, looking back to the king. These sorts of exchanges had grown common between them, little squabbles that were often petty in tone. "Anyway, to my report," he said briskly, moving things along. He looked over the small pieces of parchment again, took a moment to compose his thoughts, and then continued to delineate the latest dispatches.

It went on for a while. It always did, largely due to the many questions the king posed, digging into details as though he thought that was what a good ruler should do. He seemed to think it made him seem shrewd and venerable, when in reality all he was doing was wasting everyone's time. Elyon's mind drifted. That always happened too. He shifted sideways on the windowsill and stared out over the lands. The army was in camp just outside the fortress, twenty thousand swords, a larger Vandarian host than Elyon had ever seen. Yet they were only a fraction of the full yield of men that the kingdom could muster. Elyon's father had told him that during the war, the Vandarian army swelled to almost two hundred thousand strong at its zenith. The Tukorans added a further hundred thousand to that number, and the Rasals - when they finally joined their northern allies - added many tens of thousands more. The full weight of men boggled his mind.

Imagine seeing a battle of that scale, he thought, staring over the darkened plains, trying to picture such a thing. There had been over two hundred and fifty thousand men at the Battle of Burning Rock, some estimates said, a number swollen by the southern forces and their horses and dragons and mounted beasts; the sunwolves and starcats that the Lightborn of Lumara rode. It had gone on for hours and hours, the slaughter unimaginable, and in the end, it had all been for nought. The battle. The war. Nothing had come of it but death. Some lords and kings rose, and others fell, and a few territories and tracts of lands were won, lost, then won and lost again. In the end, everyone ended up largely where they'd started. It was futile, and yet… *and yet here we are again, falling back into the very same trap, approaching another Renewal.*

The sound of scraping chairs drew Elyon's attention and he found the members of the privy council standing. His thoughts had taken him through the end of the meeting, though thankfully, it hadn't lasted as long as usual. Sir Dalton stalked quickly from the room, trailed soon after by Killian and Lord Kanabar. The hefty old lord had his arm over Killian's shoulder, and was in uproar about something, belly-laughing as he went. *Probably sharing an anecdote about Borrus,* Elyon imagined. Killian wasn't short of them, and despite his quiet voice, had a knack for telling tales.

Vesryn remained seated, along with Sir Nathaniel. They looked to be going over some final matters before parting the following day. That left Rikkard, who made a beeline for Elyon as soon as he'd gathered his cloak. "You looked enthralled there, Elyon. Truly riveted. Getting bored of these daily meetings perchance?"

"Am I that obvious, Uncle?" Elyon said, weary.

"You couldn't have been more obvious if you'd thrown yourself from the window. Don't worry, we all feel it. Wars sound fun and exciting in theory, but for the most part, it's a lot of old men talking. Talking and waiting and then, finally…the fight!" He hooked an arm over Elyon's shoulders and began pulling him toward the door. "And after the fight, then we drink. We drink, we laugh, we dance and sing and find women to warm our beds." He grinned. Rikkard had an eye for the ladies, and why wouldn't he, handsome and roguish as he was. It was only ever talk now, though. He had a wife and young children back home in Ilivar, and would never act upon his lascivious suggestions.

They continued toward the door, as the attendant handed Elyon his cloak. "Speaking of which, how are you faring with that fine Lady Melany?" Rikkard continued. "Still off the girl, are we? You hardly spend any time with her at all, Elyon. And I must warn you - I've seen Lancel and Barnibus sniffing around, hoping to turn her eye." He peered at Elyon as they continued down the stone corridor, escaping the sweltering heat. "You don't seem unduly concerned. I thought you were more serious about this one?"

Elyon was thinking of Melany's lips, the curve of her bust, her hips. He was thinking of the time they'd shared in her bed. But more than that, he was thinking of the conversations they'd had. It had been about much more than the physical side with her.

"She's returning to Ilithor, Uncle," Elyon said eventually. They began working down the spiral stone staircase, heading for the great hall. "We decided back in Varinar that furthering our courtship would be pointless on the road. It was only ever a dalliance. We both knew that from the start."

"Yes, I suppose you did, and more than ever now that you're heir to House Daecar." A coldness bled through Elyon's veins. *I never wanted that. I never wanted any of this.* "I'd wager your lord father wishes to pair you with someone more suitable. I don't suppose you'd ever consider Princess Amilia, were she offered to you?"

Elyon might once have ripped off his own sword arm for the pleasure, but the idea stirred nothing but sadness in him now. "She was promised to Aleron. He loved her, and she him. I'd never try to take his place, nor would Father ever ask me to."

On they went, until the noise of the feast began to spread through the corridors. Eastwatch was lively that night, and the hall was heaving with men set to march to war. It was to be their last great feast before they reached Rasalan and they were sure to make the most of it.

"I meant no insult, Elyon," Rikkard said, after a minute of silence had passed. "Perhaps it was insensitive of me to bring the topic up so soon."

"It's OK, Uncle. I took no offence."

He didn't want to talk about it. He turned forward and made that clear enough, though Rikkard continued to watch him. "You're becoming more like your father every day," he then said. "He ran from his grief when my sister died. I tried to speak to him about it, many times I did, but he would never open up. I suppose only Lythian managed that." He softened his voice. "Don't be the same, Elyon. I love and respect your father enormously, but that part of him…" He shook his head. "I don't consider it healthy to bottle everything up. So…if you want to talk, I'm here. I suppose that's all I'm saying."

Elyon stopped and turned to him, looking into his twinkly brown eyes. The likeness to his mother always startled him when he really looked for it, and they were alike in spirit too. Caring to the core. Generous and noble, and unerringly kind. "I appreciate it, Uncle, truly, but I'm fine," he said. "I know how that sounds; like I'm trying to dodge the issue, as Father had, but it's true. Aleron sits with Varin now, and I'll see him one day soon. Just… hopefully not too soon." He unleashed a grin. It didn't feel so natural anymore.

"No, not for many years yet, Nephew. You have a long and illustrious life to lead first, before you recount it all in your death." Rikkard shook Elyon's arm, smiled and strolled on, the noise of the great hall growing more boisterous as they went. "But just so you know, talking isn't the only way to let off steam, or unburden a weight from one's shoulders. There are other crutches we can lean on." They entered into the feast hall, pushing through the thick oak doors, and looked upon the gathering. This was no feast, really, but a party, an event for drinking not eating, with little formality to it at all. Through the mass of bodies, Rikkard's eyes searched, and a moment later he found his quarry. "This may be your last chance to be with her, Elyon. Don't deny yourself the opportunity."

Elyon followed Rikkard's gaze across the hall, to where Melany stood with several other ladies, keeping their own counsel, and fending off the approaches of the men around them. They swirled like vultures above a kill, but seemed to be getting nowhere, as Mel stood amid the buffer of ladies, eyes down, in quiet thought. Elyon stared at her. She looked stunning, yet demure, mournful as she stood there. "Let off some steam with her, Elyon," came a final word from Rikkard. "By the gods, you both look like you need it. Don't waste this night down here, getting drunk with the men. Enjoy one another. Just one last time. I promise, you'll feel better for it in the morning."

He smiled, patted Elyon on the back, and strolled away, leaving the young Daecar to ponder his advice. And so Elyon stood there amongst the revelry, assaulted by the smell of ale and the tuneless crooning of drunken men, and caught eyes with her for the first time in days. Those beautiful blue eyes, sparkling beneath that waterfall of golden hair. He stepped forward, unable to resist it, driven by Rikkard's words. Barnibus and Lancel were there among the vultures, circling, and ready to swoop. Elyon pressed forward and moved past them, through all the men, through all the women - he'd walk through a stone wall if he had to - and stopped before her.

He dipped his head, setting forward his right foot, bowing as a gentleman should. Yet the first words to exit his mouth weren't gentlemanly at all. Nor were the thoughts pushing up from the darkness of his mind. "One more night," he said, and his meaning was quite clear. "We have one more night, Mel." He smiled. "Let's not waste it here."

When she smiled back, he felt alive again.

For the first time in weeks, he felt alive.

5

Lythian

Captain Lythian Lindar waited patiently upon the balcony of his prison quarters within the eight-faced Palace of Eldurath, looking to the murky skies. It was a muggy night, the air thick with a damp mist, visibility poor. Below, five floors down, the sprawling sandstone city stretched out, melting into the soupy fog. It was late, dark, and almost unnervingly quiet. Eldurath was sleeping, but Lythian was not. He had important work to do.

"Where is he?" whispered Borrus, standing at Lythian's side, eyes scanning skyward. "The night is on the wane, Lythian. We won't get a better chance than this, not with the fogs so thick."

Lythian drew a breath, anxious. "He'll be here, Borrus. Be patient."

A shift in the fogs above drew their attention, the air rippling, swirling, before suddenly a flock of birds rushed through in a burst of flapping wings. It wasn't what they were hoping to see. A rather larger winged creature was meant to be paying a visit.

Borrus vented an impatient sigh. "You don't think they've backed out, do you?" the Barrel Knight suggested. "I'd not put it past them to bottle it at the final moment. If they'd wanted Prince Tavash dead this much, they'd have done it themselves a long time ago. Screw their oaths of honour. What honour is there in having us do their dirty work?"

"There is no *us*, Borrus, not tonight," Lythian reminded him. "You need do nothing but sit here and wait. When the palace falls to chaos, you'll know I've done my job."

My job, he thought. *My job of killing a foreign prince.* That had been the deal they made, two weeks ago, when Kin'rar Kroll and Ulrik Marak, the infamous Lord of the Nest, had come to them seeking their aid. The bargain was simple. Lythian was to assassinate Prince Tavash, and free the kingdom from his warmongering grip. In return, the brewing conflict between north and south would be averted, and Lythian and his companions would be provided safe passage back to Varinar.

"Your job," Borrus muttered, shaking his head. "A job you should never have been assigned. You are a captain of the Knights of Varin, Lythian, not some seamy cutthroat. Honour? Please. What honour is there in killing a man as he sleeps? That is murder, no more, and they should never have put this burden on you." His eyes scanned above them again. "And where the bloody hell is he!"

The slick Skymaster was an hour past due and each minute lost was one they'd never get back. Lythian needed the cover of night and mist to make good on his part of the deal. He'd been provided the details he needed to see the job done, and had put into place his plans. Unfortunately, he'd be able to do nothing without his godsteel dagger. And that was where Kin'rar came in.

"Maybe he didn't manage to get into the armoury?" Tomos suggested. He was wearing his rich red jerkin as though expecting trouble, and had fashioned a short spear from the wooden leg of a chair. It wouldn't do much against men bearing steel, but still, Lythian appreciated the endeavour. "He might have been caught trying to fetch your dagger, Lythian. It'll be as heavy as a broadsword to Kin'rar, and not easy to sneak away with."

"He assured us himself he'd manage it. I have no reason to doubt him, Tom."

"Then why the delay?" asked Borrus. "Has he got lost in these mists or something?"

"I don't know, Borrus. He'll be here soon."

"Well he'd better. Because if he's caught, then it won't take long for them to find out what he's been up to, and our part in all this seedy business will be quickly unveiled. Do you have any idea how they execute people here in Eldurath, Lythian? They make creative use of their dragons, let's just put it that way."

"Like what?" asked Tomos, his ears pricking up. He looked worried and understandably so. Borrus was quite right. If Kin'rar was captured, they'd all be executed for collusion and conspiracy. *But that hardy alters our fate,* Lythian thought. He was of the strong belief that all three would be executed shortly anyway. This plan was all they had, and ignoble as it might be, Lythian had no choice but to see it through if he wanted them all to get home.

"Do you really want to know, Tom?" Borrus asked him, a few beads of sweat glistening on his bald head. "I'm sure you can guess at least one."

Tomos though a moment. "Burning by dragonfire?"

"Yes, that's the easy one, and the best we can hope for. It's quick, at least. Horrible while it lasts, but it doesn't last long. Like you beneath the sheets, Tom."

Tomos ignored the quip. "The others are slow then, I assume?" he quivered, glancing over the edge of the balcony. Lythian knew what he was thinking. *Better to throw myself off this terrace and be done with it, rather than suffer a slow and painful death.*

"Oh yes," Borrus said with a note of wicked glee. "One in particular is *terribly* slow. They have a wrought iron dragon here in the Golden Square; we passed it when we arrived...however long ago that was now. Anyway, it's hollow inside, and there's a small hatch at the bottom. Can you see where I'm going with this, Tom?"

Tomos was either being uncharacteristically doltish or simply didn't want to say.

Borrus continued. "What they do is...they force some poor bugger inside, lock the hatch, and then have a dragon blow fire on the thing until it gets nice and toasty. Everyone comes to watch and they bet on how long it'll take for the chap to roast to death. They use it for torture too, I'm told. If you see anyone shambling about with great welts and burns all over their body, you can probably guess where they've been."

Tomos looked over the edge again, with a little more intent this time.

"Then of course there's their own particular brand on flaying and dismembering, using dragons of course. They get some of the smaller ones to...well, putting it simply...to eat you alive. They start by stripping off ribbons of skin and flesh, nibbling on fingers and toes and ears and the like. Then, onto the bigger parts. And all the while, those fiendish little lizards will blow fire to cauterise the wounds so you don't bleed out. Makes it last longer, you see, Tom. They're remarkably skilled at it, or so I've heard. Smart creatures, really, to understand all that. I never appreciated just how intelligent they were until we came here."

"Everyone knows that dragons are bright," put in Lythian. "They're just as clever as many humans, some say, and a great deal more so than others." He didn't mention it, but imagined there were a few winged beasts out there that could best Borrus in a game of wits. "I'm curious, though, as to where you're getting all of this from? I've never known you as a scholar of Agarathi culture, Borrus."

"No, but I've a macabre interest in all the devious ways people devise to kill one another. I heard about these ones during the garden parties we attended with all those flowery, perfumed nobles. They were only too happy to share the particulars of their torture and execution methods with me. I can't think why."

He smirked wryly and scratched at his chin, which was sprouting with a patchy rusted beard. Borrus was oddly accoutred when it came to bodily hair. He'd gone completely bald in his early twenties, just like his father Wallis, and had never been able to grow a full beard, yet had a great thatch of hair upon his chest that more than made up for it. "So Tom, tell me - which would you choose?" It seemed he wasn't quite done with the topic. "Obviously, the burning by dragonfire is the clear winner if given a choice, but what of the other two? Slow-roasted alive in the belly of an iron dragon, or feasted on living by a litter of little drakes?"

Tomos looked reluctant to answer, but to Lythian there was

absolutely no debate. "Roasted alive, surely," he said, finding himself drawn into Borrus's game. "You'd probably pass out from the heat relatively quickly, and that would be that. I can hardly imagine the terror and agony of being slowly eaten alive."

He felt a shudder move up his spine. *Blasted Borrus, making us think of such things*. But that was his way, and it was a bumpy road. He often posed questions like this to entertain himself during the long days of boredom they'd endured locked away in their fine quarters in the palace, and to be fair to him, many of them had been welcome. Just not this one. And certainly not right now.

Lythian turned away from the two of them, taking a step toward the edge of the balcony, as Borrus continued to elucidate several other torture techniques involving the inventive use of dragons. He was only just getting started when Lythian's ears caught with a distinct *whumping* sound, away in the eastern skies. He turned and looked up, narrowing his eyes, and there in the fog he saw it; the shadow of a dragon in flight, beating its wings, speeding their way.

Borrus's voice was swiftly cut off as the others turned to watch. Neyruu came fast, pinning her wings back a little, forming into a graceful, streamlined shape as she reached the right altitude and came swooping down toward them. Astride her was Kin'rar, a grey shape on her back, low down to reduce drag, his cape flapping dramatically in the winds. Lythian had come to admire the pair and the obvious bond they shared, and seeing them now, he couldn't help but smile. *About bloody time, Kin'rar. Pushing it a little close, aren't we?*

They arrived within mere moments, gliding right over the balcony in a flash, cutting a path through the fog as the air parted and swirled in their wake. Lythian caught sight of a glint of silver clutched within Neyruu's curved, eagle-like talons. The claws opened up as she passed overhead. Her aim was true. The package fell swiftly and landed, *thumping* heavily onto the stone floor. And then, just like that, dragon and rider were gone.

"Well...that was all very efficient," Borrus said appreciatively, as Lythian sped forward to pick up the sheathed blade.

His fingers gripped the hilt of the dagger, and he drew it out with a gentle *ring*. A breath of profound comfort...of *relief* escaped him as he looked upon the eight inch length of misting, mystical metal. There was nothing...absolutely nothing like the touch of godsteel. Not since he first trained with it as a boy had he been denied its embrace so long. *I missed you, dear friend. Oh how I missed you.*

His vision cleared. His ears opened. Across the city, sights and sounds bloomed to life. Lythian, like all great Bladeborn, was blessed with finely attuned senses when bearing Ilithian Steel. Combined with his extreme agility, speed, and balance, they made him uniquely adapted to stealth.

He looked up, searching the edifice as it rose a hundred floors into the curdled skies. There were balconies on almost every level and with godsteel to hand, the building would be scalable. There was no time to lose. He swiftly attached the sheath to his belt, gripping the handle tight between his fingers. He'd spent days charting a route, and with the intel Kin'rar had reported, knew exactly where to go.

He turned to the others. They were looking at him anxiously; even Borrus appeared subdued. No words were shared, nor were they needed. Lythian gave his two companions a bracing nod.

Then turning to the outer wall of the palace, he began the climb…

The route grew more perilous the higher he went. The balconies that gave him rest became fewer, the facade sheer, as though sanded smooth by the increasingly violent winds as they whipped and blustered about him. Below they'd been tame, no more than a soft breeze rustling through the fog, but up here they blew hard and unrelenting, pulling at his clothes and limbs as though aware of his illicit intentions.

He clung like a limpet, refusing to part ways with the stone, and on several occasions thought he might have been bested...but no. Each time he found salvation in his godsteel, and the preternatural sense of touch it gave him. In his fingers there was strength, strength enough to hold his weight without effort. He needed but a crack or crevice in which to slip a single finger, and there were enough of those, even in the most difficult sections, to keep him going in the right direction.

Don't look down, he thought, recalling the mantra of all those who found themselves in high, precarious places. *Just don't look down, Lythian...*

He failed. On far too many occasions, as he ventured higher and higher, did he send a glance toward the foggy nothingness below, trying to remember how many floors he'd scaled. There were over a hundred, he knew, but even with his sight enhanced by godsteel, there was no seeing through this suffocating smog. Below and above, the building bled into the void. It looked to go on forever, as though he was climbing to the very heavens themselves, before eventually, after what seemed like an eternity, he broke through the veil and came upon a quite astonishing sight.

He stopped for a moment to take stock, clinging to the side of a high balcony toward the summit of the great tower. The palace was so tall it broke through the sea of fog, the final two dozen floors soaring above the soggy canopy that coated the city below. A few other buildings were of wondrous verticality too, their peaks poking out from the dun-hued mire like the tips of icebergs from the frozen sea. But none took to the skies as the eight-faced palace did, towering imperiously above all others. And at its summit the great golden dragon of Eldurath perched, its red jewelled eyes ever watchful against the clear, star-strewn skies.

The view was breathtaking, an ethereal world above that which lay below, yet he couldn't let himself be drawn to its wonders. His eyes swept across the night skies, up into the twinkling firmament, where the crescent moon glowed pink and pale. Within the mists he'd been safely concealed, but up here he was vulnerable. Guards patrolled these high passes of the palace and would commonly stand watch at the balconies. Yet there was a more pressing threat: dragons. Lythian had heard a few that night, their echoing calls ripping through the air. They seemed to keep a strong vigil over the city and palace, swooping past night and day whether carrying a Fireborn rider or not.

He took a moment to scan and listen for the distinctive sound of beating wings, but heard nothing. Pulling the hood of his cloak over his head to better conceal himself against the sandstone wall, he continued on. The cloak was tan in colour and a close match for the building, offering some level of camouflage. With a growing haste, he moved up toward a large balcony, a sprawling extension jutting from the outer palisade. It was another garden terrace, a colourful haven of flowers and plants and trestle walls coiling with vines. He clambered up and onto the terrace, taking a short break. A purple glow of predawn light was now edging upon the eastern horizon. Lythian drew a breath to steady himself. Dawn would bring the city to life and Prince Tavash with it. He had little time.

Scanning the route ahead, he saw that the final few floors would be the most difficult of all to pass, a sheer cliff of burnished stone without any noticeable imperfection. Tavash's private quarters took dominion over a large section of the palace, two levels down from King Dulian's personal apartments at the very summit, where he lived and held court beneath the palace's cone-shaped roof. A private balcony extending from Tavash's chambers would be Lythian's way in. He spotted it now, hoping his judgement was correct; Kin'rar had been assiduous in making sure Lythian knew exactly where he was going.

He narrowed his vision, searching for any flaw that might lend his fingers sufficient purchase to pull himself up. There were fewer blemishes here, the wearing effects of time seeming to have had no impact upon the stone. Yet above him, some twenty feet up and over halfway toward Tavash's balcony, he saw a single crack, a few millimetres wide, where two large blocks of sandstone met. It would have to do.

Dropping into a crouch, he drew upon his strength and thrust up in a powerful leap. With his left hand reaching for the fissure, he dug in with his fingertips, taking hold. At the same time, he stabbed with his right, plunging his godsteel dagger into the stone facade for additional support. Hanging there, suspended some twenty feet above the garden terrace, he turned his eyes up. A further ten foot gap remained to Tavash's balcony.

With the fingers of his left hand embedded into the narrow crevice, he pulled out his godsteel dagger, reached several feet higher, and drove it back into the wall. Hauling his weight up with his right hand, he withdrew his fingertips from the crevice and manoeuvred his left foot into the narrow gap instead. From there, he pushed upward, clearing the final stretch, and took ahold of the balcony wall, scrambling over the side and landing on the stone, panting, in a rather clumsy heap.

Standing, he shifted himself back into a more dignified stance and brushed himself down, refusing to look over the edge or offer further thought to how far he'd come. Instead, his eyes were drawn east, where the light was blossoming, those purples infused with vibrant shades of red. *Red for blood. Red for death,* Lythian thought, as he moved stealthily toward the arched entrance into Tavash's personal quarters. Without further delay, he crept inside, ghosting with a growing urgency to his target's bedchambers.

He moved down darkened corridors seared into his memory, turning left, right, left again. He knew the layout well from Kin'rar's reports and quickly confirmed he was in the right place. He took another turn into a larger room, fit with rugs, chairs, tables. He passed through, turning right, venturing down a wide corridor. The double doors at the end were open and there, right ahead, he could see the grand four-poster bed within the prince's bedchamber. The drapes were drawn around it, a deep crimson, yet light enough to show the shape of a figure within.

Lythian padded forward, silent as a shadow, driven by a single sordid task. He would deal with the distaste at assassinating a sleeping prince later. It went against his every ideal of honour and integrity, yet what choice did he have? To kill Tavash would install his sister, Talasha, as Queen Protector and how many lives might that save? If the edge of his blade should help avoid war, so be it. *My honour be damned,* he thought, as he stepped forward and drew aside the curtain. He brandished his knife, looking down at the figure beneath the blankets. *My function is to protect Vandar. And this man is a threat to us all.*

He moved into place to strike. The body was tucked up beneath a quilt of deep maroon, only the head and tangled charcoal hair visible above the blankets. Yet there was something...odd about the body position. He lay almost entirely prostrate, his face buried into a nest of soft silken pillows.

Lythian paused.

The figure wasn't breathing.

And then he smelled it. The iron. The blood. A frown carved itself across his brow and in an instant he was reaching and drawing away the quilt, pulling the body over, unveiling the terrible, horrifying truth. He stumbled back in shock. "My gods...no...no..."

Before him lay King Dulian, his throat sawn open, his bed soaked in scarlet. His atrophied legs were little more than bones covered in sallow skin, poking out from his night-garments. The once-white clothing was soaked red, the burning scent of blood surging now up Lythian's nose, rich and powerful and fresh. He had been killed only recently; it took him but a moment to realise by whom. And when the sound of movement came, Lythian knew that he'd been tricked.

He turned. Down the corridor, an armoured host were rushing, bearing their long black spears, their bodies wreathed in red and gold. Lythian darted his eyes around the chamber in search of some other way out. There was no exit but for the one clogging with guards, flowing swiftly into the room and taking position around him. There were a dozen, two, three. Too many to count. *Too many to kill.*

"Drop the knife!" called out their commander. "Drop it, Vandarian. There is no way out."

Lythian ignored the request. Like mist he moved forward on the attack as those long black lances came thrusting. Under them he went. Around them he went. With his godsteel knife, he cut them through and sent them clattering to the floor, spear shafts shattering, men calling out. He thrust and jabbed and punched his knife through breastplates and helms, and before anyone knew it, four were on the floor, dead, and the stink of iron burned hotter, and the cries of battle rung out through the chamber. Lythian took down another pair in an instant, yet still more came, bunching in the corridor, pressing forward, fearless.

He took pause, backing away a step. Shadows bled around

him, filling the space he left. There would be no way out. He sensed that quick enough. *But by the gods I'll take a few with me!* Several more suffered the sting of his blade, as the ring of steel sang out, and before long the floor was coated in blood and gore, guts and limbs. Lythian wasn't like Borrus; he had no interest in such grotesquery. Yet in him roared a rage unquenchable. *I have been tricked,* he thought, again and again, as he hacked and slashed and stabbed. *Was this Kin'rar's plan all along? To deceive me....to give them motive to start a war!*

He didn't know, nor would he likely find out. *There are too many. Too many for me alone.* The flood continued, the banks broken. The soldiers were swarming now like flies to the flame, pressing forward into the room. Spears were thrusting. Swords jabbing. The tip of a lance caught Lythian in his right thigh, and an abrupt bark of pain erupted from his mouth. He pulled back, leg leaking red, limping rearward. The grim-faced Agarathi soldiers closed in, as Lythian's back met the rear wall of the bedchamber. There was nowhere left to go. Nowhere left to hide.

"Well come on!" he roared, unleashing a lupine snarl, blazing eyes darting from one soldier to the next. "Who wants to kill the Knight of the Vale! Who wants to earn that honour!"

The men formed a barrier, unmoving, several paces away. Their pitch-dark, dragonsteel-tipped spears poised menacingly, but didn't move.

"Well? Come on! Finish it! What are you waiting for! Finish it!"

The men held their ground, and behind them came a voice. "No no no, Captain Lythian, I think you deserve a rather...*slower* death, for the heinous crimes you have committed." Lythian looked up, through the bulwark of bodies. He could hardly see beyond them, but didn't need to. He knew whom the voice belonged to, and in it, there was triumph. "You have murdered our great king, oh Knight of the Mists. Do you not think that the people deserve to see you fall?"

"I have murdered no one, Tavash..."

Tavash laughed, the sound echoing unpleasantly from the rear somewhere. *Might I get to him?* It was a fanciful thought. He might slay a few more should he attempt it, but unarmored and with nothing but a dagger to hand, would never make it far.

"Truly?" cackled Tavash. "All these dead men at my feet say otherwise, wouldn't you say? As does our noble king, lying dead in his bed..."

"*Your* bed," snarled Lythian. "These are *your* chambers, Tavash."

"My chambers? Yes," he laughed. "My chambers. My palace. My city and my kingdom. All are mine now, Captain Lythian, and soon perhaps the north will be mine too, thanks to you."

"Cur! You gods-damn bastard!"

"Oh come now, don't turn to cursing, my friend. I think all this is only fair. You started the last war in much the same fashion, after all, with the spreading of your filthy lies. And now...now it is *our* turn." He paused, and for just a moment, the sea of men parted to reveal him. He stood in intricate dragonscale armour, the very same once worn by his uncle, Dulian. And on his face, beneath his dark red eyes, he wore a smile of deepest pleasure. "You, Lythian Linder, Captain of the Varin Knights, have come to Eldurath to murder our king. Now, we will retaliate in kind." His grin spread broad and wicked, and he turned, waving a hand as he strolled away. "Take him."

With those simple words, the breach between the men filled in with armour and sword and spear. They did what their new king commanded.

6

Jonik

Jonik watched from the port side of the ship as it came aground upon the shingle-strewn beach. They'd been drifting for an hour or so since dawn, drawn along by the currents and the tides, hoping to make land. With the sails so badly torn up by the thrashing of the kraken, they were at the mercy of the elements. That mercy had brought them here, to this rugged stretch of land, clothed in a swamp of wet grey mist.

"Matmalia favours us!" Brown Mouth Braxton had bellowed as soon as the shape of the island came into view. He was up in the crow's nest for a better vantage, displacing Grim Pete from his perch. "She has guided us to safe harbour! We have our absolution, men!"

The cheer that went out was best described as muted. Muted by the fact that there were so few of them left. Only Braxton, Captain Turner, Grim Pete, young Devin, Soft Sid and Jack o' the Marsh remained of the original crew. It was less than a third of the contingent that had sailed from Green Harbour, the rest taken down to Daarl's Domain, first by the storm, then by the rapacious devil it summoned.

Captain Turner strode down from the quarterdeck, his tan leather coat hanging heavy against his burly frame. He looked drawn out, his eyes heavy with fatigue, carrying his bulk with a ponderous, plodding gait. No captain liked to lose so many men, nor the full use of their beloved ship. The vessel wasn't entirely beyond repair, but it was badly damaged and would likely take a good deal of resources, and time, to make it seaworthy again. Money, as Jonik had discovered, wasn't something Turner had in abundance.

"Looks like we're beached here for the time being," the captain said listlessly, as the men assembled before him at the foot of the forecastle. "Brax, best you head inland and try to find out where we are. With luck there'll be a settlement nearby who can help us. The rest o' you, gather provisions to make camp. There's a flat spot over yonder past them rocks," he pointed through the mists, to a grouping of craggy rocks higher up the beach. "We can set up there, where there's a bit more cover. Jack, see to the horses, and get 'em safely off the ship. Everyone else, with me."

The men moved into action, fetching the gangplanks to provide passage to the shore. Jonik, rather independent from Turner's command, elected to go below decks to help Jack o' the Marsh with the horses. Jack wasn't the crew's intended stablehand but with so few of them left, was best suited to the role.

"So why do they call you Jack o' the Marsh?" Jonik asked him, as they began opening up the stalls and leading the horses, one by one, up onto the top deck.

"I come from the marshlands north of Mudport," Jack said in a genial voice. "Down in southeast Vandar. Not the most creative name, but it stuck. The boys like it, anyway."

"You been with Turner long?"

He nodded briskly. "Four summers if memory serves." He wasn't so coarsely spoken as many of the others, yet had a rough readiness typical of the men of east Vandar. They grew them big down there and Jack was a strapping young man, packed with muscle and with a strong, deeply stubbled jaw. "Joined his crew when I was just out of my teens. Fished the marshlands before that around Celaph's Mire. Not a safe place with that monster always lurking in the back of your head, so was happy enough to get work on the seas. Turner took a chance with me. Good man, I've always thought."

"He seems more concerned with keeping his ship healthy than his men," Jonik noted, as he brought Shade up onto deck. The Rasal thoroughbred was being characteristically nonchalant about the entire affair, trotting along without noticeable concern for their plight. Which of course he fully understood.

"This ship's his livelihood," Jack said, "and any sailor knows the risks of the seas. We go in with our eyes wide open, friend. It doesn't serve for a captain to grow too fond of his men. Only leads to heartache when something like this occurs. And disasters are all too common at sea."

Jonik considered the argument. "I suppose that's fair," he said quietly, reaching the grey pebbly beach, where he left Shade to supervise the rest of the horses they'd brought out. "You must be only twenty two or twenty three, then? Don't take this as an insult, but you look a lot older."

Jack smiled pleasantly. "If I had a half sickle every time I'd heard that, I'd be a rich man by now," he laughed. "I'm old before my time, they say, but only because I've been forced to be. I'm the oldest of six - two brothers and three sisters - and had to help take care of them when my father was killed in a local dispute. I was only eleven at the time...been working ever since, dawn till dusk. Looked a man at fourteen, I did, bearded and burly. And you? You're about my age too, I'd say."

Jonik nodded. "About the same."

"And forgive me, but I've not yet heard your name. I think after last night, it's best that we hear it. You go through something like that, and you all become bonded like brothers. A miracle, it was." He looked at Jonik with a quietly awed expression. "What you did, I mean. I could tell that story a thousand times at a thousand taverns, and no one would ever believe it."

They walked along in silence for a moment as Jonik pondered his position. He'd woken shortly after being struck by that swinging tentacle, and was under no illusions that the remainder of the crew had seen what he did. Some of it, at least. He'd been invisible when he leaped off the boat to duel the sea-beast, but had quickly re-materialised when he'd lost his grip on the Nightblade. Which, of course, he'd quickly re-sheathed upon waking. But not before they'd all had a good long look at it, he imagined, while he lay on the deck unconscious.

"So?" Jack pressed, once the silence had become a little too uncomfortable. "You gonna give me your name, or..."

"Jonik."

They stopped, as though neither had truly expected him to oblige. "Jonik?"

Jonik nodded. "Jonik," he repeated. It felt good to say it. Too good, for such a simple thing. "That's my name."

Jack o' the Marsh's lips dressed themselves up in an affable smile, as they stood up on the main deck beneath the slate grey skies. "Jonik," he said once more, pursing his lips. He nodded in consideration of the name. "Suits you, friend. Better than Shadow, anyway."

Jonik frowned.

"It's what some of the men have been calling you," Jack explained. "Though, they're all dead now, so if that affronts you, well, not much you can do about it." He grinned in a waggish way, his red-tinted hair catching some early morning sunlight as it pierced the soupy mists.

"I take no offence," Jonik said, in a curt voice. "I grew up in the shadows, so I suppose it fits." He shrugged, standoffish, and looked away.

Jack observed him for a moment. "Huh," he said, lifting his wide chin. "So..." He paused, as though unsure. "The Shadowfort?" he then asked, showing an impressive percipience. "My father told me about it once. Said it was an ancient fortress where assassins and dark knights were trained, masters of stealth and the like. Not heard anything since then, mind you, and my father was full of tall tales, but..." He peered at Jonik again, taking him in. "I suppose it makes sense, to look at you, and knowing what you can do. And that blade you carry..."

He said it in such a way as to suggest he knew exactly what it was. Now it was Jonik's turn to peer at him. To judge him. To consider his intentions. Over the past couple of hours, he'd wondered whether he might just slaughter them all when he reached land, in order to cover his tracks, yet the idea held no great appeal. He knew these men now, and had no desire to slay them. *The Shadow Order will find me anyway,* he thought. *I can't outrun them forever, and do I even want to? Why should I fear them, after all? I bear a blade forged from Vandar's Heart, and with it, I enact his will...*

They continued in their work, leading out the final horses, until all of them were gathered outside under Shade's command. Jack looked at the sleek black steed, regally holding court as though king to the rest, and it seemed to further confirm his theory. "Rare horse, rare skill, rare blade. There's a great deal of mystery about you, Jonik. And your sudden appearance in Green Harbour." His fingers curled around his shadowed chin in thought. "Now, the others aren't so keen as me, perhaps, but I think I have a theory..."

Jonik braced. "Go on."

"Well, before we set off, I heard another tall tale, very much in the vein of those my father used to tell me. I'm fond of them, you see. Perhaps they're so ingrained in me from my youth, I don't know, but I tend to seek them out. And taverns are a wonderful place to hear them." He smiled, as though intentionally trying to be disarming. "I never said anything to you before, partly because we haven't really had much chance to speak, but now that we're alone, and given our predicament, well...I thought I might as well ask."

"Ask? I thought you were expounding some theory, Jack o' the Marsh."

"True enough. But I feel like I'm blabbering, and would rather not irritate you, knowing what you can do."

"I'm not irritated."

"No? You seem it. Or is that just how your face looks?"

"Don't push your luck, Marshlander."

Despite the jape, Jonik found that he was rather enjoying himself. It was about the most natural conversation he'd ever had; a rather pathetic indictment of the life he's led. Still, Jack had an instinctual charm that made him easy to talk to, and a part of

Jonik, perhaps a rather larger part than he'd realised, had had enough of keeping his own dull counsel.

"Force of habit, I'm afraid," the fiery-haired man said. 'If you don't push your luck, how do you know where your limits lie?"

"Doesn't that depend on who you're dealing with?"

"Yes, that's true, and so that's precisely what I'm doing with you. Who knows, we might be stranded here a while, so it's best that I know where we stand." He looked up the beach, to the rocks where the camp was being established. "And I suppose that's another reason why I'm bringing this up. I consider these men close friends, near kin to me in truth, and don't want to see them come to harm. So I guess you could say I'm sounding you out. Before the storm hit, there was no need, but now that we're stuck with one another..."

"You want to make sure I'm not a threat?"

He nodded and clipped his fingers. "Got it in one. So are you?"

"To you, and them?" Jonik looked toward the others. "No, not so long as you don't get in my way."

"Ah. Of course. And which way are you going?"

That question stumped him. Jonik's plans went no further than Greywater, and even those had been dashed. "I...I'm not entirely sure."

"I thought as much. A man on the run rarely knows where he'll end up, I suppose." That glint returned to his eyes, a pale green, far too keen for a lowly fisherman. "You *are* on the run, aren't you?" Jonik didn't nod, but didn't need to. Jack saw right through him anyway. "Another little tick in the 'correct' column of my theory, then." He reached out and placed a hand to Shade's muscular flank. The fact that the beast allowed it said a lot. "So let me get it off my chest. And you'll promise you won't kill me?"

"I promise," Jonik said, in a thin, slightly careful tone.

Jack reached out a hand and Jonik obliged. "By godsteel?" the muscular Marshlander said. "Promise by godsteel and I'll know we can all trust you."

"Those promises are meaningless. And you're not Bladeborn."

"Do I need to be? I thought only the one making the promise needed to be Bladeborn?"

"It depends. Some say yes, some say no."

"Then let's go with those who agree, shall we? Make the promise, Jonik. I see you're an honourable man, and not likely to go against it. Promise you'll not harm us..."

"I already told you I wouldn't," Jonik broke out with a flicker of impatience. "Why would I harm you after saving all your lives?"

"Well, I suspect your motivation wasn't to save us, so much as yourself, but that's by the by."

Jonik shrugged. "True enough," he rasped. "But I want a promise from you too."

"Of course. Anything," Jack said earnestly. "As you just said, you saved all our lives. We owe you, Jonik, down to the last man, and more than we'll ever likely be able to repay. Just say the word. What do you need?"

"Your trust," Jonik said, fixing him with a glare. "Same as you. Your word - all of you - that you'll not betray me. Break that bond and I'll break mine. I'll see whoever crosses me to the worms."

Jack clapped his hands together. "Fair enough." He wiped them briskly and reached out, to take Jonik's grasp once more. "On godsteel, then. Or just an oath of honour between men, if it pleases you. We'll not betray your trust, and you'll not slaughter us where we stand. Sound fair?"

Jonik nodded, then reaching to take hold of his godsteel dagger with his free hand, shook a single time. It was a version of a godsteel oath anyway. Truth be told, all this was new to him. *And I'm hardly afraid to break my oaths either,* he thought. *Doing so led me here, after all.*

"So, this theory of yours?" he said, growing weary of the wait. "Am I finally going to hear it?"

"Oh, I think we all know what it is," Jack o' the Marsh said, as he took the reins of one of the horses and began walking toward the camp. Jonik reached to take Shade's bridle but the horse gave him an indignant look and began leading the other horses on without him. Jack laughed. "They're truly as spirited as they say," he said. "Did you ride him all the way from the Shadowfort to Rasalan when you attempted to assassinate Amron Daecar?"

Jonik hardly reacted. He knew it had been building to this, though Jack delivered the words with a note of flair. *He's a confident one,* he thought, *to ask me so brazenly.* But somehow he liked it. It felt like what he needed - something wholly different to what had come before.

"And when you rode to Varinar to pose as that Ludlum fella? And defeated Aleron Daecar in the final of the Song of the First Blade? Tall tale indeed, one would think, but by your face it's true as the sea."

"Not quite," Jonik said, souring. "I didn't defeat Aleron. I...I murdered him."

Though his facade didn't change, internally he cringed. Against the sight of spurting blood pulsing from his half brother's cleaved neck. Against the horrified baying of the crowd, echoing through the dark spaces of his mind...

"You did what your duty commanded, so far as I can figure," Jack offered in a gentler voice. "But you've broken away now, haven't you? You're trying to do some good? There may be hope for you yet, Jonik of the Shadows. Just last night, you saved six souls, so mayhaps you've found a new path to tread?"

New path, he thought. He was walking one for certain, but just where it would lead, he didn't yet know. "You sound like an evangelist," he huffed, side-eying Jack as they went, "though I can't tell what religion you're preaching."

"I'm preaching goodness, and righteousness, and the turning of a man from a dark path, to one of light. I offer no religious context to it. Just the simple matter of right and wrong."

"And how much right must a man do in order to correct all the wrong?"

"Oh, you can't. You cannot turn back time, Jonik, or erase the things you've already done. But you can start a clean slate and by appearances that's what you're trying to do." He breathed out, smiling broadly as they went. "Gods, I've wanted to say this for days. That blade. The Nightblade. I knew what it was as soon as I met you, but seeing you wield it yestereve...that was something I'll never forget."

"I was under the impression I was invisible," Jonik put in, feeling oddly relaxed about being able to speak on the topic so openly. *And without judgement,* he thought. *That is most refreshing of all.*

A crack of laughter passed Jack's lips. "True, though you returned to form when you landed on the ship. And even before then, I saw you. Or, I saw the damage you were doing to that blubbery terror, at least. It's not common for the eyeballs of krakens to split open without reason, my friend. It was as if King Lorin himself had risen from the surf and taken vengeance on the creature that took him. But now my mind swells with curiosities about just how you came to hold the blade. Via the Shadow Order, no doubt, but how *they* came to have it is something I would greatly like to know."

Jonik grunted quietly beneath his breath, as they rounded the edge of the glistening black rocks and came into view of the hastily arranged camp. "You're not the only one," he said. "They never told me anything, but for who to kill."

Jonik's voice quietened as the others came into earshot, and Jack got his meaning. "You'd prefer to keep this between us?" he asked, as they looked upon the camp. "I suspect most have worked out some of what I have, given the rumours coming out of Varinar. Cap's not short of wit and Brown Mouth's got his head screwed on right too - though not enough to take proper care of his teeth. They'll put it together eventually, if they haven't already. Might as well come clean, if you want my opinion."

"You seem to give it anyway, whether I want it or not. I didn't know you were such a talker."

"I'm better in smaller groups. With twenty plus men aboard, I can struggle to find my voice. I'm not so much like these men, really, not a born waterman in the same way they are. It's hard to get a word in edgewise the way they talk sometimes."

"I find that hard to believe, after listening to you jabber on." Jonik considered things. "But fine, if you think they should know, why not. That dark path you mentioned - I've had enough of it. I don't rightly care who knows anymore." On a whim, he drew his hand into his cloak and pulled out the Nightblade, causing the air to stir and flee. "I hold a fragment of Vandar's Heart in my hand. What do *I* have to fear?"

Jack's face was in a glowing grin and his eyes reflected his wonder. "What indeed?" he mused quietly. "Not much, I would say, though it would seem you're fleeing from something."

The others were taking notice now, stopping in their work. Turner and Grim Pete looked on curiously, young Devin with large, childlike eyes, and Soft Sid with the only expression he ever managed to muster. An inexpressive one.

"That's something you should also be aware of," Jonik said, looking down the length of the misting black blade. "The Nightblade isn't strictly mine. I stole it from my masters, after what they made me do." He turned to look at Jack, finding an alliance in the man's eyes. "They want it back, and won't stop hunting me until they get it. Anyone I come across...anyone who helps me, or supports me...will get drawn into that storm. Best you arm yourself with that knowledge, Jack." He nodded forward. "You and all the others. I've got a head start, but they'll not take long to find me. And they'll start with people like you when making their inquiries."

"I see." The man from the Marshlands scratched his chin once more, thoughtful, though looked in no way perturbed by the reveal. "No wonder you've been keeping all this quiet, then. To protect those you encounter. If nothing else, that shows you have a kindness to you, Jonik. Wouldn't you say?"

"I'd say I'm thinking of myself, as I was last night when I cut up that foul beast. But twist it as you wish. I'm not a good person, Jack."

"I don't think you know what sort of person you are at all. If all you've ever known is darkness, how can you possibly know whether or not you'll flourish in the light?"

"You don't know the half of what I've done."

"What you were *forced* to do," Jack said, reading so much between the lines. "There's a clear distinction there, my friend."

Jonik rasped out a sigh. "Words. That's all they are. And you're full of them."

Jack continued to smile comfortably, despite Jonik's darkening countenance. *If I am the darkness, he is the light. What must it be like to look upon the world so fondly, as he does?*

"Words are valuable currency when spent wisely." Apparently Jack wasn't just old looking for his years, but wise beyond them too. "But I can tell I'm starting to push that luck we spoke about, so will leave you be."

Jonik re-sheathed the Nightblade as they rejoined the others, leading the horses up the beach toward a small grouping of stout old trees, huddled amid the mists. Beyond the rugged beach the lands stretched away, soggy and brown, rising into a set of low lying hills beyond.

"I don't suppose you know where we are?" Jonik asked, as they started tying the horses up to make sure they didn't wander off. Jonik doubted they would, now that Shade had taken charge of them, but it would be hard to convince the captain of that.

"Could be any number of islands," Jack said, as he nimbly strung the ropes together into sailor's knots. "I got the sense we were drifting east so hopefully we'll be within range of Greywater. We can't have gone too far."

Jonik looked away into the hills, no more than shadows in the distance. "It's grimmer here then I thought it'd be. And more rugged. I thought the Tidelands were more exotic than this."

"Depends where you land and what the weather's like. There are some nice beaches that I've seen, but don't go expecting palm trees and white, powder-soft sand. You'd have to travel to the Golden Isles for that, just off the Crystal Bay."

"Have you been that far before?"

"Me? No, never so far south as that. Always wanted to, though. Hear it's a land of plenty down there, full of bounty whatever your vice. If you're looking for somewhere to lay low, my friend, you could certainly do a lot worse."

"Than the Golden Isles? I'm not sure I'd be suited to such a place."

Jack o' the Marsh expressed another mirthful laugh. "You'd burn to a crisp, it's true! I'm not sure I've ever seen anyone so pale as you."

"And you'd take on a golden glow, would you, Marshman? You're hardly suited to the sun either with that red hair of yours."

"I daresay I've seen more sun than you, my friend, living in the Marshlands and out at sea. Now, if you'd grown up somewhere called the Sunfort or Lightfort, I might say otherwise, but I suppose Shadowfort suggests a rather drab and unwelcoming place."

Jonik didn't like the memories that passed through his head. "Drab and unwelcoming is putting it lightly."

He turned away, leaving Jack to complete the work with the horses, and returned to camp. The young Vandarian came loping up beside him shortly after, taking no offence. "Horses all taken care of, Captain," he said, as Turner stood arranging a few provisions. He looked to be paying close attention to their stocks of food, which wasn't especially encouraging. "What else do you need?"

Turner looked down the coast. "Hike up to that headland there. It'll give a good view out onto the water, and further down the coast. Might spot a ship or settlement. We'll get a fire going here for signalling, should we need it."

"Aye aye, Captain."

Jonik continued in Jack's company, as they ventured down the coast and up toward the promontory. It was a half mile or so away, growing more visible as the morning mists cleared, and rising a couple of hundred metres high upon a jutting cliff of rock. They worked inland a little bit in search of a safe route, as Jack made the jovial suggestion that Jonik might as well just make the climb himself. "It'd be a lot quicker, wouldn't it? I'll bet you could climb these cliffs quicker than I can run up there. Hmmm, I feel a wager coming on. How about it? Race me to the top?"

"I'd rather not."

A laugh interrupted the quiet, morning air. "Thought as much. You're coated in grimness, Shadowknight. But don't worry, I'll chip away at you. There's sure to be a bit of laughter in you somewhere. Maybe a smile, locked away behind those rigid lips."

Jonik glared at him with sufficient malice to persuade Jack o' the Marsh to forego any further quips, as they climbed up toward the high ground. The still air started to swirl in the breeze as they went, and the thick mists continued to melt away as the sun arced higher across the skies. By the time they'd reached the summit, they had a mostly clear view left and right up the coast, and away inland as well. It didn't reveal much, save the craggy lifelessness of the shoreline, and the scrubby, brown-green plains that swept away into the hills at the rear.

That was, until Jonik saw the body.

He pointed, further down the coast, guiding Jack's eyes to the figure flopping in the surf. Jack squinted for a time then spoke. "Polver," he said, eyes creasing. "I recognise his cloak." It was a faded yellow, whaleskin and waterproof. Polver had been one of the two men dragged overboard by the storm before the kraken crawled up from the depths. "We should fetch him, bring him back to camp. Best send him off properly, in the fashion of his faith."

Jonik made no argument. He felt happier when busy and set to some task than brooding on the twisted route his life had thus taken. *Even hauling a swollen corpse half a mile is better than the alternative,* he thought, as they made their way down the headland, and onto the beach on its opposite side.

The corpse was not yet festering, though it was hard to tell if the bloat had set in, given Polver's natural proportions. He was a short man of rotund build, and looked far from dignified in death, lying face down in the grit, all covered in seaweed and sand.

"Was he a friend?" Jonik asked, looking down at the body. A few crabs had started to get at him. "He seemed a decent enough man to me."

"He was a lout." Jack said it with a smile. "But some of the best men are." He whispered a prayer to himself, and drew a sign on his chest, running three fingers horizontally from right to left.

"A sign for Rasalan?" Jonik queried. He knew many of the gestures of faith to the gods, but not all. Seafaring folk in particular worshipped a great many spirits and nymphs.

"For Matmalia, Spirit of the Waves," Jack said, as they picked up Polver's body and began hauling him back to camp. "For bringing him back to us, so we can say goodbye properly."

"And how will you do that?"

"I'm not sure, but Captain Turner will know. Each man who boards his ship is required to give preferences for funeral rites, should they die under his command. Most elect to be buried at sea, weighted with stones and sunk to the Ocean Halls of Rasalan."

"And how many get picked apart by sharks before they get there?" Jonik asked.

Jack took no insult at his irreverence. "Many, I would say, but that is all for the good. It is only the spirit that ventures beyond this corporal plane. The body remains, to feed the fauna of the seas, as per the great spiral of life, and death."

"You speak as a priest," Jonik noted. "It seems you missed your calling."

"I missed nothing, my friend. I heard that calling loud and true, but chose to ignore the invite. My father...he was the priest. He was born to the Marshlands and never left, but that path was never for me. I bring my faith on the road, and try to marry it with adventure, where I can."

Jonik looked at him with a shade more interest. "You said your father was killed in a dispute."

"I did. And he was. He had a penchant for proselytising and I suppose that's where I get my evangelical spirit. It tended to rub some up the wrong way, and eventually led him into a heated affray with a group of heathens and heretics. I don't think they intended to kill him, just rough him up a bit, but alas he caught a fateful blow to the temple and that was enough for him."

"I'm sorry," Jonik said. "It sounds like he was only trying to do some good."

"And in that he accomplished a great deal, living full before his passing. He was a charitable man, well loved within the local communities, but never travelled beyond his homeland as I prefer to do. Now that my younger siblings are older and can take account of themselves, I permit myself these adventures." He smiled and filled his lungs with fresh sea air. "And you, friend? Pray tell of your father. What is he like?" It took no more than a heartbeat for Jack to realise the folly of the question. He sighed and shook his head in apology. "Forgive me," he said. "I suppose you know not of your father, given your upbringing."

Jonik wasn't ready to speak on that, though a part of him wanted to commit to the full truth. He chose instead to remain silent, turning solemn for a time as he pondered his own faith. He was not a spiritual man, not like Jack o' the Marsh, who was far removed from the simple, meat-headed deckhand Jonik had first taken him to be. *Perhaps it is that faith that gives him his light,* he wondered, glancing across at him. There were many forms of the afterlife, many worlds beyond this one that people crossed to at their deaths. They provided comfort for generations of lost souls, knowing their existence on this plane, however unpleasant or fleeting, was but part of a larger journey they were to take. Yet Jonik had only ever seen darkness in his death. To fall into the *Long Abyss*, and tumble forever, for all the wicked things he'd done.

Might I change my fate? he wondered, as they pressed on down the coast. *In this life, and the next. Might a lighter, more virtuous path now lead me to a brighter future, when I pass to the next world?*

He looked at Jack again, tempted to ask him, to seek his wisdom, but stayed silent. Instead they walked in personal thought until they reached the camp, and placed Polver gently to the earth. "Washed up beyond the headland," Jack said, holding his hands together, bowing his head. The others gathered around. Whispered prayers passed the lips of Turner, Grim Pete and Devin, while Soft Sid just stood there, picking at his ear and staring vacantly out to sea. He'd been dropped on his head as a child, Jonik had been told, in explanation of his dull wits.

"Matmalia returned him to us," said Devin, echoing what Jack had said. He was barely sixteen, but had been at sea since a pup, and in Turner's service for many of those years. Three fingers were drawn across his chest. "What shall we do with him, Captain?"

Turner took a moment to himself before speaking, then said, "Polver was Rasal, out of the Lowplains off the Crescent Coast. Their custom is to cremate their dead. They believe the ashes are soaked into the clouds, to be rained down upon the seas."

Jack was nodding. "A gift to feed the oceans," he said. "His spirit will find its way to Rasalan's halls."

"That it will," said Turner. "All true men o' the sea make it to the Ocean Halls and Polver was an honest sailor, so he was. We'll need to build a pyre, to set him to the flame. Might those trees where you hitched the steeds provide enough lumber?"

The question was for Jack, who pondered it, then nodded. "Should be plenty, Captain. Perhaps Jonik might cut lengths of timber using his blade. It would speed matters no end, I feel."

"Aye," said Turner, looking to Jonik. "So Jonik, is it? That's your name?"

Jonik nodded, offering Jack a quick glare for unveiling it. Turner had been calling him 'boy' and 'lad' thus far.

"Well it's a pleasure to be meetin' you officially then," Turner went on. "Jonik, o' the Nightblade." He smiled. "Aye, I know what the blade o' yours is. Ain't no other that fogs black like that and turns a man invisible, leastways not one I've heard about."

"There is none other," Jonik said.

"So it's true?" asked Devin, staring at Jonik's black scabbard. "You hold the Nightblade, Jonik? Truly? The one King Lorin lost to the seas?"

"It wasn't lost to the seas, whelp," cackled the cadaverous form of Grim Pete. "Else Jonik here wouldn't be holding it."

"Some Seaborn might've swum down and fetched it," offered Devin in retort. "You can swim deep, can't you Cap? A hundred metres, you say, and more if you pushed yourself I'm sure."

"Aye, could go deeper than that if I willed it. But the seas are mighty deep in places, lad, more than any Seaborn could go. And even so, they'd not be able to lift the Nightblade if they reached it."

"It is inhumanly heavy," Devin agreed, as though he'd tried to lift it. *Which he probably did, when I lay unconscious,* thought Jonik, as Devin turned to him. "So how did you come to have it?"

The eyes of the group swelled interestedly. "It was given to me," Jonik offered.

Devin's eyes were biggest of all. "By who?"

"My masters."

"Your masters..." Devin nodded eagerly. "And who are they?"

Jonik rubbed his eyes. "The Shadow Order," he said, enervated. He'd fielded enough questions from Jack o' the Marsh and had insufficient energy to deal with Devin's enthusiastic interrogation right now.

"The Shadow Order." Devin whistled through his teeth. "Sounds mysterious."

"So it does," Turner broke in, saving Jonik any further questioning, "But that mystery shall remain veiled for now." His eyes moved to the corpse at their feet. "Let's see Polver to the flame first, and if Jonik should wish it, he can tell his tale once we're done." Devin looked mildly disappointed, but offered no complaint. "With luck, Brax'll be back by the time we've forged the pyre, but if not we'll get started without him. Come, lads, let's get to it. Sid, with me. We'd best fetch some rope from the ship for lashing."

Soft Sid lumbered unthinkingly after Turner as they made for the beached vessel, and the others saw to the wood. Devin watched with wide-eyed wonder as Jonik sliced through the trees with the Nightblade, cutting clean lengths of timber for the fire. He might have used his dagger, but why not give the boy a treat? With a flurry of swings and sweeping hacks he'd compiled a fine pile of logs and lumber, and ever Shade watched on from the side, making a soft snorting sound as though unimpressed by Jonik's grandstanding display.

The pyre was thus built, and the sagging frame of Polver set atop it, wrapped in white linen from the ship and dispossessed of any items of value he'd had on his person. Jack suggested that they wait for Braxton's return before lighting the flame, but Turner brushed it off. "Brax and Polver never saw eye-to-eye, so no sense in delayin'." Jonik imagined the captain was rather more keen to get started on the brandy, but made no point of mentioning it.

The flames took well, despite the dreary damp in the air, and as the body burned so the men took turns in story and song. It was no great surprise to Jonik that Jack o' the Marsh had a handsome singing voice, though Turner's rich baritone was rather more unexpected when he saw fit to unleash it. Soon, the brandy came out. It was passed around the group, and as each man held it, so they were required to say a few words about Polver, or Jakken, or Lazy Lord Larry, or Whilton, or Pip the Pincher, or any of the others lost the previous night.

When the bottle reached Jonik's grasp, all looked to him eagerly. He knew none of the deceased and had nothing to say of them, yet none present expected him to. *They want to hear of me,* he knew. *Of my tale. Of how I came to be here.*

He took several swigs to loosen his tongue, and across the flames, Jack o' the Marsh offered him an urging look. *So be it,* he thought, nodding back at the Marshlander. *I said I'd unveil the truth of me, so here goes.*

So he spoke. Of the Shadowfort. Of the task his masters had set him. Of Amron and Aleron Daecar. Of his crippling of one and killing of the other. *My father and brother,* he thought darkly, and that information he kept private. He made no mention of it, but the rest flowed free from his lips, and as it did, so a weight lifted off him. Was he endangering these men's lives by revealing too much? Quite possibly, yes, but none of them seemed to care.

"We live dangerous lives, Master Jonik," Turner said, speaking for the group, "so knowing you won't much change that. And besides, we'd all be dead were it not for you, so by my reckoning we've livin' on borrowed time."

The others nodded. "We'll say nothing of what you've told us, save by your permission," Jack said. "Perhaps you joining our crew was fated, Jonik of the Shadows. It might just be that our journey together is only just getting started."

More nodding. Jonik looked around the group and sensed a strange shift among them, in the way they looked at him, in the way they seemed to brace when under his gaze. *They revere me,* he realised. *They see me as something more than just a man. And am I not? Am I not in part divine, to have so mastered this blade?*

He stood before them, holding that bottle of brandy, and once again, an urge struck at him, deep and true, and he pulled out the Nightblade with a flow of black mist. Perhaps it was the liquor now coursing through their veins, or perhaps some other force drove them, but as one all five men bowed and fell to their knees before him. Low they went, heads down, men of faith genuflecting before a god. *A god. Am I? No...not a god, but divine...perhaps.*

And as they knelt, so a shadow appeared from the growing gloom, and the panting form of Brown Mouth Braxton reemerged from the hills beyond the camp. The moment passed like the final flicker of a dying flame, and the men stood, turning to him, blinking through the shroud.

"Braxton, you return," Turner said. "What news, old friend? Do you know where we've made land?"

Braxton plodded wearily forward and the bottle of brandy was immediately passed on to him. The man with the lopsided jaw chugged for a few moments, wiped his mouth with his filthy sleeve, then unveiled his nightmarish grin. "Fine news, Cap'n, fine news indeed. Ran into a herder out in the hills and by his account, we're on Passway Key, right up on the northeastern tip, no more than a day's ride to Greywater." His appalling set of teeth looked more brown than ever in that low light. "We've been given another reprieve men. Our fortunes are on the turn!"

He raised his bottle and cheered, and so bellowed the others too.

"A reprieve it is," Turner called out, snatching the brandy from Brown. "And another stroke of luck." He took a swig. "I might forgive myself for thinking you're a good omen for us," he said, toasting Jonik. "Now come, let us drink ourselves to oblivion! On the morrow we make for Greywater."

They drank, they laughed, they sang.

And Jonik remembered nothing of it.

7

Saska

"This here's the place," said Roark, as they rode over the lip of a hillock and came into sight of the village, straddling the Marshway River.

There were two old stone bridges crossing the water, with a rickety wooden mill turning between them. A little south of the village, a stout keep stood guard, set among the marshes and accessed by a half flooded causeway. A handful of men stood upon the battlements, though they wore the garb of farmers, not soldiers. All were looking their way now as they ventured over the hill.

"There are no real soldiers here," Saska said, looking back at them. She ran her eyes over the remaining villagers. “Why haven't they left yet? Wouldn’t it be safer for them to flee north to somewhere better fortified?”

"Hope can kill,” Marian told her. "It keeps people rooted to perilsome places long after they should leave."

"And bravery too," offered Roark, a half horse behind them. "Courage is the biggest killer of all. In every war, in every land, thousands die by its hand."

They went another few paces down the slope, before Marian thought it best to call out. "We come as friend, not foe," her voice rang, announcing their arrival. "My name is Lady Marian of House Payne, niece to Lord Tandrick Payne. Who takes charge here?"

From the keep a man came bustling, bearded and breathless. "Lady Payne, thank the gods." His eyes moved across the small troop. "We have been praying for aid for days, what with these rumours of Greenbelts in the area. You are most welcome, truly you are. The gods have seen fit to answer our call."

It was almost a shame to let him down, though Marian had no choice. "My apologies, sir, but we're not here to stay. We are here on a mission of particular importance and you'd best heed what I tell you."

"Oh. I...I feel quite the fool." He shuffled uncomfortably. "Of course, you'd not concern yourself with so humble a village as ours. What mission do you speak of, my lady?"

Marian slipped off of Stormwind and gestured for Saska to follow. The rest stayed saddled upon their steeds, ready to make a swift departure.

"The Greenbelts are coming," Marian said, in a blunt voice that said time was running short. "They'll be here within the hour by our estimates, and you'd do well to let them take what they wish and leave. If you raise arms they will slaughter you all. Offer no resistance and you may escape with your lives at least."

The man gaped. "You...you say this freely, my lady? That we should let them take away our livelihoods?"

"Better your livelihoods than your lives. Yes, I say this freely. We've passed many such places where the men chose to fight, and the result is ever the same. You will die, and not well." She looked over the small settlement. "Where are all the villagers?"

"Many have fled, my lady." The man held a sharpened hoe for a weapon. *If that is all they have, they'll not trouble even the weakest Tukoran soldier,* Saska thought, looking at him pitifully. "They've ventured north in search of safer pastures. Only a few of us remain, us men willing to fight..."

"All the women have gone?" Saska asked. It wouldn't serve if she was the only one there, when the men came searching for Bladeborn. *Too suspicious,* she thought. *The ruse mightn't work so well.*

"Most yes, but not all," the man said. "One or two of our womenfolk bear arms too and are willing to die if they must. We've got nought here but our livestock and what little possessions we have. If we lose them, we'll not survive through winter when the snows set in."

"You'll not survive through today if you don't put down that hoe," Marian said sharply. "The Greenbelts raiding these lands are led by a cruel young knight who will see you to a slow end should you resist. If you wish to see your innards cut from you while you're still alive, by all means try your luck, but believe me, it isn't a nice way to go."

She was laying it on thick, yet it seemed to be doing the trick. The bearded farmer looked suddenly doubtful. "Will they not slay us anyway?" he put forward, glancing into the hills. "We hear bystanders are being murdered whether bearing arms or not. Are these mistruths we're hearing?"

"No, only truths twisted. Bystanders have been cut through, yes, but only once hostilities have been stirred. If none of you offer a fight you should come away unscathed. It's the best you can hope for."

The man gave a relenting nod. "Fine," he said, tossing his hoe to the ground. "I'll instruct the others to lay down their arms. But I can't promise they'll agree. We've some hardy women here who'd sooner die by the blade than be dragged off for befouling."

"They won't be hurt," Saska said firmly. "I'm the one they want."

The farmer looked at her quizzically. "And who are you, if you'll permit the query?"

"I'm your servant," Saska said, and behind her the men began to laugh.

The bearded man looked at them, then back at Saska, giving himself time to work out her meaning. Sure enough, he failed. "I...I'm not sure I understand."

"This here is our mission. Her name is Tilda," Marian informed him, giving the fake name Saska was to use along with her fake identity. "When the Greenbelts come, they'll gather your womenfolk outside their homes and test them for Varin blood.

Tilda here is Bladeborn, and will thus be taken by them. That is all you need to know."

The humble farmer looked at Saska with a hundred questions burning in his eyes. Along with her false name, she'd developed a false appearance, one that would serve to entice Lord Kastor, while making sure he didn't recognise her. She'd used ointments to subtly darken her skin and had taken a potion to alter the hue of her eyes, turning them a hazel brown. Her hair had been dyed jet black, cropped short, and she'd developed a passable southern accent with an Aramatian twang. It would be plenty to flummox Kastor and his men, should she come across any she knew.

"You're some spy, then?" the man said eventually. After a half minute of thought it was all he could come up with.

Saska shook her head. "No, I'm but a lowly maidservant in your house," she said, softening her voice, adding that Aramatian lilt. She dipped her head in submission, as all good house servants did. "I've been serving you for two years since coming from Aramatia in search of honest labour. You found me at market in Shellcrest and offered me a fair wage for fair work. I've been happy here in..." She paused, and her real voice came back through. "What's the name of this village?"

The man blinked from his reverie. "Baymoor, my...my lady."

"And your name? Best I know of it, seeing as I've been serving you for two years."

"Westham. Um...Albert Westham."

"A noble name," Saska noted. "Nice to meet you, Albert Westham of Baymoor."

"Aye, and...and you."

"Now you do understand what we're saying to you, Mr Westham?" Marian asked. It seemed as though he needed clarification. "Most likely, you'll not be troubled with questions, but in case you are, remember what Tilda here has told you."

He nodded, thinking things over. "Right. That I...I found you at market in Shellcrest. Offered fair wage for fair work and have had you here in Baymoor some...two years?" He finished with a question and Marian gave her confirmation.

"Very good. Recollection under stress is never easy. You've

done well. Now best tell your people to unhand their arms. I can hear the thunder of hooves at the edge of my hearing. The Greenbelts shan't be long."

Albert hustled away at that, calling out as he went, and Marian turned to Saska. "I'll be watching from the hilltop," she said. "Should the Greenbelts seek to slake their bloodthirst here I'll intervene." She paused, and that familiar crease furrowed her brow. It had come more often, a show of doubt at this course. "This is your last opportunity to back out, Saska, should you wish it. I know what I'm asking of you. This is a mission fit for one much more experienced, and I'm loathe to ask you to fulfil it, with so little..."

"I'm ready." Saska's voice was firm, measured. She held her hands behind her back, already dressed in her maidservant clothes, stained and frayed and fit for a place like this. She had no godsteel dagger now, no fine grey cloak, no finery at all. She was as she'd always lived. A simple servant and no more. "I'll see him dead, Marian. I promise you I will."

Marian inhaled long and slow and breathed out the same. "I'll be watching, such as I can," she then said. "I may yet be able to pose as a Greenbelt myself and..."

Saska shook her head, a single, brisk motion. "It must be me," she said, and her voice held a strong conviction. "You'd never get Kastor alone yourself, Marian, and besides that, I want this." She closed a fist. *By the gods I want it. To see his blood gush, and the light fade from his eyes. To make him suffer as he has so many others like me.*

Even Marian's way of nodding had a slow grace to it, and away went those keen blue eyes, thoughtfully looking into the distance. "So be it," she said, in a quiet, smokey voice. "You are dear to me, Saska, more dear than I would like. I am not in the habit of caring too deeply about those I take under my wing, but you..."

"I feel the same." Saska's voice was close to catching. She smiled wanly and looked to the men, huddled on their horses a little way off. Lark was tearful, Braddin furtively wiping the mist from his eyes. Quilter's flattened face was a shade less grim than normal and Roark held a warming smile to send her on her way.

"And you," she added. "I care about you all. But I'll see you again soon," she told them, not knowing whether that was true. "Just...don't have too much fun without me. I'd not want to miss out."

Their lips cracked into smiles, and Lark sniffed loudly. *Such sweet burly men,* she thought. *I'll miss them. As I do Orryn and Llana and Del...and Leshie and Astrid and Ranulf. I wonder whether I'll ever see any of them again? Might I die? Might they?* She turned from the thought as Roark's ragged voice broke out. "Go get 'em, Princess," he said. "You cut that fiend from ear to ear and get free of that foul place. We'll be ready to extract you, whenever you need."

The others nodded in hearty agreement. "I'll write a song for your return," Lark said in his lyrical voice. "A dozen verses, one for each o' your virtues and triumphs."

"You'll need more than a dozen then, Warbler," said Braddin, nudging the younger man so hard he near fell from his horse. "Now don't go selling her short."

"Two dozen then," said Lark. "Or as many as needs be to do you justice."

"That's sweet, Lark," smiled Saska. "But I fear I'm being oversold."

The men wouldn't have it. All four of them began denying her statement fervently, until Marian raised a hand to silence them. "OK, that'll do," she said. "I might make the point that I don't hear myself be complimented with such unbridled enthusiasm, but I suppose I'll let it pass. Saska is a special soul, as we've all seen." She leaned in, so the others couldn't hear. "And King Godrin's seen it too, child. You'll come through this unharmed, I'm sure of it. Let that thought keep you warm, when you suffer through the bitter nights. If there comes a time when all seems lost, do not lose hope. This is but the start of your journey."

She drew back, and took Saska's shoulders, turning her toward the village. "Best get going," she said, gently urging her forward. "Now go, child, and do not look back. Trust the process. Trust your fate."

Saska firmed herself, nodded, and began moving off down the

hill. *Go and do not look back.* They were the same last words that Master Orryn had given her.

She heeded them once more.

The echoing rumble of pounding hooves arrived a short time later, as Saska sat quietly within the home of Albert Westham, mentally preparing for what was to come. The plates rattled in their racks and the ground began to shake, and within moments the clipped voice of their commander came ringing through the deserted streets.

"Whoever remains in this squalid little rat-hole, emerge from your hovels now. I give you the count of ten as a mercy, before each and every one of them is put to the torch."

Saska stood, following Albert out into the rain. The skies had grown gloomy in the time she'd spent waiting and a thick sheet of grey cloud had amassed above. *It had been a fine morning too,* she thought, glancing up the hill to where she knew Marian and the men to be, but she could see nothing from this distance without godsteel. From the other wattle and daub buildings the rest of the villagers stepped out. There were a count of twenty, perhaps, most men but a small handful of women too, a miserable lot to be sure, and not one of them carried a weapon.

"Obedient today, very good," snivelled the young knight at their lead. Saska took him in, and saw the Kastor family resemblance, and the bear print on his crest. He looked much like Lord Cedrik, only half his age, a pup of only twenty odd leading a hundred swords. Dark curly hair ran down to his shoulders and there on the right side of his neck, Saska spotted the nasty scar that Father Pennifor had mentioned.

Saska had to remember to stay in character. She'd heard of what he'd done. How he'd had the young boy, Mattius, hung from a tree and filled with quills and quarrels for sport. How he'd ordered innocent men, nothing but bystanders, cut down for no reason at all. This man was no noble knight, but a criminal clad in steel. He turned his eyes down the line, his brows cut to cruel slants, and drew a godsteel dagger from a gilded sheath at his hip.

"Let's have the women line up, shall we?" he said. He pointed with his blade to the ground before him. "Right here, in this big brown puddle." The men laughed in ragged breaths, the air fogging around them. "Come, on your knees. Or else I'll have you bent over instead and every one of us will have a go."

Saska inched forward, keeping her head down. The other women gathered where the tracks of wagons had rutted a crater, filled with fetid water. The young knight loomed above them on his black destrier, his steel breastplate gleaming in the light rain. He sniffed the air theatrically, then pinched his nose. "Oh my my, you stink, every last one of you. A bath will do you good. Come, in you get."

He slipped from his horse, and Saska sensed several other men gathering. Others went for the vacant homes to search for loot. Several hurried off to check the stone keep should there be soldiers hidden there, waiting to spring a trap. Men stepped behind her and the other three women, pushing them forward. The puddle was deeper than it looked, the water cold enough to steal breath. She was violently thrust to her knees, and the others splashed down beside her. One was sobbing, a girl still in her mid teens. She seemed to think she was set to be executed right there in the mud.

"Someone shut her up."

A slap caught her square on the cheek and she went over, falling face first into the filth. The knight stepped to her, as a soldier took a fistful of her sopping hair, pulling her back upright. The godsteel dagger was summarily thrust into her grasp as she spluttered for breath.

"Can you hold it?" asked the young knight, as he released it from his grip.

It pulled her right down, splashing into the puddle. "I...I'm sorry," she wheezed. "I...I can't..."

"Take her from my sight." The knight reached to take up his dagger as the girl was dragged off, sniffing and sobbing and soiling herself by the smell of it. Saska had to fight to keep her eyes down, to stick to her duty. *Might I just cut him through when he hands me the dagger?* It would be so joyous, so easy. But what then? *Bigger picture, Saska. Don't react. Don't...*

The young knight moved to the next woman, a stocky figure

who looked like she could heft a sword well enough. "My gods, look at this great wench!" he laughed. "It seems they breed with the cattle out here. Do you speak the common tongue, my beauty, or only converse in moos and grunts?"

The stocky woman looked directly up at him and that was her first mistake. Her second was to spit. Her third was how good her aim was. A glob of saliva caught the man square on his sneering lips and he near fell in the mud from the shock of it. He stabilised, turned to her, snarled, and then swung with his blade. In a flash her head was cleaved from her neck in a single, clean strike. It teetered, then toppled forward, peeling off her body and splashing into the puddle. Then came the blood, spurting like a geyser, hot and red and steaming against the bitter grey skies.

"Insolent bitch," snapped the young man's voice. "See what happens when you defy me!"

Saska didn't look. She couldn't, lest she react. She stared down and tried to ignore that rain of warm blood landing on her left shoulder, as behind her, a few screams went out from the watching men. This woman had been someone's wife, someone's mother. It sounded as though several of the villagers were being restrained and gagged, and all the while, that cruel laughter clapped through the village and out into the misty hills.

The young knight wiped his mouth of the spittle the woman had shot at him, then continued down the line, as though nothing had happened. There was only one last woman huddled beside Saska now, the others dragged off or dead. "Are you Bladeborn?" he asked her in a grunt.

She seemed unable to answer, staring wide-eyed at the decapitated head of her friend, poking up through the puddle. A deep crimson was inking through the water, blackening it. "You...you killed her..."

"And you'll follow lest you answer me. I have no time for this." He nodded to the guards behind them and they pulled the woman up onto her feet. "Here." He pushed the dagger into her grasp and it slipped straight through her shivering fingers.

"You killed her. She's...she's dead."

"You're a bright one. But no Bladeborn. Take her off."

The guards did as bidden, dragging the woman away to join the men, all huddled and gagged outside their homes. The few that weren't were too stricken to make a peep. A few had been knocked unconscious; Albert looked to be among them.

"Another fruitless day, it would seem." The Kastor knight sounded bored, and more cruel than Saska had let herself believe. She kept her eyes down, as he turned his attention on her. A short delay followed, before his voice crept back out. "Well, what have we here..." He was right before her, standing atop the rutted track, a rich brown coat at his back. "A southerner, goodness. Stand and look at me."

She did so, and his sneer appeared before her eyes, that black hair framing his pale, narrow face. "Now what are you doing here, so far from home?" He might have been handsome in another life. "A servant? Or does one of these philistines take you for a wife?" He laughed at the notion. "Or pleasure girl more likely. Yes, you'd be good at that, I would say." He looked her up and down, desirous. "Is that what you are to these men?"

"I'm a house servant," she offered in her false accent. "I cook and clean."

"And that's all, is it? Or do you polish swords too." He laughed at his little joke.

"No, my lord. I just cook and clean."

"Hmmm, well trained," he noted, "unlike this headless wench here at my feet. Well...let's get this over with, then." Out came his godsteel blade. It was all a formality to him, a box to be ticked. Finding Bladeborn women hidden away in places like this would be rare. Finding one of southern heritage a great deal rarer still. "Come on, then, try to lift it."

"I...I cannot," she said. "This is...it is godsteel."

"Just bloody well take it. I want rid of the sight of this great cow's corpse. It insults me. And the stink…"

He sneered and thrust the dagger into her grasp, ready to see it drop, and retrieve it. Yet when the hilt graced her fingers, she held it firm and didn't let it slip. Her eyes bloomed into false shock, to match her false name, false look. "I..." she whispered. Her hand began shaking and she let the dagger slip to the floor, recoiling. "I'm...I'm so sorry, my lord. I don't know what happened, I..."

Her words were cut off by his laughter. "Goodness me, I didn't expect *that.*" He looked up. "You see this, men? A southerner with Varin blood. It seems some Bladeborn got frisky on a visit to the south! My uncle will be most interested in you."

"Your...uncle, my lord?" Her voice quivered. *I'm in shock,* she kept telling herself. *Show it on your face. Let him hear it in your voice.*

"Yes, Lord Kastor, you may have heard of him. He has a particular interest in girls like you." A big greedy grin exploded onto his youthful face. "He may just reward me for this. Give me more men to command." He spoke to himself, nodding, then looked up at the men around him. "Bind and gag her, so she'll not wail on the road. We ride for my uncle's camp."

When the soldiers came for her, Saska got her first proper look at the villagers gathered behind her. The blood told her that others had died during the commotion, and that those unconscious men weren't unconscious at all, but dead, and that poor Albert Westham was among them.

She felt cold. So cold as she was handled by the men, as her wrists were tied, and her mouth gagged, as she was hauled up onto a horse to ride in front of a big brawny soldier, clad in mail and boiled leather and musty wet fur. She could smell him, and he was smelling her too. "Southern stink," he said, sniffing long and deep at the back of her neck. "We love a bit of that where we're from. We're all gonna love a bit of you too."

She could feel him stir, as he pressed himself forward in the saddle, prodding at her all the while. And for the hours they rode that day, she endured him and his stink and his stiffness. *A test,* she would tell herself, *that is what this is. I cannot react, nor will I. Not until my job is done.*

She entered a place of calm, and knew that Marian would be proud. And that was enough to satisfy her. The imagined pride of a would-be mother.

8

Ranulf

Ranulf Shackton could hear them again.

The grunts and bleats of pleasure, the tumble of bodies, the laughter. Vincent Rose was with the sultry Lumaran twins and enjoying them both at once in his living chambers next door. It was a daily occurrence that Ranulf was largely used to now, as he sat within the office of Rose's quarters, with no more than a thin veil of wood separating him from their unnecessarily noisy passions.

"Come, Ranulf, join us!" came Rose's chuckling voice through the wall. "You work too hard, my friend, and I'm more than happy to share."

The Lumaran twins giggled, and even that was quite audible too. "No thank you, Vincent. That is one adventure I'd rather not take."

"Ha! Well you're missing out, dear man. There is no greater adventure than the one between the sheets."

Ranulf ignored him and carefully turned another page. He'd perfected the art, after turning hundreds of them, and had come to see that the Book of Thala, despite its great age, wasn't quite so delicate as he'd first thought.

"Have you discovered anything new?" Vincent called. Then he laughed loudly, and the twins giggled, and Ranulf could only imagine what they were doing to him. "Anything exciting, anyway?"

Ranulf didn't answer.

"Well? Just remember whose ship this is, Ranulf! Untangle that tongue of yours and speak!"

"You know I don't like to talk to you like this, Vincent. It makes me terribly uncomfortable."

"Well bloody well join us then and break the ice. The twins are desperate for your company."

"Yes, I'm sure they are. But I'd rather not spend time in yours in this condition."

"Condition! Oh your words ever entertain." Rose's guffawing could often be heard all through the ship when he was in this sort of mood. "Nephys, my dear, why don't you entice him in."

Oh gods not again...

The door opened, and Ranulf begrudgingly turned to find one of the twins standing naked in the doorway, her dark skin gleaming with sweat, her cat-like eyes glowing a vivid emerald green. "Will you come, Master Shackton?" she asked in a beguiling voice. "Maybe Vincent would leave us for a moment, until you are more comfortable." She stepped forward a pace. "You don't need to be nervous, you know. It can just be you and I, if you'd prefer."

Her grasp of the common tongue is truly excellent, Ranulf thought, refusing to let any others nudge their way into his mind. "I thank you for the offer, Nephys, but tempted as I am, I really must continue in my work."

"Are you sure? Or would you prefer my sister, Tephys? We are not entirely identical you know. Her breasts are a little larger, if that's your fancy?"

Ranulf knew that. Rose had sent both girls to him in the nude a handful of times already, and he was quite well accustomed to the minor differences between them. "That's quite all right," he told her, turning back to the book. "But thank you for the kind offer, as always, Nephys." He forced himself to read on until he heard her light footsteps patter away. A moment later, the door closed. *Damn you, Vincent, and these rotten games you play.*

He refocused on his studies, such as he could, as the chaotic lovemaking continued next door. It didn't much help that most of what Ranulf had unearthed in the Book of Thala so far had been of little merit or use. It was a compendium of events for the most part, those that had been foreseen within the Eye of Rasalan, and subsequently inscribed here in the book by the serving Rasal monarch. Those events had since become part of historical record, and contained little insight into the sorts of mysteries that Ranulf had long been a student of.

I might as well be reading a series of historical tomes, he thought, idly turning another page. He was onto a section written during the time of King Baldrin the Younger, a reign that lasted some thirty years, half a millennium ago. As a scholar himself, Ranulf was well acquainted with every major Rasal king and queen stretching all the way back to Thala and the founding of the queendom, some three and a half thousand years ago. Baldrin the Younger was hardly the archetypal Rasal monarch, and where others were well known for their wisdom and wit, he was famed for being quite the converse. *Baldrin the Brainless*, history had cruelly called him, for his absent powers of perception. His entries into the book had thus been quite banal, confirming to Ranulf that history had labelled him not cruelly, but correctly, and he had little foresight at all.

He ran his eyes over one such account, reading aloud to overcome the noises next door. "I have seen it, the greatest of joys," he recited. "I will have a son, by my good wife Elspeth. He will be strong and wise, as I am. He will rule for a hundred years, and throughout, there shall be peace, and prosperity, a golden age for our people."

Ranulf scoffed lightly, noting the date of the entry; the year 3021 of the Age of Man. If he remembered correctly, Baldrin's wife Elspeth had been with child at the time, so it was hardly a profound prognosis to foresee the coming of his boy. *And nor did his son reign for a hundred years,* he recalled, *but a mere half dozen. And not one of them were peaceful or prosperous either.*

He stood, needing a short break, and stepped over to a side-table to pour himself a cup of wine. He drank the first cup more quickly than he'd have liked, grunted at the door - the affair was ongoing and, by the sounds of it, reaching a dramatic crescendo - and then refilled his silver goblet.

"Just what is he hoping to find in there?" he grumbled to himself, turning to look at the book. He began pacing to stir his mind. "Two weeks and I've found nothing at all but historical accounts and fatuous nonsense."

Though it had been Vincent Rose who arranged for the Book of Thala to be stolen, its final destination was meant to be Ilithor, and the halls of King Janilah Lukar. But quite what the Warrior King expected to find, Ranulf couldn't work out. A prophesy? A secret? Something that might help him win the war?

Rose had taken a prosaic view on it, when they'd discussed it over dinner one night. "I don't rightly know, and I don't rightly care," he'd said, with that unbreakable confidence of his. "It is not for mere mortals like us to question the motives of kings, Ranulf. It's probably just Janilah swinging his manhood in Godrin's face, that's all. Their feud has been going on for decades. This is nothing but a game."

It sounded plausible, though Ranulf imagined Janilah's motives were a little more shrewd than that. *I must comb through every page and decode every word to find what he is looking for,* he thought now, pacing. *That is my purpose here, to unveil the truth for king and country. Whatever Janilah is searching for, it must be me who finds it first.*

Next door, the climax had come and gone and a silence had settled on the room. A moment later, the door into the office opened up once again, and Rose wandered in, dressed in a purple satin robe that hugged his softish figure unpleasantly well.

"Vincent, please, would you cover yourself up properly."

"Don't be such a prude, Ranulf." He paced forward languidly, taking a long, pleasured breath, mopping the sweat from his thinning hair as he went. "My gods those girls have stamina to spare. I can hardly keep up these days." He smiled foolishly and poured himself a cup of wine, gulped it down, poured another, then turned. Ranulf remained standing near the centre of the small room, cup in hand, rather more appropriately dressed in white cotton hose, cream shirt, and navy doublet. "I thought you were working?" Rose noted, seeing that Ranulf had vacated his usual position at the desk. "I'm not paying you to guzzle down my wine and shirk your duties, my friend."

"You're not paying me at all," Ranulf returned, trying not to look at the swollen bulge between the man's legs, which hadn't been given time to settle.

"Am I not? Then what is that wine you're drinking if not payment? Or the fine cabin you inhabit? Or the free passage from Thalan I have most generously provided? And I'll not even mention the carnal joy I've offered you more times than I can count. Believe me, the twins will take you places you never knew existed, Ranulf, yet for reasons I cannot fathom, you continually rebuff them."

"There is much about *you* I cannot fathom, Vincent, so permit me the same courtesy." Ranulf moved to sit at the desk, setting down his wine, looking away. "I have asked you repeatedly not to try to lure me with those girls, yet still you play your tiresome games."

"Games? Please. I try to open the mind of a friend, and you come at me with these sordid accusations. For such an adventurous man, you can be tremendously dull." He stepped forward, turning his eyes to the book, laid out splendidly at the centre of the large wooden desk. "Now, tell me what else you've unearthed today. There must be a nugget or two in there for us to use."

"Us? You still haven't told me how you intend to use any information I extract."

"The same as you. To satisfy my curiosity, that's all."

"Spare me, Vincent. You intend to sell the information. Just admit it."

"Admit it?" Rose repeated, affronted. "I don't like the suggestion there, Ranulf. It makes it seem as if I'm doing something terribly untoward."

"You stole an ancient tome from a king and killed dozens of people in the process. Untoward is putting it lightly."

Rose lifted a finger. "First, *I* did none of those things," he said, with a little prideful smile on his lips. "I was merely the middleman, the go-between, if you will. And second, I had no choice. Janilah's people came to me with this request, and it was not the sort you say no to. Given the risks, I see no reason why I shouldn't profit from the endeavour too."

The ship rocked a little on the gentle waves, and Ranulf adroitly took up his cup to stop it from spilling. The noonday sun was streaming in brightly through the port-side window, the waters off the Solapian coast a sparkling, turquoise blue.

Ranulf took a sip to settle himself. These sorts of disagreements were common with Vincent Rose and they'd spent many dinners aboard his ship embroiled in impassioned, though typically good-natured, debate. "You *are* profiting, Vincent," he went on. "You told me Janilah is paying you handsomely for your efforts. Or did I hear you wrong?"

"No no, you heard quite right. The good king is compensating me well, it's true, but if I can profit twice, I will. Information is currency, Ranulf, and currency can be traded. Should I find something that I think will appeal to one of my associates, I'll offer it up for a price." He smiled greedily and looked out over the waters. "Janilah will have received my crow by now and will be sending men to fetch the tome. That gives us a month, maybe a little more if we're lucky, before his soldiers take it off us. It would be an awful waste if we didn't find anything before then, wouldn't you say?"

"I'd say, Vincent, that you'll be lucky if those same soldiers don't cut you down as part of the bargain. Say what you will, but Janilah commissioned you to bring the book directly to him, and you have betrayed that trust." He looked at him straight. "Have you met the man before?"

"Janilah?" Rose shrugged, nonchalant. "I can't say I've had the pleasure."

"It's no pleasure, believe me. I found that out when I spent time in his dungeons in Ilithor. He'll take this as a slight and will not forget it. Cross him at your peril."

Rose flicked a bangled wrist. "Yes yes, we all know how ruthless the Warrior King can be. But I'm a businessman, Ranulf, and sometimes transactions don't go as smoothly as one would like. That is the nature of the beast, and Janilah's savvy enough to understand this. I explained it all in the letter I sent him, so you need not worry about me, my friend...though I find it awfully sweet that you do."

He smiled playfully and put an end to the topic there, stepping over to Ranulf's side. His eyes scanned the book. "King Baldrin the Younger," he said, raising a questioning brow. "Now who is he?”

"No one worth mentioning. He's rare as Rasal monarchs go, and was quite the fool. None of his entires have any merit, lest you desire a chuckle."

"Save them for a dinnertime telling, then," Rose said in a humoured voice. "But no matter. So far as I can tell, you haven't gotten to the good stuff yet. My interest lies in the more recent entries, likely those written by Godrin's own hand. I want something usable, Ranulf, and nothing written a thousand years ago is likely to have any bearing on how things are now. Outdated information doesn't interest me."

"No, I suppose it doesn't. Though my personal interests are rather different from yours."

"Oh I know, I know, and for that I feel awful, dear friend. I do hate to see you so dispirited. It hasn't lived up to billing, has it? The mysteries you'd hoped to unravel. The ancient sects and secret societies and all those funny old artefacts that so interest you. Was there truly nothing from Queen Thala about any of that? Or the other ancient monarchs?" He patted him on the shoulder, all the while, in a manner somehow reassuring and condescending all at once.

Ranulf sighed, shifting a little in a bid to dislodge Rose's stroking fingers. "Nothing that I don't already know," he said, with a tipple of fatigue and a rather larger dose of resentment. “Many pages are frustratingly difficult to decipher, whether through writing I simply cannot comprehend, riddles that have little meaning to me, or coded messages that I'm missing. It might well be that there are a great many secrets hidden herein that I'm not seeing, but with a mere month to study the tome I doubt I'll have time to unveil them."

"Or perhaps they're just not there?" Rose offered. He stepped away to refill his wine. "I have a sense about people, Ranulf, and know an obsession when I see one. Best let this one lie, else it will consume you, hmmm?"

"I'm not obsessed."

"No?" Rose turned, his near see-through robe doing little to hide his decency. "You were once interested in nothing but the next great adventure, as I recall, yet now you're no more than a shadow of that man, hiding down here below decks, feverishly poring through these pages night and day. If that's not an obsession, I don't know what is." He swilled his wine. "You ought to spend more time up top. The old Ranulf Shackton I remember would have slept on deck if he could, watching the stars blink awake in the night skies, listening to the waves and the winds, not hunkered at this musty old desk alone. Where has that famed socialiser gone? You've hardly spent any time with little Leshie or the crew. Where are the stories, the gripping tales? You'd once have gathered us all around each night and regaled us of your adventures, but no. Nothing. You're no fun at all."

He was starting to grate now, truly grate on Ranulf's nerves. "The bloody gall of it," he muttered, standing from the desk, stamping off down the short set of steps and across the room, wine cup in hand.

Rose watched on, bemused. "Oh, have I offended you?"

"Most of what you say is an offence, Vincent," Ranulf bit. He made for the table, took the flagon, and hastily filled his cup. "Honestly, you have some nerve to say all this to me. You've near shackled me to this desk with orders to find you something you can use in that blasted book, and now you're telling me to spend more time up on deck? I've never heard anything so hypocritical in my life."

"Well excuse me for caring, Ranulf. True, I've requested you unearth something useful from that old tome, but shackled to the desk? Come on, my friend, that is nonsense and you know it. I've come to you with daily urges to broaden your horizons on this ship, yet those too have been brushed aside." His voice then caught with a rather less jovial edge. "Now I'd caution you to take a better account of your tongue," he said. "You are dear to me, Ranulf, but my generosity has its limits. I hope I don't have to remind you of that."

Ranulf sighed heavily, took a long breath to calm himself, then nodded in quiet thought. *I am obsessed,* he knew, *on that he's telling no lie. And Vincent can intimidate when he wills it, there's truth in that too.* Ranulf was not in the habit of being unmanned by threats, yet it didn't serve to stoke a man like Vincent Rose's ire. *He calls me 'dear friend', but nothing is truly dear to him but profit and gain...and should I threaten that, I'll see the other side of him. A side best avoided, as others will attest.*

"You're right," he said eventually, pulling another breath into his lungs. A sense of contrition came upon him. "I am being unfair, Vincent, and perhaps have taken your hospitality for granted." He looked at the book, and felt its pull. *Just one more page. Just...just one,* he thought. *Who knows what I might find hidden in the next account? A clue to Janilah's purpose, or the mysteries I strive to solve...*

"It's OK, Ranulf," Rose said, stepping forward. He laid an arm over his shoulder, and the sweaty reek of his sexual adventures swept up Ranulf's nose. "We'll be arriving in Miren by this evening, and you know how lovely the Solapian coastline is. Why don't we enjoy the view from the quarterdeck, with the sun of our faces, and as much wine for company as we can take? Some time away from this office might do you some good, allow you to return to the Book of Thala refreshed and reinvigorated." He tugged at him. "So? How about it?"

Ranulf began to nod. *An afternoon off might serve me well. And he's not wrong about the coastline here. This is a truly beautiful part of the world.* "You might be right," he relented. "But...permit me a favour first." Rose raised his eyes, and Ranulf crinkled his nose. "Do wash first, for my sake, and that of the crew. Your congress with the twins has left something of a stink on you, my friend."

Rose grinned dreamily, and wafted his own scent up into his nostrils with a wave of the hand. "My favourite fragrance," he purred. "But I understand it's not for everyone. So be it."

He placed down his wine cup and moved for the door; there were washing facilities in his bedchambers. Ranulf hurried back to the book, sat down, and continued.

Just one more page, he thought. *To satisfy my obsession.*

9

Jonik

They reached Greywater at dusk, after a long day's ride, and not once had the rains abated. They'd come down relentlessly, sometimes light, often heavy, but never moving off for good, cloaking the entire island of Passway Key in a thick blanket of fog.

It hadn't made navigation easy, but Braxton proved a fine helmsman, aided by the information the herder had given him the day before. As they ventured further inland and toward the western coast, the features of the island became more recognisable to the men.

"I know that ridge yonder," called young Devin excitedly at one point. "You recall it, Cap? We went there to trade with those cattlemen once. They took four of our horses and at a good price too. I wonder if they're still there?"

They'd diverted to check if the same cattlemen were in the market for mounts, but had found their settlement deserted. "Must've moved off for better pastures," Turner said, looking around the tumbledown shacks that appeared to have been abandoned some time ago. "No matter, we'll flog the steeds when we reach Greywater. There's usually demand for 'em there."

Jack o' the Marsh and Jonik had been put in charge of leading the horses. Beyond the five steeds being ridden - they'd left Soft

Sid and Grim Pete back at the camp, should some scavenger come by to try to pick at the ship - another seven were unsaddled, with two loaded instead with whatever goods Turner thought they could trade. "If we're to make sail again, we'll need good timber and canvas for repairs," he'd said. "I got some coin, but not enough for what we'll need." He'd grumbled something about gambling debts, before trailing off.

Of course, the horses were the most valuable trade goods they had, which created something of a conundrum. "How do you expect to get back to camp once you've sold them?" Jonik had asked. It was a full day's ride on horseback, and would be a great deal longer and more arduous on foot.

Turner had clearly thought of that already. "We'll not have trouble hiring horse and wagon, Master Jonik," he'd said, in the reverential tone he now used when addressing him. "We'll need a wagon or two to haul the supplies back to camp anyhow, so will be able to hitch a ride on those."

"I don't suppose you'd consider selling Shade, would you?" Jack o' the Marsh posited, riding a broad-necked courser that fit the brawny Marshlander's proportions. "He alone would cover everything we need."

Jonik gave him a withering glare, and Jack nodded with a smile.

"I'll take that as a no, though be forewarned, my friend, Shade may not like it should we venture further south. He's conditioned to highlands and bitter winds, not sand and balmy climes."

"Don't put words in his mouth," Jonik returned. "If you'd like to know what Shade wants, just ask him. He's right here."

Jack's little grin stuck fast to his lips. "All right." He veered a little closer, as they trotted over the squelching moors. "So, Shade, does the sound of sun, sea, and sand tickle your fancy?"

Shade side-eyed him, then chuffed, flicked his mane, and expressed a great, echoing neigh that rang out over the misty hills.

Jack didn't know what to make of it. He looked at Jonik in beseech. "A translation would be most appreciated, if you don't mind. I speak horse well enough, but Shade here has a broader vocabulary than most."

"It means he's amenable to exploring new lands, as I am, but by that sideward glance he gave you, I'm thinking he didn't like the notion that I might sell him." Shade nodded fervently. "And do you know why, Jack o' the Marsh?"

"Please enlighten me, Jonik of the Shadows."

"Because he isn't mine to sell." Jonik ran his hand down Shade's sleek, muscular neck. "He is not property, and never will be, not while I draw breath. He is in my company by his own choice, and that alone. Should he ever desire to part with me, that is his choice too."

The horse stamped his feet in unfettered accord and galloped off at dizzying speed, the winds pulling at his mane and Jonik's black hair and cloak alike. And that was when they came into sight of Greywater, as they stampeded ahead of the group, up and over the final stretch of moorland, and the port came into view, huddled against the falling rains and the closing pall of night.

The others caught up a few moments later, falling in atop the hillside, looking to the dreary town. "Gods be good, we're here," said Turner, venting a wearied sigh. They dismounted their horses and gathered into a circle, Shade taking charge of the steeds to one side. "Right then, let's be quick about this, if we can. We'll see to business first, then we can gather for a brew or several and warm our bellies with some hearty grub." He shivered against the soggy cold air, pulling his coat tighter. "I know a few rough ol' places that'll suit us nice for the night. Hopefully we'll find one to accommodate us."

The others looked greatly appealed by the prospect, rubbing their hands together, grinning eagerly. *After all we drank last night, they want more? Do they not wish for a break from it?*

"Jack, Brax, you two come w'me to the docks. The market won't be open long, but with luck we'll have enough time to shift our wares, or most of 'em at least, before they close up shop."

"And the horses?" asked Jack. "You think we'll find a buyer there, Captain?"

"I can pay old Lady Shark a visit, if you like," put in Brax. "She's always eager for good mounts for her men."

Turner nodded. "Right you are, Brown. Go see her, and

report back to Jack 'n me at the docks. We'll get the steeds penned at a stable in the meantime."

"I'll go with him," Devin said. "I've always wanted to meet Lady Shark."

"Then you'll be the first," Braxton laughed. "She's mean as that name of hers makes her sound, and she'll lick her lips at a sight sweet as you. She likes making little boys cry, you know, so best you avoid her, Dev."

"I'm not a little boy." It was the first time Jonik had seen Devin looking upset. "I'm almost six feet tall, and not far off seventeen summers neither."

"Not far north of five feet, more like," teased Braxton. "Don't worry, kid, you got time to sprout yet. You'll not be a dwarf forever."

Devin snorted and looked angrily at the ground, prodding at a piece of moss with his foot. "I'll knock that wonky jaw of yours back into place, if you push me," he said, under his breath.

"You what?" Braxton was suddenly much larger than normal, and much closer to the boy than a moment ago. "Say that again, boy. Go ahead, see what happens."

Jack o' the Marsh dropped a mollifying hand to Braxton's shoulder and gently drew him back. Other than Soft Sid - who was a veritable giant - Jack was the biggest of them all, and these weren't a group of small men. Turner and Braxton were burly old sorts and Devin wasn't so short as Braxton was making out. *Closer to six feet, certainly,* thought Jonik, mentally measuring his height. *And strong enough for his age too.*

"Come on now, Brax, best chill that tongue," Jack suggested. "You're near three times his age."

"Age has nought to do with it, Jack. Some feisty birds need their wings clipped to keep them in line...that's all this is."

"Violence isn't always the answer. Better to solve disputes through words than rough action, if you can."

"Jack's right," Turner said. "Leave off the boy, Brax. Ain't no need to be threatening him, not in such company." He gestured to Jonik. "Apologies, lord. I'm sure you think we're awful petty, behavin' as such."

"I'm not a lord, Captain Turner. You really don't have to call me that."

"You're lordly in my eyes, to be holdin' that blade." He looked at the black scabbard, which Jonik kept on full show now. "You got the spirit o' Varin in you, demigod blood, and strong stuff too to master a Blade o' Vandar. So lord it is, or master if it pleases you. But sure enough you deserve some title when dealin' with lowly folk like us."

"You stood up to a kraken, Captain Turner, you and all the men. That took great courage. And courage makes one noble."

Jack o' the Marsh might have said that, but sure enough it came off Jonik's tongue. He even unleashed a smile to go with it, which didn't feel especially natural...and he didn't imagine looked good on him either...but he did it all the same.

"You flatter us, young lord," Turner said. He shifted as though about to drop to his knee, and swear his fealty all over again, but merely let his chin dip into a bow. "You have my ship, as I told you last night. Once we get it fit for the water, I'll take you wherever you want to go. I'm in your service till you see my life debt fulfilled. Me and every one of these boys."

All nodded. Jack o' the Marsh looked quietly delighted with how things were turning out. Jonik remembered now that Turner had said something similar last night. He couldn't recall how he responded, however. *Just say thank you,* he thought. *That will do for now.*

"Kind words, Captain," he said, still trying to sound grand. "I imagine I'll want to head south. Jack mentioned the Golden Isles. Perhaps I'll go there."

"A fine choice, should it become final. But you need not tell me now. The ship won't be ready for some days yet, so should you change your mind, say the word. Far as you like, south or north, east or west. I'm a man o' my word, Master Jonik, as these 'ere men will tell you. Twas a miracle you comin' aboard my boat, and that ain't so easy to ignore, not for us men o' the sea, god-fearing folk as we are. So for fear o' ramblin', I'll say it once more." He paused and took a breath. "You have our service, till you see fit to sever it. And our loyalty...you have that too."

A ringing sound came echoing up from the town, the chiming bells telling of the turning of the hour. The rains continued to fall, light now, little more than a misty mizzle, and all across Greywater, lamps and lanterns were starting to wake. Jonik found himself touched by Turner's words. *I got him wrong,* he thought. *He is a good man, as Jack o' the Marsh told me. They all are...decent to the bone.* And then came an unexpected thought. *I rather like having them around,* he realised, as he looked from one man to the next. Turner with his craggy grin and Devin with those big bright eyes, and Jack o' the Marsh, cheerful and full of wit, whose presence he enjoyed most of all. *Even Brown's smile doesn't offend me so much anymore. Might be that I'm getting used to the company of these men.*

"We ought to get going, Cap," Braxton put in, as the silence between them lingered too long. "Dev, you, er...you come with me if you like. It was wrong of me to snap at you as I did. Sorry, kid. You know I'm sensitive about my jaw." He rubbed at the side of his pockmarked face, jutting out a little to the right.

"Might want to be more sensitive about those teeth o' yours," Turner said, with a grim smile. "I ain't so sure what drove that kraken off - the sting o' Master Jonik's blade, or when you smiled at it, Brown."

The men laughed loud and rough, and even Brown took the insult well.

"Anyhow, fine as that apology was," Turner went on, "I got other plans for Devin. Better that you mosey on down to town with Lord Jonik, lad. See if you can find us lodging for the night and then fetch us a table for meat n' mead. You'll find the best taverns down by Squatters Square."

Devin appeared happy enough with that. "Aye, Cap'n. I'll give his lordship a tour."

"Only if he wants it. Don't be taking advantage of his good manners, should he be too polite to tell you where to go." Turner looked to Jonik. "You'll be OK in the lad's company, lord? I can swap him about with Jack if you'd prefer?"

"Should be fine, Captain," Jonik said. "It is still your crew to lead."

"Aye." Turner nodded, respectful. "Just checkin' to make sure."

Their conference atop the hill ended there, as they split to see to their separate tasks…

Greywater fit its name.

The place was dank and musty, the wooden buildings slung low and tightly packed into warrens set back from the rugged, rocky coast. There, the harbour spread out, supplying the town's primary purpose. Many of the buildings were built on stilts to cater to the annual tides, sweeping in for half the year and then pulling back out for the rest. Through winter, the tides were in, so most of the stilts were submerged.

"It's much more obvious over in Stiltport," Devin said, as they strolled down near the docks, heading for the cluster of taverns set a little further inland around Squatters Square. "The way the tides change the look of the town, that is." Jonik hadn't asked, but Devin had clearly noticed him looking at those stilts, and spied a chance to speak. "They're stronger there, up on the northern Tidelands. The water levels change by over ten metres some years, I've heard, and the whole of Stiltport is built on stilts, which I suppose you can guess from its name." He grinned and looked inland. "Not like here. The island rises up higher from the coast, so even when the tides are in, most of the town is protected."

"Just not down at the docks," Jonik said.

"Yeah. Exactly, yeah."

He skipped on, as they entered the grubby, tight streets leading toward Squatters Square. The air was thick with the scent of mould and fish and salt, and everywhere the ramshackle buildings looked in dire need of restoration. *It's rotten,* this place. *Rotten to the point of collapse.*

"So who's this Lady Shark you wanted to meet?" Jonik had been intrigued by the name. "Does she govern the town?"

"Not officially, but might as well," Devin told him with honest enthusiasm. "Got her hands in everyone's pockets, and nose in everyone's business. And when you poke yours in hers, she cuts it off, I've heard. I've seen lots of men about with flat faces 'cause of her."

"She sounds lovely. Why Lady Shark?"

"The name? Oh, what Brown said."

"Because she's mean?"

"That and her face, shark-like as it is. Pointy nose, black eyes, sharp teeth. Maybe that's why she cuts off people's noses when they cross her?"

"Because she's got a long one?"

He shrugged, showing his age. "Sure."

A crowd of men were blocking the street ahead, not intentionally it didn't look, but simply because the lanes were so tight. They were laughing raucously and drinking from clay bottles, five of them, a couple big and burly. Devin seemed to see an opportunity by the firming of his jaw, and the sudden speeding of his gait. He stamped toward them and, without asking them to move, barged right through, calling "away, cretins," as he went.

Jonik almost gawped, it was so unnecessarily impetuous. The men seemed similarly shocked, until they weren't, and then they were angry, then furious. One had tripped over and fallen flat in the sticky mud, soiling his coat. He stood up with filth plastered all over his hands and face and bellowed fumes. "Shit-eating whelp!" he roared. "I'll flay you living!"

He went for young Devin in an instant, charging like a bull, swinging hard and knocking him flat with a powerful hook to the face. The boy went several feet sideward before settling face-down in a puddle, unmoving. "Serves you right you puss-filled boil," spat the man, before levelling Devin with a firm boot to the ribs, then actually spitting on him. He snorted, spun, and stomped away to the company of his friends, to continue drinking and clogging the alley.

Huh, Jonik thought, bemused by the suddenness of it all. He moved casually through the crowds - several others had naturally been drawn to the commotion - and prodded Devin with a black leather boot. "You all right?" he asked. "You alive?"

A few bubbles popped on the surface of the puddle, suggesting he was still breathing at least.

Jonik leaned down and took a grip of Devin's collar, pulling him back to his feet with a groan. The left side of the boy's face was already blackening, his cheek possibly fractured, eye preparing to balloon. Though all of that was hard to see through the mud. "Are you still with me, Devin?" He looked into his eyes, and saw a foggy cognisance. "Can you walk?"

Devin nodded feebly, then cringed and rubbed his cheek where the brute had struck him. "I'm...I'm fine," he stammered. "I'm not...not hurt."

"You sure?"

He nodded, tried to stand upright, then keeled over. Jonik was quick enough to catch him. "Right, let's get you sat down somewhere."

He looked around. The alley had opened out into a wider street, and at the end of it, it opened further into a bustling square. *Squatters Square,* he imagined. The town wasn't large enough to have more than one busy quad. He wrapped his arm around Devin's waist and set off, supporting the boy through those early first steps, as he stumbled like a fawn from the womb. When they entered the square, his eyes were beset by revelry. Seafaring men were fond of a drink and liked to make the most of their time when in port. That explained the scantily clad women, too, and the tasteless makeup, and all the sordid propositioning going on. Each timberframe building around the square looked like a tavern or brothel or both, and business was booming in every last one of them.

Jonik sighed. He'd hoped it would be quieter than this, but here he was, so off he went. At the far edge of the courtyard, on the inland side, a darkened corner offered a bit of respite from the roistering. A swinging sign - painted, by some coincidence, with a kraken attacking a ship - suggested a tavern, so he made for it, pushed through the black wooden door and stepped inside. *This'll do,* he thought, looking around. The tavern wasn't so busy as he'd feared, lit at one end by a burning hearth, and with a broad mahogany bar at the other. He made for a spare table at the far wall, manoeuvring Devin through the tables and chairs and the cloaked men, clustered in their groups around the bar.

"Oi, we're a reputable place here, and don't want no trouble," came a crackly old voice, as they took their seats. Jonik looked up, to find an old bartender shuffling toward them with more speed than one might expect for a figure of such decrepitude. "Out, the both of you!" He waved a withered hand. "Come on, out!"

"We're not here to stir trouble," Jonik said, as politely as he could manage. "We mean only to have a drink and enquire over lodging, if you have any?"

The old man seemed to reconsider things. It appeared Devin's bloodied face had given him cause for concern. "Lodging, you say? For how long?"

"Just for the night."

"Quick stopover, then." He said it like it happened a lot, giving the two young men another scan. "You don't look a sailor to me," he said, in reference to Jonik, whose black cloak, lined with fur at the shoulders and neck, was hardly typical seamen garb.

"I'm just passing through," Jonik said. "A kind captain gave me passage."

"And this one?" Devin still looked groggy, hardly able to contribute to the conversation. The old innkeeper studied him a moment. "What happened to him? The two of you looked like you were coming in here to escape something, and I'll not have some rowdy group of thugs barging in here to find you."

"You need not worry," Jonik said, softening his natural rasp such as he could. "The boy is just clumsy, and found himself in the way of a startled horse. Got knocked over and hit his face against a wall." He pursed his narrow lips. "Nasty business. But unless that horse - or wall - should be looking to further the fight, you don't have to worry about anyone coming to find us."

An ugly gargle of laughter crawled up and out of the man's short wrinkly neck. "Then it seems I had you wrong, and for that I'll beg your pardon," he said, seeming sold on the fib. "I try to nurture a well mannered clientele here, such as I can, to retain the fine ambience we have."

He gestured with pride across the inn, which did have a warm rustic feel to it. The crackling fire and gentle din of conversation presented a pleasant backdrop, and no one was speaking especially loudly.

"We understand," said Jonik. "By the looks of things, all the hooligans are outside in the square."

"Aye, too true. Busy time of year with the tides in. And the Shark's men are causing no end of trouble."

"I hear she likes to cut off noses."

"Oh sure, and that's if you're lucky. Many get more than a chopped snout."

Jonik didn't seek details. He pulled a small pouch of coins from his cloak and placed it on the table with a clunk. "So how about that lodging?"

The man's beady little eyes judged the weight of the pouch, the clink of the coins within. "Mayhaps we have a room or two going spare," he said. "Just the two of you, is it?

"Five. Three others will be joining us shortly."

"Aye. You'll need some more chairs, then, for the table. And something to fill your bellies on a cold wet night like this. But drinks to start, yes?" He laid a shrivelled hand on Devin's shoulder. "This one looks like he needs one, and something strong too. Whiskey? And a nice big mead on the side for afters?" He was glancing at the pouch of coins all the while, with an avarice all innkeeps shared.

"Just the one whiskey," Jonik told him. "For the boy."

"Right you are. Whiskey and two meads, coming up."

They had their drinks a few moments later, as the innkeep hustled about, fetching chairs, and bringing Devin a rosewood soaked rag to help with the swelling on his face. He wiped it clean of muck and blood, pressed it to his cheek, and quaffed his whiskey, and once all that was done he looked a great deal better.

"So, are you going to tell me what that was about back there?" Jonik asked him, taking a sip of his mead.

Devin's eyes went down to the wooden table. "Nothing. I...I was just being stupid."

"Trying to prove something to yourself?" Jonik could read it well enough in his face. "After what Braxton said about your size?"

A shrug pulled at the youngster's shoulders. "Maybe," he admitted. "I guess I just..." He stopped, shaking his head.

"Go on."

He glanced up. "Well, I...I thought I'd be OK, you know...with you there." His eyes dropped again. "To back me up," he added in a faint voice.

Jonik might have been more angry were Devin not so contrite. He looked feeble enough, sitting there with that rag to his cheek, mumbling to the rutted table, without a scolding to add to his woe. "You provoked those men," he pointed out in an even voice. "What did you think was going to happen? That I'd come ghosting in with the Nightblade to cut them through?"

Devin shook his head. "I don't know. I wasn't thinking. I know you're trying to go unnoticed."

"Where possible."

Jonik gave the inn another quick pass with his eyes, a habit he'd grown conditioned to. He'd become somewhat recognisable in Varinar, when portraying Fitzroy Ludlum, and could never be sure when someone might notice him. *And thus I'd be better served going south, and then further south still,* he thought. *The fewer northern men around me, the better.*

The occupants of the tavern appeared to be keeping their own counsel, mostly, though a couple had glanced their way. Jonik's general demeanour tended to do that, though just as likely they were being drawn to young Devin's battered face. Yet there was one, a man of interesting disposition, sitting alone at the bar. He had before him a mug of ale, quill and parchment on which he was writing something. There was a studiousness to his expression, an erudition, yet he had the framing of a warrior too, broad-shouldered and black-bearded, with a bearing that men carrying godsteel tended to possess. Jonik's eyes stayed with him for a moment, until the stranger lifted his gaze from his work, and looked directly at him. It was a curious thing, that of a man sensing in another some similarity, and being drawn to them by an unconscious whim. For several long heartbeats they looked across the tavern at one another, before the man reworked his lips into a smile, nodded affably, and returned to his writings.

"Someone you know?" Devin asked, interrupting the moment.

Jonik shook his head and returned his attention to the boy. "I've never seen him before."

"So he's not one of those Shadowfolk tracking you?" He said it with far too much volume, and with far too little fear.

"Not one I recognise, if he is, and you'd do well to keep your voice down."

Devin bit his lip. "Right. Um...sorry, milord."

Jonik glanced at the stranger again, as he dipped his quill, and continued scratching away at his scroll. *Was he here when we arrived?* He hadn't noticed him, if so. And that gave life to a more concerning prospect - that he'd followed them in, set up the quill and parchment as cover for his true intentions, and had been watching Jonik all along.

Then he had a thought. "You want to make it up to me?" he asked, looking to Devin, who seemed desperate for such a chance.

"Anything." The boy was like a hound, big-eyed and loyal, but not always so easy to control.

Jonik leaned in. "Go grab two more meads from the bar. There's space next to that stranger there, for you to make your order."

Devin was quick enough to get it. "You want me to see what he's writing?"

"Yes. Furtively. Can you do that for me, Devin?"

Devin was already on his feet, though looked a tad unstable. "Aye, milord, no problem at all."

He's overeager, Jonik realised too late, as the boy moved carelessly into position next to the stranger, lacking any discernible tact in his investigations. It was almost amusing, and so said the stranger's face, one side of his lips gripped in a knowing grin as Devin fumbled about, trying to get a clear view of his work. Yet he returned triumphant all the same, utterly oblivious to how poorly he'd performed.

"Got a good look," he said, puffing his chest, and passing Jonik his fresh ale. "He had no idea. None." He grinned, boastful, and gulped his drink.

"And?" Jonik had no heart to tell him otherwise. "Did you see what he's writing?"

"Oh, nothing I could understand. He was writing in another language. Something southern, I think."

That softened Jonik's suspicions somewhat, though quite why he was so suspicious, he couldn't rightly say. *Because you're paranoid,* he told himself, *and still not so comfortable as you think you are, carrying about that godly blade.* The idea of someone taking it from him brought a sharp edge to his thinking that made everyone a threat.

He had little time to consider it, however, as the door was flung open and Jack o' the Marsh paced inside, bringing the howl of celebration with him as the merrymaking continued in the square beyond. He took one look around, spotted his companions in the corner, expressed that broad smile of his, and then called out across the quad for Turner and Braxton - who'd evidently been checking the other taverns - to join him.

A few moments later, all three of them were gathering at the table, having fetched tankards of ale from the bar.

"Is Shade well settled?" Jonik asked Jack, as he sat down beside him at the small circular table.

"You do worry about him so." Jack took a long swig, then wiped his mouth of the froth. "He's fine. I think he rather likes supervising the other steeds, if I'm honest. Though I'm not so sure he's happy about the prospect of selling them on."

"Would you be? It's slavery, as far as he sees it."

Jack gave him a quizzical look, then let his eyes run over the room. "Might you be giving Shade a little too much credit, perchance? He's smarter than most mounts, true, but I'm not sure he understands the moral complexities of slavery, my friend. You'd need a human intellect for that."

"Depends what human we're talking about." Jonik might have thought of Soft Sid, but Devin's bumbling behaviour that evening had brought the youngster to mind.

"So did you meet Lady Shark, then?" Devin was asking Braxton across the table.

The crooked-jawed sailor emerged from his tankard and gave Devin a grim, frothy smile. "Indeed I did, lad, and good thing you didn't come with me too. She was in a foul mood, worse than normal, though why I couldn't say. Didn't want to talk business, so I'll have to head back tomorrow and try again." He didn't look particularly appealed by the idea.

"What about the other wares?" asked Jonik.

Turner plonked a bag of coins on the table. "How does that answer your question, lord? We done all right, didn't we Jack?" He slapped the man's muscular back. "The lad could sell seawater to a seaman, so he could. Who knew Jack o' the Marsh had such a knack for barterin'?"

Jonik hardly found the news surprising, though didn't offer Jack any favour by saying it. "Enough for what you need to repair the ship?"

"Once we sell the mounts, perhaps, though we'll have to hope Brax here can sweeten up old Lady Shark first. Maybe don't smile next time, Brown. You'll have her running off like you did that kraken."

He seemed to enjoy the 'bad teeth' jokes more than anyone else. This time Brown wasn't quite so amused. "Well how's about you go visit her next time, and we'll see if you fare any better?"

"Can't fare much worse." Turner sunk his beer in one, then called out for the barkeep to bring another round. "That old fossil behind the bar tells us you secured beds for us all, lord?" he then said, giving Devin a firm glare. "That were meant to be your job, boy, yet I'm supposin' that mangled face o' yours has something to do with it."

Devin glanced at Jonik. "I...got run over by a horse," he said, repeating Jonik's lie. "Hit my face on the wall. Nasty business."

No one looked particularly convinced, nor did they look particularly interested either. As Turner set about ordering a tableful of chicken, bread and pungent cheese, Jack gave Jonik a little nudge. "You see that guy at the bar?" he said, glancing to the stranger. "He's writing Lumaran. You find that odd for a northerner?"

"Lumaran," Jonik repeated. Jack must have taken a quick peep when he'd arrived and ordered his drinks. *With rather more success than Devin too. I hardly even saw him get near the guy.* "Devin said it was southern, so he got that right at least. How can you tell?"

"The symbols are pretty easy to spot, if you've ever seen Lumaran before. Have you not? I was of the impression Shadowknights were trained in mind as well as body?"

"We are, but not in everything. Depends what contracts we take. I know a little about southern languages, but not much."

"Right. And what was that about Devin?"

"I sent him up there for me, to get a look at what he was writing. He recognised it as southern, though nothing more specific than that."

"*Sent*? Seems you're settling nicely into this leadership thing, my friend." Jonik ignored the waggish grin. "So, can I infer that you're suspicious of him? He seems out of place here, doesn't he? There's a gravitas to him. Do you think he's Bladeborn?"

"He is. I can tell."

"How?"

"Same as you. Bladeborn often carry themselves in a certain way, which the keen-eyed can observe."

Jack nodded. "They do seem to possess an inner weight to them, it's true. Perhaps I'll go and have a word with him, see what he's about."

"I'm not sure that's smart."

"Why not? I'm a personable chap, and can read people well enough. I'll feel him out for you, no trouble."

He'd left before Jonik could further his protestations, moving through the increasingly crowded inn with a sleek grace unusual for a man of his size. *He could be confused for Bladeborn himself,* Jonik thought, watching him go. It seemed a shame that a man like Jack o' the Marsh had been born common, with no noble blood to his name. The great houses were all blessed with Varin blood, and beneath them were many dozens of smaller houses who boasted weakening bloodlines, or no Bladeborn links at all. Jack o' the Marsh had been sired by no such house, nor had he been born to the rung below, or the one below that. He was the son of a priest and a milkmaid, a step or two from being penniless, and yet by judge of character alone, felt more noble to Jonik than many of the great lords and knights he'd met.

And what of your father? came a dark whisper in his ear. *Is he not noble, Jonik? And his son, his heir, his echo, destined for greatness, and now gone, because of you….*

Jonik cringed against the thought. *I did it for you,* came his reply. Because that whisper, he knew, it came from the blade he bore. *I had no choice, lest I lose you. And I'll make them pay for it. One day, I will.*

Then why do you run? Because they'll not stop chasing you. Is that what you want? To run, and hide forever...to be alone until the darkening of your days?

Jonik shook his head. *I'm not alone. I...I have these men with me now...*

He could almost hear the laughter, deep in the darkest shadows of his mind, but that wasn't the Nightblade…no, that was himself, the darker side of himself that he was trying to leave behind. Companionship was not a part of the codes he'd been weaned on. *Closeness is weakness,* he remembered. *Bonds, when broken, can break a man too.* There had been no space for friendship in the Shadowfort, not between the men born and bred there. "If you forge a bond with another, then what if they should not return? What if they should fail, or betray the order? What if you should be called upon to hunt them, Jonik? Could you? Could you kill a man you called friend?"

Shadowmaster Gerrin had taught him that, one of a thousand lessons Jonik still recalled. *And now, is it he who hunts me?* he had to wonder. *He who raised me, trained me, as a father might a son?* Their relationship had been cruel and violent, as was customary in their order, but had there not been a bit of tenderness too? An occasional kind word. A smile. An urging nod.

Jonik could remember a few such instances, as patches of thawed green grass on an endless snow-draped plain. They stuck out to him because they were so few, and he wondered whether Gerrin might recall them too. That look of pride he gave him when he first began to master the Nightblade. The shadow of concern he'd seen in his master's eyes, when he sent him on his path to assassinate Amron Daecar.

And yet he knew, he thought. *He knew what he was making me do, that he was sending me to kill my own father, my own brother, my very own family.* Jonik's fist closed firm around his mug. *Might he be the worst of them all, for that? Might I not seek to kill him first, for that?*

His thoughts wandered. He had no clear path still, no sure way forward. He drew a sip of ale and looked at Turner, Braxton, Devin, laughing at some joke. Away at the bar, Jack o' the Marsh was making inroads with the stranger. They were laughing too, Jonik saw. *How does he do that? How can he shift a man into mirth so soon after meeting?*

I am not like him, and never will I be, he knew. *And this new path of mine...this path of light,* he snickered. *Is it lightness to want to destroy the order that made me? Is this lightness, Jack, that fills my veins, when I imagine the Nightblade moving through them, one after another...when I look to that great fort and see it in flames?*

He'd loved it once, or whatever version of love he felt. Those high passes. The winds. The storms. But now he saw it was no different to how a captive learns to love his cage. It is the familiar fighting the unknown. Safety fighting doubt. And broken from its weighty shackles, he saw only the darkness he'd left behind. The darkness that needed purging. He'd lived a lie and only now did he know it. And what of all those who remained? All those other Bladeborn bastards, slaves to the cruel will of the council? *Do they not deserve to break free, as I have? To taste life beyond that cold, lifeless place?*

He sat in cold counsel with himself, sipping his ale, until the large frame of Jack o' the Marsh returned, bearing a grin. "Well that was an interesting discussion.," he said, dropping back into his seat. Jonik looked over to see that the stranger was now packing his things up at the bar, offering the group a congenial glance as he moved off to the door.

"Aye, saw you chit-chatting over there," said Turner, leaning back in his chair, and cradling his mug against his belly, looking about as content as a man could be. "Who was he, Jack?" He began rocking. "Making new friends, are we?"

"More than just a friend, if he's to be believed. He might just be our salvation."

The group shared a series of interested looks. "We're gonna be needing more than that, kid," said Braxton. "Who is he?"

"Someone who's in the market for precisely what we've got," Jack said, picking up a leg of chicken. "Namely horses and transportation. Lost both in the storm, apparently - his ship fared worse than ours, and is down in Daarl's Domain now with half of its crew. The rest managed to cling to some debris and got picked up yesterday morning by a passing fishing boat...but not before most of them were taken by sharks." He took a big bite of chicken, as demonstration.

"Aye, cause they didn't have Lord Jonik here to ward 'em beasties off," Turner said.

Jack swallowed his chicken, facilitating its journey with a great swill of mead. "Indeed. And that leaves our new friend rather stranded, much like us, lest we help one another out. He saved his valuables in a waterproof satchel and has money enough to get us back on the water in no time. All he asks is that we give him transport, and we can forget having to deal with Lady Shark and her cutthroats too."

"Transport where?" asked Braxton. "Somewhere north by his look." They glanced up, but the man had already departed. "Why didn't you invite him over, so we might all get a read on him?"

"Too much too soon, Brax," Jack said, continuing his feast. "I've told him to meet us tomorrow, once we've had a chance to consider the offer."

"Aye, and so where's he headed?" Turner pushed, rocking back and forward on his chair. "We ain't going nowhere lest Master Jonik agrees to it. I've made that pledge already, and won't be backin' out."

"I'd never suggest that, Captain. Yes, he's a northerner - out of North Tukor by his accent - but he's not stepped foot on the continent in years, he says. Plies his trade south now, down in Lumara mostly. Says he has people there who're always looking for good horses."

Turner thought on it a moment. "We'd be passin' the Golden Isles, lord, were we to head that way. So I suppose it wouldn't hurt us, not if that's where you want to be goin'."

Jonik still wasn't sure. "It remains your ship, Captain, and your choice. If this will speed our departure, that suits me."

"Seems it would, if he's as flush as Jack makes out. What of this rest of his crew? Those not chomped up by them sharks and the like?"

"He made no mention or anyone but himself." Jack had devoured the chicken leg and started on a chunk of bread. "I don't think it was his ship. He was just hiring it, so he has no connection to the crew."

"Aye, that makes things easier. This man got a name?"

"Emeric Manfrey."

"Manfrey? Now why does that ring a bell?" Turner brushed through his bushy blond beard in thought.

"You'll be thinking of Sir Oswald Manfrey, Captain," said Jack. "One of the greatest ever Varin Knights."

"Aye, that'll be it," he chuffed. "Use to love that tale, when I was a young-un. Manfrey and the dragons. His hike to Vandar's Tomb." He smiled wistfully. "I wonder if they're related."

Jack was smiling too. "Distantly, maybe, and wouldn't that be a thing? Sir Oswald died hundreds of years ago, but it's possible." Jack looked to Jonik at that, speaking to him directly. "He had a godsteel sword in his cloak, and didn't care to hide it. But...he seemed honest, if my judgement means anything to you. Might be that he's more than he seems, but I saw nothing to suggest he was part of the order trying to hunt you."

Jonik had already come to the same conclusion. "Let's put it to a vote," he said, though already he could see that the others were sold. "Who wants to include Emeric Manfrey on our journey south?" He looked across the table, a part of him rather enjoying being in charge.

"Can't hurt to have another Bladeborn aboard, should we run afoul o' pirates and such," said Turner. "Not to mention the other perils down there, of which there are a fair few."

Jonik didn't look for him to elaborate. He knew how Turner liked to go on. "Braxton?"

Braxton shrugged. "As Cap'n said, having another sword in the company ain't something to sniff at. And we got these men hunting you too, who're more likely than pirates or any other peril to catch up with us, the way you told us last night."

It was another thing Jonik didn't remember clearly, though he must have said it straight and true. All he had was his head start, but it wouldn't keep the wolves from the door for long. He nodded and looked to Devin. "Dev?"

"Yeah...sounds good to me," the boy said. "I mean, whatever everyone else says."

"You know where I stand, lordling," said Jack, having his turn. "Emeric seems an interesting character to me, and the sooner we're back on the water, the better. Those shadows you're running from...they'll spread here soon enough, and we'd best be gone by they time they arrive."

It seemed settled, and so Jonik raised his mug to the heart of the table, and four others came to kiss it. They all looked at him as though expecting a speech, and truly he had no idea what to say. "To...to our onward adventure," he offered, finding a few words that worked.

They worked for the men too, who all smiled.

Their crew was to swell by one.

10

Saska

It was dusk when they arrived at the Kastor warcamp, somewhere between Harrowmoor and Shellcrest upon a rise out on the plains. A sea of tents and pavilions had been established, of Tukoran brown and green, and above them fluttered banners and flags of the houses under Kastor rule.

Firepits were covered in tarps on poles. Men sat round them swilling grog and munching on hunks of stale bread as the force of a hundred horses stamped on through. They seemed to go on forever, wending down streets between the portable canvas city, as Saska tried to calculate just where they were, how far they'd gone, and how she might get out.

Eventually, they came upon a pocket of larger pavilions erected within a cluster of old stone ruins. There had been a castle here once, though for whatever reason it had been abandoned and left to crumble. Two towers stood apart, their upper battlements collapsed at their roots, and between them the foundations of the outer wall and gatehouse still poked out from the mud. Beyond them, the pavilions stood, their canvas coverings beaten by the rain, and by their stately grandeur Saska guessed that this was where Cedrik Kastor would be.

They dismounted outside the ruins, somewhere at the heart of the sprawling encampment, Saska figured, as the stablehands came forth to tend to the horses after their ride. The malodorous soldier with whom Saska had ridden swung a great, mail-clad leg and dropped to the softened ground, then reached out to pull her off his whickering horse.

"Now now, be careful, Borgin," said the Kastor commander - whom Saska had heard called Sir Griffin during the ride - as he slipped with more grace from his fine, padded saddle. "She's precious cargo, and not to be manhandled so. My uncle shan't be pleased to find her in poor condition."

Borgin grunted, and set her down with more care. "I'll be seeing you again," he promised her, and for the first time she got a good look at him. He was as foul of face as he was of smell, his scraggly hair hanging limp and thin from his halfhelm, several scars rutting his ugly face. One wound looked fresh, a festering gash on his cheek that he'd probably won during the coastal assault some weeks back. "Maybe I'll be put on watch with you, girl. Get some time alone in your tent..."

"No, there'll be none of that." Sir Griffin Kastor stepped forward and pushed Borgin away, who staggered sideward, before righting his footing with a grunt. "Fear not, girl, that lout won't lay a hand on you. We don't allow low men like him to bed our precious breeders. You'll be tended well enough here."

"B-breeders?" Saska repeated.

"Yes, and it's just as it sounds. Not particularly nice, I wouldn't have thought, but in truth our breeders live well. Certainly a great deal better than in that village we found you in," he scoffed. "But you'll need to be tested first, of course. The stronger your Varin blood, the better."

He placed a leather-gloved hand to her left shoulder and turned her toward the central encampment. Behind, the captain of his guard was calling orders and the men were dispersing, none more grumpy than Borgin as they did, wet and cold and ready to count out their daily spoils. "Come along, you'll be housed here. There's an area near the rear curtain wall set up to accommodate you and your sort. Lady Cecilia will take you under her care."

They moved past the old moat, though it was hardly dug deep

anymore, filling in over the years and now no more than a shallow ditch. Across it, however, a short stone bridge offered passage, as they entered the skeleton of the fort, and came into sight of the dozens of marquees arranged tidily within.

"What is this place?" Saska asked, in her soft Aramatian accent. "It looks like it was grand, once before."

"Grand?" He repeated the word with a chuckle. "Hardly more than a low lord's keep to my eyes, but my eyes have seen a great deal more than yours, I'll wager. You'll know grand if ever you should travel to Keep Kastor, where I grew up. This place is a hovel by comparison."

Oh I've seen Keep Kastor, Saska thought, *and the palace in Thalan, and Northgate Castle, and Harrowmoor too. I've seen more than you're ever likely to know.* Tilda wouldn't say that, though, nor even think it, so Saska kept her eyes big and bright as she gazed about the broken stone walls and towers, imagining how they might have once been. "Did a king live here once?"

He glanced at her, as though she was so very simple. "This was a castle of the old Lowplain Kings, if I'm not mistaken," he offered, in an indifferent voice. "Which one I don't know. Morlan the Third, or Fourth, I think." He finished with a bored flick of the wrist.

Saska had heard of the War of the Lowland Lords from Father Pennifor, though wasn't sure if these kings were the same men. *Unlikely,* she thought, *given how old the place is.* Rasal history was rich with infighting and civil conflicts, and though there had always been a monarch in Thalan, other great lords had often called themselves king and separated themselves from the crown, for a time.

"How long ago did they rule?" she asked, looking at a part of the inner wall still standing. It rose about fifteen feet high, topped with a narrow walkway, and some of the crenels were still intact. *Not so large at all, really.* The walls at Harrowmoor and Northgate were several times as grand, and near thick as they were tall besides.

Sir Griffin glanced at her once again, wondering whether to continue humouring her queries. "I don't know. A thousand years, perhaps. I'll not pretend I'm an expert in Rasal history. And these kings, they were hardly kings at all. King of a hill or two, but little more, squabbling over these empty moors." He grinned at how pathetic it sounded. "Though let me ask you something, girl."

She dipped her eyes to the ground. "Of course...my lord."

"Your name, for one. Where you're from, for another. I find myself curious as to how you came to be here in these lands. But more so that you're Bladeborn. Do you know who your father was?"

She shook her head. "I never knew him. My mother was a simple housemaid, as I am, in Aram. She worked in the estate of a merchant when she had me. She never told me who my father was."

"No, she wouldn't. I suppose a northern lord must have bedded her during a profit seeking venture with this merchant. Against her will, most likely, judging by how you look. A pretty thing, for sure, and no doubt your mother was the same." He spoke with such a casual disdain for her and how she might have been sired. "And your name?"

"Tilda."

"Tilda? Doesn't sound much like an Aramatian name to me."

"My mother wanted me to live among northerners, so gave me a northern name. It was not safe where I am from."

"Ha, the irony. And it's safer for a southerner here, is it?"

"In Rasalan, yes. They treat southern people well here. I was kindly treated by Master Westham. And now...now he is dead."

"By his own hand," Sir Griffin was quick to point out. "When my men are threatened, they are sure to respond fiercely. If he'd stayed quiet and not caused a fuss, he'd have been just fine."

"You had just beheaded a woman dear to him. It is hard not to react to that."

The knight stopped, and his temper spoiled, that lazy disdain in his eyes sharpening to anger. "That hulking cow spat in my face. *Me*. Nephew to the Lord of Ethior and honoured knight of House Kastor. She's lucky I didn't lengthen her end and see her suffer for that. And now your master is dead too, for which she is to blame, not I. These little people need to know when they're beaten."

He snorted and spun on his heels, marching away, as Saska followed in his wake, wondering just why she was antagonising him. Would Tilda do so, this browbeaten servant girl from the south? It wouldn't serve her to be too outspoken, nor stoke the fires of this impetuous young knight. *He might just let Borgin in with me, if I aggravate him*, and that thought alone was plenty to seal her lips.

They continued to the rear of the derelict castle, passing what was once the main yard, where the largest pavilions had been set up. One looked fit for Lord Kastor, guarded by a brace of Emerald Guards, with their tall godsteel lances and shields, and rich green cloaks hanging sodden at their backs. Their presence suggested he was in there now, though Sir Griffin hardly gave the place a glance as he marched on through to the rear, beyond another cluster of shelters intended for the cooks and armorers and medics and scholars here to record affairs, and offer counsel to the lords, where needed.

Further back still, another tower sat crumbled in the rear left corner of the outer battlements, and a part of the postern gate still stood, though its iron bars had long since fallen to dust. There, the final tents had been arrayed, a series of a dozen or so pavilions lined up in a neat row.

Sir Griffin looked to have calmed by the time they reached them. "You'll be staying here, for the time being," he told her, waving at those tents. Then he led her to one set aside from them, a private pavilion of modest proportion, its canvas door held open on a hook. A timber decking had been laid inside, and two braziers near the entrance offered light and warmth. Saska got a look beyond them as they approached. At the rear, an attractive middle aged woman sat at a dark wooden desk, laid with heaps of parchment, scribbling with a quill by candlelight. She lifted her gaze as Sir Griffin approached, her rich brown hair tied up in an intricate braid. *Llana would be impressed,* came a thought. *She was always so fond of doing up her hair.*

"My Lady Cecilia, I have another for you." He paced forward, ushering Saska in beside him like a prized cattle at a show. "And a rare one too, as you can see."

The woman offered little reaction to the proud little grin on his face, as she took Saska in with a pair of keen jade eyes, setting her quill aside to announce that she had her full attention. "Your name?"

Sir Griffin nudged Saska forward, and her head fell into a bow. "Tilda, my lady."

There was a pallet bed to one side, coated in furs, and several small tables arranged at the walls, set with candles and small stacks of books. The rain continued to fall outside, a constant drizzle chasing them across the plains through the afternoon. It pattered against the sloping canvas roof as Lady Cecilia continued her observation. "Age?"

"Eighteen."

The woman nodded then took up her quill again, scratching notes. "Where were you taken from, Tilda?"

"Some godsforsaken village a few hours from here," began Sir Griffin. "She's southern, Lady Cecilia, look." He seemed a child all of a sudden, excitable in her company. "From Aram, she says."

"I noticed. Now please let her speak, Sir Griffin."

That silenced him. Saska could hear him drawing back a pace, and had to work to conceal her smirk.

"Go ahead, child. Continue. What is the village called, where Sir Griffin found you?"

"Baymoor, my lady."

"And you're from Aram originally?"

"Yes, my lady. I came here two years ago, to find work, at my mother's urging."

Lady Cecilia observed her quietly for a moment. "So you lived in Aram until you were sixteen years old?"

Saska nodded.

"You learned the common tongue, then, while you were there? Your grasp of it is excellent. Even your word usage is typically northern."

"My mother taught me."

"Your mother? And what did she do?"

"She was some house servant," said Sir Griffin, still lingering behind her. "Plowed by a lord doing business with her master, I figure..."

"There is no need for you to be here any longer, Sir Griffin. Please leave us."

"My lady? I am only trying to help."

"You're not. You are interrupting my work. If you're concerned you'll not be given credit for this one, fear not, you will. I've already recorded in my notes that you were the one to bring her in."

"Yes, well...good. I think my uncle will be particularly interested in her, given her heritage. And she's strong too. Took up my blade easily enough, before dropping it to the mud. But that was shock, I think, rather than weakness. I'd hope to be credited with finding her, Lady Cecilia, when she comes to his attention."

"I'll be sure to mention you. But remember, these girls are not Kastor property. They are in the service of the crown. I will decide where they go, not your uncle."

"By who's order?"

"The king's." And with that the boy was silenced again. "Now please, do let me work, Sir Griffin. I'm sure you have pressing matters to attend to, what with the siege of Harrowmoor to be planned."

Saska still didn't turn to look at him, but imagined he was lifting his chin and trying to seem important. But truly, he was of little significance here, and would be less so when the Vandarians arrived. Saska knew they were coming, though how far out they were remained to be seen. *I must get to him before they come,* she thought. *My task will be doubly hard with a great host of Varin Knights in camp.*

"There is much to be done," Sir Griffin concluded. "Should I come upon more cattle for your pen, I'll return in due course, my lady."

The boy playing at being a knight left with that, and Saska found herself in the company of an adult instead. "I apologise for him," Lady Cecilia said. "You are not cattle, Tilda, nor will you be staying in a pen. Do you know why you've been brought here?"

Saska bit her lip, and glanced through the opening, as Sir Griffin marched vaingloriously away. "He said something about...breeding? I...I don't know if I fully understand."

"It means you will be given a great opportunity, to be in the service of a great king. Does that sound appealing to you?"

"I...I don't know. I am just a house servant. I cook, and I clean."

"Like your mother?"

"Yes, my lady."

"Who knew the common tongue, well enough to teach it to you?"

"I...have improved, I think, since I came here. But she taught me the basics, yes."

"And where did she learn it?"

"From a former master, when she was young. She would tend to his guests, sometimes, and they were often from the north. It was better that she knew how to speak with them."

"Tend to them? And what do you mean by that?"

"I...I think it was just serving them. But..." She looked away. "I don't know for sure."

"Of course."

A silence fell upon the room. Short, but telling, as Lady Cecilia continued to observe her in her own time. She spoke again after some ten seconds that felt a good deal more. "And this simple life you lead. Cooking, and cleaning. Does it satisfy you?" Saska's eyes were drawn back up, in time to see her smile for the first time, and how beautiful she was when she did. And what was the point, of course, to make her more inviting...less a threat, more a friend.

"I have never known anything else."

"As say most girls who come to me, seeking something more. But they know not who they truly are, and where they truly come from. I am the link, to bring them back to where they belong. You are Bladeborn, Tilda. Do you know what that means?"

"I can hold godsteel. I...I have the blood of Varin in my veins."

"You do." She purred the words, then stood, moving around the table, as her deep green robes fell down behind her. She was of medium height, her figure of shapely form, the sort to turn heads and stir movement below. She came close, then faded past, around her back, observing her all the while. When Saska shifted, she told her, "Don't move. Just stay still, and let me look at you."

She did, for a minute, maybe two. And then her hands slipped out through her silken sleeves and began moving over Saska's body. Across her belly. Over her bust. They gripped at her hips and moved down past her thighs, and Saska could do nothing but stand there, and try to stop from flinching, as her fingers worked to her inner thighs, then up, up, up...

"I...I don't feel comfortable with this." She shifted away.

Lady Cecilia stood. There was a knowing look on her face. "You've never been with a man, have you?" she asked. "Or a woman?"

Saska's eyes dipped in answer. That was real. She didn't need to be in character for that.

"Has anyone ever tried to force themselves upon you?"

"I...um, no," she whispered. "No...never."

"You're lying. Who was it, Tilda? Your employer in Baymoor?"

She shook her head. "No. He would never have..."

"Is this why you left Aram? Did someone mistreat you?"

"No, I...I came to find work, only. I..."

"It's OK. You don't have to tell me now." She took a couple of paces away, and for a moment Saska could breathe. *Control yourself. Focus. Do not think of...them.*

But she couldn't help it. They were there. They were *always* there. Lord Modrik Kastor. Lord Quintan. The two men who'd tried to rape her in the past, and who'd both ended up dead for their trouble.

"He says you're strong," came Lady Cecilia's voice, as she returned to her desk. "I'd like you to show me." She turned, and in her hand, she held a five inch godsteel dagger, its hilt gilded and encrusted with glittering green jewels. "Hold this, for as long as you can. Do not feel nervous, Tilda. It is but a blade, nothing more. To those like you and I, godsteel is just...metal. You need not look at it as anything more than that."

She came forward, brandishing the misting blade. It looked a priceless weapon, and Lady Cecilia held it well, exhibiting the strength of her own bond to the steel. "Come, it won't bite," she offered to lighten the mood. "Ignore the mists. Before long, you hardly notice them."

She placed the dagger in Saska's palm, and stepped back, watching. In her head, Saska was counting. *One, two, three, four*...Marian had told her not to reveal too much of her strength. "Count to five, then weaken," she'd said. "Begin shaking. Grit your teeth. Let it slip through your grasp to the floor when you reach eight or nine. Do you remember how you first felt when you held my blade, Saska?"

She'd nodded. "How could I forget."

"Then you know how to act." Saska could hear her words now, see her kind thin smile. "Just...don't hold it too long. Long enough, to make them interested. But not *too* long. You understand?"

She did. And now standing before Lady Cecilia, she acted just as Marian had described. She held it to five, then shook, strained, blinked, breathed a heavy pant, and let the blade drop to the floor, hitting the wooden deck with a clunk.

Now she waited. She waited for the woman's words, for her reaction. When it came, it was simple. "Good," is all she said, leaning down to pick up the dagger. "Very good, Tilda." She returned the blade to the table, placing it onto the wood. With her back turned, she spoke once more. "Are you sure you have never held godsteel before?"

Saska's pulse ran quicker. "No. Never."

"You're certain? Quite certain?"

"Yes, my lady. I have never been near godsteel before."

"That isn't true."

Her heart hammered. "My lady?"

Cecilia turned, sharp and sudden. "You were near godsteel when your father pumped you into your mother's womb," she said, and there was a note of spite in her voice. "He must be of a powerful bloodline to have sired a girl like you." The words came bitter, and it felt another test. "Who was he? Your mother must have told you."

"She never..."

"Who was he, Tilda?" The blade was in her grasp again, and her eyes were burning jade.

"I don't know. I...I promise I don't."

She moved forward, ghostly, her long green robes flowing all about her. "You're not lying to me, are you? You know what will happen if you are."

"I'm not. I promise I'm not."

Lady Cecilia smiled. "The promise of a stranger is meaningless, child." Her knife shimmered in the candlelight, a series of emerald gemstones running up the golden hilt. She raised it to Saska's neck. "I will ask you one more time." She stared, long and deep into Saska's fake hazel eyes. "Do you know who your father is?"

The colour of her eyes was false, but the tears gleaming upon them were all too real. "No," she said, her voice shuddering. "I do not know who my father is." *I don't. I really don't...*

"Hmmmm." Cecilia drew back, an inch, then another, until she was two feet away and turning once more, placing the knife back on the desk. "No, I don't think you do." Her words fell cold from her mouth, until she spun again and that fire in her eyes was gone, doused to warm embers, and her voice was warm again too. "I am sorry, Tilda. I must ask these questions, with anyone who passes through this tent. You will forgive me, won't you? You understand?"

Saska's lips trembled, tasting brine. "Yes, of...of course. I...understand."

"Good. That is good, child. Now come, let me show you where you'll be staying. I have a comfy berth, just for you."

She moved forward and took Saska's hand, leading her as a mother leads a child out of the tent, and through the light rains. "This wretched weather, it seems never to end," she laughed, hurrying them along. "Mind the puddle there, Tilda, and the mud. Are you getting too wet? Oh, no matter, we'll get you into something more comfortable in a moment, don't worry."

They passed along the line of tents, most glowing within, others dark and cold and empty...until they reached one half way down, and pushed inside through the fabric door. The interior was warm and soft, all reds and deep browns, with cushions and drapes and rugs, and a table set with food and wine, and a snug bed laid with pillows and wools. It was larger than Lady Cecilia's quarters, a palace to a peasant, and therein lay the appeal. The air seemed soaked in scented candles such was the aroma in the room. Saska sniffed, and did so deep, and for a moment she even closed her eyes to better take it in.

"So, how do you like it? Doesn't it smell divine in here?"

Saska nodded quietly. "It's...just for me?"

"Oh of course, yes, it's just for you. You're here to relax, Tilda, to enjoy the fruits that you've been denied all these years. You are Bladeborn. You are noble. You should have spent your youth in grand castles and fine estates, not hidden away in some moorland village." She laughed, so light now, so breezy. *So kind,* Saska thought. *But this is no more than a show, and it's not just me who's acting.* "This is how we make it up to you," she went on. "So indulge yourself, and your every whim." She gestured to a little bell, set atop a table near the entrance. "If you ever need anything, just give it a little shake. A servant or guard will come running, you'll see."

She stepped over to a broad chest, positioned to one side of the room, and opened it up. The craftsmanship was fine, like everything else here, and atop the chest was carved the crossed mallet and sword of Tukor, set upon a broad shield. *The royal standard,* Saska thought, *not the sigil of House Kastor* - the paw-print of a bear, black on a background of green. It furthered what Lady Cecilia had said - that the breeders were not in the service of House Kastor, but the crown, and though that would be fond news for most, it was a little more troubling for Saska.

I must get his attention somehow, she thought, *else my being here will be pointless.* Lady Cecilia seemed disinterested in pandering to the Kastors, and if she'd identified Saska as a prize, might not let her be despoiled by the venereal whims of their lord. Cedrik Kastor would not, after all, wish to sire a child by her, or use her as Lady Cecilia and the crown intended. He'd put many a babe in many a girl, but each time it had been duly aborted, to save him the disgrace of fathering a half-breed bastard from one of his southern slaves.

She's knows about that too, I'll bet. Saska watched Cecilia, as she rummaged through the chest. *She'll prefer to preserve me for someone else, and that won't do, not for me.* She found her eyes moving back through the opening, out through the rains, toward the larger pavilions away across the ruins. *I need to get to him somehow. By invite or no.* And then she thought of Lady Cecilia's dagger, and a plan began to take shape. *Might I retrieve it somehow? While she sleeps, perhaps? Use it to sneak into Kastor's quarters and slit his throat as he dreams...*

She let the thought trail off. There were hurdles to that, and perils too numerous to ignore. No doubt Lady Cecilia kept the blade hidden at night, and besides, even if she thieved it from her, she'd have to get through those Emerald Guards too, and they'd be far more than a match for her.

"OK, let's get you out of those wet clothes, shall we?" Saska's thoughts dispersed as she saw Lady Cecilia coming forward now with a richly embroidered tunic, shaded a dark green. "It's comfortable, I assure you, and plenty warm for these bitter nights. Now come, undress. Let me get a look at you."

A shot of anxiety bled back into Saska's veins, and all thoughts of her plans were gone. "Might I not...dress in private?" She hated exposing herself to others. She'd had to do it before, and those memories still haunted her.

"No. I want to see you." She had firmed again, and there would be no way to convince her.

"Yes...my lady."

Saska peeled off her maidservant clothes, one garment at a time, trying to forget, to forget all those times she'd been stripped bare and sent naked to her cell, starved and beaten and whipped bloody.

"Good. Keep going. Everything, Tilda. I want to see all of you."

She battled to hide those memories, and managed to keep the worst of them at bay, and before long her clothes were bundled in a dull soggy heap before her. Her hands pulled up and over herself, covering her modesty, but Lady Cecilia just tutted and shook her head. "Now come on, Tilda, don't be shy. Remove your hands. Let me see you."

Saska's hands slid off her soft, bronzed skin, falling to her sides, as her chin fell too. She shivered despite the warming caress of the braziers and lamps, as her shoulders pulled in, trying not to question her decision to come here. *I am doing this for Marian. For my duty to Rasalan, and King Godrin. I would be dead but for them, and this is a small price to pay.*

"What a fine figure you have, child. So soft. So ripe." Cecilia moved forward, as she had before, around her back, studying her. She remained there for some time before she spoke again. "My, what happened here?" Saska felt a finger move softly down her back, tracing the diagonal line of a scar. "These scars were made by the lash, child. Who did this to you?"

Does this ruin me? she wondered, with a strange flicker of hope. *Might I not be fit for a prize anymore?* It was a foolish thought, really. *It is my blood they need, and my ability to bear children. They'll have some knight put a babe in me and then keep me locked away, till I'm ready for another.*

"My master was cruel in Aram," she croaked, letting her mind fill now with all the dreaded things she'd faced. "He would beat, and starve and flog me until I bled. He was not a nice man, my lady."

"No, I can see that." She remained behind her, allowing some tenderness back into her voice. "But he never abused you? Sexually?"

She shook her head. "He would...pleasure himself, sometimes, when he beat me, and stripped me. His son would too. He was as cruel...just as cruel....but they never crossed that line."

She was thinking of Lord Modrik. She was thinking of Cedrik. And everything she was saying was true.

"This was before you came here to Rasalan? Is that the reason you left?"

She moved now, stepping back around in front of Saska, handing her the tunic. Saska took the clothing eagerly and covered herself. "Yes."

She didn't elaborate, for she didn't want to extract any further pity. It wouldn't serve her ends. *I do not need her sympathy, nor do I want it. I need her to leave. I need Sir Griffin to bring news of me to his uncle, so I get the summons I'm here for...*

Lady Cecilia went quiet for a moment, as Saska pulled on her clothes. *I wonder...was she once a breeder too?* Saska observed her now as she looked off to the side in thought. *It would fit, wouldn't it? Who better to tend to these girls than one who'd been through it all before.*

"I hope this has not been too distressing for you, Tilda," Lady Cecilia went on eventually. "The first meeting is typically the worst, though it is not my intention to make you uncomfortable. Far from it, in fact. Your life will be one of great comfort and pleasure from now on. All that darkness in your past is behind you."

Saska stayed quiet. *Go. Please...go now, so I can breathe...*

"I can see you have plenty to ponder. I like to give all newcomers a chance to adjust to their new surroundings and conditions. So take these days for that, but do make sure you stay within the tent, and yard space outside. There are a great many untended men beyond these old castle ruins, and perhaps some within them too, who will be best avoided by a pretty little thing like you. If you should wander off, I may find it hard to protect you."

She let those final words hang in the air, before shifting through the curtains in a billow of emerald robes. And yet they were the only ones that truly mattered to Saska. *I am allowed out of this tent,* she thought, almost gleeful at that basic liberty. She'd expected to have been confined to these canvas walls, but that changed things enormously. *Maybe I'll see him, outside his own tent? Tomorrow, once the rains have died. Maybe I'll see him then?*

It was something. Hope. A horrible hope, really, but that's what she was working with. A dark prayer that the abominable Cedrik Kastor would spot her, feel that stir in his loins, and summon her to his privy quarters before Lady Cecilia could stop him.

And then...

She didn't want to think about that.

Moving to the rear table, she filled a silver chalice with fine summer wine, then took a seat in a cosy pile of cushions. The rains pattered a soothing song on the roof, and the firelight flickered warmly from the braziers, and that wine, it went down better than she'd expected. It was as snug a setting as she'd ever enjoyed, here at the heart of the Kastor warcamp, with her target hardly more than a stone's throw away, and that thought, despite all the horrors around her, almost made her laugh.

So she sipped her wine, and sniffed the scented air, and listened to the rains fall. And all the while, the clock was ticking. Ticking toward the toll of Cedrik Kastor's death.

Or her own.

11

Elyon

Elyon mused on the last time he'd crossed the Links, as the army passed along the ancient stone bridge. *Father was still himself, full and whole,* he thought, as he trotted atop Snowmane beneath the drizzling rains. *Aleron was alive, just starting his courtship with Amilia. The world...the entire world was different then. And yet here we are.* He glanced back along the great train of bodies, pushing through the fog. *Marching to another man's war...*

The Knights of Varin made up the vanguard, with Lord Wallis Kanabar and his personal host among them. Behind, the twenty thousand men of the Riverlands and Lakelands followed, marching ten abreast, all dressed in leather and mail and rain-soaked hauberks and surcoats atop them. Many wore the coat of arms of Vandar - the skyward-pointing blade, framed by a mountain behind - but others were crested in the sigil and colours of House Kanabar, or those of the other houses of the Lakeland Lords, and the Marshlanders who dwelled in East Vandar, bearing banners and standards to match, flapping and flowing in the easterly breeze.

The procession of man and steel bled into the mists, and back there, some miles away, followed the wagons and wains, hauling camp supplies, and the servants and scribes and other attendants among them. Even further back, a rearguard had been established, though it was a small host only, with no threat of being attacked from there. Yet Lord Kanabar liked to do things right, and so posted men there all the same. After suffering King Ellis's feeble attempts at leadership on the march from Varinar, it had been a mercy to have a man of Lord Kanabar's experience taking charge of the host.

"Will these blasted rains ever relent?" the bulky old lord called out now, cursing the dreary skies. He shook a fist for comedic effect and gave Elyon a playful grin through his thick rusty beard. "We'll all bloody well drown by the time we reach Rasalan at this rate. Seems those prayers of theirs work. Have you heard the Song of Storms, Elyon? Awfully dreary, but effective it would seem."

"I can't say I have, Lord Kanabar. They murmur it, don't they? It isn't really a song at all."

"No, but Song of Storms sounds better than Murmur of Storms, so I can understand why the name caught on." He glanced skyward again, muttering. "Three days, and we've had nary a break in the clouds. It'll slow the wagons for certain when we cross the Lowplains. It's boggy enough there as it is."

"I hear the snows are falling hard to the north as well," put in Rikkard, who was riding with them.

"Oh yes. Bogs to the south and great snowfalls to the north. And people wonder why Rasalan is so damned hard to win. Forget the foresight of their kings and queens. They have the luck of the elements too."

"Not so lucky, when you worship a pantheon of water gods, my lord," said Elyon. "Do they have one for constant rains like this?"

Kanabar gave a little grin at the comment. "Probably, but if they don't, they can just as easily invent one. Call me a cynic, but I hardly think that every one of those spirits and sprites of theirs is real. We've only a handful of gods in Vandar, and how many have they got? Dozens upon dozens, so far as I know. That hardly seems fair, does it?"

Sir Dalton came trotting up behind them on his sleek steed. "I never took you for a heretic, Lord Kanabar." He was dressed in his full godsteel regalia for their arrival in Rasalan, clad in the exquisite Ilithian armour worn by the heir of House Taynar. Most of the other Varin Knights were in their standard-issue breastplates and gauntlets, though a couple of others who had full suits of godsteel armour were similarly accoutred as Sir Dalton. "Do you imagine we invented some of our gods too?' he went on. "What of Hugarus, who kept Vandar's armies so well fed during the War Eternal?" He took a passing look at Lord Kanabar's ample belly, half hidden by his great red beard. "By looks alone, I'd say you worship him most enthusiastically, my lord."

"Well, I see Dull Dalton has a bit of wit to him after all," returned Lord Kanabar. Hugarus was the god of plenty, so it was a fitting enough jape. "I might advise you to say a prayer to him from time to time, my man. You're wasting away beneath that fine armour of yours, enough to make one think you're ill, Sir Dalton. Perchance that might be true? Might the stress of this war be unduly affecting your health?"

"We breed our men lean and tough in the Ironmoors, my lord. Excess is considered an ill-favoured trait there."

"Yes, well you can live as you wish, I suppose. But do remember that Hugarus keeps Varin's Table fully stocked too. He may not look upon you favourably when you take your seat, should you continue to denounce him."

Sir Dalton gave out a little grunt, and then continued on, with his nephew, Sir Rodmond, trotting along beside him. Elyon had often felt a little sorry for Sir Rodmond. He was about Elyon's age, and was far more genial than his bitter uncle, yet by dint of kinship, spent most of his time in his dour company.

"Do you think I offended him?" Lord Kanabar posed. "He might want to pick his fights with more care, if so."

"He's been surly since Vesryn took up the Sword of Varinar," Rikkard said, watching him trot away. "Thinks it should have gone to him."

Wallis Kanabar's large ruddy nose pushed out a snort. "Nonsense. These are exceptional circumstances, and Vesryn is the right choice. Were Lythian here, perhaps he'd get my vote, but he isn't." His mood soured a little, for reasons that required no explanation. They'd still heard nothing of Lythian and the others, and though he was of a stoic persuasion, Lord Kanabar was quite naturally concerned for his son. "You'd have been a good choice, too, Rikkard," he went on after a time, in a more subdued voice. "You have the favour of the men, at least, which is more than can be said for Sir Dalton. He is a fine knight I'll not deny, but too mean spirited to be an effective leader. And besides, I'd be wary of him holding the reins to the Varin Knights, with his father sitting the throne in Varinar in Ellis's absence. That is too much power for a house like Taynar to wield."

Elyon nodded his agreement. There was a lot to be wary about, so far as he could see, and still he'd not spoken a word of his doubts about Vesryn. His father had told him to be patient, to keep his own counsel where he could, to watch, and to wait. "This villainy will out," Amron had said, soon before Elyon had departed Varinar. "In time, all will become clear, and we'll unearth the full truth of it, son."

How long that would take, Elyon didn't know, but he'd followed his father's wise guidance thus far. *And now he's returning home,* he thought, *for the time being at least.* He'd received news a couple of days ago from Jovyn that his father, sister and auntie were setting out for Blackfrost, and their ancestral lands around the North Downs. The news had been gladly received. There was too much plotting and scheming going on, and with Lord Taynar holding court in Varinar, he felt happier knowing his family weren't there.

I made the right choice leaving Jov behind, he concluded. His squire had been training Lillia well, as he'd hoped, and kept watch over his father besides, such as he could. "There remains a shadow over him, Elyon," Jovyn had written. "He still struggles with his grief. I think this trip to Blackfrost will do him good."

It would do them all some good, Lillia and Amara too, and Jovyn himself had been invited to accompany them. *They'll not be far away from Blackfrost now,* he mused, as Lord Kanabar and Rikkard continued in their discussion. A good part of him wished he was there too. He'd not been home for a couple of years now and, while he enjoyed life in Keep Daecar, and had taken advantage of the pleasures of the capital's social circuit, there was a simple charm to the North Downs that he greatly missed at times.

A rustle of noise reached his ears, coming from the dozen or so Varin Knights riding ahead. Elyon peered through them, to see the shape of the Eastbank Fortress coming into view, marking the end of the Links and passage into the Kingdom of Rasalan.

It was devastated.

The gate, thick and broad, had been knocked in, hanging askew in a tangle of iron. Above, the gallery and hoardings were completely destroyed, and either side, those soaring black towers had been knocked down to piles of rubble, the wreckage spreading out onto the plains beyond.

Elyon gave Snowmane a spur, as a number of the more eager knights sped on toward the fort. They passed through the iron gate, mangled and battered by the Tukoran war machine, as further signs of the carnage came into view. The skeletons of siege weapons, turned over in the mud. Discarded swords and lances and random bits of armour, tossed away as the defenders fled. Not all the dead had been burned, or buried, or otherwise laid to rest. Where the Tukoran men who fell here had been gathered, many of the Rasals had been left to rot. Arms and legs poked out from the rubble, crushed when the towers came down, and over the edge of the cliffs bodies could still be seen snagged among the rocks, a banquet for the crabs. And there were ships there also, many ships Elyon now saw, dashed against the crags or sunk in the Sibling Strait, with only their masts now visible above the waves.

A quiet fell upon the host as they worked through the rubble, clearing away a few bits of debris to allow the wains and wagons through. The stink was unbearable, a noxious stench suffusing the air. Men had to hold their hands to their faces as they worked, and others shot off, retching and heaving, as they unearthed another putrid corpse. Sometimes the scavengers had been at them. Others were more maggot than flesh. Elyon saw a head sitting alone, hacked clean from its body, parts of the skull already emerging through the rotting brown flesh. It was not the only severed body part littering the wreckage, left as nothing but carrion for the crows.

"They're calling it the Battle at the Gate." Vesryn had come up beside him, upon his golden brown destrier, Sunsilver. "Used a battering ram called Tukor's Fist to smash their way in. The entire head was coated in Ilithian Steel, so only their Emerald Guards could wield it." They looked to the wreckage of the gate. "A regular ram may never have broken through. It'll come in handy when we reach Harrowmoor."

Elyon continued to look out over the rubble and ruins. "Could their godsteel swords not have cut though the gate?"

Vesryn shook his head. "A gate that thick, of reinforced iron? Not without considerable effort."

"And that?" Elyon's eyes were on the Sword of Varinar, affixed to Vesryn's hip in its gilded sheath. *He begins to bear it well,* he thought. *Though he'll never master it like Father.*

"The Sword of Varinar can cut through anything, Elyon. But chopping through a fortress gate, or thick castle wall, is no job for a blade, no matter which it is. We have our engineers for that, and the siege weapons they forge. It is an art to which the Tukorans take particularly well, shadows of Ilith as they are."

Elyon nodded, though the blood of Ilith was all but spent now. Galin Lukar had made sure of that when he conquered Tukor three hundred years ago, wiping out any of the Forgeborn houses who didn't swear fealty and bend the knee. Those who now remained were responsible for building King Janilah's siege engines and smithing his armour and weapons, using their unique power to rework godsteel as only Forgeborn could. The armourers and swordsmiths at the Steelforge in Varinar were all Forgeborn, and there were some here with the army too, but the direct line of Ilith had long since been severed now.

They were quiet for a time before Vesryn spoke again. Their exchanges had become like this; a little cold, a little distant. "So...how are you? You never forget your first battlefield, even if you weren't present during the fighting. The sight of the bodies. The smell. It can take some getting used to."

"I'm fine, Uncle. I've seen death before."

"Yes...of course." The quiet lingered a moment further. "Your next test will be participating. Contributing to what you see before you. Are you ready for that, son?"

I am not your son, stabbed a bitter thought. Vesryn had always offered Elyon shrewd counsel and guidance and it had always been well received. But that had changed now. *He tries to sound like Father, but it just isn't the same.* He missed his Father's presence, and could tell most of the other knights did too. Vesryn was trying his best, but he wasn't Amron Daecar. *There is only one Amron Daecar,* Elyon thought, *and he is far from here.*

"I suppose I'll find out when I get there," Elyon said. "I have no way of judging that yet."

Vesryn regarded him. He looked saddened by Elyon's reaction, by the lack of warmth between them. *Perhaps I'm being unfair,* Elyon wondered. *Maybe my suspicions about him are unfounded.* "I know you don't want to be here." There was a tenderness to Vesryn's voice, an understanding. "I will keep you from the van when we strike at Harrowmoor, Elyon. I'll keep you from the heart of the fighting, when it comes. I'll not force you to kill Rasalanians. We have plenty of others for that."

"I don't want to be treated any differently from the other knights," Elyon returned. He knew how that would look. He knew how every other young knight of his age was eager for their first taste of blood. To begin their story. Write the first verse of their song. Heroic deeds awaited, they knew, that would force Varin to take notice. It was what drove all of his knights to seek glory, to seek war...that chance to sit near him at his Table, to listen to his stories and songs, and have a chance to share their own.

"You'll get your measure of blood soon, Elyon," Vesryn went on. There was a cold pallor to his skin that told of ill news. "It won't be long before Agarath attack. You need not redden your blade here, if you don't wish it. This war...we'll need to end it quick, and spare as many fighting men as we can on all sides. If King Godrin is as wise as they say, he'll open his gates and let us through, and surrender before this day is out."

A frown rutted Elyon's forehead. "What's happened, Uncle? What have you heard?"

Vesryn shook his head. "Not here," he said. "We'll make camp tonight where the Rasal warcamp was...the one you visited with your father. Killian says it's a little way inland. I'll explain during the evening brief."

He turned on Sunsilver before Elyon could press him, and shortly after, the army was moving once more.

Elyon could think of little else for the remainder of the day, though he was distracted for a time as they arrived at the sloping valley where he'd been some months before. As the army assembled and the camp was pitched for the night, Elyon left Snowmane with the stablehands and took a quiet walk alone.

Signs of the previous occupation by the Rasal army were rife. The earth was churned, the grasses browned, detritus littered everywhere. You could see where the tents and pavilions had been pitched, where the larger thoroughfares had been established through the camp. Old fire pits sat soggy and black. Around the encampment, atop the hills surrounding the valley, the wooden watch towers the Rasals had constructed were still standing. Soldiers were ordered to man them, and a guard was set to keep watch. "We are on Rasal soil now, enemy soil!" Lord Kanabar could be heard bellowing to his men. "Expect ambushes and attacks at any moment! If I hear of any man falling asleep on watch I'll have them hauling the wains with the workhorses, do you hear me!"

Elyon made his way to the southern side of the valley, as the Vandarian camp was set up a little to the north. A few lengths of canvas had been left behind there when the Rasals packed up, whalehide, Elyon saw, torn when the pavilions were taken down. Other refuse peppered the ground. Some timber here. An old, cracked cooking pot there. Elyon knew this was the place, by the arrangement of the tents, and their position beneath the shadow of the hills to the south.

This is where we stayed, he thought. *This is where Father lost the use of his arm.*

He could still remember that night, more clearly than he'd like. That ripple of black smoke, as it passed by his tent. The roars of his father only a minute or so later. The sight of him, hacked apart like a piece of butchered meat, lying there in that pool of spreading blood with the Sword of Varinar beside him. Elyon gulped to lubricate his throat. It still felt raw sometimes, for the scream that had ripped through it when he came upon his father's corpse.

Because that's what he was, he thought. *A corpse. There was no way anyone could survive that.* And yet... he had.

"Elyon?" The voice was behind him, a whisper only. He turned, and there was Killian, his golden hair darkened by the drizzle, face grim. "I thought I might find you here."

Elyon nodded. "You came for the same reason?" Killian had been there that night, one of only a few.

"Your uncle has called a meeting," he said, stepping to Elyon's side. Then he looked over the earth, browned as though soaked with blood. *And might it be? There was so much of it...*"This is where it happened?"

Elyon nodded. "Somewhere around here."

They stood in silence beneath the rains in private thought, as east came the thunder, a distant rumble in the air. "I wonder where he is now?" Killian then said. "The boy...the assassin."

The Shadowknight. My brother...

"A long way from here," Elyon whispered. "There are rumours he's gone south. Some say he will look to hide somewhere in the Tidelands."

"He'll not hide for long, if that's what he's intending." They all knew now. That the fake Ludlum was a Shadowknight. That he'd stolen the Nightblade and abandoned his order, murdering that Whisperer and all those men in Russet Ridge. That he was a hunted man now, trying to outrun them. *And everything he did,* Elyon thought, because they didn't know it all. *That it was his very own father he maimed, his very own brother he killed.* That detail had stayed with Elyon, for his father and his family's sake. It didn't serve for people to know that it was Amron's own bastard who had attacked him and killed his son. *What would it change? It would only sully Father's honour, and right now, that is not what he needs...*

"They're calling him the Ghost of the Shadowfort," Killian went on. "It's one name I've heard, anyway."

Elyon had heard that one too. Yet there were others, those spoken in private circles among the Vandarian host. One of prominence was 'Hadrin's Horror', in reference to the widely acknowledged theory that it was Prince Hadrin of Rasalan who had unleashed the man upon the Daecars, and caused such turbulence across the Kingdom of Vandar. A theory Elyon didn't subscribe to. A theory that was far too convenient for him.

"Let them chase and hunt one another," he said, not wishing to dwell too much on it until further proof came to light. His words came dour, empty of feeling. It was always the same when the Shadowknight was mentioned, or his father's crippling, or Aleron's death. "I hope they find him and he cuts every last one of them down. I hope they devour one another like the two headed snake they are."

Killian had a mind as keen as his eyes and knew it wasn't a discussion to further. He turned toward the encampment. "We'd best be off, Elyon. I hear Vesryn has some troubling news."

It was enough to switch Elyon's mind back to more immediate concerns. "He seemed... anxious," he noted, "when I spoke to him earlier. Do you know what this is about?"

Killian was already moving. "I suppose we'll find out shortly."

They arrived at Lord Kanabar's command tent a few minutes later, joining the rest of the Varin Knights who made up Vesryn's privy council, comprised of the heirs to the great houses. That was the reason for Elyon's inclusion, if any of the other knights might grumble about nepotism. Several other lords of the Lakelands, Riverlands, and Marshlands were also in attendance.

The tent was of no particular luxury, given their temporary stay, and was thus furnished to a simple standard. Braziers burned around them, and at the heart of the room, a table had been set up upon the hastily laid out deck. There Vesryn stood, hands to the wood, head down. The rest stood in their cloaks and heraldry, sharing looks, waiting for him to speak.

When he did, his voice was blunt. "King Dulian is dead." A short silence followed as the room digested the information. Elyon gave Killian a look. It didn't sound like the ill news they'd been promised. "He was murdered in his bedchamber by an assassin, some five nights past." Then came the punch to the gut. Then it all made sense. "They say that Lythian was the killer."

The air stilled.

"No, that...that cannot be." Rikkard looked around, head shaking. "Lythian would never..."

"It's what I'm told, Rikkard," said Vesryn.

Lord Kanabar had visibly paled. "Borrus...my son. Do you know..."

"I know nothing of their fate, Wallis," Vesryn said. "Just that Lythian plotted this from the start, by the order of my brother..."

"That isn't true," Elyon broke in. He stared at his uncle in dismay. "None of that is true. How can you say that?"

Vesryn raised a hand. "I know, Elyon, of course I know that. But what I know, or you know, or any of us know doesn't matter. It is what the Agarathi believe that counts."

"He was set up," said Killian, resolute, an angry clench to his jaw. It was the only thing that made sense. "Lythian lives by the codes as closely as any one of us, and would not betray his honour like that. He would never consider murdering a king, and certainly not one who invited him into his city under banners of peace."

"He was never invited," put in Sir Dalton, keen to remind them all of that. "Amron sent him there on a whim and look at where that has gotten us. We know how close he and Lythian are. How do we know they didn't conjure this plot at the hearthside one night? Maybe this was their intention all along."

It was an ugly claim and an absurd suggestion and Elyon showed his displeasure with a glare. He prepared to speak, but never got his chance. Killian was that little bit quicker.

"I was there, Sir Dalton, when Amron decided upon this plan, along with Elyon and Borrus besides." A shade of anger burned around the edges of his smokey voice. "Amron sent Lythian and Borrus to bring a message of peace, that is all, and should you suggest otherwise again, I'll see that you feel the sting of my steel."

Sir Dalton licked his lips. "You'd challenge me to a duel, Killian?"

"I'd challenge you to nothing, because it would be no challenge. You are limited, Dalton, and always have been."

"Says the man who was too frightened to enter the Song of the First Blade."

It was a cheap shot. Everyone knew why Killian didn't enter, and fear had nothing to do with it.

"Enough," boomed Lord Kanabar's voice. "You feud and squabble like children, and now is not the time." He looked directly at Vesryn. "What else do you know, Vesryn? How did this happen? Where?"

"In the palace in Eldurath." Vesryn had a scroll before him, yet didn't need to look at it, so sparse seemed the detail. "It appears Lythian scaled the palace from his quarters on the lower floors and cut Dulian's neck as he slept."

"But...how?" asked Rikkard, disbelieving. "That palace is some hundred storeys high, is it not? A marvel of Ilith's design. It could never be scaled without godsteel, and even with it..."

"Lythian had his dagger, Rikkard."

Rikkard's frown deepened. "They didn't take their weapons from them?"

"I'm uncertain. There are rumours they had help."

"Help?" asked Elyon. "From whom?"

"I'm not entirely sure."

"And who exactly is your source?" queried Sir Dalton. "Whose hand is that scroll in?"

"Lord Pentar put quill to parchment...

"And how did the the Lord of Redhelm come by this information?"

Vesryn closed his eyes, growing weary of the badgering. "You know full well the answer to that, Sir Dalton. Porus Pentar is charged with defending the Black Coast and is often the first to hear of matters coming across the Red Sea. He has merchant spies in Eldurath who relayed the information. It is all across the city."

"And all lies," snapped Rikkard. He slammed a hand on the table. "Lies! They have set this up as a mandate to go to war, and will stir the entire south against us..."

"It's retribution," Elyon said, quiet, introspective. "For King Storris." He looked around. "They always claimed they never killed him, and that our retaliation was unwarranted. Now they're doing the same to us."

The men in the room nodded.

"Who takes the throne in Eldurath now?" asked Lord Fullerton, one of the Lakeland Lords. He was short and toadish, of middling influence, though had raised two thousand experienced swords for the army at Lord Kanabar's behest, so had earned his spot at the table.

"Dulian had a son before the war, as I recall," said Lord Kanabar. "Teth..." He waved a hand. "Tethlam or....something. This'll be his revenge, for what Amron did to his father..."

"Revenge? For sparing him?" Elyon never liked the notion that Dulian had been festering on his throne, waiting for his chance to get vengeance on his father. It didn't add up. "My father showed Dulian mercy, when he might have killed him at the Burning Rock, my lord. Why would he seek vengeance for that?"

"We're not talking about Dulian, but his son, Elyon," Lord Kanabar explained. "He will have grown up watching his father waste away, and gods know you younger generation yearn for war. It's true here, and no doubt it's true there too. The Agarathi lust for battle just as much as we do, despite what they say."

"Not all of us from the younger generation yearn for war." Elyon shook his head. "Why do I keep hearing that?"

"Because it's true, Elyon," said Killian, with whom he'd argued about this before. "You have shown a lack of faith about Varin's Table in the past. That isn't a view most of your age share."

Sir Dalton was staring at Elyon with an indignant sneer on his lips. "You doubt the scriptures?" He looked personally insulted by it, and grievously so. "You question Varin's very own teachings, Sir Elyon?"

"I doubt anything that cannot be proven," Elyon said, without thinking. A few of the group raised their eyes; it wasn't a popular opinion. "I'll remind you all that Aleron was set to be the finest knight of our generation, and yet he died without ever taking a man's life. Without ever fighting a war, or a battle, or a gods-damn skirmish with bandits. Nothing." He could feel his blood boiling. *Calm, or else you'll say something you'll regret.* "I just...I just think that's unfair. That he should fall without a glory to his name, when another lesser man might live a hundred years and win a hundred battles..."

"Then that would not make him a lesser man," interrupted Sir Dalton, curt and cold as ever. "Varin does not only reward talent, but grit, and longevity, and..."

"My brother was *murdered*, Sir Dalton," Elyon said, his voice filling the tent. "Tell me, does Varin account for that? For a man whose time was so cruelly cut short?"

"Your brother, Sir Elyon, was bested by a better man. It was not murder. He began to believe in his legend, and thus did he pay the price..."

Elyon couldn't stop himself. Before he knew it, he was going for Sir Dalton, reaching wildly for his neck, and Rikkard and Killian had to swoop in to hold him back. The haughty chuckle that came from Dalton's narrow mouth was grating. "He's feral, this one. You might want to reconsider letting him in here, Vesryn..."

"And you might want to reconsider your tongue, Dalton, lest I have it cut off." Vesryn looked at him, eyes narrow. "Killian has already had to threaten you during this meeting, and I'll be damned if I have to do so too. You rile, you rankle, and ever you provoke. Think on your words, man. Elyon has just lost his brother, and you have the temerity to speak to him like that?"

"I spoke nothing but the truth."

"Oh for Vandar's sake, you truly do lack in tact." Lord Kanabar shook his fleshy neck, beard swinging side to side. "You're as insensitive as your lord father, and that's no mean feat, I assure you. Unfortunately, being a bloody awful shit isn't a trait Varin cherishes. If you think it'll nudge you further up his Table, I'd say you've got another thing coming."

"I've achieved enough already to be in sight of him, to hear his tales," said Dalton, lifting his chin.

"Oh yes, after all those bandits you killed, defending your father's lands." It was Rikkard's turn to get at him, and though Elyon appreciated their support, he knew he'd reacted poorly.

"I killed as many Agarathi as you did during the war,

Rikkard." Sir Dalton's eyes were glancing about now, seeing the group close in. He had few friends here, though that was how the Taynars liked it. They had alliances, but not friends. There was a big difference between the two.

"Truly? I didn't realise we were keeping count? Though of course, if Killian might permit it, I'd gladly take his place in that duel you have planned and knock you on your skinny backside."

A few more lances were thrust between the pair before their verbal joust abated, once more by the booming order of Lord Kanabar, who looked like he'd had quite enough. "I'm having blasted flashbacks to the war," he announced. "I recall you two as scrawny little teens getting at each other's throats even back then. It seems time hasn't done much for your sense of camaraderie."

"Nor Sir Dalton's miserable demeanour," Rikkard said, looking for one final insult. "He was dreary then and has only gotten worse. You might want to smile once in a while, Dalton, and stop being such a bore. People may like you more."

"I care little for who likes me."

"Spoken like a true Taynar."

"Enough!" The word came fierce off Vesryn's tongue, trying to get a handle on things. *Trying to be like Father,* Elyon noted, and it was a passable job, as he stood there, glaring, a sizeable man himself. He was shorter than Amron, true, but taller and more broad-shouldered than most. "This rancour among us has to stop. I'll admit I have had my part in it, but no more, not after today. This news from Agarath is grave, more grave than one might think to look at us." He shook his head, a frayed edge to his voice. "We can consider it certain that Lythian will be executed for this, and Borrus and Tomos may too, should they have been involved. These are sons of ours." He glanced at Lord Kanabar. "And dear friends." His eyes were on Elyon, Killian, Rikkard. "Their loss is personal, and tragic, and yet there is a bigger framing to this picture. War with Agarath has only been speculated upon thus far, yet we can be certain now that they'll unleash their hordes, their dragons, and all the southern allies they can muster."

He vented a sharp breath, then looked at the short figure of Lord Fullerton. "You asked who ruled now in Eldurath, my lord?

It is not Prince Tethian as Lord Kanabar suggested, but Dulian's nephew, Tavash, who now sits the dragonthrone. He has already styled himself king and will be officially coronated in the coming days. King of Agarath. Divine Protector of the South. We all know what this means. We know that the old allegiances run deep there, and that the nations of the Lumaran Empire, peaceful as they now proclaim to be, may well rally in the face of this offence." He took another pause for breath. "Tavash is a hawk, a known war-monger among the Agarathi high nobility, and with him at the helm we can be certain he'll strike soon..."

"Then we must pull back," said Lord Shorton, another of the Lakeland Lords, who had his seat in Lakeheart. "We leave the Tukorans to their war and make haste to Dragon's Bane. Should they march on Death's Passage in force, they could penetrate as far as Rustbridge before we stop them."

"We have a strong garrison at Dragon's Bane," said Vesryn, thoughtful. "How many men, Lord Rammas?"

"Five thousand," came a deep, calm voice. Lord Rammas was the Lord of the Marsh, young, square-jawed, and thick-chested. "That is the standing force there, but some thousands are available to join them if they must."

"They must," said Lord Kanabar. "Send a crow to Lord Morley of Mudport to see to it, Rammas. We must reinforce our borders."

Lord Rammas dipped his chin. "My lord."

Vesryn continued. "Lord Pentar has already been doing the same along the Black Coast, in response to the dragon sightings over the past several months. I will instruct him to redouble his efforts. The rumours coming from Agarath suggest the Wings are beating hard, sending more and more drakes to be bonded up in the Nest. That the Fireborn ranks haven't been in such rude health in decades...and all the while, we're here fighting amongst ourselves. In this tent. Out there." He flung a hand to the tent flaps, as the wind picked up, causing the canvas to billow. The thunder was still lumbering from the east, and the rains were lashing hard. "This war between us cannot persist. We *must* try to mediate a peace, and fast, lest the entire north fall to ruin."

As Father always said, Elyon wanted to add, but of course he didn't. Now wasn't the time, and his mind was shot with worry, and a growing, throbbing grief. *First Aleron, now Lythian,* he thought. *What has happened to you out there, my friend?*

The discussion was going on, the tent a blur of voices, of noise. Elyon hardly heard the next few comments as his thoughts swirled, and his heart thrashed, until Killian's soft voice cut through the bluster. "Does Janilah know of this?" he questioned. "Ellis? Godrin? These are our kings, Vesryn. They are the ones who decide our fate, not us here in this room."

"I despatched crows to King Janilah and King Godrin before I called you here," Vesryn said. "The news may well have reached them already, but if not my birds shan't take long to arrive."

"And Ellis?"

The reaction within the room said it all, the energy sapped. No one had much faith that King Ellis Reynar would affect affairs in any meaningful way, no matter that he commanded the largest army, and most powerful Bladeborn order, in the north. "I have scribed a note for him too," Vesryn confirmed. "Therein I have beseeched him to persuade King Janilah to end hostilities immediately. But I think we must appreciate that it will not be an easy task, not even for the King of Vandar."

King of Vandar, Elyon thought. *Ellis was never a king, but a puppet on strings, dressed in a crown.*

"And what do you propose now, Vesryn?" asked Sir Dalton, his spat with Rikkard and the rest forgotten. "We know what sort of man Janilah is. He will prefer to drive home his victory before he tucks tail and turns from a fight."

No one would deny that. "We have little choice but to press on to Lord Kastor's warcamp. Prince Rylian will be there shortly, and is rumoured to have already questioned this conflict among his privy council. This news may tip the balance, and he will likely have a great deal more luck in convincing his king father of the folly of this war than Ellis."

"That is assuming Ellis will even try, or wants to," said Killian. "If his orders are for us to support Janilah's armies, we will have no choice but to remain in Rasalan until the war is won. An alliance has been struck and it is not one Ellis is likely to renege on."

Vesryn was considering, his eyes away to one side. It was a lot for him to take on, so early in his tenure as First Blade. *More and more his absence is felt,* Elyon thought. *What will he make of it when he learns of this? Might you come join us, Father, to offer counsel, if not your blade? And when you hear of Lythian...*

"The war will not be won quickly," the new First Blade said after a time. "Even if things go well, sieging Harrowmoor, marching to Northgate, crossing the Forks, invading Thalan..." It was but part of the list that needed doing to win a kingdom. "None of that will happen fast, not at this time of year, not with the Rasals digging in their heels." He continued thinking, then came to a decision. "We have a hundred Varin Knights in the company. A hundred of our best, promised to Janilah, but I'll not in good conscience have them so far from our borders at a time when our oldest and most fearsome enemy is blowing air on the embers of war." He looked around. Men were nodding. "I'm going to send fifty knights to Dragon's Bane. We have others dispersed around the coast, and in Varinar and the other major cities, where they'll stay, but it is Death's Passage that needs our attention most of all at this time. The rest will continue to the warcamp, under my leadership, along with the army Lord Kanabar has assembled. I'll not break it up; that is the mandate of the king, but the Varin Knights are mine to command by the Steel Father's will. And this is my decision."

The assembled lords and knights took that well. No one liked an indecisive First Blade, especially not at times of war, and Vesryn was proving himself capable.

"I'll take the evening to consider who will be sent to the coast," he went on. "Lord Rammas, it may be better for you to accompany them south, to help muster the Men of the Marsh to Dragon's Bane. A garrison of five thousand will not do, not now. I'd like to think we can double that number, without weakening our other defences. Can it be done?"

"Yes, my lord." Rammas was a man of few words.

"Good. I would also urge you to contact your fathers and see them call their banners." That was for Killian, Rikkard, and Dalton, heirs to three of the great houses. "I'll write your Father, Elyon, and request the same."

"You'd need to send the crow to Blackfrost then, Uncle. Father rides there as we speak."

Vesryn didn't seem aware of that. "Is Amara with him?"

"I believe so, yes."

Vesryn frowned, perhaps expecting a crow to bear him the news. He blinked and shook his head. "Fine. Once we muster our full force, having twenty thousand men absent in Rasalan won't be such a sting."

"No, though these are twenty thousand of our best," put in Lord Kanabar. "They may not all be Knights of Varin, but we have other lesser Bladeborn in the ranks, and even our regular soldiers and men-at-arms are warriors through to the bone. So believe me, Vesryn, as soon as I hear a whisper that an Agarathi horde is marching on Death's Passage, I will turn them all around, no matter how far north we are, no matter whether we're in the middle of a battle or a gods-damn siege, and make for the south at haste, with or without King Ellis's consent."

"I understand..."

"And should those heathens have murdered my son, for some plot they concocted to bring war to our shores, so help me gods, I may just march on their lands myself!"

"Of course, Lord Kanabar. But let us not lose all hope." Vesryn drew the man's eye, urging calm. "Borrus and Tomos are both worth more to them as hostages. You may see your son again yet." He made no mention of Lythian, because with him the die had been cast, and in truth none were ever likely to return. "Until we know more, I think it's best we put this aside for now. Fogged though it is, we have our course, and will follow it until a clearer path reveals itself." He looked around. His words sounded final. "Good." Then he turned to his nephew. "Elyon, a private word."

The two stepped away to the side of the tent, as the others dispersed out into the misty night. The squalls were coming hard now, and had been unrelenting for days, barrelling violently into the canopy above them, roaring a backing song as Vesryn gave his nephew a bracing look. "We'll need strong knights, strong leaders, manning the fort at Dragon's Bane, Elyon," he said, "and I'll likely send Killian and Rikkard there to take charge. Your good grandfather Lord Amadar will not be short of capable men in his muster, and if some travel south to the border, it'll be better if Rikkard is there to lead them. Same with Killian and the Oloran banners."

Elyon was nodding. "I agree, Uncle. It is a wise course."

"And that brings us to you. If you wished it, I could request that your father send a host of Daecar men south from the North Downs, to be taken under your command. I am giving you that choice, my boy. If you'd prefer to keep your sword sheathed in Rasalan, a posting south may better suit you."

He stopped, giving Elyon a moment to digest, and consider. "What about Sir Dalton? Might it not be better to send him, given the difficulties he's causing?"

"Difficulties that I hope are behind us, after today. But a wise man once told me to keep my enemies close, so that is what I'll do."

"Then I'll stay," said Elyon, coming to an abrupt decision. "I'll stay to support you, Uncle."

For the first time that day, for what seemed like weeks...months, Vesryn smiled. He placed a hand to Elyon's shoulder. "I'd hoped you would, son. Gods know this is more than I ever expected, and though we've shared little time together of late, your presence here...it gives me solace...during difficult times."

Elyon saw the man he held so fond then, looking at him, with that warm smile, those silver-blue eyes, webbing with lines. He hardly liked the thought that Rikkard and Killian would be gone, but he took some solace too in that look on his uncle's face.

"You're doing well, Uncle. Father would be impressed."

Vesryn looked sideways, with a soft smile. "I would hope to carry on well in his stead," he said. "But I do wish he was here, bearing this blade."

They both looked at the Sword of Varinar, set to one side. Vesryn still had to take it off sometimes, when its weight grew too heavy to bear.

"We all do the best we can, in the circumstances we're given," Elyon said. "And I'd not want anyone else in the role than you."

Vesryn looked touched. "That...means a lot to me, Elyon. You probably don't realise how much."

"I can hear it. In your voice." He smiled.

The fog between them seemed to lift, and as ever all it took was a few quiet words to do it. Yet that shadow of grief hung, and returned anew with Vesryn's next words. "This business with Lythian..." He was close to the Knight of the Vale too, as many of the senior Varin Knights were. "I curse that it ever came to this. I am so sorry, Elyon. I know how much he meant to you."

He speaks as though he's already dead, and might he be? If not, he won't last long. Elyon wasn't going to give himself that hope, nor lend it thought if he could. "I just hope Father doesn't take it too badly, when he hears. He should never have sent him south. I fear it will gnaw at him."

"I fear it too."

They stood together, silent for a moment, before a strong gust of wind tore the tent flaps apart, pulling them from their fastenings. It was the break they needed, before their words became too mournful. Vesryn lifted his lips to a smile to favour his nephew, and send him out into the winds and rains. "I'd best get on, Elyon. Fetch some sleep. We'll ride hard tomorrow and the next, and should be at the warcamp by then, should the weather not hinder us so. I'll pray to the Steel Father that we go no further than that."

Elyon hoped the same, but something in his head warned otherwise. He remembered that look on King Janilah's face, when he met him at the banquet. That look in his eyes. Resolute. Unmoved. That tone of his voice when he spoke of Rasalan, so full of spite and loathing. *He will not fall back in this war,* he realised, *not unless Godrin should surrender the rule of his kingdom.* And that felt just as unlikely.

And so he fell asleep with a horrid thought.

We may be in for a long war yet.

12

Amron

Amron Daecar rode through the vitalising, wintry air, a broad smile clinging to his black bristled cheeks. Ahead, the snow-draped hills that formed the southern edge of the North Downs spread away to the distance, a blanket of pristine, sparkling jewels, gleaming under the afternoon sun.

Nestled in at the bottom of those hills, was the city of Blackfrost, though calling it a city was a stretch. It was no Varinar, nor was it comparable in scale to the other great cities elsewhere in the kingdom, but that was the very reason why Amron liked it so much. Large parts of the town were constructed of rich brown timberframe, and triangular, thatched roofing, and at winter, it was especially beautiful, when those roofs were padded with snow, and Blackfrost Castle - one of the few stone buildings here, where Amron had been born and raised - sat so stately beyond.

"I half forgot how rustic and charming it was," said Amara, grinning as broadly as Amron. "And the pine..." She sniffed the air. "You can smell it already. "Isn't it funny how a scent can stir such fond memories?"

Amron gave out a nod in agreement, as the two rode along, side by side. Amara liked to ride, where she could, rather than travel in the carriages, and never looked anything but demure and graceful on her fine palfrey, her slim figure clad in a silver lambswool cloak to beat off the winter air.

"I always thought the little thickets and copses had been artificially placed, they were so perfect," Amron put in. "They frame the town so splendidly, wouldn't you say?"

Parts of the North Downs were clothed in pine and spruce, and they grew in patches either side of the town. It had inspired a great many paintings that hung upon the walls of Blackfrost Castle, commissions that the best artists in the region had fought for over the years.

Amara offered up a playful grin. "I never knew you were so romantic, Amron. I have always thought the same, and with the castle there, at the rear, looming over the winding streets and quaint little homes. Splendid is the word. Splendid indeed."

"Well I'm glad you agree, and I have my moments of romanticism when untethered from my duties with the blade. Kessia used to say I had a poet in me, just trying to get out. We'd take walks through the hills often, enough to inspire a line or two."

"What a handsome picture, and a handsome pair you were. Though you needn't have looked beyond Kessia's beauty for inspiration, Amron, as I'm sure you know. I do not believe I've seen a face so divine as hers... though Lillia will surely compete, when she comes of age."

"She is the spit of her mother," Amron agreed. "And her auntie is of fine appearance too."

Amara laughed the compliment off. "A poet and a charmer, it would seem. I judge myself to have a certain allure, but not to Kessia's vaunted level. That would be like one claiming to match Varin with the blade. No one would dare declare such a thing. Not even you, Amron."

I certainly wouldn't, he thought, *though others might draw the comparison.* They had, in fact, and often, and even his famed fight with Vallath and Dulian had been named The Echo of Titans as a tribute to the legendary battle between Varin and Eldur several millennia ago. That fight had taken place at the momentous Battle of Ashmount, and as Amron had killed Vallath and spared

Dulian, so Varin had done the same with Eldur and his dragon Karagar, spawn of Drulgar the Dread.

They rode on for a time, their host made up of a few attendants and Daecar men, and a local lord or two whom they had picked up along the way. Among the protective guard were a few Bladeborn, though those of middling blood who'd never been skilled enough to join the Varin Knights, and Jovyn, who was the most gifted among the company with godsteel, despite being only a squire. Amron had watched him training with Lillia a few times when they'd stopped along their route at night, and had been quite impressed by how well he moved and danced with blade in hand.

"It would seem my son has taught you well, Jovyn," he'd told him several nights past. "You have a nice way with the blade, and a bond to godsteel that will continue to flourish if properly nurtured." The young man could hardly look at him. *He's shy, but respectful,* Amron had thought, *and that earns my favour too.* "Elyon told me that he made you a godsteel promise that you'd become a full Varin Knight one day, is that true?"

"He did, my lord, at the warcamp in Rasalan," the boy had said. "The morning after you'd..."

He didn't need to say anymore, though Amron took some joy in how he squirmed. "A sour day for some, but uplifting for others," he offered with a smile. "I am glad for you, Jovyn of House Colborn. And I'm glad you're here with us now. I had my doubts - I'm man enough to admit that - but you have been excellent with my daughter, and have instructed her well." He'd leaned down and given the boy a friendly smile. "Keep that up, and perhaps Elyon's godsteel oath will come true. I may not be First Blade anymore, but I still have some clout among the Varin Knights. Plenty enough to see you sworn in, if I wish it."

Jovyn was with Lillia now, riding a little way behind them, forming a firm friendship that seemed to extend beyond the training yard. *Keep her safe,* he thought, *and I might let you take her hand one day too.* He was of a lower Bladeborn house, but Amron had learned his lesson now. *I'll not sell Lillia off like a lamb for slaughter. She'll marry whom she pleases, and could do a lot worse than this boy.* It was a thought for a happy day, a rare one amid the sea of gloom that had near drowned him, and perhaps it wouldn't last. But still, it felt good to think more laterally for a change. To escape the confines of his life as a great lord, and imagine a more simple, fair world, where people had a little more choice in how they lived.

They continued to trot along the High Pass - the track that stretched from Varinar to Blackfrost, and all the way up to Northwatch on the edge of the Weeping Heights - as a small host came riding out of town toward them. Amron took a grip of his godsteel dagger to get a better look. "It seems my cousin is coming to greet us," he said "He rides with some haste, it would appear."

"You've not returned here for some time, Amron," Amara pointed out. "No doubt Sir Gereth is just excited to see you."

"I would say that's unlikely. He is not a man prone to excitement."

Sir Gereth Daecar was Amron's cousin on his father's side, a former Varin Knight who'd been badly injured during the War of the Continents, and had taken up the post of Warden of the North Downs, when Amron became First Blade. He'd resided here in Blackfrost ever since, a quietly spoken and thoughtful figure of fifty who'd governed with distinction, and was well-liked in the region. He had once had a typically Daecar look, though now his hair was mostly silver, and his formerly broad physical shape had atrophied with age, lending him a slim and scholarly appearance.

Amron gave his great destrier Wolfsbane a little spur and set off into a canter to meet Sir Gereth, as Amara followed. Alongside Sir Gereth were a trio of other knights bearing the Daecar sigil - the gallant rider on horseback, misting blade held aloft - whom Amron didn't recognise.

"Cousin Gereth, so glad to see you," he called out as he came quickly upon them. "You look well in the saddle. How's the leg?"

"Troublesome, my lord, as it always is in winter. I am already pining for the coming of spring when the ache is more bearable." Sir Gereth had been mauled by a sunwolf during the war, an encounter that had left him with a badly shredded left leg, and a horribly crooked gait. "But I might ask you the same, Cousin.

How fare you? Your leg and arm? I have been lending you my prayers these last months, and have had all the city doing the same."

"I remain in recovery, Gereth. It is a long road, as you know, and not one that always ends well."

Gereth nodded his understanding. "You are still early upon yours. I will continue to pray that the gods see fit to return you to full health." A pause occurred between the two, as Gereth expressed a mournful smile. "And...about Aleron. I am glad you are here, Amron, so I can offer you my deepest condolences. His death has rocked us here. A terrible tragedy, truly terrible."

"My thanks, Gereth." He dipped his chin. "And that is largely the reason I have come - to show strength at a time when our family has been so gravely wounded. I wish to shore up confidence, and keep any more of our vassals from wavering."

"Yes, of course, my lord, and in that you have had some success, if word is to be believed."

Amron nodded. "We spent last night in the company of Lady Crawfield, and the night prior with Lord Rothwell in his castle. Both seemed reassured by what I had to say."

They were two of the houses that occupied the lands east of the North Downs, and bannermen of the Daecars. Amron had heard a rumour or two that Taynar men had been creeping about, trying to turn their heads, but those fears had been put to rest by his visit.

"I would say the other houses will be similarly reassured, my lord." Sir Gereth shifted in his saddle, as the carriages came rattling up behind, with Jovyn and Lillia trotting alongside them. "I do not believe you have anything else to worry about, not on that front. Other concerns have come to light that take precedence."

"What concerns?" Amron asked.

Gereth looked to the youngsters coming into earshot. "Concerns that are best spoken privily, Amron. I have had your solar prepared in the castle, and the hearth lit within. It should be plenty warm by now."

"Fine. Lead the way, Gereth."

The convoy trotted on.

Amron had little time to indulge in any sense of nostalgia, as he arrived in his lord's chambers toward the summit of Blackfrost Castle. Lillia had gone off to show Jovyn around, and many of the most prominent members of the city, and surrounding estates, were beginning to gather for the feast that Sir Gereth had planned.

That was all of secondary concern now, as Amron took a seat behind the grand pinewood desk that had once been his father's, and his father before him. Sir Gereth planted himself opposite, and Amara, also present, relaxed into an armchair to one side, an old threadbare thing that Amron's famous grandfather and former First Blade, Balion Daecar, had liked to sit and ruminate in when Amron was a child.

He drew a breath as he settled. Though his cousin had been warden here for many years, he never sat in this seat, or slept in these chambers. They were reserved for the Lord of House Daecar, and at Amron's death, only Elyon would be entitled to use these rooms. "So, Gereth, what is this news you wish to tell of?"

Sir Gereth had politely waited for Amron to ask, as was custom, before speaking. "Ill tidings, my lord," he then said. "A crow came by your brother's hand earlier this afternoon, flown all the way from Rasalan. He has reported the death of King Dulian and the ascension of his nephew, Tavash, soon to be crowned as King of Agarath and Divine Protector of the South."

Amron stared, taking a moment to process the news. "I...I had no idea Dulian was so ill," he then said. "We have heard much about his ailing mind, but nothing of his physical state. But...pray tell, Cousin, is this report from Lythian? Has he finally sent word of how he fares?"

The shadow upon Gereth's face told enough of a tale in itself, and Amron's nascent hope was doused. "I'm afraid not, my lord, and I would advise that you brace for what I'm about to tell you." He paused then went straight into it. "Dulian did not die by illness or any natural cause, but by a throat cleaved open by godsteel, your brother says. He was assassinated, Amron, and by Lythian's own hand. Vesryn reports little more than that, except to warn that Agarath are likely to hasten hostilities on account of this treacherous regicide. He wishes for you to call your banners, and set the Daecar lands to muster. The entire kingdom is being put on a war footing."

The news brought a slow, twisting nausea to Amron's gut. He stared forward for a time in reflection, thinking of his dearest friend, of what could have possibly befallen him, as Amara shifted from her armchair and hurried to a side table. She poured three glasses of whiskey and sped to the desk, setting them down. "Drink it, Amron. It'll help settle the shock."

The worry in her voice was clear, and he didn't refuse. He thought nothing of his newfound sobriety, as he threw the burning brown liquid down his throat. Then he looked his cousin straight in the eye. "Is there more?"

Sir Gereth answered. "Only that Vesryn is planning to bolster the forces at the fortress of Dragon's Bane, and has called for a widespread reinforcement of our borders."

"That has already been occurring for some months, has it not?" asked Amara, standing by the desk. "Word of war with Agarath is not new, Sir Gereth."

"No, my lady, but this puts it in no doubt at all. The fear is that the murder of their king will rouse their southern allies to the fight. And all at a time when the north is at war with itself."

"Then this ridiculous war must end," she said, knocking back her own whiskey with a practiced hand. "Amron has fought for that very thing for well over a year, and it's high time everyone else listens."

"I think your husband agrees, by the tone of his message, Lady Amara. One would hope that Janilah and Godrin are similarly inclined."

Amara gave out a huff, as was customary when her cousin was mentioned. "Janilah will not be so easily convinced, not with the blood-soaked strides his armies have been taking. If he withdraws now, he will have achieved nothing in this campaign, and that will be far too onerous for his mighty ego to take."

Gereth was quite aware of Amara's thoughts on the matter and didn't offer any retort, for fear of getting into a debate with her. "You know better than I, my lady," he said, showing his tact, then turning back to Amron, added. "I can draw up the orders, my lord, to have our banners called. Might you lead them yourself? Your experience would be invaluable, and your presence a great boon to morale, I feel."

"I am not sure, Gereth."

He wasn't sure of anything at that moment, except that burning sense of shame he felt. *Lythian, my dear Lythian...I...I am so sorry. I should never have sent you there. I should never...*

"My lord? The orders. I would need your confirmation, before I..."

"Yes." He looked to his glass of whiskey, and Amara swiftly went to refill it. "Draw them up, Gereth. Have them sent immediately. A full war muster, if that is what my brother suggests."

"He does."

"And it comes from Vesryn, not the king?" queried Amara, stepping back over and placing Amron's glass down. She'd refilled her own, though Sir Gereth hadn't touched his. "Is that typical. I was under the impression that only the king could make such an order."

"He will seek Ellis's confirmation if he hasn't already," Amron told her. "But there would be no reason for our king to question it. If all this is true, what little hope we had of calming tensions with the south will be gone. Ellis will have no choice but to prepare for a full invasion."

"*If*, my lord? You imagine these reports from Agarath may be false?" asked Gereth.

"I know they are false, Sir Gereth. Lythian would never assassinate King Dulian. This is but another treachery to befall this kingdom, and we have lost another of its finest sons." He sunk his whiskey. "And my finest friend."

The second taste of whiskey went down with an eagerness that gave him pause. He could feel it, the desire, the need to soften his grief. His shame. *What have I done? This...it all started with me. Ellis was right to cast me aside for sending Lythian there so recklessly.* He cringed visibly, and looked to his glass, wishing only to see it refilled, but forced himself to push it away. *No, I'll not fall again. Who will it serve?*

What will it achieve? He cast aside the thoughts, firming, and looked at his cousin, who was watching him with a thoughtful expression. "What of Borrus and Tomos? Any mention of them?"

Sir Gereth quietly shook his head. "None, my lord. I have the scroll here, if you'd like to take a look."

Amron nodded and Gereth drew it from his navy doublet, embroidered with Daecar heraldry upon the chest, and handed it over. A quick read confirmed that it was indeed by Vesryn's hand, though there was nothing more that Gereth hadn't already enumerated. "We'll see these lands to muster immediately," he said. "How many might we mobilise, by week's end, Cousin?"

"Hard to be sure, my lord. At full force I'd expect our banners to bring in some fifteen thousand, perhaps a little more."

Amron considered it. Fifteen thousand sounded about right, though most of those wouldn't have seen blood at the edge of their blade before. Many of the common soldiers and knights who'd fought in the war twenty years ago were either dead, maimed, or too old now to fight effectively. "The other great houses should command similar forces," he said, quietly musing, as he glanced once more at his empty glass. Amara took that as a request for more and reached out to refill it. He lifted a hand and shook his head. "I shouldn't, Amara. We both know where it leads."

"Yes, I suppose you're right." She drew her long fingers back. "A brace to settle the nerves, but I agree, best leave it there."

"Yes, best leave it there." He looked longingly at the glass for a moment more, feeling that deadly tug to drown his grief, then forced his eyes back to Sir Gereth. "And that goes for this meeting as well," he decided. "I will speak personally with the lords and knights come for the feast. It has proven opportune my coming here, if only to oversee affairs. Send a crow to Vesryn, pledging the full support of House Daecar. You say he has reached Rasalan?"

"I know only what is listed in his note, my lord."

Amron ran his eyes over it again. *I write from Rasalan,* it said, offering no further detail, but Amron already knew of the army's intention and rough location from other correspondence he'd received. "He will be making for the warcamp of Lord Kastor," he said. "I would hope they'll be able to come to a parley with the Rasals, for the greater good of the north, but should that not happen, we must prepare to defend our borders. It seems Vesryn has acted quickly on that account, to our benefit. But we must rely on ourselves first and foremost, as ever we do."

Gereth was standing, taking up his walking stick. "Very good, my lord. I shall scribe a note for Vesryn without delay. Might I also make a suggestion?"

"Go ahead."

"Write King Ellis as well, by your own hand. He will be affronted should you circumvent him on this."

Amron wasn't so swift in his assent this time, and Amara came forward with a quiet word. "I agree with Sir Gereth," she put in. "Much as I dislike the spineless little weasel, he will not take kindly to you and Vesryn running this kingdom without his input. And you know he'll blame you, Amron, not my dear husband, for going behind his back."

I care not for who Ellis will blame, came his first thought, though he didn't utter it. Instead he nodded to their wise counsel and told his cousin that he'd see it done.

"Excellent, my lord. Shall I summon the others here, or...?"

"I'll speak to them over the feast," Amron told him. "And thank you, Cousin. I find myself indebted to you, as always, for running these lands so well in my stead."

"It is my unending pleasure to serve this house." He bowed and stepped away.

Amara lurked for a time, as Amron withdrew the necessary items from his desk and began writing his letter to Ellis. "Yes?" he said, after a minute had passed. "I can see you watching me, Amara." She was sitting in his grandfather's armchair again, pensive in her gaze, cradling her whiskey. "What is it?"

"Nothing. I'm just waiting here should you want to talk, sweet brother."

"Talk? About what?"

"About Lythian. He is your closest friend. And Borrus wasn't far behind. If you need another drink to..."

"Why are you trying to get me to drink? Do you have some motive I'm not privy to?"

"My only motive is to see you open up. If it requires a few whiskeys for that to happen, then perhaps that's a risk worth taking."

"You'd see me fall back into that spiral?" He frowned at her. "And for what, exactly? So you can see me cry? Because it seems that's all you ever linger about for sometimes, to prod and poke at me until my eyes begin to leak." He set down his quill, shaking his head. "Believe me, you're wasting your time, Amara. I wept my last when Aleron passed and shan't be doing so again. This obsession with me showing emotion...I confess I have never understood it. I've heard it all my life and still it vexes me. What good is me speaking of this going to do, Amara? Aleron is dead. Lythian is dead, or will be soon, and by gods it won't be pretty. They like to humiliate the men they execute in Agarath, debase them and rid them of all their honour before they give out...and does that make me want to cry? To think that my most loyal friend, the only man to ever truly understand me, is going to die like that?"

He set his eyes on her, and had no answer for his own question. Because it did. By Vandar it did. Yet he shook his head and firmed his jaw. "I feel shame, and anger, at myself, and at the world. I want to rage, not weep, and yet I can do nothing with this rotting arm of mine, hanging off my blasted flank."

"You can," she returned, and she did so with more force than he'd expected. She was on her feet in an instant and marching toward the desk, setting down her whiskey glass with a heavy clunk. "Gods, Amron, you have so much more to give than you think. Whichever course you now take will be for the benefit of us all. You are Amron Daecar, for goodness sake, and yet you whine and bleat like a lost sheep. Enough! Enough doubt, enough darkness. When you asked me to come on this trip, I was delighted, and do you know why?"

She didn't wait for him to answer. "Because look where we are." She pointed to a map of the region on the wall. "Look, Amron," and then she was marching toward it, pointing, jabbing her finger to where Blackfrost sat, clutched amid the hills of the

North Downs. "We're half way there, Amron. If you leave tomorrow, who knows, you could be in Northwatch within a week, and then halfway across the mountains in another. The snows will slow you, true, but that's no reason to lose heart. It is heart that you need. *Heart*, Amron. Courage. Honour. These are words that define you. These are the qualities that will save you."

She paused, perhaps seeing the confusion in his eyes, and gave him a moment to untangle her words. "You think...you think I should go to Vandar's Tomb?" he asked, quite sober in his tone, but as he spoke she nodded and stepped back toward him, back to the desk where he sat.

"Yes. Yes I do, Amron! I wholeheartedly do!"

He couldn't understand her. Amara had her moments of bewilderment, her particular opinions that seemed intentionally against the grain, but this..."I can't do that, Amara. We talked about it with Artibus. We were all in agreement that it would be suicide. And Lillia..."

"Lillia will be fine, now that she has Jovyn to look out for her and keep her company. With you and Elyon absent, she'd be the sitting Lady of House Daecar. I think she'll rather enjoy that, if I'm honest."

"No, Amara, she will not be fine. Not if I don't return, she won't. And I wouldn't...I see that now, the folly in it, the madness." He shook his head. "I'll not leave my daughter an orphan."

"You will not die, Amron," Amara reassured him. "You will make it there, and you will make it back. And when you return, gods help those who have wronged us, for you'll have your retribution."

She continued to confound him. "Gods, Amara, what is this? Another game of yours? Are you so idle without Vesryn to torture that you'll turn your tart tongue on me?"

"Hurtful, Amron. I am only trying to help."

"Well you're not. I lived and breathed this nonsense back in Varinar, but have moved past it. Artibus put his case perfectly. There is no man living who has been to that mountain and returned to tell the tale, not for hundreds of years..."

"That isn't true." She had a look on her face, cunning as a vixen. "I know of one such man, in fact."

He blew a breath though his nose. "Another of your tall tales, no doubt."

"No, this one is quite real, I assure you." She walked toward the door.

"And just where are you going?" The conversation didn't feel as though it had been satisfactorily concluded. *It's another of her tricks, to have me dwell on it. Blasted woman.*

"Oh, to check on Lillia and Jovyn, see that they're not getting up to any trouble." She paused at the threshold, with an aggravating look on her face. "I'll see you at the feast, sweet brother. Do what you need to do, consulting with the lords and knights, but spare some time for me, if you will. There may be someone I'd like you to meet when you're done."

With those frustrating words, she slipped from the room, soft and silent, leaving him to brood on them alone.

13

Jonik

"OK, lads, what are we thinking?" asked Captain Turner, standing before the others beside their little camp up the beach, where they'd been based for almost a week now. He gestured to the ship, newly repaired and fitted out, sitting at anchor a little way offshore. "After all she's been through, she needs a fittin' name. Jack, you're good with this sort o' thing. Come on, what's in your noggin?"

Jack enjoyed his position as the group's resident thinker, not an especially hard feat, true, but something he clearly liked all the same. "Stormmaster," he said, after a short consideration. "How about that?"

The name was greeted by a few pursed lips and bobbing heads. Not exactly the glowing reaction he'd expected. Sea-faring vessels, Jonik understood, were commonly given female names, though that wasn't always the case. Still...*Stormmaster?* Somehow it didn't work.

"Anyone else?" asked Turner.

"Sally the Unsinkable," offered Devin in a grand voice, the left side of his face still black and blue after the beating he'd taken in Greywater. "

That got a better response. "Hmmm, not too bad, lad," said

Turner. "Not too bad at all. Had a lover named Sally once, though she was far from unsinkable at her size." He laughed to himself. "I like it. Who else?"

Brown Mouth Braxton cleared his throat. "Invincible Iris," he said. "My mother was called Iris, and she was invincible too...until she died, that is. Proper strong woman, she was. Worked hard as any man I've ever known, and raised a litter of kids besides. It'd be a nice homage to her, Cap, to paint her name on the side of your ship."

Jack was smiling in his charming way. "That's nice, Brax," he said, laying a large paw on the man's shoulder. "I never knew that about your mother."

Braxton shrugged. "I don't like to talk about her much, if I can avoid it. Some things are best kept to yourself, you know."

Turner looked around the group, wondering if Grim Pete, or Soft Sid might have a suggestion, but seemed to conclude it was unlikely. "Well, I'm happy enough with one o' those, unless you got somethin' to offer, lord?"

Jonik shook his head. "Nothing that's better than those already mentioned."

"Not the creative type, huh," put in Jack, never short of a tease. "Though, you might want to consider asking Emeric, once he gets here, Captain. Without him, we might never have gotten back on the water after all."

Turner didn't seem sure of that. "Nah, he'll not mind. Fine benefactor though he's been, this here is our ship and we'll be the ones who name her." He looked around. "So, Iris or Sally? Let's take a vote." The next half hour involved a fair amount of squabbling, and a deeper debate than the topic was worth, but in the end, Invincible Iris came out the winner for Braxton's touching story. "Well, nice to get that sorted," Turner said in conclusion. "Grim, break out the brandy for a toast, then we'd best get all this packed up before Master Manfrey returns."

It hadn't yet crossed midday, yet these men were hardly restricted as to the hours they chose to drink. Emeric Manfrey had proven himself quite beneficial to that end, supplying not only timber and canvas and other materials for the ship, but a cask or two of ale besides for the crew. If there was a quick way for a man like him to endear himself to a group of sots and drunkards like this, it was through the judicious supply of alcohol. And on top of that, he'd been cordial, courteous, and hadn't been averse to helping with the repairs, for the two or three occasions he'd come by.

Smart, was Jonik's overall conclusion of the man, *but not threatening.* They'd met him six mornings past in Greywater, and throughout, and since, Jonik had been watching him closely. The bargain that Jack o' the Marsh had brought to them that night in the inn had been simple. Emeric Manfrey would purchase their horses and supply materials, and in return, they'd give him passage to Lumara. That accord had since been followed and largely completed. The horses were back, and loaded into the cargo hold, the ship was repaired and ready to sail, and now all they needed was for Emeric himself to return, so they could set off south, and fulfil the bargain.

And yet, he wasn't here.

"When'd Manfrey say he'd get here, Cap'n?" complained Grim Pete, who whined about almost everything. "You know how I get when on land too long. I want off this rotting rock, I do, and soon."

"Then take that box o' odds and sods and bugger off to the ship, Grim," snapped Turner. "How many times are you going to ask me that? He'll be 'ere when he's 'ere, all right!"

"Fine...I'm just saying." Grim's bony shoulders tucked in. "He said he'd be here earlier, is all. I'm worried about him, Cap."

An unpleasant fit of laughter burst from Turner's throat. "You? Worried about *him*? Never heard anything more ridiculous in all my days, Grim. You worry about nothing but that sallow skin o' yours. Now take that scrawny bag o' bones you call a body and keep on packing the ship, you hear?"

Jonik watched Grim Pete scuttle off down the beach, as Soft Sid lumbered after him, hauling a stack of supplies. "That was a little harsh, wasn't it, Captain?" Jonik said. "Pete isn't exactly wrong. Emeric should have been here by now."

"Aye, mayhaps that's true, lord, but Grim...he just gets on my nerves. I can bear the man at sea when there's a big old crew as a buffer, but here, with just the handful of us? He's grating on me, to be sure."

Jonik's pale lips crept into a smile. "Yes. I've noticed."

"Aye, hard to miss, I'll bet. You seen that scar he's got across his left cheek? You know, between all the wrinkles and scabs and welts and all the rest? Well, I gave that to him." He said it with a curious pride. "We ran aground once in a storm, not unlike the one that got us stuck here, and were there for two long weeks. The man near drove me to despair, he did, with his bleatin', and one day I just snapped. Put my fist through his face and broke that cheek o' his right open, splitting the flesh atop it. Sounds a bit base, I know, but twas one o' the most satisfying moments o' my life."

A short rusty laugh broke from Jonik's chest, a feeling he was getting more accustomed to. Before meeting these men, he wasn't sure if he'd ever laughed, but these last days had changed all that. "I can understand that," he said. "It can be rewarding, putting things right." He was thinking of those men in Russet Ridge, and that odd creature he'd slain. *That demon,* he thought, *with the magic in its voice.* He'd never felt so good as he had that night, when he'd lopped that monster's head free of its neck. He looked up. "Have you ever killed anyone, Gill?" he asked.

"Killed? Well, er...no, lord, I can't say I have." Turner looked at him with a shadow of concern. "You...you fond o' it, are you? I say it without judgement, lord, just interest, if you follow me. I'm supposin' it's natural to take some pleasure from it, given what you were trained for."

"I take no pleasure in killing, Captain," Jonik assured him. "Not in the act itself, necessarily. But in taking life? Yes, there can be some joy in that, if a man's passing is well earned."

"Aye...aye, I see the distinction." Turner brightened anew. "I'm not short of men I'd want to see dead, lord. Whether I'd have it in me to take a man's life, though...well, that's another matter."

"It isn't so hard as you think," Jonik returned. "Like anything else, it just takes some getting used to."

The camp was duly packed up, all supplies loaded to the little rowboat they used to reach the ship at anchor. Jonik and Turner strolled down to the beach, as the work continued, to join Brax and Jack o' the Marsh who were in conference there. As ever Grim, Sid, and young Devin were required to do most of the manual labour.

"He's coming," said Jack, as they joined. He pointed off to the hills. "Emeric. Spotted him coming over a hill a few minutes ago. He'll not be long."

"Aye, good." Turner looked to the others. "Get that lot over to the ship," he ordered, gesturing to the supplies. "And bring the boat back quick as you can. Winds are good for a getaway, and best we don't waste this weather. Come on, quickly now. Brax, how's about you lend a hand to speed things along."

"Aye, Cap'n."

They pushed the boat out onto the water, crunching over the shingly shore, and began rowing hard for the ship, some seventy or so metres out. That left Jonik, Turner, and Jack o' the Marsh on the beach, waiting for Emeric Manfrey who soon appeared in view. On foot.

"He's not on horseback," Jonik pointed out, surprised. "He's hiked all this way from Greywater?"

"Aye," bobbed Turner, cheerful. "He told me he was plannin' to, since we got all the horses here in the hold. Said he'd walk the island in two days and make camp somewhere over night. Might explain his tardiness. Hard to be exact when dealing with long distances on foot."

They continued to wait, as the rowboat reached Invincible Iris, and the supplies were hauled aboard. Seeing as it would only take two of them to row the boat back, Turner called out for Brax and Devin to start making the ship ready to sail, leaving Pete and Sid on the oars.

"Bit of a mismatch there, Captain," Jack o' the Marsh pointed out, seeing the giant figure of Soft Sid sitting beside the skeletal Grim Pete. "If they both pull to their strength, the boat will just go in circles."

Turner cackled out a laugh. "There are few weaker than

Grim, to be sure. And few stronger than Sid. I suppose that's why I like puttin' them together. They make a comical pair."

The two men were laughing, and looking to the boat, but Jonik's eyes were inland. Yet not on Emeric, no. It was the dozen riders galloping over the hills who had caught his silver eye.

"We may have trouble," he said, looking that way. "Seems Emeric has picked up a tail."

The others turned, squinting to the distance. After a moment Jack said, "Look like Lady Shark's men." He had good vision for a regular man, Jonik had noted. "Not port officials out of Greywater, certainly. Stink of cutthroat to me."

"Well then I'm guessin' this has to do with them horses," Turner suggested. "I'll bet she feels maltreated, us sellin' to Master Manfrey instead o' her."

"She never showed any interest in those horses, Captain," countered Jack. "Brax told us she turned him away, as soon as he tried to discuss selling them."

"Aye, but that's not how her mind works. She's a shark and does what she pleases. Brax was gonna head back over and try again the next morning, remember, but you sparked up that bargain with Emeric and he never needed to bother. That's no offence to you or me, but her? Aye, she'll have found out and clearly ain't happy. Not much happens in that town that she don't know about."

It seemed Emeric himself had taken note of his pursuers now, glancing back occasionally, as he moved into a light jog. He was a man of strong build, with a short, neatly cut beard, piercing golden eyes, and a full head of dark brown hair, cut short to require minimal management. Jonik had found him to have an unhurried way about him, a composure that he rather admired, and as he looked back now, he seemed in no way troubled by what he saw.

"Captain Turner," he called out, as he reached the top edge of the beach, and began walking across the pebbles toward them. "Nice to see you've gathered a welcoming party for me. Jack. Jonik. How are you all?"

Jonik hadn't given his name to the man as yet, though no

doubt someone else had let it slip. It pinched at him, that measure of control he ceded when giving things up to other men. *The more men you take into your confidence, the more men there are to betray you*, he thought.

"Fine, yes we're all fine here, Master Manfrey," said Turner. "Just loadin' the ship for departure. Got little 'n large coming over with the skiff, as you can see."

"Ah yes, good. And Braxton and Devin hoisting the sails. Very good."

He stepped in and gave each man a hearty handshake, his cheeks a little flush from his travels. Then he turned and addressed the matter of the incoming men. "It would appear others have come to see us off, Captain Turner. Do we know who these riders are?"

"Some of Lady Shark's throat-slitters, we figure."

"Of course. Our transaction has not gone unnoticed, it would seem." Emeric Manfrey had done business in Greywater before, Jonik knew, and was versed on the stranglehold Lady Shark had on the town. "Well, I suppose I ought to handle this, seeing as I poached all those fine horses of yours from under her pointy nose." He unloaded the pack from his back, and straightened himself out.

"You really needn't, Master Manfrey," cautioned Turner. "If we're swift, we might just get to the ship before they reach us..."

"No, Captain, no need to rush. I'm sure this can be smoothed over easily enough." He turned to Jonik. "Perhaps you might come with me, Jonik. As backup, should we see trouble?"

He must know I'm Bladeborn too, Jonik thought, though that was no surprise. They hadn't explicitly mentioned it, but both men were quite aware that the other had Varin blood. *And strong blood too, the way he carries himself. And that name?* Even Jonik knew the famous tale of Sir Oswald Manfrey, one of the greatest Varin Knights to ever live. The once famed house of Manfrey had since faded, but perhaps there was an ember or two still burning?

Jonik nodded his agreement and the two men took a few paces up the beach. Behind, Sid had noticed the coming of the riders and was rowing harder in a panic, with Grim powerless to keep up. The boat was thus spinning, though Turner wasn't laughing. "Harder, Grim, come on! You feeble stick o' a man, pull harder!"

Ahead, the riders were moving with haste over the plains and fast approaching the beach. "It's rumoured Lady Shark has some Bladeborn in her sellsword ranks," Emeric said, in that low measured voice of his. "If she's identified who I am, she'll have sent them all." It was the first public acknowledgement that he was Bladeborn himself. "Are you ready for a fight?"

"I was trained to be ready," Jonik said, acknowledging something of his own.

"Yes, I know."

The stampede of hooves was soon upon them, a snorting parade of muscular beasts ridden by grim-faced men. At their lead was a shaven-headed thug, long jawed and grey-cloaked with a glitter of mail beneath his mantle. It said it all. They were here to fight. And at his hip Jonik could see it, the faint mist of a godsteel blade, breathing to the salty air.

"You here are trespassing on these lands," he called out, looking at the pair before him, and to the others down the beach. "All who pass this way must pay a tax to Lady Greyskin, and word is you've been here over a week." He paused, a sneer curling on his scarred lips. "We hear you have a dozen good horses aboard your ship, one a fine Rasal thoroughbred. We'll be taking those as payment for your passing. Bring the ship ashore and unload them, else you'll feel the sting of our swords."

The ring of metal sang across the beach, a dozen silver blades catching the sunlight through the clouds. Half of them were misting.

"Well, that escalated rather quickly, friend," said Emeric, quite calm, his hand resting on the pommel of his sword, his dark green cloak fluttering in the light breeze. "Are these all the Bladeborn Lady Shark has? Just the six of you? I was hoping for more of a challenge."

The leader bristled. "Six is better than one, Manfrey, and challenge aplenty for the likes of you." His eyes shot to Jonik, having ignored him until now. "Or two, is it? This boy a Bladeborn bastard like the rest of us?"

Emeric ignored the question. "You've given us your side of the bargain, now let me give ours." He smiled. "Turn around, right now, and ride back to Greywater. Inform Lady Greyskin that we were already gone by the time you arrived. Do this, and you will live. Do it not, and every single one of you, Bladeborn or not, will redden the pebbles of this beach this day."

The man laughed, as the five other Bladeborn sellswords in his ranks moved forward on their steeds, lining up. "Six on two are odds I'm happy with. We'll see to you, Manfrey, and the rest of my men will deal with your companions. Is it worth it, for the sake of a few steeds? This needn't turn to violence, lest you make it."

"I fear my young friend here is rather attached to his Rasal," Emeric came back, gesturing to Jonik. "The horse is his. I fear he'll not take kindly to you trying to steal it."

"As if I care," howled the cutthroat. "I'm here on the Shark's bidding, and just following her orders. Do not confuse me with someone who has a choice. We'll be taking those horses, Manfrey. Resist and we'll take your lives as well."

The leader dismounted, and the five Bladeborn at his flanks did the same, leaving the other half dozen behind them in the saddle. Their godsteel blades were a mix. One held a shortsword, another a curved scimitar. The biggest of them bore a greatsword, five feet long, and the smallest had been given two lengthy daggers. A motley crew of Bladeborn bastards who got what they were given. Godsteel wasn't easy to come by, after all, even for a woman as resourceful as Lady Shark.

"Unlike me, you have a choice, Manfrey," came the thug's final words, brandishing a standard longsword. "I advise you make it now, and not do anything stupid. Think of these men. It's not worth..."

Emeric Manfrey drew his sword, signalling his intent. "Let's just get it over with, shall we? We really don't have time for this, good man."

The words came with a genial tone, yet the actions that accompanied them were hardly what one could call friendly. In an instant, he was speeding forward and engaging the lead figure, who blinked in surprise and threw his longsword forward in a defensive parry. A loud clang of godsteel gave out, echoing across the beach, higher in pitch, and cleaner than the clash of regular steel.

The overture was enough to force the others into action. They split into two groups and rushed forward, though only two came for Jonik, thinking him less able, leaving Emeric to contend with the other four. *Now that won't do*, Jonik thought, as he unsheathed the Nightblade without a sound, and the mist of silver and soft blue was joined by black. The two men approaching him were too enthralled in the fight to take pause, the brute with the greatsword swinging at him with a two-handed grip in a bid to hack him in two. Behind, the killer with the dual daggers followed, half his size, twice his speed, ready to zip in and punch a few holes through Jonik's cloak should he avoid the first strike.

He did. Easily. With an athletic duck, he moved under the swinging blade, emerging behind the man wielding it, who stumbled forward from the motion, slipping on the shingly ground. The smaller man followed, crouching, zagging side to side with a decent flow. *He has some skill,* Jonik noted, though of course the pair would offer him no challenge. He engaged the assailant, fending off his first strikes with a languid swipe of the Nightblade, leaving a trail of glittering black smoke behind. Glancing at Emeric as he did so, he found his new companion fencing the four attackers with a broad smile on his face, moving easily through the stances from Blockform to Strikeform to Glideform and back. *He fights well,* Jonik thought, observing him, as he lazily beat back another attack. He could see the subtle change in Emeric's movements, the gentle shift from stance to stance, the ease with which he dealt with his assailants. It took a great deal of training to achieve all that.

His own fight continued, though Jonik was hardly focused on it anymore. Only when the two men came at him at once did he pay them the proper attention and decide their time had come. With a swerve and a swish, he befuddled them both, and pressed the Nightblade through one dark heart, then another. And dark was the blood that pulsed from their wounds on that grim grey day, spitting out to stain their shirts and mail. Both men dropped where they stood, one, then another, landing on the beach.

"G-ghost!" came a call. "It's him. The...the Ghost..." Jonik looked up, as the six mounted riders began turning on their steeds, pebbles flinging underhoof, clods of mud going with them. "Back," shouted another. "Back to Greywater. He'll slay us all. Back!"

The six mounted men spun and fled, galloping off toward the hills on their horses in the short blink of an eye. Jonik gave Emeric another swift glance to find that he'd taken down two of the other Bladeborn sellswords, and was fast settling matters with the pair that remained. The rest of the horses had bolted, scattering off down the beach, or else heading inland, spooked by the commotion and the ringing shriek of steel. Jonik began making for the nearest one, but Emeric's voice held his stride.

"Let them go," he called out. "They can do us no harm." He parried a thrust, then swung his sword through the penultimate man's neck, severing his jugular, and leaving the leader to last. "Fool," Jonik heard Emeric say, as he bore down on the backtracking man. "You know my name, but not who I am. You damned fool."

"I'm sorry, Master Manfrey, I...please, don't kill me...I don't want to die...I don't..." The man held his hands up before him, slipping and sliding on shingle, as Emeric came.

"Too late, friend. Far too late." With a final dart and thrust, Emeric Manfrey put his sword through the man's heart, dropping him where he stood. A calm took hold for a moment, as Emeric drew out a cloth and began wiping down his sword. "You're gifted, Jonik," he then said. At his feet, the leader's blood was reddening the pebbles as he'd warned. "I'm glad to have had you with me. I'm not sure I'd have been able to take them all alone."

Jonik shifted the Nightblade back into its sheath, though knew full well that Emeric had identified it. "I doubt that, Emeric. Another two swords would not have troubled you, judging by what I saw."

There was a rugged smile on his cheeks. "You are too kind. I may be almost twice your age, but we never forget our training, do we? And, well, I've been required to recall it, from time to time. More often than I would like, perhaps, but it's all in the name of justice."

Jack o' the Marsh and Turner came hustling up behind them, breathless. "Well that all happened quickly," said Jack through a pant. "Are you OK?" He scanned both men. "Hard to tell, the way you move. Neither of you are injured?"

"We're quite all right, Jack," said Emeric. "These sellswords rarely have any official training. They can swing a godsteel blade, but duelling is about a great deal more than that. They're no real match for men like Jonik and I." He turned to the shore, where Pete and Sid were waiting to launch the rowboat. "Well, shall we? Best not miss the winds." He smiled and strolled away.

"Um, well...er..." Turner started. "I..."

"I'll gather the godsteel blades, Captain," Jonik told him. "They're worth a great deal more than those horses that started all this."

"Aye, yes...good idea, lord." He frowned, trying to catch up. "Will the rowboat take their weight?"

Jonik considered it. "Not all at once, no. Godsteel's a fair dozen times heavier than regular steel and that greatsword alone will weigh the boat down. Best ferry Emeric over first, and come back and fetch me after."

"As you say, lord."

It took several trips in the end, before the godsteel blades could be safely assembled aboard, Emeric lending his support in stowing them away below decks. The rowboat was brought up as well, then the anchor raised, and with a groan and a pull, the sails began filling with wind, edging Invincible Iris out into deeper waters.

The crew gathered up at the quarterdeck as Captain Turner took to the wheel. "Feels better than I can rightly say, to be clutching at these handles again," he said, hardly able to contain his joy. "Now Brax, what's our headin', you think? East down the Agarathi coast, or west out past the Blue Hole?"

"Best keep away from Greywater if we can, Cap'n. The Shark

might just have ships out on the waters there, looking to hunt us down. Best we avoid that channel."

"Aye, true enough. That good by you, lord?"

"It's your ship, Captain, and your course."

"Aye. Master Manfrey, any thoughts?"

"As young Jonik says, Captain Turner. I'm but a humble passenger aboard your fine vessel, and will leave it to your good graces to lead me back to Lumara."

Turner seemed delighted by that. "Well then, let's see Iris to the winds, shall we? Get praying to Matmalia men, for safe passage from here on out. I think we deserve a break, don't you?"

The ship cut through the shallow waves, as Jonik took a final look to shore. The half dozen riders had galloped from view now, but a half dozen other horses grazed about upon the plains, showing no distress at the litter of bodies spread across the beach. Bodies, Jonik knew, that would not go unnoticed.

Another crumb, he thought, with a strange smile on his lips, *for my former masters to follow.*

14

Amron

"This had better be worth it, Amara," Amron grunted. "If I find that this is another of your games, so help me gods, I'll..."

"Oh quiet down, Amron. I have known Walter for years and believe me, he's the real deal. Now enough fretting. I'll have you keep an open mind and hear him out. If you still have your doubts afterward, then fine, I'll leave you be. But I'm hoping you'll be convinced."

"Convinced," he muttered under his breath, as they continued on away from the castle and down the cobbled street, covered in a thickening sheet of snow. "I had convinced myself this was the right course before you and Artibus helped me see otherwise. And now you come and spin me around like this..."

Amara had taken a few paces away. "What was that?" she asked, turning. "Did you say something?"

"Nothing," he grunted, using his walking stick to stay stable on the slippery stones. "Just that I forget how much of a deathtrap these cobbles can be in winter. I dread to think how many hips have been shattered on them over the years."

"Well mind that you don't shatter your own. Did you not think to bring Artibus's crutch with you?"

"I don't need it anymore. The walking stick is just fine." He paced on, his right leg still uncomfortable, though a great deal less than it once was. He had a minor limp, but it didn't hinder him as egregiously now, leastways not when he was walking. Anything approaching a jog would remain problematic and likely quite painful, should he try it. "So tell me, dear sister, just how exactly do you expect me to scale the Weeping Heights and find my way into Vandar's Tomb if you're worried about me slipping on these cobbles?"

"I could ask you the very same question, Amron. You ruminated for weeks about the prospect of travelling to Vandar's Tomb, knowing full well how tricky the route would be. So clearly you had some plan to cross the mountains yourself."

"I was grieving, and not seeing things clearly. But believe me, my eyes are open now. So? Does this man we're to meet have some miraculous flying machine that might have me soaring over the mountains to the very foot of Vandar's Tomb unscathed?"

She slowed enough for him to catch up. "Now wouldn't that be a thing," she offered with a smile. "But no, Walter has no head for inventions like Artibus."

"So, what then? How do you expect me to climb a mountain range in my condition?"

"Oh, I think a healthy dose of luck should do it." She grinned, then walked on, widening the gap between them so he couldn't question her further.

"Confounded bloody woman," he grumbled, shaking his head, pulling his black bearskin cloak tight around himself. He always looked particularly colossal when returning to Blackfrost for the winter, cladding himself in great animal hides to beat off the plunging temperatures. It widened his frame to an excessive degree, and often had young children scuttling for the lanes and alleys to escape him, as though he was an actual bear stalking his way through town.

There were few people out tonight, however, given the lateness of the hour, and coming of the heavy snows. Amara had skulked around patiently during the feast, running a few laps of the social circuit as she liked to do, waiting to see whether Amron would bend and pay a visit to this mysterious man of hers. Eventually, he'd relented, if only because he knew he'd never hear the end of it, and so here they were, beating through the blizzard and blustery winds, as everyone else stayed warm and comfortable inside.

"How much further is it, exactly? You said a few minutes from the castle."

"Oh, not far to go now. He's staying at an inn at the end of Slipper's Way." She stopped, and laughed. "Oh, I just got it. *Slipper's Way*. Because people slip all the time on the icy cobbles. How silly of me. I'd never worked it out before." Her laughter tinkled through the winds.

Amron gave a gruff smile though didn't mention that he'd never thought of that himself. "Right, yes, very silly. But they might as well call every street in this town the same, in that case." A few ideas came to him. "Faller's Avenue...Stumbler's Street..."

Amara smiled and took it up. "Tripper's Terrace," she said. "Or...Skidder's Lane."

They chuckled together, managing a couple more as they carried on, taking care as they reached Slipper's Way which did seem to be rather more perilous than the other paths. It took them down a slight hill at a gentle descent, covered here and there in a glaze of black ice. One wrong step would be plenty to have either of them toppling to the cobbles. "Here, take my arm," Amron suggested. "If one of us falls the other can stabilise them."

Amara gave him a doubtful look, studying the sheer mass of the man. "You must weigh about four times as much as me, Amron. I'm not sure there's anything I'll be able to do if you should take a tumble."

"I'll be sure to let you go, Amara, fear not. This is more for your protection, not mine. I'd not want you to lose your dignity here on the streets of Blackfrost."

"I lost my dignity when I married your brother," she said, grinning. "I think we all know that."

"Yes, well..."

"So, did it go well tonight?" she went on, as they linked arms and began navigating the perils of Slipper's Way. "Did you men all beat your chests and call your banners and do all that manly stuff that manly men do?"

"We set our lands to muster, yes, if that's what you're trying to ask."

"Oh, no beating of chests? No measuring of...well, you know."

"Amara, have some propriety. I find you in such a strange mood tonight. What has caused it? Mustering men for war is nothing to joke or laugh about."

"Maybe it's just the word 'muster'. I've heard it so often it's started to drive me mad. Might you not use another term, from time to time? Like assemble or summon or rally? You know, just for the sake of variety."

"I suppose I could, if it should please you."

"There are other things you might do to please me, Amron." She looked at him suggestively, though of course he had no idea what to make of it. "I do miss Vesryn so, and well, you are brothers, and you do look quite alike you know..."

"Amara, stop it." He made to withdraw his arm, but she clung like a limpet, nearly hauling them both over as she did so. "I do hope you're joking. And even then, it's entirely inappropriate."

"Well, I'll leave it to you to judge, Amron. You know I have my appetites."

"I know of no such thing."

"Oh? You haven't heard us? I've been told my voice carries when in the throes of passion, even so far as that lonely nest of yours atop Keep Daecar."

He shook his head, turning silent for a moment. "Thank you for reminding me that I no longer have someone to warm my bed. We're not all so fortunate as you and Vesryn."

"Well yes, I..." She trailed off, as they reached the end of Slipper's Way, managing to conquer the treacherous path without incident. "I didn't mean to make you think of Kessia, Amron," she said once she'd released his arm. "I'm sorry. It was insensitive of me."

She was fine with her apologies, as skilled as with that acid tongue of hers. This one drew an accepting smile to his lips. "That's OK. Your jests can go a little far sometimes, is all."

"Indeed. And as ever, I'll blame the wine."

The end of Slipper's Way revealed their quarry, a quaint little timberframe inn sitting at the corner of an intersection of cobblestone lanes. Amron looked to the sign, frosted white from the snows. "The Stag," he said. "Seems a pleasant place."

"Isn't everywhere pleasant here?"

They stepped toward the door, Amron taking the lead as he pushed inside, out of the cold. It was quiet within, a few figures remaining before closing, finishing up their drinks. A man of thirty-something worked the bar with a cloth, polishing it to a sheen with a practiced determination. He looked up when he heard the door go. "We're just closing up here, I'm afraid. Served last orders some ten minutes ago."

"We're not here to drink," Amara said, stealing a step on Amron, as he plodded forward, shaking the snow from his cloak. As soon as he'd pulled back his hood, the bartender's lips unloaded a swift apology.

"Oh, Lord Daecar, I'm so sorry, I didn't realise it was you." He placed down his cloth and stood to attention. "There were rumours you'd come to town, but I didn't...well, no matter. What will it be, my lord? Anything, and on the house, of course."

"I just told you we weren't here to drink," Amara said. She looked mildly displeased to have been ignored, but was hardly as important as Amron here so seemed willing to let it pass. "But, since you're offering, I'll have a large glass of mulled wine to warm me on this cold winter's night."

"Um...we're a little short on mulled wine, Lady Amara. I'm expecting a new stock in tomorrow, but for now our stores are dry."

"No mulled wine? During winter? If that is not a crime punishable by death, I don't know what is." She sighed dramatically. "But nice to see that you recognise me, at least, young man."

"Oh yes, of course. Your beauty and grace comes afore you, my lady, if it's not too bold of me to say."

"Bold indeed, but quite well taken." She smiled, easing. "Just fetch me a sweet port, then, if you have some of that."

"We do, my lady. And you, my lord?"

"Nothing for me, thank you. I doubt we'll be staying long." The barman nodded and diligently set about his work, as

Amron looked around. "So, which of these men is this Walter?" he asked his sister-in-law. "Let me guess, that portly drunk over there in the corner. Or...how about that one, speaking to the wall? Come to think of it, they're all sots here. Is that why you've brought me really? For some therapy for my drinking. Show me where my life will take me if I'm to continue down this path?"

"Oh stop." She pushed him in the arm, and scanned the room, pleasantly lit by the hearth and a few lanterns ensconced on the dark timber walls. "I confess I cannot see him. He must be in his room." She turned to the innkeep, raising her voice. "Bartender!"

The young man turned, as he drew a bottle of rich red port from behind the bar. "Yes, my lady."

"You have a Walter Selleck here, staying in one of your rooms. I'd ask you to go and inform him that we have arrived."

"Yes, of course. I'll see to it immediately. Please, do take a seat wherever you wish." He poured her glass, stepped around the bar to hand it to her, then turned to the others. "And the rest of you...drink up and be on your way," he called out. "I want you all gone by the time I get back."

A few grumbles came from here and there, as Amron and Amara took a seat at a small rectangular table near the crackling hearth. The barman appeared to have some authority, however, as the remaining handful of drunks did as ordered, draining their drinks and shambling out into the frigid night, looking entirely disinterested in the esteemed pair as they did so. Within a few moments, they were alone. "So, does he live around here? This Walter Selleck?" Amron asked.

Amara unburdened herself from her grey fur coat and revealed her slender form, sitting upright and dignified before him. A quick sip of her port revealed it to be of decent vintage, given the appreciative look she gave the glass, before setting it down. "Well if he did, I imagine we'd be meeting in his home, not a tavern, Amron," she finally said.

"Fair point. Though I wasn't referring to Blackfrost in particular. I mean these lands. Is he a man of the North Downs?"

"He's a little more northern than that. From Lakeside originally."

"Hmmm, so not far off, then. And just how have you come to know him?"

"Oh, he's something of an itinerant. You know the sort. Those who seek adventure, and hate to stay idle. I know one or two people like that." She gave him a look.

"I wouldn't call myself adventurous, if that's the implication. I am dutiful. I don't seek adventure wantonly."

"No, I suppose not."

"And? You met him how?"

She supped her port. "On a visit of his to Varinar, some six or seven years ago. He was on a mission helping the poor, down in the Lowers, lending himself where he could. He's quite the generous soul, is Walter, and lives only to help others. That's why I suspect he may be interested in helping you."

"So you wrote him, did you, before we came here? You had this in mind all along?"

"I sent a crow as soon as you told me you wanted to pay a visit to these lands, yes. By some good fortune, he happened to be at his home in Lakeside, and returned my message with a warm interest in hastening here to meet you."

"Good fortune indeed."

"You'll find that good fortune follows him around, Amron," she offered, with a mischievous twist to her lips.

"I see." He turned toward the door that led into the visitors' quarters, as a pair of figures came creaking down the stairs. It was starting to add up. "He knows the way then, I presume? To Vandar's Tomb?" He looked back at her. "He's been there before?"

"Well, I think it would be impolite of me to tell his tale. I'll let Walter have that honour."

A few moments later, the barmen stepped back through the door, trailing a rather unremarkable man with an untamed head of scruffy brown hair, patchy beard, and drowsy eyes that suggested he'd been awoken from his sleep. The great yawn he gave out as he entered confirmed the theory. "My Lady Amara," he said, as she stood, grinning, to greet him. "I hadn't expected you tonight. My sincere apologies. You caught me napping, I'm afraid."

He spoke with a mildly common accent, marking him as lowborn, and his shirt and hose were both relatively poor, a little frayed at the edges, and in dire need of the attentions of a needle. Amron spotted at least two missing buttons, and an entire pocket looked to be absent. He frowned, rather expecting someone more fitting of the adventurer label, and when Amara reached him and drew him into a hug, the man's height was put into stark contrast too. He wasn't exactly tall, nor was he particularly slim. He had a rather stout framing, a bit of a paunch, and there was the clear curve of an extra chin hiding beneath his short, shabby beard.

"My dear Walter, so good to see you. I do apologise for the lateness of the hour, but, well, I didn't want to wait."

"No no, of course not, nor I, my lady." He looked past her, to Amron, who remained seated at the table. "So, here he is then. Lord Daecar, what an absolute pleasure it is to meet you, sir." He spoke in a sort of offhand way, though seemed polite all the same. Amron made to stand, but Walter hastened forward, shaking his head. "No, you need not stand on my account, my lord." He drew forward with a crooked smile and dropped to a single knee before him. Then he glanced back at Amara. "Is this right, my lady? Or should I be bowing? I always forget etiquette when meeting lords and the like."

"Oh forget all that, Walter. Just sit." She giggled. "You are silly, always playing the fool."

Amara continued to chuckle, as they sat, the barman hovering nearby. Amron looked at him directly. "Perhaps I will have a drink after all. An ale, please." *I think I might need it.*

"Oh yes, one for me too, Bernie, there's a good lad." Walter settled with a smile, seeming a great deal more lively all of a sudden. He looked at Amron for a long moment, lips pursed. "What an honour," he then said. "The things I've heard about you, Lord Daecar. The names. The legends. Is it true you got that great scar on your face from Vallath? He ripped it half off, some say, though you're still a handsome man to be sure. More so than

I'd have thought, actually. And bigger too." He leaned back, eyes bulging. "What a terrifying sight you must be, charging a battlefield, fully armoured and armed with that great golden sword of yours. Terrifying indeed, oh yes!"

"Former sword," Amara put in, laying a hand on the man's forearm to calm him. "It is held by my husband now."

"Right, right." He nodded several times, then looked up, eager, as Bernie came with the drinks. "Perfect. My thanks, Bernie." He took up his tankard, raised it to the barman, then gobbled down half its contents. And all the while, Amron just watched, entirely bewildered by Amara's choice of friends.

"So..." he said. "Amara has told me a...a few things about you, Walter."

"Not too much, I hope." He set down his mug and wiped his mouth, his grin never departing.

"Hardly anything, actually. She likes to be mysterious, as you may know, and said she'd leave it to you to tell me just who you are."

"Oh?" Walter looked to Amara, who sat beside him. "You've not told him, my lady?"

She shook her head. "I thought it would be better from the horse's mouth, so to speak. Go ahead, Walter, tell him."

Walter sat up a little, straightening himself out. A look of pride moved onto his face, and though his next words were quite ridiculous, he spoke then with a profound sincerity. "I, my lord, am the luckiest man in the world."

It was hard for Amron to miss the amused frown on Bernie the barman's face as he stood at the bar, idly polishing, though really listening to their exchange. It rather reflected how Amron felt, though he managed to keep his facade placid to avoid insulting the man. "I see," is all he managed to say. "That is a claim many men might make, Walter. I might once have done so myself, some years ago."

"Oh yes, I'll not deny it. Luck and good fortune can be considered subjective, I suppose. A man with a beautiful wife and family, a strong calling, a fine home...well yes, that man might very well lay claim to the title, but only subjectively, if you understand me."

"And yet you are somehow...different?" he asked, a little more intrigued. "There is some science behind your luck, is there?"

Walter smiled, leaning back. "Not science, no. More like...magic."

He left it there, for Amron to ponder, and a picture started to form. He found himself more drawn to Walter, as he shed the image of the bumbling fool, and sat there quietly, seeming to rather enjoy Amron's puzzlement. "Magic, you say?"

"Aye, magic. A gift, you might call it, my lord. A blessing, bestowed by a... a higher power."

Amron might once have stood, downed his drink, and marched from the bar, laughing. Only some months ago he'd have done that, and then gone to Amara later, congratulating her on the prank. It was quite absurd, really, and went against all he knew. *But just where has that gotten me?* he had to wonder. *Might it not be time to keep an open mind, as Amara asked?*

"OK," he said, sitting back in his chair, as it creaked under his great weight. "You have my attention, Walter." He took another pause, and another small sip of ale, conscious of making sure this remained the only one. "So, you made it, did you? To Vandar's Tomb? You're telling me that the legends are true. And not only that...that you, a rather unspectacular man, if you'll forgive me for saying so, managed to brave the wilds, and the darkness, and the cold, and all the perils of the north, and made it into the presence of a fallen god? That's what you're telling me?"

"Every bit of it, yes."

"And you did this alone?"

"All on my lonesome, true."

"And you...spoke with him? With Vandar? Or somehow...communicated?"

"Yes, communicated would be a better way of putting it. Speaking suggests talking, doesn't it? And Vandar said not a word, least not one that was vocal. I suppose...I suppose it was all in my head, and my heart. Even my soul, if you believe in such things." A light came on his face as he spoke, one given by neither hearth nor lantern, an inner light that seemed to glow about him as he recounted the first details of his experience. "I cannot truly put it to words, Lord Daecar. It was a...a spiritual and transcendental thing, something one must experience themselves, to truly understand. I felt...changed, from that moment on, from those minutes, those hours, I spent within that hallowed hall."

"Hours? You were there for...hours?" Amron's voice had been reduced to a whisper. He was leaning forward now, little by little, trying to imagine it.

"Hard to say really. The tomb is deep, my lord, so deep you think you might never find your way out. There's no light that penetrates so far, nothing save what you bring with you, and even that...even that seems dimmed down there."

"And yet you found it? How?" It wasn't just finding the sacred tomb itself, deep within the mountain, but facing all the terrors it took to get there. "There's no one who's been there for hundreds of years, Walter, not since the way was shut."

"The way was never shut, my lord, just...forgotten. I went there to escape. To...to die, really. At least, that's what I expected. I had nothing. I'd lost everything that was dear to me. Family. Friends." He paused, as if knowing that would strike a chord with him. "I sought a way to change my fate, or die in the attempt if I had to. It wasn't easy...I'll not lie...but I made it. By some miracle, I made it...and that miracle, I think, has brought me here to you. I believe I was given this gift for the task that lies ahead. For you, my lord. I believe we were always destined to meet."

Amron was somewhat struck by that, as he stayed leaning forward, staring at Walter for several long moments, trying to spot the lie, the trick, but there was none. There was an honesty in his face, a probity in his words, and their delivery, that had already convinced him. Were he to have stumbled upon the man from nowhere, his doubts would certainly remain, but he hadn't. Amara had brought him here, and he trusted her with his life.

"This gift of yours," he asked. "This blessing. It is luck you sought? That is what you asked for?"

He nodded. "I wished for good fortune, for lightness, not the dark that had consumed me. I cannot tell you how many times I have been a part of something good since that day. How many perils I have avoided, by some unlikely stroke of luck that, if taken once or twice would be remarkable, but when repeated again and again, endlessly..." He shook his head. "It becomes proof."

"And you've faced these perils on your adventures, have you?"

He dipped his chin, and on his face was a fondness for the memories that came. "I was never especially adventurous, not before my blessing. One might say going to that mountain, to that tomb, was an adventure but...well, to me it was desperation. A last chance, to which I had little true hope of salvation." He smiled, exposing those crooked teeth once more. "But since...I've become rather more fond of living, and not just existing. I take to the seas. I explore distant lands. I try to bring hope and a smile where I go, and everywhere, Vandar's light goes with me."

Amron thought a moment on those words. They might have been spoken by a priest, or by a madman, and truly, many would look at Walter and see just that. *But I don't, and what does that say about me? Might I be going mad myself?* He almost laughed at the thought, but rather kept his face straight, peering at Walter as he continued his probe. "And this manifests how?" he asked. "I can see where this is going - that with your luck and knowledge of the lands beyond the Weeping Heights, you will be able to lead me to Vandar's Tomb, to implore his spirit to restore me to full health. But...I remain cautious of my own disabilities, Walter. I am not so great a warrior as I was, and those wilds...they will be perilous for me, no matter how lucky you are."

"A fair concern, my lord, though one I'd like to set aside, if I can."

"Please do."

He smiled. "My luck is not limited to my own experience. The light that Vandar bestowed upon me - it extends to those around me, and will give us both the good fortune we need to see this quest fulfilled." He smiled again, and though his teeth were rather ugly, the shape of his grin had a charm to it, Amron noted, that drew a gentle smile to his own lips. "I could recount a dozen occasions where those in my company have escaped almost certain death by dint of being near me," he said. "Many who would be in the Eternal Halls instead cling a little longer to this mortal coil."

"Might you describe one of these occasions?" Amron glanced

to Amara, who sat by, watching. "I do not doubt you, Walter. I only wish to better understand this...strange power of yours."

"Of course..."

"I know of one," Amara put in, sipping at her port. "You asked how I came to meet Walter, Amron, and I told you I came across him as he worked with the poor in Varinar. Well, that very same day I was almost killed. I didn't tell you that, did I?"

Amron raised an eye. "What happened?"

"A building happened, Brother. You know how they can get down in the Lowers, during the wetter months. They collapse from time to time when their foundations rot and sure enough, one came down right on top of me as I was strolling by that day."

"Gods..."

"Yes, quite right. Gods indeed. And by the light of our greatest god, so I was saved." She smiled at Walter, who dipped his chin in mild abashment. "Walter here sped from nowhere, flew his arms around me, and...well, the rubble came down all around us, but not brick nor chip of it grazed our skin. A few others, regrettably, weren't so lucky, and were crushed in the collapse, but there we were, amid it all, perfectly, and miraculously untouched."

Amron's brows pinched tight. "Why have you never mentioned this before, Amara?"

"Because of that look on your face. I didn't want to worry you or anyone else. There seemed no need to trouble you, not at that time."

"Did you tell Vesryn?"

"Absolutely not. He'd only have stopped me going to the Lowers for my charity work, and that wouldn't do. It was a freak accident, and wasn't worth mentioning. At least, not until now. And I'm delighted to have finally been able to tell you, and give Walter the praise he's due. There is a reason I adore this scruffy little man, Amron, and it all started that day he saved my life."

Amron looked at Walter, who seemed quite diffident when taking the praise. "And for that you have my heartfelt thanks, Walter. I do hope Amara repaid you for this."

"I care not for material possession or gain, my lord," he said. "I think my appearance is enough to tell you that. Lady Amara's friendship was payment enough, and more than I could have asked for."

"Oh you are sweet, Walter." Amara gave him a little kiss on the cheek, and from where her lips touched, spread a shade of blush.

"You clearly value Amara's friendship a great deal, though curious that I've never heard of you," Amron said, running a finger down his scar, and to the shallow dent in his wide chin. He thought for a moment. "These occasions, these miracles, they've happened often to you, you say?"

"Oh yes, too often to mention, really. There are many others like Lady Amara who would support what I've told you. Men and women from all across the world, my lord, who've been touched by my light."

A curious smile moved onto Amron's lips, and he indulged in another short swig of his ale. "It is strange, Walter, how you seem to be selling this to me. Should it not be the other way around? What do you have to gain from this quest, I wonder?"

An earnest frown clutched at Walter's brow. "To see you restored to your former glory, my lord. To see Vandar prevail in his war with Agarath, the War Eternal that still rages, to this day. They are not gone, the gods, not truly. First Varin and Eldur fought in their stead and now it is us who do their bidding. But it comes from them, my lord, always. They still pull the strings, and I..." He lifted his chin and nodded. "I must continue to do my part in this Renewal, and my part is helping you."

Amron observed him in silence for a moment. *He is a great deal more thoughtful than he first appeared,* he saw, *and there is some strange magic to him, a warmth that feels somehow... divine.* He favoured him with a smile, and then lifted his tankard in toast. "Well put, Walter, and your sense of duty is most admirable." He paused for a moment longer, thinking on what he'd heard, before continuing. "And you...you know the way?" he then asked, as a new tension gripped at his voice. "Truly? You can find your way there, through the mountains, through the snows, the wilds...down to the tomb itself?"

"I know the way, my lord. I will get you there, I promise it."

Amron turned to Amara. "And you're certain this is the right course, Sister? For me to journey to that mountain?"

"I do," she said with a whisper, reaching across the table to grip his hand. "We need you, dear brother. *All* of you. We need you whole so you can strike at those who have wronged us. Only you can stand up to him, Amron." She set him with a firm stare. "You know of whom I speak."

He turned his eyes down, thinking a moment, nodding to himself. Then he spoke again. "I'd not want to come to such an abrupt decision now," he concluded. "Give me the night to ponder it." He was speaking with Walter, who dipped his head in accord. "I'll return on the morrow with my decision."

"I am at your service, Lord Daecar," Walter told him. "With *luck*, you'll see the *light*."

He grinned with those playful words, and they were the last of their exchange, as Amron and Amara returned to the castle. The snows had grown a little lighter and the winds less fierce, yet not so in his mind. In a fashion, he'd started to settle upon his decision to stay, to be a good father to Lillia, to be Lord Daecar, first and foremost, as his father-in-law, Lord Amadar, had urged. But now...how could he not take this chance? He would live forever in regret, if he didn't, and would always ask, *what if?*

And thus those two words simmered, boiling away at the back of his mind, as they moved through the castle and up to his chambers, where he sat once more at his father's old desk, and Amara settled into the armchair his grandfather had so often enjoyed. Neither of them spoke for a time, as the hearth warmed the chill in their bones, until Amron dipped his head into a single nod and spoke. "I'm going," he told her. "I have to, don't I?"

She lounged, cross-legged, across the room, a fresh chalice of wine to hand. "I'll not make the decision for you, Amron. If you have doubts, sleep on them, and see whether a brand new morning brings the focus you need. I know you don't like to make decisions without due thought. You have never been reckless."

"No...not until I sent Lythian off," he said, turning his eyes aside. "I'll regret that forever, Amara. He and Borrus and

Tomos...they might all be sat at Varin's Table by now because of me."

"You had no way to know what might befall them down there." Her voice came with a firming edge that brooked no interest in self-pity. "It is important that you look forward now, not backward. What wrongs have been done to us can never be righted, but they can be avenged."

"And you think I might do so? Fight the world, as I once did?" He sat heavy and weary in his chair, feeling old all of a sudden. "The world thinks more of me than I deserve, Amara. I am not Varin. I do not truly know how much difference I might make."

She expressed a tired sigh. "This is dull, Amron. Hearing you speak like this..." She shook her head. "I'll not indulge your moping anymore. How many times do I have to tell you just *who...you...are*. Varin? No, but you're the closest we've had in generations. And seeing you restored, seeing you return? Do you truly not see how that will affect our people, as war encroaches upon us once more? To see their greatest hero reborn? As Varin himself was, again and again, by Vandar. No, you may not be a demigod, but let them think that you are. You never know, Amron…it might just win us a war."

He contemplated those words for a time. There was a wisdom to them. A deep wisdom he couldn't ignore. "And our personal enemies?" he asked, hunched at his desk. "I know you think that your cousin is behind all this, Amara. Would you have me slay him too?"

"I would have you slay all those involved, Amron." The red wine had darkened her lips by now, making them look almost bloody in the dim light. "Yes, I believe that Janilah set this into motion, but he is not the only enemy we have. I may not have been born of this house, nor contributed to this family with a child of my own, but that does nothing to lessen my desire to protect it. I am a Daecar, Amron, as much as any of you. And I will do anything to protect those I love, and destroy those who threaten us."

Now there's that lioness, he thought, enjoying that look on her face, the fierceness in her eyes. He knew she'd protect Lillia with her life, and Jovyn was here too for that now, as loyal and as trustworthy a companion as he could hope for his daughter to have. *She doesn't need me, not now,* he decided. *In time, she'll understand.*

"We would need to do this quietly," he said, as Amara's facade softened, and she settled back into her chair. "It would not serve us for our enemies to know where I've gone, and that includes the great lords of this land."

"Yes, I agree. Most will not understand, not without meeting Walter and feeling his light." She noticed the look on his face. "So, you did feel it, then? Even besides what he told you, you sensed that...magic of his?"

Amron could hardly deny it. "He does have a certain...glow to him, yes."

"He's a special man, and so humble too. He might have sought fame or riches with his gift, but so few people know of him. That, too, will serve us well, but you'll need a story to cover your departure. People will ask questions if you just disappear without cause."

He was acutely aware of that, and had already considered what he might do. "I will travel to Northwatch," he said, "in a day or so, under the guise of briefing the men stationed there. With these lands rallying for war, my leaving should not cause a stir. Lord Borrington commands the fort at Northwatch and is a close friend; he'll help provide Walter and I passage to the Weeping Heights in secret."

"That should do, though the longer you're gone, the more questions will be asked."

"I doubt it. Not with everyone's eyes turning south. I'm hardly being considered of great consequence right now, Amara."

"True, you are rather pathetic these days, hardly worthy of one's consideration." Her lips pulled into a puckish smile and she further reddened them with wine. "But it does bear thinking about. I can't imagine you'll be back for some months, and a lot can happen in that time. I won't be able to conceal your true purpose for long, sweet brother."

It put it in context. *Months,* he thought. *And how might the world look when I return?* It added an extra urgency to his thinking. "Do what you can," he said. "I trust you to share this with only those you're confident we can rely on. But should word get out, so be it. That isn't something we need worry about now."

"Then it seems you have come to your decision." She sunk her wine and stood. "We can continue in the morning, once you've slept on it, and let the quiet hours confirm your course. I'll leave you to your thoughts, unless..." She gave him a little look. "Unless you'd rather I stay."

"No, Amara, I wouldn't."

"Oh, I know. Just...testing you, Amron, that's all."

She swirled away in her cloak, leaving him alone. And when he took to his bedchambers, his dreams came vivid as he slept, and in them, Amron Daecar flew. He soared above the mountains, the snows, the beasts that lurked below, and down through the tunnels and caves and caverns of that lonely mountain, deep into Vandar's Tomb.

Where he stood before the embers of a god, basking in his wondrous glow.

15

Jonik

The sky was a glittering sheet of stars unlike anything Jonik had ever seen, not a cloud to blot them, not a breath of wind in the air. He stood at the forecastle in silent contemplation, enjoying the strange sensation as the ship sat almost entirely motionless upon the waters, waiting for the winds to pick up. They'd sailed through afternoon and some way into the night on a light breeze, but now the air had stilled to sleep, leaving Invincible Iris temporarily becalmed on the light sloshing waters amidst the Islands of the Tides.

Apparently it was a common problem here. "Happens from time to time," Jack had told him a little earlier, with the confidence of a man who'd experienced it all before. "I've heard of ships getting stranded for days, or even weeks out here, but that won't happen to us, don't worry." He added a grin, and put that paw of his on Jonik's shoulder, gripping through the furs. "We'll be up and running by morning, you'll see."

Jonik gave him a doubtful look. "How do you know?"

Jack o' the Marsh's brawny shoulders bobbed into a carefree shrug. "What Captain said earlier. We deserve a break, right? The winds will be blowing again soon enough."

He'd patted him on the back and strolled off to sleep at that, leaving Jonik to his thoughts, and the peace and quiet of an empty deck. Well, it wasn't entirely empty - Brax remained on duty to stern, lounging at the wheel - but otherwise Jonik had Iris all to himself.

At least, until Emeric Manfrey arrived. He came without invite or warning, catching Jonik off guard as he appeared at his side in his worn green cloak. It would have once been fine, but was now a little frayed, a cloak bought at market in Greywater, Jonik imagined, after he'd lost most of his possessions when his ship went down in the storm. "Fine night," Emeric said, in his smooth low voice, eyes out to the twinkling seas. "Enough to inspire poetry, wouldn't you say? Is there a poet in you, Jonik?"

Jonik glanced at him. "I wouldn't think so."

"No, of course not. Not with the life you've led." He paused a moment, then said, "I know who you are, you know. I thought it best I tell you that, lest you think I have some hidden motive for being here. I'd not want to make you feel uncomfortable around me."

Jonik kept on looking at the waters, as the starlight danced upon them. He thought back to the fight on the beach earlier, as the half dozen men on horseback had fled. "One of those men...he called me the Ghost," he recalled. "I figure people have begun talking about me by now if I'm being given nicknames like that. So you knowing who I am...it doesn't surprise me."

"The taverns and squares do swell with tales of you, it's true," Emeric agreed. "The Ghost of the Shadowfort. That's what they're calling you. That's the full name. And one to inspire fear, wouldn't you say? That can only be a good thing, for a man like you."

Jonik turned to look at him, and saw a sparkle in those keen gold eyes. "I'd rather have no name at all," he contested. "I'm not out to seek glory, Emeric."

"No, and that's why you're venturing south? To escape it all? The names." He paused. "And the men who hunt you?"

"I see you know about that too." Jonik turned to look at the shadows of the islands, laid out upon the horizon. "Who told you? Jack? One of the other men?"

A smile warmed Emeric's rugged black-bearded cheeks. "I don't think Jack would betray your trust like that, from what I've seen, nor would any of the others. Not unless you gave them leave to. They seem loyal to you, and quite protective of your identity. Simple men often quell under the light of a powerful Bladeborn like yourself. And, well...you're a little more than that."

He took a quick glance at Jonik's black scabbard, and the black hilt and pommel emerging from within it. "And in any case, it's been easy enough for me to deduce who you are from the whispers and rumours I've heard. I grew up in the shadow of the Hammersongs as a boy, you know, and heard many a hearthside tale about the Shadow Order from my dear sweet grandmother. They were a brutal sect, she would tell me, hunting any man who abandons them, ruthlessly protecting their secrets. What you've done is crime enough already for them to hunt you, without adding a stolen Blade of Vandar into the mix."

Jonik had no reply, but to remain silent, to listen to the gentle slosh of water against the hull, the surprisingly tuneful whistling of Braxton as he stood at the helm, keeping watch for passing ships. There was one, off in the distance, a shadow gliding slow and silent upon the horizon, though it was a long way away, and going further still. The seconds gathered to half a minute as Jonik watched it, and still he spoke not a word.

Emeric got his meaning. "An uncomfortable topic for you, I'm sure," he said, dipping his head in apology. "Forgive me if I'm being too forward, Jonik. I'll leave you to your thoughts."

He took a few slow paces away, as Jonik watched him go through the corner of his eye. *He is only trying to get to know you,* he scolded. *And if you're to sail together, it isn't such a bad idea that you make the same effort.* "I have a question for you, Emeric," he said, causing the man to stop in his stride. "Seeing as you know about me, I'd wish for the same courtesy from you."

Emeric spun around and drew back toward him a step, seeming quite amenable to the proposition. "I agree, Jonik, and stand before you an open book." He opened out his arms. "Please, ask away."

There was a great deal Jonik wanted to know about the man,

but one question came first to mind. "Sir Oswald Manfrey," he said. "We've been wondering if you're related to him, have Jack and I. After what I saw of you today, you're clearly a talented Bladeborn. And the name? It adds up."

Emeric took another step forward, his cloak hanging limp from his wide shoulders, deep brown leathers layered beneath. He placed his hand to the pommel of his sword, carved with intricate precision in the shape of an eagle's head, with a silver cross-guard of feathered wings. Jonik took it in with little more than a glance, but Emeric didn't miss it. "It was my father's sword," he said. "The ancestral sword of my house, bearing the great eagle of Manfrey. He fell during the war, my father, as so many others did, leaving me this sword, and the command of a dying house when I was nothing but a teen." He spoke in a soft voice as he thought of those days, a melancholy in his tone. "House Manfrey is little more than rubble now, Jonik, and with me the name will be lost. I claim no title of lord anymore, not since it was stripped from me, along with my lands, my home, my honour..." He turned his eyes out to sea, a clench to his bearded jaw. "I have only this blade now, the blade that Sir Oswald himself once bore. It is...dear to me, yet a reminder, also, of a time long gone. And now...now it falls upon me to see my house fail. A once great house, fading like the dying light of a sunset, never to rise again."

A ripple of wind moved through Jonik's long black hair, no more than a stir before settling. Emeric's words had made him think of his own past, of the house he'd never been a part of, the family he'd all but destroyed. "What happened?" he whispered. "Who stripped your life from you?"

Emeric released a long held sigh and stepped toward the bulwark, staring to the horizon and the shadows of islands leagues away. "We were once of Vandar," he started. "I suppose you know that. After Sir Oswald rose to prominence, and led the Varin Knights with such esteem, he was awarded a lordship by the king and given lands in East Vandar on which to settle, beneath the banner of House Lukar. When Galin Lukar assembled his army, and marched on Tukor, House Manfrey was sworn to support them. Of course, Sir Oswald was long dead by then, so it fell to his grandson, Bedrik, to stand beside Galin when he stormed Ilithor, and took the kingdom for his own. And in return for his loyal support, the newly crowned King Galin gave Bedrik lands in the north of Tukor, to replace the lands in East Vandar he abandoned by supporting Galin's claim."

"I never knew that," Jonik said, listening intently. "So the Manfreys became Tukoran, only two generations after Sir Oswald established his house?"

"Yes indeed, but as with anything that burns so fast and so bright, the light of House Manfrey soon dimmed. By the time my grandfather became lord, we'd been reduced to nothing but minor vassals of House Kastor, tucked up in the wilds of North Tukor, forgotten as the great house we once were."

He raised a smile, as if to counter the sadness in his words, and drew a breath of cool night air. "Which I suppose, brings us to me. A forgotten lord of little power, living off a dying name." He turned. "That's what I was, Jonik, before Lord Modrik Kastor labelled me an outcast, and forced me into exile, taking my lands and everything else. And do you know why he did all that? Why he took what little I had left, and cast me out into the cold?"

Jonik shook his head. "I don't know, Emeric."

"Love." He let the word hang for a moment. "It was love, my friend. Love for the wrong woman. Not his sister, no, nor his daughter. I didn't fall in love with his wife, or sully someone he held dear. Oh no. Just a girl who worked in my household, an angel between my walls, who was reviled for one reason, and one reason only. The tone of her perfect skin."

A great sadness washed over him then, such that he had to turn away, and on his face Jonik could see the weight of the hate he felt. "It wasn't long after the war, when tensions were high, when innocent southerners who'd made their lives in the north suddenly found themselves spat on in the streets, and driven from their homes. And those were the lucky ones. The ones who lived. Many more were killed, tortured, raped and abused. They suffered untold horror, living their own nightmare, their own war, and none more so than those who lived under the shadow of House Kastor."

His hand was in a fist, pressing against the wooden railing of the gunwale. "I sense your hate for the order that used you, Jonik," he said. "I understand it, because I have lived with hate all my life. Hate for the Kastors. Hate for Tukor. Hate for lofty men who sit in high towers, casting judgment on those beneath them..."

His words graduated to a growl, low, bitter, and those golden eyes of his seemed lit by the stars as he stared forward across the world. To Tukor. So far away. To the people who destroyed his life.

"Did you ever wish to get vengeance?" Jonik asked him. "Did you ever try?"

His voice softened. "Modrik Kastor was killed some years ago," he said. "I wish I could say it was me, but it wasn't. Just a drunken accident, a fool slipping in his own filth and cracking his head on the hearth. It was a good day...and a sour one. To see him gone...yet to have never had the chance to kill him myself..." He shook his head and trailed off.

Jonik continued to watch him, study him, understand him. "And his house? Might you seek a...a broader retribution?"

Emeric smiled, and gave out a little laugh. "I do not hold a Blade of Vandar, as you do. And even were you to hand me that blade, and let me seek the justice I crave, I'd never be able to wield it." He looked at it now, but there was no desire for it in his eyes. "I am but a faint shadow of Sir Oswald, a distant echo of his voice on the wind. A few weak Bladeborn I can handle, but little more than that."

"I don't believe you."

He turned, eyes raised. "Oh? Which part."

"You're stronger than you claim, Emeric. Your house may have fallen on ill times, but you might just restore it, if you ever try to reclaim what's yours."

"Reclaim what's mine? You mean go to King Janilah's halls, fall on my knees, and beg? I have my pride, Jonik, and know just how that meeting would go. The Lukars are little different to the Kastors, rotten to the core. The only way I might reclaim what is mine is through their ruin, and the rising of a new more moderate king. I wait, as ever, with bated breath," he finished with a sardonic huff.

Jonik decided not to question him further. *It is our first night on the waves,* he thought, *and we have time to revisit this if we wish.* And he did wish it, just not now. There was something about Emeric that appealed to him. *He is more broken than he outwardly seems, those wounds that cut so deep. And his ancestral lands are not far from the Shadowfort, if I'm figuring this right. It might be that we can help one another out, one day.*

"Anyway, it's a dreary tale," the exile went on. "And I've long since learned to love the south, over the many years I've spent there. The lands are not without fault, nor the people, but there is a greater sense of community, of compassion about them. If you're running, Jonik, and seeking to find solace somewhere, you could do a lot worse."

"I am yet to decide where my path will lead me."

"A wise course," he told him. "I'm sure it will reveal itself, in time."

Jonik offered him a nod, in thanks, as he felt the first pull of his bunk. "I ought to get some sleep," he said. "Take advantage while the ship's still. I don't much like the motion when the waves pick up."

Emeric's smile was fond. "You'll grow used to it." He turned to him fully, looking every bit the noble lord in the way he swirled his cloak, and dipped his chin. "I thank you for listening, Jonik, as I have spun the bitter weave of my life. It is a tale I seldom share, but you...well, I thought you might understand."

He gave him a final smile before turning again to look upon the world, standing silent, standing pensive, at the bow of the ship. Jonik left him there, stepping down from the forecastle, past the soaring masts, and to the stairs that led below decks. Turner had tried to give him his private cabin, but Jonik was having none of it. There was plenty of space in the communal quarters, now that most of the crew were dead, and he no longer had to contend with the stink and noise of a score of sleeping men. A bit of snoring and heavy breathing he could handle. And a half dozen was much better than twenty.

He returned to the Shadowfort that night as he slept. He and the Nightblade, his great companion, his guide, the whispering voice in his head. *We will destroy it together*, it said, as they looked toward the great fortress. *You and I, Jonik. All of us.*

Jonik looked to his sides. There was Jack, on his right, and Emeric Manfrey on his left. Brax and Turner came next. Then Devin and Grim and Sid, and beyond, a dozen grey shadows, a score, a hundred...more and more lining up, with Jonik at the heart of them. A roar gave out, building, spreading, rattling the frozen rocks beneath his feet...and all through the peaks, the tumult grew, louder and louder still, all singing out his name.

This is your destiny, Jonik, whispered the Nightblade, so clear to his ears amid the great din. *You were never born to follow, but to lead. It has started now, but this is not the end. The Ghost of the Shadowfort...*The blade smiled, rippling black, curls of fog twirling, dancing. *That is what they will call you now, but it is only one...one of a hundred names you'll have.*

Jonik looked toward the blurred black peaks before him, and the thousand shadows at his sides. They were staring at him, all of them, waiting now, silent. Jack and Emeric and Turner and the rest. An endless chain of blurred faces, watching him, waiting...waiting.

Now you lead, the Nightblade said. *Lead them, Jonik. It is your fate.*

Tucked up in his bunk, with the Nightblade resting beside him, Jonik smiled as he slept. As he slept, as he dreamed, he smiled like never before.

16

Saska

Saska stood at the edge of her tent, just within the flaps, watching as the young girl from three tents down was marched without ceremony out of the camp. There were two surly guards either side of her, and her weeping was wetter than the rains, endlessly drizzling from the iron-grey skies.

She was the third girl Saska had seen leave over the last six days, though the first of the trio to have done so in such abject misery. The first two had left in quite different circumstances, beaming from ear to ear as they strolled away, garbed in luxury linens and wools that Lady Cecilia had granted them as a parting gift, escorted by servants holding parasols to protect them from the soaking skies. They were off to start their new lives, Lady Cecilia would have told them, a life of comfort and excess, of dashing knights and gallant lords and banquets and balls...and beautiful dresses and grand private quarters with flower-lined balconies overlooking wondrous, unending views.

So off they went, enraptured by the promise of a comfortable life, believing all the lies they'd been told. *But they'll soon find out different,* Saska thought, *when they arrive at that castle and find it cold and bleak...and are taken to their meagre room which is little more than a cell...and that handsome gallant lord turns out to be a sixty year old drunk, ruddy-cheeked and reeking...lumbering into their room each night to flop on top of them, pump a few times, and stumble back off to his feast.*

That was the truth of it, though the picture wasn't so pretty. So Cecelia painted a different one. One of bright lights and colours and comfort. *One of fantasy,* Saska thought bitterly. *Of fairy-tale. That is what she sells them. Nothing but a rotten lie.*

She felt pity for these girls, pity that they hadn't been taken in by Marian instead, though in reality most would have preferred this life anyway. *Perhaps I'm being unfair? Perhaps it wouldn't be as bad as I imagine.* Saska had to think of the ends. What was all this for? To produce strong, healthy children, boys who will grow into men, men who'll grow into warriors. If that was the end, then it served them to keep the mother happy too, didn't it? A happy, healthy mother would breed a happy, healthy son, after all.

But either way, the girl being marched out of the camp right now would be given no such life. There was no parasol to cover her, no handmaids to escort her. She wore simple white garments, sodden with rain, sticking to her skin. Saska could see the clear shape of her bottom and bust and the dark circles upon her breasts, pressing through the fabric. She could see all the watching soldiers too who'd gathered to see her off. A score of them had assembled, staring at her with avaricious eyes and cawing out unpleasant remarks, hot-faced at the sight of her fine, womanly form.

The girl was young, pretty, and terribly confused, her shoulders hunched tight and eyes darting as the crowd bleated and cackled around her. Saska could only guess at what had happened. She'd arrived just yesterday, her stay lasting little more than a day, and clearly that was perfectly long enough for Lady Cecilia to conclude that she wasn't suited to life as a breeder. Maybe her blood was too weak. Maybe she couldn't bear children. There might have been a dozen issues that made her ineligible, but in the end the result was the same.

So here she was instead, being marched out amid the leering, jeering men, likely to be taken to one of the camp brothels instead, where her fate would be a whole lot worse. And down the line of tents, several other breeders-to-be were peeking from the flaps, watching as the bawling girl was hauled away. It was a loud and pitiable public display, and that served a purpose too - to show these girls the other side of the coin...to make it clear what would happen to them should they fail to satisfy Cecilia's demands.

As Saska watched the commotion, she spotted Sir Griffin emerging from the network of tall pavilions established at the heart of the castle ruins, dressed in his leathers and furs. He took a look around, spotted what was happening, let out a bellowing laugh, and began sauntering over to observe with his men.

His arrival had caused several of the other girls to disappear back into the safety of their tents, but not Saska. She stayed where she was, shifting a little to draw Sir Griffin's attention, opening the flaps wider so he'd spot her. Her attempts to be noticed had thus far been fruitless, and the constant rains hadn't helped, keeping her confined to her tent for most of the last six days and giving her almost no opportunity to draw the interest of Lord Cedrik Kastor or his haughty unpleasant nephew. Now time was running short, and from what she'd managed to glean from her eavesdroppings, the camp was about to be moved northwest to begin the siege of Harrowmoor. *By which time it might be too late*, she thought. *If I'm going to do this, it has to be soon. And curse these damned rains! Will the skies ever stop from weeping!*

The drizzle was light now, elsewise Sir Griffin wouldn't have ventured from the warm dry comfort of his pavilion, and Saska chanced herself by taking a step out, colourfully lit in a dress of light green lace. It was the most eye-catching garment she could find in her chest, a scanty nightdress best suited to private use, and as soon as she appeared a number of the men took note, eyes popping, tongues lapping like the flea-ridden curs they were. She ignored them, drawing a long, full breath of fresh air into her lungs as she looked to the skies. It was a bold move, but it worked. And along came Sir Griffin Kastor.

"Hot in your tent, is it?" he sneered, stepping across the

muddy yard toward her, as the girl was taken away. "What was your name again? I forget..."

"Tilda, my lord." Saska drew back out of the rain, though didn't pull the flaps to cover herself. She smiled, less coy now, more sultry. *I can't afford to be shy anymore.* "Yes, very hot in here. I needed some fresh air. This rain..."

"It's been rather unrelenting, hasn't it? Though I should say - I'm not a lord, but a knight. So sir will do."

"Oh. I am sorry, sir. The lord is your uncle, yes? Lord Cedrik?" She glanced toward the grand pavilion looming over the rest, a little way off. "He must be a great man, to run an army this size."

"He is. Oh yes, a great man indeed." He looked at her, seeming to have forgotten about her entirely over the last week. "I took you from that little backwater village with the roundtower and flooded causeway, didn't I?" he said. "The girl from Aram. I've been so busy planning the siege of Harrowmoor that I'd all-but forgotten about you."

Saska doubted he was playing any part in the planning of the siege at all, but didn't say it. "The village was called Baymoor, sir," she said instead. "You were surprised to find a southern girl with Varin blood there." She dipped her eyes and gave another suggestive glance toward the heart of the ruins. *Your uncle, you dumb whelp. You said he'd be interested in meeting me, remember? Remember!*

"Oh yes, you are a rare one." He frowned and looked toward Lady Cecilia's tent, in which she was currently taking shelter from the rains. "I wonder what she has in mind for you? You're hardly suited to breeding among our more esteemed bloodlines, not with your colouring. Any son you bear will be part southern and no such man would ever be permitted to join the ranks of the Emerald Guards, or lead a host of men like I do. Gods forbid." He scoffed at the notion. "A spy, perhaps. Yes, that might do for a spawn of yours."

Or me, Saska thought, as she let the stupid boy speak, glancing all the while toward the heart of the camp. He went on for a time, spilling more vitriolic bile, before finally seeming to remember how he'd wanted to introduce her to his uncle. "Have you left this yard since arriving here?" he asked, and as he said it, he was looking away toward the taller pavilions. "My uncle...he hasn't come by at all, has he?"

She shook her head.

"Hmmm, I did mention you to him, I think. The night I brought you here. Though I'll admit, I was on the ale that evening with the men, so I can't be sure. And he is a terribly busy man." He glanced again at Cecilia's tent, then ran his eyes over Saska's lace-clad body. "He'll like you, I think. My uncle. You're just the sort he enjoys spending time with, to..." He smirked to himself. "To blow off steam, and unwind." The smirk remained, growing yet broader. "Would you like to help him unwind, Tilda?"

Got him. "I...I am not sure," she said. "Lady Cecilia does not allow us beyond the yard. The soldiers, they guard us, and stop us from leaving..."

Sir Griffin flicked a wrist. "Those men are regular footmen, and beneath my command. And Cecilia?" He huffed. "She can coddle you all she likes, but my uncle far outranks her here. Come, follow me. He's alone in his pavilion right now."'

Saska dipped her eyes, feigning nerves, and turned to the side of her tent where the clothes were stored. "I should change into something more appropriate, I think. To meet a great lord is an honour, and I'd not want to displease him by wearing something so indecent."

That horrid little smile clung to Sir Griffin's lips, as though he was in on some big secret. "Oh, I think what you're wearing now is just fine, Tilda. You look lovely."

"I do?"

"Oh yes, very lovely. Come."

She trailed him out into the light rains, ignoring the ogling of the remaining guards, wondering just what she was getting herself into. It was still daytime, though dusk was fast approaching, and attempting to assassinate Cedrik Kastor now would be little short of suicide. But what choice did she have? The long days here had made her desperate, and one way or another, she had to get the man's attention. She tried not to think beyond that as she marched through the tents intended for the cooks and scribes and squires, and into the old quad where the command pavilions were arrayed. "Just this way, Tilda." Sir Griffin was almost skipping he was so happy with himself. "Are you nervous? Don't be. He's a kind man, my uncle, a good man. He'll make you feel comfortable, you'll see."

She could hear the sound of the whip, feel the sting of the lash, smell the iron scent of the blood as it dribbled down her naked back. *No, don't think of all that,* she scorned. *If you do, you'll lose control. You are Tilda, the girl from Aramatia. You do not know what sort of man he is. Believe what you're being told. He is kind, he is good, he will make you feel comfortable.*

She smiled, and walked on.

There were a pair of Emerald Guards on duty at the front of the tent, their tall spears held straight, tips piercing the sopping skies. "I'd like to see my uncle," said Sir Griffin. "I have a gift for him."

The men gave no reaction, though one turned and slipped into the pavilion, returning a moment later with a nod. Saska stilled her breathing and brightened her eyes and painted a timid smile onto her lips. They stepped inside, out of the rain, and the large internal space came into view. A central room broke off into separate chambers, one for lounging, one for sleeping, though the heart of the pavilion was intended for the functions of command. A large oaken table was at its centre, laid with maps and plans, and around the room were warm braziers and separate trestle tables loaded with whiskey, wine, and assortments of food. And there, at that thick wooden table, stood Lord Cedrik Kastor, accoutred in rich brown leathers stamped with the bear print of his house.

"Uncle, I hope I am not interrupting. I brought..."

Lord Kastor cut the young man off with a raised hand. Sir Griffin stopped mid-sentence near the entrance, with Saska at his side, and for an age Cedrik seemed to peruse the maps before him at his leisure, before finally standing straight and turning to them.

"Nephew," he said, and that voice sent a chill up Saska's spine. It was as rich as his leather tunic, clean, clipped, *perfect.* Cedrik

Kastor was looked upon in Tukor as the archetype of the ideal lord, the very sort of dashing figure that Lady Cecilia would be promising these poor ignorant girls. Yet like his father, his private and public face were very different. This was his mask to hide the monster beneath. "I'm told you have a gift for me?"

Sir Griffin shoved Saska forward. "Here, Uncle. Her name is Tilda. I believe I mentioned her to you..."

"Yes, you did." Cedrik gave Saska a cursory look, though there was nothing to suggest he recognised her. "She's one of Lady Cecilia's girls?"

"Yes, from Aramatia, Uncle. They're your favourites, aren't they?"

Lord Kastor studied Saska for a moment longer, ignoring his nephew's question. And there she saw it, the creeping shadow of cruelty inching upon his face, the desirous sneer pulling back his top lip. "A pretty thing," he said. She wasn't a person to him but an object. A plaything with which he could do as he pleased. "Where did you find her?"

"Some rotting old village out on the moors. Had to take the head off an ugly old sow for insubordination." He laughed at the recollection, though his uncle looked less than interested in the boy's murderous antics. "I imagine Lady Cecilia will find her a suitable posting soon though. If you want to enjoy her, now would be the time, my lord."

"Yes, thank you for your generous advice, Griffin," Lord Kastor dismissed. He seemed to hold his nephew in disdain, much as Cecilia did. *And the boy's men,* Saska thought. She'd noticed that they hardly liked him either, and could quite easily understand why. "You didn't think to bring her to me sooner?"

The young knight stiffened. "I...well I told you about her, my lord. And since then, I've been busy. What with the..."

"You forgot," cut in Lord Kastor.

"No, I didn't...I..."

"Oh stop blabbering, Griffin. You forgot. I forgot. It doesn't matter. I have no time for this right now." He seemed angry all of a sudden. "Can you not see I have a war to run? Stupid bloody boy." He turned back to his maps. "Take her back to her tent."

Griffin hesitated. "But Uncle, I...I'd hoped you might..."

"What?" Cedrik Kastor turned, staring at his nephew with those deadened brown eyes. "Reward you? Gods, boy, ever you grovel and fawn. It's pathetic and unbecoming. If you want more men to command, then fight well and climb the ranks by merit. I'll not hand you a hundred more men in exchange for a base southern whore..."

"I'm not a whore," Saska broke out, setting a flare of anger to her eyes. She needed to do something to get his attention, and if this was the way, so be it. "I have never been with a man. Not once. Not ever. And I am not here for that." She shook her head, resolute. "I will not be touched by you, my lord."

A hand caught her on the cheek with a swift, fizzing slap, causing her to topple momentarily to the side. "You'll hold your tongue here! How dare you speak to him in that way."

She stood back up straight, cheek burning red, eyes shining with a coat of tears. Through the blur, she saw the twist of Cedrik Kastor's lips, as Sir Griffin rose his hand to strike her once more. "Now, Griff, let's not redden her cheek any further," the Lord of Ethior said. "I like a girl with spirit, you know that."

Saska knew that too, and she knew how to stoke his interest. A virginal Aramatian with Varin blood? How could he resist? "I came here to meet you," she told him. "I do not want anything else. Not...not that. Lady Cecilia will not allow it..."

The familiar sound of Cedrik Kastor's grating laughter filled the pavilion. "You put too much faith in her, girl. If I desire it, I'll take you from that little nest she's feathered for you and have you chained up here for my pleasure." Even speaking of such things was stirring him, Saska could see. *The outspoken ones were always his favourites. The ones who tried to fight back.*

"I'll take her to your bedchamber now if you wish, Uncle," said Griffin, sticking his nose further up his uncle's rear. "I'll tie her to the posts for you, and gag her so she can't call out."

Cedrik took a time to consider it, and in that moment, Saska wondered whether she might be forced to strike right now. *I could grab Griffin's dagger and have his throat cut easy enough,* she wagered, *but covering the ground to Cedrik and seeing him to the same fate?* It would be folly, and she knew it. *He'd have his own blade unsheathed before I could blink*, she realised. Much as she hated the man, there was no denying how gifted a killer he was. It was said only Prince Rylian outmatched him in Tukor and lest she take him completely off guard, she'd have little chance of killing him, let alone doing so quietly enough so the guards outside didn't hear.

So she put the thought aside, and stood there, praying now that Lord Kastor didn't follow through. The seconds stretched out, long and longer still, as his lips twisted up, ugly and cruel. Yet just as he opened his mouth to speak, and seal Saska's fate, the sound of approaching men rustled the air outside. His attention was drawn to the exit, and any thoughts of his dark perversions were instantly dismissed. "See what's happening, Griff," he commanded.

Sir Griffin marched to the exit, but before he could step out, one of the Emerald Guards posted outside came pushing through the flaps. "My lord, the lead host from Vandar have arrived," he said. "They approach through the ruins, a half dozen lords and Varin Knights in sum."

"So soon?" The change in Cedrik Kastor's expression was immediate, his sneer smoothing off, a strained smile taking its place. He took a moment to straighten himself out, fetched his cloak, and fixed his sword belt and sheath to his waist. "Lead the way, Sir Wenfry." He took a final moment to compose himself before marching outside and into the light rains. "My lords, welcome to my warcamp," Saska heard him call out over the pattering on the deerhide roof. "I hope your ride was not too arduous?"

"Arduous, no. Just long, slow, and bloody wet," came a heavy, resounding voice in reply. The shuffling of bodies and clinking of armour swelled, as more men grouped outside. "Is this your command pavilion, Lord Kastor? We're soaked to the bone and tired and all crave warmth and wine. I'm assuming you have both within?"

"Of course, Lord Kanabar." She could hear Cedrik's hesitation. *He will not want me found in here.* "Would you not wish to get settled in your private pavilions first? I have some set up for you to the east side of the castle ruins..."

"Later. Wine and warmth first."

Before Lord Kastor could argue, a huge great man with a bushy red beard and bald head was tramping through the flaps and into the pavilion, turning his eyes around. Sir Griffin immediately drew Saska to the side, out of the way, in an effort to conceal her, but seeing as they were the only two people inside, they were impossible to miss.

"And who is this, then?" Lord Kanabar asked, rainwater dripping through the thick, twisting hairs of his beard. Behind him, several other Vandarians followed him in, dressed in gleaming godsteel breastplates and deep blue cloaks. One was fully accoutred in godsteel armour, clad from heel to neck. A couple of others were dressed more moderately in leathers and furs as Lord Kanabar was, marking them as lords, not Varin Knights. All crowded into the pavilion and made quickly for the braziers to warm themselves, fetching wine, shaking the rains from their cloaks as they drew them off to hang.

The young knight offered his answer as it all unfolded, standing stiff in the presence of the incoming men. "Sir Griffin Kastor, my lord," he said. "I am nephew to..."

"No, not you. The girl." Lord Kanabar turned as Cedrik stepped back inside. "So this is how you've been spending your time is it, Lord Kastor?" he accused. "Here was I thinking you were planning the siege of Harrowmoor, yet we arrive to find a scantily clad girl in your company. And southern, besides. I'm supposing the rumours about you are true, then?"

That made Cedrik Kastor noticeably uncomfortable, though he attempted to hide it by stepping over to pour himself a cup of wine. "She's just a servant, my lord," he said. "I'd give no mind to spurious rumours. They crop up like weeds, but wither and die soon after."

"Yes, I'm sure." Saska liked this Lord Kanabar immediately, though kept her eyes down as he turned to her. "What happened to your face, child? That looks sore."

She gulped, but before she could answer, Sir Griffin did so for her. "She's a clumsy one, Lord Kanabar," he said. "Slipped in the rains and..."

"I wasn't asking you, boy." Lord Kanabar towered over him. He must have been deep into his sixties, but even stooping a little, soared well beyond six feet tall. "They're not mistreating you here, are they child? Has someone struck you?" He shot a dark look at Sir Griffin, rightly imagining it was him.

Saska was half tempted at the moment to tell the man everything. To abandon her mission right now and flee back beneath the safety of Marian's wing, wherever that might be. *This is too much for me,* she thought. *I may never get Cedrik alone, and even if I do, how am I supposed to kill him and get away without being caught and killed myself?* She might have been angry at Marian for asking her to do this, but in truth her mentor had given her plenty of opportunity to back out. And only now was she realising how unprepared she was. *There are too many of them. Too many soldiers, too many Bladeborn, too many things that might go wrong. Even a seasoned spy and assassin would struggle to see this job done, and yet here I am, right in the thick of it, and I can hardly gods-damn breathe...*

She said none of that, though her temporary silence was telling. Eventually she shook her head and whispered, "No, n-nothing like that, my lord," but the damage had already been done.

"Poor thing's scared stiff," said another figure, coming forward. He was tall, distinguished, with salt and pepper hair, a square, dusted jaw, and silver-blue eyes. At his hip, Saska spotted a great gilded sheath, a faint golden mist fogging from the blade stored within. "Is this how you like to run your camp, Lord Kastor. We were greeted as we arrived by a half-naked girl being dragged through the mud, trailed by a crowd of leering men. Did you know about this?"

"Of course not, Sir Vesryn. Or is it *Lord* Daecar now that you're First Blade?"

"Whichever makes you more comfortable."

Lord Kastor nodded and moved his eyes to his nephew. "Find out what has happened with that poor girl, Sir Griffin, and report back to me immediately. It is a disgrace to treat a young lady as such. I'll have all those responsible flogged, I assure you, Lord Daecar."

"Does that include yourself, Lord Kastor?" asked another man. Saska took him in with a glance, though found her eyes lingering on him a little longer. *Elyon Daecar?* she wondered. She knew the Daecars all shared a particular look, and this young man looked much like the new First Blade, only a quarter century younger. He also had a reputation for speaking his mind, and was living up to it, judging by the comment.

"Excuse my nephew, Lord Kastor," Vesryn said, easing forward. "He is protective of those who cannot protect themselves, and we're all weary after a long ride. I'm sure you had no part in this."

"No, I didn't," said Lord Kastor in a stiff voice, giving Elyon Daecar an equally stiff stare. And that was true. The girl had been dismissed by Lady Cecilia's order and Lord Kastor had had nothing to do with it. "I would not expect to have to suffer these accusations in my own warcamp, and by a knight, no less."

"Elyon will one day be Lord of House Daecar," Vesryn reminded him, "but as of right now, you are quite correct. Forgive us all our harsh words. The rains made the journey particularly troublesome, and much of the route had us battling the wains through bogs and broken-banked rivers. But we're here now and ready to begin talks." He looked around. "Where is Prince Rylian? I was told he would arrive today."

"He is on his way," Lord Kastor said. "He wishes to take part in the siege of Harrowmoor and will not be long."

The Vandarians shared a series of glances. "So you anticipate the siege will go ahead?"

"Of course. Why would it not?"

"You know why," boomed the bearded Lord Kanabar. "Agarath is stirring and we can ill afford to be squabbling among ourselves. King Janilah must know this."

"His intention, I believe, is to continue as planned."

The Vandarians seemed in equal part shocked and confused by the news, and in the ensuing silence, Lord Kastor gave Sir Griffin another firming look, demanding he lead Saska away. The young knight dipped his chin, gave Elyon Daecar a curiously bitter glare, and then marched back out into the drizzle, with Saska once more trailing behind him. As soon as they were out of sight, he reached out, gripped her upper arm hard, and dragged her through the encampment to the rear. His anger disquieted her, as did the force of his grip and within moments he was tugging her behind a tent, beyond the peering eyes of several watching guards, turning on her. "You stupid bitch," he snarled, shadows lengthening his narrow face. "Embarrassing my uncle like that. Stupid bloody bitch!"

"I...I didn't say..."

"You said enough." He threw his open palm at her once more, slashing her across the cheek. "Be glad I don't close my fist, you filthy southern whore." Rageful, he slapped her again, and as her head twisted sideways, quickly reached out and grabbed her by the throat, pushing her against a support pole. His spare hand gripped his godsteel dagger, giving him unnatural strength, and up she went, off her feet, his grip like the gallows, suffocating, squeezing. "Bitch," he repeated, his breath fogging the air. "I might just throttle you dead right here for that." He spat in her face, and her legs began to kick and squirm. *He's just like his uncle,* came a horrified thought. *Just as sadistic. Just as cruel.*

"Drop her this instant!" The voice surged from nearby, enough to relax Griffin's grasp as he lowered her back to the boggy earth at their feet. Saska took her own weight again, doubling over as she rasped a breath into her burning lungs and caught sight of Lady Cecilia, marching toward them in a warm brown bear-hide coat. "How dare you touch her, you stupid nasty boy! Just what do you think you are doing?"

Sir Griffin snorted a breath and then came up with a swift excuse. "I caught her fleeing," he said. "Thought I'd better teach the girl some manners." Saska was wiping the spit from her face and the tears from her eyes, shivering. Dressed in that sodden green lace she must have looked a sight. "She's wild, Lady Cecilia, and don't tell me you're surprised. If I were you I'd cut this one loose. There's no sense in having a southerner as a breeder anyway. What would you do with a mongrel son of hers?"

Lady Cecilia continued toward him at pace. "So she tried to run off in a lace nightdress, did she? In this weather? At this time? How stupid do you think I am?" Before Sir Griffin could answer, Lady Cecilia swung, whipping him across the cheek with a gloriously loud *clap*. "Stupid child! Don't you dare touch her or any one of my girls again!"

Sir Griffin righted himself, blinking wildly in shock. "You...you can't do that..."

"Can't I?" She swung again, though this time he blocked the blow, but more of them came, another swing, another swipe, swatting at the cruel boy as he backed off, defending himself from her flailing attacks. "Now off with you. Go! Find some poor animal to torture, or whatever else gets you stiff. You perverted little wretch. Get out of my sight!"

He dodged a couple more attacks, then seeing no other way out spun, snarling, and fled into the hazy mists, almost slipping in the mud as he went. Within moments he was out of sight, though Saska could hear his manic yells as he took his anger out on a couple of nearby guards. Cecilia stood listening with a sabre-sharp glare. "He's always been dangerous," she said, shaking her head as she looked off through the tents. "Spoilt little highborn boys like him often are." She turned to Saska and a motherly softness came over her. "Are you hurt, child? He didn't try to force himself onto you, did he? Come, let me see you." She moved in and began looking her over, inspecting the flare of red skin blazed across her cheek.

"I'm...I'm fine, my lady." Saska's voice was brittle, though she managed to maintain her Aramatian lilt. "It was a...a misunderstanding, that's all. I went out to see that...that girl leave. He thought I was trying to run, but...I wasn't. I was just watching, that's all." She let out a sob and covered her eyes and hoped it would be explanation enough.

"Well, it won't happen again, I promise." Cecilia curled a gentle coaxing arm around her back, and began leading her to her tent. "Soon you'll be under the protection of a great lord in Ilithor, and that cretinous little goblin will be hundreds of leagues away. You'll never have to see him again."

Saska glanced across at her, eyes hooded. "I-Ilithor, my lady?" she croaked.

Cecilia smiled. "Many of my girls go there, yes, and I have hopes that you will too. The city is rife with noble lords and knights whom any girl would be lucky to bed. And I live there myself, you know, within my father's halls, so will be able to keep an eye on you, make sure you're comfortable and happy. Would you like that, Tilda? To go and live in a white tower at the heights of the Sky City?"

"I...I think so."

"And you'll know so, as soon as you see it."

They reached the tent and stepped inside, out of the light rains. Saska gingerly removed her muddied slippers, wiping the flecks and clods off her ankles with a rag. "When would I leave?"

Cecilia poured Saska a cup of wine to ease her nerves. "Oh, of that I'm not yet sure. It is my job to pair my girls with the right man, and it can be more difficult in cases like yours." She handed her the chalice, and Saska took a deep sip, needing it more than she'd realised. "My enquiries are ongoing, though I have a few who may be interested. For the time being, however, you'll be staying here with me."

Saska wasn't sure what to think. *Janilah's in Ilithor,* she knew. And however much she wanted to see the light drain from Cedrik Kastor's eye - and Sir Griffin's too now, certainly - she knew full well that his death wasn't going to stop the war. *But Janilah?* She set the thought aside. *You're struggling to get close to Cedrik, and he's hardly a stone's throw away. How do you think you'll have a chance against a king, and succeed where so many others have failed?*

"We'll be moving camp tomorrow," Cecilia went on, "now that the Vandarians have arrived. Once assembled, the army will march to Harrowmoor, and for the time being, we'll be staying with them." She moved around the tent, fluffing cushions, making things nice. "Get out of that lace nightdress, Tilda. You must be freezing." She walked to the trunk of clothing, bringing out something more suitable. "Here, put this on."

As Cecilia continued to tidy up, Saska peeled the sodden fabric from her frame and drew on the warmer woollen garments she'd been given. Her clammy skin prickled with the heat of a nearby brazier, and soon enough, Cecilia had set the tent back to order. "Good, much better. A tidy room is a tidy mind, I always feel. Now is there anything you need, gentle girl? Would you like me to stay a while, or leave you alone? And fear not, I'll instruct the guards to let me know if Griffin comes prowling around again tonight. He'll not trouble you anymore, I promise."

No, but with some luck Lord Kastor will, Saska thought. She'd not expected Cecilia to interject and kind as the woman appeared, needed her to keep the hell out of it. *I just have to hope I've done enough to spike the man's interest, and get that summons. But with the Vandarians here now? And with the camp moving to Harrowmoor?* She had no idea what might happen next in this chaotic mess her life had become. *A tidy mind,* she thought. It was easier said than done. "I'm OK, my lady. I think I just need to rest."

"Of course." Cecilia moved for the flaps. "Oh, and Tilda?" She turned, that neutral smile fixed to her lips. "Don't lie to me again, child. I know Sir Griffin came to bring you to his uncle. I know what he intends."

"No, I..."

"You need not protect them. When we reach Harrowmoor, I'll have us set up nearby to my brother's pavilion, if I can, and you'll not have to concern yourself with another Kastor lord or knight or man-at-arms again. Believe me, my brother holds Cedrik Kastor in no high regard and you'll be perfectly safe under his protection."

For most those words would be music to their ears, but for Saska they were the dreaded drums of her plans being shattered, boom boom boom. "Your...your brother, my lady?"

"Prince Rylian," she said, offhand. "Oh, you didn't know?" She laughed, seeing the shock on Saska's face. "He's my half-brother, really; we share different mothers. And alas being born out of wedlock meant I was never a princess, thus you find me here tending to this duty my father gave me, rather than wed to some god-blood lord."

"Your father." Saska's throat was tight, her heart hammering a beat. "You're the daughter of..." She could hardly say it. "Of..."

"King Janilah, yes. One of several, actually, though I'll not make you curtsy, don't worry; a polite bow will do just fine." Her laughter came again, and she tossed her wrist to the side, sleeve billowing, dismissing her illustrious parentage. "I was born out of wedlock, the product of a dalliance of which my father had a few in his youth, so was never a legitimate Lukar. My mother was Lady Jeyne of House Blakewood...not a major house, but one you may know. I took her name."

Saska swallowed to moisten her throat, lest it close up entirely. "I've heard of it," she managed to say, the name ringing an old rusty bell. "So you live..." She could barely conjure words, and already her accent was threatening to slip. She gulped again. "You live in your father's palace?" *Her father's halls, she'd said. King Janilah's halls...*

"I have a set of chambers there, yes, though they're situated to the southwest and quite low down, where the views aren't so fine." She cocked her head, playful. "But I can hardly complain now, can I? Even the worst quarters within the White Towers of Ilithor are far greater than what the Blakewood estates could offer me. Perhaps you'll see yourself when we journey there, Tilda? I might just be able to sneak you in for a tour, if you're lucky."

Those words tugged at a faint hope, but for the most part Saska's head was sawdust. She couldn't think, nor forge a possible plan out of this mess. She could sense her skin paling, feel the blood draining out of her flesh. *How will I get to Cedrik Kastor now?* roared a question in her head. *Will I truly be taken to Ilithor? Might I get a chance yet to put my blade to Janilah's throat?* That last thought remained ludicrous, and her focus had to be on her task. *My given task. Marian's task.* King Godrin himself was privy to it and she had seen the deep wisdom in his eyes. *The foresight,* she thought. *Has he seen something else in my being here? Is this not about Kastor at all? Is this all just a part of something else?*

The questions exhausted her, and Lady Cecilia Blakewood could see it. The king's bastard daughter stepped to her again and gave her a firming little hug. "I can see this is a lot to take on, and won't weigh you with anything more. Try to relax, Tilda." She smiled and had her in another delicate embrace. "Try to sleep."

Then she stepped away, and as soon as she had, Saska's first instinct was to follow. To chase her down and grab her godsteel blade and abandon her duty and run. But she didn't. She just stood there, closed her eyes, and thought of her mentor. *Trust the process,* she thought. *Trust your fate.*

Some way, somehow, her opportunity would come. *And when it does, I'll know it.*

17

Elyon

Elyon stood to one side of the large oak table, clutching a goblet of wine, as Lord Cedrik Kastor took them through the proposed plans to siege the great fortress of Harrowmoor.

On the table before him were arranged a series of maps and hand-drawn pictures depicting the fortress and its battlements. One diagram portrayed the fort in its entirety, a bird's eye view complete with the layout of the lands around it, the depth and height of the walls, the width of the moat and thickness of the gate, the number of towers and defensive weapons and a whole lot else besides. Other lengths of parchment were drawn with specific designs, or listed notes on soldier types and numbers, weapons inventories, formations, and more.

Right now, Lord Kastor was drawing a line with his finger upon the largest sketch, tapping on the gatehouse. "We'll use Tukor's Fist to batter through the gates, and have our trebuchets rain fire in the meanwhile," he said. "Ladders will go here, here, here..." He was pointing at a variety of points now, "and we have lighter catapults to distract their scorpions and ballistas. The Rasals love their tricks and so we've conjured our own, with half our siege weapons nothing but empty husks to draw fire. The aim is confusion, gentlemen; to overwhelm their defences while we knock in the gate. Once through, we'll have little trouble slaughtering those inside and forcing a surrender, with the numbers we have."

"Slaughter isn't a word I'd like to hear right now," grunted Lord Kanabar, standing opposite Kastor across the table, thick-fingered hands planted to the wood. "Every Rasal man slaughtered is one less to hold back the Agarathi when they come. The fewer we have to kill the better."

Lord Kastor seemed unconcerned. "There is no reliable intelligence to suggest an Agarathi attack is imminent, my lord. The murder of their king changes little. We must still bring the Rasals to heel lest the north remain divided."

"Divided?" Kanabar laughed. "I've never seen us so divided, Lord Kastor. Not in all my years, and I'm a bloody old man."

"A temporary division, until Rasalan comes under our joint control."

"Temporary..." Kanabar pressed himself upright, the table groaning against his weight. "Yet another word I don't much like in these times. Temporary can last months or longer if you let it, and that won't do. I'll have to remind you that it is we who protect the north's borders, not you. I suppose that allows you and your king to be flippant, doesn't it? Knowing we'll hold the Agarathi at bay while you dither and deliberate and decide when to join the fight."

Lord Kastor gave him a quizzical frown, and drew on his wine. "I hardly think that's fair, Lord Kanabar. Tukor and Vandar have been close as kin for generations and stand shoulder to shoulder in every fight."

The Lord of the Riverlands seemed unwilling to concede the point. "It takes but one occasion," he said.

"And King Ellis?" Kastor looked to Vesryn, who stood studying the maps and designs, with Sir Dalton at his side. Lords Fullerton and Shorton of the Lakelands were with them too, though Killian and Rikkard had left them two days past, riding south to the fortress of Dragon's Bane along with Lord Rammas of the Marsh, and a host of fifty Varin Knights besides.

Vesryn looked up, bedecked in his Varin cloak and gleaming

silver breastplate, marked with the crest of the First Blade. "What of him?"

"Well, if you have doubts about joining us in this siege, it might be better to petition your own king to abandon plans, rather than mine." Lord Kastor broke eye contact with him, then turned to the other Vandarians present. "King Janilah is committed to this course, at this time," he told them. "When Prince Rylian arrives, he will say the same, I can assure you. Until we perceive a real, imminent threat from the south, our orders are to continue driving forward in this invasion until Rasalan is won. It will be to the benefit of us all in the end."

Elyon didn't like the man. He didn't like what he'd heard about his family. He didn't like the fact that they'd arrived here in camp to see that poor girl being debased, and harried, and heckled as she staggered through the rains, dressed in nothing but see-through linens. He didn't like that there had been another girl here in this pavilion when they'd stepped inside, a pretty southern girl, scantily clad and red-cheeked from a recent slapping, shivering in fear. There was so much he didn't like about being here right now, but in the end, those words of Cedrik Kastor's were hard to deny. They were on this track now, and lest Ellis should grow a backbone, there would be no getting off it.

He drew to the side table as the meeting went on, mulling things over, pouring himself another cup of wine. *Don't use it as a crutch,* he warned himself, knowing the weakness to it his father had shown. A weakness he never knew about, or considered a problem until now. Yet men often turned to alcohol during wartime, amongst other vices, and he could understand why. It wasn't just the stress of it, but the boredom. His life for the last month had become a tedious routine of riding and meetings and sleeping and little else. The rare breaks he'd had from it - the drinks he'd occasionally shared with Rikkard or Killian on the road, or the last, blissful night he'd had in Melany's bed - were distant shadows now, shapes on the horizon behind him. But now Melany was back in Ilithor, and Rikkard and Killian were travelling south, and here he was, surrounded by these doltish, chest-beating Kastor men, who by the evidence of the villages they'd passed to get here had been raping and pillaging their way through these lands without restraint.

And it all starts with him, Elyon thought, giving Kastor another glare. Elyon was hardly puritanical, but understood the difference between bedding women consensually and doing so by force, and doubtless the Rasal women of the Lowplains had suffered enormously since the invasion began. His father had warned him not to react when encountering such behaviour. *It will happen*, he had told him. *Men turn to monsters in war, son, and you cannot police them all.* He'd advised him, even warned him to follow official channels if he came across anything of that sort. *But what if their leader, their most powerful lord, is culpable,* he wondered now, staring at Kastor, quietly seething. *Who should I go to then?*

He knew the answer. There was no one to go to, lest Prince Rylian wish to step in, and even then a man like Cedrik Kastor could do as he pleased. *Turn a blind eye,* he told himself. *Don't look for it, and he'll not show it. He'll have the decency to keep his antics behind closed doors, at least.*

The rains were draining from the skies still, a relentless deluge that refused to wilt. The last three days had been the worst of their journey from Varinar, a slog through swollen rivers and streams, bogs and mires sodden by the storms. They'd lost too many wagons and wains to count, their wheels sinking deep into the filth and refusing to budge, and what was meant to be a two day trip had stretched to three. And all the while, Elyon thought of Lythian, who he'd meet again only at Varin's Table now, if at all. And Aleron. And his father and sister, and Melany too. He still couldn't help thinking about her, a balm to soothe his aching heart when he needed it most. Now gone.

He looked again at the knights and lords gathered at the table. Their voices were background noise, a blur, mixing, blending as they debated their plans. *Will anyone miss me if I just leave?* he wondered. He offered so little in these meetings, green as spring grass as he was. He had no experience of battle and war and Varin knew he'd hardly paid much attention to it all before. *That was Aleron's path, not mine, and how he'd be relishing this.* He smiled, wistful, as he pictured it. Pictured his mountainous older brother standing at the table, fully engaged and engrossed. *It should have been him here, not me,* he thought. *It should be me entombed beneath the Steelforge, not him.*

He turned from the thought and drifted toward the exit, needing some time to himself. He hated it when his mind took him to such places, when it went wading through this swamp of dark, unhelpful thoughts. They didn't do him any good, but he could hardly help it either. Every day he grew a little colder, a little harder. *And one day soon I'll be impenetrable,* he thought. *What a gift, and a curse, that will be.*

No one noticed when he slipped outside into the rains, or perhaps they did, and just let him go. He stepped through the yard toward the crumbled gatehouse and old moat, looking out over the camp, laid out over a gentle decline on all sides. Dusk was starting to fall and with it, the edges of the camp grew blurred and indistinct. Away to the south, Lord Kanabar's army was spreading out upon the moors, doubling the size of the warcamp. Elyon stepped to the skeleton of the gatehouse, and out of the ruins, dressed in his breastplate and Varin cloak, lit with the silver sigil of Vandar at his back. There were several guards stationed outside. "Where would a young knight find himself a woman around here?" he asked them.

They turned to him. One had a great scar cut across his face, splitting his nose, recently inflicted and poorly sewn. He would never have been a handsome man, but now looked truly grotesque. The voice that crawled out of his throat was similarly unpleasant. "Just keep on down the hill, you'll find one," he rasped, revealing a mouthful of rotten teeth. "Ain't hard around here, Son of Varin."

The men snickered, as Elyon nodded his thanks and continued on. He had no interest in finding a woman. He just wanted to get a sense for what a real warcamp was like. Not like those he'd visited before the invasion. There were no spoils then, no raids, no ransacking. No blood had been drawn. No battles had been fought. But here? How many tents were loaded with bounty? How many poor helpless women had been stolen away from their homes, their families, for the sordid pleasure of these base bawdry men?

He stepped down the hill, through the central thoroughfare between tents. A few taller pavilions dotted the camp but for the most part they were slung low, brown and green for Tukor, earthy and wet. Some had collapsed, falling apart in the rains, and several small streams trickled along through rutted paths and tracks, cutting their way down the hillside. He reached a large fire pit, burning warm and bright, around which a full score of common soldiers sat on logs, hunched over and covered in dark cloaks against the drizzle. They spoke in grumpy, grunting tones, sharing sordid stories and several gave Elyon rough scowls as he passed. One had the gall to call out, "About time you lot arrived. We've been waiting here weeks for you, Vandarian." Grumbling laughter fogged the air with that, and a few others offered assenting remarks, buoyed by the first man's brazenness.

Do they even recognise me, in the darkness, in these rains? Elyon wondered. He felt momentarily possessed by an urge to draw his godsteel blade and instruct them in etiquette, but had the good sense to ignore them instead, continuing deeper into camp where the darkness swelled, and the fire pits and braziers began to pop and glow amid the dusky gloom. All were surrounded by shapes and shadows and grunting men. And grunts came from inside the tents too. Grunts and yelps and moans of pleasure...of discomfort...of pain. Some left their flaps untied, not caring who might walk past and see. And the further he went from the old castle ruins atop the hill, the worse it got, as the camp brothels came into view; large felt tents like great longhouses, glowing from within as shadows and shapes in fevered fornication writhed and rolled about.

Elyon pressed on, away from it, passing rowdy groups gathered around casks of ale, playing drinking games and breaking out into fights. One brawl started just as Elyon passed, emerging from a tent as two half naked men came crashing out, falling dangerously close to tumbling into a nearby fire. A woman followed them, completely nude and the source of their conflict, screaming. No one helped break them up. Every man close enough to bear witness to the commotion just laughed loudly, pointed, and downed their drinks, enjoying the free entertainment.

Elsewhere the fighting was more coordinated. In a training yard set between tents, opposite a stables, a larger circle of soldiers stood, creating a ring. Bets were being taken, and the latest participants chosen. Those who had just fought were bloodied, bruised, though in good spirits. One was being attended by a medic, inspecting a nasty gash above his eye; another's nose was badly broken, snapped sideways and leaking blood. Elyon stopped a moment to watch. He liked a brawl himself on occasion, and an urge took him to partake...but at the last minute he resisted, with a single thought in mind. *I am heir to House Daecar now. I cannot be seen embroiling myself in these things anymore.* So on he went.

Darkness was fully upon him by the time he reached the extremities of the encampment, and here the fire pits flickered feebly, and men drifted about like ghosts. Elyon took a closer look at them, and saw that most were boys, teens labouring into the night. Some were chopping trees for timber at a nearby patch of woodland. Others were sorting laundry, washing, scrubbing the filth from armour, leathers and furs. There were a few cooking over pots, stirring a watery stew. Only a few were practicing with weapons.

"Who are all these boys?" Elyon asked the nearest man he could see, a soldier on guard at the camp border, warming himself beside a fire. "Are they servants? The sons of some of the soldiers? Camp followers?"

The guard gave a lazy shrug and shake of the head. "They're all enlisted men, sir."

"Men?" Elyon knew Janilah had begun a program of conscripting boys into the army to swell his numbers, but some here looked even younger than the fourteen year old threshold he'd heard tell of. "They were never enlisted to fight?" he asked. "These boys are labourers, not soldiers."

"It's where we train 'em, sir. They all take turns with sword and spear, but sure, we have 'em working camp duties too. Toughens 'em up. Elsewise most would just be sitting about idle." The man let out a little snort. "And an army's always gotta have some fodder for the archers, ain't it? Some lads are good for nothing but drawing fire, so real soldiers can do their work."

Elyon turned on him. "And you'd be one of them, I'm guessing," he said without pause.

"I'm a fine soldier, sure."

"No. Fodder for the bowmen. You look more like fodder to me."

The soldier gave a shrug. "If you say so," he said. "I'll not argue with a Varin Knight, though you look pretty young yourself, I'd say." He took a closer look at him. "Fought in many battles, have you sir?"

Elyon allowed a little smile, nothing but a quick tug of the lips. "I take your point, Tukoran. And you? Do you consider pillaging the local towns and villages here battles?"

The man's nose twitched. "Wouldn't be my definition, no, but we do what we're told. If one of the lords or knights tells us we've been in a battle, then we've been in a battle. It's as simple as that."

Elyon looked back toward the camp. The castle ruins were clearly marked by the fires burning within, up the hill, and the rainfall had calmed to a faint mizzle. "And the rest?" he asked. "We saw a young woman being humiliated and harassed earlier, when we arrived. Is that normal here?"

The man grew more grim at that. "Happens," he admitted. "Might be that she earned it. Or not, more likely. Some men don't care either way. I ain't that sort, though, if you're asking. Got a wife and three girls back home, I do. And these here..." He gestured to the camp. "They're all someone's wife, someone's daughter, someone's mother as I see it. I can't get past that...makes me think of my wife and girls." He began poking at the burning coals of his fire with a stick, eyes down. "I don't much like seeing them treated so poor, truth be told, but these things...they happen in war..."

Elyon inched forward, and took a perch on the log on which the soldier sat. It was quiet out there, away from the busier parts of camp. Calm, despite the boys labouring nearby. "Do you miss them?" he asked. "Your family?"

The soldier glanced over, seeming surprised to find him sitting.

"Course. Always." He prodded at his fire. "But I got a duty to be doing, so here I am till it's done. Got no choice in that, so what's the sense in missing 'em? Ain't likely to make it easier, is it?"

"I don't think you have much of a choice in that," Elyon suggested. "You can't help how you feel...or who you miss."

The man took him in again. His gleaming breastplate. His rich blue cloak. He didn't seem in any way uncomfortable in the presence of a Varin knight, sitting there with his scruffy hair and weary eyes, skinny-faced and sullen. But Elyon liked his energy all the same, more than most others he'd seen. *This man doesn't want to be here,* he could tell. *Just like me. And how many others are the same? How many thousands of men and boys and poor, abused girls are here for Janilah's pride, and nothing else? How many are suffering, dying for his war?*

"Maybe you've got a point." The sullen soldier's shoulders' bobbed. "But you can learn to control it, I guess. Try not to think about those who are gone. Family. Friends. Lovers. I've lost many over the years. You get used to it...eventually."

Elyon looked out toward the boys, cooking at the pots a little way off. "I lost my mother when I was about their age," he told the soldier. "And my brother...I lost him recently too. And my mentor...just days ago I learned of his death." He gave no detail, no names. He wasn't even sure why he was telling him all this. "I'll take a while to get used to all that, I think."

"It's that time again," the skinny-faced soldier said, poking at the bed of coals, nodding pensively. "You'll be hard pressed to find anyone who ain't lost someone dear to 'em soon." He looked over, a measure of kindness in his gloomy brown eyes. "I'm sorry for your loss, sir. I lost a brother too, when I was a lad. Joined the bodies at the Bloodmarsh Isles, back during the war. Saw him hacked down by them Agarathi, right before my eyes. Hard thing to forget, but he died fighting, at least."

Elyon let a moment pass before speaking. "So you were there? You fought in the war?"

"Was hardly much older than these lot here," the soldier said, looking over at the boys. A couple of older ones were sparing with wooden swords, clacking as they kissed and parted. "That comment about fodder for archers..." He shook his head in self-rebuke. "It was ill of me to say so. And I hope it turns out to be untrue."

Elyon nodded, hoping for the same. A bitterness sharpened the edges of his voice when he next spoke. "Your noble leader Lord Kastor is already talking about trickery and deception for the upcoming siege," he said, glancing again up the hill. "He's got fake catapults and siege weapons being made to distract the Rasals and draw their fire, so who knows, maybe he intends to do the same with these kids."

The notion was even darker than the treatment the Rasal smallfolk were having to endure, and the soldier didn't look too keen on furthering the topic. "You, er, you been meetin' with him then?" he asked to break the short silence. "Lord Kastor?"

"I walked out," Elyon admitted with a grunt. He gave the man a closer inspection. "Are you a Greenbelt?" He couldn't see that particular garment that marked out the Kastor soldiers. "Or do you serve another lord?"

"Another," he said. "And glad for it too. I live out near Broadway, a little farming village you'd not have heard about. Lands are Lord Caldlow's, but he's sworn to Kastor's northern army so here I am. Name's Don Mears, if you're wondering. Though you're probably not."

"I was actually," Elyon retorted. "It was the next question on my lips."

"Aye, sure. And yours?"

"Elyon. Elyon Daecar."

The man's face twitched, but otherwise gave little reaction. "So the brother you spoke of..."

"Aleron, yes."

Don nodded, staring out over the darkened moors. He sat still and silent for a full half minute, to let the awkward moment pass. "You'll forgive me for speaking out of turn," he then said. "I, er, I didn't take you for someone so important."

"A Varin Knight isn't important enough for you? I need to be heir to a great house too?"

Elyon didn't imagine he'd ever speak like this with an Emerald Guard, or any commander, Bladeborn or not, within his own army. He was a simple footsoldier only, a veteran of a world war, a candle burned right down to the wick. There didn't look much left of him, but to sit here and lament days done by, and wonder how he might fight his way through another global conflict. So all he did was give another listless shrug and say, "Been on duty all day and night, Sir Elyon. Guess I'm just tired, is all."

Elyon looked out across the camp perimeter. The other guards scattered about along the border looked similarly relaxed as they sat alone at their little campfires, idly gazing out into the darkened plains beyond. "Lord Kastor isn't worried about an attack, then, I'm guessing? The defences seem a little lacklustre here, if you don't mind me saying."

"True enough, sir. But I don't think anyone's concerned about a Rasal ambush here."

Lord Kanabar won't be so careless, Elyon knew. *Even only staying here for a single night, he'd have the borders of his own army well watched.* "Have you lost many men over the last few weeks?" He'd heard the daily reports, of course, but it was always smart to seek another viewpoint.

"Here? Not many, no. Seen the odd man put to the ground or burned on a pyre for his gods, but not many of late. We've been sat here on our hands mostly, waiting for you, though a score or two might have been lost clearing the way to Harrowmoor. Lost a fair few when we landed, though, but that was expected. Been quiet since then."

"You took part in the coastal assault?"

"Aye, came into a little bay north of the Links. Had a good view of the siege there at the Eastbank Fort when my ship pulled in. Brought me back to the olden days, seeing all that. And not in a good way. I'm a fine soldier as I told you, but hardly a warrior born like you god-blood folk. If I make it through a second war I'll be counting my lucky stars, one by one, I will."

Elyon favoured him with an encouraging dip of the chin. "You'll make it through, Don," he offered, thinking it was the right thing to say. "Who'll take care of your wife and girls if you don't?"

A small chuckle coughed from Don's throat. "You ain't met my wife, young sir. Believe me, she can take care of herself without my miserable arse moping around."

Elyon laughed at the man's bleak humour. "So you're miserable back home as well, are you? I thought it was just being sat on watch all night in these rains that did it."

"Oh aye, I was miserable from the womb," Don said. "I prefer it that way. Being a cynical old grump fits me nice, it does."

Elyon's lips kept to a smile. "Well in that case, I'd best leave you to your watch. I've heard misery loves company and I'm not sure that's healthy for me right now." He stood. "Nice meeting you, Don Mears. I hope to run into you again."

"Aye, and you Sir Elyon. Best be getting back to your high table now, hey?" He dropped a genial wink, then his sullen scowl returned, as he resumed his idle prodding of the fire.

Elyon took the man's advice, though when he reached the castle ruins the meeting had long since ended. He strolled through the camp atop the hill, the rains so faint they were little more than mist now, and spotted Vesryn outside a grouping of pavilions near the old foundations of the east wall. He was pacing, hands behind his back, the Sword of Varinar embedded in the mud nearby. The red flush on his cheeks suggested he'd been practicing with it. "We missed you at the meeting, Elyon," he called out, stopping as he saw his nephew step forward. "These aren't duties you should be shirking, not if you want to learn how to command an army of your own one day."

Elyon felt contrite all of a sudden, and foolish for having left. "Sorry, Uncle. I just..."

"You needed to step away?" He gave him an understanding look. "I saw how you were glowering at Lord Kastor, son. You looked damn near ready to draw your sword on him so perhaps you made the right choice." His eyes moved away toward the camp beyond the ruins. "So, how is it out there? As bad as I fear?"

"Worse," Elyon grunted. "It's a gods-damn disgrace how these Kastor soldiers are behaving, Uncle. If their tents were kennels I'd understand but they're not. You'd be appalled."

"Oh I don't doubt it, but it won't be anything I haven't seen before. The men of North Tukor have a wild streak to them which can make them particularly unruly, but it fosters a strong fighting spirit in them too. And that can be useful when properly channelled. Sometimes in war you have to compromise, Elyon."

"I draw the line at rape," he bit. "And not much of what I saw down there looked consensual."

Vesryn gave him a placating look. "Things will change when Prince Rylian arrives," he promised. "You know him. He's not the sort to tolerate this sort of behaviour in any camp under his command, and it'll stop when we leave for Harrowmoor."

Elyon hoped that would be the case, though didn't imagine it would stop entirely, nor was he so foolish as to think that his own countrymen would be entirely virtuous when their blades started swinging, and the blood started spraying, and all their lusts were stirred. There would always be ignoble elements within any army, and the larger it was, the more there would be.

"So how did the meeting go?" he asked, putting the subject aside for the sake of his own sanity. "I'll, um...I'll not miss another one, Uncle, not after today. You have my word on that."

"Save your word, Elyon, until you can be sure you'll keep it." His uncle knew him well enough to judge that, and Elyon didn't deny it. "But so far as it went? Well enough, given the circumstances. I'll want to talk to Rylian when he gets here, to confirm his father's position, but it sounds as though we've got little choice but to push on with this siege."

Elyon nodded. A number of protests went through his mind but he decided not to be contrary for once. "And our king's position?" *Is it still beneath Janilah's boot, or has he managed to squirm away,* he wondered.

"Ellis has yet to return my crow, but I'm quite sure what he'll say, if and when he does." He made sure there were no further questions in Elyon's eyes, before turning to look at the Sword of Varinar, planted deep in the earth, misting gold against the filthy skies. "Join me in a sparring session?" he offered. "I feel I need to shake off some rust, and Sir Dalton seems disinterested. So, what do you say?"

"With *that*?" Elyon looked at the Blade of Vandar, doubtful.

"Father never sparred with the Sword of Varinar. One good swing and you'd have me in two."

"I'll be gentle."

"Uncle, no. You're joking, surely? You..." He saw the spark in his eyes. "You are joking!"

Vesryn broke out laughing. "Of course I am. Gods, Elyon! No, no, best we use regular steel unless you want to suit up in your armour? No? Good. I for one am in no mood for that. Now be kind, Elyon. I'm getting old and you're fast approaching your prime. I'd not want to be embarrassed in front of all these Tukorans."

Elyon looked around. There were a few Kastor knights ambling about, a handful of guards stationed a little way off at the front wall, but no more than that, and none looked to be taking notice of them.

And so they fetched a pair of regular steel swords, and set to their dance in that muddy yard outside their tents. It felt good to swing a blade, even one that wasn't godsteel, and better still to do it with his uncle. They used to spar often back in Keep Daecar, but hadn't done so in some time, and Vesryn had always been generous with his wisdom, his encouragement, his praise. So clash and clang they went, for ten minutes, twenty, thirty, until the rains began to gather and fall again, thick fat drops making the floor too slippery to go on. They shared a look. Another few minutes? They both wanted it, so on they went. *He needs it, as I do,* Elyon realised. *The stress weighs on him, the responsibility, heavy like a great wet cloak.* But the kiss of steel helped shed it, their stress sloughing from them like a serpent wriggling from its skin. And only when both of them had slipped not once, but twice apiece, and Elyon had near impaled himself on his own blade, did they decide to call it a day.

"I needed that, Elyon," Vesryn called, as the rains flooded down in sheets. "By the gods I did. I'll sleep well tonight now!" He slapped him on the back. "Get inside, get dry, and get some sleep. We have some big days ahead."

He left looking lighter by half, but when Elyon escaped to his private pavilion, hoping to sleep well too, he found himself assailed by a familiar set of dreams. His father's butchered body.

His brother's open neck. They were there together, side by side, drowning in a sea of thick crimson blood. And all around them whirled shadows, shapes in copulation. Muffled screams and grunts blended to a roar, growing louder, louder...and in those shapes Elyon saw himself, saw every girl he'd been with, every one of them but Mel. And one of them was bronze, draped in green lace, and her cheek was red as the blood into which his family sank...

Elyon's eyes flew open, every pore on his body weeping wet, and still the rains were falling, heavy and loud on the roof. *That girl...*came a cloudy thought, as he searched the dying embers of his dreams. *The girl in the lace dress.* There had been something unusual about her, something he couldn't place. *But enough to steal a place in my dreams?* He settled back down and put the thought aside, but still she lingered, colourful and clear as the rest of his dreams faded off like cinders, red to black, hot to cold. *But why her? Why?*

A weariness gripped at him again and he knew he'd find no answer tonight. Or ever. His dreams had come vivid and dark for weeks and half the time they made no sense, a twisting, twirling blend he'd never be able to unravel. But as he fell asleep again, so the southern girl in the lace dress returned, standing to the side in Lord Kastor's tent. Yet her dress was not silky and sodden this time, but misting, fogging, fading, rising. And a light, bright and pure, began to glow about her, and as her dress faded to mist, so her form faded to light.

A light of silver.

A light of blue.

18

Janilah

Janilah Lukar had always sat the throne well. It took a certain man for that, a certain grandeur and force of command. *Not like this man,* he thought, staring down at Ellis Reynar, who was waving a scroll of parchment in his hand and proclaiming the need to end the war with Rasalan. *This man has no command. This man is no king.*

"My new First Blade is intent, Janilah, intent that the fighting conclude," he was bleating. "I have considered it all night and believe he…he may be right. Do you not think we should begin talks with King Godrin? With Agarath hurrying toward our doorstep, it might…"

"Good King Ellis…" Janilah stood, his voice spreading out through the hall, regal jade cloak rolling out behind him. "I have never been one to bow to rumour and am not likely to start now. Let the Agarathi do as they please. My war goes on." He paused, and a brief smile clutched at one corner of his grey-brown bearded lips. "*Our* war," he corrected. "Our war goes on."

The Vandarian king shuffled on his feet. "Right, of…of course," he snivelled. "But…should things change…should we hear word that the Agarathi are coming…we…we will have your support, will we not?"

How feeble he is, how weak, Janilah thought, as he began pacing across the dais and down the steps to where Ellis Reynar stood, layered in an excessive number of silver and blue robes. *Even the chill air up here is too much for him. The air!* He almost laughed, as the Craven King stood shivering at the foot of the steps, trying to hold his gaze.

"Ellis, of course you'll have my full support." Janilah's sturdy callused hands fell upon the man's narrow sloping shoulders, gripping through the layers of fine fabric to his puny frame beneath. "We'll win Rasalan first, then deal with those swarthy southerners." He gave him a firm shake, and leaning in close, revealed a rare, dead-eyed smile. "Yes? Does that sound OK to you, King of Vandar?"

Ellis couldn't hold eye contact long, not for more than a few short moments. He nodded and his eyes were on the floor, the white mottled marble at their feet. "If…if you're sure, King Janilah. Then yes…yes of course…I'll…"

"Good man." Janilah's grip eased. "Now was there anything else?"

The little man stuttered where he stood, shaking his head, no more a king than a submissive servant here to deliver a message, and be summarily dismissed. "No…um, nothing, King Janilah." He slid back a little, to give him room to breathe, and finally managed to raise his milky blue eyes. "I will retire, and leave you to your thoughts. It…it seems you have everything in hand."

"Gracious of you to say, good king."

"Then good day to you. I shall see you tonight, at the feast."

Ellis shuffled back, almost falling to a bow as he did so, before remembering he was, in fact, a king himself. He fixed his crown - fitted with miniature godsteel blades atop it - and spun, hurrying off toward Sir Nathaniel Oloran, who waited at the exit to the throne room with a clutch of other Greycloaks. Oloran had been installed at the head of Ellis's guard now, a curious appointment, Janilah had thought, but a welcome one. *He's almost as craven as his king,* he mused, watching the two shuffle off. At least Godrin had the good sense to appoint the Wall to his side, and Sir Ralston was worthy of the name, a brutish bulwark encircling the Rasal king that few would ever be able to breach. But Ellis had always lacked sense as much as he did courage. *They'll be no obstacle…good,* Janilah thought. It was one matter he could relax on, as several others remained unresolved.

He turned and moved back to his throne, drawing a full breath of bracing winter air, as a member of his own palace guard entered the grey-white room, lined either side with tall circular pillars. Janilah turned and settled back into his seat as Sir Owen Armdall stood to attention, bowed, and spoke. "My king, are you ready to receive your granddaughter? She waits in the antechamber for your summons."

Janilah had given that summons, though it wasn't Amilia he was so interested to see. "Her Lady-in-Waiting is with her?"

"Yes, Your Majesty."

"Send them in."

Sir Owen turned in his striped white, green and brown mantle and rustled his way through the arched doorway and into the antechamber beyond. A few moments later, he returned trailing Amilia and Lady Melany, the latter following a pace behind to Amilia's right. "Princess Amilia of House Lukar and Lady Melany of House Monsort," the sworn sword announced. Then he bowed and swept away, feet clanking lightly against the stone.

Janilah studied his granddaughter as she stepped through the room of silver and white. "Sweet child, come forward," he called, favouring her with a genial tone, if not the grandfatherly manner that he'd never once known how to portray. Fatherhood was a job to him, not a joy, and grandfatherhood the same once removed. "I pray you feel better this morning after a long salutary sleep? The air here invigorates and restores all ills, does it not?"

She moved up the stairs, and put herself into a bow before him, wrapped in soft green satin and hazel brown wool. "Grandfather," she said, curtsying. "I slept well. One misses their own bed when absent from it too long."

She's lying, he could tell, seeing those bags beneath her eyes, the fading pallor of her skin, the lack of gloss to her typically lustrous hair. Janilah had been told that she'd lost interest in her glamour and frequently turned her handmaids away when they came to do her hair and make up, or dress her fine for the road. *It will not do,* he thought. *Her beauty is her weapon and it grows blunt. No, it won't do at all.*

"I understand you've neglected your routines," he said. "That you rode in your carriage all the way from Varinar and not once took to the saddle, as you like. It isn't healthy to ignore your habits, Amilia. You will only lose your way if you linger on the Daecar boy too long."

"I know, Grandfather. This languor will not last, I promise." She tried to look cheerful but could hardly muster a spark, let alone a sparkle, to her once-bright emerald eyes. It wasn't just losing Aleron, but the life that came with it. The boy was young, handsome, gallant, and mostly importantly inexperienced. A perfect fit for a pretty young coquette who liked to be in control, but now a new match awaited, and not one she was likely to favour. She could probably sense that too, as she looked at him now, filling his high-packed, shield-shaped throne, a cloud of apprehension fogging her eyes. *But is now the time to tell her?* he wondered. *She is so pitifully despondent she might just throw herself from the balconies should she suffer another setback.* It didn't seem a risk worth taking and there was no need to inform her yet. *I'll correct her course later*, he concluded. *Once she's regathered her wits and her strength.*

The princess gave out a little cough, to break the silence, and shuffled on her soft slippered feet. "How does Father fare, my lord?" she asked, in a voice so sweet and small it hardly reached his ears, sitting but a pace or two away. "And my brothers, Rob and Ray? Are they well? I have prayed for them these last weeks, and they have been in my thoughts always, but I've heard so little of them since the invasion began."

"They prosper, such as I'm told," Janilah said, "and have both claimed their first kills and triumphs. Robbert in particular has expressed an instinct for heroics, it would seem. He duelled a Suncoat during the storming of Shellcrest and came away the victor, I hear." He managed a little proud smile at that, and Janilah had always preferred Robbert to Raynald. He was the older of the twins, by a few minutes only, but enough to make him Rylian's heir and thus second in line to the throne.

Amilia gave a quiet nod. "That is good to hear. Both will

become famous warriors, I know it, just like Father and you, my lord. The dragons of Agarath beware, now that two more Lukars have come of age."

Those words were well spoken and he gave them the favour they deserved, blessing her with a smile and a nod.

"I have also heard that the Vandarians want to parley with the Rasals," she then said. "Is that what you were in discussion with King Ellis about?" She glanced over at Melany, who stood demure to the side, hands clasped before her, head slightly down. "He looked rather flustered, as he left. I take it any request he made to cease the fighting was duly dismissed."

Good, he thought. *She retains a sharpness to her wits, even if her beauty has thus suffered through her grief. But nothing a little polish won't correct.* "Ellis will continue to support us," he told her, his voice carrying through the grand stone chamber with an icy stillness. "He cannot withdraw now, lest he lose a hand on the Rasal crown when I take it from King Godrin's head. It will not take long to secure the east, not if my plans take root and spout as I wish." She gave a questioning look, though knew better than to probe, and he wasn't going to tell her any more than that. "I suppose you know what has the Vandarians spooked, Amilia?" he asked. "The assassination of their Crippled King."

"By Captain Lythian, yes, I have heard," she said, frowning and shaking her head. "I do not believe he would have done such a thing. Not the man I travelled with to Varinar. He seemed a noble knight, not a murderer. The rumours speak of a trick, to stir all the south to war."

"A trick it was," confirmed Janilah, "and in such treacherous ploys and plots, the Agarathi are well versed. Your assessment of Lythian Lindar is quite correct - there are few men more committed to their oaths of honour than he, and there is no doubt in my mind that he was somehow set up. For years I have spoken of a rising tide of warmongers there, but did anyone listen to me? Did anyone heed my warning?" He grunted out a 'no', though in truth this twist of events in Agarath suited his own ends. "Had others paid my foresight the attention it warranted, the whole north might have been fortified by now, but none did...and if the

Vandarians find themselves assailed at their borders then they have no one to blame but themselves."

The young princess nodded to his words. "This is the fault of Amron Daecar," she said. "If he had supported your claim earlier, Rasalan might have already been won. His honour was his curse. It blinded him to the realities we face."

Janilah liked that. His granddaughter had always been a Lukar to her bones; ambitious, practical, and unsentimental. She was, in many ways, tougher than her own father, and thus Janilah had found himself so surprised…so disappointed…to learn of her recent melancholy. *But perhaps, returning here, she'll move past it now,* he hoped. *There can be no space for sentiment in what we all must do.*

"Yes indeed," he said, letting his sonorous voice fill the chamber, "but by our good fortune, King Ellis is far removed from Amron Daecar in all the ways that count. He has shown some spine in ousting Amron from his court but beyond his own borders he remains nothing but a craven fool. He'll follow where I lead. But onto other matters." He turned his eyes to Lady Melany, the golden haired girl standing motionless a little to the side in an ankle-length blue gown, warm for the winters here. "I'd like a moment alone with your Lady-in-Waiting, Amilia. Please, step outside to give us privacy. We can continue our discussion later, when we feast. I will expect to see you radiant, child. Can you do that for me?"

Amilia expressed a faithful smile and a little more light glowed about her. "Of course, Grandfather. I will summon the royal couturier and have my maids freshen me up. I already feel more sturdy of spirit, having spoken with you, great king."

"Then let me further furnish your spirit and health this evening, child. Your Lady-in-Waiting will not be long. She will meet you outside within a few moments. Wait there."

Amilia nodded, bowed, and swept away, giving Lady Melany a little glance as she departed. Janilah waited until her fluttering satin robes had left his sight, before turning to Lady Melany and ushering her forward with a gesture of the hand. She moved right before him at the bottom of the stage, and he spoke. "How is she?" he asked, moving his eyes briefly to the exit. "This sorrow of hers. Has it been real?"

The young lady dipped her chin in affirmation. "Quite real, Your Majesty," she answered, in that calm smooth voice of hers. "She didn't expect to fall for him as she did. It will pass soon, I'm sure."

"It must," Janilah told her. "I'll do what I can to coax her back to good spirits, Melany, but you'll need to play your part too. Take her on walks. Get her moving. Find some handsome young men to attend her if you have to. I want her sparkling like a jewel when she leaves for Rasalan, do you understand?"

"I do, my king. She'll recover quickly now that she's back home. If anything, her heartache will serve her well, going forward. She'll not let it happen again, I assure you."

"It never should have happened in the first place. Lukars wed for blood, not love, and she knows that as well as anyone. At least, I thought she did."

"She does," Melany asserted.

"And you?" He studied her for a short time, though the girl had proven herself quite inscrutable over the years. "I trust you didn't make the same mistake as she did," Janilah went on, "with the second son? It seems these Daecars have a way with women, and the boy Elyon is known for his charms. I would hope you have come away from your time with him without the burden of feelings to weigh you down."

"I have no feelings for Elyon, Your Majesty. I did only as you requested."

His eyes moved to her midsection, though there was no discernible bump there, not after so short a time. "Are you with child?"

She shook her head, just once, and spoke without inflection. "I fear not," she told him, maintaining eye contact. "No child ever took, despite my best efforts."

"A relief for you, I'm sure," he challenged, staring at her, but the girl had developed a strong skill in deceit and deception and was not easy to read or unnerve. "I know you never wanted to bear his spawn, Melany." She remained quiet, looking slightly down with those cool blue eyes. "I'm told you had no further relations with him on the road. What happened?"

"We had one final night together," she explained, her voice never wavering. "Some ten days past, at Eastwatch. But he showed no interest in me elsewise, not after Aleron's death."

"Then you might still be carrying? You'll know during the next moon."

"It's possible. But unlikely."

His lips cracked into a smile. *She has grown yet colder since I last saw her. Such a change from the teenage girl who first came into my service.* That was some years ago now, a bargain she struck in order to further the fortunes of her family. Her brother, Sir Mallister, had become an Emerald Guard off the back of it, and her lord father, Derwin Monsort, granted new lands and mining operations that had brought the family a regular and reliable stream of wealth. They had been on the brink of collapse before she intervened and Janilah liked that about her. She was willing to do anything for her kin and that made her a precious asset; loyal, committed and unyielding in her service.

"I may have more time with him, if I cross his path again in Rasalan," she put forward. "But it is possible he is unable to bear children…"

"Or you are." A frost crackled around Janilah's voice, though really he had other plans now for her than to birth a boy with Daecar blood. It was powerful, he knew, and a great deal purer than most, but Melany would be better served remaining at Amilia's side for now. "Perhaps this works out for the best," he said, after a time. "I can have another bed the Daecar heir, and it just so happens he's perfectly situated now for that. So fear not. I won't require you to take him between your legs again, child." Was that a flicker of disappointment he saw? Was she being entirely truthful with him? He watched her carefully for a few long seconds, before speaking again. "You're to continue in your service of my granddaughter. She will need your support more than ever now."

"I understand, Your Majesty. I will keep watch on her and see her through this, such as I can. It was…unpleasant, watching

Aleron fall as he did. The horror in the arena was quite palpable." She paused, showing the first signs of discomfort. "He suspected me," she then said. "Amron Daecar. He challenged me that very night, after his son was slain."

Janilah shifted forward a touch on his throne. "Challenged you? How?"

"Accused me, I should say," she clarified. "He believed I poisoned Aleron before his fight, weakening him so that the Shadowknight could strike him down." Janilah's stare stiffened, but she didn't drop her gaze as the coward Ellis had. "He was desperate, drunk, and seeking someone to blame, my lord. But I handled it. He and Elyon have no reason to suspect me."

"You're certain of this?"

"Quite certain," Lady Melany said. "I spent the next days in the company of them both, and no further accusation came. I poisoned Aleron's water jug in the arena, not the one down in his changing room, as Lord Daecar had accused me of, and made absolutely sure no one saw me. Amron was driven by grief, nothing more and his accusations were baseless, as he quickly realised." She paused. "But…he will link you to this eventually, Your Majesty. He and others. It's just a matter of time."

Janilah was aware of that, of course, but knew Amron Daecar would never act without proof. And finding it would not be easy, not with the efforts Janilah had made to compartmentalise his plot, and use different agents for different tasks, never letting anyone in on the whole. A small circle he could control and trust, but a larger one? No, his preference had always been to keep his own counsel, where he could. "Amron Daecar should prove no hurdle," he concluded, with a firm voice that brooked no further discussion on the issue. "He is tucked away in Blackfrost, seeing to the muster of his lands, and has other matters to concern himself with now."

He shifted in his throne, moving his eyes to the side, and Melany knew not to speak. There were a number of matters he wouldn't tell her about, matters that remained of profound frustration, and currently beyond his control. *The boy Jonik. The Nightblade. The Book of Thala.* He'd expected to have all here in his halls by now, yet all remained beyond his grasp. Those were the hurdles that concerned him, not the faint suspicions of a crippled lord whose attention would now be on defending his kingdom from the threat simmering to the south. *A threat that is my focus too,* he thought, *and has been all my life*. It was the unending goal of the Lukar kings to rid the north of that menace once and for all, and now it fell to him. *To me,* he thought, as he filled his stone throne, grand and regal. *By my blade, the dragons will fall…and when I hold Vandar's Heart in my grasp, I'll do what even Varin could not…*

He drew from his thoughts, and set his eyes again on Melany. "Return to my granddaughter's side, and tell her nothing of any of this," he instructed. "Protect her, and guide her, and your family will continue to flourish. Do it not…" He said no more, as the other side of the sword no longer needed showing. She knew it already. With one hand he offered riches, and with the other he brandished his blade. It had always been an effective way of maintaining loyalty among his subjects. Wealth and power, or the death of every person you loved. There really wasn't much choice.

"I will do as you command, Your Majesty."

She dipped her head and slipped away at that, as he sat for a time in his throne, falling back into the deep musings that had consumed him. It had all started with King Galin three centuries before, and it would end with him in the short years to come. *And one day soon*, he thought, *when I've won his war, and rid the world of Agarath's winged spawn, Vandar will grant me a Table of my own*. Alone now, he could let his smile spread broad and free, gripping at his bearded cheeks, pulling them apart. "Janilah's Table," he said, his voice but a whisper, echoing silently across the hall. And then again, louder. "Janilah's Table!"

It was heresy, he knew, but here alone he didn't care. *If I fulfil King Galin's promise, it will be mine, I know it. And where the Varin Knights rise to the Steel Father's table, so the Emerald Guards will rise to mine. And there I'll sit at its head, immutable, timeless…*

Divine.

His laughter ran out through his lips, and out through the balcony behind him. Down through the city, the valleys, it ran.

19

Lythian

It was the worst time of day.

Mid-afternoon, when the sun was at its hottest, when it beat down in ceaseless, unforgiving waves. There was no shade, nowhere to hide. Not until it edged off toward the west would its unbearable attentions begin to wane.

"Water," croaked Tomos. "Water. Please..."

Through the teeth of their cell, a guard cackled on his platform, though his voice was barely audible above the cacophony below. It was the worst time of day for that too. There were several hundred of them now, half a thousand perhaps, calling out their jeers and taunts, throwing rotting fruit and filth and worse. The stink was as bad as the heat and the noise. The fetid reek of refuse and waste and the layered filth on their burned, blistered skin. The sun had been so unrelenting that they'd even lathered some of that filth onto themselves to act as a block, though it hadn't much helped. Now they sat, a beleaguered trio of proud Varin Knights, stripped to filthy hose and not much else, waiting for their summons, waiting to die.

I wonder what will take him first, Lythian wondered, as Tomos pressed his face against the carved stone teeth of their cage, begging once more for water. "Please, sir...please. My throat, my tongue...I can...I can hardly swallow...please..." He rasped a few more words, but the guard paid them no mind, and Tomos flopped forlorn back onto the rough hewn floor of the great dragon-maw in which they'd been penned.

It was large enough to fit them all, but only just, and lying flat or sleeping had been difficult for the week they'd been there. Attached to the inner side of Eldurath's northern border wall, the cell was forged of sandstone, carved to the shape of a roaring dragon head and raised some fifteen feet from the ground. It was a high enough leap over the front set of teeth to snap a spine or neck should they dare it, and the open square below was continually watched by guards, while another stood on perpetual vigil to the right side of their cage, occasionally passing them meagre portions of food and water to keep them living.

"Kingkiller!" ripped a fierce male voice from the mob. Not many of them taunted them in the common tongue, but this particular word was well enough known by now. "Kingkiller! Kingkiller! Kingkiller!"

Lythian's new sobriquet spread through the bustling throng, swelling into an ugly chant as a fresh assault of spoiled fruit and vegetables came splattering their way. Borrus raised his large arms to protect himself and Lythian shifted in front of poor Tomos to shield him from the barrage, as rotten tomatoes, onions, leeks and lettuce, figs and dates and grapes came flying. They burst on impact, sending old clods of putrefied flesh and pips and seeds spraying everywhere, coating the great dragon's maw in a fresh layer of soft stinking slop.

It didn't take long for the men to start picking through the waste for chunks of edible pulp, as below the chants of 'Kingkiller' were swallowed by a din of heckling laughter. Lythian didn't care. He ignored them all as he searched for hunks of flesh, passing most of what he found to Tomos and keeping little for himself. "Here, Tom," he croaked, his voice raw, his lips parched and cracked. "There's some moisture in there. It'll help. Eat it."

Tomos could hardly eat after eight days of growing thirst, but managed to suck some water from a few handfuls of mulch. Only when the guard upon the platform next to them roared for the crowd to stop did they relent in their bombardment. Then the pebbles and little stones came instead, biting at their skin, leaving cuts and weals and welts. A larger rock found its way past the lower teeth of the cell, cracking against Borrus's patchy-bearded jaw and knocking out a tooth. Blood spilled from his lips and he fell fuzzy to one side, too weak and weary to call out a response. More rough heckling clouded the humid afternoon air, as several other soldiers bellowed orders to the crowd. Lythian could only pick up a few words, but got the gist. They weren't to throw a rock that might kill or seriously maim them. Only small projectiles, small pebbles and stones. Tavash had other plans for these men.

The day stretched on, much like the last and the one before that, and that, and that. They'd been dragged here through the city in chains the morning after Lythian's capture, pelted with filth as they went, spat at and mocked, and it hadn't stopped since. Only in the dead of night when the crowds thinned and the air cooled did they find respite, but it never lasted long. The people were relentless, the crowds gathering at dawn and dispersing beyond dusk, endlessly swapping in and out. *There must be a waiting list to be here,* Lythian had thought, *judging by the numbers crowding the alleys and streets nearby*. They were being corralled by guards, eager for a look at the Kingkiller and his co-conspirators, though the square could only hold several hundred in any comfort.

But today was slightly different. Today Lythian had heard that Prince Tavash was to be crowned king. Even from out there on the northern extremities of the city he could sense the swell of excitement further in. See the bunting blowing. Hear the trumpets and drums. He'd seen dragons too, a dozen of them at least, swooping past, gathering for the coronation. *And perhaps that's what he's been waiting for,* he thought. *To be crowned king before he kills us. To command his first executions as a monarch, not a prince.*

They didn't know when that would be, not yet, but first they were to endure this long humbling humiliation. That was the Agarathi way, Lythian knew, and Varin Knights were most likely to suffer a long ordeal. "They will keep us living for some time," he had told the others several nights past. "They will try to rob us of our dignity, strip us of our honour, and deny us our place at Varin's Table. They believe that by degrading us, Varin will forget our triumphs and see only the disgrace with which we fell. That he will at worst deny us our seat, and at best move us far beyond his sight where our tales of woe cannot be heard." He'd looked to each man in turn, and taken a grip of their shoulders. "We cannot let them. Borrus, Tomos. We *will not* let them win."

Tomos had looked most haunted by that. He was already worried about dying without a triumph to his name. "Is that all true, Lythian?" he'd asked on a whisper. "Will Varin deny us our seat for this?"

Lythian didn't have to lie when he next spoke. "I have never believed so, Tomos," he said. "How a man dies is but another test, another opportunity. Do so with dignity and Varin will know it. I see a chance here to improve our place, not remove it. We do not wilt. We do not yield. We are Knights of the Steel Father's order and will die as we have lived. With honour. With pride. Do not let them break you."

Those words had steeled Tomos's spirit but the thirst was still starting to get to him. Lythian had warned him not to beg. "That is what they want, Tom. They will not let you die of thirst. That will not be your end here." But these last two days, he'd been unable to help himself, crawling to the edge of their cage and pleading for water as his dehydration became unbearable. It had become a mission now in securing their passage to the Eternal Halls and denying their captors the pleasure of seeing them fall. There was no talk of escape. No thought of rescue. They were alone now, abandoned to their fate. Abandoned to their suffering. Abandoned...

Through the streets now, a growing swell of noise broke out as the scarlet sun arced away west. There were few tall buildings out here to block its light, leaving them hopelessly exposed throughout the day, yet now it was cooling. Lythian shifted, sweeping away a few small pebbles from beneath him and turned his eyes toward the south. A procession seemed to be coming their way down a central street, a parade of colour and noise, and in the air, several sleek dragons were gliding, spinning, roaring.

"He's coming," Lythian said, turning his eyes back to the others. "Their new king."

Borrus roused himself, rubbing at his swollen, bloodied jaw. "About time," he growled. He held the rock that had struck him to hand. "I've got strength enough yet to bloody his smug face at least. Soon as he gets close..."

"You'll do nothing, Borrus," Lythian said. "It won't change anything."

"Change? I've been shitting in my bloody breeches for a week, so don't talk to me about change." It was another side of humiliation they had to suffer, relieving themselves here in the open, though there was a hole at the rear of their cell that acted as a sort-of privy shaft at least.

The trumpeting procession continued toward them, as those red-cloaked guards with long black spears spread into the square, forcing the crowd to part. From the skies, the dragons came, three of them, four, five, an array of colours and sizes and shapes, landing upon the walls and rooftops set around the square. Atop them were their bonded Fireborn, coloured as their winged steeds. One wore a fluttering cape of dark maroon, mottled with spots of black like the leathery beast he rode. Another was garbed in rough stripes of deep blue and burnt orange for his dragon, another a purply black. Lythian turned his eyes upon them as the horses and carriages came trotting and rattling down the avenue. Borrus and even Tomos were looking too.

"Do you see them, Captain Lythian?" Tomos's feeble voice was just about audible above the din. "Kin'rar? Marak?"

Lythian shook his head. He could see neither Neyruu, Kin'rar's sleek young drake, nor the great bonded beast of Ulrik Marak, Garlath the Grand, among the host, and didn't expect to. "They have likely fled," he said. "Or else they're being kept in another cage, further down the wall."

Borrus gave out a derisive grunt. "Or they're sipping fine wine and toasting their trick as they watch from some flowery terrace. I said all along that Kin'rar was using us, Lythian..."

"To kill Tavash, yes. Not to frame us for Dulian's murder and spark a war."

"Details. I never trusted him. Never. And Marak? Gods, the man has made his living killing Varin Knights. How could we have been so damned foolish? The next we see of them will be during our executions, no doubt. I'm sure Neyruu wants to take a bite out of me and she'll have to get in line. Marak will get there first, I'm certain, when he runs me through with the Fireblade. The bastard. Both of them. Treacherous gods-damn bastards!"

Lythian wasn't going to re-enter this debate. He'd had enough time to reflect during his imprisonment and felt it more likely that Kin'rar and Marak had also been betrayed. *They were sincere in their desire to see Tavash removed,* he thought. *And Marak would never have had a hand in Dulian's death. That would be like me having a hand in Amron's. Never.* He shook his head. *Never...*

The wailing trumpets and banging drums came louder now, as the procession continued into the square. Lythian watched on as the host spread forth, and there at the heart of them he saw him, riding a fine white palfry with a black-gold crown atop his head, flanked by a score of dragonknights. Those rusty red eyes shone out from beneath it, the crown shaped in the likeness of a ring of dragons, standing snout to tail, their wings arched skyward into points. *Eight points,* Lythian saw. *Eight dragons. Eight wings. For Eldur and his brood.*

The crowd lost themselves to rapture as their new king came, falling to their knees, as Tavash and his guard trotted through, trailed by a tail of nobles and knights. Among them Lythian spotted faces he knew. Perfumed men and women from the garden parties that seemed a lifetime ago, grinning triumphant as if they'd played a hand in their fall. And as they came so called a loud voice, splitting the air, clean and clear. "Hail King Tavash! All hail the King of Agarath. All Hail the Divine Protector of the South!"

The crowd erupted, the air thundering his name as the new king approached the square. He was wrapped in sumptuous silks of gold and red above his dragonscale armour, a thin smug smile on his face. A hand slipped off his reins and emerged through his sleeve, quietening the crowd. "My friends, my friends, you honour me," he called, using the common tongue, which many didn't speak. “But let us take a moment to remember my noble uncle who reigned so long and so well."

A deep long hush stilled the air, lasting a full minute before Tavash slid from his horse, and landed light on his ceremonial sabatons. Several servants rushed forward with long brooms, sweeping away the refuse left by the smallfolk, but Tavash waved them off. Over spoiled fruit and filth he walked, moving to the heart of the square alone. He looked to the dragon maw cell, then turned. "These men conspired to kill our king," he called. "These men of Vandar, these men of Varin. For too long we have let their insults fester, their crimes go unpunished, but no longer. When the Knight of the Vale slew my uncle, it was not only a king he killed, but a messenger of Eldur, our great founder. That is a crime beyond all. It was not mere regicide, but deicide. Deicide, friends, that he attempted, to try to silence Eldur's voice."

He paused and turned around, and a deep heavy silence compressed upon them. "My friends," he whispered. "My brothers, my sisters, my kin. The Knight of Mists failed. He stole my uncle's life, it's true, but Eldur's voice will not be stilled. And it is I, now, whom he speaks to, I who communes with the Founder." A murmur came, boiling, brimming through the square, as Tavash closed his eyes a moment, nodding slow and quiet. "I hear him now, friends," he went on. "I hear him, our father, our founder, our guide. I hear him..." His voice grew small, and smaller still. "Eldur," he whispered, as all the crowd inched forward, hushing. "Eldur...what do you command? What is it of us you wish?"

The hush went on, and on and on. Lythian and Borrus and Tomos all watched. Not one of them spoke, not a peasant nor knight nor lord. A cold madness had gripped them all.

And then the whisper came, a sweet long hiss on the air. "War," he said. Then he nodded, and said it louder. "War..." The crowd began to murmur. Men returned to their feet. "Vengeance," he said. "Justice." The trickle became a flow and soon it would be a flood. Tavash sensed it and his voice grew grand, spreading through the square a roar. "War!" he bellowed, and the mob were all to their feet. "Eldur wills it! WAR! WAR!"

The chaos that followed reminded Lythian of who these

people were. It sparked memories of Agarathi mounted charges, of the noise they made, the thunder of a hundred thousand hooves. Their war cries were unlike any other, matched only by their southern cousins and the giant golden wolves they rode. And so they bellowed now, and in their eyes Lythian saw the flame, bright and wild and wanton, as around the square the dragons stood tall and beat the air with their wings, shrieking.

And all the while, King Tavash Taan smiled, and up his hands went, up and up in orchestration. Lythian almost admired him in that moment. There were many types of leader, but all the best knew how to inspire. Some through fear like Janilah. Others through heroism like Amron, or deep wisdom like Godrin. And here was Tavash, the great conductor, twisting the narrative with his lies.

"The dragons will feast and flame," he called now, above the thunderous din. "They sense the time is right, and have flocked in force to the Nest. The Bondstone sings, my friends, it sings to them! Agarath's Soul burns bright!"

It was a frenzy now, chaotic. Not a man or woman looked quelled by the thought of it, by the great war their new king craved. *Fools,* Lythian thought. *Every one of them has bought his lies.* He sat listless, exhausted and weak as the noise expanded. "Have faith," he found himself whispering. "Have faith in Vandar. Have faith in Varin."

"It's the next Renewal," managed Tomos, huddled beside him. "The War Eternal...it stirs again."

It had been renewed so often, that divine war, and never once had it truly ended. *Nor will it now,* Lythian thought. For thousands of years it had come and gone, sweeping in, fading out like the tides. How many had died for it, how many millions? One might see a Renewal once every few centuries, and yet here they were, set to see another not two decades since the last.

"We'll prevail," nodded Borrus, defiant, his cheeks stung with burns and blisters. By some irony, he'd complained less this week than any other, despite their hopeless fate. "The north will prevail. They must."

They must, thought Lythian, giving a short weak nod. *Without us.* It was a doleful thought, and as it came, so Tavash's voice swelled again. "The Sons of Varin will fall. They will fall in flame and fear as our dragons swarm their lands!" His finger pointed them out in their cage, sitting silent, sitting hopeless. "We have here with us three of their kind, treacherous to the bone, kingkillers! They will be the first to feel the fire, but not the last. They will be but the start of what is to come!"

There within the jaws of the dragon they sat as all of Eldurath cursed them. And when the first pebble came, a thousand quickly followed, fizzing through the teeth of the stone drake toward them. Borrus heaved his bulk ahead of Tomos to shield him, as Lythian turned sideward, tucking his head among his arms. The rocks struck and stung and the derision swelled, all the square laughing, and all the streets leading off it, and all the city beyond, it seemed.

"Varin Knights!" he could hear Tavash shouting over the din. "Ha! Look how they cower to pebbles and stones! Look how they weep and wail!"

Lythian might have stood tall and proud if he could, but he couldn't. He just crouched there where he was, taking it. And in his head he prayed. *I will not yield, Steel Father. Oh Varin, I'll not yield, never...never...*

He didn't know how long it went on for, before the stones settled, and the air stirred with the sound of hooves and rolling wheels. Battered and bloodied, he lifted his eyes and saw King Tavash upon his gleaming white palfrey, set among his host as they moved off east to continue on his coronation parade. Around the square, dragons spread their wings, flapping, rising, and into the dying light they went, as Lythian looked to his companions to find them both unconscious. The Barrel Knight's body was blackened by bumps and lesions, flopped atop of Tomos, who lay laboured in his breathing, rasping ragged breaths.

And thus Lythian broke his own rule, his own promise, as he shifted to pull Borrus off him. He looked up to the guard upon the platform, and begged, "Water. Please, sir...water..."

20

Ranulf

"My daughter will die," read Ranulf. "She will die by the last month of this year by a child of great consequence. My sweet Atia. I have seen your death, but I can do nothing to change it. By Varin's blood you'll sire a boy. And this boy, I see, must be hidden..."

The passage ended there, trailing off, and by the fractured nature of the writing, Ranulf could tell just how difficult it had been to write. He frowned as he pondered it. The passage was scribed by the hand of King Astan, Godrin's father and predecessor to the Rasal throne. *Atia...she was his fourth child and second daughter,* Ranulf recalled. *An uncelebrated princess who was said to have died of tuberculosis when she was only in her teens. But this account...*

He took a step away, pacing around the spacious library in which the Book of Thala had been placed. It was on the second floor of Vincent Rose's sprawling estate outside the coastal city of Miren, with ranging views down to the white-stone harbour and sparkling sea beyond. The change of setting hadn't much changed Ranulf's fortunes, however, and his search for Janilah's purpose remained an ongoing cause of frustration. *But this?* He returned to the book and looked over the passage once more. *This suggests that Atia died in childbirth, delivering a boy. And by Varin's blood?* He considered that a moment longer, trying to remember just when Atia had died. By his recollection, it was roughly forty years ago, about the same time as Varin's last direct heir, King Lorin, had perished during that fateful leviathan hunt, losing his life and the Nightblade with it.

Ranulf was moving again to stir his thoughts, pacing up and down the sumptuous red carpeted room, framed by great tall bookshelves all around the walls. *Might King Lorin be the father of this child?* he wondered. *By Varin's blood you'll sire a boy...* He continued pacing. Varin's blood could refer to any Bladeborn, in theory, though it was certainly possible that Lorin had had a secret lovechild too. The man was known for his appetites, after all, and had an interest in women to match his profound mastery of the Nightblade. It was said that many babes had been pulled from wombs on account of his lusts, though never from a princess. *And if true...*

His thoughts were momentarily interrupted by the sound of movement outside. The snorting of horses and stamping of hooves, coming from the front gate. Ranulf ignored it, busy in his thinking. *If Lorin had a son, and that son was hidden...*His heart thrummed into a steady beat. *This child would be the true King of Vandar, a secret worth hiding for many. And a secret worth getting hold of too, perhaps?* He was thinking of Janilah, of course. *Might this be what he seeks? Some lost heir who might rise to threaten him, as he tightens his grip on the north?*

He continued to pace, musing, as a light creak sounded behind him, and Leshie stepped into the room, light and quick on her feet. She wore a fine little suit of embroidered red-leather armour, a slim fit for her petite, girlish frame, and at her belt was a silver sheath and misting godsteel dagger gifted her by Rose. Her eyes went straight for the doors leading to the balcony. "There's a troop incoming," she said, pacing straight across the room. "Vincent says I'm not to interfere. I don't think he trusts me, Ranulf." She sounded bitter. "Do you know who they are?"

Ranulf followed her toward the balcony, as she pushed the doors open, stepping out into the balmy afternoon air. A light coastal breeze rushed through Leshie's strawberry blonde hair, and her impudent eyes sped over the stone railing. Below, a force of some two dozen men were cantering up the track on horseback, arriving from the path that wended down to the port. Ranulf caught sight of rawhide scale-mail armour beneath some of their cloaks, coloured light in white, blue and green, and scimitar swords at their hips. Others looked to be carrying regular longswords, falchions, and even cutlasses. And their colouring was varied too, some dark-skinned, others tan or even fair. And behind came crates and barrels, pulled along on a pair of horse-drawn drays, with a short order of white-shirted servants running along beside them.

"So, who do you think they are?" Leshie asked. "I saw their ship coming in from the north, so I'm thinking they're from the mainland. Business associates from Aramatia do you think?"

Ranulf had another thought, though didn't care to share it with Leshie. He'd come to learn that she was too impulsive to be trustworthy with information of any import, and he could never be quite sure where her loyalties lay. With Marian or Rose or herself? It could be any one of them, or all at once, for all he could tell, and in truth he had long since given up taking a close account of her. *Saska may have requested I watch over the girl, but my purpose here has grown beyond that now,* he thought. *She's quite old enough to determine her own course. I'll not let her interfere with mine.*

"Well?" she gave him a nudge, pressing through the fabric of his sky blue linen shirt. "Must be something criminal if he's told me to come join you here." Vincent Rose was now striding out from the central entrance hall below, arms open wide in greeting, calling, "My friends, so good to see you," as he went.

Leshie's lips bunched in annoyance. "He won't tell me anything, you know. I've tried to get him to open up, but he won't. Not about all his underhand stuff anyway. Even in bed he won't. He's not like other men."

Ranulf glanced sideward at her. She'd taken to Rose's bed almost as much as the Lumaran twins and he doubted her only reasons were to extract information. "Perhaps you're being too obvious, Leshie," he offered. "Vincent Rose has not amassed all this power and wealth by being stupid. He isn't likely to involve you or I in any of his nefarious enterprises."

Leshie gave an amused little grunt. "No? Well what about that?" she pointed in through the balcony doors toward the Book of Thala, opened up on the splendid light-wood desk at the far end of the room. "He only brought you on board the ship so you could decode it, didn't he? And he killed how many dozens while stealing it? He'll be a wanted man in Rasalan forever if his part in all that gets out, and only you and I and a few others know about his involvement in stealing it." She looked down as Rose marched out across the gleaming marble courtyard below, dressed in a rather more modest outfit of dark blue hose and jacket today, though he held his tally stick to hand, as he liked to, tap tap tapping on the floor as he went. "Doesn't that worry you?" she went on. "We're loose ends, Ranulf. I'm not sure either of us are ever going to leave this place."

It was a rather more insightful and troubling comment than he'd expected from the girl. *She sees things more clearly than she makes out, it would appear. But kill us?* He knew just what sort of man Vincent Rose was, but hadn't exactly thought that far ahead yet. *Though she may have a point,* he reflected. *I'd not put it past him to cover his tracks, should he be worried we might connect him with the crime.*

"Yeah, you see. You're worried about that too." She gave him a knowing look, then looked down at Rose. "He's keeping me around because I'm a novelty to him, and you because you're good at combing through that book. I'm under no illusion that he cares for either of us, Ranulf. Once we've served our purpose..." She let the thought fester a moment. "So yeah, we're in this together, so far as I see it. You watch my back, and I watch yours. Isn't that why Saska asked you to come along in the first place?"

A smile swung up in the corner of Ranulf's mouth. "So you know about that, do you? I didn't think..."

"You didn't think I would figure it out? Come on, it's obvious. Those first few days you were watching me all day long. I thought you had a thing for me, until Vinny unveiled the Book of Thala, and since then you've only had eyes for that tome." A smile emerged on her cherubic little face. "She asked the same of me, you know. To keep an eye on you, keep you safe..."

A half dozen creases deepened on Ranulf's brow. "Saska? But I thought..."

Leshie shook her head. "Marian. Saska and I...well, we never got a chance to say goodbye, with how quick everything went, but Marian...she asked me to keep you safe when she gave me this mission. Don't think I'm not keeping my word on that, Ranulf. I'm not falling for Vinny's charms if that's what you're thinking."

"And yet you call him Vinny," he teased. "I can't say I've ever used the name, and I've known him quite some time."

"He likes me to call him that in private. Just slips out sometimes, that's all."

"Well please try to correct the urge around me, if you can..."

"I'll do it if you stop keeping things from me," she said in an instant. She narrowed her eyes on him. "You've found something, haven't you? In the book. I thought you looked a bit shifty when I walked in. What is it?"

"Nothing of interest, I assure you."

"Or nothing you're willing to tell me?"

"It's not like that, Leshie. Just..."

She stepped away before he could finish the sentence, taking a grip of her new godsteel dagger to speed herself beyond his reach. Before he even knew it, she was at the desk some dozen metres away, scanning the page he'd left open. "My daughter will die," she read out. "She will die by the last month of this year, by a child of great consequence..."

"Leshie, hush!" Ranulf followed her in, ignoring the greetings going on below as Rose met with his guests. "Be quiet. There are guards who may be listening..." He reached her and grabbed her shoulder, pulling her away, but the girl was a great deal stronger than him with that dagger in her grasp. She drew it out now and pointed it at his neck.

"Hands off," she hissed. "Don't make me prick your throat, Ranulf."

"Oh stop." He brushed her arm aside, recognising the false threat. "You just said you were sworn to look out for me and now you're pointing a dagger to my neck? Please, Leshie, put it away. It isn't a toy."

She drew it aside, though slowly, and with a suspicious little look on her face. Then with a skilful twirl she flicked the dagger between her fingers, spinning it around, and dashed it into her polished silver sheath. "Fine," she then said. "But my point stands. You're keeping things from me and I don't like it. If we're to work together, we should be sharing, not censoring. Now what is this passage about?" She looked at it again. It was one of several short accounts by King Astan written across the double spread, but by his rotten luck, Leshie's eyes had gone right for it. "Who's Atia? And this child, from Varin's blood? To be kept hidden..."

Ranulf closed the book. "Enough, Leshie. It's not important."

"No? So why did you just do that? Why are you so flustered? What are you hiding from me, Ranulf? What?"

"My gods, child, you sound like Vincent. I'm hiding nothing. Atia was daughter to King Astan is all. She died in childbirth, bearing the son of a Varin Knight. That's all it means..."

"You're lying. Why are you lying?"

"I'm not lying."

"You are."

"I'm bloody well not." He stormed several steps away, as Leshie reached to pull open the book. She did so far too forcefully. "Careful, for goodness sake, Leshie, be careful! Do you have any idea how old this book is?"

"About three and a half thousand years, or something. Seems in pretty good condition to me." She flung it open at a random page, the open flap landing with a heavy thump. "King Astan came before Godrin didn't he? He was his father. Have you not got to Godrin's chapter yet?" She was flicking forward, page after page. "I thought Vincent wanted you to check his accounts most of all?"

Ranulf marched in angrily. "Leshie please! Handle it with care. It's more delicate than it looks."

"And you're more skilled at avoiding questions than you look, Ranulf."

"Well if you just gave me a chance..."

"Fine." She stepped back, opening out her arms, dramatically presenting the book. "I know it's precious to you. To me it's just a silly old book full of arcane nonsense, and perhaps that's even true. I'd know if you told me. And believe me, I'll keep asking until you do."

Ranulf looked at her, utterly dejected. "Yes, I can see that."

"Good." She leaped deftly up onto the desk, crossing her legs. "Go."

Ranulf expressed a slow breath, if to do nothing but give himself a moment to think. *Is there any harm in it?* he wondered. She didn't seem devious enough to be tricking him, and Ranulf had known enough of those sorts to tell the difference. *She's just bored,* he decided, *and looking for something to do. And what exactly have I discovered anyway?* Not much was the honest answer.

"The bit you just read," he started. "Well, what I said is true...sort of. Atia was King Astan's daughter, though not particularly well known, being the fourth and all, and dying young as she did. As far as having a child with a Varin Knight...well, I'm not sure. That could be true. Or it could have been someone else...anyone else, really, with Varin blood..."

"Or..." She leaned forward.

"Or...maybe the account refers to King Lorin." His shoulders went up and down. "I'm not sure. The timings line up and Lorin was known as something of a womaniser, as well as a great adventurer besides."

"You must like him then."

“It's so. For the adventuring, anyway."

"Yes, that's what I meant. You don't seem interested in women. Vinny...sorry, Vincent told me that he's offered you time with those Lumaran twins many times over and you always refuse. Some would say you're mad for that."

"And others would say I'm noble. But I've never much cared for what others think of me. In any case, it's possible King Lorin and Atia coupled and had a child, a child hidden away by King Astan."

"Right." She didn't look especially interested. "And remind

me...King Lorin was the one who lost the Nightblade at sea? The last of the Varin line?"

"Yes. Though there are many different accounts about all that, of course, and the recent return of the Nightblade clarifies that it was never truly lost."

"Yeah, that Ghost guy. What are they calling him?"

"The Ghost of the Shadowfort." They'd heard that a couple of days ago, Rose bringing them news over dinner. So far south as they were, it took time for news to filter, though all that had rocked Varinar and the Daecar family could hardly be contained. By now half the world knew of the assassin who'd maimed the Crippler and killed his gallant son. It was even said he was headed south himself now, hunted by the order he'd betrayed.

"So you think the Varin line might not have been broken?" Leshie probed, sitting forward like a child, elbows to knees, chin cupped in her palms. "That his heir is out there somewhere still, in hiding?"

"It's possible."

"So he'd be what, forty years old or something? And powerful, no doubt. Why would he have stayed hidden all these years? Do you think it's part of some prophesy, that he'll emerge and retake his place as king?" She almost swooned at that thought, growing more eager. "How exciting! Do you think that might actually happen?" She inched a little closer, those big brown eyes unblinking. "Do you, Ranulf?"

He had to remember how young Leshie was. *Just seventeen,* he recalled, *though she looks a fair bit younger.* Even in that scarlet armour and with a godsteel dagger at her hip, she still had the countenance of a girl hardly into her teens. He couldn't help but smile. He enjoyed recounting tales, after all. "It's possible, I suppose," he said, with a purse of the lips and a dip of the head. "Though if there's a prophesy about the reforging of the Varin line, I've not heard it."

"Could it be one of Queen Thala's? Vincent told me that most of her accounts are coded or too hard to read. Perhaps she keeps her most important accounts hidden? I'd do the same - design riddles that were almost impossible to unravel, so the secret never got out."

"If you were ever worried about the book falling into the wrong hands, then yes, that would be the wise course, and one that several other kings and queens have chosen to follow too. I've managed to decode some of their passages, though those that I have unravelled have proven rather uninteresting anyway. It seems some of the old monarchs liked to cipher their accounts purely for their own sense of personal fun, rather than to hide something important. A little challenge, perhaps, for future kings and queens to untangle their accounts before reading them? Who knows. The Rasal people are prone to whimsy, so I'd not put it past them. But in the end, most of what I've uncovered is already known to historical record. And the vague prophesies I've found have long since expired...or never came true in the first place."

Leshie had a frown on her face. He was never quite sure which part of what he was saying she was picking up. She looked to lose interest rather quickly when he went on for more than a few moments. "I thought the Eye of Rasalan was a window to the future?" she said "How can these prophesies not turn out to be true?"

Ranulf offered an avuncular smile. "Because the truth can be easily misread or misinterpreted, Leshie. Not all Rasal monarchs have been able to master the Eye of Rasalan, as not all Vandarian monarchs have been able to master the Blades of Vandar. Imagine looking through a dirty window to a crowd of people outside. You might spot someone you think you know, but how can you be sure with their features so blurred? The Eye works in a similar way. The more one masters it, the clearer the image becomes, and the more accurate the account or prophesy."

Leshie looked at the book for a long moment, chewing on her lower lip."So half of what's in there is just someone looking through a blurred window and guessing at what they see?"

"Well, yes I suppose you could put it like that."

"Well no wonder you've been frustrated by it then. How disappointing. But this lost heir...I guess that's interesting at least. Do you know where he might be?"

Ranulf shook his head, and gently turned a clump of pages, searching for the correct account. "Remember it is only speculation, Leshie," he was quick to remind her. "It might very well be that this child of Atia's was the son of another Bladeborn lord or knight, and not the lost heir at all."

"Then why would King Astan write about it?"

"Because it involves the untimely death of his daughter. Can you imagine searching the Eye of Rasalan and seeing that? Your own daughter dying in labour? It has always been considered both a blessing and a curse to possess the power to see into the Eye, and none more so than at times like that." He continued to flip pages, turning them over with care.

"Yeah I...I guess." Leshie bunched her lips and turned her eyes to the side. "The only thing worse would be seeing your own death, I reckon. Do you think they do? See how and when they die?"

Ranulf had wondered that himself, and had even asked King Godrin about it once, though had received only a riddled reply. *Such is his way,* he thought with a note of melancholy, *and it seems many of his forebears were of a similar persuasion, judging by their coded accounts.* "I don't know for sure," he answered. "I've not seen any account like that. If any monarch had seen their own death, then it seems they didn't wish to write about it."

"Nor would I." Leshie shuddered. "Unless I found out that I was going to die warm in my bed with a bellyful of food when I was withered and old and grey, then no thanks. It would be on my mind all day, every day. I could never live with that burden."

"As I said. A blessing and a curse."

She nodded and unfurled her spindly legs, sliding forward off the desk. Ranulf watched her a moment, hoping her questioning was over, and sure enough she paced away toward the balcony again, taking a look outside. She returned a moment later. "I might go have a listen, see what they're talking about. I want to know who they are."

The Patriots of Lumara, Ranulf might have told her - for he was quite certain that's who they were - but he didn't. The varied assemblage of men and armour and weapons made it likely these were from that militarist, warmongering group, though Ranulf couldn't be entirely certain, nor did he know why Rose would be meeting with them. *Trading weapons or armour or other valuables, no doubt. Anything to further his ends.* He said nothing of that, however, but simply asked, "Are they down there still?" He couldn't hear anything coming from outside, no talking or rustling of men and mounts and wagons. Just the twittering of birds and the distant voice of the sea, as it jostled about down by the shore.

Leshie continued toward the exit to the library, speaking as she went. "Some of them are. Just guards I think. The important ones have gone inside."

Ranulf nodded. He would rather she leave him so he could continue working in private, though didn't want to see the girl come to harm. "Just...be careful, Leshie," he warned her. "You seem to have identified what sort of man we're dealing with, so I'd caution you to tread lightly."

"Oh I will. I'm very quiet and quick with godsteel, Ranulf. I'm getting good with it, actually. Marian might make a proper spy of me yet."

"Just be careful," he reiterated. "And act natural. You don't want one of Vincent's men catching you snooping around."

"I'll be fine." She moved to the door with impressive speed, as if to show how sleek she was. "The soldiers here know I'm one of Vinny's bodyguards so who are they to bother me? And you...get working. I want to know more about this lost heir."

So do I, he thought, as she dashed off out the door, though he didn't imagine he would. Still, he clutched to some vague hope as he settled back into his chair and returned to the page he'd left. He ran his eyes over King Astan's tragic words, turned the sheet, and continued on. The following passages offered nothing further on the matter, as expected, and unlike his forebears, Astan had no interest in complicating or coding his accounts. He'd been a sombre king, and had died shortly after the death of his daughter - of a broken heart some said...and perhaps that might have been true?

And then came Godrin, Ranulf thought, as a flutter of nerves flew through him. He was about to enter the final chapter, the accounts of the current king. *Is this the reason I'm here? To find the secret in Godrin's personal accounts?* "There's no better place for you, my friend," the king himself had said to him, that fateful day in the palace...the very day the Book of Thala had been stolen. He had let those words drive him these last weeks and yet much remained unravelled. Besides this vague note on the lost Varin heir, he'd excavated little of worth or interest. *Nothing to appease Vincent, certainly. And Janilah? Just what is he searching for? What...*

He turned the page.

Godrin's hand came into view.

His eyes scanned the words, and...they made absolutely no sense at all.

A dull throb of despair shambled through him. *It's another language entirely,* Ranulf saw, and not one he'd ever read. He went to turn another page. *Just this first account,* he hoped. *That's all. He's playing a game for the next monarch to follow; his son, most likely. Yes, this is a game for Prince Hadrin.* He smiled broad and full and let the page fall flat. *Oh Godrin, so full of whimsy. What a funny old king you are...*

Then the page landed and the next account fell into view, and his smile quickly slipped away. It was just the same as the last; entirely unintelligible. A creeping dread came upon him, as he racked his brain for all the languages he knew, or had heard about or seen, but never once had he seen such symbols. He turned another page, and another. His head was starting to shake, and he was cursing himself for not having checked Godrin's chapters earlier. *I should have looked forward. I should have known.* He didn't imagine Vincent Rose was going to be happy about this. Ranulf had assured him he'd already begun searching Godrin's accounts and had thus far unearthed no value. *Lies on lies on lies,* he thought. *He'll not enjoy being deceived.*

But Ranulf had no intention of telling him. He flicked another page, and another and another, looking forward two dozen pages, but all his accounts were the same. It might take him an hour to decipher this secret language, or a day, or a week, or a lifetime. He had no idea until he got started. No idea at all.

He reached out and drew up a quill and new piece of parchment. There were many others already filled with scribbles and notes across his desk. On some he'd successfully decoded a monarch's messages. On others he'd failed and failed again and ended up moving on. He must have left at least a tenth of the book like that, untranslated, and no doubt those were the best parts. *Janilah will have time to pore over it all and extract what he needs, but me?* According to Rose, the Warrior King's men were but a few short weeks away, perhaps no more than a fortnight...*and that is no time at all.* He could feel the sweat on his brow, the heat on the back of his neck. *I must find what he's looking for...I must. That is my purpose. That is my task.*

He flicked back to the beginning of Godrin's chapter, quill poised and inked, and began to decrypt his king's words.

21

Elyon

The Rasalanian host rustled across the broad stone bridge, a mounted troop of blue and yellow and silver beneath the slate-grey snowy skies. There must have been a full score of Suncoats, and a score of their best, accompanying the high lords as they pressed forward for the parley.

Among them Elyon spotted Lord Paramor, leading with a brace of noble knights at his flanks. *Two of his sons,* he imagined, seeing the arms of their house - the blade-wielding merman of House Paramor - emblazoned upon their chests. Other lords came with them, bearing their standards. Several were Seaborn, Elyon could tell, for the leviathans and krakens and sea-serpents they took as sigils, and the rough whale-hide armour they wore. Others were from Bladeborn houses migrated to Rasalan many centuries ago, garbed in misting godsteel armour and mail, and with an array of Ilithian blades and axes fixed to their flanks and backs.

"A show of strength," said Prince Rylian, sitting atop his tall destrier in godsteel breastplate and rich umber cloak. The sorrel steed was a match to his rusty reddish beard, named Flame for his fiery hide. "They seek to give us pause, it would appear."

If that was the aim, it wasn't the host that would do it, but the great towering fortress behind them. Though Elyon had seen the maps and sketches of the fort of Harrowmoor, seeing it in person was rather different. Its walls were solid dark grey stone, tall and deep, and protected on all sides by a wide flooded moat. At its heart soared a huge tower atop a bailey, with walkways and bridges giving quick access to some of the other mighty battlements. It looked impenetrable, laced with steel and iron in places, the entire fort sitting atop a slight rise as the moors swept away to the south and east and west, with a rugged sweep of rocky land to the north that bled into a great oak-tree forest. *It shan't be so easy to siege*, Elyon realised, as the huge fortress loomed before him, filling his eyes. The upper battlements were lined with ballistas and catapults and there must have been a thousand ace archers inside. *And thousands more spearmen and axmen and armoured knights besides,* he thought. *No, it shan't be so easy at all.*

"Well come on, let's get this done." Rylian kicked his spurs and his destrier trotted forward, Lord Kanabar and Lord Kastor and Vesryn at his sides. Behind, Elyon took up his reins and urged Snowmane on, with Sir Dalton gliding alongside him, and a mingled host of Varin Knights and Emerald Guards at their back, including Sir Rodmond Taynar and Sir Brontus Oloran, and the titanic figure of Sir Taegon Cargill. Rylian's twin sons, Robbert and Raynald, were there too, as was Melany's brother, Sir Mallister. *We show a strength of our own,* Elyon mused, as the two delegations converged just beyond the bridge and moat, lining up in a tense exchange as the light snow whirled about them. Many were familiar with one another and would be friends at another time. The lords and noble knights of the northern kingdoms often came together for banquets and feasts and tourneys, and many were bonded by marriage besides. Elyon could feel that in the air. It was as though no one wanted this, and yet here they were anyway, about to fight over a great heap of stone and shed a thousand bathtubs of blood.

Rylian was the first to speak, mustering a gentle smile as he did so. "Lord Paramor, you look well." His eyes went to the heavy iron gate beyond the thick stone bridge, bordered by the massive towers of the barbican. "I envy you your halls and hearths in this weather, my lord, and the comforts they surely bring. No doubt you wish to keep them..."

"And no doubt you wish to take them." Paramor's voice iced the air. Elyon had known him as a jovial and genial man, but he looked anything but right now. He stared with those blue-gold eyes, webbed by deep wrinkles. "Turn your army around and return to your lands, Prince of Tukor. Turn your eyes south. That is where the true threat lies, so you say, not here at this fortress, nor further north of these lands." Rylian made to speak, but Paramor raised a wizened hand to cut him off. "King Godrin wishes an end to this conflict. He laments that it ever began. Oblige an old man this blessing, and take your men west across the strait. Do that and my king will engage with yours in talks. He will sign a treaty of support against Agarath, and promise to aid in the defence of the north. Is this not what your father always wanted, Prince Rylian? A united northern continent? We offer it now on a platter. You need only reach out, accept, and go home, and much bloodshed might be spared."

A silence stilled between them and Rylian's short smile was gone. All looked to him, and yet the prince looked steadfastly forward. "My father has long been fed King Godrin's lies and has no appetite for them anymore, my lord. I see this platter you offer, and it is laded full of them, fetid and spoiled. Should we march from here, you'll renege on your word, and take the chance to fortify your borders. You will sit and hide as you have always done as Agarath blows its fire, and let your northern brothers burn."

"Then I can see your mind is set," Lord Paramor said in a sabre-sharp voice. He looked older than before, older when not smiling. His rough tanned skin was paler, and his short grey-white beard had grown whiter still, a match for the snow swirling about them. "Why did you send a messenger for this parley if not to even consider our terms?" he challenged. "Or do you have a counter to them, good prince? Go ahead, find your father's scroll if you need to recall his orders. It is clear you have no agency of your own."

Rylian ignored the taunt. "My father is my king, Lord Paramor. Of course it is he who directs our course, as Godrin does yours. But if it's a counter you wish for, how's this..." His tall flaming horse took a short pace forward, inching away from the rest. "Open the gates of this fortress, throw down your arms, and empty out onto the moors. No harm will come to you or your men, of that you have my word. Do this, and it will show us that you are serious in your wish for peace."

"So you think me dulled by age, do you?" There was some bristling behind him, and to his left and right, as the lords and knights of Rasalan stirred. "I'd not leave our men open to treachery, good prince. This offer is an insult, no more."

"It is no insult, and you'll suffer no treachery. You may hold my father in disdain, but I'd hope you consider me a man of my word, Lord Paramor."

"In other circumstances I might, but not when you have a host of fifty thousand at my door." Paramor peered through his tired old eyes to the distance, to the siege camp being erected some half mile away. "This army of yours..." His voice turned heavy, curdling with a quiet rancour. "We've had thousands come this way with tales of how they've suffered by your hand, Prince Rylian. There have been horrific accounts of mass rape. Of boys being hacked up for sport, or hung from the trees for the practice of your bowmen. Graves have been despoiled for trinkets. Livestock slaughtered for no reason at all, but to see our smallfolk starve. Are these the actions of a people I can trust? Is this not treachery, noble prince?"

Rylian took pause for a moment, then said, "These are the actions of small bands of base men for whose behaviour I can only apologise. They do not represent this army. They are outliers and shall be duly dealt with." He gave Lord Kastor a short stiff stare at that, though nothing more. Elyon knew Rylian had reprimanded him in private for the behaviour of his army already, and wasn't likely to do it again in the presence of an enemy host.

Paramor nodded in a slow thoughtful way. "You have Rasal women in your warcamp, taken from their homes," he said. "I would have them released as a show of good faith."

Rylian considered it, then nodded. "It shall be done, my lord.

I'll assign a team to scour the camp for your women and have all who wish to leave returned to you."

"Many might wish to leave but be too frightened to admit it," Paramor said.

"Then it will be for them to judge. Not all of your women came to Lord Kastor's camp by force. Some came seeking work, for which there is plenty. I can only ask and give them a choice. Does that satisfy you?"

"It will have to." Paramor's voice was tight and terse. "I might also ask that you bring us some of these base men you speak of, so they might face their reckoning..."

"You'll get not a single soldier from our camp," cut in Lord Kastor, pulling forward on his charcoal grey steed, the bear print of his house blazoned large on his fluttering cloak. "These are my men, men of North Tukor, and will be punished according to our laws, not yours."

"These are criminals of war," Paramor returned. "And you most of all, my lord. The rot in your army starts at its core, and you'll have your reckoning too."

Lord Kastor's cruel handsome face tore into a smile, the air fogging as he laughed. "You Rasalanians are so very sensitive; no wonder you quiver and flee at our coming. But spit your slurs elsewhere, or you'll feel the edge of my sword." He drew out a few inches of steel for effect, as several Emerald Guards did the same.

"You'll do no such thing," Rylian told his brother-in-law, wedded as he was to Cedrik's sister, Clarris. "Sheath your sword immediately, Lord Kastor. We are here to parley not part limbs."

Kastor sneered and pressed his blade back into its gleaming scabbard, as the air thickened with tension and snow. Elyon glanced around. Half the knights on both sides were gripping hard at their hilts now, eyes darting from behind their helms. Some were fully garbed in godsteel, others in breastplates, gauntlets and cloaks as he was. Most of the lords, Paramor and Kanabar and the other Rasal Lowland Lords, were draped instead in leathers and furs, and would be no good in a fight. The laws of the parley forbade that, of course, but with such bile being spat, who knew what might happen. Lord Paramor seemed to identify this, deftly pulling a breath into his lungs and adding a smile to his lips. Then he looked directly at Elyon.

"How does your father fare, Sir Elyon?" he asked him, more genial. "He has been often in my thoughts since the attack last summer. I only wish he was here with us now, to add a calm to proceedings."

Elyon hadn't expected the conversation to turn to him, sitting in his fine leather saddle a little off to one side. He sat up straight as the attention of the host came upon him. "He retains much of his strength, my lord," he said, breath misting the cold wintry air. "I have been told he's able to walk well enough now without his crutch, and has some feeling back in his left arm. Much of that is thanks to you and your surgeons, and the quick action you took to revive him."

"Of course." Paramor dipped his chin, courteous. "I only wish we could have done more. Perhaps then we'd not be facing off like this, on opposite sides of a war."

"It is regrettable, my lord," agreed Elyon, choosing his words well. It was a sentiment shared by most, though to convey the true depth of his dislike for this conflict wouldn't be so wise.

"And Sir Vesryn," Paramor moved on. "It seems you have taken up Amron's reins well. The Sword of Varinar suits you, though of course it would...it has always looked well at the hip of a Daecar."

"My thanks, Lord Paramor." Vesryn dipped his chin, as some tension bled from the group. A few niceties could go a long way in soothing sore tongues, it seemed. "I still have hope that my posting as First Blade is temporary, and that my brother resumes in his duties, in time." It was a courtesy, Elyon knew. No one thought that Amron Daecar would retake the role. Nor was he certain his uncle wanted to give it up either.

"We can hope, of course, though I'm sure you'll follow him well if not. Yet I must confess, I was disappointed to hear that King Ellis had pledged his support for Janilah's ugly pride. What grounds does Vandar have to aid in this invasion? By honour's sake you should be standing beside me right now, not holding a knife to my throat." His eyes moved subtly sideways to Lord

Kanabar. "I have known you for almost fifty years, Wallis, since our early days on the duelling circuit, and you've always been a man I could trust...a man I considered a close friend. Now I find you here with a host of twenty thousand Rivermen and Lakemen for company. Does that sit right with you? With your honour, old friend?"

"Little sits right with me anymore, Donal," Lord Kanabar said without mirth. "You know that war is never personal."

But it feels it, especially now, Elyon thought. Was this Lord Paramor's ploy, to tug at the heartstrings a little and sew doubt among their ranks? It might not take much for a man like Wallis Kanabar to renounce his king's order and turn his army about, and indeed he'd threatened that already once or twice, with the sting of Borrus's fate still raw.

"I might once have agreed, Wallis," Paramor said regretfully, "but what is this war if not a reckless exhibition of one man's ego and pride? This is personal for Janilah, believe me. A personal, long-term attack on our king and our people. None of us should be here. None." He shook his head and a loud sigh blew through his rumpled old lips. "We should be supping together and sharing fond stories, not standing two sides of a siege. Gods, Wallis, I named my firstborn after you." He looked to the mounted knight beside him, garbed in blue-dyed godsteel from heel to helm. "You remember him, don't you. It hasn't been so long, has it?"

"Long enough for my ailing memory," said Lord Kanabar, "but of course I'd not forget." He looked at the younger man. "How long has it been, Sir Wallis? It must be a decade at least?"

"Some dozen years I believe, my lord," said Sir Wallis Paramor. He was much like his father in look, not especially handsome or large, but with a kind openness to his face and a twinkle to his blue-gold eyes. "You came for the celebration of my twenty first birthday, as I recall. I have since spent much time in roving, training young knights for occasions such a this."

“I'm sure you trained them well, sir."

"Wallis is one of our finest knights," said Lord Paramor proudly. "I would say he'd offer even you a decent match, Prince Rylian."

"I'm sure," said Rylian, with grace. "And this is another of your sons, by his look?"

He was referring to the knight on Paramor's other flank, though he carried a more disagreeable disposition. Still the resemblance was enough to make the connection, as was the fine godsteel plate he wore. The Paramors were one of the richest families in Rasalan and could garb many of their members in full suits of Ilithian armour. "My third, yes. Sir Brendan. Equally gifted as his brother," their lord father said generously.

"Then you have sired a fine brood, Lord Paramor. I will hope to avoid both of them should we find ourselves on the field."

"As would I," said Sir Wallis. "For my own sake, at least. We met once, Prince Rylian, at a tourney in Ilithor, do you recall?"

"Of course," said Rylian without hesitation. The fact that he didn't elaborate suggested otherwise, however.

Sir Wallis raised his eyes, shining from behind his upturned faceplate. "I had the honour of fighting you, Your Highness," he went on. "I was only young, not yet beyond my teens, and you sure taught me a thing or two." He smiled in an agreeable sort of way. "I would hope to have improved a great deal to stand a chance against you, should we ever cross blades again."

"Which you have, I imagine. And for my part, I've surely slowed." A smile was emerging through Rylian's rusty-bearded lips, as the meet grew more cordial. "I would say you're in your prime, Sir Wallis. Thirty three, you said you were?"

"Yes, Your Highness."

"Then you have over a dozen years on me. And those years, I'm sure, have seen you through great improvement and me the reverse. Your father may just be right."

Elyon didn't imagine so, not from what he'd heard. By all accounts, Rylian had not held back in battle during the siege of the southern coast, and had proved quite imperious and unstoppable thus far. Sir Wallis Paramor might be a fine knight, but a challenge to the Prince of Tukor? It seemed unlikely.

A stiff breeze began to pick up, blowing in hard from the east. Half the assembly craned their necks westward, turning against the blast of wind and snow. "Snowstorms grow strong this time of year," called out Lord Paramor over the squall. "I hope you'll be warm enough in those tents of yours. The winters can be awfully bitter, even so far south as this."

"We'll have your fine castle soon enough," Lord Kastor put in, his black hair frosted with flakes. "I hear you have a hundred hearths in there, and enough wine to redden all the waters of the world." He rubbed his hands together as the winds calmed. "I'll raise a toast to you, my lord, once we've driven you out. I'll even take your chambers for my own, I think. I'm sure they're the finest in all the fort."

"Then those chambers would go to me." Rylian gave him a humourless stare. "But I suspect our good lord rests elsewhere. The lord's chambers will be occupied by Prince Hadrin, I would wager." He paused and looked to the towering fort, grey and black against the white snowy skies. "Where is he, Lord Paramor? I had expected him to lead these talks."

Paramor gave a swift shake of the head. "Our prince is indisposed."

"Indisposed? Or too craven to face up to what he did?"

Paramor wasn't certain of his meaning. He raised his eyes in question and Rylian offered explanation.

"It is well known that Prince Hadrin was behind the attempted assassination of Amron Daecar, and by extension the disgraceful murder of his son." He spoke short and sharp and with complete conviction. "He is doubtless afraid to ride out with Vesryn and Elyon among us, and might just want to concern himself with me as well. Amron is a dear friend, and Aleron had been set to wed my daughter, and become my son by law." He closed a gauntleted fist with a crunch of steel, staring at the thick iron gate. "This treachery will not go unpunished, Lord Paramor. So ask again why we're here. Ask again of my terms."

A tension renewed its grip on the group. Men were starting to reach for their godsteel blades. "I will not entertain such talk. These are lies..."

"Have your prince marched out here," Rylian interrupted in demand. "Better yet, have him dragged out here at the tail of a horse to answer for his crimes. Have him cry and confess before us, my lord, and perhaps then I'll consider your proposal."

Lord Paramor glowered. The levity had not lasted long. "He has nothing to confess. This is a fallacy, a fabrication, and no more, designed to secure Vandarian support in this war. If there is a plot here we know full well who is behind it." He looked to the First Blade. "Vesryn, you must know. Tell me you know the truth of it."

Vesryn stared, lips fixed to a line. "I know only that Hadrin masterminded the plot against my family," he said, voice rigid as the walls beyond.

"No." Paramor shook his head and rattled his reins in despair. "You do not believe that, Vesryn. Nor you Elyon." He looked to him. "You don't believe this, I can see you don't. Wallis, Sir Dalton, Lord Fullerton, Lord Shorton..." He went through several others, looking to the Vandarian knights and lords in turn. "Not one of you truly believes it, and yet here you are anyway. You say craven, Prince Rylian? Craven are those who cower to your king, and I see many such men before me. Gods, let me spell it out for you all, if you're too fearful to say it. It was Janilah. Janilah! He is behind this mess, as he has been from the start. All of this has been him. All of it, my lords. And yet here you are, dancing to his drums..."

The ring of steel sung loud and clear as Rylian drew his blade. "Silence, Paramor! You'll not sully my father's name! You'll not sully his honour with your lies!"

"Lies? Lies, you say!" Paramor laughed, an old croaking sound. "Blind. Blind and deaf, and dumb, every last one of you!"

More swords came to meet the frosty air, scraping and scratching from their silver scabbards. Horses were stamping now, snorting, shuffling and turning. Behind him, Elyon could hear blade after blade being drawn by the host of Varin Knights and Emerald Guards at his back. *Madness,* he thought, drawing his own. *This is madness.* But as he thought it, so a voice roared out over the winds, Kastor's voice, clean and clipped. "Slay them," he roared. "Slay them all!"

Before Elyon knew what was happening the meet was

descending into anarchy. Men were charging in on their mounts, swinging, or leaping from the saddle to engage. The old Lowland Lords bolted for the bridge, flinging up clods of snowy mud in their wake. Beyond, archers were rallying above the gate, setting their bows into crenels, or gathering in the hoardings. Lights flickered about the windows of the towers as men passed by the fires inside to grab spear and sword and shield.

"Protect Lord Kanabar!" he heard a voice bellow. "Get him out of here!" It sounded like Vesryn, though in the chaos he couldn't be sure. A moment later Kanabar was turning on his huge great horse and galloping back for the siege camp, a brace of Varin Knights at his side, and Lords Fullerton and Shorton too. Lord Paramor was doing the same, charging for the fortress gate with the rest of the Rasal lords. His eldest son Wallis was calling orders to the Suncoats. Several were closing in on Prince Rylian, who'd dismounted Flame and stood in Strikeform to greet them. Two Emerald Guards charged to join him, lances to hand, likely his sons Rob and Ray though Elyon couldn't be sure in the rush of it. One punched through the pauldron of a Suncoat, bursting through his shoulder in a shower of blood, as the two knights leaped from their steeds to join the fray.

A heavy impact caught Elyon in the side, as an unmounted horse barged into him in a bid to flee. Snowmane neighed and bucked, throwing Elyon from the saddle. He reached to cling on but the reins slipped through his gauntleted fingers, landing hard on his back in the sodden snow. Two Suncoats were on him in an instant, swinging as he spun and clambered back to his feet. He managed to right himself, straighten out, and drop into Blockform to fend off their first attacks, as away at the fort he heard a bellowing call, "Nock!"

He glanced that way. The bowmen were fitting their shafts, pulling their bowstrings taut. *There'll not fire with their own men here,* he knew.

He was wrong.

"Loose!"

The arrows came flying, half a hundred of them, and half looked tipped with godsteel. All men sensed them on a heartbeat and turned, seeking cover, or dashing away as they surged. Elyon had keen enough eyesight to track their trajectory and rush for safety behind the low stone wall of the bridge. A moment later a half hundred quarrels were plunging into the earth, catching a couple of wayward horses which cried out and bucked and galloped from the fray.

Elyon expected to hear the command to retreat, but no such order came. He turned his eyes out, as more arrows began to fly down, aimed at his allies. The bowmen above the gate and nearby battlements were skilled and close enough to take aim. This was no random assault. It felt almost planned.

The chaos continued, as Elyon looked out through the squalls of snow, the steam of three dozen fighting men. The Suncoats were a score in number and facing a brace more than twelve, doubling up on each man they faced. Sir Dalton, Sir Rodmond, Sir Brontus and Sir Taegon were all fighting two apiece. Rylian had three to himself. His sons were man on man with a pair of others and Sir Mallister the same. Lord Kastor had hunted down Sir Wallis Paramor and looked intent on ending the heir. Vesryn was being avoided by everyone, as he held the great Sword of Varinar to hand.

Elyon stood from the side of the bridge and sped forward to his uncle's side, but as he neared sensed movement to his right. He turned. A knight was coming at him in Strikeform. He recognised him only from his armour; Sir Brendan Paramor, the lord's third son, wreathed from top to toe in perfect interlinking godsteel plate. He came forward in Elyon's favourite stance as a few loose arrows punched into the ground at his feet. Elyon braced in Blockform, one eye on the skies for shafts, the other on the knight. He shifted several steps sideward, moving away from the host. The clang of steel rang out, and the whoosh of quarrels blew, and over it all, he could hear his uncle shouting now, "Sheath your swords! Sheath your swords!"

But no one seemed to be listening. No one seemed to care. Sir Brendan was closing in. "You needn't do this," Elyon warned him. "I am friend to your father, Sir Brendan. You needn't..."

Sir Brendan either didn't hear him or didn't care to listen, as he surged forward in Strikeform in a pattern Elyon knew well. Elyon swung his blade in defence, once, twice, thrice, knowing where Sir Brendan would strike next, parrying with a graceful ease. It was a flurrying set of moves, high to low, low to high and finishing with a long-arm jab to the heart, and Sir Brendan executed well. *But the wrong move,* Elyon thought. *Why end with a strike at my breastplate when I'm undefended above the neck?* He had a habit of analysing duellists' strike patterns, something he'd done for himself and his brother during tournaments, but now wasn't the time. *He is trying to kill you,* he reminded himself. *You're not in the training yard or duelling ring, but the field. This is a battle, your first damn battle, and he'll hack through your neck if you let him...*

The thought centred him. After fighting a hundred friendly duels you forgot that sensation of fear, but now it rose up high and thick in his throat, swelling. He gulped it down. *This man is trying to kill me.* Sir Brendan came again, remorseless, striking hard, striking fast. The adrenaline in Elyon's blood was such that he'd never felt, throbbing and rushing fast as a river swollen from the autumn rains. He wore only leather at his arms and legs and a good strike there would see him lose a limb. *But I must stay close to him, lest an archer put an arrow through my eye,* he thought. The bolts were still raining down, darting into the dirt. As a gap opened between he and Sir Brendan so a sudden flurry came, one narrowly missing him, another glancing off his breastplate as he spun and backed away. *Closer, damn it. Closer!*

He moved to his favoured form, striking with speed and precision. A low slash to the legs put his opponent off balance, and a high swipe got through his defences, clanging hard against his godsteel pauldron. It left a dent but no more, as Sir Brendan swung the momentum, surging forward. Clang came the kiss of steel as he went for Elyon's left arm, and the young Daecar parried. Clang it went again as he changed stance and thrust for his neck; again, Elyon was wise to the strike and battered his attentions away. He drew away a pace as he did and glanced to the fray. Men were dead, at least four of them in their gold surcoats, and a brace of Emerald Guard too. It looked like Sir Rodmond had taken a godsteel-tipped quarrel to the flank, which had punched through his plackart and into his abdomen. Sir Taegon was seeing to him, hauling him onto his enormous shoulders and lumbering away to the camp. Sir Dalton and Sir Brontus were fighting back to back. Rylian had two dead men at his feet. Vesryn was still calling the retreat...

But no...not Vesryn, Elyon realised. It was Sir Wallis Paramor, he noted, backtracking quickly from his contest with Lord Kastor. "Fall back!" he called. "Fall back to the gate!"

Several of the Suncoats took heed, though Sir Brendan didn't seem to hear. He came again, as Elyon recalled that one of Paramor's sons was born half deaf in one ear, and completely deaf in the other. Suddenly it made sense. "Your brother has called the retreat," he called out, as loud as he could. He pointed to the bridge and gate beyond. "Go, Sir Brendan. Go!"

The man neither looked nor listened. His blade struck hard for Elyon's neck and the young Daecar parried, spun, and thrust at his back. He drove his blade with such force it went a full inch into his plate, and came out dipped in blood. Sir Brendan made his first sound - a great bark of pain - as he staggered forward a step, and from the skies a volley of arrows came down. Snap snap snap they went, cracking into the earth at his feet. Elyon looked up in time to spot one whirling right for his face, ducking beneath it as it whistled through his flowing black hair. "Elyon!" he heard a call. He saw Vesryn launching himself forward, trailing the Sword of Varinar. "Elyon, watch out!"

He sensed the swinging blade before he saw it; a tickle of wind at his back. By instinct he dropped down, just as Sir Brendan's broadsword swung over his head. The Rasal knight had committed to the strike and lost his balance as Elyon dodged, toppling forward to the snow. Blood was draining down his back now; Elyon's stabbing strike had cut deeper than he thought. It reddened the churned white-brown snow as he leaped back to his feet and turned.

"Sir Brendan, seek aid!" Elyon shouted at him. "Go!" He pointed again. His allies were in full retreat now. "You don't need to die..."

He still didn't listen. *He's maddened, bloodlusted*, Elyon thought, as he prepared to defend again. Sir Brendan rushed at him, swinging, and Elyon held fast to Blockform. His enemy was weakening, the crimson leaking down his leg. He stumbled, and Elyon struck, though his swing was only half-hearted and bounced feebly off his plate. Still the man didn't relent. Still he came. Elyon moved side to side, protecting his flanks, parrying here, countering there. His foot caught on a rock hidden beneath the snow as he moved back, tripping him. He stumbled and fell and braced as Sir Brendan swung...

The strike never landed.

When Elyon looked up, he saw the Sword of Varinar punched through the mute knight's back, exploding through the front of his breastplate. Blood ran off its edge, its mystical glyphs glowing gold in the ashen afternoon light. Vesryn stood over his shoulder, a pale grim look on his face. He gave a pull and the blade slid easily through the knight's body and plate, flesh and bone. Sir Brendan fell dead to the earth with a dull lifeless slump.

And in the distance, Elyon was certain he heard the shrill desperate cry of an old man, watching his dear son die.

22

Saska

Lady Cecilia Blakewood was fussing again as the camp was set to order. She liked it all a certain way and had a slightly obsessive way about her. "No no no, not there, you silly boy," she said as a servant who wasn't a boy at all began setting up a tent, apparently in the wrong place. "Come here, come stand beside me." The man hung his head low and trundled over to her. "Now look," she said, pointing. "Does that seem right to you?"

The other tents were lined up neatly, with perfect six feet gaps between them. The one he'd been pitching was a little askew, however. Nothing major, but enough for someone as discriminating as Cecilia to notice. "No, m'lady," the browbeaten man murmured. "Sorry, I'll...I'll correct it for you."

"For me, yes, and also for yourself. What's your name young man?"

"Martus, m'lady." He looked about forty.

"Well, Martus, this is a lesson you'd best learn." She smiled, looking quite radiant in that rick green cloak of hers under the falling white snow. "If you're neat and tidy in all you do, you'll never find yourself troubled. Do your job and do it well and you'll please your master. Do it not, and you may just feel the lash." She delivered the sermon with a pleasant smile. "Now we wouldn't want that, would we?"

Martus shook his head. "No, m'lady. I'll not displease you again."

"I'm sure you won't. Now back to it, Martus. Let's see you pitch the perfect tent."

The pressure of those words sat heavy on the man, as he set about his task with a meticulousness he'd probably never possessed till now. Cecilia took that as a triumph, addressing Saska and the other girls as they stood huddled to one side in their quilted fur coats, waiting for their tents to be prepared. "You see," she told them. "A nurturing word and look, young Martus is setting to the task with great care and assiduousness. That's something we all can learn from. Be diligent in all you do, and the world will bless you in return. No matter your station, you'll reap the rewards of your efforts."

The girls rather liked that. There were six of them currently, Saska included, who were waiting to be assigned their postings, and the other five lapped up everything Cecilia told them. She seemed to have a way with them, a skill at making them forget all the possible unpleasantness associated with their upcoming life, and see only the joys it would bring. True, they might be well kept, live in pleasant castles and estates, wear fine clothing and have servants of their own...but they'd have to carry and birth children for all that, and worse, have them ripped from their breast and given to the wet nurse as soon as their babe drew breath.

Were they prepared for that? Did they truly understand how horrible that would be? Saska had learned that Cecilia never took on girls who'd already had children. In fact, the poor young thing she'd seen harried and heckled through camp a few days ago was likely driven out for that very reason. A woman who'd been through that would never agree to give up their child so willingly, Saska knew. So Cecilia chose youngsters who were more stupid and less cynical, and wound them around her finger. It wasn't so hard, really, when you were selective. And the girls around Saska now had been well chosen, a grinning flock of birds, tweeting excitedly about what was to come.

She sighed, the chill snowy wind assaulting her. Across the camp, it was falling harder as the afternoon progressed, making the labour of setting up camp rather less fun. Many of the servants and soldiers wore gloves, but not all, and even those who did were constantly rubbing their hands together and blowing on their fingers to unthaw them. It was hard work, by the looks of it, driving those poles into the earth, digging ditches and trenches and fire pits, erecting the pavilions and tents and raising wooden palisades around the encampment to fend off sallies and surprise attacks. Not far off, a more permanent timber longhouse was being set up, to double up as a command post for the siege camp leaders and a feast hall for when the days went well. How many days they'd lay siege to Harrowmoor, Saska wasn't sure, but she hoped it would be a few. *The longer I have to find a way to slit Kastor's throat, the better,* she thought grimly, furled like a bat in her brown fur coat.

It took Martus a good quarter hour to finish the tent, as Cecilia hovered about, watching like a hawk. Eventually she seemed satisfied. "Very good, young man," she said to him, persisting with the 'young' when they were clearly about the same age. "Now see the braziers lit inside and make sure all the furnishings are put right where they should be. Then make the beds and scrub the chamber pots. I want things spick and span for my girls, understand?"

He mumbled, "Yes, m'lady," and continued, as Cecilia fluttered about elsewhere, checking on the other servants. In the meanwhile, Saska took her chance to scan the camp as best she could and lock its layout into her memory. Their cluster of tents were being established on a shallow rise a little south of Prince Rylian's pavilion and those of the Vandarian leaders. On the other side, the Kastors would be housed, some hundred or so metres away. Cecilia had thus been good on her promise, making sure that her princely half brother formed a buffer between them. "Now you will tell me if Sir Griffin comes snooping around again, won't you Tilda?" she'd asked earlier, when they'd first arrived from their two day slog through the marshes and moors. "I don't imagine he will now that my brother is here, but do tell me if you see him skulking about."

"I will, my lady," she'd lied. In truth she'd do nothing of the sort, but Cecilia didn't need to know that.

The king's daughter looked at her for a long while after that, her thoughts entirely her own, assessing in that curious way of hers. Then she asked, "Are you ready to lose your maidenhead?"

The question came quite abrupt. "My...maidenhead?" repeated Saska, playing dumb, as a shot of anxiety ran through her.

"Your virginity, child." Cecilia gave a little chuckle. "You're quite old to still be in possession of yours, you know, and in a sense I suppose that's admirable. Some girls are carted off to wed when hardly into their teens, so the fact that you've almost escaped yours without feeling the thrust of a man's sword is impressive, especially looking as you do." She pressed her palm to Saska's cheek and smiled. "But I think it's time, sweet girl. There are many noble men here who will be gentle with you, for that first time, and all the better for when you travel to Ilithor. Best break the seal before then, wouldn't you say? I'll come see you about it later."

She'd made no further mention of it over the last few hours, and nor did Saska know what 'later' really meant. *Tonight? Tomorrow? Two days from now?* It wouldn't be longer than that, she didn't imagine, and the thought was a dull weight in her gut. *But should it be?* she had to wonder. *Have I not overthought all this?* Her virtue had become unduly important to her to the point of being prudish. Yes she'd suffered. Yes she'd beaten off the lurid advances of unpleasant old men. *But is that enough? Enough to wear this chastity belt forever?* She didn't believe that, of course. She only wanted choice. The man Cecilia brought to her might be a fine man, a kind and handsome and noble man, but he wouldn't be of her choosing. She wouldn't know him, not well enough for that. That's all it was. *I want to choose. I deserve to damn well choose.*

She took a few paces away from the other girls, warming her stiffening bones. *None of them would mind,* she thought, *were Cecilia to have them practice on a handsome knight.* They reminded her of Leshie.

Innocent in look but not in experience. *And then there's me, tight as a drum, rigid and cold and dull.* She paced on, kicking at a few loose stones. *Might it not be best to get it over with? I may want a choice but I'm hardly going to get one. Not unless I run, and I can't do that, not now.* She'd thought about that a lot, but whenever the temptation rose, she thought only of Marian, and the words King Godrin had whispered into her ear.

You have endured more than anyone of your age ever should, he'd told her back in the palace some weeks ago. *And yet there are more trials to come. Be strong, Saska. Be fearless. And always remember this - you are exactly where you're meant to be.*

Those words had become her crutch and guiding light, and continued to give her confidence when all those dark doubts closed in. And so they came to her again, as she idly shuffled about the yard. *I'm exactly where I'm meant to be,* she thought. *Does that include being in the company of a strange man? Does it include taking him between my legs?*

Her innards still coiled at the notion, though she tensed and braced against it, trying to remain relaxed. She might plead and beg with Cecilia to spare her that, but what good would it really do? She knew her new mistress had short limits to her kindness and had witnessed that firsthand already. *To deny her might just lead me down a far less pleasant path,* she knew. *In the end, what can I do but comply? Comply and trust in my fate.*

A little further down the slope, a light commotion caught in the air, distracting Saska from her discomforting thoughts, and the other girls from their giggling. Cecilia paced over, looking through the growing forest of pavilions toward Harrowmoor in the north. From their position upon that low rise above the rest of the encampment, they could see the shape of the fortress up the slope, some thousand yards away. The blustery weather and snow obscured it, but its shadow was clear enough, a great black beast dominating the northern skyline.

"Is something wrong, Lady Cecilia?" asked one of the girls. Gurta her name was. A narrow-shouldered whippet of a girl who'd arrived only a few days before.

Cecilia was clutching her godsteel blade, looking north. Saska wasn't certain whether her eyesight or hearing were enhanced by her blood-bond, but given her parentage, both seemed likely. "I hear a battle," she said, turning her head sideways. "The clang of steel and thunder of horses."

Saska raised her eyes. Her hearing was quite something, then. "A battle?" repeated Margo, another of the breeders-to-be. She was a little more stout, though prettier of face than the others. "But...why would there..."

"Shut up, Margo. I'm trying to listen." Cecilia stayed quite still for a moment, shutting her eyes, then opened them up and relaxed. "I can't say what started it but it seems they've come to blows." She sounded less than worried. "Just a quarrel, that's all. It shan't last long, I wouldn't think."

At the northern edge of camp, Saska could see men mustering and mounting their horses, charging off to join the fray. There must have been a hundred of them, some Bladeborn, some not. She watched as they thundered into the mists, fading through the snows after a few hundred metres. Only then did she remember that Lord Kastor was among the group gone to parley with the Rasal leaders. *Maybe he's been killed,* she thought, hopeful, *and I can get the hell out of here?* It seemed unlikely. Kastor was a killer born and if there was going to be a last man standing, he'd be in with a shout.

"They're returning," Cecilia said after another minute or two had passed. Through the light fogs several figures were coming back to camp, though by no means the hundred who'd charged off a few moments before. "The Vandarian lords," she added, peering to the distance. "They're cloaked in furs and poorly armoured. It wouldn't be safe for them in a fight."

The wait went on a little longer before the full contingent appeared, cantering down the slope and across the flattened moors. Saska squinted to the distance, though was unable to make out anything much beyond the blur of equine shapes and the silver-suited men atop them, their backs fluttering with their green and blue and dark brown capes.

Cecilia continued to scan. "Seems a couple have been slain," she said. "There are a pair of Emerald Guards slung over the backs of their horses. And a Son of Varin...he looks to have taken a bolt to the belly."

"That's all?" asked Saska.

Cecilia gave her a little look. "Sir Griffin isn't among the dead if that's what you're hoping for, Tilda. He's neither important nor gifted enough to have been invited, no matter what he'll tell you." She looked again. "His lord uncle has come away unscathed it would appear, however, as has my brother, but of course there's no surprise there. As I thought; a bit of bluster and no more."

The puffing parade of nobles and knights soon trotted back up to the heart of the camp, though Saska could see little from their position tucked up in the rear of the shallow hillock. She could hear the noise, though, that was clear enough, as men dismounted horses and clanked in their armour, and great hosts of servants and squires came busying in to attend them.

"Well then, I suppose I'd best go find out what happened," Cecilia said. She extended an arm across the snowy grasses. "Your tents are ready. Take whichever you like, girls. They're all exactly the same."

Saska was quick to choose hers, barging a tall towheaded girl called Effy away as she made for the tent with the best view. From inside the flaps, she could see the entrance to the timber longhouse by a fortuitous arrangement of the camp, giving her an indication of the comings and going to the command centre. She removed her fur cloak, hanging it on a hook on one of the inner support poles, then took position at the entrance, peering through the hide flaps.

From there, she watched. It was how she spent most of her time, though rarely did she see much of interest, but that was the old camp. This one was new and the wheels of war were starting to turn more quickly now. Ahead, Cecilia was marching briskly across the yard, down the little alley between pavilions, heading for the longhouse set upon an open patch of land. Builders and labourers had been sent ahead of the host to erect it, along with many of the watchtowers and the outer palisade wall, and it was already standing by the time they'd arrived.

Outside, a group of figures had gathered. Varin Knights in

silver and blue, and a small host of green-clad Emerald Guards with their tall thin silver spears. Saska noticed Elyon Daecar appear alongside his uncle Vesryn, easy to pick out for the great golden blade he bore. She stared at it, transfixed, as he passed the other men. Ranulf had told her all about the Blades of Vandar, to the point of tedium at times, but actually seeing one up close had made her understand his obsession. She felt herself drawn to it, as she had each time she'd spotted Sir Vesryn over the past days. On a few occasions during their march from the Kastor warcamp, she'd found him riding nearby to the carriage she'd travelled in with the other girls, and had been unable to tear her eyes away. The others hadn't cared so much, but her...she'd been around plenty of godsteel blades by now, not least the sleek sword Marian carried, and had even had her own dagger for a time, but the Sword of Varinar was different. *A piece of Vandar's Heart,* Ranulf had told her. *And the greatest piece of all.*

She watched, temporarily ensorcelled, until Vesryn and his young nephew stepped away into the longhouse, flecked with blood and grit from the fight. Others were following them in, and among them was Cecilia, pressing right after them, disappearing through the arched wooden door.

Saska escaped her reverie, pulled up a chair and sat down, watching.

She sat, she waited, and she watched.

23

Elyon

The interior of the longhouse was much larger than it looked from outside.

Around the edges, braziers burned and lanterns sat in sconces on the walls, protected by brass housings. There were a full dozen tables, long in length, arranged for feasts, and Tukoran banners and drapes were hung about, bearing the kingdom's crest.

Lord Kanabar was already waiting when Elyon and Vesryn arrived, sitting with the toadish Lord Fullerton and lithe Lord Shorton, and a great tankard of ale affixed to his paw. He drained a great gulp, and slammed the iron container onto the wood as the longhouse began to fill.

"Now what the bloody hell was that?" he bellowed out. "That was a parley! A parley!" He crashed his cup back down again, shaking the entire table, as ale sloshed from the rim. "You have a lot to answer for, Kastor," he growled. "What in Vandar's name were you thinking, man!"

Lord Cedrik Kastor had just arrived too, red-cheeked from the rush of the fight. He removed his frosted cloak and threw it to a boy, who hustled off and placed it neatly on a hook on the wall. "I know you don't like me, Lord Kanabar, but it's churlish to lay the blame of this at my feet." He clipped his fingers and that same boy came forward to help him remove his breastplate, fiddling with the straps at the back. "Lord Paramor was goading every one of us with that ugly acid tongue of his. If you have to point a finger, point it at him, not me."

"Slay them all," Kanabar returned sharply. "That's what you said. Don't think we didn't all hear you, Kastor. It was those words that sparked the affray, not the taunts of a prickly old man."

Kastor dismissed it, reaching out his hand as a server came forward with a steaming cup of mulled wine. "It is your right, of course, to think what you wish, my lord. But in this case your accusations are ill-aimed. If memory serves it was my brother-in-law who first drew his sword, and rightly so, after Paramor's filthy slurs. My words came after, once violence had been incited. And I'll not be judged by you." He supped his wine.

Rylian hadn't arrived yet, having stayed down at the northern edge of camp when they'd returned, so had no chance to put in a word. Sir Dalton was absent too, likely having his armour removed by his squire and seeing to his wounded nephew, though others were arriving to find out what happened, knights and lords and other courtiers among them. And a woman, Elyon noticed, as he took a seat beside Lord Kanabar, looking out across the large hall. He'd seen her around a few times though wasn't certain who she was. A handsome woman of forty-ish who had a resemblance he couldn't quite place. She moved inside, looked around, and then began following after Lord Kastor as he stepped away down the hall.

Elyon watched them go. "I don't much like him, but he's got a point," he said, as Vesryn removed his sheath and set the weighty Sword of Varinar aside. "The meet was never far from tense and something was always likely to spark it off. You could tell that from the beginning."

"A few taunts and drawn blades are not the same as an order to kill, Elyon," the Lord of the Riverlands reminded him. "Kastor wanted that fight, you could tell. He has a murderous look in his eye, that one."

Vesryn sat, nodding, as an attendant came to fill his cup. He waved him away and took the jug of ale. Even as First Blade,

Vesryn Daecar preferred to serve himself. "What's done is done," he said, in a tired voice. "We lost a few men, and so did they. It about evens itself out in the end."

Elyon sat quiet as Vesryn filled the cups. He could still hear the faint wailing screams of Lord Paramor as he watched his son die, that air-rending roar in the distance. *He must have rushed right up to the parapets,* he thought, *once he'd passed through the gate. Rushed up to watch...only to see his beloved son fall.*

"I tried to tell him," Elyon said, listless, as Vesryn passed him a tankard. "Sir Brendan. He didn't seem to know the others were retreating. I tried to tell him, but..."

"Sir Brendan is dead?" asked Lord Kanabar. He looked over. "You killed him, Elyon?"

"I did," said Vesryn. "It's not a kill I'll cherish by any means, but one that had to be done. I hope Donal accepts that, if we find ourselves allies again. He saw what happened. He knows."

"He was watching?" asked Lord Fullerton, recoiling. His toadish face bunched in dismay. "What a ghastly thing to witness. Why did he not retreat, Elyon?"

"I don't think he could hear me."

"Sir Brendan was hard of hearing." Lord Kanabar refilled his cup, shaking his head as flakes of melting snow dripped from his bushy red beard. "Let's raise a toast to him. A full goblet for the lad. He wasn't of Vandar but had the blood of Varin in him regardless. Let's help see him to the Eternal Halls." Once they'd raised their drinks and swallowed down their contents, Kanabar asked, "Did he die well?" He placed down his tankard and gave the Sword of Varinar a glance. "I take it he didn't put up much of a fight, not with you wielding that thing."

Vesryn gave a slow dispirited shake of the head. "I drove it through his back," he said, his words coming without triumph or pride. "An ignoble kill, but a necessary one. Sir Brendan was swinging for Elyon's head, it looked to me, and I had no choice."

A silence followed. There were ways to die and ways to kill, and even in battle, no noble knight wanted to end a man like that. Lord Shorton was next to speak. He was rare as East Vandarians went and thin as a pole, with a long pointed nose and a nasally voice to go with it. "You did the right thing, Vesryn," he said charitably. "I would do the same, if it meant protecting my family."

"It was a foul affair all round," agreed Lord Kanabar. "Had I known we'd cross swords I'd have arrived clad in steel myself. There's no shame in what you did, Vesryn, given the circumstances. It was Kastor caused all this, no matter what he says. Sir Brendan's blood is on his hands."

And the rest, Elyon thought. Two Emerald Guards were dead and a few other Suncoats too, and Sir Rodmond's fate remained uncertain. Vesryn nodded and busied himself with refilling their cups, then took a long drink. He didn't look too interested in hearing any more on it. "So Lord Paramor named his firstborn after you, did he Wallis?" he asked, shifting the subject. "I knew you were friends, though wasn't aware you were as close as that."

Kanabar allowed a nostalgic smile, though it looked a little forced. "We had a wager when we were young," he told them. "Donal and I met often at tourneys and became rather competitive, placing bets on how far we and others would advance. We reached the finals at a joust in Shellcrest once, and agreed that the loser would name their firstborn son after the winner. Needless to say, I won."

"And a good thing too." Vesryn tried to summon a smile, but failed. "I'm not sure Borrus would have suited a name like Donal."

Elyon could tell well enough that Lord Kanabar wasn't interested in speaking of his son. It was still too raw and, for Elyon's part, thinking of Borrus and Lythian and Tomos's rotten fate wasn't what he needed right now either. "So...what do you make of Prince Hadrin's non-appearance?" he decided to ask. "Might he be unwell as Lord Paramor suggested?"

"I suspect he wasn't even there," said Vesryn through a grunt. "He has probably retreated to Northgate by now, or even Thalan, if he's smart. He isn't much of a military commander and has no Bladeborn blood. There's no sense in him hiding in Harrowmoor as we lay it to siege."

"They're worried we'll take it quickly," claimed Fullerton, with those bulging eyes and long flat lips. "Better Hadrin runs now than later." He gulped down a swig of ale, then added, "What Donal said...about Janilah. Do you think he may be right?"

"No," said Vesryn without delay. "Hadrin is behind this, and there's no sense in us thinking otherwise." He turned his eyes down through the hall. At the far end, Rylian had arrived now through another door, and was in conference with Lord Kastor. He didn't look happy. "You saw how he reacted when Donal smeared his father. If one of us were to do so it might just spark a slaughter. We cannot afford that right now, whatever we might believe. It's exactly what the Rasals want."

The others looked in agreement on that point, and in a fashion Elyon was too. Was Hadrin behind this? No, he didn't think so. But there was no sense in unveiling his opinion on the matter. *Watch and wait,* he thought. *And keep your own counsel.* His father had been clear on that, and Elyon wasn't about to let him down. *I'll watch, Father, as you instructed. I'll not do or say anything without proof.*

The discussion had no time to develop, in any case, as Rylian ended his terse exchange with Lord Kastor and came marching their way across the hall. His scowl fled as he did so, reshaping into a smile. The Prince of Tukor, quite unlike his father, knew how to soothe a man with words and was a practiced hand in diplomacy. "My lords, please...don't stand." He gave a gesture for them to stay seated, smiling handsomely through his short rusty beard. His godsteel gauntlets and breastplate had been removed, his shoulders heaped in thick warm furs. "Let me apologise for what happened earlier. I'll admit I lost myself a moment, though never expected that. Lord Kastor has been told. He knows what he did was wrong, and for my part, so do I. I hope that satisfies you, my lords? I'll not let it happen again."

His words were primarily for Lord Kanabar, who carried the most influence among them having mustered the majority of the Vandarian host. "Well said, good prince." He stood at Rylian's words and dropped his great bald head into a bow. "Let the gods squabble over who started the affray. They can judge it when we fall." He raised his cup. "To those who redden the snow. May they find their way to the Eternal Halls, whichever it is they seek."

Rylian didn't hold a cup of his own, but that was shortly dealt with as a servant hurried over with jug and goblet. Once filled and taken to his grasp, he raised it, and the others at the table stood to do the same. Another full cup was thus sunk. And it didn't look to be the last. "Let us drink tonight, and feast," Rylian told them. At the far door, men were arriving with harps and lutes and lyres, pipes and horns and handheld drums. "I've been a week on the road from the coast, in all, and feel the need to make merry. We can debrief on the morrow and sharpen our plans to bring Harrowmoor to its knees. But for now..." He turned as the musicians arranged themselves in one corner. "Begin," he called out. "Something lively to start. Let's be loud so they can hear us. Hear how the men of the west lay a siege."

It was a turn Elyon hadn't expected, though he wasn't going to complain. *And a smart move,* he thought, *to tighten bonds between our armies.* They were like to spend the whole winter together, going from Harrowmoor to Northgate to Thalan, and these divisions wouldn't serve. Thus the pipes started skirling and the drums started pounding and the strings were plucked and thrummed. Elyon sat again, refilling his drink and those of the others. And as the music picked up, more flooded in, until the room was heaving and heavy with men in green and blue and brown.

"Ah, there's Dalton," noticed Lord Kanabar. He raised a paw. "Dalton! Come here, man!"

Sir Dalton had stripped out of his godsteel plate and arrived wearing leathers and a fine beige doublet. He moved sleekly through the crowds toward them, though chose not to sit, rather preferring the company of others or no one at all.

"How's Sir Rodmond?" Kanabar asked him, as the Taynar heir stood stiff and still beside the bench, right where Vesryn had place the Sword of Varinar. He eyed it with avarice, something Vesryn didn't miss, as Lord Shorton filled him a cup of ale.

"Should live. The surgeons are seeing to him now." Dalton took the cup and supped a short sip, turning his eyes through the hall. "I thought we were gathering for a debrief, not a feast." He didn't look happy about it, though Dull Dalton Taynar wasn't happy about much.

"Tomorrow," Vesryn told him, over the music and murmuring. "Rylian seeks to make merry tonight."

Dalton nodded and took another look at the Sword of Varinar. "Then I'll see you in the morning," he said, and stepped away.

He was replaced soon after by Sir Lancel and Sir Barnibus, who came to hear what had happened. Elyon had always liked them both, and perhaps more now than ever. They'd become too sycophantic around Aleron, nodding and bleating to his every word, but without him had lost that habit and become more straightforward and serious. "We hear Lord Kastor started it," Lancel said, tall and willowy, with pale green eyes and tousled blond hair. "Sir Brontus told us he shouted 'kill them all' and charged Paramor swinging his blade. Almost took his head off, he said, before his eldest deflected the shot."

It wasn't strictly true, but accurate enough.

"It's madness," added Barnibus. He was broader than Lancel, if a shade shorter, and a great deal less handsome, with a flat nose and podgy cheeks that made him look fatter than his frame. "The gods will curse him for this. You don't bring violence to a parley. It's an affront to all good laws of honour."

"He'll have his reckoning," Lord Kanabar said, pouring a pair of ales. "Donal Paramor told Kastor that and he's right. There's a strain of sickness in that family." He pushed the two tankards down the rough oak table. "Lord Modrik was the same. I heard rumours for years that he gathered southerners to his keep in Ethior to torture and rape and kill. Passed that onto his wicked son and seems it's spread through half their house as well. And you know how good Lord Modrik died? Slipped in a puddle of his own piss and cracked his head on the hearth." He looked off down the hall, a sour old grin on his face. "A fitting end for a miserable old drunk who'd long since lost his honour. And if the gods are just and good, they'll take Cedrik the very same way."

But the gods aren't good, Elyon thought, as men banged their mugs on the table in accord, *else Modrik wouldn't have reached such a ripe old age, and his son would have been cut down a good long time ago.* And others too. So many others would have seen their wickedness repaid in horror and blood, and that was but one side of it. What of the other? Elyon thought again of Aleron, and Lythian, and all the virtuous knights who'd fallen before their time. *There is no goodness in the gods*, he thought, taking a sharp sip of his drink. *They left this place long ago...left it to the wicked whims of man.*

The music grew louder, the drums booming and shaking the wooden walls, the pipes shrieking out their tune. The Tukorans liked all this. More than most they did. They grouped at the braziers and tables, downing their meads as the meat and bread and cheese came out, carried by servants holding large wooden trenchers. Elyon spotted Sir Mallister nearby, and couldn't help but think of the man's sister. He was a few years Melany's senior, and they shared a strong resemblance with those clear blue eyes and that straight golden hair. Sir Mallister saw him and strode over, as Elyon stood and took a few paces from the table. They locked arms. "Well fought today, Sir Elyon," the Emerald Guard said in a pleasant voice, as the feast hall rumbled and swayed about them. "I saw you paired with Paramor's son. Not an easy challenge without full plate."

"Nor that storm of arrows in the skies."

"No indeed." Sir Mallister smiled. *It's the same shape as hers,* Elyon thought, smiling back. "Your uncle put the Sword of Varinar though him, I saw. I was curious as to why Sir Brendan didn't retreat at his brother's call."

"He's deaf. Couldn't hear the command."

"I see. A shame." He let out a short sigh. "I lost a friend," he then said. "Sir Warren, of House Condor. He took a bolt in the neck."

"I'm sorry to hear that, Sir Mallister."

He raised his cup. "Join me in a toast to him."

Elyon obliged again, and was starting to see how drunken these occasions could become. During the larger battles in the great war, dozens of highborn knights could fall in a single day, he knew. At the Burning Rock, Elyon remembered, a full forty two Varin Knights alone had succumbed to blade and blaze - a devastating proportion of their remaining numbers at that point - and there were similar numbers dead among the Emerald Guards and

Suncoats, and the sundry other Bladeborn soldiers not affiliated with either order, sellswords and mercenaries and bastards and the like who'd joined the north in their war. Then there were the regular knights, those without Varin blood, who accounted for legions more. And the other men-at-arms, and the spearmen and axmen and bowmen and all the rest. You couldn't drink to them all, of course, but when a Varin Knight fell, those among the order who survived were honour-bound to toast them, talk of them, sing of them such as they could.

Elyon's grandfather Gideon had fallen at the Burning Rock, and so had King Storris, and they demanded most time of all when it came to the stories and songs. *What of the rest?* he'd often wondered. With those two leading luminaries to toast, many Varin Knights would have been given short shrift or forgotten entirely. Did they sit in a less illustrious seat now, at Varin's eternal feast? Wouldn't it have been better for them to die at another battle, when everyone might remember to toast them?

Elyon had always been cynical of all that. Now he could only think of how fortunate Sir Warren Condor had been to fall today. And Sir Brendan too. And the other handful of knights who'd died. All would be honoured tonight, without having to share time with hosts and hosts of others. *Lucky them,* he thought. *How lucky to die today, with so many of us to toast them.* But he said none of that, of course, because there were few who shared his views and Sir Mallister wasn't likely to be one of them. "To Sir Warren," is all he said, raising his cup. "May he find his way to the Eternal Halls."

"The Hall of Green," Sir Mallister added, clinking. "Let him meet his father William there upon the grasses. And all those who came before." It was where the Emerald Guards went at death, it was said, though it was nothing like Varin's Table. Elyon had heard it described as a garden rather than a hall, a beautiful garden between lakes and mountains, a place for reflection not merriment, in the manner of Ilith. It was one thing the Lukars and their allies lost when they conquered Tukor; the chance to join in Varin's feast. The Hall of Green was no equivalent.

"I hear my sister plans to come here to Rasalan soon," Sir

Mallister said, once they'd finished their drinks, and a server came hustling over to refill them. "I received a crow from her this morning, though she didn't say exactly why. I imagine Princess Amilia has grown tired of Ilithor already and seeks to join her father and brothers here in camp. Melany will be with her, of course. Perhaps you might further your courtship, if so?"

Elyon liked Sir Mallister's sense of chivalry. They'd brawled over Melany's honour when they'd first met, and now here he was, trying to make her honest. "Well I'm...I'm not sure, Sir Mallister," he said. "Mel and my coupling was always intended to be short - or not intended at all, if I'm being honest with you - and I'm not entirely certain..."

"Say no more," Sir Mallister cut in. "Of course, you're heir to House Daecar now. Too lofty for us Monsorts. It was improper of me to suggest it." There was no spite in his voice, just a firm grasp of how things were. "We are growing wealthy, however, if that might make a difference," he then added. "My father continues to prosper in his mining operations and I am rising through the ranks in the Emerald Guard too; I would seek to become captain in the coming years. In time our house may become a great one. And a match with House Daecar would greatly..." He gave a wry smile and cut himself off. "I'm overstepping," he acknowledged. "Forgive me. I shall leave it to your good graces to determine your course. You and your lord father."

Elyon nodded, courteous. "Did she say when she might be leaving?" he enquired.

"She didn't, I'm afraid. Her message was quite vague on that account, really, so I might be wrong. She wanted to tell me of our father most of all, and his recent successes, but added that she might be upon Rasal soil soon. I'll admit I inferred the rest. I shall return her crow and seek clarity."

"Please keep me informed, Sir Mallister. It would warm me to see her again, even if only as friends."

They parted at that, doing so with a cordial grip of the forearm, before Elyon returned to his table with a soft hopeful smile on his lips. He didn't have any intention of resuming his relationship with Melany, yet still the thought of her stirred feelings in him he'd tried to ignore. *And failed,* he realised, *because I love her still. That hasn't changed, no matter how much I might want it to.* The others were in conversation as he retook his perch beside Lord Kanabar, though Vesryn - sitting opposite him - broke away as he sat down. "You seem pleased about something," he saw, as Elyon gestured for a server to fill his tankard. "What did Sir Mallister want?"

"Nothing to concern you, Uncle." Elyon watched the boy give his tankard a generous complement of ale, nodded his thanks, and then drained a good portion of it. The longhouse was growing louder now, a song breaking out down the hall. Men were standing before the band, arms over shoulders, swaying and drinking and crooning a tune.

"Well then it must be Lady Melany," Vesryn identified, not looking so festive. "Else you'd not be so defensive."

"Melany and I are over." He looked his uncle in the eye. "I thought that had become clear on our travels from Varinar."

"It was. Until you climbed back into her bed in Eastwatch," Vesryn returned with a disapproving look. "Yes, I know about that. Rikkard shouldn't encourage you into relations that have no future. I warned you of that before, Elyon."

"Yes I know. You said one thing. Rikkard said another. But either way it matters not. I'm my own man and will do as I please."

He swigged his ale, as Lord Kanabar gave out a barking laugh, turning from the others. "The boy's got some gumption it seems," he said, giving Elyon a hearty slap on the back. "Good on you, Elyon. Keep that up and you'll lead your house well one day, and plenty enough to do your lord father proud. Who knows, perhaps you'll follow in his stead and become First Blade too. What do you say, Vesryn? Do you think the boy would fit the role?"

"A question you needn't ask, Wallis. Elyon would excel in it, I'm sure."

"Well let's see, shall we?" Lord Kanabar placed his cup down with a thump and looked right across at the Sword of Varinar. He seemed in jolly mood now, having massacred a full dozen ales.

"Let's see if you can lift it, Elyon. If you can heave it to your shoulder then I'll..."

"Name your firstborn after me?" Elyon said with a keen smile. "I think it's too late for that, my lord."

"A sharp tongue I see. I'd heard you had one." Kanabar's bush of a beard shuddered as he laughed. Elyon half expected to see birds fly out of it. "Now come on, stand up and take ahold of it. I've got a few granddaughters running about. And pretty ones too if you're wondering. Lift it, and maybe I'll give you one of those."

Elyon looked at the blade and stood in preparation. There was enough ale in his blood by now to see him rise to a challenge, though Vesryn didn't look best pleased about it. "Sit down, Elyon," he said, with a weary note of displeasure. "The Sword of Varinar is not a toy."

"Worried he'll bear it better than you, Vesryn?" teased Kanabar, all ruddy cheeked from the mead and growing heat within the hall. "Come on, there's no harm in it. Elyon, take it up. Let's see how..."

"I said no." Vesryn's voice was curt and loud enough for several people nearby to look over. He set a stiff stare on Lord Kanabar. "Maybe Elyon will get his chance one day, but until that time comes he's not to touch it...and nor is anyone else but me."

Kanabar eyed him with a quiet concern. "Careful now, Vesryn," he cautioned in a low voice. "You know what sort of power a Blade of Vandar holds." He glanced at the sword, propped grandly to Vesryn's side. From the top of the gilded scabbard a golden mist was rising, swirling about the ornate two-handed hilt. "Do you hear *his* whispers yet, I wonder? Do you imagine the blade speaking to you, son?"

Vesryn waved it off. "Of course not. I've held it barely more than a month."

"Then what is the trouble exactly?" the Lord of the Riverlands challenged, sharpening. "Your father Gideon let me try to lift it once or twice when he possessed it, you know. And I imagine Amron did the same with Lythian and Borrus and the like. And you?" He looked at Vesryn. "Are you to tell me Amron never let you try to lift it, just for fun, when you were younger men?" He didn't let Vesryn answer. "Rufus Taynar even made a game of it when he was First Blade four centuries past. He'd line up every knight in the mead hall and challenge them to lift the blade off the ground. The man who raised it highest, or held it longest, or carried it furthest would be rewarded, the legends say. Sir Percival Mantor even found himself a wife by winning one such contest. Rufus gave him a young niece of his, it's said, and a prize beauty too."

"I know the legends and don't need a sermon from you, Wallis," Vesryn cut in. "And no, Amron never let me hold it, nor anyone else as far as I know."

"Be that as it may." Kanabar took a gulp of his ale. "I see the way you look at it, and it worries me. You'll lose yourself to it if you're not careful."

"I understand intimately how seductive a Blade of Vandar can be," the First Blade dismissed. "My father and grandfather held the Sword of Varinar for many years and my brother the same. None fell to the blade, and I won't either. I am a Daecar lest you forget."

"Yes you are, a Daecar in blood and bone, but the strength of they alone won't save you. You doubt yourself, Vesryn, and doubt is dangerous. We only have to look at this Ghost of the Shadowfort for that..."

"Do not compare me to that man." A darkness came upon Vesryn's face as he barked out the words. "He is nothing like me, Wallis...nothing. I'll not have you suggest otherwise."

"Then why do you react with such venom?" Men were starting to quieten in their conversations to watch. Down the table, Fullerton and Shorton and Lancel and Barnibus had all gone silent. "You doubt your right to hold the blade," Lord Kanabar said. "You never took it by merit, Vesryn, and I can see it weighs heavy on you. That doubt...it makes you more vulnerable to its lure. We've seen it before, when men have disputed possession of it. You mustn't let that gnaw at you, son. For your sake, and ours, you mustn't."

"I won't." Vesryn was resolute, and by the look in his eye he'd reached the end of his tolerance for the subject. He shook his head and blew out a sigh. "I thought I had your support, Wallis. Gods know I've not got it within the ranks of my own order. I hear the snickers and snide remarks, don't think I don't." He swung his eyes out to a number of Varin Knights, watching and whispering beyond them. Those loyal to House Taynar and House Oloran continued to dispute Vesryn's claim, and though he might have sent them off south he'd kept them close instead. It had seemed wise at the time, but Elyon was starting to see different. Vesryn could have kept Rikkard here instead of Sir Dalton, and Killian to keep the Oloran clan in order, rather than his cousin Sir Brontus, but he didn't. He'd been brave and perhaps a little foolish. And now the pressure was starting to tell.

"You have my support Vesryn," Lord Kanabar assured him. "You know you do."

"Do I? And yet you rile and rankle, the very day I stabbed a man in the back, and the son of a friend no less. It wounds me to have done so. I dishonoured Sir Brendan and I dishonoured myself. That is what weighs heavy on me, Wallis, not the lure of this bloody blade."

Those were the last words he spoke. He gave a grunt, finished his drink, and then stood and marched away, snatching up the Sword of Varinar as he went. It was inadvisable, perhaps, with his dissenters watching on, though he didn't seem to care, shoving past a few of them as he pressed through the hall.

"Uncle..." Elyon stood to follow without hesitation, ignoring the suggestion of Lord Kanabar to do otherwise. "Uncle, wait..."

He made it only a few short paces into the crowd before a voice smooth as silk stopped him in his tracks. "It seems your uncle needs some time alone, Sir Elyon." A woman stepped before him, blocking his path. The woman he'd seen earlier. "I'd let him go, if I were you. You've been drinking, as has he. Best let things simmer down, wouldn't you say?"

He took pause as he looked at her, standing out like a rose amid thorns among the tall jostling knights around them. "You...know my uncle?" he asked her, as she stood there in a fine jade tunic and cloak, quite fetching against her styled chestnut hair.

"Sir Vesryn? Oh yes, from a long time ago. Though I'm not sure he remembers me."

Elyon looked past her, as Vesryn continued out into the night,. "I really think I should..."

"Join me for a drink? Oh, I wholeheartedly agree." She moved in and at once her arm was coiling around his, and with a short tug she turned him, drawing him away from the Vandarian contingent and toward a quieter part of the hall. "I knew your father too," she went on as they walked. "Though like your uncle I doubt he remembers me. It was so long ago, back during the war. I spent time in camp, and it seems not much has changed." She laughed heartily, a charming sound, and waved for a server boy to come over. "I have a fondness for whiskey. Do you, Sir Elyon?"

"I...well yes, from time to time."

"More than time to time, as far as I hear." She grinned in a disarming sort of way and gave a brisk order to the server boy, who hustled off to fetch their drinks. "You're quite the charmer, I'm told, sir. The social circuit in Varinar just isn't the same without you present, they say."

"I'm not sure about that anymore, my lady. But even if I'm considered a charmer, I'm clearly not a gentleman to have not yet asked your name?"

"Lady Cecilia Blakewood."

He took her hand and kissed it, bowing and setting forward his right leg.

"Well there you are, gentlemanly duties complete," she said. "Now put them aside, young man. I sense you're far more fun without them."

He nodded though was starting to wonder how to extricate himself from her attentions. Beautiful though she was, she was old enough to be his mother and with all this ale in his blood...well, he didn't want to wake in the morning with another throbbing regret. "I really ought to check on my uncle, Lady Cecilia," he said. "One drink and then..."

Her laughter broke him off. "Fear not, dear boy, I'm not trying to seduce you. No no, dashing though you are I think you're a little too young for me. I've had my sample of Daecar before and don't need another."

He was about to ask her who when the server boy bustled back over with two short cups of whiskey in hand. Lady Cecilia was quick to take them off him. "Bring another," she said. "One cup won't do."

"Really, I should only have the one," Elyon said. "I've had plenty of mead as it is, my lady..."

"Nonsense." She thrust the cup into his hands. "Drink."

For whatever reason, he did as she bid him, in part because he did rather enjoy a good whiskey, and more than that, he could hardly say no. She was probably right in that Vesryn needed time to himself, and besides, he'd been intrigued by this woman for some days and now had her all to himself. Feeling a little more loose tongued, he decided to enquire further into her knowledge of the Daecars. "You said you'd sampled a Daecar before," he said, as a warm wash came over him from the strength of the whiskey. It had a curious taste too. He gave a little cough to clear his throat. "Who, if you don't mind my asking?"

"Why would I mind?" She gave another waggish little grin. "It was your first cousin, once removed." She thought for a moment. "Well I think I'm getting that right. I'll not pretend to be an expert in the Daecar family tree."

Elyon was thinking too, though one candidate seemed most likely. "Sir Gereth?" he asked her.

"Yes, that one," she said. "Though it was before his leg went lame, of course, and nothing but a short dalliance. I hear he commands from Blackfrost now in your father's stead?"

"He has for as long as I can remember," Elyon said. He was fond of Sir Gereth, a wise and unassuming man, and once fine knight before his crippling. "My father is likely with him now. He has travelled to Blackfrost to muster our lands."

"Yes, I've heard." She turned as the boy came back over. "Wonderful. Bring another."

"No. No really, I shouldn't..."

"Just one more." She handed him his second drink, and dolt that he was, he threw it back in time with her. "Come, Sir Elyon, let yourself relax. Your uncle will wait till morning. There are pleasures to be had tonight, should you let yourself have them. We have many pleasures here."

The room was beginning to swim, as her comely face blurred before him. He blinked. She looked younger all of a sudden, more inviting. *A trick,* came a short thought, though it was dulled half a heartbeat later, then gone. Then he thought, *No, just the whiskey. That is all this is.*

"I hear you're broken-hearted." He looked at her again, at the sympathy in her pale green eyes. She pressed forward and her scent wafted up his nose. A warm, alluring aroma. "You needn't suffer, sweet boy. We have ways of taking that pain away." *Pain,* Elyon thought. *Melany*. He felt a longing for her, stronger than before. *But she's coming here?* He smiled and there was another cup in his hand. "Drink," the woman said. "Drink, and she'll be with you."

"She?" he managed to whisper, confused. The longhouse was a writhing swirl of colours and motion now, but Lady Cecilia stood before him, still and smiling. "Who?"

"Whoever you most desire, Sir Elyon. Who is it you most desire?"

"Melany," he whispered. He could think of nothing else now but her. "Melany. I...I miss her."

"You needn't. She's right here."

"Here?" He looked around, trying to compose himself, but his thoughts were a fog, and his eyes were a blur. "Where?"

He felt her arm around his once more. "Come with me. I'll take you to her."

He had a vague recollection of Sir Mallister saying she was coming. *But when was that? Was she already here?* He felt a flutter as he stepped out into the bracing cold. *But...we're finished. We were never meant to be. We can't...*

"Melany will take all your pain away, Sir Elyon. Just lie down and she'll take it away. You needn't do anything else."

The cold didn't wake him, nor the wind nor the falling snow. Out across the camp he walked, until he could remember nothing more.

24

Saska

Saska was woken with a whisper. "Tilda, wake up. Tilda, it's time." She opened her eyes, and saw Lady Cecilia before her. It took her a moment to realise that she was still in her chair, having nodded off during her vigil. Out through the camp, the sounds of the festivities still swelled from the longhouse, the drums thudding, pipes wailing, men calling and shouting and singing. Steam poured from within, from the bodies and braziers, clouding in the frigid night air. "My lady?" Saska croaked, shifting up. "I...I must have fallen asleep."

"In this chair? You know I don't like it when you rearrange the furnishings, Tilda." Saska could smell the faint scent of whiskey on her breath. "Why did you put this chair here?"

Saska looked around. "I just...wanted to watch," she admitted. Cecilia turned to see that the main entrance to the longhouse could be seen from where they were. "I like to look at the knights and lords, my lady."

"You're worried Sir Griffin might come?" Cecilia deduced, ignoring Saska's explanation. "I understand, child, but you needn't worry about that anymore. Stand up now. How is your breath?"

Saska was still shaking the fog away as she stood. "My...breath, my lady?"

Cecilia sniffed the air around her mouth. "Hmmm, a tad stale." She stepped over to the table and poured a large glass of rich red wine, infused with flavoursome spices. "Drink this. It'll freshen your breath and relax you." She handed it over. "Come, drink it up." As Saska was doing so Cecilia looked her up and down in appraisal. "No, that won't do. Let's get you into something prettier, shall we?"

Saska sipped on her spiced wine and watched. Her eyes had grown hooded, a drum beating hard at her chest. "Where am I going, Lady Cecilia?" She feared she knew the answer, but liked to play dumb as Tilda. "It is late, and I am tired. Should I not get to my bed?"

Cecilia ignored her questions. "Take off your clothes."

Saska felt a tightening strain of panic. *It's happening,* she thought, glancing out through the tent flaps. *She's here to give away my maidenhead...to some drunken knight from the feast.* As Cecilia rifled through the trunk of garments, Saska felt her eyes pulled to the blade hidden beneath the lady's cloak. She took a determined pace toward her, ready to take it and cut her throat and run, but just as she did Cecilia turned with a shimmering blue dress to hand, lace and scanty. "This is perfect. He'll like it, I think." She smiled. "Put it on, Tilda, and no arguments. It's time you became a woman."

Saska stood her ground a moment.

"Tilda. Come now, don't make me tell you again."

"But I...I'm tired. I...I don't want..."

"You don't know what you want, silly girl," laughed Cecilia. "Now remove your clothes and put on this dress. I will not ask you again."

Saska had little choice. She started slipping out of her clothes, trying to think logically. *He'll be Bladeborn,* she thought, *and will have a godsteel dagger nearby. If I have to, I can take it...take it and kill him and flee...* The thought made her feel a little better. It was late now, and with much of the siege camp romping and roistering escaping mightn't be so difficult. *The defences are weaker to the south,* she knew. She'd seen that when they arrived that day. *I could escape there, out into the moors, and find my way to Harrowmoor. Maybe Marian's there now, to help organise the fort's defence?* But thinking of her mentor set only a cold hard feeling of defeat inside her. *Can I return having failed in my task? After she saved my life twice...can I let her down like that?*

The questions swirled as she removed her clothing and pulled on the light lace dress. All the while, Cecilia watched with an approving twist to her lips, admiring Saska's svelte young form. "Beautiful." She pressed her hands to her chest, purring. "What a vision you are, child. Now don't look so worried. I know the first time can be scary, but you'll soon see there was nothing to fear."

Saska's skin was prickly, every hair standing on end. She drew long slow breaths to compose herself as Cecilia moved to fetch her cloak from the support pole on which it hung, and draped it over her shoulders. "It's cold outside, but the walk isn't far. Just over yonder, among the Vandarian tents."

Vandarian...Saska had expected to be handed to a Tukoran man. "Who...who is it?" her voice quivered, as they stepped out into the cold dark night. "One of the Varin Knights?"

"Elyon Daecar," she replied, offhand. "He's had a drink or two so may seem a little dazed, but I'm told he is a fine lover, and gentle with the women he beds. The Daecars have always been as such. His father was the same."

Saska didn't press her on it, but the news was welcome. Being led to the tent of some unknown man was what scared her most, but Elyon Daecar...she knew the name and had even seen the young knight once or twice. The first had been in Lord Kastor's tent when the Vandarians arrived to join them some three days gone. As with his uncle Vesryn and the red-bearded Lord Kanabar, Elyon had shown a firm dislike for finding Saska there, with her cheek raw from Sir Griffin's palm. *And that girl...they'd seen her marched through camp as they arrived,* she recalled, *and hadn't much liked that either.* She wondered if Elyon Daecar might remember her. He didn't seem the sort to want to take a frightened servant girl to his bed.

"What if he doesn't like me?" is all she asked. "Sir Elyon. He...he has seen me in camp, I think. He might think me a servant. He may not like southern girls."

"Oh you don't have to worry about that, Tilda. Elyon will see what he wants to see. And your name is Melany tonight, not Tilda, understand? Melany."

Saska didn't understand. Cecilia was making little sense. "My lady?"

"Don't ask any more questions, child. Sir Elyon will take you atop him, I assure you. All you need to do is climb on, and he will do the rest."

They crunched over the freezing snow, as flakes glittered down about them, moving some way from the longhouse. The noise was not abating, nor was it likely to for a while. *A cloak should I need to escape,* she thought. But she hadn't imagined it would be Elyon Daecar she'd be sent to. She could slice the throat of a Kastor man, but the heir to House Daecar? Then she had another thought, one that fit well with her purpose here. *She hopes he'll put a child in me,* she realised, sparing a quick glance at Lady Cecilia. *A child with Daecar blood.* It was richer than all the other great houses, some people said. First Balion, then Gideon, then Amron Daecar had been First Blade. *And Aleron had been expected to follow before his untimely death.* She knew that too. *And now Vesryn holds the berth. And Elyon, he's just as gifted, they say...*

She walked on in thought, but didn't expose them to Lady Cecilia. She'd remained insistent that a noble knight awaited Saska in Ilithor, but perhaps that wasn't the case. *But whether he's here to break me in, or give me his seed matters not,* she concluded. *It all amounts to the same thing in the end...*

Within moments the blue Vandarian pavilions were coming into view, arrayed in a neat arrangement nearby. It was quiet, though inside the tents the braziers were burning, and for a second Saska thought she spotted Vesryn Daecar sitting solitary in his own quarters, stroking the Sword of Varinar as it lay atop his lap. But it was a glimpse and no more, as a second later they passed toward another of the central tents, and Cecilia pressed toward the flaps. "There's wine inside, Tilda," she told her. "If it'll help loosen you, do partake. But...not him. It may cause an imbalance." She reached in and pulled the flap aside, her words continuing to confound her charge. *Imbalance? What is she talking about?* Saska had no further time to consider it as they stepped within, and Cecilia called out, "Sir Elyon. I've found her, your beloved Melany. She was wandering the camp, taking in the view of Harrowmoor. Come along, Melany." She gave Saska a brisk glance. "Your noble knight awaits you."

In they went, out of the stinging cold, as Elyon Daecar's large private pavilion spread out before them. It had a decking and a desk and a table and chairs, and to one side was his bed, plenty large enough for two, set upon a rich brown rug. Elyon Daecar lay atop it, dressed only in a pair of short breeks to cover his modesty. The rest of him was exposed. That chest, curved and carved and muscular, and sprinkled with black twisting hair; his arms, thick as pythons, and legs three times their size.

"Sir Elyon?" Lady Cecilia stepped toward him, though at a glance he looked unconscious, lying spreadeagled on the mattress with his head rolled sideways. "Gods, he's asleep. Sir Elyon!" She spat out an irritated breath and stamped forward to give him a shake. "Sir Elyon, wake up. I have Melany here for you. Sir Elyon!"

He groaned and his eyes flickered open, taking her in. "M-Melany," he said in a thick slurry voice. "Mel..."

Cecilia clipped her fingers for Saska to approach. "She's right here. I found her wandering outside." She turned to Saska. "Cloak. Off," she hissed. "Now."

Saska removed the garment and laid it on the back of a chair. A cool air swum in through the part-open flaps, chilling her, as Elyon Daecar frowned and stared through the blur atop his eyes. "M-Mel...is...is that you?" he said. His words were heavy and plodding, as Cecilia gave him another shake. He turned to look up at the older woman. "Mel?"

"No, not me. For goodness sake." She released his dense meaty arm and stood up straight, then turned and marched across the room. "Stay there," she told Saska. "He'll come around soon enough." She set about preparing some tonic to revive him as Saska quietly observed the young man. *Would it be so bad?* came a thought she'd not expected. She'd never seen a man shaped like him before, and certainly not like this, lying atop those furs and blankets with nought but a thin piece of linen across his groin. It hid his manhood well enough, though not perfectly, and Saska found herself more curious than she'd anticipated. *He thinks I'm this Melany,* she thought. *A girl he knows...maybe one he loves? So it wouldn't be me, would it? I could be her, for just tonight, couldn't I?*

As Cecilia marched back past her, so the notion soured and fled. She broke from her temporary trance and her thoughts closed back in. *No. I must find a way to avoid this.* Finding him sleeping was fortuitous, but she needed a little more luck. Cecilia tipped the tonic down his throat and turned, as Elyon spluttered and coughed and settled again. "It'll take effect in ten or fifteen minutes. Maybe a little more, given his size. Take the time to get used to him." She stepped closer. "Explore him, Tilda," she whispered. "You'll not find a better match, believe me. Think yourself lucky for this chance."

"I...I do, my lady."

She allowed a smile, and even took her into a hug. "I'll return at first light," she said soft in her ear. "You'll be naked in his bed, won't you? If I see otherwise, I'll consider it a betrayal. I'll know, believe me." And then came the cold threat to finish. "Fail me, and your next match won't be so kind."

She left the tent with that, as Saska pulled the flaps tight, latching them fast behind the king's bastard of a daughter. An anger boiled in her sudden and fierce. "Bitch," she hissed, snarling, as she watched Lady Cecilia saunter away through the snow. "My virtue isn't yours to give out." She turned and looked back to make sure that Elyon was still locked in his delirium, before checking his tent for weapons fast as she could. A swift sweep of the pavilion unveiled none, though there was a large trunk set aside, chained and locked, where she suspected his blades and armour would be. In a way she was glad for it. Finding a godsteel dagger now might have her running for the hills. *But how can I? How can I let Marian down like that? To run from my duty like a coward, when all I'm being asked to do is bed this boy...*

She turned again to look at him, hovering over his bed. He was groaning occasionally, though his eyes remained closed, tossing and shifting on the bed. Whatever tonic she'd given him looked to be working. In one moment, his glazed eyes peeled open again and he looked at her, frowning. "Mel?" he asked through a tight ragged voice. "Mel, is that...is that..."

"Sleep." Saska moved forward, not sure what else to do. "Sleep, Sir Elyon. Just relax."

He settled with those words, though only for a moment, mumbling to himself as he tried to get comfortable. Out through the camp, other noises filled the night air. She could hear them singing for their prince in the feast hall now, a clamouring chorus of Rylian the Brave. It was a song for the Prince of Tukor's heroics in the war, and in particular at the Battle of Burning Rock, where he'd slain a dragon and gravely injured another. Of course, Amron Daecar had killed Vallath and crippled Dulian that same fateful day, earning a number of monikers for his trouble, and now she could hear his own famed tune crooning out in competition, bellowed from the Vandarians. *The Echo of Titans,* she thought, listening. She'd always liked that one. *And now here I am with his son. What an odd twist of fate that is...*

"Melany..." The young Daecar croaked again, as Saska looked out through the flaps. She ignored him a moment, hoping he'd settle. "Mel...I was told...is that...is that you?" She turned. He was propped up now on his elbow, blinking at her. "I...where am I?" He looked around, a fraction more lucid. "Who...who are you?"

"I'm Melany," she said, in an awkward voice.

"Melany," he whispered. "Come...come here. Let me..."

"Wine?" she asked, cutting him off. "Would you like some wine, Sir Elyon?" Cecilia had told her not to feed him any, so that's exactly what she'd do. She stepped to the table of drinks. *Please go back to sleep. I need more time to think...*

"I...your brother...he said...he said you'd come." She found him smiling when she turned, a winsome look on his face. "When...when did you get here?"

"I've...always been here." She had no idea what else to say. "Here." She stepped over. "Drink this. It'll help."

He took it, rubbing his eyes as he sat up, his toned torso straining and twisting above his breeks. One sip had him spluttering all over again. "This...this is *wine*?"

"Of course. Just drink it."

His eyes continued to flutter a great deal as he forced the concoction down his neck. It was more whiskey than wine, though he didn't need to know that, and she'd added in some brandy and rum and vinegar too. *He'll see what he wants to see,* Cecilia had told her. *If I can pass as this Melany then perhaps whiskey can pass as wine...*

He almost brought it back up a couple of times, though with some coaxing from Saska, gulped it all down. "I'll take that, Elyon," she said once he was done, reaching out and taking the goblet off him. "Would you like some more?" She took a pace away, as he watched her with a puzzled expression.

"I...no I...I don't think so." He looked queasy, as he slid back down onto the bed. "What...what time is it?"

"Late," she told him. "You really ought to be sleeping."

She retreated further, waiting for the cocktail to kick in. With luck it would counter whatever Cecilia had given him, and knock him back out. *Unbalance him,* she'd said. First light was a few hours off. *I'll have to strip and climb in bed with him when she comes and hope the ruse passes muster.* It was a long shot, but what else did she have? *Go through with it,* was all she could think. She turned and looked at him, a rippling mass of muscle on the bed, a rain of lustrous black hair flung about on his head. She lost half a breath at the sight. *Would it be so bad?*

"I...like your dress." His smile was a little languid and lazy, though sweet all the same. "Come...come a bit closer, will you. I can hardly see you over there." He rubbed his eyes again, as she continued her retreat to the counter. "Where are you going?"

"We're celebrating, Elyon. The entire camp is celebrating. It calls for another drink, doesn't it?" *Damn you, sleep! How much alcohol can you take?*

"Celebrating what?" He looked around for the hundredth time, still gathering his bearings. "Have we taken the fort?" He gave a hissing sound. "How many did we kill? How many good men fell?" She turned and found him cringing on the bed, gripping feebly at the blankets. "Tell me at least that Kastor's dead. Tell me that, Mel."

Saska paused, as Elyon huffed and snarled, legs stretched out before him, arms hanging limp to his sides. He looked half paralysed, though through all that, his deep dislike for Cedrik Kastor came through. She kept her eyes on him, curious. "He's...still alive, I'm afraid," she told him. "But...maybe he won't be for long."

She watched and watched close, as he gave a brisk nod to those words. "Sooner the better," he said. "Wallis...Wallis says he should slip in his own piss and crack his head on a hearth like his father...would be just, but...but what justice is there in this world?" His head shook side to side, swaying, his eyes down between his outstretched legs. "Aleron should be alive...and...and Lythian too. I should...I should have known. I could have stopped it. My brother. I should have stopped him. I should have done more..."

He was rambling now, though far from falling back to sleep he seemed to be coming around. He smashed a fist into the bed, then looked about once more. His eyes blinked, though only once or twice, as he looked across the room at her. And for a good long while he stared, with a track of ruts on his brow, before his expression soiled and his eyes narrowed and asked her again, "Who are you?"

When she replied, "Melany," she felt even more awkward and idiotic than before. She could see it wouldn't work anymore. That noxious brew had countered the tonic, sure, but not in the way she'd hoped. Whatever potion Cecilia had given him was fading now, and fast. An accusing look flushed on his face. "You're not Melany," he said. The veil upon his eyes was melting away, like a morning mist under a hot summer sun. And through that mist he saw her. He saw her for who she was. "That servant girl," he said. "You...you were in Kastor's tent. You..." He looked aside, as a memory came to him. "You were in my dreams. That night we came to camp, I...I saw you in my sleep..."

Saska frowned at that, though said not a word. He still seemed part delirious.

"I saw you," he was going on, whispering to himself. "You were wearing that lace dress. The green one. It faded to mist and...and you faded to light. Silver and blue." He looked up and asked again, though softy now, "Who are you?"

"I'm no one."

His eyes weren't blinking so much anymore. He looked groggy, a little intoxicated perhaps, but the enchantment had withered away. "You are," he said. "You're...you're someone." He leaned forward on the bed. "Who?"

"A prisoner." She'd not expected to say that word, but out it came anyway, bursting through her lips. Elyon Daecar frowned. "A breeder," she then added, deciding to take a chance. "That's what they want of me. They want a child from you, Elyon. At least...I think they do..."

He stared. For a full long minute he stared, and behind his eyes something was turning, something was falling into place. "That's how they did it," he said after an age. "My father...they...they must have tricked him. Sent a breeder to take his seed...just as they've sent me you." He looked aside again in private thought, and blinked slow and hard to clear his mind. "Water," he said then. "Please...water."

Saska turned and fumbled about at the counter, wondering whether to hand him another cocktail instead, but that ship had sailed. She took a few slow breaths and then brought him a jug and fresh goblet. "Here." Then she fled back across the tent, keen to stay near the exit, as he poured himself a cup, and another, and another, gulping each down in turn.

His eyes were a great deal clearer once he was done. He regarded her once more, though remained on the bed. She saw no threat in him, no reason for fear. "You...work for that woman?" he then asked. "Lady...lady..."

"Cecilia," she told him, and saw that he remembered the name.

"She brought you here?"

Saska nodded. "Told me my name was to be Melany tonight. I suppose she must have given you a potion of some kind, at the feast, to make you believe it."

His brows hung low over his silvery blue eyes. "Whiskey," he whispered. "She gave me...whiskey."

"Must have poisoned it, or maybe it wasn't whiskey at all?" Saska watched him, wondering how much of this he'd remember come morning. "She said you'd see what you wanted. That you'd think I was this Melany."

He looked at her in befuddlement. "But...you look nothing like her. She's blonde and pale and has blue eyes. But you..." He rubbed his eyes once more. "Where...where are you from?"

"Aramatia," she said.

"But your accent..."

And then it dawned on her. *Shit,* she thought. In the rush of it she'd given up on using her Aramatian lilt. "I..." She couldn't think of an explanation, not on the spot. "I..."

"You spoke differently before," Elyon went on, searching through the waning fog in his head, looking intently at her face with his deep set eyes. "When we found you in Kastor's tent...when we first arrived...you had an accent. A southern one. But now...you sound Tukoran." There was a spreading confusion on his face. "Who are you?" he asked her again, shifting as though trying to stand. "What are you doing here really?"

She flung her eyes at the tent-flaps, wondering whether she might make a dash for it, godsteel or no. But something kept her where she was, something in Elyon Daecar's eyes. She studied them and somehow she knew. *I can trust him,* she saw. *I can trust this man to keep my secret.* So she stepped forward, moving closer to him, as he watched half-naked from the bed. She kept on coming, closer and closer still, until she was perched close enough for her whisper to be heard.

"I'm not who they think I am," she told him, so quiet he had to lean forward. "They think I'm from Aramatia, but that isn't true. I was born there - at least I think I was - but raised in Tukor a servant. That's been my life from the cradle. And the worst of those years were spent in Keep Kastor."

She paused and observed his reaction, but he gave no reaction at all. All he did was nod and say, "Go on," and so she did.

"I heard the hate in your voice, when you spoke of Lord Kastor. Believe me, I know all about that. You've heard of how he treats his southern slaves? I was one of them." In a sudden move she was standing and turning and pulling the lace straps from her shoulders. She let the dress drop to her waist, holding her arms across her breasts, as the scars of Lord Kastor's whip were unveiled before his eyes.

"Lord Modrik did this," she said, looking over her shoulder, "when I was only a child. But I was one of the lucky ones. Others suffered worse than me. Many aren't alive to tell of it." She began pulling the dress up, setting it back into place, and turned. There was a cold dull horror on his face. "I was sent here to put that right, Sir Elyon. I'm no breeder, but a killer come for Kastor." It sounded more impressive than it was, but on she went anyway. "I've come for him, for myself as much as anything. And I can see you wish him dead too - you said it yourself only minutes ago." She moved forward again. "I'm not asking you to help me. I'm just...I'm asking you not to interfere. Not to give me away." She looked to the flaps. "Lady Cecilia will return at first light. She wants me naked in your bed and that's all I need from you. Just tell her you took me atop you. Tell her Melany gave you a good night. Honestly, tell her anything. Just please, don't give me up."

As she looked into his eyes, she felt no fear, no stress, no creeping apprehension. All she saw was a man who understood. A kind man who was as his father born; as noble and highborn as they came, but a champion of the commonfolk all the same. The Daecars were known for it. And Elyon's mother had been too. *Kessia Amadar,* she remembered. As a young child, when Saska spent her days chopping onions and carrots and potatoes down in the kitchens of Lord Caldlow's estate, she'd heard all about Lady Kessia. The kitchen wenches and scullery maids would gush and swoon over her all the time, telling of her beauty, her kindness, her charity. But she remembered the day they learned of her death most of all, when that rider had charged into town cawing of her death on the birthing table. Even there at the heart of Tukor, a thousand miles from Varinar, the women wailed and wept and prayed and lit candles for her passing. It had stayed solemn for some weeks after, as though a cold shadow had fallen across all the world, sucking some joy from it such that it would never be the same again. Amron Daecar might have been the Hero of the North, but Kessia Amadar was its heart, its darling. And here before her sat the product of the two of them. A man, she saw, who'd not betray her. A man whom she could trust.

Elyon Daecar reached out and took her hands into his. They

were large and strong and more rough than she'd expected. He gave her a look, firm and bracing and from his lips came a promise. "I'll say nothing of what you've told me," he said. "And I'll help you where I can."

Warm tears crawled out of her eyes at that. She couldn't help it. Day on day she'd waited and watched and wondered what would happen next. She'd sat in cold counsel with herself, doubting herself, hating herself, wishing she wasn't here. But sat before her she had an ally, born of a place she'd never expected. *I'm not alone anymore,* she thought, and so her tears came hotter and stronger still, rolling down her cheeks...and before she knew it she was in his arms, those strong muscular arms, and his heart was beating through her. "What is your name?" he whispered.

"Saska," she said, sniffing. Then she laughed, a soft sobbing sound. "I'm sorry. I just, I haven't said my real name in a while. And I'm...I'm quite new to all this."

"I can tell." He drew back and smiled and turned his eyes around. Spotting his shirt, he lumbered over to fetch it, looking a little unsteady on his feet. "I can take it off again before dawn, if it'll help convince Lady Cecilia," he told her. "Just...for now, I...well it's more appropriate if I'm dressed."

"Of course," she croaked. "And...they know me as Tilda, I should say."

"Tilda." He nodded, securing the name to his mind. "Would you like a drink, to pass the time?" He gestured to the table. "What was that you gave me? Whiskey? I'm having a little trouble remembering." He scratched his head. "It's all a bit of a blur."

"I was hoping you'd pass out," she admitted. "I didn't expect it to counter the potion or wake you up. It was whiskey, mixed with wine...and a few other things. Mostly whiskey, if I'm being truthful."

"You've been plenty truthful, Saska. A little more than I expected, I'd say."

"And me." She giggled like a girl, like she hadn't done in years, wiping the warm tears from her cheeks. "I'll have some wine, if you're offering?"

"Of course." He retuned a moment later with a goblet, and

settled down beside her on the bed, though kept to water himself. Outside the festivities were still unfolding. If anything they were growing louder. "That'll go on for some time yet," he said. "The Tukorans love a feast. Though I suppose you know that."

"I've served at a few," she told him. "They often come to blows, I've seen."

He had a fond smile on his face. "I know. I got into a brawl myself, some months back, at one such occasion. It involved Melany, actually." A quizzical frown furrowed his brow. "Did I truly think you were her? I vaguely remember calling you by her name, which sounds ridiculous now."

"You did, a few times. And Cecilia too."

"Really?"

"Really." She nodded and took a little sip of wine. "Must have been a strong elixir. I learned a little about alchemy and witchcraft at the academy in Thalan, and can brew a few potions myself. I'm...I'm actually on one now."

"*On* one?" He frowned. "How so?

She pointed to her eyes. They were a warm hazel right now, an effect of the Rasal potion that Mistress Tufnell had taught her to brew back at the university. It would fade eventually, though not for some weeks yet, lest she take a tonic to counter it. "My eyes are blue normally," she explained. "And my skin, it's usually a bit lighter. I used lotions and ointments to darken it a bit, and my hair..." It was coal black now and cropped short. "It's actually brown, and long, to my chest. Lord Kastor, he knew me once. This is my disguise."

He looked fascinated, if a little drunk still, though given how much he'd been drinking that was no surprise. "The Rasals like their tricks," he said, with a smile. "But...you're Tukoran. I'm a little confused. Why are you..."

"Long story." She was thinking of all she'd been through. It would take all night to tell of it.

Elyon Daecar seemed to be thinking the same. "We have time, you know, if you're to stay here till dawn."

"I suppose that's true."

She thought for a long moment, then decided to give him the

broad strokes of it. *I've revealed so much,* she concluded. *Why not tell him a little more?* So she spoke of how she'd worked for the Kastors once, but managed to escape, and came to the care of Master Orryn in the shadow of the Hammersongs. How she'd been attacked only months past by Lord Quintan and killed him in defence and gone on the run. How she'd met Marian, and learned she was Bladeborn, and sailed to Thalan to be trained. How her task was to be taken into Kastor's warcamp, get him alone and slit his throat and be gone by the time anyone knew. That was the sum of it, and she said no more. Not of Lord Modrik's death, and how she'd caused it. Not of Ranulf's claims of her dubious heritage and links to the Aramatian Duchy. She told him only what she felt comfortable unveiling and all the while he listened quietly and said not a word in interruption.

Only when he identified that she was finished did he ask her a question she'd heard a thousand times before. "Do you know who your father is?" Outside, the revelry was pouring through the camp, as men left the feast hall and made for their tents, or lumbered drunken to the brothels to slake their thirst for flesh.

She shook her head. "Some lord in Ilithor, I'm told."

Elyon Daecar didn't look convinced. "Not a Vandarian?" he asked her.

In truth she wasn't sure, though the short details Ranulf had unearthed pointed to an Ilithoran lord being her father. "I don't think so. Why would you say that?"

"That dream I had," he said. "You...you faded to light. Silver and blue. They're the colours of my country." He shrugged. "It's just a thought."

Saska wasn't about to give credence to a dream, though it remained a possibility. "Maybe," she conceded. "I'm told he's from a powerful house, and I took to godsteel well when first tested. That's all I know for sure."

Elyon remained in private thought for a time, before emerging from his musings. "Does it enhance your senses?" he asked. "Your hearing and sight and touch?"

"All of them," she said. "I'm still training to improve them. Or was before I came here."

"Huh. That's...unusual." He looked to have a long list of questions labouring through his mind, which remained a little addled. "Is that why you were given this task? You seem a little inexperienced for it."

"I am. That's why I've gotten nowhere. I've been in camp nearly two weeks now and have met with Kastor just once. That time you saw you me in his tent, with Sir Griffin," she explained to his questioning look. "That was the only time."

"You were going to try to kill him then?" There was something approaching rebuke in his voice. "You'd never had gotten away with it, Saska. What were you thinking?"

"I wasn't. I was just..." She didn't really know what she was going to do. It had been desperation that drove her, not some neatly thought out plan. "Trying to get his attention, I guess."

"And you'd risk being abused and assaulted? Being..." He could barely say the word, though Saska knew just what he was thinking. *And might he think I've been raped already? No doubt he does, given the life I've endured.* "You shouldn't have to put your body on the line, not like that. No one should have asked that of you. No one."

Hearing it from another person put it into bitter context. She knew it herself and Marian had been doubtful in sending her away. But what other option was there? "I wasn't going to let him." She said it firm and tried to look determined. "I'd sooner put a dagger through my heart than let that man lay a hand on me."

"Yet someone did. On your cheek, at least. Was that Sir Griffin did that to you?" He saw the answer in her eyes, then stood, and began pacing. "I should have cut his neck clean through when I had the chance," he grunted to himself. "No doubt he's as cruel as his uncle..."

"He is," she said on a breath, thinking of all his monstrous deeds. "He took a woman's head when they found me. It was a village called Baymoor, on the Marshway River. He cut it clean off and that was that. And hung a boy, Mattius, too, at another village we passed. Strung him up in the trees and had his bowmen use him for practice. And others have suffered as badly at his hands. There's a kill order on him among the Suncoats, a price on his head. I've a mind to finish him myself as well if I get the chance."

"But you won't." He turned to look at her, a blue blaze in his eyes. "How would you? He or his uncle? Or any of the other rotten men in their family? You're a prisoner at the heart of an enemy warcamp, Saska. There's no way you can do this without help."

"Then help me." The air stilled. Outside, a few men were carousing through the Vandarian camp, singing as they went. "Get me alone with him, Elyon," she whispered. "That's all I need. Get me alone with him and I'll do the rest..."

He was shaking his head. "You won't. Do you have any idea what sort of man you're dealing with?"

"Of course I do." She was on her feet and marching across the tent toward him, looking up into his bright silver-blue eyes. "It was his father put these scars on my back, but Cedrik was witness to half of them. He sat and watched and laughed as I lay naked and bleeding and trying not to cry out. I was a child, Elyon, a child. Believe me, I know exactly who I'm dealing with."

He said nothing for a few moments, letting her calm, as the men's loud singing voices trailed off outside. "You've suffered, I can see that. And I want to help however I can, Saska." He moved his eyes to the flaps a moment. "You and all the other Rasal girls taken from their homes. Rylian has promised that all who wish it can leave. I believe him. He's a good man, and he'll right the wrongs that have been done here, such as he can. But Cedrik Kastor is a killer, quick and deadly as they come. You may want him dead...that may be your task...but whether I can get you alone with him or not doesn't matter...you'll not see it done. He'll see it coming and make you regret you ever drew breath." He took her narrow shoulders, pressing light but resolute against her soft bronze skin. "It doesn't have to be that way, Saska. I'll help you. I promise you I will. But only to escape this place, nothing more. I'll not let you die for that man."

"Then kill him yourself," she bit back at him. "Cut him down during the siege and say it was a Rasal knight that did it."

"Dishonour myself? I'll not. Never."

"Then what good are you?" She shook from his grip and marched away, though regretted those words a heartbeat later. "I'm sorry, I didn't mean..."

"It's fine." When she turned she found no injury in his eyes. "I can only imagine how difficult all of this has been for you. You've earned a few harsh words, and for my part, I'm happy to take them if it helps."

She didn't know what to say to that. How lucky had she been to be paired with this man and here she was, berating him for not aiding her further. For not abandoning the oaths of honour he'd sworn and murdering a highborn lord. *Mind your words,* she scolded herself. *You've no right, no right at all, to speak to him like that.*

"I don't..." She vented a breath, and found herself slumping into a chair. "I don't know what to do." Through the slit between the tent flaps, a cooling air slid through, fresh and clear as it kissed her skin. She breathed in. The pavilion had grown warm with the dual braziers burning bright and her skin was starting to weep. Elyon noticed and poured a cup of cool water. He handed it to her.

"It'll cool you down. Drink."

She'd not realised how hasty her heartbeat had become, her pulse pressing hard through her veins. It was all too much, living like this. Wondering what the next day might bring. Or the next hour or minute besides. Cecilia was unpredictable, and her prodding and probing made Saska more uncomfortable than she could say. Every time the king's bastard daughter left her, she'd sit and review the exchange. *Did my accent slip? Does my story line up? Has she figured out who I really am?* She was afraid every moment of every day that Cecilia would come and have her stripped, and force-marched through camp to the brothels to the leers and jeers of the men. The woman terrified her in the turn of her tongue. One moment kind and motherly and sympathetic. The next cutting and callous and cruel. For the most part she'd been agreeable and warm but that made it all the worse when she wasn't. It reminded Saska of life under Kastor's roof, that never-ending dread and tension. *But can I just give up? Can I let Marian down?*

"You shouldn't be here, Saska," murmured Elyon's voice. "Your mentor...she should never have sent you. It wasn't fair." He stepped forward, and perched on the end of the bed, opposite where she sat. "What do you hope to achieve by killing him?" he asked. "Are you doing this for you? For your mentor? For Rasalan?"

All of the above, she might have said, but she just sat and said nothing.

He leaned forward. "Killing Cedrik Kastor won't change anything in this war. If that's your aim, you're wasting your time. For that King Janilah would need to die, not Kastor." He bunched his fists. "And that...that's something I might just see to myself."

Now she looked at him, her attention gripped. Her voice crept out, quiet and curious. "You'd...kill him?" she whispered.

Elyon Daecar stood, his floppy white shirt flapping against his broad back as he stepped away. "He's behind this," he said, looking off. "I know that now. It's all been him."

She wasn't sure what he was referring to. "The war?"

"Everything. Everything that's befallen my family. My father's crippling. My brother's death. Both were by his order." And so he repeated, "I know that now."

She stood and stepped a little closer to him across the decking. It was quiet outside now, and their voices needed tending. "The Ghost of the Shadowfort," she whispered. She'd heard that name used for the assassin who bore the Nightblade. "He works for King Janilah?"

"He's my brother." Saska stood in confusion as Elyon turned. His eyes had sharpened to scimitars, curved and deadly. "My father's bastard son, born during the war," he went on. "I wasn't sure how that happened before, but now I am. Now I know."

The pieces were coming together in her mind, completing some part of a puzzle she never knew existed. "They used a breeder on him?" she breathed. "They...they stole a son from him?"

"As you've been sent to steal one from me." He marched to the tent flaps and looked out through the gap to make certain no one was nearby. "Dawn isn't far off." He turned, and went to the bed.

She followed as they huddled to a corner. "I didn't know it until tonight," he told her in a clandestine whisper. "My father...he denied it. He said he'd never have dishonoured my mother by bedding another woman, but..."

"He thought the woman who came to him *was* her," Saska said, realising. "Just like you thought I was Melany?"

"Yes. He must have been slipped a potion, as I was, and awoken thinking it all a dream...or some fragment of a memory." He clenched his square bearded jaw. "As I might have, had you not fed me that brew to wake me."

"Does anyone else know?"

"No one. And they're not to." He turned to her. "This stays between us, Saska. You and I, and no one else. Do you understand me?"

"I understand."

For a long moment they looked at one another, sharing in one another's secrets, their fears and hopes and dreams. *Is he why I'm really here?* Saska wondered. *Is this not about Kastor at all, but the heir to House Daecar?*

He broke his gaze off and moved it to the thin slit between the tent flaps once again. There was an early suggestion of the coming of dawn, and the air outside had turned silent as death. "It'll start getting light soon," he said. "We'd best get into bed." He stepped away and moved around to the far side of the bed, stripping off his loose-fitted shirt as he went and tossing it aside. A moment later he was climbing beneath the blankets. Saska stood on the spot all the while. "I'll not look," he assured her, as he settled. "I promise. See." He turned his back to her, rolling over under the quilt. "Just climb in and cover yourself up. I won't look," he said again.

You can, if you want, came another thought, and it was another that she kept to herself. Instead she reached to the lace straps at her shoulders and drew them aside, letting the scant blue dress fall from her frame, and settle to a small little bundle on the wood-deck floor. She took a pace forward, keeping her eyes on him all the while, and slipped beneath the coverlets. Her pulse quickened anew, and her lungs grew greedy, filling and emptying with a ready eagerness. "OK, I'm in," she whispered, once she'd pulled the covers over herself, leaving only her shoulders bare.

"Are you sure?"

"I'm sure."

He turned around, and settled, lying on his thick broad back. Beneath the covers the shape of his legs extended almost a full foot beyond her own, and thrice as wide. "So...we're just to lie here, then," he said, filling the short silence. "Until Cecilia comes to fetch you?" He glanced over at her. "How is she to know if we've...well...you know."

"She expects to find me naked in your bed." She'd told him that already. "I...well I guess she's going to peek through the flaps and see."

"Right...right." He seemed a little uncomfortable. "You have...been with a man before, haven't you?" he then asked, careful not to offend her. "You just seem quite nervous to be here with me. It isn't a reaction I'm used to."

She thought a moment about lying, but realised there was little point. "I'm a virgin," she told him, staring up. She shrugged. "Since we're giving up our secrets, I suppose you might as well know..."

"Right." He said nothing for a prolonged moment, then asked, "And Cecilia...she knows this?"

"She said it was time I became a woman. The whole thing about you putting a child in me...I guessed at that. But with what happened to your father, it makes more sense now." He had a concerned frown on his face. "What?" she asked him. "What is it?"

"There are ways of testing whether a woman's lost her maidenhead, you know," he said. "You...did know that, didn't you?"

She went suddenly dizzy, the colour draining from her cheeks. "No...how?"

He looked like he'd rather not say. "Well, um, typically a midwife would...well, she'd inspect you. Down there. They can tell, most of the time."

She was staring now, off to the side. What he'd said rang a bell. *Llana,* she realised. *Llana had spoken about that once.* Her eyes snapped back to him like a whip. "Would...would she do that? Would Cecilia check?"

"She might. It's quite common, with chaste brides when marrying, to make sure they've not been with anyone else. There is bleeding sometimes too, the first time." He raised his eyes, speaking softly. "I could stain the sheets, if you'd like? Cut myself and bloody them. That might work."

"Would...would it?" She wasn't sure, and was far too stressed to thank him for the offer.

"If she saw them, yes, though that's not certain."

"But checking between my legs is?"

"Well...yes. Certain enough, anyhow."

"Gods." She groaned, sitting up, clinging to the quilt as she did so. Her thoughts were running wild, and worst of all was the idea of having Cecilia put her through something so invasive. She'd had her naked many times now and put her hands to her too, but not like that, not there. She felt the bed shift as Elyon sat up a little, and gave him a glance. "Would you..." She stopped a moment to think some more, but there seemed no other way out, lest Cecilia perform her inspection and determine she'd failed, and march her to someone greatly less forgiving. "You'll be gentle?" *She told me he was gentle. She said that, didn't she?* "You will, won't you?"

"Gentle?" He got her meaning a moment later. "Of course, Saska, but we don't need to..."

"We do. What choice is there? I can't let her do that to me. She threatened me, Elyon. She told me she'd give me to someone else. Someone less kind. I can't let that happen. I won't."

She reached across to a side table, took up a goblet, and gulped down all the wine she could. "What are you..." he started, but she didn't let him finish. In a flash, she turned, and giving in to a reckless thought let the quilt fall free from her body, exposing her breasts to the glimmering firelight. Elyon's eyes shot to them and back up. He drew away a fraction. "No, Saska...you don't have to..."

"I do." She reached out and pressed her hands to his shoulders, pushing him down onto the feather-stuffed mattress, climbing atop him. "I've got no choice. Just...be gentle."

Her fears were gone now; this was necessity, life or death, even, she told herself, and she could do a great deal worse. *Could I do better?* She wasn't sure of that. But Elyon was still protesting, and that wasn't helping. "Saska, please. Just think a moment. There may be another way..."

"There isn't."

"I could tell her. Tell Cecilia we were intimate. That's what you wanted, isn't it?"

"It won't work." She was straddling him now, and feeling him stir beneath her. *It's the only way,* she told herself, again and again she said it. *She might check me anyway, but at least she'll not find me chaste. I can't be sent to another man. I won't...*

Elyon shifted sideward, but she wouldn't budge. "Why not?" he asked, trying not to look at her breasts. "We don't..."

"I didn't have the facts then," she cut in. "I do now." She leaned in and pressed her lips to his. Her first kiss. All she could think about was how much his short beard tickled her, how warm and wet his lips were. She pulled back, giggling.

"What? What's funny?"

"Tickles." She went in again, and that swelling between his legs kept rising. And soon his hands were rising too, and sliding through her short black hair, and the quilt was falling off her, exposing her soft nude body to the air.

"Saska," he was saying between breaths, between kisses. "This...this is crazy."

"Why?" She drew back again. "Do you not find me attractive?" She was thinking of the white scars on her back, the shade of her skin. *Why did I have to show him? Why?*

But when she looked at him again she saw only an earnest light in his eyes, and through his lips came a whisper. "No, I...I find you beautiful, Saska." He ran a hand over her unburdened back, across the thin sleek lines of the lash. "All of you."

Her smile was soft and shy, the smile of a girl who'd never done this before, who'd never heard words to make her swoon. A light flutter went through her chest and she had to blink the mist from her eyes. *This has to happen,* she thought as she looked at him. *I...I want this to happen.*

Her thoughts melted one into another, and what happened next she could hardly recall, a series of kisses and strokes, then a flurry of movement as he rolled her over onto her back, and their lips were locked as one, and a hand was beneath the covers, and his breeks were coming off. He loomed above her, a sculpture of meat and muscle, the hair atop his head flowing down in a thick black sheet of waves. He flung a hand through it, wiping it aside, and beyond was a face crafted of the gods. And it was the gods she thought of now. *Gods...it's happening*, she thought, as she smiled back, and laid down flat. *It's...it's really happening.*

She thought not of her past. Not of Kastor. Not of Quintan. Not of the parades of lurid men who'd leered at her across the years. She thought of nothing in particular, nothing but relief as Elyon Daecar kept to his promise, taking her gently, and stopping and whispering all the while. "Are you OK, Saska? Does...does it hurt?"

It didn't. A mild discomfort, perhaps, but in the rush and flush of it she didn't care. "Just...be quiet," she told him, gripping his neck, tasting his lips. "No more talking, Elyon," she panted, as he lay down atop her. "No more..."

He kept to that promise too, and didn't say another word. And if he proved one thing that night, it was that Cecilia had been right.

There really had been nothing to fear. Leastways not from a man like him.

25

Amron

The horn started blowing as soon as they came into sight of the fortress, sitting sprawled across a rugged hillock in the foothills of the Weeping Heights. Either side of it, the Banewood spread out, clothing the southern side of the mountains as they spread high and endless into the distant ash-grey skies.

"I suppose they've spotted us, then," Amron noted from atop Wolfsbane as he stared toward the battlements. Men in sooty silver cloaks were standing guard along the parapets and up at the summit of the Infinity Tower, the great Horn of Haldar was blowing loud and long, a deep vibrating bellow that rang out for miles around. "Have you visited Northwatch before, Walter? Quite the sight, isn't it?"

"Aye it is, my lord, and a sight I've seen once or twice, if never from this close," answered the luckiest man in the world, trotting alongside him on a stubby-legged garron that rather matched the man's stout and paunchy proportions. "Not been beyond the gate, though. You'd have to be a lord or knight or listed man for that."

He was right, of course. The fortress of Northgate was the northernmost of all the Vandarian strongholds, a military outpost not intended for the use of commoners, standing vigil against wildmen and raiders and other things more foul that might seek to pass south across the mountains. For a thousand years the men of Northwatch had seen to that solemn duty, though in recent centuries they'd grown idle in their work. It wasn't for want of trying, no, but a lack of threats to busy them. Rangers still ventured into the Weeping Heights, if not beyond them, but rarely came back with any report to trouble those who slept warm in their beds.

"Quite the racket too," Walter Selleck said, as the horn continued to rumble. "Does it blow like this every time someone gets this near?"

They were travelled along the final stretch of the High Way, though much of it was buried under a foot or so of snow. Still, Amron knew the route well, leading them along the winding track through the low foothills to where Northgate loomed. "If someone approaches, yes, the horn will blow," he said. "It shouldn't last much longer." Even as he said it, the noise trailed off, leaving a light ringing in his ears. "Ah, you see. Blows a lot longer if someone comes from the other side."

"I suppose that doesn't happen often."

"Not for some time, but for when a ranger returns. They have different sounds for those, though. There's a whole series of signals they use to give warning of who approaches."

Walter pulled at his left earlobe, and wiggled his shaggy-bearded jaw. "Leaves a bit of a ringing, doesn't it," he said. "Must be a big old horn to make a sound that deep."

"You haven't heard of it?" Amron was surprised by that. Walter was a fairly learned man, and profoundly interesting besides. They'd shared much about their adventures during their ride from Blackfrost, though it was Walter did most of the talking. "The Horn of Haldar? It doesn't ring a bell?"

"Ring a bell," Walter repeated, with a rough guffaw. "Very good, my lord."

"Oh, yes." Amron laughed. He hadn't intended the pun.

"But yes, of course, I know the name. King Haldar. He built the fortress, as I recall, some thousand years back."

Amron nodded. "He was a heedful king, and did much to secure Vandar's borders. Built Eastwatch too, out near the border of Tukor, commissioning some of Ilith's descendants for the work. He liked to hunt as well; that was another side of him, a rather less cautious side you might say. Often went into the Banewood and Icewilds for that, seeking a beast to match him. Took the horn from the head of a *bovidor*, and a mighty large one too, if you get a chance to climb the Infinity Tower and look at it. Must have been some dozen feet tall at the shoulder, and twice as long. All muscle and bad manners."

Walter gave a laugh. "Bad manners," he repeated. "True, *broadbacks* are like that." It was another name for them, a common name, and quite apt too. The bovidor was a bull-like creature, only about ten times as large, with a single great horn at the centre of its reinforced rock-like forehead. It was thought near extinction now, though, as with many of the other superfauna that once roamed freely across the north.

*But then...*Amron gave Walter a curious look. "You haven't seen one, have you? You sound as though you've had experience of that rotten temper of theirs?"

"I have, as it happens," he said in that blithesome way of his. "One came for me in the foothills, oh, not so far from here I wouldn't have thought. Must have stumbled past its den or something and disturbed it. Frightening sight, I'll tell you, seeing ten tons of muscle coming at you."

"And? What happened?"

"What do you think? I got lucky." His crooked yellow teeth peeked out from behind his lips."I happened to be by a river when he came charging. Heard the splash of a waterfall nearby, so made a dash for it and leaped over the edge without looking. Could feel the lumbering beast behind me all the while, getting closer with every thundering step, but made it just before it had me gored and gutted. Jumped over the edge and hoped for a soft landing and by gosh was I lucky to get one. The drop was some forty feet, all rocks and jagged stones at the base, but I managed to slip right between them. Landed in a pool of water just about deep enough to cushion my fall. A foot left or right and I'd have been smashed to smithereens, but in the end all I got out of it was a nice refreshing bath. And a much needed one too."

Amron had heard many such tales of good fortune now, so reacted with no great surprise. Still, any encounter with a broad-back was worth hearing, uncommon as they were. "I take it this was after you'd visited Vandar's Tomb?"

"Of course. It happened on my way back, actually. Hence the need for a bath." Then he sighed and shook his head. "Poor beast wasn't so lucky, though. Lost its footing as it came after me, and fell into the rocks just as I was swimming away. Heard a horrible crack, a rending of meat, and when I turned around, the entire pool was black-red with blood. Wretched beast lay there moaning and dying, but what could I do? Never knew such a monstrous thing could look so helpless. Sad sight, that was, sad sight indeed."

"Yes," Amron said softly. "I...I can imagine."

At the top of the craggy slope, the portcullis gate was grinding up on its winches, and beneath the dagger-like blades at the bottom of the grille several soldiers stepped out. Northwatch held a standing force of some five hundred experienced men, though only about a hundred of those were rangers. The rest were regular soldiers trained with sword and shield, draped in grey where their more rugged, roaming counterparts wore garb of green and black. As a military outpost, the fort had no ancestral loyalty, and the incumbent commander was always drawn from among the Varin Knights, both serving and retired. It was the same with Eastwatch, the Twinfort, Dragon's Bane and the sundry other forts under the running of the crown.

As they approached, a final figure stepped through the gate, bearing a broad smile beneath a floppy mop of greying hair. Lord Robert Borrington was the reigning commander, a former Varin Knight who'd sought to end his serving years in the relative quiet and calm of these distant wintry climes. He arrived in his Varin cloak and leathers, looking well fed and full of face. "Amron, dear friend, how fare thee?" he called out in his merry voice, crunching along the packed snow in his heavy black-leather boots. "I was delighted to receive your crow and hear of your coming. You travel light it seems. No escort? No attendants?"

Robert had always been a voluble man, and unerringly positive, even after he'd had half his body melted by dragon fire during the war. Amron could see the scarred skin running up the right side of his neck, his disfigured ear poking out from beneath his lanky grey hair, though knew that was just the tip of it. He'd spent most of the war in recovery, and had near talked his nursemaids to death it was said, chattering all day long from his bed. Still, despite all that, he was a man of discretion too, and one Amron could trust. "We're on an errand of secrecy, Robert," he said, as Wolfsbane pulled up at the gate. "This is my travelling companion, Walter Selleck. We plan to stay the night only and leave at daybreak." He shifted from the saddle, as the stablehands came out to tend the horses. "I'll bring you up to speed privily."

"Say no more, Amron." The two gripped forearms. "And Walter. Well met, friend."

"Aye, Lord Borrington, tis a great pleasure." Walter waddled forward, giving a polite bow. "A great pleasure indeed." He looked characteristically scruffy, his padded leathers full of small snags and tears, his head a nest of tangled, unkempt hair. The cold had turned his cheeks a bright pink and the furs he draped on his shoulders were old, musty, and falling apart.

Robert Borrington missed none of it. "We have store rooms full of spare cloaks and warm furs, Walter," he said, looking him over. "Feel free to update your garb, if you wish it. Any friend of Amron's is a friend of mine."

"Much obliged, my lord. Very generous of you. I may do just that."

"Well then." Robert waved for a boy. "Show Walter here to the storehouse," he instructed. "And then up to my solar once he's done. Lord Daecar and I shall be in consultation there. Shall we, Amron?"

The solar was up in the Commander's Tower, situated opposite the Infinity Tower on the northeastern side of the fort. Amron moved to the broad stone window looking northwest as he arrived to take in the view, where the Weeping Heights spread out, grand and foreboding. Below, the postern gatehouse gave access into the foothills, peppered with pine and spruce, and flanking the gate were two tall towers built in the likeness of armoured men bearing shield and sword. The Bladed Barbican it was called, those blades held aloft, shields to the front in a pose reminiscent of an early Blockform stance, guarding the kingdom of Vandar from the perils and threats that lurked beyond.

"You move well, Amron," Lord Borrington noticed, pouring two cups of mulled wine at a table near the flickering hearth. "You seemed to have little trouble with the stairs, and there are a fair few of them, to be sure, to reach these chambers." He stepped to the window to join his lord, handing him a steaming cup. House Borrington were bannermen of the Daecars, hailing from the top of the North Downs, though Robert wasn't the lord of his house, only this fortress. It was his older brother Randall who was busy mustering their men for war. "I'd heard your leg was improving. It's heartening to see so in person, I must say."

The two men clinked cups in toast. "It's usable," Amron said, his eyes meeting the mountains once more. "It's my left arm that most troubles me."

"It troubles us all, old friend, with war afoot. I take it that's why you've come?"

Amron took a short sip of his wine. It would likely be his last in a while. "Yes. At least, that will be your answer should anyone come asking."

"I see. Errand of secrecy, you said. Pray tell of your true intention?"

Amron looked through the window. He'd trekked the foothills of the Weeping Heights on occasion in the past, though never ventured to the towering mountains beyond them, a perilous labyrinth of ridges and scarps in which the uninitiated could fast lose their bearings, and never find their way out. "There's a hundred ways to die out there," his father Gideon had once told him, when he'd first climbed this tower as a boy and looked out through this very window. "If the cold doesn't catch you, then starvation just might, and the beasts, Amron...oh the beasts. They lurk there in their legions. Ancient terrors of an older time. Only the bravest men venture there, oh yes. The brave...and the foolish." He'd had a playful smile on his face, Amron recalled, but there had been a truth in his words too. *And which am I?* he wondered now. *Brave or foolish...or perhaps a bit of both?*

"I plan to head north into the mountains," he said at last, as a brisk wind blew through the window, rustling through his salt and pepper hair. "I'll need you to fit Walter and I out with suitable provisions, enough for some weeks, Robert. I cannot say how long we'll be gone, but would prefer to be well stocked." Carrying it would be the problem. They could take horses for a time, but beyond the foothills would need to continue on foot. "Walter will ride his garron until we reach Scarfall Pass," he went on. "I'll need a mount of my own, one strong enough to bear me and my blades. Wolfsbane is not fit for tricky terrain, even in the low hills. You have horses bred to bear godsteel, yes?"

Robert Borrington gave a short nod. "There is one who'll suit you, a strong upland pony we call Brute. He'll be able to carry you and your blades, but no more, so best you laden Walter's garron with your supplies."

"That was my thinking, yes. Brute will know the way back, will he? I'd hope for him to lead Walter's garron here to be stabled. Wolfsbane will remain with you too, until my return."

"Brute knows the way, better than most of our rangers I'd wager. I'll assign you a brace of those too, Amron..."

Amron was already shaking his head. "Just Walter and I. We need no further assistance."

"You...intend to carry all your provisions yourself? Amron, forgive me for saying so, but I see no wisdom in that." He looked to the mountains, fading in the distance as the daylight began to wither into a purply dusk. "It is winter, I'll need not remind you, and the snowslides and icefalls can be most troublesome this time of year. Some of the passes may be closed, or else too treacherous to travel. You'll need someone who knows the Heights, someone to redraw your course should it need correcting. Let me send one ranger with you, at least." He thought a moment. "Rogen White-beard, he's my best, and don't let the name fool you; he isn't so old as he sounds. He'll help you plot the climb and make sure you don't get lost."

"We don't need him. Walter knows the way."

The Lord of Northwatch frowned. "Does he? Which way? And how many, might I ask? There are a dozen twisting routes into the Heights, and you might find eleven of them shut from the snows. Lest Walter knows every one of them you'll need a ranger who does." He shook his head. "I'm sorry, Amron, but I'll not permit your passing lest Whitebeard goes with you. A friend you may be, and a dear one, but..."

"*Permit* my passing?" Amron continued to look through the window, as a light snow began to fall. "Let me remind you that I am your lord, old friend. I need no such permission to pass."

"That isn't true, Amron. At least, not anymore," said Robert Borrington in a careful voice. "Only the king or First Blade may overrule my authority here, as you well know, and tragic though it is, you no longer hold the latter post. You know what my job is, Amron. It falls to me to defend this border and that includes keeping men from venturing north. Ever do our patrols scour the Banewood and foothills for such folly, yet still desperate souls seek to cross to the mountains to weep for those they've lost, never to make it back. Hardly a week goes by when our rangers don't come across a new corpse frozen stiff to the marrow, and I'll not have you join them if this is your design."

Amron gave out a short huff. He'd grown so used to having his word obeyed without question, and this sort of dissent...it prickled at his ire. "My design is not to weep or mourn, but to restore myself to health. I make for Vandar's Tomb, to seek conference with his spirit. That is my aim, Robert. Restoration, and vengeance."

Amron didn't look at him, for fear of seeing the curdling shock on his face. Robert Borrington was a man he could trust to keep his secret, but convincing him of it in the first place mightn't be so easy. *And he isn't wrong about his authority here either,* he thought dismally. Here at Northwatch the commander's word was law, and Amron Daecar no longer had the rank to rule against him.

"Amron..." The man's voice was a whisper, stocked with worry. "You...you seek to travel the Icewilds? I had thought this was about Aleron. That you were to scale the mountains to grieve him. Why did you not speak of this in your letter? You might have given me a chance to consider it."

"I didn't want it falling into the wrong hands, Robert. And I'd hoped you'd trust an old friend."

"Trust? This is not about trust, but risk, Amron. And there are a great many out there."

"I know of the risks. And I know what I'm doing. Walter may look an ordinary man but believe me, he is not. There is no one better to guide me."

"Because he's been there before?" Robert inferred.

"Yes."

"And you believe him?"

"I do."

"When was this?"

"You'd have to ask him. Some dozen years past, I believe."

"And why? Why did he go? To convene with Vandar's spirit, as you intend to? He returned a man blessed? That's what you're telling me?"

Amron stared out for a moment in silence. He knew how it all sounded. *He thinks me desperate,* he thought, *and more than a little mad.* It only served to shine a light on his own doubts, and that made him uncomfortable. Looking out now, he even felt a shudder of fear. *So far,* he thought. *So high. So cold and wild and dark. Might I not just turn around, and return to Blackfrost, to Lillia and Amara and dear Cousin Gereth?* The notion held an appeal, more powerful than he'd like. He needed Walter here with him, needed his spirit and his light. The man had been a reinforcing presence, ever optimistic and enthusiastic and cheerful on the road. *But when we pass into the dread and the darkness, what then? Will his light truly follow him back there? Will it keep us warm, keep us safe?*

He let out a breath and turned his eyes from the window, looking into his friend's worried eyes. "I had hoped you'd be less cynical, Robert," he said, in a soft weary voice. "But if you were willing to let me pass with Rogen Whitebeard into the Heights, then what reason do you have to renege on your words now? The risks are manifold whether I visit the mountains only, or venture beyond them. One equals the other."

"No, it does not." Robert took a hasty step away to the counter, and refilled his cup of mulled wine. "We're well acquainted with the mountains and the perils therein, Amron. Our rangers venture there often, but the Icewilds?" He shook is head. "No. That frozen wasteland is beyond our bounds and beyond our wish to revisit. What terrors lurk there we hardly even know anymore. Only a handful of our men have ever travelled beyond the Heights, and never so far as Vandar's Tomb."

"But Rogen Whitebeard is one of them?" Amron asked.

Robert sighed and dipped his head into a reluctant nod. "Well...yes. Of all our rangers, he's roved the furthest."

"And if I agree to take him with us? Will that satisfy you, Robert?"

"Satisfy me?" He gulped his drink, looking altogether unhappy at the prospect. "It would satisfy me to know that you're going no further than the foothills, and with a host of rangers at your side. Or better yet, that you'd merely come here to see an old friend, and check on our borders with war a-brewing. But Vandar's Tomb? By Varin, Amron, I never expected such recklessness from you."

"And I never expected to be chopped apart like a slab of beef on a butcher's table, Robert," came his sharp, biting reply. "I never expected to watch my son's neck cleaved open, to hold his body in my arms as his blood soaked the sand scarlet at my knees. There's a great deal I never expected to happen but here we are, and this is my intent. Now if you'll not trust me to know my own mind, and steer my own course, then let me remind you of something, old friend." He set him with a steely blue stare. "You draw breath because of me. You stand here as lord of this fortress, because of me. I drove off the beast that melted you half to death, and gave you this posting once you'd convalesced. Without me you'd have been sat at Varin's Table two decades ago...and more distant from him than you will be now, of that I'm decidedly sure. So if you'll not permit my passing on my request alone, then I'd demand you do so in repayment of a debt. I saved your life, and now you'll help me save mine. And let that be the end of it."

It was the end of it, he could see, as he stared blazes into

Robert's umber eyes, which dipped to his feet, and then his chin followed as his head fell into an acquiescing bow. "You're right, Amron," he said with a whisper. "Of course, I...I owe you everything, and more than I could ever repay." He looked up. "If this is your wish, then I will help you see it done." He looked to the door. "I shall speak with Whitebeard presently, and see to the other preparations. If I have displeased you, for that I apologise. I hope you know it was not my intent."

"You haven't displeased me, Robert, and I'm quite aware of your intent." Amron stepped toward him. "You wish to keep me safe from harm, and that is worthy of my thanks." He closed in and placed a hand to the man's shoulder, drawing a smile onto his black-bearded lips. "Now let us not quarrel over this anymore. I would have us laugh and reminisce, if I can, and share stories of fonder times. It's been how long since I've seen you? Some two years, at least. Now a lot must have happened in that time, old friend. Let me hear of it over another cup of wine. You can pay your visit to Whitebeard later."

The strain between them eased as Robert gave out a laugh. "Two years, you say? Well, let me see...what has happened in the meanwhile?" He began counting on his fingers. "Well, there's not much...nothing at all...a whole load of nothing..." His eyes glinted in the firelight. "Need I go on?"

"Oh it can't have been that dull? Walter told me he encountered a broadback not too far from here. None of your patrols have come across it?"

"He said that? Really?" Robert Borrington rubbed his double chin. "Interesting. There was an old broadback lair we came across some winters past, though the beast was long since dead. Found its bones at the base of a frozen waterfall nearby." He stepped back to the window, pointing into the darkening skies. "It was out yonder, some fifteen or so miles off, in an area few ever tread. We took the horn, of course, and have it down in the crypts now. I'll show you, if you'd like?"

"No that's...that's OK." Amron was thinking of Walter's story a little earlier. He enjoyed a hunt but had never much liked the plaintive sounds animals made when dying. The idea of seeing such a mighty beast as a broadback in that state was quite saddening, in truth. "Walter was there when it died," he told him. "It had chased him to the lip of the waterfall, and fell in after him. It was right after he returned from the Icewilds."

"Huh. And he went about a dozen years ago, you said?"

"Yes, I believe so."

"Well then it lines up. I had the remains examined and was told the bovidor died about that time. But..." He frowned, thinking back. "How did Walter survive the fall? There were a great many rocks at the base, as I recall. It'd be madness to jump from the top."

Amron smiled. "He must have gotten lucky, I suppose."

"Well yes. Very lucky indeed." Robert had a frown on his face, as though he was starting to see that Walter was as Amron said; no ordinary man at all. "I'll hope to speak to him about it later. I'd be most interested to know which route he took to Vandar's Tomb."

"You sound convinced he went, old friend," Amron teased.

"I...well, I'm *more* convinced, certainly." He offered a faithful smile. "I trust your judgement, for what it's worth. You've never been prone to gullibility and your faculties seem quite intact. And anyway, you'll have Whitebeard with you. So if this Walter turns out to be a charlatan then at least you'll have a seasoned ranger at your side."

Yes, though it wasn't what Amron had wanted. The way Walter had explained it, he only had so much 'light' to go around. "I'm as a man walking with a torch in the darkness," he'd told him. "Those who remain close to me will benefit most from my light. Those who step away into the shadows will only expose themselves to peril."

It was a fine analogy, though not one to take entirely literally, and having one extra man along shouldn't cause undue problems. *I really ought to be happy,* Amron realised, giving himself a gentle scolding. He respected the rangers greatly for their courage and keen survival instincts and having the best of them with him was no bad thing. *Just so long as he makes it out alive,* he thought. *I'd not want Robert to lose his best man on this foolhardy endeavour of mine.*

With all that, he realised it was time for some gratitude.

"Rogen's presence will be most welcome," he said, with as much courtesy as he could bundle into his voice. "I had not wanted to place any of your men in danger, if that explains my reluctance for him to join us."

"It does. But what good is a ranger if not to support the Hero of the North in his great quest? Though I must give you fair warning, Amron. Rogen Whitebeard is a solitary sort, sullen and more grim than most. All good rangers enjoy their own company, but he does rather take it to an extreme. Disappears for months, sometimes, on his rovings, coming and going as he pleases. I allow it because he's a damn fine ranger, but I'll admit he can aggravate me sometimes."

Amron raised an eye. "Might it not be better to assign me someone else?"

Robert's head went side to side. "No," he then said, having mulled it over. "There's none who know the mountains better than Whitebeard, nor what lies beyond. And in winter, even more so. That said, I'd best go see him now, lest he sneak off on one of his unsanctioned trips before I can collar him. I shan't be long, Amron." He took a pace toward the door. "Would you like to eat with the men tonight? I could have a feast arranged for the senior rangers and officers, if you'd like?"

"Thank you, Robert, but that won't be necessary. I'd rather spend tonight with you, old friend. We can eat here if you'll permit it?"

"Of course. And that was my preference too. I'll see the food brought up."

He didn't return for some thirty minutes, during which time Walter arrived, led up by the boy instructed to attend him. He stepped inside cloaked in black bearskin and wearing a self-congratulatory smile. "Fine stocks they've got here, my lord," he said, greedily pouring his own cup of wine. "Outfitted myself in a whole new wardrobe fit for the wilds, with a hunting knife and bow besides. I'm not much of an archer, in truth, but sometimes I get off a lucky shot." He grinned. "As you can probably imagine."

"Yes, no doubt you'd have killed that broadback with a single arrow if you'd had a bow to hand."

"Through that thick skull of theirs? Please. I'm not *that* lucky." He turned and looked to the west facing window. "Fine view," he said. "Having any second thoughts?"

Can he see into my mind too? Amron had to wonder, as Walter stood there with a knowing little grin. "It wouldn't be natural not to, Walter. Even I can admit that."

"Good. Just testing you, my lord. I like an honest man. Those who deal in deceit aren't so worthy of my light."

Amron nodded, and supped his wine. Walter's rhetoric could be a little sanctimonious at times, though it was a small price to pay.

"And how'd it go with good Lord Borrington?" the man from Lakeside asked, looking out into the brisk wintry night. "Did you tell him everything, or..."

"Most of it," Amron said. "I kept a few details to myself, though perhaps they'll come out when he returns. As with Amara, I'll let you tell your own story. I'd rather like it if you could convince him, as you did me."

"Well's how about I throw myself from this window as proof of my powers? I see a pile of hay down there in the yard. No doubt I'll land in it nice and safe."

"Now I'm sure it doesn't work like that," Amron scoffed. "You cannot willingly put yourself in danger....can you?"

"No, probably not, though in truth I've never tried. Best I don't test the theory, with our adventures just beginning." He took in a full breath of air, smiling happily. "We feasting tonight then? Lots of interesting men downstairs I'd be keen to get to chatting with."

"You'll have to satisfy yourself with Robert and myself. We'll be eating here in his solar."

"All right then, no trouble. And he's...he's happy to let us pass, is he? I know a bit about how it works here, my lord." He leaned out of the window, a little too far to be safe, then returned with a covering of frost clinging to his patchy beard. "If not, we can just work around through the Banewood. Tis how I got through the first time, after all. They'll not catch us, I'm sure."

"No, that won't be necessary, Walter. Robert has agreed to let us pass and has given us his best ranger to help guide us." He looked at his companion. "I hope that doesn't offend you? As you might imagine, he's a little sceptical."

"No no, I take no offence." Walter turned from the window, with one of those funny little smiles on his lips. "And his best ranger to guide us, you say?" His grin stretched just a little wider. "Well...aren't we lucky."

26

Jonik

Jonik sat sipping at a cocktail of fruit juice and rum, served from a carved coconut husk that was all the rage around here. The heat had forced him to unburden himself of his black cloak and cowl, though he retained his coal-coloured undershirt and breeks, tied up at the knee, in keeping with his character.

Everyone else wore shades of white and cream, yellow and blue, in silks and satins and loose fitting linens. Apparently, lighter colours were better at reflecting the sun and keeping one cool, though for that Jonik merely kept to the shade as best he could, sitting beneath the fronds of a waving palm as he looked out over the powdery white beach. Beside him, Jack o' the Marsh reclined on a cushioned lounger, bathing beneath the sun, wearing not black nor white nor any colour at all, but the pinky white shade of his skin.

"You might want to turn over at some point," Jonik advised, giving his friend's reddening skin a glance. "You'll be two-toned by day's end otherwise. Red and white." They were probably the colours of some great noble house, though for the life of him he couldn't think of one right now. "Are you sure that lotion you lathered over you is working?"

Jack wore a languorous grin as he lay down on the lounger, a damp cloth draped over his eyes. "I've got a plan, Ghost, don't you worry. I'll give my front a nice bronze kiss before turning over and letting my back have a smooch. It's beneficial to soak up some rays once in a while. You might want to give it a try."

"And go crimson like you? You're not getting a bronze kiss, Jack, but a scarlet slap. You look ridiculous."

Jack seemed unconcerned. "Trust the process, friend. First you go a bit pink, then it matures into a nice golden brown. Better to fit in around here, wouldn't you say?"

"We fit in fine. There are plenty of pasty northmen here. So I'll stick to the shadows, thank you very much." *They're where I belong, after all.*

They'd landed that morning, a short time past daybreak, on a small but lively island called Lizard's Laze in the west of the Golden Isles. It hadn't taken Jonik long to see why it'd been so named. Even now he could spot at least a hundred grey-green lizards, lounging down by the rocks nearby in a manner much the same as Jack o' the Marsh. "So how are you finding all this then?" the Marshlander asked, as he stretched out his thick strong arms and expressed a leisured sigh. "The slosh of the sea. The smell of the beach. The gentle din of happy people." He smiled and looked over. "Not so bad, is it?"

"I suppose not. If you like that sort of thing."

"And you don't?"

I don't like much of anything, Jonik thought, though he didn't say it. He was trying to be less dark and brooding where possible and affect a more pleasant demeanour. "It's nice," he managed, in a stiff voice. "I can see why people would like to live here."

"But you're not one of those people," Jack identified, cupping the back of his head in his hands. "In truth I don't think any of us imagined you would be. Turner says he's been here a few times before, but only stays a handful of days on each occasion. Any man with much ambition starts to get itchy when idle too long. Not once did I think you'd want to settle here."

That had been one of the reasons for their short layover - to give Jonik a chance to see what life was like here, should he wish to remain. He didn't, and that had been clear to him long before he even arrived. In fact, he didn't want to find anywhere to stop and hide and while his days away. Nor was his intention to run either. His mind had been settled on that account, and in the likes of Jack and Turner and Emeric he had allies he could count on. *I know my path now,* he thought, *and it doesn't end here with these lazing lizards.* The Nightblade had shown him the way, whispering, ever whispering to him in his dreams, and sometimes through his waking hours too. *To lead,* he thought, *and no longer to follow. That is my path and purpose. That is what I'll do...*

"You know I think you may be right," Jack said, interrupting his musings. Jonik turned to find his friend sitting up now on his recliner, running a hand over his sizzled skin. He cringed. "Mayhaps I've misjudged this. That girl did give me the right lotion, didn't she?"

It was nice to see the burly, red-headed Marshlander in discomfort for once. He did so little wrong, that when he made a mistake it was an occasion to celebrate. Jonik watched with amusement as Jack turned, cringing again as the skin of his chest and stomach twisted and tightened, and called for the girl attending them from the beach shack nearby.

"Yes, sir," she said in a silky sweet voice, gliding barefoot across the decking that gave access up the beach. She was only in her late teens, with a deep rich tan and lustrous brown locks, radiant against the white of her short linen tunic. They were a striking lot here in the Golden Isles, though of course the prettiest girls would be hired to entice such men to these venues. "Did you want another rum cocktail?" She smiled at Jonik, as he hid in the shade on his reclinable chair, and it was enough to have his eyes fleeing her. *Damn you,* he thought to himself. *I can butcher my father and kill my brother and slaughter a dozen Bladeborn men in a fight, but I can't lock eyes with a simple server girl.*

He'd never been trained for that, of course, nor had there been any female presence among the tall black towers of the Shadowfort. Jonik recalled back to his fight with Elyon Daecar, when he'd found the young knight in his changing room prior to his semi-final bout with Sir Dalton Taynar. "I even hear they take your balls up there in the mountains," his tall dashing brother had goaded, as they wrestled about on the dusty stone floor. "Is that true, eunuch? Are you even a man at all?"

There had been some truth in his taunt. Many of the Shadowknights were gelded as boys to guarantee compliance, and avoid certain distractions that might interrupt their training. The best of them, however, weren't subjected to that, should they be called upon to breed later and furnish the ranks of the order with their sons. Instead, they were treated with a form of chemical castration while in the service of the order, to temporarily restrain their sexual desires and avoid associated diversions. Only when they grew too old to fulfil their contracts, or graduated to become masters, did this chemical treatment discontinue. Jonik, by dint of his powerful blood-bond to godsteel, had been included within the latter group. And by his stirring reaction to this pretty young girl, the drugs he'd been given looked to be wearing off.

Of course, Jack o' the Marsh suffered no such difficulties when conversing with the fairer sex. "What's your name young lady?" he asked her in a well structured voice, big and broad as he was. And that smile was big and broad too, plenty to make a girl swoon.

"Sapphire, sir, for my eyes." The girl smiled back. "That is my public name."

"Your public name? You have another in private?"

"Yes, as is custom here. The private name is only given to family and friends."

Jack smiled winningly. "Then say no more, Sapphire. It's not a custom I've heard of, but in any case Sapphire fits you well. You have beautiful eyes."

She giggled. "Was there something you needed, sir?"

"Just a question, if you'll permit me." He gestured to his freckled skin, which was growing increasingly red and prickly. "That lotion you gave me earlier. It was to help keep my skin from burning, yes?"

"Yes, sir," she said with a neat pretty smile. "But...well, you are quite light of complexion. And have been in the sun some time now. It might be time to add another layer."

"Or better yet, take to the shade," Jonik said under his breath.

The girl heard. "Yes, or that." She looked at him again,

though his eyes didn't hold her gaze for long. "I can put more lotion on you, sir, if you need," she said, dropping her eyes back to Jack.

"Well there's an idea." He stood, towering over the dainty young girl, as his wide pale back caught the light, glistening with streaks of sweat. "If you'd be so kind as to apply it to my back, Sapphire. I'll try to even out the tan first, before fleeing to the shade."

"Tan." Jonik gave a rough laugh at that. "Would you call that a tan, Sapphire?"

"I would prefer it if the kind sir would not force me to answer that question."

Jack's guffawing rang out down the beach. "OK, well it seems I've been humbled. Let's just say I want to be evenly burned, then. A nice shade of red all over. Now..." He lay down on his front, grimacing all the while as his scorched skin rubbed against the cushions. "Do give me a liberal spread, Sapphire, to ensure I don't blacken to a crisp. And perhaps you have some ointment for after-care? I can't be the only northman foolish enough to misinterpret the fierceness of the sun down here?"

That giggle tinkled from out of her again as she raised a delicate hand to her mouth. "It happens often. But we have a broad selection of salves and balms to soothe you after. The red skin will settle quickly, do not worry."

She speaks so beautifully, Jonik thought, trying not to stare at her. The Golden Isles were an independent state and despite their geographical proximity to Agarath, often welcomed northern sailors and merchants when passing down this way. The locals had learned the common tongue as a result, and many spoke it well. *She is one of them,* he thought, as she set about applying the lotion to Jack's thick brawny back. *A voice as pretty as she is. And those eyes...that skin...* They called them the Girls of Gold, and to many they were the most beautiful in the world. For a moment the thought of staying here held a stronger appeal, until Jonik turned away and looked back over the seas, and remembered his solemn duty. *To free them,* he thought, staring at the soft lapping waves, and the immensity beyond, endless and blue, sea and sky. *He called me a slave to their will, and he was right.* Elyon Daecar had said that too, when they'd brawled beneath the arena in Varinar. *But it isn't just me.* There were over a hundred Shadowknights living in that ancient fortress, thralls to the will of the masters as Jonik had once been. *Did they all deserve to die? Might I not try to save them, as I have been saved myself?*

When Jonik escaped his short reverie, he found that Sapphire's application of the lotion had evolved into a full massage. Jack was making a light groaning sound, a dumb look on his face as he lay there sprawled on his bed. "Now this really...is the life," he moaned in a lazy voice, barely bothering to move his lips. "You'll want her hands on you next, Jonik. The girl's a magician, truly."

"I would be most happy to oblige," Sapphire said, smiling across at him, working her hands up and down Jack's meaty flesh. There was a coquettishness to her that suggested she offered other services too.

Jonik once again averted his eyes. "No, thank you," he said to the seas. "I am perfectly relaxed as I am. Maybe another time."

"Of course." The girl smiled and continued to work. "Are you here long in Lizard's Laze?"

Jack glanced to Jonik. "That is for our lord master here to decide."

Her thin brown brows lifted up, crinkling her little sun-kissed forehead. "You are the master, my lord?"

She sounds surprised, Jonik thought. *Do I project no authority at all?* "I am," he said, giving her a single affirming nod.

"You are very young. Are you from Tukor? And you...you are Vandarian, from the east," she said, rolling her knuckles over Jack's spine, as he rumbled out another groan.

"You have an ear for accents," Jonik told her, trying to break free of his quiet rasp, and speak with more presence. *Like the father I crippled. Or the brother I killed.* Those bitter thoughts came occasionally, a constant rebuking reminder of what he'd done. *And what I will one day do, to secure vengeance for my family.* He looked the girl in the eye, and found a gleaming allure within them. "You are correct. Jack here is from the Marshlands in East Vandar. I hail from the north of Tukor."

"And the others from your ship?" Sapphire's gemstone eyes were out on the turquoise water, where the ship was at anchor within the wide protected harbour. The island was shaped as a vague crescent moon, with soft sand beaches along the outside and the harbour and town established within the inner curve. Jonik had heard it took only a few short hours to traverse from one side to the other, and that on the outer seaward side, facing west, great black flying rays could often be seen, surging from the seas and skimming upon the water.

"They're from a few places," Jack told her. "All northern, though. We have another Tukoran lord in our company, as it happens. Lord Manfrey. He's well known in the south, so perhaps you've heard of him?"

The girl gave a brisk nod. "I have heard the name Manfrey." She offered no explanation as to whether it was Emeric she'd heard tell of, or his famed forebear Sir Oswald, which seemed more likely. "A shame you're to depart so soon. The gold banners will be raised for the Day of Dawning in a few days. It is an occasion of great importance here, and one of much fun. All through the Golden Isles we drink glittering wine and wear silks and satins of the finest gilding. But at night many of the girls do away with them. They frolic naked on the sands and skinny-dip in the waters, and when the silver moon shines down, they take a drink of the seas in thanks for her endless bounty."

"Is all that true?" whispered a voice. Jonik turned to the source and found Devin standing wide eyed beside his smooth-trunked palm, taking a moment in the shade. Unlike Jack his skin took a tan well. "The girls dance naked?" His lips tore into a beaming smile. "Truly?"

"Truly," Sapphire told him, taking the boy's sudden arrival in her stride. He'd been further down the beach, speaking to some other girls, the last Jonik saw. "They say the girls outnumber the lizards on the beaches. It is a feast for the eyes. A fine spectacle for young men like yourselves."

Devin looked like he was imagining it, with his mouth half agape. "And the boys? Do...do they go naked too?"

"It is not custom. Most of them are too frightened, I think, to expose themselves. But later, yes, some join in. You would be welcome to if you wished it. All of you. You'd hear no complaints, I'm sure."

Devin was almost bouncing he was so overjoyed. "Foreigners are allowed? I didn't think..." He turned to Jonik. "We have to stay, milord. We have to. What man in his right mind would leave? With the girls...and the nakedness...and..."

"Calm, Devin," Jack said. "You'll only overexcite yourself." He turned back onto his front, sitting up. His short time tanning his back hadn't much evened out the burn. "When is it?" he asked Sapphire. "If it's only some days off, it might be worth sticking around." He looked over to Jonik, and gave a short shrug. *No doubt he's wondering whether Sapphire herself will disrobe.* Jonik gave the girl another glance. *Not an unpleasant sight, I wouldn't think...*

"Then you should stay." The girl was looking at Jonik again. "The Day of Dawning is but three days from now. Within two the island will be dressed for it. Streamers from the palms. Banners on the beach huts. The stone houses in town will be transformed, you'll see. Everything becomes golden. Everything."

"Even the girls?" Devin asked. "Do you wear paint...on your bodies?"

"We don't need to," the girl said, smiling at the boy. "Our skin is gold already."

"Mine will be as well soon," Devin announced proudly. Then his eyes burst open. "I could invite Kulia and Salma." He spun around, looking down the beach. There were a pair of girls sunning themselves in the distance, dressed in scanty linens across their bottoms and busts. "Will they come?" He turned again. "Do you know them?"

"I do. I know everyone here," said Sapphire. She favoured him with a pretty smile. "You must have made an impression, for them to give you their private names." Devin didn't seem to know what she was talking about.

"Kulia kissed me," he said, looking smug about that. "Not on the lips or anything, but...it counts. The cheek counts, right Jack?"

"Toward what, Devin?"

He'd not expected that response. "It counts," is all he said. "But I'll get more next time. At the party. I'll get more then."

"If we stay," said Jonik firmly. "I may yet decide to leave."

Three days, he was thinking. It was a long time to sit under this swaying palm, with all these pretty girls around, reminding him of what he'd never had. And wouldn't seek, he knew. The pleasures of the flesh were an irrelevance to him right now. At least, that's what he told himself. *I have other matters of greater import to see to. I'll not be swayed by the idea of frolicking girls, dancing nude in the moonlight.*

Devin looked dismayed by the suggestion. "What?" He stared at Jonik with a welling worry in his eyes. "Why would we...why would we leave, milord? Is there reason to rush?"

"There may be. I haven't decided yet."

"But..." Devin was on his knees all of a sudden, clasping his hands together in prayer. "Please, lord. Kulia...you haven't met her. She's..." He pointed down the beach. "I can't describe her. Even in her bathing clothes she looked..." He was breathless, and quite unable to form proper sentences. "You have to let us stay. It's only a few days. Please, Master Jonik. Please, I'll do anything..."

Jonik found himself in something of a quandary. He was quite enjoying the praising eyes of the girl, as he mulled on it, yet he had a fondness for Devin too and didn't want to let him down without cause. "I'll talk it over with the others when they return," he said, giving his decision. "I can say no fairer than that, Devin."

"So we'll take a vote?" Devin was doing his calculations, and probably coming to the conclusion that a host of red-blooded sailors would likely opt for all the nudity and drinking.

"No," Jonik told him. He gave the girl a glance, to check the approving twist of her lips. "I will listen to everyone's thoughts and then make my decision." He checked her again. "And that will be that."

When Devin had grudgingly accepted and moved down the beach, and Sapphire gone to tend other customers, Jack o' the Marsh leaned over and said, "She likes you, Ghost. Why not ask her onto the ship for the night? Maybe even show her the Nightblade to get her hot under the collar?" He had one of those playful grins on his face, the type he used when probing for a reaction. "There's more than one way to get some colour in your cheeks, you know."

"I'm aware." Jonik preferred to avoid this sort of topic entirely. "But I have no time for that sort of thing. And she likes my power, not me."

"Same thing." Jack took up his coconut shell and drained his rum and pineapple juice. "Half the women across the northern kingdoms marry for power not love, and it's the same down here I'm sure. And besides, you're not awful to look at. A bit miserable, true, and you could probably do with washing your hair a bit more often, but there's enough good on your face to entice a fair lady."

"Flattering as always, Jack."

The Marshlander grinned a broad grin. "Well then why not? You told me you've not been gelded, so I'm not seeing any excuses there."

Jonik was growing uncomfortable now. *I shouldn't have told him all that.* "I don't want to talk about it."

"Why not? It's my job to break you out of your shell, isn't it? To bring you into the light? Well, sometimes a few hard questions need be asked for that."

"Not these ones." Jonik was on his feet in an instant, marching from the Marshman's company. He made it about two dozen paces before he ran into the returning pair of Turner and Braxton, who'd gone to the nearby market to fetch supplies. Both were carrying rattling wooden crates and sweating profusely from their labour. "Captain. Brax," Jonik said in a grunt. "Did you get what you needed?"

"Rum," is all Turner said, giving his crate a shake. "They brew it best here and it's cheap too. We're gonna get it loaded on old Iris and then head back for more."

"Right. I'll come with you," Jonik said, eager to put more space between him and Jack and all his bloody questions.

They'd fastened their rowboat at a short jetty in the bustling harbour, paying a small tax for the pleasure. Loading the precious cargo inside, they climbed in, Brax and Turner taking the oars. Jonik took position before them on an old wooden bench. His instinct had been to pull an oar himself, but he needed to let go of that. "If you wish to lead then leave the labour to others, Jonik," Emeric Manfrey told him some days gone, as they sailed south from the Tidelands. "That doesn't mean be idle. It means identifying when to involve yourself and when not to. It means showing your men who's in charge." Jonik had since tried to do just that, and the transition had been easier than he'd thought. "Be decisive," Emeric had advised, and Jonik had obliged. He was trying now to take decisions quickly, to listen to the points of the others, weigh the balance of what he'd heard, and then give his orders. Emeric had told him about that balance too. "A good leader doesn't bend to the will of his men, but he does take time to listen to them. Do not let them sway you more than you'll allow. But know when not to go against them, to avoid the fester of resentment. It can only lead to mutiny and betrayal, and that you cannot allow. It is the balance you must judge, Jonik. Always remember that."

When they reached Invincible Iris, Grim Pete and Soft Sid were waiting up on deck to help with the rum, which was unloaded as briskly as they could manage. In the meanwhile, Jonik moved below decks to check on Shade and the other horses. It was one reason to continue as soon as possible. The horses were stalled and confined and Jonik could sense their discomfort. It was humid too, down in the hold, though he'd given orders for Grim and Sid to make sure they were well watered and attended at all times. He gave Shade's rippling black flank a stroke. "If we decide to stay longer I'll take you for a ride on the beach," he told him. "We can lead the other horses. Get you out of this stifling stall for a while."

Shade gave a peevish swish of his mane and looked in no way happy about lingering here too long. It was plenty to bend Jonik's thoughts toward the prospect of an imminent departure. To him, Shade's wishes were just as important as anyone else, and in some cases, even more so. So he gathered the men on deck once they'd finished loading the cargo to pick their brains. "There's talk of staying for the Day of Dawning," he said, as they assembled on the main deck before him. "I'd like to hear your thoughts."

"My thoughts are simple enough, lord," Turner said first,

already sampling the rum. "Tis a good ol' rollicking day and night, but only fun if that's what you're seeking. I'm not sure if it'd be your scene, if I'm bein' honest with you. People get stupid. They drink and strip and let go o' their thoughts for the night, and for most that's fine but perhaps not for a man like you. With those shadowfolk on your tail it might only make you vulnerable. If one's lurkin' hereabouts then there'd be no better time to strike."

Jonik nodded. It was a fair point, though he felt quite certain that his head start remained ample for the time being. Still, there were other considerations now. With his notoriety spreading, it was possible that independent assassins and sellswords might have picked up his scent. The Shadow Order weren't in the habit of outsourcing their work, but that wouldn't stop a resourceful cutthroat from seeking him out anyway. *Kill first, ask questions later.* Many such men operated like that.

"It'd be unwise to let your guard down," Brown Mouth Braxton agreed, taking the rum from Turner and gobbling down a swig through his lopsided jaw. He wiped his mouth with the back of his sweat-stained sleeve. "And I'd say that goes for all of us, after what you and Master Emeric did to those sellswords back on Passway Key. We'll all be wanted men now after that. Lady Shark will have put prices on our heads, and I don't want to lose mine to some cutthroat at the beach."

"Aye," said Turner. "The Shark's fond o' her grudges, it's true, and each o' us are known to her. We might be safe o' her grasp once we reach Lumara, but not here." He looked around the harbour. "Might be that one of these ships is full o' her men, creeping about looking for us. Not a thought to make me want to celebrate."

"And you, Grim?" asked Jonik, looking to the scrawny hollow-cheeked man. Soft Sid towered next to him, at least four times his measure, gazing dully out to the harbour and chewing on something like a cow does cud. "Sid? Any thoughts?"

It was more a courtesy to ask Sid, who just grinned and bobbed his head, as Grim Pete gave answer. "Shame to miss the nudity and such, real shame, but can't disagree with what's been said," he replied in that grating scratchy voice of his. "I rather fancy staying alive for now. And there were those ships after us, you remember, a few days back." His sunken fearful eyes were looking over the boats. "Maybe one's caught up."

"You recognise any of them, Grim?" asked Turner.

The cadaverous little man didn't seem sure. "Might," he said. "The Shark's ships raise dark blue sails, and she likes sharks for her figureheads too. He pointed. "That one, look." There was a ship some way off with furled sails of deep navy and the suggestion of a fish-like creature sculpted at the prow.

Brax was peering forward. He shook his head. "Nah, that's a merman, not a shark. Not one of Lady Greyskin's. And anyhow, those ships behind us were too far off to have caught up by now. Mightn't be till evening that they get here."

"If they come here at all," said Turner, taking back the rum. "This ain't the only island to entice seafaring men like us. And they might think we've passed right by."

"She'll have sent birds too," Grim said. "You know she will, Cap. She'll have every rotten killer in the region looking for us." He spat a sharp breath. "Why'd Manfrey have to kill those men? It's only courted us more trouble."

"We had no choice," Jonik said. "If we hadn't killed them, they'd have slaughtered every one of you right there on the beach."

"I wasn't impugning you, my lord," Grim said, quick to drop his beady black eyes. "No, twas Manfrey caused that affray."

"*Lord* Manfrey," Jonik corrected. "He is lord of an ancient, noble house, Grim. You'll refer to him as such."

"And you'll not pass blame neither," said Turner, adding to the reprimand. "Lord Jonik's right. Those men needed killin', just as that beastly kraken needed drivin' off. So show some thanks, Grim, and some respect besides. Every breath you suck down that wrinkly old gullet o' yours is a blessing, d'you hear? By rights you should be dead twice over."

Jonik wasn't interested in furthering this. Grim Pete had a tendency to whine on when he got going, and Turner's rebukes could get nasty. "I've heard enough," he said. "We'll set off tomorrow morning, and sleep on the ship tonight, no exceptions.

Two men on watch at all times. If a skiff comes near, and neither Emeric or I are awake, see to it that we're roused immediately. Lady Shark's men will know what Invincible Iris looks like, so they'll try to creep aboard and slaughter us as we sleep." He thought for a moment. "Might be best if either Emeric or I are up at all times, just in case." He didn't imagine they'd be attacked, not with the Ghost of the Shadowfort aboard, but could never know for sure. "Gill, is there anything else you need in town or at market?"

"More rum," answered Braxton for him. He shrugged and looked at Turner. "You did say you wanted a second load, Cap."

Gill Turner nodded. They'd seen off half a bottle between them already and those crates only held twelve apiece. "Twas my thinking, lord, if you'll allow it."

"Of course. Go ahead and get what you need. Grim, stay here with Sid. Where's Lord Manfrey now?"

"He ran into some associate in town," Turner said. "Someone he knew from Lumara. Think they're catching up on the gossip."

"I see. Then I'll come with you, see if I can track him down. Once you're back from market, fetch Jack and Devin back to the ship. Devin will whine about it but ignore him. I want everyone gathered aboard by nightfall."

"Aye, lord, we'll see it done."

Jonik found Emeric Manfrey outside a whitewashed mud-brick tavern, sitting alone at a table and nursing an ale. He'd arrayed the wooden setting with parchment, ink pot, and quill, and was busily writing a letter. Along the sandy streets, men were selling wares from carts, costermongers calling out their latest deals in a range of languages. As Jonik passed by a wain loaded with fruit, the vendor turned quickly to the common tongue, transitioning mid-sentence from what sounded like Agarathi. "Dates, apples, pineapples, oranges, we have it all sir. We have more, much more. Take a look. I give you good price. A good deal for a good man. Are you a good man, sir?"

That last question was a little unusual, though Jonik took it for a simple mis-translation and didn't offer answer, as he pressed right past and the vendor's Agarathi resumed. Elsewhere, children were rushing about with trinkets for sale, bakers' boys were peddling cakes and tarts and sweetened breads, and all about the streets and squares, entertainers were busking and singing and dancing, charming snakes, juggling knives, eating fire, and doing a whole lot else besides.

It was such a bustle of noise and activity that Emeric Manfrey didn't notice Jonik's coming before he was a short metre or two away, looking entirely lost in thought. "Ah, Jonik," he said, once he'd spotted him pressing through the crowd. "You found me." His thick, neatly cut black beard spread into a smile. "It's rather hectic here, isn't it? Seems the festivities are already beginning for the Day of Dawning. Have you heard about it?"

"There's a lot of drinking and nudity." Jonik pulled up a chair and sat down, excavating a space for himself among the throng. "Who are you writing?"

Emeric set down his swan-feathered quill, and took up his ale instead. "Miss Brewilla," he said. "She's the head housekeeper at my estate. Would you like an ale?" Before Jonik could answer he'd summoned a boy and a wooden tankard was being plonked down ahead of him.

Jonik took a short sip. He rather preferred the taste of rum and fruit juice, though wasn't like to admit it. "Gill told me you'd run into an associate of yours," he said, as Emeric paid the boy, slapping a half sickle into his hand with a grateful smile. "Did he report anything interesting?"

Once the boy had dashed off, Emeric's smile soured. "Interesting and troubling," he said. "The man's a merchant I know by name of Dax'or Zin, come for the festivities, and like to stay a while after on account of the war. He's wealthy enough that he can hide here for a dozen lifetimes if he wishes it."

"Dax'or Zin," Jonik repeated. "Sounds like an Agarathi name."

"It is. He's from Videnia off the Askar Delta but plies his trade all over. As with all good merchants, he likes to keep his ear to the ground. As far as he tells me, Agarathi agents have been heading into the Lumaran Empire in great abundance, trying to secure support in the war. The more militaristic types across the Empire are stirring, he says, and that is cause for concern for a man like me."

Jonik had to think a moment to put it together. "You think you're under threat, being a northerner living in the south?"

"I don't know as yet, but it's certainly a worry. I'm instructing Brewilla to hire more security for my home and staff. I am well known in those parts and my workforce might be targeted by association to me."

"Then we oughtn't stay here any longer," Jonik said. "We must return to your home as soon as possible, Emeric."

"I had hoped you'd say that, my friend." He favoured Jonik with a warming smile. "But there is one other consideration."

"Go on."

"The route." Emeric drew into his satchel and pulled out a map of the south, laying it down on the table. "At any normal time, travel between the Golden Isles and Lumara is simple enough. Most choose to give the Wings a wide berth, sailing south around them." He traced an arc with his finger past those feared islands, tapping when he reached the city of Solas, where his estates were situated. "If time is more pressing, and dragon activity is minimal, then others might choose to travel through Dragonwatch Pass. It is quicker by half, depending on the weather, but at a time like this, comes with risk."

"Dragons," Jonik said.

"Yes. By Dax'or Zin's account, they have never been known to be so wild. Many have flown to the Nest, lured by the Bondstone to be saddled by Fireborn riders, but there are dozens of others that remain untamed and feral. The Wings grow restless, it is said, and many dormant dragons stir. There have been numerous reports of ships being attacked, and some have even taken to eating livestock, rather than the fish and sharks and whales they typically prey on. This is troubling indeed, Jonik. It makes any route east most perilous."

"But necessary," Jonik said without delay. "We must return to your home, Emeric, whatever the dangers. What other option do we have?"

Emeric let out a sigh. "Stay here for a time. Hope things calm. Then sail east when we hear that the dragons have settled."

"Is that likely to happen?"

"Not from what I've heard."

"Then there's no sense in waiting. The others are concerned about Lady Shark's men and the threat of cutthroats on our tail, and are keen to leave as well. I've spoken with them, and given my orders. We'll leave tomorrow, Emeric, if it suits you?"

"It does." Emeric Manfrey gave him an appreciative look. "You're fast becoming a leader, as I'd hoped, Jonik." He drained his drink, folded his map and parchment, and set the topper to the bottle of ink. "Now I'd best send off this letter. Will I meet you back at the ship?"

"That'd be best, I think. There's some concern that we'll be set upon tonight. If you're willing, I'd have you take a time on watch yourself." He looked at the exiled lord. With the others he could give instruction now, but not Emeric. As far as he saw it, they were somewhat even in standing. One a banished lord, stripped of land and title, the other a bastard of an ancient house, and bearer of the Nightblade.

"I'd be happy to," Emeric said, with a warm smile. "By my mind we're perfectly safe here, but if it'll give the men some succour, so be it."

"Then it's settled." The men shook hands. "I'll see you back on the ship, my lord."

Emeric Manfrey smiled. "And I you. My lord."

The concerns of the men turned out to be unfounded that night, though Jonik determined to forgo his own bunk just in case. For much of it, he wandered around on the moonlit deck, looking out to the glittery lights of the island and listening to the roistering going on at the beach bars and taverns that lined the pretty shore. Only Devin seemed grumpy about his confinement, muttering about his blissful night with Kulia that would never now transpire. As far as Jonik was concerned, it probably never would. Devin was a handsome lad, but a puppy to these girls, and that peck on the cheek was likely no more than politeness, if not pity.

When he wasn't wandering about the deck, Jonik was in

conference with whomever was on watch, and with all the noise and celebrations going on, no one but Sid found it easy to sleep. At one point, he entered into discussion with Emeric and Turner about which course to plot. It seemed like folly to make for Dagonwatch Pass, though shaving another week or more from their trip was tempting enough for them to consider it. "We'll have some days before we need to choose one or t'other," Captain Turner concluded, and in matters of navigation, his voice still held great sway. "So we needn't decide now. But my instinct is to take the southern route. Seems needless to risk the pass."

It was the general consensus, and even Emeric, despite his haste to get home, agreed. "There would be no sense in us speeding through the gap if only to be set upon by a hungry drake. That's not to say the south will be free of risk, but it seems the more sensible course."

"Dragons don't like to fly at night, so tend to stay relatively close to land." Jack had joined them and made that point. He didn't like to miss out on these brainstorming sessions if he caught wind of them. "If we sail far south of the wings we should be OK. I assume that's what most ships are doing."

Emeric liked Jack o' the Marsh as much as everyone else. "It is, Jack. You're quite right." He gave the burly man a smile.

"Just so long as we don't go too far south," Turner put in. "Some say you might just tip over the edge o' the world if you stray down there..."

"A northern belief," Emeric told him. "No one south of the Red Sea thinks that."

"Aye, true, Lord Manfrey. Just pointin' it out is all. But the sea beasts are all too real, and those we do need to watch for. We'll have to keep an eye on the skies and the seas. Further you go from the coast, bigger the monsters get."

"Well swell," said Jack. "Dragons to the north and leviathans to the south."

"Aye," Turner laughed. "Tis all about threadin' the needle, but no matter, we'll be fine." That confidence was for Jonik's presence among them. "No harm'll come of us with Lord Jonik here. Not to lessen your worth, Lord Manfrey, but you don't wield a Blade o' Vandar like he does."

"I take no offence, Captain Turner. My thoughts are much the same."

Jonik had to leave them at that lest the compliments become too distressing for him, stepping away to the stern of the ship to keep watch alone. Checking no one was near, he drew the Nightblade from its lightless scabbard, as the mists lifted and swirled from its edge, lit by the distant orange blur of the torches away on the beach. "And what is it you say?" he whispered to it. "Is it south we should go? Or through the pass?"

The mists changed, ever so slightly, shifting and roiling in answer. He found he could understand them. And in his head, he heard them. *South,* came that deep distant whisper. *You will go south, Jonik.*

Jonik nodded to the voice and moved to the rail, looking out onto the shore. He lay the Nightblade atop the wood, one hand holding light at the ancient black hilt. And standing there alone, he entered into another conference.

A conference in his mind.

A conference with a god.

27

Lythian

The crowd roared and jostled about them, a swarm of violent swarthy faces. The chains were tight at Lythian's wrists, cutting into his skin, as he staggered behind the horse drawing him along. He wore a suit of filth from heel to head, blood, mud, and spit. The only true fabric upon him were his tattered breeches, the rest of him bared to the blasting sun as he shambled barefoot along the sooty cooked cobbles beneath the blazing midday sky.

The heckling ahead of him continued, and along the streets the Agarathi commoners were packed, pointing and laughing. Borrus was their focus. Despite their long starvation, his belly remained ample and thick with fur, wobbling left and right as he hobbled along the scorching pavestones, tripping on his legcuffs to a chorus of rattles and howls. "Curse you!" he roared, scrambling back to his feet. "Curse you curs! I am the heir to House Kanabar! God-blood fills my veins!" It did him little good to fight, earning him nothing but a volley of dung and stones, but by this point he didn't seem to care. "The Steel Father slay you all! May he cut down every last one of you, man, woman and child!"

The mob were only spurred by his bellicose bellowing, their jeers and boos growing louder. Some men tried to break through the crowds to get at him with sticks, but were duly held back by the crimson-caped soldiers lining the route. Behind, Lythian could hear Tomos coughing. He glanced back to find the younger knight doubled over, hacking into the rusty-red dirt, as several guards kicked and prodded at him with the blunt ends of their black spears. "Up, up, up!" one ordered. "Stand up! Stand up!"

He can't, thought Lythian, *with you all crowding about him.* He'd said not a word on their forced march through the city thus far, but now his voice ripped free. "Leave him, damn you! Let him stand...give him space!"

"Be silent!" The order hissed from ahead, spat through the thin tight lips of the mounted dragonknight leading him. "You'll not speak again, Kingkiller! Not a word from you!"

Lythian ignored him. "Leave him," he called again, as the soldiers continued to jab and kick at Tomos. "He has nothing to do with this. Nothing! Leave him be..."

"Silent!" the dragonknight growled. "Silent or you'll get the lash!"

"I'll not be silent! I'll not!"

"Then you'll be flogged!" rippled the dragonknight's voice. "Let us see the colour of your godly blood!"

A tall bearded scourger was following behind him, wearing nought but a pair of black breeks, waiting patiently for his chance. Lythian had just enough time to see the grim eager smile on his lips before he pulled back his sinewy brown arm, and unleashed his black leather whip. The lash *cracked,* cutting a ribbon of red across his bare back. Pain shot through him. Violent. Searing. "Another!" roared the dragonknight, and the scourger happily obliged. "Another," he said again, and a third gash opened up. "You'll get more if you speak again, Vandarian! Be silent!"

Lythian staggered from the blistering pain but managed to keep his footing. His eyes watered, and down his back he felt a warm trickle of blood. But behind him Tomos was still being beaten. He set a clench to his jaw, blotted out the pain, and turned. "Stop...leave him..." he called, weak now, but defiant. "Leave him be..."

"He wants more," laughed the dragonknight, grandstanding for the throng. "Give him eight! Eight for Eldur! Eight!"

The crowd hooted and shrieked at that, and the scourger set forth to his task. Once, twice, thrice came the whip, as Lythian's head grew blurred. By the fourth he was losing consciousness, from his hunger and the heat and the pain. He stumbled at the fifth, dropping a knee to the hard hot floor, but up he went again as the sixth stung his skin. "Harder!" the dragonknight called. "Harder! Harder! Harder!"

The last two Lythian hardly remembered. They felt like they cut to the bone. He went forward again, his manacled wrists hitting the hot dusty road with a rattle and a clang. The crowd jeered, but his ordeal wasn't over. "Yah!" the dragonknight called, as he kicked his spurs. "Yah! Yah!" The slack length of chain separating Lythian to the horse quickly tautened, hauling him off his feet. He landed on his stomach, taking a mouthful of dry copper dust as his chin jutted into the cobbles. "Yah! Yah!" The horse set off into a gallop, dragging the Varin Knight down the uneven pavestone street, their blunt edges punching against his shoulders, arms, hips. And the crowd roared their pleasure. They laughed and cheered and roared.

When he finally came to a stop, the Knight of the Vale was only semi-conscious, a blur of gold and red and black shapes around him. The soldiers hauled him to his feet in a daze. "Stand! Stand!" He was pulled up, slapped hard across the face. "Stand or be dragged again!"

He took a ginger pace to test his footing and near stumbled once more, though a firm hand steadied him. A moment later, a swift shadow passed overhead, blotting out the sun. He glanced up. *A dragon*...It screeched as it passed, an ear-splitting sound, trailing a billowing cloud of red grit. The horde cheered again, giving name to the winged beast. "Malathar!" they called out. "Malathar! Malathar!" Lythian blinked against the blinding sun and saw the dragon wheel away, gold glittering on its coal-black scales. He recognised it, the name and dragon both, a short-winged, thick snouted brute that had lived through the war, slaying a dozen Bladeborn knights in the process with his famed Fireborn rider, Vargo Ven.

Lythian squinted at the figure saddled atop the beast, tiny

upon its broad scaly back. *Is that him now?* It was hard to tell as the dragon arced and turned, swooping over the hollering horde, heading toward the shape of a vast arena ahead. "On! On!" came a call, and the parade started moving again, the shackles at Lythian's wrists pulling tight as he stumbled forward amid the snorts and jeers. His eyesight cleared further, and he soon saw that the arena was shaped in the likeness of a great, sleeping dragon, its body curled to a circle, tail looping about itself and resting under its chin. Through its yawning jaws men entered, and upon its huge inner scales they sat on tiers and terraces. *The Pits of Kharthar,* Lythian remembered. *The famous fighting arena of Eldurath.*

He'd always wanted to see it, though never like this. They used to battle dragons here to determine hierarchy among the Fireborn ranks, he recalled, though in recent centuries it had played host to gladiatorial contests and executions too. Above the gaping dragon-maw entrance, two nostrils snorted fire, and either side men were working great bellows. The air rumbled as though the arena itself were breathing, and from within the drums were beating like a heart...ba-dum...ba-dum.

"Vargo Ven, Lythian. Did you see? It's Ven and that stout-nosed beast of his!" Borrus's voice was a blur behind him now, faint among the noise. "Lythian? Can you hear me, Lythian?"

"Shut up, Bloated Knight! Or feel the lash!" spat a man.

"Lash me raw if you wish it," Borrus returned. "What more can you do to me?" The whip cracked and cracked again, shortly followed by Borrus's laughter. "You'll have to do better than that. Give a real man that lash and perhaps I'll feel something. If there is a real man among you."

"I'll strip the fat off you, hog!" Borrus's personal scourger had another go, though the Barrel Knight's laughter only ended after the fifth or sixth strike. *Even he will break eventually,* Lythian thought. *But no matter. It's time now...time to die.* He looked up as he stumbled along. *Steel Father, give me strength. Let me die well, my lord. Let me not cry out...*

The drums were still playing ahead, ba-dum, ba-dum, as the stadium loomed close. Above, several drakes cut through the skies, shrieking. Others were perched atop the stands, their talons clutching at the scales on the great dragon's back. Malathar still whirled, larger than the rest, and older and grimmer besides. He had a great many godsteel-inflicted slashes and gashes across his scaly black-gold hide, but no Bladeborn had even been able to permanently maim him. And now it came back to him. *Borrus...he duelled him during the war.* It had been at a skirmish not far from Blademelt in the first year of the conflict, and a few of those scars were from Borrus's own blade.

Trumpets came now, added to the drums, wailing an ugly tune. The procession slowed and then stopped, as men came forward to unshackle the Varin Knights from their fetters. They were corralled together at the tips of black spears, lined up side by side. Borrus looked beaten but not broken, a lattice of gashes across his bloodied back. Tomos teetered where he stood, wheezing, though in his kind blue eyes there was steel.

"So what now?" Borrus asked, finding some further defiance as he stared at the dragonkinghts before them. "Here's an idea...give me my godsteel blade and let's see how good your dragons are." His eyes moved up as Malathar passed over. "I have unfinished business with Ven. You hear that, Vargo!" he roared. "Come face me like a man!"

The black dragon was wheeling their way, its hide glittering gold in the sunlight. The crowd parted like scuttling ants as Malathar came down, lining up and landing vertically with a heavy, shuddering thump, the dusty air fleeing in its wake in a great billowing cloud. And when it parted, so Vargo Ven appeared, calmly unclipping himself from his saddle. "This one always had a big mouth," came his low growly voice as he slid down off Malathar's wing. "Even as we fought he couldn't shut that great blubbery maw of his."

He landed smooth on the stone cobbles outside the Pits, garbed in black dragonscale armour of fine, rich detail. His shoulder clasps were gilded dragon claws, gripping at his blended gold-black cloak, and on it Lythian saw a dragon clutching a misting blade in its sharp, hooked talons. *The crest of House Ven,* he knew. Every great house in Agarathi bore a dragon on their crest.

"So good to see you again, Vargo," Borrus said. He gave a

bow, showing the licks of red criss-crossing this back, trying not to cringe against the biting pain. "I'm a little underdressed compared to when we last met, but I hope you'll not hold that against me."

"You're perfectly dressed for a man like you, covered in spit and shit." Vargo Ven was from one of the richest houses in Agarath and had the accent to match, more refined than most of his kin when speaking the common tongue. "And I do not imagine your armour would fit you anymore. You're twice the size as when I last saw you."

"Oh this?" Borrus shook his shrinking belly, plastered with spittle and dung. "Believe me, it was a great deal bigger a few weeks ago. I've wanted to shed some weight for years, so I suppose I can thank your benevolent new king for that. We haven't been fed especially well, you see, since moving quarters. But no matter. All the better for my appetite when I join Varin and his feast."

Vargo Ven gave out a gruff guffaw. "You'll eat even Varin's table clean. No god can contend with your appetites, Sir Borrus."

"How kind of you to say."

"It was not meant as a kindness."

"Then you'd best refresh yourself of our culture, good man. In East Vandar we take pride in our size."

Vargo Ven laughed at that, and then the dragonknights followed, then the soldiers, then all the crowds about them. A cacophony of ugly noise swelled and spread and all the while, Lythian peered past them into the stadium. Through the entrance of jaws and teeth, and across the sands and dirt, he could see the vague form of King Tavash Taan sitting in his private balcony, beneath a rich red canopy, sipping at a golden goblet. Girls in scant white cloth were waving great fans to cool him, and colourful nobles stood in their layered robes mingling and smiling and laughing and toasting.

Lythian felt a boiling in his blood at the sight of them, puffed up and pompous in their fineries. He had so much reason to hate them. They were an insult to every ideal he held dear. Honourless. Unscrupulous. A parade of fawning sycophants bowing to their new tyrant king. *Do they not care?* he thought, staring. *Not care that their new king is leading them to war? That hundreds of thousands of their countrymen are set to die for nothing but his vanity and pride?*

He felt a shove as a dragonknight swung his spear and pushed him in the shoulder. "Focus!" he spat. "When Lord Ven speaks, you listen! Or you'll have another kiss of the whip!"

Lythian didn't have to look at the scourger licking his lips behind him. Each of them had a man at their back, bare-chested and cruel and keen to do their work.

"There will be no need for that," Vargo Ven said with a smile. "I see these men are broken already."

"You'll never break us." Lythian gave the man his full attention. "Knights of Varin do not break, nor yield, Lord Ven. If this is your intention, you have failed. You and that murderer you call king."

"Murderer, is it? Now how is that, Captain Lythian? I see but one killer here. A kingkiller!" He turned to the crowd. Not all could speak much of the common tongue, but they knew and liked that word. So their voices came together again. *Kingkiller! Kingkiller! Kingkiller!* Vargo Ven watched with a smile as more stones and fruit and shit assailed them, until he raised a hand and called for silence, lest he get caught with a stray load of muck. When some calm was restored he said, "Now who's to go first, I wonder? Captain, you seem fond of killing. I think I'll let you choose."

Lythian stared the man in the eye. "I'll not."

"No? You who hold your honour so dear? Might you not spare your friends and step forward? Or are you not so courageous as they say?"

"Let it be me." Borrus Kanabar stepped forward a half pace as the dragonknights swung their spears to stop him. "Give me my blade, Ven, and then speak of courage. You think yourself so mighty? Prove it." He slapped away several spears and snarled. "Show yourself a man and make it a real fight. Or be called coward forever."

Vargo Ven stared with black gold pits for eyes. "Your words are empty and meaningless. It would be no challenge..."

"Then I call you coward!" Borrus bellowed. "Coward! Coward! Coward!" One of the dragonknights drove the butt of his spear into Borrus' heavy gut, punching the air from him as he doubled over, wheezing. Vargo Ven gave a dismissive nod and several other men surged in, kicking and beating the man while he was down.

"Now, where was I?" Vargo Ven said, as Borrus was battered at his feet. He had to raise his voice over the baying crowd to be heard. "Ah yes. You were going to choose, Sir Lythian. Or refusing to." He smiled. "Well then, I'll take the decision from you if you'll not step forward." He flashed a wrist at Tomos. "This one. See him prepared."

A second group of men now descended, grabbing at Tomos and dragging him away. "No..." Lythian was moving, struggling, as hands came to restrain him. "No, Lord Ven. He is innocent of this. Sir Tomos has done nothing. Nothing. He's not killed a man before nor took part in our plot. Keep him as a prisoner. Keep him for ransom. It's Borrus and I you want."

"This is true," Ven was nodding, "but neither of you are broken yet. This boy Tomos is. And perhaps his death will see you crack."

"Lord Ven!" Lythian called, but his voice could hardly be heard now. The Dragonlord was turning and walking away, leading Tomos and his handlers to the arena. Others crowded forward around Lythian, returning the hot heavy chains to his wrists. There was still punching and kicking to the side of him, and Borrus was somewhere in that huddle. "You're making a mistake, Vargo!" Lythian called out. "Take me! Let me speak to Tavash! Stop..."

Vargo Ven didn't answer, but merely swished a hand and called for the soldiers to end Borrus's beating. "I want him conscious. I want him watching. These men have more suffering to do."

Everything was a blur. Of noise and colour and movement. Borrus was hauled to his feet, his head drooping forward, blood running from cuts on his lips and nose and cheeks. A man stepped forward and thrust something beneath his nostrils to revive him, and his lungs suddenly wakened, pulling in a long ragged breath. A few orders ripped through the din in Agarathi and Lythian felt himself bundled forward at Borrus's side. The Barrel Knight blinked and spat blood and asked through swelling lips, "Where's Tomos?"

Lythian couldn't answer. *Be brave, Tomos,* he was thinking. *Be brave. Die with dignity. The Steel Father is watching.* He hoped the Red Knight of the Helm was thinking the same, he prayed for it as they went. But that hope had dwindled like a dying flame during their incarceration. The hope of rescue. The hope of salvation. He had known all along that he and Borrus would be targeted for killing so many Agarathi during the war, but Tomos? He'd never even drawn his blade, and was worth so much more to them alive. He caught sight of the royal balcony as they were dragged across the arena, to the heckling chorus of ten thousand voices. "King Tavash!" he called out. "Please, hear me, King Tavash! Hear my plea!"

But he was too far away, and the stadium was too loud, and the dozens of dragonknights bustling around him continued to block his view. He saw glimpses of the arena through them, the tiers towering high in black and red, shaped to create plates of scaly armour. Each one teemed with spectators, on their feet, throwing fists and cursing and drinking. At the highest points the Fireborn riders perched atop their dragons, watching. There must have been a dozen, two, encircling them now.

"Tomos, Lythian?" Borrus was saying. "Where...where's the boy? Where is he?" There was a dull dread in his voice. "They're not to kill him? No...they can't..." He tried to struggle but there was nothing left in him now. It was all he could do to keep walking as they were marched beneath the lowest stands, where a series of wrought iron cages awaited in the shadows. Both were shoved inside as the doors were chained, and the dragonknights took position either side, holding the points of their spears through the bars. "You watch," they were told. "You watch him die. Do not turn away. Do not close your eyes. Watch or we stab you. We stab where it hurts most."

From the shade now they looked out, across the arena. Borrus dropped to his knees, exhausted and too weakened to stand. The spears came for him, jabbing and stabbing. "Stand! Stand!"

Lythian helped him to his feet. "Hold the bars, Borrus," he said. "Hold on."

There was so much blood coming from Borrus now that Lythian wondered if he too would die right here in this cage. He'd been cut in a hundred places from the spears and fists and whips and his skin was paling beneath all the blood and filth. "He needs medical attention," Lythian pleaded, to anyone who might listen. "If you want him to stay alive then you need to see to these wounds." His own back would need attention too, lest the lacerations get infected. He didn't imagine that's how King Tavash wanted them to die, beyond the sight of the braying mob. Only a public execution would do.

"After," growled one of the older dragonknights. "You will be treated after." It was the best Lythian would get.

Across the arena now, figures were reappearing, led by the exalted form of Lord Vargo Ven. He strode with purpose toward the royal balcony, draped in black and gold, as Malathar swirled and wheeled high above him in the dusty skies. Behind came an organised cohort of crimson-caped dragonknights in fine, dark leather armour. Tomos was among them, stumbling as he went. They'd dressed him in something. Something shiny and silver. From a distance it looked almost like godsteel. Little silver and light blue ribbons had been attached to the arms and legs, trailing as he walked, as if to mimic the mists. Lythian's hands gripped the bars, squeezing. *Have faith, Tomos. You'll be with the Steel Father soon. He is watching you, waiting for you. Have faith.*

The crowd were laughing at the sight of the prisoner. He held in his hand a blunt blade, silver and large and long. Ribbons trailed from that too. "Here comes our valiant Varin Knight. Look how grand he is. How tall and proud." Even from the distance, Vargo Ven's cruel voice was clear enough. "The Red Knight of the Helm, he is called. He is thought one of the greatest swordsmen in Vandar. Let us see. Let us witness his prowess. Let us sit in awe of his might."

The dragonknights started to disperse, spreading out toward the sides of the arena. Tomos stood his ground at its heart, as the hordes watched on from the stands, and the bellows were blowing and breathing, the drums thudding ba-dum, ba-dum. All else was murmurs and whispers now as the crowds settled into their seats, and as they did so King Tavash stood from his throne. Before him, Lord Vargo Ven dropped his head into a deep bow, his blended black-gold cloak fluttering in the breeze. The murmurs and whispers shrivelled into a deep silence, and the drums went with them, beating quiet and slow, ba-dum...ba-dum. For an age it went on, and for a moment, Lythian felt a stirring hope as Tavash stared down at Tomos. *Might he show mercy? Might he let him live?* But it took no more than a single word from the Divine Protector to sever that hope. He filled his lungs and said loud and clear, "Begin." And so it did.

They came from the tunnels built into the sides of the arena, scurrying forward, snarling. Some were spitting fire and smoke. All were black and stunted, kept in the darkness and the dungeons. Dragons grew to fit their surroundings, they said, and even those that might become mighty would be forever small if kept confined. But these weren't dragons, not really. Their wings were weak and underdeveloped, unable to bear their weight. Some looked malnourished, skinny and sunken around the ribs, starved for occasions like this. As they scampered into the open, the noise became deafening. Across the arena, several of them made for one another, snapping and biting and fighting like dogs until their handlers rushed in with whips, slashing to force them apart. Several others made straight for Tomos, who spun and wheeled about with his blunted streaming sword, fending them off as they came. He seemed to find some energy, sidestepping, slashing, gliding left and right, back and forward. The crowd jeered at each move, and cheered when the drakes lurched in, snapping and prowling about him. Lythian could hardly watch. Borrus was clinging onto the bars, white-knuckled, a ghostly pale look on his face. His eyes glimmered in the shadows. It was a tragic, wretched thing.

It didn't take long for Tomos to tire. There was only so much he could do. Once all dozen drakes had surrounded him, there was no way for him to fend them off. But still he tried. Left, right, back, forward. He spun and slashed and swung at them, but nary a strike left a mark.

"He knows Varin is watching," Borrus whispered, a single tear crawling out from his eyes, cutting a clear glistening line down his cheek. He managed to smile through his bloody swollen lips. "Vargo Ven was always a fool. He gives him a chance for glory. This *is* glory, Lythian," he insisted, looking over. "They'll sing of this at Varin's Table. They'll welcome him proudly for this."

It didn't make it any easier to watch, and soon the beasts were closing in. They'd been trained to toy with their prey, and at the sides of the arena, Lythian could see their grim ugly handlers calling out in Agarathi words he didn't understand. But he didn't need to; he could translate by way of the creatures' movements as they darted in and out, nipping and biting and taunting their prey. It was a slow sorry dance, a horror to witness never mind endure, but still Sir Tomos Pentar fought on, still he blocked and swung and swiped and did as he was trained to do too. *But when the flood-gates open, there will be no stopping them,* Lythian knew. *They will slake their hunger on his flesh...they'll eat poor Tomos alive.*

The first bite that drew blood had the crowd gushing and rushing back to their feet. From the side, a tamer roared out a command and in went one of the beasts, snapping at Tomos's ankle, ripping flesh and skin from the bone. Tomos gave out a short sharp piercing roar, but rose back to his feet in an instant. The blood trailed from his leg, red on the sand. If anything it revived him for a few moments, a false dawn that wouldn't last. As here came the second attack, to his right arm now. Several fingers were chomped off as Tomos bellowed and slashed, catching the fiend in the eye, and the dwarfish drake yelped and snorted fire, backing away. It looked like Tomos had blinded it, cutting a gash where it was soft and weak. Blood came bubbling out from the socket and several of the other creatures took note, sniffing, flapping their malformed little wings excitedly, pouncing on their new prey. The handlers were roaring out and rushing in with whips, but it made no difference. Within a few short heartbeats the wounded dragon was beneath three or four others, as they ripped and tore at its flesh, quenching their craving for blood.

Tomos took a chance and backed away, hobbling on his good foot, dragging the other. Blood dripped liberally from his severed fingers. A couple more dragons rushed in for the feast, as the handlers slashed with their whips in a bid to break them up. One was particularly insistent and the misshaped little monsters didn't like it. Three turned on him, and soon the buffet had doubled. The rest of the handlers backed away lest it be tripled, and that had half the arena laughing. The stands shook and rumbled overhead, and still the bellows were breathing and the drums were beating, louder now and louder still, BA-DUM...BA-DUM...BA-DUM.

"They're his, Lythian...they're *his* kills," Borrus said through a weak slurry voice. He looked close to passing out, his bloody hands slipping on the bars. "He killed a dragon, Lyth. That was him. And...and an Agarathi soldier. They count as soldiers, those...those handlers." He smiled. "They'll be cheering up above. Louder than this. They'll be cheering for him, Lythian."

Lythian didn't think it could get any louder. He'd never heard anything like it. His brain felt like it was swelling in his skull. *It's the thirst, the hunger, the heat,* he knew. But still Tomos was fighting. Still he was defying them. *How...how is he doing this?* He'd been at death's door for days, hardly clinging on. But this...

The Red Knight had some space to himself now. He fixed his footing such as he could, as one of the pygmy drakes loped toward him, slathering like a dog. It launched itself from the sand as it neared, but got only a mouthful of steel for its trouble. With the precision of a surgeon, Tomos thrust his long dull blade down the creature's throat, plunging it through the back of its neck in a burst of black red blood. "Another," Lythian found himself blurting out. "He's got another, Borrus!"

Borrus's eyes flickered and a weak smile simmered on his lips. "He can be proud now," he whispered. "He...he need not fear...his death."

No, he need not. Lythian felt Borrus begin to slide, so wrapped an arm about his thick waist, holding him up. "We watch," he urged "We watch him ascend together."

Borrus nodded, finding some final strength, and out in the

arena the beasts were closing in. Tomos had done enough, and he seemed to know that now. He'd spent his strength, and so faced his end with courage, putting himself into Blockform, blade forward, waiting.

And when they came there was nothing he could do. Four of them rushed in together, charged together, pounced together. There were no handlers nearby to call orders or halt them; the blood drove them now, the scent of flesh, the feast. And so Tomos crumbled beneath the weight of four ravenous ill-formed dragons. They snapped and tore and feasted, and so passed the Red Knight of the Helm.

Rising, proud now, to take his seat at Varin's Table.

28

Elyon

Elyon stood within the private pavilion of Prince Rylian Lukar, looking out through the tent flaps as the womanly form of Lady Cecilia Blakewood approached. She moved through the pale midmorning sunlight in a warm green gown and brown fur over-coat, her leather boots sucking at the light coating of churned snow and mud that now blanketed much of the camp.

"You wished to see me, Your Highness," she said, stepping inside.

"Let's dispense with the titles, Cecilia," Rylian said, sitting at his oak desk. He waved her forward, and she moved into position before him. "You know Sir Elyon Daecar, do you not?" Rylian went on, gesturing to him. "I understand you met him at the feast some nights past?"

Cecilia turned her eyes to the right, where Elyon stood beside a drinks counter, accoutred in his typical Varin attire. "I had that very pleasure, yes," she replied with a balanced poise to her voice. "And I'll confess I've seen you since, Sir Elyon, though only from afar. You have been most busy sieging the fortress after all."

Elyon responded to the smile she gave him with one of his own. "Not so, my lady," he said in a cordial tone. "As yet I have had no hand in the assault. We remain in the early overtures, testing the defences and the range of the Rasal defensive weapons. I am not required for that part. I'll be called upon when the siege proper begins."

"Well consider me duly educated, Sir Elyon. You must have been busying yourself with other matters, then."

"I have, my lady. Namely the freeing of innocent Rasal girls from this siege camp."

The air tightened.

"Ah, I see." Cecilia's smile fixed itself to her lips, unmoving, as she turned her attention back to the prince. "And pray tell why I've been summoned, Rylian? I fail to see what..."

"You know why you've been summoned, Cecilia," Rylian cut in. "I made a promise to Lord Paramor that all captive Rasal girls within this camp be offered a chance to leave, without fear of harassment or reprisal. By my honour I'm duty-bound to follow through, and Elyon here has been supporting the cause with much enthusiasm."

"Of course. I'd expect nothing less from the heir of House Daecar." Lady Cecilia favoured Elyon with a smile, but there was a tension behind her eyes. "However, I am still struggling to see why I've been called for, Rylian."

"Cecy, don't play dumb." Rylian was on his feet, waving a hand in frustration. "You know full well that I've never much approved of that sordid little programme you run. Well it seems the secret is out, if it was ever a secret at all. The Vandarians are demanding that your girls be released, lest they withdraw their support. I don't have to tell you how insistent Lord Kanabar can be. He is old and singleminded and in grieving at the loss of his son. That makes a man inflexible, and it's my job to smooth over any cracks between us and make sure they don't widen to fissures."

"Have you written to our father about this?" she asked, quite calm.

Rylian grew as stiff as his rich leather jerkin. "This is not his decision. Father does not run this army, Cecilia. I do."

"Of course." Cecilia dipped her chin, acquiescing. "I only wish to point out that this is his initiative, not mine. I am but his humble servant, as you are. We all live to serve him."

Rylian didn't much like that. Elyon could see his jaw clenching beneath his rusty beard, a vein beginning to thicken and throb in his neck. "Father is ageing, and absent, Cecilia. It may be that I sit the throne soon, and when I do, his breeding programme will be the very first thing to go. It has never sat right with me, never...and believe me, I've told him so. We need not resort to such methods to augment our Bladeborn ranks."

Cecilia remained perfectly still before him, hands neatly clasped at her waist. "That is not for me to say."

Rylian let out a short grunt and turned to Elyon. "You see what I'm dealing with, Elyon? My father has all of Tukor wrapped around his little finger. And me too, you probably imagine."

The thought had crossed Elyon's mind, but of course he wasn't going to say it. "I've always thought you were your own man, my lord."

Rylian gave out a short barking laugh. "Well chosen words, sir, and gratefully taken. I have always thought it incumbent on all good sons and heirs to support their fathers, where they can, and I have done so for the most part. This war, for instance. Do I feel comfortable slaying northmen? Do I enjoy sieging their cities and castles and forts? No, of course I don't, but I do it because I agree that Rasalan needs to be brought to heel. That has long been my father's course and it's one to which I agree. But other matters..."

He shook his head firmly and set his eyes on Cecilia. "Father's ambition is praiseworthy, Sister, and in keeping with the tradition of our house. But there is something in him that is broken. An obsessive fixation on matters of which he will not speak. Do not tell me you haven't seen it. He keeps almost exclusively to his own counsel, and has built a wall around himself that I have been unable to penetrate. By the gods you'd need the Sword of Varinar for that, and even then who knows what you'd find if you cut through."

I know, Elyon wanted to say. *I know what you'll find. Nothing but a sick old man who has plotted and schemed and abandoned every single shred of honour he has in his ugly pursuit of power.* He wanted to march before Rylian, look him in the eye, take him by the shoulders, and tell him the whole filthy truth of it, because it was clear the prince didn't know. But did this sly vixen he called sister? Did Cecilia know of Janilah's tricks and treachery? She ran his cursed breeding programme, true, and had blackness in her blood so far as Saska said it, but did she know more? Did she hold her father's counsel, where Rylian, his firstborn and heir, had been denied it?

"My lord," he found himself saying, eager to push things along. "You were instructing Lady Cecilia of what would be required of her."

A little smile paid a visit to Cecilia's full smooth lips. "Indeed, it is as Sir Elyon says, Brother. What is it you need of me?"

Rylian had to take a moment to compose his thoughts. "The girls," he then said, grunting the words out. "Your breeders. You're to let them go. Send them home. They're not to be part of your schemes."

"Unless they should want to," she retorted, in a tone as light as air. "I understand that the girls here in camp are being given the choice as to whether they wish to leave. Some are here to work, after all, and would prefer to stay. I hope the girls under my care will be given the same opportunity?"

Rylian sat back in his chair, mulling it over a moment. "Fine." He waved a hand to the exit. "No doubt you've worked your silver tongue on them, and they've bought into all your fine gilded promises...but let no one say I haven't tried." He turned. "Does that satisfy you, Elyon?"

Elyon gave the man a grateful nod. "It does, my lord. So long as they have a choice, that will pacify Lord Kanabar, I'm sure."

Cecilia was looking at him with a slow simmering suspicion, but Elyon had expected that. Giving the other girls in Cecilia's care an opportunity to leave was but a cover for his true purpose; releasing Saska. They'd come up with this plan the morning they'd shared a bed, after the night in which their lives and bodies had become so tangled and intwined.

"She will expect you to remember nothing of this," Saska had whispered to him, as they lay beside one another, sweaty and flush from their congress, the purply predawn light beginning to spread through the camp outside. "You can give her no indication that you recall me being here, Elyon. I'm Melany, remember. This has all been a dream to you. If she thinks we're plotting something..."

Well, they were plotting something, and by the look on Cecilia's face, she wasn't being so easily deceived as they'd hoped. *But with luck, it won't matter,* he thought. Because Rylian had one further order to give.

"Elyon will speak personally with each of your recruits, Cecilia," the prince told her, looking eager to return to more pressing business. "If any wish to leave he will take them into his care, and see them duly returned to their homes, or provided employ elsewhere. The rest will travel with you when you leave for Ilithor. I have instructed a carriage and protective cohort be gathered for departure. You'll leave this afternoon."

Cecilia took the news passively, uttering not a word.

"This displeases you," Rylian identified. "You would prefer to remain with the army?"

"I would prefer to be able to do my duty, as assigned by our king father."

"Then do it. Just not here. There was need for you to be here whilst Lord Kastor was scouring the lands for these Bladeborn girls of yours, but no longer. The practice will not continue in any army I oversee. Tell that to father when you see him, if you must. He knows my mind. It will not surprise him."

No, but it was surprising Elyon to see Rylian so defiant. When he'd sat next to the prince during the feast at his former warcamp, he'd spotted an unmistakable deference whenever his king father spoke. *But perhaps being away from his shadow has unshackled him?* he wondered. The only question was - would it last?

"If these are your orders, then I will of course obey." Lady Cecilia Blakewood bowed low before her princely half-brother, then swept her cloak and turned. "Sir Elyon, shall we?"

They stepped together into the cold morning air, rustling with the distant sound of the siege. It had been going on for a couple of days now, though as yet little progress had been made. Despite Lord Kastor's fine detailed plans, Rylian had decided to pursue a more deliberate, guarded course at first. That meant wheeling out the great groaning catapults and trebuchets and seeing what damage they could do from afar. Not much, it seemed. The defensive weapons atop the battlements of Harrowmoor, coupled with the elevated ground on which the fortress had been built, gave their own artillery an impressive range. The snows didn't help either, making the movement of the siege weapons cumbersome and slow. Several had already been targeted during their placement and destroyed, sitting now as busted husks of wood and iron on the slopes south and east of the fortress. Several others had found blindspots where the Harrowmoor defences couldn't reach them, but had nothing but ten foot thick walls, laced in places with iron and steel, to aim at. They could bombard those for months and still they'd stand tall.

Undermining was an option too, and one under consideration. So was a possible sneak attack through the sewers and tunnels on the northwestern side. There were several others being discussed at the daily war meetings, but in the end, it seemed likely that they'd fall back to Kastor's plans eventually. A full assault. Artillery battering the battlements, breaching towers and scaling ladders for the walls, Tukor's Fist smashing at the gate. They'd use the mock siege weapons Kastor had devised to draw fire, and attack at night to cause greater confusion. With tens of thousands of men scrambling about the walls, Harrowmoor would soon fall, it was thought. It would cost lives - thousands of them, no doubt - but allow them to take the fortress and turn their eyes north to continue the conquest. It was a balance, in the end, between bloodshed and haste, and to achieve the latter you'd have to sacrifice much the former.

"Do you remember much of the other evening, Sir Elyon?" asked Cecilia as he accompanied her through the camp. She took his arm, as she had that very night, to secure her footing in the more slippery sections. "You had consumed rather a lot of alcohol, it seemed to me."

Elyon drew her around a large stretch of slushy snow, keeping to the driest sections of the track. "Several men had been killed when violence broke out at the parley," he said. "We were drinking to their memory, to send them to the Eternal Halls. I don't have to tell you, Lady Cecilia, that these occasions can become quite bacchanalian."

"They can," she agreed. "And I should have known better than to call for that whiskey. I hadn't appreciated how much you had already imbibed, Sir Elyon. My mistake."

"It's OK. I'm quite well acquainted with the sensation of misplacing my faculties some way through the evening, and waking the next morning in a fog, quite unsure as to what transpired. Half my life in Varinar was like that, I'm ashamed to admit."

"Oh there's no shame in it, sir. Why not use your name and position to enjoy yourself."

"That was my thinking, my lady. Though things are rather different now, with my brother slain, and the north in such peril. I ought to take a better account of myself. I have a vague recollection of meeting you, but no more. The next thing I knew, I awoke nude in my bed some hours past dawn." He let out a short laugh. "Though thankfully, alone. I can be grateful for that at least."

She looked at him a moment, then chuckled and said, "Grateful? I imagine that would be wholly disappointing to a man like you."

He judged not to respond to the comment, as they walked on, weaving around sumps of snowy mud and through the ordered network of tents. Elyon couldn't be sure if Cecilia was buying his lies, but felt assured that he was doing the best he could to deliver them. After a time, they passed the infirmary pavilion erected for the use of the highborn men of the company. Cecilia gave it a cursory glance as they passed. "How fares Sir Rodmond?" she asked. "I understand he was injured during the affray outside the fortress gates."

"My thanks for enquiring, Lady Cecilia. He fares well, and should return to full health in the coming weeks. The arrow that struck him did no permanent damage, thankfully. He'll be left with a superficial battle scar only, which all good knights cherish."

"Badges of honour, I suppose they are? Good for hearthside stories." She smiled, seeming in no way distressed by Rylian's abrupt orders. And why would she? Surely a return to Ilithor would be favoured by such a woman, with the comforts palace life would bring. "Do you have any scars of your own, Sir Elyon?"

"Only to my heart, my lady."

"Oh come now, I'm sure that isn't true. You inflict scars to the heart, as far as I hear, rather than suffer them."

"To my discredit, I have been known to do so in the past," he agreed, still playing along. "But there is one who has left a rift in me. You will likely know her - Lady Melany Monsort. She stands at Princess Amilia's side, as her lady-in-waiting. You must have seen her about the palace."

"I know her in passing, yes. A fine looking woman. I did hear of your courtship."

Elyon nodded quietly, and liberated from his lips a regretful sigh. "She is the only girl I have ever loved," he said, and that part was at least true, for now. "She is on my mind often, I'll admit. I even dream of her...sometimes."

"Oh?"

"Yes, a wretched curse, really. It only prolongs the pain of our parting, when I wake from her embrace, to find that she isn't truly there." He let out a further sigh, realising that if she wasn't convinced by that, nothing would persuade her.

"Well..." She gripped his arm tight as they walked, giving him a supportive little clench. "If any love is meant to be, it will find a way, I always feel. Perhaps you might rekindle your romance at a later time."

"Perhaps," he said, and no more.

Soon they were breaking into the yard that led toward Cecilia's personal little camp. The tents in which her recruits were kept were lined up in a neat row, some five or so feet apart, with Cecilia's own pavilion at the far right side. Elyon gave a quick count. "A dozen," he said. "Are all of the tents filled?"

"Only half. Some of our recruits have already been sent away. And whatever my brother might think, each of them was happy to be given this opportunity. He sees them only as human broodmares, but in truth their lives will be greatly improved by their new terms of service." She tugged lightly at his arm, turning him.

Her eyes went curious. "You did know he was my brother, didn't you?"

Elyon nodded. "I'd heard, yes. King Janilah's indiscretions are well known." He bit his tongue, lest he say more.

"Indeed." Her mouth opened into a glorious chuckle. "Indiscretions. Well put. But I might also take offence, Sir Elyon, seeing as I am the product of one of them."

"I would beg your pardon then, my lady. I didn't mean it like that."

"I know how you meant it, sir. My father bedded women beyond his wedlock and fathered children from them besides. No one would call that honourable, lest they know the full truth of it."

"And that is?"

"His wife was at that time incapable of tending him. And being a man, as any other - and by that I mean, imperfect - he did find himself drawn to other women. If you had ever met my mother, Lady Jeyne Blakewood, you would understand. She was a rare beauty herself, quite alluring to even the most loyal of men."

"I am not surprised, to look at you, my lady. "

Her mouth was full of sunshine, bright and gleaming. "Your charms truly come afore you, sir. See that none of my girls fall for them when you speak." She turned back to the tents, though there was a slight suggestion in her words that Elyon didn't miss. "Now, I suppose you wish to talk to them alone?"

"That would be my preference, yes."

"Afraid I might unduly influence them if I'm looming behind you?" She let out another little laugh. "I understand. I'll return to my private quarters and prepare my effects for departure. Please do come see me when you're done. Should any of my lovely girls wish to leave my company, I would rather like to say goodbye in person."

She left him with that, moving across the open, snow-patched yard toward her private tent. Elyon followed behind her a few steps, preparing to enter the tent immediately to the left of hers. "Oh there's no one in there, Sir Elyon," she told him. "Start with Margo - she's three tents down. You'll find the rest dispersed among the tents after hers."

"My thanks, Lady Cecilia. I shall return to you presently."

He found Margo sitting in a soft bed of red and brown and amber cushions, with a plate of breads and cheeses and olives on a table to her side, sipping mulled wine. She was a short girl, pretty-faced, with red cheeks and a handsome smile. As soon as she saw Elyon enter she fought her way to her feet, scrambling through the pillows, bowing before him. "Good day to you, milord. How might I be of service?"

Clearly, she'd formerly held employment as a maidservant before, judging by that reaction. She looked like she'd been caught in her lord's private chambers, guzzling his wine and supping on his dinner. Elyon couldn't help but smile. "I'm here to ask you whether you want to go home, Margo," he said. "Margo - that is your name, isn't it? I was told so by Lady Cecilia."

"Yes, milord. Tis my name indeed." She did have a very pleasant smile, and looked far too nice to be sent away for breeding stock. "But...home, milord?"

"Yes. Prince Rylian has decreed that all Rasalanian girls brought to this camp be given the choice to leave, should they wish it. I am here to deliver to you that choice. You need not be here, Margo, should you have been brought against your will. Can you tell me what happened to you?"

Her story was much the same as the one Saska had told him. Margo had been living in a small village on the moors, and discovered by Sir Griffin Kastor and his troop when they passed by to pillage and plunder. "Not sure there's much left of my home, to be honest, milord," she added. "But here's the truth - I'm glad for it. Never liked living there. My father was a drunk and a brute and my mother wasn't much better. He beat me with his belt, and she with her words. Hated them both. Was happy to be rid of them."

"I'm...sorry to hear that, Margo. But there are other safe havens to which you could be taken. Or we would be happy to help you find employment elsewhere, if you'd prefer?"

"Can I stay here?" she asked, growing brighter at the thought. "With Lady Cecilia."

Elyon frowned. "You'd wish to? Even knowing what she requires of you?"

"Oh yes, milord. Very much I wish it."

"But you truly understand what it is she intends? That you will sire children for the crown. That those children will be taken away from you, once birthed."

"I understand, milord. Lady Cecilia says we are there to help nurture the children, at first. We have time with them. Give them our love. It helps them grow strong, she says. It's important...to make sure they become powerful knights. Like you, milord."

No, not like me. Like my half-brother, he thought, who'd been birthed from such a vile practice. *Like the man ripped from his mother's breast and raised in shadow and darkness.* He let those thoughts pass right by, keeping a cordial countenance all the while. "Do you want any further time to consider it, Margo?"

"No, milord, I've had time enough here. I'm eager to do something worthwhile with my life. A handsome knight awaits me in Ilithor, I'm told. I hope he's as handsome as you." She giggled, a shade of dark blush spreading right down her neck.

"Well, I hope the same, Margo." There was no sense in destroying her optimism, he knew. *And who knows, perhaps she's right?* "I will inform Lady Cecilia that you wish to remain in her custody. Good luck to you, Margo. You leave for Ilithor this afternoon."

He left her squealing in excitement at that, and moved to the next tent, which was vacant, and the next, which wasn't. Inside was a skinny girl with narrow shoulders, a pointed nose, and hips that hardly looked childbearing. "Good morning, miss," he began, as she looked at him with curious eyes. "Might I have your name?"

"It's...Gurta, sir."

"Gurta. Well met." He set about explaining to her her options, but soon came to discover that she was just as keen to remain here as Margo had been.

"Got no family, sir. No friends. Worked as a scullery maid before coming here. Was a ghost, really. But Lady Cecilia's given me a purpose, and I'll not let her down. She's saved me, sir. I owe her everything."

It was another hopeless case, and it was the same with the girls to follow. Poppy, then Quisilda, then Effy, all Rasal girls of the Lowplains who had suffered through less than pleasant lives and saw Cecilia as their salvation. They were all young, impressionable, and easy to exploit. *Perfect recruits,* he thought bitterly, but what else could he do? Rylian had proclaimed they be given a choice like all the rest, and that was all Elyon could offer. *A choice they may not yet fully comprehend,* he thought, but it was not for him to persuade them. In truth, the rest of the girls remaining in Cecilia's care served his cause. He was here for one, and one only. That was the cold hard truth.

And so he went to her now, stepping toward the final tent, as his eyes slipped through the flaps. He could already see the shadow of her within, waiting, hoping. *I have good news, Saska*, he thought. *This little plan of ours has worked.* He drew a steadying breath and moved through inside, letting the flaps fall and flutter closed behind him.

"Good afternoon," he said, as he had with all the others, as Saska stood before him in a long linen tunic, a smile simmering on her lips. "And might I have your name, miss?"

29

Saska

"Tilda," said Saska, trying to suppress her grin. "My name is Tilda, my lord."

"Tilda." Elyon stepped inside, his face stretching into a smile that she'd longed to see for days. "A pretty name. It suits you." He moved in until he was a mere half pace away, clutching at his godsteel dagger. His eyes went sideward for a moment, then he whispered, "She's in her tent, and won't be able to hear us. We can speak freely, Saska. Just quietly, OK?"

She nodded her understanding, trying to compose herself, trying to read his face. The last few days had been tortuous, wondering if their plan would actually take shape, and for the duration she'd hardly heard from him. But now here he was, right before her. "Did it work?" she whispered, looking into those silver-blue eyes. It looked like good news. *Please let it be good news.* "Is she leaving?"

He placed a hand to her shoulder and drew her a little deeper into the tent, clinging to his godsteel dagger with the other. Then he gave her the news she'd longed to hear. "She's leaving in a matter of hours," he told her, with the barest hint of a smile. "You're free of her, Saska. It's over."

Free, she thought, unsheathing a hopeful little smile of her own. *It...it worked.* "She's going back to Ilithor?"

"Yes, and with all the other girls it seems. None have elected to leave Cecilia's service."

That didn't surprise her much, not from what she'd seen. "They've all bought into her fantasy," she said, tending his arm with a grateful stroke. "You did your best, I'm sure."

"I gave them the same choice as the rest. But their fate is their own, Saska. It is yours I worry for."

She smiled at him for that. "Did you manage to convince her that you don't remember me?"

Elyon didn't seem sure. "Hard to say. I've never pretended to be much of an actor, really, but I gave it my best shot. Either way, there's nothing she can do to you anymore." Then his voice lowered yet further, and he looked at her with a soft concern. "Did she...check, in the end?" he asked. "After our night together. That you'd...lost your chastity?"

"She didn't need to." Saska turned her eyes away, feeling embarrassed all of a sudden. "She said she could tell, just by looking at me. Something about a smile on my face. A flush to my cheeks." She gave a self-effacing shrug. "I didn't realise I was so obvious."

"It can be hard to hide from those who know what they're looking for," Elyon said tenderly. "Especially when it's one's first time. But that's good, Saska. It's what you wanted."

What I wanted, she thought. *But not you?* She wasn't going to lie to herself that it meant much to him. How many women had he been with, after all. Fifty? A hundred? And was he not in love with this Lady Melany as well? She hadn't really considered that, when she'd leaped atop him, but had pondered it since during her nights here alone. *Did I force him?* she'd wondered. *Was it even consensual?* There was a horrible irony to that, given her experience. Having suffered through the vile attentions of Modrik Kastor and Lord Quintan, she'd never expected to lose her maidenhead in such an insistent manner.

"We shouldn't linger too long, Saska." Elyon's voice came again, pulling her from her thoughts. "I want you out of here as soon as possible." He turned his eyes around the confines of her luxury tent. "Is anything here yours?"

"Nothing," she said. "The clothes I wore when I arrived in camp were taken away. I have no other possessions."

And how sad was that. She truly had nothing, nothing but the godsteel dagger Marian had given her, though she'd taken it back when Saska went off on her mission. *Failed mission,* she thought, miserably. Elyon had made it quite clear that he'd not support the murder of a great lord, no matter how much he disliked him. *But has his mind changed on that account? Now that I'm free of Cecilia's watchful gaze, might I have a chance to renew my duty?*

Elyon gave her a quick inspection. "Do you have a cloak to wear over that tunic? Something warm, with a hood?"

"I do, but it's not mine. I'm not sure Cecilia will let me keep it."

"She may. Put it on, Saska, and I'll go give her my report. She'll want to say goodbye." He took a step to the exit. "Are you ready?"

She took a long deep breath, then said, "I'm ready."

A minute or two later, Lady Cecilia Blakewood was stepping into the tent, leaving Elyon to await them in the yard outside. Saska held her eyes down to avoid the woman's reprimanding glare. "I'm sorry, my lady," sped her Aramatian accented voice. "I...I know you have done a lot for me, but I...I just feel like..."

"Oh it's quite all right, Tilda. Don't look so frightened child. What the devil must you think of me?" Saska looked up to find a handsome smile on the woman's lips. *The nice side*, she thought, before those eyes retreated to the shadow, and the threats slithered off her tongue. "You need not explain, child, don't be silly. It's your life, and your choice. What sort of monster would I be if I didn't see that, hmmm?"

She wondered if the woman's words were intended for Elyon. *Does she think he's listening?* "Um...yes, my lady. I just think...the other girls...they want this more than I do. I am simple. I am happy to wash and cook and clean."

"If that is the life you want to lead, then who am I to stop you?" The smile on her lips began to grow a little more fixed, a little more forced. "Where do you think you will go?"

"I...I am not yet sure. My master was murdered by Sir Griffin's men, and my village is abandoned. I will try to seek employment in another household, I think."

"Do you want my advice?" Lady Cecilia's eyes dulled. "Leave. Leave these lands. Go south, as far away as you can get. That is my advice, Tilda. You do not belong here."

There was a frost to her voice that unsettled her, as Saska dipped her chin to break eye contact. "Yes, my lady. I may do just that. I am not sure it is safe for me here anymore."

"No, child. It isn't." She stared at her with that flat, expressionless visage, before her entire face lit up like a lantern, swelling with a sudden smile. "But my dear, good luck to you, in whatever you choose to do." She pulled her into a hug, speaking loudly now. *For Elyon,* Saska now knew for certain. "I will miss you, sweet child. I was so hoping you'd come to Ilithor with me. These other girls..." She drew away and made a face. "They're not so interesting as you. But here we are, and you've made your decision. And that is your right, of course."

Saska didn't know what to say, so decided to remain silent. Cecilia let it linger for just long enough to make it sinister and uncomfortable, before saying, "Do you have clothes? You'll need something for the cold, and something to sleep in, and something to lounge in. And..." She smiled. "Well, maybe I should just let you take the entire chest with you? You look so pretty in everything you wear, child. It would be a shame for you to part with them."

"Thank you, my lady, but that...that is too kind. I cannot possibly..."

"Well then an item or two at least?" She looked at her. "I'm hardly likely to have you strip, am I, so you can leave in what you're wearing."

There was some knowing malice in those words, some taunt. Cecilia had forced Saska to strip before her on many occasions, after all. *But no longer. You've seen me naked for the last time, witch.* "That would be most kind, my lady. But I could not take anything more."

"Are you sure? It really is no trouble."

"I am sure. You have done enough for me already."

"Well, shall we return to Sir Elyon then? The poor man waits patiently outside in the cold, what a gentleman. And what a coincidence that it is he who has come to fetch you, child." She stepped in and lowered her voice. "After the night you spent together, I might wonder if something is amiss." She set her with a deadened stare. "*Is* anything amiss, sweet girl?"

"Nothing." Saska didn't turn her eyes away this time. She stared at her, long and hard. "Nothing is amiss, my lady."

A slow creeping smile formed on Cecilia's face, before she turned and marched through the tent flaps, crunching across the patchy snow outside. Elyon was waiting patiently in the yard when they joined him. "Now you promise you'll see her safe, Sir Elyon?" Cecilia said. She gave Saska a saccharine smile. "She is a kind and honest soul and deserves to be happy. You'll see to it personally?"

Elyon stood tall and gallant in his Varin cloak and silver breastplate. "Of course, my lady."

"Promise it." Lady Cecilia withdrew her godsteel dagger, and reached forward with her spare hand. "Your godsteel oath, Sir Elyon, that Tilda will be safe."

Elyon didn't seem especially comfortable with that, but he didn't stop it from happening either when Cecilia reached and took his grasp. "I promise it," he said, with a note of reluctance. "I promise I will see her safe, such as I can. By godsteel, I promise it."

Cecilia had a twinkly little grin on her face, as though it was all a game. As though she knew how seriously Elyon Daecar took such oaths and was having a riotous old time of it, forcing him into one. "Good," she said, withdrawing her felt-gloved fingers. "I can leave now, quite happy in the knowledge that this sweet innocent girl will be safe. Farewell, both of you. I would hope we will meet again, one day."

She bowed with those words, gave her coat a little swish as she turned, and stepped away. Saska watched her go, as her chest drummed light and airy, and a long slow sigh of relief escaped her. For the first time in weeks, she could breathe. That crushing weight...it was gone.

The pair said nothing as they moved through the encampment, but for Elyon telling her to pull up her hood and conceal herself, lest someone spot her entering his tent. A few soldiers stood guard here and there, and other servants and camp workers hustled about, but for the most part anyone of import was absent on account of the siege.

Saska got a good look at it as they went. It was a clear day, the skies unburdened by falling snow, bright and breezy, and beyond the northern palisade wall of the encampment, many men and machines were at work. There looked to be some two dozen artillery weapons scattered about upon the shallow slopes south of Harrowmoor, occasionally flinging loads of rocks and boulders at the walls in a hopeless bid to topple them. Once they'd passed into the privacy of Elyon's pavilion, she said, "That won't work, you know." She gestured out through the flaps as he fastened them, in the direction of the fort. "Those walls are like tunnels when you pass through them. A few rocks and stones aren't going to do anything."

He finished fastening the flaps and turned, moving to light the dual braziers. "I know," he said as he prodded at the coals. "I think we all know, in fact. But Rylian is nothing if not thorough. He'll try everything he can to smash his way in before risking the lives of his men."

"He seems a good man."

"He is." Elyon gave life to the brazier with a taper, setting the wood and coals burning. "And not much like his vile father." He gave out a grunt. "I long for the day that Janilah falls and Rylian takes the throne. He's a just and honourable man and will make a fine king. We need one of those right now, with Ellis at Janilah's heel and Godrin losing his mind."

Saska took umbrage with that. "Who said Godrin's losing his mind?" she demanded. "That's not true. He's just old, is all, and likes to speak in riddles. But he's quite sane, I assure you."

Elyon shrugged, as he finally got the brazier lit, adding orange peel and grapevine trimmings to help sweeten the smoke. "I'm sure you're right. It's mostly the Tukorans spreading these rumours and of course they'd try to discredit him." He moved toward the second brazier, before deciding to let the first burn a while alone. "There are drinks on the counter, and food," he pointed out. "Is it too early for wine?"

"It's still morning, Elyon."

"Right." He continued to peruse his pavilion, eyes passing over the bed. "I suppose it's best that I get a pallet bed brought in, for me to sleep on. You can take this one in the meanwhile, as we figure out what to do next." He turned to check her reaction to that, though as she looked at the bed, all she could think of was their night together. It had been such a rush, such a blur, but so invigorating all the same. "What do you think? It's probably better that we sleep separately, while you're here. I'd not want you to think I'm trying to take advantage of you."

Saska gave a sour laugh at the irony of it. "I think it was me who took advantage of you, Elyon." She looked at him with a troubled frown. "I...I didn't force you into it, did I? The other night..."

He seemed to find that quite amusing. "How could you have? You can hardly overpower me, Saska."

"No, but I..."

"Don't worry about it. Honestly, you'll not hear me complaining. But we should probably make sure it doesn't happen again. It will only complicate things, and make it more difficult when we part."

Not for you, she thought. She didn't imagine he'd care much at all, with all his experience of such matters. *But might I?* She felt an undeniable attachment to him now, and one she couldn't fully understand, but for the most part she was eager to push all that aside in the face of the larger concerns they both faced.

"I'll look into getting you more clothes." Elyon went on. "Any particular requests?"

A maidservant's outfit, she thought. *So I can pose as one and sneak into Kastor's pavilion and slit his throat one night.* But she chose not to say it. Elyon had made himself clear on that and it wouldn't serve her to bring it up. "Just simple clothing will do. Something hardy for the elements, and warm for the cold."

"Of course." He took a good long look at her, as though sensing what was on her mind. "And you'll be OK here, when I'm away? You'll not go sneaking out to try to finish your mission?"

"No, of course not."

"Saska, I'll need you to promise me that. If you try to kill him and are caught, then it will all come back to me. I cannot be seen to be involved with a Rasal spy. Even having you here is a risk, not only to myself, but to my house and family. I will host you here until I can work out how to get you safely out. But you must promise me you'll not try to murder Cedrik Kastor."

He stopped short of making her do so by godsteel, trusting her to hold to her word without it. More likely, he didn't imagine she cared for such oaths. They were typically made between knights and men of honour, not duplicitous assassins and spies.

"I promise I won't try to kill Cedrik Kastor," she told him, breaking another promise in the process. To Marian, and to her own oath of service. But her long days here had shown her that Elyon was right. Kastor was rarely out of his armour now, but for when he slept, and at such times he had at least two towering Emerald Guards standing watch at his door. It was also said that he slept with a godsteel dagger in his grasp, giving him heightened senses even then. One false step, one unusual sound, and he'd be wide awake and ready for her. It seemed impossible, and of little point regardless. *Killing Kastor will do nothing to end the war,* Elyon had told her before. *No,* she thought now, *but it'll help frighten my nightmares away.*

Elyon moved to his desk, set up at the rear of the tent. It was heaped with books on history, politics, war. She saw one about siege strategies, another on fighting techniques among the Suncoats. An old dusty tome looked dedicated to the War Eternal, and all the Renewals that had followed. Another smaller book, hardly more than a pamphlet really, had an image of dark spires and towers etched into the black leather cover. "What's that one?" she asked, as he began tidying up.

He followed the direction of her gaze. "Oh, it's about the

Shadow Order. Information is scarce about them, hence the size of the book. But there are some interesting insights." He reached out and picked it up, handing it to her as she stepped over. "It was written by a former Shadowknight," he explained. "He'd kept a secret diary when he lived there and passed it onto an associate when fulfilling a contract in Vandar. Seems he'd lost faith in what he was part of and wanted to expose them, but no one knows what happened to him. Most likely they discovered the betrayal and butchered him. Only a handful of copies were ever printed and most of those were tracked down and destroyed. This is one of only a few remaining, as far as I'm aware."

"And what have you learned?" she asked, looking over the frayed leather cover, old and timeworn.

"That the place needs to be destroyed," he told her plainly. "Or at least those who've corrupted it. Ilith built it, you know, almost three and a half millennia ago. It was meant as a refuge for his people, should war spread across his lands...somewhere for them to flee to when the dragons came swarming. Some say he had his mages work magic into the towers and peaks. It's why it's so stormy there, they believe."

"There were often storms in the west," Saska said in a faraway voice, as she gently flicked through the pages, and the brazier began to grow warm behind them. "I'd watch them with Del and Llana from the porch. And Master Orryn would tell us stories of the *black storm that never ends* up there in the distant peaks of the Hammersongs. Not many believed that people lived up there, though. They said it was the spirit of a dark god, something ancient and unknown, trapped up there in the mountains. And it sounded like that, sometimes. The thunder and lighting. It sounded almost like a voice, bellowing to be released."

"Not Tukor himself?" Elyon asked. "Isn't that a belief you have there? That the storms are an echo of Tukor's dying breath, crying out as he died."

She nodded. "It's a common belief," she confirmed. "But the black storm that never ends is different. That's not Tukor. It's something else. Something older, and darker."

"It can't be. The gods made the world. There was nothing before."

She shrugged. "That's what people say. That the gods trapped the ancient spirit in the mountains. That the world was already as it is when they came here from across the endless sea, but it wasn't theirs, not originally."

"There are many beliefs," Elyon said, reaching out to take the book back. He closed it with a snap and set it down. "It's always vexed me how these creeds can become so contrary over time. Even across the north our doctrines differ...sometimes subtly, sometimes starkly, and it's just the same in the south. Take Lumara. Some people think she was a benevolent goddess, who worked tirelessly to end the war between Agarath and Vandar. Others say she was Agarath's greatest ally, as Tukor had been for Vandar. That she was wicked and warring and despised everything and everyone north of the Red Sea." He looked to another book, one about the formation and history of the Lumaran Empire, which had only been forged after the last great war. "They still fight for her soul down there," he went on. "Even since the empire was created, elements have looked to destabilise it and rekindle war with the north, believing it's what the goddess Lumara would have wanted...that at her essence she was a warlike goddess and not the pacifistic appeaser the current rulers of the empire believe."

"Her patriots," Saska broke in, staring at the book. "Ranulf told me about them. The Patriots of Lumara."

"Yes." He picked up the tome, handing it over. "It's all in here. A good book, if a little long-winded, but there's a chapter on the conflict between Empress Valura, her supporters, and the Patriots that's of interest. Agarath will be looking for allies now and will need the support of the southern nations if they're to defeat us. They'll find willing partners in the Patriots, no doubt, and may just try to have the empress overthrown. It's been theorised for years, and it all stems from these conflicting beliefs. Just like the war here. And the great war to come. And every Renewal for the last three thousand years. People fight and die by the thousands...not just for land or power or glory...but because we look at the world through different bloody lenses."

Saska held the book between her fingers, yet her eyes remained on Elyon as he vented a sharp sigh and marched away across the tent. He stood at the drinks counter, looking tempted, but refrained. Eventually he turned back to her. "Sorry for the rant," he said once he'd calmed. "I'm sure it's the last thing you need to hear."

"On the contrary, I rather like it," she told him, and that was the honest truth. "Most men don't think so deeply about these things. You're a knight and an heir and well regarded by men in power. There's a lot of good you can do, Elyon."

"Perhaps." He began to nod, slowly, and then stepped over to his chained trunk of weapons and armour. "But for now, my focus is on making sure you're safe, as I promised." He drew a key from his leathers and opened the large chest, and from within came a pouring of godsteel mist, like silver steam from a simmering pot. He waved a hand to clear it and then reached in and drew something out, before closing and locking the chest once more.

He stepped over toward her, with a small sheathed dagger in hand. "Here, take this," he said, handing it to her.

She looked it over. The scabbard was dull brown leather, quite worn, and the hilt of simple, straight design, with a basic circular pommel and gently curved crossguard. She drew it out, and with it came the light swirling mists. "Godsteel," she whispered, half surprised to find the divine steel worked into such an unspectacular blade. "It's...for me?"

"To be kept hidden here, should you feel under threat when I'm not around," he told her. "Find somewhere safe to stash it, somewhere you can access in haste. And promise me you'll not try to use it on Kastor."

"I already gave you my word."

"I want it again."

So she gave it.

He seemed satisfied with that. "You can read my books as well, while you're here. They'll help pass the time as I try to secure safe passage for you. You said you think that Lady Payne might be in Harrowmoor?"

She'd told him all about Marian the other evening, though remained unsure of where she was. "It's possible," she said. "She suggested she'd try to stay close, but might have been called away. I don't know. I'm not sure I can rely on that."

"I'll make enquiries. If she's there, I may be able to get word to her that you're in my care, and I'm trying to get you out. But it's risky. I shall ponder it some more and see what I can do."

Saska forced herself to smile and say thank you, but all of it just made her feel hollow. What would Marian think of her, to receive such a note? To know that she'd failed, and hardly even made an effort to end the man she'd been sent to slay. That her salvation had come in the form of a courtly young knight without whom she'd be lost. It made her uncomfortable to have to rely so heavily on Elyon, yet she had to swallow down that shame and try to see the providence in all this.

You're exactly where you're meant to be, she thought, returning to King Godrin's words. She had to keep faith in them, and let her path reveal itself.

It seemed it wasn't to Kastor, after all.

But where, she didn't yet know.

30

Ranulf

"Nothing, you say?" asked Vincent Rose, sitting at the head of the long wide dinner table, some ten metres distant from Ranulf, who perched at the other end. "Nothing at all, even after all your hard work?"

"Not as yet," Ranulf said, prodding at his plate of half eaten food. "But I am only a few pages into the translation, Vincent. I may find something more interesting soon."

"How soon?" Rose twirled his wine flute, sitting cross-legged and utterly imperious in his broad-backed throne-like seat. They were dining in the inner courtyard tonight, beneath the light of the full moon. Firelight flickered from lamps set about the walls, and a balmy breeze blew through, quivering the flowers and vines that climbed up the stone pillars around them. "I don't have to remind you that Janilah's men are fast approaching, Ranulf. And your deceptions are starting to wear thin."

"Deceptions?" Ranulf was happy for the ten metre gap between them. They sat alone, but for the shadows that lurked in the corridors leading onto the courtyard, those of servants with flagons and food, ready to rush in at their master's call, and the armed guards ever on watch.

"Yes, Ranulf. Deceptions." Rose clipped his fingers and a

serving boy emerged from the shadows with a flagon of wine. "No, not that! The sapphire. Where are you?" The boy was replaced by another, who trembled his way forward, and held the jug beneath Vincent's round bulbous nose. "Yes. Good." He held out his flute for the boy to fill, watching to make sure he didn't spill any of the precious blue liquid. "Now go." He waved a hand once the boy was done, and off he went, scuttling into the darkness that bordered the moonlit marble courtyard.

Rose took a sip. "It's an excellent vintage, Ranulf. Would you like to try some?"

"I've no taste for wine tonight, Vincent. You were saying something about deceptions?"

"Yes, I was." He set down his glass and stared. It was another half minute before he spoke. "Call it a sense, but I have the impression that you're hiding something from me. You must have uncovered something of interest by now. The location of a treasure, perhaps? Or a scandal with political implications? Every king, queen, lord and lady from here to the Hammersongs has something to hide, and secrets are worth money. Or better yet...favours. I'd hoped to have dirt on every greathouse in the north and south by now, but here you are, with absolutely nothing to give me."

"I've given you plenty, Vincent," Ranulf retorted. "Have we not dined together daily and discussed what I've unearthed? There are a great many secrets that I've told you about, but you dismiss them like you do your servants, with a peevish little flick of the wrist."

"Because they're old and irrelevant." He gave one such flick now, his bangles and bracelets tinkling a tune. "What good is a scandal unless I have someone to blackmail? Preferably someone rich and powerful, who wants very much to keep that information concealed."

"If that is what you truly seek, then you might be better off finding someone else to decode the tome. I will not be party to your perverted schemes."

"Ah! So you admit it! You *are* hiding something!"

"I admit no such thing. I am just weary of your badgering, and your uncouth pursuit of power and profit. You have built an extravagant life, through ingenuity and a fine head for business, and do not need to lower yourself to these standards. They are beneath you, Vincent. Gods man, are you not rich enough as it is?"

Vincent Rose was a curious sort of man, and seemed to like it when Ranulf scolded him. He twirled his flute back and forward with a little grin on his puffy red face. "I have everything a man could ever wish for," he admitted. "More money than I could ever hope to spend. More property than I could ever visit. I've houses, Ranulf, that I have never once stepped foot in. Ships I've never sailed. Carriages I've never sat in. Horses I've never ridden. Beauties I've never bed. But in the end, there's one thing I'll always want, and never be able to attain."

"And what's that?"

"*More.*" He sat back and smiled. "More properties. More ships. More carriages and horses and women. *More* is such an inexhaustible thing."

"It's a cursed thing," Ranulf grunted. "How about more happiness? Does more of what you already have bring you that? Does it make you happier, Vincent, to have more things you don't need?"

"Oh my dear friend, you truly sound the fool when you speak like that." He chortled haughtily above his ostentatious crimson cravat, sprouting from a rich cloth-of-gold doublet. "Of course more brings me happiness. Because it isn't about the material gain, my friend, but the pursuit of it. Tell me, when you climb a mountain, which part brings you the most joy and satisfaction...the climb itself, or simply spending a few moments upon the summit? It is the journey, not the destination, that so appeals to me, Ranulf. And the hunt for more of what I already have gives me exactly that."

"Until your luck runs out," Ranulf said, finding himself unable to counter the man's point. "As it surely will soon, with your own deceptions."

Rose gave out a little chuckle. "Skilfully spun, I applaud you." He supped his wine. "But to which deceptions do you refer?"

"You know which. Your dealings with Janilah. He'll not forget what you did."

"Oh goodness, this again?" Rose waved over a bowl of fruit, and plucked a bunch of grapes. "Ever you fixate on this imagined vengeance. I'll suffer no reprisal from King Janilah, I assure you. The man has rather larger concerns to worry about than to spare a thought for little old me." He began feasting on his grapes and wine, reddening his lips with purple and red and blue.

"And the Patriots of Lumara?" Ranulf watched him carefully. He'd not yet brought this up since that motley crew of southerners had arrived some week or so before. "Is it wise to get in bed with such a group?"

"Wisdom never played a hand in the enterprise. It is all but part of the journey."

"And the destination? What do you hope to gain from this association with them?"

"What do you think? Money. Favours. Power. The Patriots are an eager organisation, and always interested in new and rare weapons and armour. I can provide that for them, given my unique set of contacts." He didn't seem too wary about revealing all that, as he popped another grape into his mouth. "You know some of them are Bladeborn?" he went on. "Southerners with some northern Bladeborn blood in them. Like that friend of yours and Leshie's from Thalan. The rather stunning girl with the radiant blue eyes. I forget her name."

"Saska."

"Yes, that's the one. Poor girl, to be entrusted into Marian Payne's domineering care. Such a horrid woman. Leshie made the right choice to abandon her and her ludicrous terms of service."

Ranulf didn't have much to say on that. Not much that would do him any favours, anyway. He admired Marian and Saska in equal measure, and a great deal more than he did this man. But saying so wouldn't get him anywhere. He smiled and poked at his chicken, pulling off a strip of meat with his fork. "So you have godsteel do you?" he inferred. "Presumably that's what you're selling the Patriots? Supplying their Bladeborn recruits with godsteel blades."

"Amongst other things," said Rose. "Godsteel isn't easy to come by, but there's enough rattling around on the black market for a resourceful man like me to sniff out. Moving it is the problem. Bloody heavy stuff. Takes several strong men to shift a single blade and I've had more than one dropped from the gangplanks before and sunk to the seabed at the harbour here." He leaned back, stretching and yawning. "Might be worth having Leshie try to fish around for them. It isn't too deep there. What I really need is a Bladeborn-Seaborn mix." He smiled. "The search goes on."

Ranulf was beginning to tire of him tonight. His eyes were so heavy he felt like his head might tip forward into his cold soup at any moment.

"You seem in ill-spirits, my friend," Rose noted, taking another long swill of his wine. "You've hardly cracked a smile all evening."

"Just weary, Vincent. My work has been keeping me up all hours, as you know."

"Right, right. And no doubt my suspicions sap your energy somewhat too? Well for that I apologise. Hopefully you'll uncover something interesting as you progress through Godrin's accounts."

"Hopefully."

"And how long might it take to translate them?"

"Some days, I imagine."

"And you're writing down the translations as you go, yes? I would like to see your work regularly, Ranulf. Twice daily, perhaps. Lunchtime and dinner."

He doesn't trust me, Ranulf thought, and that was no great surprise. It had taken him more than a week to break through King Godrin's code, and only that afternoon he'd finally done it. The cipher was quite brilliant, really. On closer inspection of his jumbled accounts, Ranulf had come to realise that every single word was written backward and upside down, and in a dizzying number of languages. It was the reason why none of the symbols were familiar to him at first glance, but he soon unravelled that part of the riddle. Then came the next step - working out whether those words, when turned around and translated, made sense. They didn't. The accounts remained entirely unintelligible and muddled, but at least he was making progress.

After that, he began the painstaking task of working out what the code might be. Following several long days of trial and error, he eventually came upon something that gave him hope. Within the words written in the common tongue of the north, he found that by replacing each vowel with the following consonant in the alphabet, he was able to solve the riddle and translate the word. It was a seminal moment, but his work was only beginning. Though Ranulf spoke several languages, King Godrin had used many others that he didn't, and for that he needed lexicons and dictionaries and alphabets. Thankfully, he was operating from a library, and with that library belonging to a man like Vincent Rose, it was of course extensive. Everything he needed now was at his fingertips. It was just a case of translating each individual account, and mining the secrets therein.

"So, twice daily then?" Rose pressed. "I'll send a man to fetch your translations for my afternoon and evening perusal. Does that suit?"

"Twice daily is fine," Ranulf said, seeing no other option but to agree. He stood from the table. "I will resume immediately. With Janilah's men on their final approach, there isn't much time to lose. Goodnight, Vincent."

He left his host at that, passing through the courtyard, down the corridor, and away into the main entrance hall. A grand staircase stood at its heart, branching off to the left and right. He stepped up the white marble steps, veering left, down a further passage, and into the capacious library he called home. Leshie was awaiting him.

"Nice dinner?" she asked, sitting cross-legged on the desk, and going over some of his latest notes. "I've been looking through your translations, I hope you don't mind. Almost put me to sleep. Gods Ranulf, could this be more dull? It better pay off in the end." She reached for the edge of the desk and pulled with her fingers, propelling herself onto the floor without a sound. That was Leshie. Soundless when she moved. She pulled back his desk chair and gestured him forward. "Come on then, there's much work to be done."

"I'm quite aware, thank you." *I need to sleep,* he thought, as he sat down. The balcony doors were shut behind him. "Would you be so kind as to open those," he asked her, nodding to them. "I need air to keep me awake."

"Sure." She sped over, doing a couple of athletic tumbles and backflips along the way. "I'm getting better," she then said, tumbling back over to the desk. "I can do summersaults even without godsteel now."

A chill wind blew in; it was always a bit cooler coming from the west. It helped revive him somewhat. "That's very good, Leshie." He picked up his quill and drew the Book of Thala before him. The first accounts he'd translated from Godrin's hand were indeed rather dull and uneventful, written some decades prior when he'd first become king. It was a pattern Ranulf had grown used to seeing. The Rasal monarchs often took time to improve their mastery of the Eye of Rasalan, and thus their accounts tended to become more percipient and provident as their personal chapters went on.

As Leshie continued to practice her gymnastics, Ranulf turned his eyes over Godrin's next passage, quill inked and poised over a fresh sheet of parchment. *A long night awaits,* he thought, setting into it, yet within only a few minutes his eyes were starting to pull shut. He stood and moved to the balcony for a breath of fresh air, but it wouldn't revive him long. Leshie came to a stop before him, landing in a fine dismount. He smiled at her. "Would you do me a favour, Leshie? Go see if you can find me something to keep me awake."

The girl nodded, breathing heavily from her exertions. She was dressed in that fetching leather armour of hers, a fine match for the colour of her hair and freckly skin. "Like what?"

"Death's Denial, if you can find any. I'm sure Vincent has some in his stocks. He has everything else."

"Right. I'll go check."

She sped away, leaving him to his work, though without some sort of stimulant it was destined to be an uphill struggle. Death's Denial was often used to wake patients from induced comas, but in small doses the smell was plenty enough to keep someone quick-witted and alert. It was harvested from the glands of deep sea serpents, lurking so low that only the very best Seaborn could catch them, and was rare and expensive as a consequence. But that's just why he'd trust Vincent to have it...and of course he did, as Leshie came bouncing back in a few minutes later, clutching at a little purple vial.

"Here. Vinny said to use as much as you like."

"Much obliged." He gave her a glance. "I'd step aside. The smell is quite pungent." It was a truly foul thing, but therein lay its wonders. With one quick sniff his fatigue was blown away like a hut in a hurricane.

"I can smell it from here," retched Leshie, crinkling her nose about half a dozen paces away. "It's gross."

"It's so. Very gross indeed. But potent too. Now, if you'd kindly keep it down, Leshie, I'd best get back to work. Stay if you wish, but do try to be quiet. I'll need all my powers of concentration tonight."

He cursed that he'd not thought to use Death's Denial sooner, as his eyes darted here and there, and the quill danced upon the parchment. Within a couple of hours he'd forged ahead some years into Godrin's reign, uncovering a passage that, at the time, must have taken the Wise King aback.

It was a foretelling of the War of the Continents, of the great Renewal that was to come. He'd seen it in the Eye of Rasalan over a decade before it began, noting that, 'the killing of a king will spark a great war, and so will come the next Renewal.'

But not the last, Ranulf thought, *as many had said it would be.* Nor did the account mention that the killed king would, in fact, be King Horris Reynar, and allegedly by the order of King Tellion of Agarath. The Agarathi always claimed otherwise, of course, citing natural means of death, but whether a coincidence or not, it had been enough for Horris's son, Storris, to raise his armies for war.

There were other passages, too, that spoke of events that would come to pass during the war. One of particular note was Godrin's divination of the deaths of Gideon Daecar and Storris Reynar at the Battle of Burning Rock or, 'the greatest battle of our age' as he'd called it. He'd also written of the 'rise of Gideon's son, Amron, and the fall of the Agarathi prince, Dulian son of

Tellion' at the same event. This account was written some years after the foretelling of the war itself - though still before the conflict had even begun - by which point Godrin's mastery of the Eye of Rasalan had become quite prodigious, and beyond most of his forebears. That was clear in the detail and the names, though much else remained obfuscated and unclear.

And yet as Ranulf worked hard into the night, translating the Wise King's words, he began to wonder whether this was, in fact, exactly what Janilah was looking for. *Might this be what he truly seeks?* he thought. *Might it not provide proof of Godrin's wickedness, as Janilah sees it...of his heartless hoarding of secrets and prophesies that might, if shared, have saved countless lives?* He could see the rationale behind it. He could see how Janilah would look at it as such. *He'll hold it up for all the north to see and proclaim Godrin a villain,* he thought. *And might the people just believe it?*

He kept on and on long into the deep silent hours of the night. Away in a corner, Leshie slept, curled up on a large red armchair, snoring soft and light. And beyond the balcony doors was the merest whistling and rustling of the wind, and the gentle caress of the sea as it sloshed down by the shore. But most of all was scratching. The scratching of quill on parchment, as Ranulf feverishly worked through Godrin's accounts, progressing deep and deeper still into the Wise King's reign.

He entered into such a trance, in fact, that he hardly even realised it when he translated his own name.

Curious, was all he thought, but on he went, translating the next sequence of words until he reached the end of the sentence and stopped. Then he frowned and read over what he'd written, blinked, blinked again, rubbed his eyes, blinked a final time, read the words once more...and nearly had a heart attack.

"My gods," he whispered. "I...I cannot believe it."

'Thank you for persevering, Ranulf,' the translation read. 'I knew I could count on you.'

He stared at those words in a state of utter disbelief. The passage was written over twenty years ago, before Ranulf had even met the wise old king. *And yet...he'd foreseen us meeting? He'd foreseen all of this?* Godrin's words came back to him then, those that he'd kept close to his heart ever since that day in the palace. "There is no better place for you, my friend." Ranulf had always suspected that Godrin knew he'd find himself in the company of this book, but...but this? A direct message to him, written long before their first encounter?

His head was swimming from the time-bending implications of it all. It took him a few long breaths to regain his composure and stop from passing out right there on the library floor. Then he turned his eyes over the words to make sure...absolutely sure...he wasn't dreaming. They were still there. *A mistranslation?* He wondered. *Might I have gotten it wrong?* But he hadn't, of course he hadn't. It was too neat, too perfect. Then the urgent nature of it began to set in. *He knew I'd be here. He knew I'd translate his words. I must uncover what he says next.* He flashed his eyes to the balcony doors, as the deep long darkness began to recede, auguring the coming of a brand new day.

Before dawn, he thought, *I must...*

31

Janilah

The wind pulled hard at King Janilah's rich green cloak as he climbed the steps built into the mountainside.

The mists below him obscured his city...the White City, the Sky City, the most beautiful city in the world, they said. Perhaps that was true, but even the most beautiful of things grew dull to the eye eventually. A man with a beautiful wife would stray. A woman would grow tired of her jewels. All things were subject to the slow decay of time. *And Ilithor,* Janilah thought, *is no different.*

The stairs were of rough-hewn rock, narrow and perilous, accessed through a network of secret tunnels and passages built into the foundations of the palace. Eventually, they came out into the peaks north of the city, through old cold caves and dripping chambers, over rifts and fissures, down long dark corridors filled with ancient statues and busts and old rusted armour.

Much of that had taken decades, even hundreds of years, to excavate, following Galin Lukar's siege of the city. But so far as Galin and his successors had searched, they'd never come upon the secret stair. *No, it was I who found it,* Janilah thought, as he continued the climb, high above the tallest spires and towers that sprung up through the mists below. For all the hard work of his ancestors, only he had taken that final step. *One by one we pass the torch,* he thought, *and now in my hand it burns.* He smiled as he approached the top, gripping his godsteel dagger all the while to steady his footing. Not once did he look down the scores of steps he'd scaled. Not once did he consider the way down. *It is not my fate to fall,* he knew. *My fate is to win this war.*

He reached the summit, his leather boots crunching upon the thick layer of snow gathered upon the plateau. A fierce wind took his cloak, hauling it westward, as he leaned the other way to fight its pull. Three strong steps and he was beyond the perilous drop, peering through the white misted air toward the open cavern before him. He remembered when he'd first set eyes upon the ancient ruin. The rush as he pulled himself over the lip. The wonder as he looked ahead and saw Ilith's forgotten forge laid out before him. For three hundred years it had sat dormant, hidden by King Neyrith as Galin Lukar marched to siege his city. The last of the Ilithian kings had ordered his engineers to collapse the caves and passages, block the tunnels, hide the route. And it had worked. For over two hundred and fifty years Galin and his heirs had searched, though as the generations passed, so the Lukar kings began to lose interest. *Until I took up King Galin's mantle,* thought Janilah. *Until I renewed the search and found the way.* He had always considered himself to be Galin's true heir, the only one to share his lofty vision. *Not my father, no, nor my grandfather. Nor those that came before. They have held the torch, but failed to light the way. But now, in my grasp, the path is clear...*

He pushed on, raising a hand against the stinging white wind as the open mouth of the forge yawned ahead of him. Inside the air was orange and red, and from within came a billowing steam. A shadow took shape. A swinging arm. The clang of a hammer. Janilah battled on across the plateau and through the entrance. "Tyrith," he said, drawing the blacksmith's attention as he stepped beyond the bitter cold. "I have come to see how you fare, dear boy."

The young man startled at the voice, and through his fingers slipped the Hammer of Tukor. It caught the edge of his anvil and clattered to the stone floor with a resounding, trembling thump. "Sorry, my king..." Tyrith scrambled to retrieve the magical hammer, lifting it back to the workbench, and setting it aside. "You caught me by surprise, is all."

"I should have announced my coming." Janilah stepped forward, brushing the frost from his shoulders. His eyes took in the Hammer of Tukor, one of the greatest treasures of the world. *A treasure only this man can bear. And that makes him precious too.* "You grow more accustomed to its weight by the day, Tyrith. It seems that your efforts are paying off."

"Yes, my lord." Tyrith wiped a hand through his damp blond hair, clearing it from his eyes. Beyond was a youthful face of twenty five, modest and unassuming in the fashion of his forebears. "It is merely a question of time," he said in a soft silvery voice. "The more I am given, the better I may wield it."

"I know all about that," Janilah said, favouring the man with a rare smile. It had always been his way with Tyrith. Kindness, he'd learned, would yield the best results with such a man. "I still find myself learning more about the Mistblade every time I take it to my clutch."

"Might I see it?" Tyrith asked. His eyes moved to Janilah's swordbelt, and the sheath half hidden beneath his cloak. "You did bring it, didn't you?"

"Of course I did, dear boy. I know how much you like it." He flung aside his cloak and pulled out the soft blue blade, swirling with a cobalt mist. The glyphs glowed radiant in the firelight. "Would you like to see me fade, son?"

"Oh yes, my lord. Very much so."

"Well then." Janilah took a heartbeat to focus, before his body dematerialised, leaving behind a hazy impression of his form. Reaching out with his spare hand, he pressed his arm right into the glistening grey rock all the way up to the elbow. "Now how's that for a trick, Tyrith?" he said in a moment of mirth.

The young man watched with a beaming smile. "A very impressive one, my lord. It's quite something."

"Indeed it is. And one of five such tricks I shall hope to master soon." Janilah withdrew his arm from the rock and let his body return to its physical form. He sheathed the blade. "Now tell me how you've been, Tyrith. Are you being well tended here? Do you have everything you need?"

The young man gave a brisk little nod. He possessed an inviting sort of diffidence that Janilah had always found fond. "I'm in want of nothing up here, my lord. Though I do worry for those who tend me. The steps look terribly precarious to me, especially when the winds are high. I'd not want to think that the servants are risking their lives bringing me food and wine and the like."

Janilah gave the man's shoulder a firming shake. "They're not, don't worry. Do you think I'd climb up and down those steps so often if they were unsafe?"

Tyrith had a doubting look on his face though wasn't of the habit of arguing with his king. In truth, dozens of servants had tumbled to their deaths upon those stairs, but Janilah wasn't going to tell him that. The man needed to be fed, after all, and there was no other way up to this forge.

"Well I...I would hope so, my lord." Tyrith stepped away to a set of wooden shelves, returning a moment later with a scroll to hand. He reached out.

"And what's this?"

"A design for a lift," Tyrith said. "One that might be installed in place of the steps, to allow easier..."

"No need, Tyrith. It is perfectly safe, I assure you. And those steps are sacred, as you know. Your ancestor Ilith would climb them himself, as did King Varin and Queen Thala when they visited. It is an honour for those who serve you to lay their feet upon those stairs. I'd not want to deny them that. Would you?"

Tyrith shook his lank golden hair. He was dressed in a stained shirt of cream, short breeches of brown. "No, I suppose not."

Janilah continued to smile, though as ever he found it hard to keep it up for too long. His visits with Tyrith never lasted much more than a few minutes lest the boy have something interesting to report. They were, however, necessary to make him feel valued. To keep his spirits up, should they threaten to sag. It was essential that that didn't happen. Only Tyrith, as Ilith's direct heir, could master the Hammer of Tukor, and that meant only Tyrith could combine the Blades of Vandar. *If something were to happen to him, my entire plan and purpose will fail,* he thought. For three hundred years the Lukar kings had kept the line of Ilith safe and secret, should their unique powers be needed, and now that power lay in Tyrith's hands alone. *He is a piece of the puzzle that I cannot risk. And soon his time will come...*

Janilah turned his eyes over the forge. It had been his express desire to keep the blacksmith busy and active, for therein lay the key. Not only was it essential in helping him master the Hammer of Tukor, but it soothed his sanity too. Ilith was known to be happiest when at his forge, hammering and singing as he styled the greatest weapons and armour the world had ever known. Weeks could go by, it was said, without him stopping to eat or drink or rest, and Janilah had discovered that Tyrith was of a similar sort. So he gave him projects and kept him busy. He gushed over the blades he forged, the armour he hammered, the swords and spears and shields. It was praise that Tyrith craved so praise was what he got, along with all the godsteel he could melt and mould and hammer to his heart's desire.

"Show me what you've been working on, Tyrith," Janilah said now, spotting a couple of new blades mounted reverently upon the rough-rock walls. "I see some fine new weapons about me; clearly you've been busy. And my armour? Have you had time yet to add a flourish to it, hammer it harder than all the rest?"

That had been Janilah's latest request; to improve his ancestral armour, reshape and rework it, make it fitting for a god. "I will need to look the part, Tyrith, when I hold the Heart of Vandar to hand," he'd told him some months ago. "Can you do that for me? Design something Varin himself would have worn?"

Set on a table across the chamber, Janilah could see that very armour now, each component set apart and misting a gentle green and gold. Tyrith drew him over, shuffling with a nervous step. He got like that, when presenting anything new to the king. *No matter that I shower his every creation with praise, he still grows agitated when unveiling something.*

"I have made a start, my lord, but there is much work to be done," the blacksmith said in a hurried voice. "Note the helm. I have shaped the visor into the likeness of the five blades. The

Sword of Varinar at the heart, with the others set aside it in their pairs." He gave him a careful glance. "I know you're not one for cosmetic flourishes, but I thought it would be a nice touch."

Janilah forced his lips into a smile. "A very nice touch, Tyrith." He studied the helm a moment. He wasn't typically enamoured with unnecessary stylistic elements like this, but could make an exception this once. "Very good, I like it enormously," he lied, looking over the breastplate and pauldrons set nearby. "Perhaps some metalwork on these. Nothing too extravagant. The Lukar coat of arms on the chest, perhaps. I would wish to bear the standards of my house when wearing it."

"Of course. I will see it done. I have also begun adding an additional layer of Ilithian Steel to all components. Very thin, and hardly noticeable to the naked eye. To any other man it would add weight, but when you're wielding the united Blades it shouldn't be a problem." He smiled up at the broad, bearded king. "You shall be as a god, my lord. There will be no man or beast to match you."

It seems Tyrith is quite generous with his own praise today, Janilah thought, as he turned once more to survey the chamber. His eyes fell once again on the shelving, stacked with books and rolls of parchment. They had all been here when Janilah discovered the ancient smith, a trove of information into which Tyrith had plunged after he'd been brought up here as a young boy. Within he'd found many secrets to Ilith's work, to his methods and his magic, but one particular scroll had been most interesting of all to Janilah.

He stared at it now, easily recognisable for the rot that had set in on the bottom third of the parchment, obscuring what had once been written there. "Have you been able to study it further?" he asked, stepping over toward it.

"Every night, my lord," Tyrith said in a silky voice, following. "I read it through before I sleep, in the hope that I will see something I've not noticed before. And I've worked hard to clean it, such as I can, to better read the final passages."

"And have you had any success?" Janilah drew out the scroll in question, unravelling the ancient sheet of parchment across a rutted stone table. The bottom third was almost entirely unintelligible, blackened by age and soot and thousands of years of decay.

Tyrith hesitated in his answer. "Some, my lord," he then said, pointing out a few words that he'd been able to uncover. "It is meticulous work, but I've been able to decipher a little more of the text, via a few methods I'll not trouble you with."

Janilah followed the tip of Tyrith's finger, though could see little that would help them. *But perhaps it will not matter?* he hoped. The scroll had first informed him that the Blades of Vandar could be combined. A secret, Ilith had written, that he denied Varin for fear he'd misuse it. 'I have forged these blades as a deterrent,' the demigod had written three and a half millennia ago. 'Against the great calamity Drulgar...the Dread that might stir and lay waste to these lands. If we hear tidings of his rise, I shall share with Varin my secret. I shall raise the Hammer of Tukor, and work the Blades together as one. But it is beholden on me to be prudent. For here I have created a calamity of my own; more powerful than Drulgar, more deadly. Only if the latter should rise, will the former be forged. That is my solemn oath.'

"An oath he broke," Janilah said, once more reading through those words.

Tyrith frowned, and drew his finger away from the parchment. "My lord?"

Janilah gestured to the passage at the top of the scroll. "The oath," he said. "Ilith's oath that he'd unite the Blades if Drulgar attacked. He broke it."

"But I will not," Tyrith told him. "I will unite the Blades for you, my lord, where my ancestor failed. Bring them to me and I promise it. I carry Ilith's shame, and will seek to make amends. I promise it, I will."

Janilah knew that full well. The boy was dutiful, and had been weaned on these stories as a child. *I made sure of that. This dedication and determination to right Ilith's wrongs come from me.* But still, he wasn't sure. His eyes moved over the parchment again, trying to see something he'd missed before. But of course he wouldn't. There was nothing in Ilith's text to suggest some hidden meaning. He made it quite explicit that the original intention of the Blades of

Vandar was to combine them, that very few were ever aware of that secret, and that in order to do so, it took a man of his direct descent, wielding the Hammer of Tukor, to achieve. Those were the critical facts, and Janilah had compiled the necessary pieces to that puzzle up in this forge.

But that final third...

It had always vexed him. The possibility that Ilith's method was hidden behind all those years of soot and grime. Was there some incantation Tyrith would need to say? A special element he'd need to apply? Did the blades need to be merged at a particular heat, or in a particular order? Which came first, if so? Or were they all to be melted and remoulded as one?

He'd laboured over those questions for more hours than he could count, and still no answers had come. Tyrith seemed confident that other texts of Ilith might provide the answer. He'd found several that detailed his methods of breaking down the Heart of Vandar, and forging the blades, but uniting them was another process entirely.

"I'll continue to clean it as best I can," Tyrith now said, sensing Janilah's glowering concerns. "It is painstaking work and the parchment is brittle, but I think I can unearth more, in time." He smiled timidly. "Or perhaps you might take it with you, my lord? I'm sure there are those better suited than I to..."

"No." The word came more harsh than he'd expected. He never liked to raise his voice around Tyrith, fragile as the boy could be. "No," he repeated, more softly. "I would not want others to look upon this scroll, Tyrith. It is our secret, remember? As Ilith kept it, so shall we. No one need know, but us."

Secrets and lies and prophesies. In truth Janilah was sick of them. *But it shan't be long before my plans take shape,* he thought. *Soon I'll have the north, and the Blades of Vandar besides. And then what will I have to fear?*

He placed an arm around Tyrith's narrow shoulders and drew him away from the scroll, past his anvil and the Hammer of Tukor, and the blades and armour mounted on the walls about them. They moved to the mouth of the cave, as the icy winds whipped and blustered and howled, and even a dozen metres away, Janilah could hardly see the edge of the precipice, nor the perilous climb down he'd have to make.

"Soon you'll be free of this place, Tyrith," he said. "Free to come and go as you please. But not until the Blades are united. Do you understand, son? I hope you understand."

"I understand, my lord. I am happy here at my forge. Just as Ilith was."

"And it *is* your forge, Tyrith. As much as it ever was Ilith's."

"And you are as Varin, great king. He who will end the war."

Janilah smiled at that, and this one didn't need to be forced. *But Varin failed,* he thought, looking out over the plateau. *He let his arrogance blind him and paid with his life. I'll not make the same mistake.*

"I will visit again soon, Tyrith." He gave the towheaded boy another amicable smile. *Grandfatherly,* he thought. *And do I not cherish this boy more than Amilia, or Robbert and Raynald, or even my own sons and daughters?* He had to think through the list of them, most of no importance or worth. Rylian was running his war and soon Amilia would do her part too, and Cecilia? She was most alike to him, conniving and clever and callous when she needed to be. *And now returning to me,* he'd recently been informed. *I stand eager to hear her news.*

He stepped away onto the plateau, out into the bitter cold wind. "Be well, Tyrith," he called out as he went. "Together we will save the world."

He didn't look back, though knew those words would ignite the boy's spark anew, and feed him until he next returned. Stepping to the edge, he looked down over the stair, plunging into the white mist. One wrong move would see him fall, see all his plans to nothing. The thought only brought a smile.

He stepped over the edge.

32

Lythian

He dreamt he was in her arms. She held him tight as they danced, twirling beneath the moonlight on a maple-bordered courtyard of stone. The soft soothing wind stirred the trees to life, their ruby-red leaves dancing in a thousand pairs, rustling and whispering as they frolicked among the branches. And in the air was a sound more beautiful than any he'd ever heard. *My son,* he thought. *My happy healthy boy.* He danced her over to him, giggling so sweet in his crib and swaddling, and she drew the child up into her arms. Together they spun and swirled upon the smooth stone as a family, their robes flowing, their smiles growing, laughing loud and long in their joyous embrace..

And then it came. A violent wind, so sudden and fierce and bitter cold, blasting from places unknown. Their laughter was swallowed in the bluster, their robes flapping and snapping about them. He felt her warmth leave him, their bodies prised apart, and when he looked up she was being dragged away. "Talia," he called, reaching out, but already she was too far gone. "Talia!" The wind took her, pulling her across the stone, and the baby was in her arms, screaming. "No, Talia!" He pushed against the howling living wind but it fought back, wrestling him off his feet. "Talia, hold on! Hold on, I'm coming..."

He fought his way back up to his feet, but suddenly the wind turned black and dark and dreaded, wreathing her, engulfing her, strangling life from lung and limb. "Talia!" He battled on and forced himself forward, but all was black now about him. Her voice echoed out, calling for him as he spun...but each time he turned it came from behind him. "Talia!" he called, but he couldn't hear his own voice. He bellowed again, louder and louder... *Talia! Talia! TALIA!*...but nothing. A panic seized him as he rushed through the void, weeping hot harsh tears as he groped in the blackness, but she was nowhere to be found. "Talia," he roared, and again and again he roared it. But no answer came. His wife and son were gone.

He woke to the fetid stench of his cell, curled up within the stone dragon's jaws. A thick black rain was falling through the darkness, driving the crowds back to their sandstone homes. It was a short respite only from their unremitting abuse. Soon the rains would abate and they'd flock back to the square, stocked with pebbles and stones and rotting fruit.

Lythian shivered and sat up. A half inch puddle of rain had pooled in the bottom of their cell, though it hadn't been enough to wake Borrus. Lythian turned to his left, where the proud knight lay, rasping and wheezing through an uneasy sleep. His body had been dressed in linen wrappings, the worst of his wounds sewn and sutured and tended by healing balms, and Lythian's lacerated back had seen similar attention. It seemed a kindness, but in truth it was cruelty. *These men have more suffering to do,* Vargo Ven had said. And he'd make sure they were fit to endure it.

Lythian shifted up, sliding to the elevated edge of the dragon's jaws where the water hadn't yet reached. As he set his back against the teeth of his cage, he heard a voice behind him, breaking through the patter of rain. "What were you dreaming of, Captain?" Lythian turned and looked through the bars. A figure stood upon the platform beside their cell, tall and solemn in a sodden crimson cloak. His greasy black beard was cut into a triple braid, surging south of his chin like a trident. Lythian stared and Sir Pagaloth stared back. "Was it Sir Tomos?" the dragonknight asked in his rough Agarathi voice. "Is it for your friend that you weep?"

Lythian blinked through the rain and the darkness. He'd seen nothing of the man since his time in the palace, when the dragonknight had been assigned as his escort. He cleared his throat, and said, "My wife. And my son. I dream of them often."

"As you saw them in the flames," Sir Pagaloth said. "I remember, Captain. A terrible loss to bear."

Lythian took a second to unravel his meaning as he fought through the fog in his memory. Then it came to him. He'd seen Talia and his son that night they'd stopped on their journey here across the Drylands. At that camp held sacred to those who passed through. They'd sat around the firepit on smooth flat stones and looked into the rippling blaze, recalling those they'd lost. And there he'd seen her, dancing and twirling. In shadow and in flame.

"Do you believe you will see them again?" Pagaloth was looking down at him with those dark brooding eyes, rivers of rain streaming down his face. Through the pall of night Lythian could see some shame in him. "When you take your seat at Varin's Table, are you permitted visitors? Can you visit loved ones within the halls?"

"We can leave...for a time," Lythian said. "Else joining Varin's feast would be not a blessing, but a curse. All knights are allowed to visit family and friends. But their seat at the feast...that cannot be changed."

Pagaloth gave a short nod. "A curious belief," he said. "Why can the Knights of Varin not move about the table? Would it not be better that way? To allow more stories to be shared, by those who haven't yet heard them?"

Lythian gave a wince as he sat up a little straighter, pain flaring across his back. "Varin explained it all in his scriptures," he said, grunting a little. "He decreed that a knight must gain the honour of sitting near him by great feats and deeds upon this mortal plane. It is what drives us to feats of heroism and gallantry. If a man could merely swap seats, then what would inspire them to join the Varin Knights at all?"

"To protect one's nation," Pagaloth posited. "To defend the

weak and the helpless. To gain honour for one's family and friends. There are many reasons, Captain."

Lythian gave the man a nod, because of course there were many such reasons, not least those he'd listed. He'd always been somewhat troubled by that particular decree. Many of its detractors had argued that it did nothing but incite men to seek war for the sake of glory. Time upon this ephemeral plane was, after all, fleeting. But the afterlife? They were called the *Eternal* Halls for a reason, and it was not beyond the designs of some to stir conflict and war when living, to guarantee a richer and more prosperous death.

"And where do you suppose you will sit? All this...what they are putting you through. I would hope it does not degrade your position."

"Then you're one of the few, Sir Pagaloth. And truly, I know not where I'll settle."

"Near Varin, I believe. I do not imagine there have been many knights more noble than you, Captain."

"You would be surprised. What nobility is there in trying to murder a prince?"

Pagaloth didn't speak for a time after that, turning his eyes upon the city, cloaked in rain and shadows and mist. Eventually, he said, "Sir Tomos fought well. He honoured himself and fell with pride." He moved his eyes over the yard below, as a couple of soldiers walked by through the deluge. "I do not favour what is happening to you, Captain. What King Tavash is doing..." He turned again as the pair of guards moved off. "I am sorry it has come to this."

Another shadow of guilt crossed his eyes. Lythian climbed to his feet, looking at him through the jagged stone bars. "Was it you?" he asked, looking at the man directly. "Was it you who betrayed us, Sir Pagaloth?" He had wondered that, of course, during his long incarceration. They had been in league with Kin'rar and Marak only, but Sir Pagaloth was often standing vigil outside their door, and might have come to learn of what they were plotting. "I don't blame you, if so," he said quietly, seeing something of an answer in the knight's deep dark eyes. "You had a duty to do, to your country, and your king. I do not hold you to account, Sir Pagaloth. Do not reproach yourself for what you did."

Pagaloth looked away. "Marak and Kin'rar have fled the city," he said in a quiet sombre voice. "As soon as they'd learned your plot had failed they fled the net before it fell. Vargo Ven has been promoted to Lord of the Nest, and stands watch now over the Bondstone. It is...a dark time here, Lythian. I feel shame...great shame for what I have done."

"You had no choice." He might have scorned him, cursed him, but he didn't. "You were protecting your kingdom, Pagaloth, and your people..."

"I was protecting myself." Pagaloth's eyes were lit with a cold burning remorse. "Kin'rar told me of what you were doing. He had no choice, lest I grow suspicious. He took me aside and told me, Lythian, and asked me that I trust him. He told me that Tavash was your target. He told me it all, and yet..." A sigh slipped through his lips. "I was a coward. A frightened boy, and no more. He only asked for my silence, that is all, and I couldn't even give him that. I betrayed him. I betrayed Lord Marak. And you, Captain. I betrayed you."

Lythian could feel the man's seething hate for himself, a hate that would live with him always. He wanted to help, such as he could. *Because he is a good man,* he thought. *And need not suffer along with us.* "You did what you thought was right. Were I in your shoes, I might have done the very same."

"No, you..."

"Believe me, Sir Pagaloth, I wrestled with this choice myself. To kill a man while sleeping would have disgraced me. And a prince? Within his palace and his city? I would have cursed myself to a life of dishonour and debased my standing among the order. Tavash thinks what he is doing to us will degrade us to lesser seats at Varin's Table, but that isn't true. No, I would have done that myself had I killed him." He looked the dragonknight in the eye. "Do not wallow in self rebuke over this, Sir Pagaloth. You did what you needed to, as I would have done myself. To me, the shame of what I attempted was worth it...to save my friends, to help stop a war. But how long would that have lasted? How long can war be kept at bay when it is the gods themselves who continue to incite it? There have been two dozen great Renewals and may be two dozen more. That is the world we live in. One built on conflict and war..."

"I do not deserve these words, sir," Pagaloth said, as a distant clap of thunder shook through the turbid night skies. "You try to assuage my guilt and in doing so prove your nobility once more. But let us be clear. I am complicit in helping bring about war. The blood that King Tavash will spill is on my hands, and it has started already with Sir Tomos. His parting has cut me deep...deeper than I would ever have thought. I liked him. He had much to give and should never have died like that. Nor should you, Captain. Nor even Borrus. I see a dignity in his defiance now, as I have always seen a dignity in you." He took a sharp breath and turned away. "I will never forgive myself for this."

The skies were roiling now, what light there was giving shape to the thick black clouds as they gathered and churned overhead. The rain fell heavier, harder, washing against Pagaloth's pitch black hair, crashing against his shoulders like waves on rock. He stared out over the city in the direction of the palace, hidden within the swirling black squalls. And when the lightning came Lythian saw the tears upon his eyes, silent as they slipped down his rain-soaked cheeks. And his face was stuck fast in a grimace that would never now be far from his lips.

"You show your honour in your reaction, Sir Pagaloth," he said, after a long sullen minute had passed. "You do yourself a great service. And you have my forgiveness, if that is what has brought you here."

The dragonknight gave a slow nod, still looking out. "I doubt Sir Borrus will be so kind. And nor can Tomos now have his say."

"Tomos fought with courage, and saw to the slewing of two juvenile drakes. He will have advanced his cause greatly. And Borrus?" He turned his eyes behind him, as the puddle in which Borrus slept continued to fill. "He has had his war, as I have. Do not grieve for our loss or our suffering here, Pagaloth. We both go willingly to the Halls."

Whether his words were helping, Lythian couldn't tell, but if he could do one good thing before he died it would be to palliate this poor man's guilt. *He is a victim as the rest of us are*, he thought. *Victims of Tavash's vanity and greed.*

"Your words give me some solace." Pagaloth managed the smallest of smiles, as thanks for Lythian's kindness. He took a short pace across the platform, looking through the teeth at Borrus. "Your time here will not last much longer," he said, as Borrus coughed and stirred, shimmying in his sleep out of the cold wet puddle. "You will be returned soon to the arena. To fight one another, I have heard."

Lythian looked sharply down at his dear friend. "We'll not raise swords against one another, Pagaloth."

"I know this." Pagaloth's trident beard dipped, rainwater flooding down it and pouring from the triple tips. "They will offer life to the victor. This is what I have heard." He looked into Lythian's gentle amber eyes. "You will not do so, I see."

"Not were I to live a hundred lifetimes would I kill a brother for the pleasure of a tyrant."

He needn't say anymore than that, for Pagaloth knew so already. *If that is what they wish of us they will be sorely disappointed,* Lythian thought. *It is no more than another taunt to shame us.* Another crack of thunder split the air above them, closer now as the storm came for the city. They were rare here, he knew, though welcome. *Might it linger through the day, give us a little more peace?* Soon as the rains abated the mob would be back, heckling and hurling and howling their abuse. *Was all of Agarath of a mind?* he wondered. *Do they all hate us so?*

"If you ask it of me, Lythian, I will help you escape." Pagaloth was looking out to the square. It was empty save a pair of soldiers hiding beneath an awning. "Say it, and I will see it done." He took a grip of his hilt. "I will right the wrong I did to you."

Lythian was already shaking his head. "You would get yourself killed. There is no sense in you throwing your life away, Sir Pagaloth."

It felt like the knight had to offer, whether feasible or not. Because escape wasn't possible, not from here. Lythian had long since given up on such a fancy. *The only escape will be death,* he knew. And a part of him longed for that now.

He drew away from the bars, away from the dragonknight beyond them. The rains crashed wild and unrelenting as he slipped to the rear of the cell, settling down beside Borrus. His mind was back with his wife. *Talia,* he thought. *My dear sweet Talia. I will see you again soon. We'll be together...as a family.* Yet to the side Pagaloth was still watching, as though unsure of what else to do. *He has my forgiveness. There is nothing more he can do now. Nothing more for us.* "How long does your vigil last, Pagaloth? Do you have more time on watch?"

"A bribe," the knight told him, staring through the stone bars. "I have paid to be here, Captain. It is not a duty for a dragonknight, yet I had to come. To explain and...to see you again."

"And you've seen me."

Lythian wanted to be alone, wanted to lose himself to his thoughts. Return to his dreams, to Talia, to his son. To the moonlit courtyard where they danced and laughed and sang. The black wind would come again, he knew, taking them away from him each time, but didn't care. The dancing was enough, and the sweet giggling of his boy. It made what was to follow worth it. And so it always had.

Sir Pagaloth understood. "I will give my excuses to the guards below, and have one of them replace me." He took a long final look at the two Varin Knights, shivering within that cold wet cell of stone. He seemed like he had more to say, yet no more words came through his lips. He just stood there, mournful, staring quiet and staring still.

And when Lythian next looked up, the dragonknight was gone.

33

Jonik

The seas stretched out around them, a strange eerie calm in the air. *Blue,* Jonik thought. It was all he could see. A glimmering azure blue for the sea, and a lighter brighter tone for the sky. Behind him, stretching away to the west, the sun was lazily forging into its slow descent, and above was not a wisp of white, not a blot of cloud upon the endless ether.

A clang of metal rattled from the main deck. "Nice Devin, very good young man. Now let's try combo four, you remember it?"

Jonik turned to watch as Emeric Manfrey took the lad through his daily routines. The exiled lord had offered all the men the chance to train under his tutelage while at sea, and both Devin and Jack o' the Marsh had taken it up eagerly. The rest weren't so interested. "I'm Seaborn, not Bladeborn," Turner had told him. "Ain't never gonna be much of a soldier." Brax had contested that he was a decent fighter already, and had fought in the war under Taynar banners, while Grim Pete was hardly strong enough to hold a cutlery knife, let alone a sword. And Soft Sid was, well...he was Soft Sid. Teaching him anything beyond his deckhand duties would likely be more work than it was worth. *Though I'll bet he can cleave a man clean in two if given the chance,* Jonik thought. The giant had strength enough in him to lift godsteel alone and that was saying something.

Jack strode up to the forecastle as Manfrey took young Devin through his paces. "He's a quick learner, isn't he?" he said, gesturing to the boy, as he defended a sequence of attacks from Manfrey, parrying left and right. "Think he wants to be your bodyguard, Ghost. Even you need good honest men to watch your back, you know. You have to sleep some time."

Jack was dressed in a stained white shirt and short sailor breeks, his face as red as his flaming hair. Despite the aftercare ointments Sapphire had given him his skin was still amusingly raw. Not that he seemed to care. "I love it when I mess something up," he'd confessed. "It only teaches me what not to do next time. Isn't that how one becomes wise, Ghost? By making mistakes and learning from them." He'd clearly made a lot of mistakes in his life, because he seemed to do everything else so bloody well. Manfrey had been taking him through drills ever since they left the Tidelands a couple of weeks back and to absolutely no one's surprise, he'd excelled with sword and spear.

Jonik watched as Devin worked through the same routines. He didn't have Jack's natural spacial awareness or precision of movement, but was energetic and determined and making fine progress of his own. "And you?" he asked. "Do you want to be my bodyguard as well, Jack o' the Marsh?"

"I'll be what you wish me to be, my friend." The Marshlander nodded to the collection of men scattered about the decks. "I think that's become clear of all of us by now. We all fear the day that you sever our service and judge our life debts fulfilled. I believe that they're all rather enjoying this new adventure you've taken us on, you know."

"An adventure that will probably get them all killed," Jonik said. "The Shadow Order won't take long to track me, Jack, not with all this noise we've been making. I can defend myself well enough, but the rest of you?"

Jack gestured toward Devin as he ducked a swing from Emeric and came up the other side, beaming. "Well that's why this training is so important. I'm not saying the likes of Devin or I will be able to fight off a Bladeborn Shadowknight, but it can't hurt to know a few tricks." His eyes settled on Lord Manfrey a moment. "Do you imagine he might stick around with us for a little while? I'd like to think we've picked up another powerful ally in this great quest of ours, my friend."

Jonik still wasn't sure about that. They'd been over a week on the water since leaving Lizard's Laze and were another week at least from landing in Solas. Right now, Emeric's priority was in returning to his estates and ensuring the safety of his staff. They'd entered into few discussions as to what might happen beyond that, and in truth Jonik's own forward course was hardly crystal clear. He gave Jack o' the Marsh a curious look. "And what great quest are you referring to, exactly?"

Jack smiled. "This very one we're on, Not all quests need a defined outcome, do they? I'd say that some of the best adventures unravel as they go." Then he gave Jonik a look, and his eyes dipped to the Nightblade. "But I suppose you've got some idea, don't you? The two of you." He raised his eyes. "I've heard you whisper to the blade, you know. Is that Vandar you speak to? Might it be the lord of gods that lights your way, and ours?"

Jonik turned away from him. The man was as insightful as he was direct, and knew how to read Jonik far too well. Before he could give answer, however, a bleating call sounded from above them.

They turned as one and looked up. "What the hell's got into Grim now?" grunted Brown Mouth Braxton as he fiddled about with some rigging beneath the foremast. Grim Pete was in his typical perch in the crow's nest, staring concernedly to the north and pointing. "What?" bellowed Braxton. "Come on man, speak, what d'ya see?"

"I...I'm not sure," came the panicked call above them. "Something in the sky...I think...I think it might be a..."

"DRAGON!" roared Turner from the quarterdeck, a monocular set to his right eye. He pulled it away. "To arms men! There be terror in the skies!"

Jonik was reminded of the kraken, of the febrile fury that had engaged the crew as soon as it was spotted, lurking about around them, slithering with its thick slick arms. The same thing happened now, as Brax rushed to fling open the crates full of javelins and spears, handing them out. Jack and Devin and Sid were there in an instant, clutching at lances and pikes as they sped for the portside gunwale. Manfrey was already in position, the ancestral eagle-blade of Sir Oswald misting to his side. But there was something different about those mists. They were puffing out thicker and faster, swirling as though agitated. Vandar's soul they were said to be. And they sensed the spawn of their greatest foe.

Jonik pulled the Nightblade and marched to join them. The magical black metal was pulsing, its glyphs cast lightless along its length. "Can we fight it off?" he asked Manfrey.

The exiled lord was staring, narrow-eyed, toward the growing shape on the horizon. "It may not come for us," he said. "They have been known to fly this far to feed." His eyes darted over the side of the ship, to the frothy white waters churning at the keel. "There are sweet treasures down there that the drakes like to feast on. They can fly far from the Wings to find them."

"Does the beast have a master, Lord Manfrey?" bellowed Tuner from the wheel. "I judge your eyes are better than my monocular. Might be scales o' a Fireborn rider atop her, I can't tell."

Lord Manfrey gave answer. "No rider, Captain. This one's wild and free. And big." He looked back. "Bigger than most I've seen."

Grim Pete was in a panic up in the nest. "What do we do?" he squawked, flapping his skinny arms to get their attention. "Lances and spears'll do nothing to that thing."

They had some crossbows too but they'd be even worse. More accurate, true, but the bolts would bounce off a dragon's hide sure as day followed night.

"Might you call it for a duel, Lord Manfrey?" bleated Devin, his face shredded by fear. The boy was brave when it came to the terrors of the deep, but this was something different. All northerners feared dragons more than anything else. It went primal...and it went deep. "Knights challenge them, don't they...and you were an Emerald Guard once." He stared out with big white eyes, his hand shaking as he clutched his spear. "They have honour...they...they honour the duel..."

"*Fireborn* honour the duel," Emeric said, a tight clench to his jaw. "Unbonded dragons are wild animals, Devin. They honour nothing but the growl of their stomach. We'd best pray it isn't hungry."

The dragon was coming fast, its wide red wings beating the balmy air in slow, languid waves. Jonik could see its underside sparkling with a gemstone mix of blue and green, scales glinting as they caught the reflected light from the sea. It's jaws were clamped shut, narrow and sleek, its eyes of black obsidian. *A beautiful, deadly thing,* he thought, staring as it came.

"It's gonna kill us all. Burn us living!" Grim Pete was shrieking as the menace neared. "It's Drulgar born again! Fills the skies it does!" He flung himself over the side of the crow's nest, leaping from the barrel in a moment of panic, and began scrambling down the mainmast.

"Get back up there!" roared Turner. "Back to your post you craven fool!"

Grim wasn't listening. He clambered down in such a rush that he lost his grip on the rigging, falling backward. It looked for a moment like he'd go tumbling down to deck and snap his neck, yet at the last second his foot got caught in the nets and ropes, arresting his fall. "Help!" he cried out, blubbering and flailing his arms. "Someone...help!"

Brax was on the case at once, surging up the mast. "Leave the fool," Turner called to him. "He aint' no good in a fight anyhow. Leave him!"

Away to the north the dragon was still coming. Jonik stood side by side with Emeric in quiet discussion. "If she attacks it'll be down to us to drive her off, Jonik," Emeric said. "If one can draw her down to the deck, the other might be able to leap atop her from the masts. I see no other way. Do you want to go up or stay down?"

"Up," Jonik answered without a moment's delay. "I can go black without it seeing me. I'll have the Nightblade through its skull before it even knows I'm there."

"Then there's no time to waste." Emeric turned to Devin and Jack, the latter of the two speaking a prayer to keep the boy calm. "Men, with me."

Jonik turned to the mainmast, heart smashing against his chest as he shut his eyes, focused, and fogged into a rippling black mist. The wind swirled at the wisps of smoke, tugging them away until only a few gentle curls remained. He'd not mastered complete invisibility in daylight yet but it would be good enough. A third of the way up the mainmast, Brax was working to free Grim. The shrunken haggard man was rasping in agony as his ankle twisted and caught. "Quiet with your whining," Brax demanded. "And hold still...hold still, Grim, gods-damn you, and let me cut you free!"

Jonik passed them by, blowing past like a puff of wind. Neither seemed to notice. Within moments he was reaching the crow's nest and leaping inside. Below, Emeric and Devin and Jack were pulling down the sails at the foremast and jib. The exile looked up, having to imagine where Jonik might be. "You'll have a clear sight of it, Jonik!" he bellowed. "I'll lure it to the prow. Be ready!"

Jonik had thought the mainmast would be best but now realised the folly in it. Below him was a sea of white sails and ropes and rigging. *It'll never fly through here*, he knew. He climbed to the lip of the nest and faced forward, teetering on the edge. With a powerful thrust he bounded across to the foremast, clearing the wide gap and catching at the folds of the fore topsail. Below, Manfrey was calling orders for Devin and Jack to retreat, as he sped out now to the bow and leaped up onto the figurehead. "Hey! I'm right here!" he called out. Jonik turned his eyes north. The dragon was looming. He scrambled up to the top of the foremast as it stretched its maw wide and released a primal shriek. The hairs went up on the back of his neck, a tingle rushing through his limbs.

Below him, caught in the flapping sails, Grim was still crying out. Jonik spotted the shapes of Devin and Jack speeding down the main deck to cover, clutching at silver-tipped spears. Turner remained at the helm, refusing to hide. There was a strange calm to the man as he clutched the wheel and watched. Was that acceptance? Such men were defenceless against a terror like this. *Maybe he's just struck dumb...*

"Come here, my beauty....yes, come to me!" Emeric was calling out in his rich deep voice. "I hold the blade of House Manfrey, look! The blade of Sir Oswald who slew Karlog the Knight Killer and Bagazar the Brute, your kin! Come seek your vengeance; I await you! Feast on me if you dare it! I taste better uncooked, I swear it!"

He's trying to goad it, Jonik saw. *Goad it into eating him without using fire.* One blasted breath from the drake's jaws would have the whole ship in a blaze, and there'd be little they could do about that. The beast was a mere seventy yards off now, skimming low over the water. Jonik stilled his breath. It was heading in the direction of Manfrey...sixty yards...fifty... Then a sudden strong beat of its wings had it rising. Another. Another. Three strong flaps and up it went, thrusted high and higher still into the burning blue skies. Jonik craned his neck, as the fiend swept skyward in a near vertical climb, before suddenly twisting, turning, plunging. It took but half a heartbeat for it to shift the other way, diving directly down toward the shimmering water, some thirty yards off. A split second later it was cutting through the waves a mere stone's thrown away, folding its wings and pulling back its scaly shoulders into a dart-like streamlined shape. The splash was minimal for such a beast. The waters parted and swirled and frothed as the dragon disappeared, and all across the ship there was silence.

A moment passed. Another. Ten seconds. Jonik turned his eyes down to Emeric, but the man couldn't see him. At the stern Turner started laughing. "It's fishing. She's fishing is all! Twas a coincidence her comin' here." His laughter spread loud and long until a bursting surge of water and waves filled the air to starboard. Everyone spun and looked out as the beast broke back through the sea, great streams of salty water running off its huge red scaly back and wings. It flapped several long heavy beats to get airborne, hauling its great bulk beyond the surf five metres, ten, twenty, until it could fall into a smooth swift glide. Jonik stared in shock. Between its jaws was a massive shark, dark grey and white underneath, with black pins for eyes and rows of sharp white teeth. The dragon sailed off on the air, angling its wings to the left, picking up a breath of wind. It rose a little more before flapping again in sequence, rising each time as it wheeled and flew away north.

Jonik watched on, marvelling at the magnificence of the beast. But a voice came in his head. *No, Jonik. This is not a thing to marvel at. It is a spawn of Agarath, evil and corrupted. None of them can be trusted. Remember that. None...*

"She heads north to the Wings," called Turner. "She came to feed but not on us. And why would she? Us skinny morsels ain't so nutritious to her. Just a shame she didn't eat Grim."

She, Jonik thought. Both Turner and Emeric were saying that, though how they could tell the difference he had no idea. Already the dragon was fading into the white-blue skies a hundred yards gone, two. Jonik looked down and saw Devin and Jack crawl back out from their hiding places. Sid was standing below the mainmast, ready to catch Grim Pete should he fall, and still Brax hadn't gotten him loose.

Turner moved down from the quarterdeck. "I said leave him, Brax. All that bleatin'." He grunted and shook his head. "I've half a mind to leave you tangled in them ropes all night, you wretched poltroon. Why I put up with you I don't rightly know."

"I think my ankle's broken, Cap," Grim was groaning. "And my head...it aches horribly it does."

"Maybe it wouldn't if you didn't shriek so loud!" Turner continued fore, past Sid - who he tended with a genial pat on his muscular broad back as he passed - and up to the forecastle to join the others. He counted out his crew. "Where's Lord Jonik?" He looked around. "You hidin' hereabouts, lord?"

Jonik remained quite silent for a moment, watching as the dragon bled into the distance. Before long it was a spot of red on blue, making for the Wings some hundred miles north. Only when he was sure it wouldn't wheel about and return, did he let his form ripple back into sight in a gathering cloud of black fog. "I'm right here, Captain."

All eyes arched up to him, high above them at the summit of

the foremast. Turner let out a gruff guffaw. "Now what are you doin' up there, lord? Frightening that flying beasty off, no doubt."

"You think it sensed the Nightblade, Cap'n?" asked Devin, a buzzing thrill on his face. "Lord Ghost scared it away?"

"Aye, these dragons are smart as they say, boy. Got senses we'll never understand, they do. Some say they all have a link to Agarath, that the fire god still commands 'em. And look up there, Devin - what do you see in Lord Jonik's hand? A piece o' Vandar's Heart, oh yes, and a mighty strong piece too. Mayhaps the beast sensed it." He grinned. "Mayhaps it frightened her off."

"Or perhaps it was just hunting," said Emeric, sheathing his blade. He strode from the prow in his deep green cloak. "You said it yourself, Captain. We may have just misjudged its intent."

"Aye, that too, my lord. I'm supposin' we'll never know."

The experience had shaken Jonik a little more than he'd realised as he climbed down to join them. That was relayed to him by the trembling shiver in his fingers as he clutched at rope and rigging, at the thud thud thudding in his heart that wasn't going away. His ears still rang with that ancient other-worldly screech, like a thousand tiny knives pricking at his brain. But it was more than just him. *The Nightblade,* he thought. *Vandar feels it too.* There was an agitation in the blade, part eager, part feared. He felt the same as he reached the deck and Jack o' the Marsh said, "You're even more pale than normal, friend."

"And you're still red as a lobster." He pushed past him, lest Jack look deeper into his eyes and see his disquiet. He didn't want anyone to see that. *I need to lead these men. I can't do that if they see me quiver.* "Rare for a dragon to come out this far, isn't it?" He stepped to the gunwale and looked north so no one might see the strain on his face. His hands clung tight to the rail.

"Rare but not unheard of," said Emeric, stepping beside him. He gave Jonik a quick glance. "A shame it didn't attack. I was looking forward to see what you could do." The man was calm as a breathless sky, smiling fondly. "If you can handle a kraken, there's no reason why a dragon should trouble you."

"A huge disappointment all round," agreed Jack, stepping to his right flank.

Turner followed. "Aye. Would have been a sight for sure."

Then there was Brax, coming in beside Emeric. Then Devin bounded over. Then Grim shuffled to join them, dragging his twisted ankle, Sid following behind should he fall. All lined up and looked north, and Jonik's thoughts turned back to the dream he'd had the night they'd left the Tidelands. He'd stood and looked upon the Shadowfort with a thousand shadows at his flanks. To his right had been Jack and his left had been Emeric. Then Turner and Brax and the rest. And so they stood now, looking to the endless sea. *But north,* Jonik thought. *North to the Shadowfort, thousands of miles away.*

He'd have a long way to go if he ever meant to return there, but more and more he did. *Let the world have its war and I shall have mine,* he thought, but the Nightblade said different. *You're part of this world and this war, Jonik,* it whispered. *You're to be a champion in this Last Renewal.*

Jonik nodded and didn't question the voice.

Because who was he to argue with a god?

34

Amron

Amron sat in the shadow of a shallow rift, its bare rock wall giving shelter from the bitter winter winds. Beside him, Walter Selleck was barely visible within his bundled furs, his straggly-haired head poking out from within his rimy cowl. They'd managed to get a fire going, though it wasn't especially large or warm. Beyond the foothills, kindling was at a premium and anything more substantial than that was dearly difficult to find.

Walter turned the spit. It was rudimentary, stuck through a white-furred coney that Rogen Whitebeard had expertly snared that morning. They had food enough in their packs to not have to worry about hunting right now, though any fresh cooked meat would be welcome. "Looks roasted through to me," Walter noted, giving the sinewy meat a swift inspection. "Might we have a bite or wait for Whitebeard to return, d'you think?"

"We'll wait." It would be rude to feast on the thing without its trapper present, not that there was much meat on it. *About a mouthful or two each,* Amron imagined. Hardly worth the effort, really, though Whitebeard liked to live off the wilds wherever he could, he'd learned.

He'd been gone for some two hours now, checking the pass ahead to find out if it could be crossed, or whether they'd have to backtrack and find another route. "I'll go alone," the ranger had told them in his rough whispery voice. It sounded rare-used, as though his throat had rusted through inactivity and Amron had found that to be true. He'd spoken perhaps two dozen times all through their expedition thus far - mostly to tell them he was leaving to hunt, or checking the route ahead, or where they might safely stop to make camp - and had been excessively ungenerous when discussing anything personal, though Walter had unearthed a few theories the morning they'd left Northwatch. "Some say he was born to the wilds," he'd said as they ventured west from the Bladed Barbican on a bright sunny day, the snow-draped lands shining brilliantly beneath the skies. "That he was sired by an ancient tribe living in the foothills on the western side of the Heights, or even from the Deadwood. I heard that too."

There had been theories more fanciful than those as well. That Rogen Whitebeard was a half-breed, born of man and beast. He had the look for it. There was something lupine in his face, with that thin long nose and chin, upturned orange eyes, and the dark grey whiskers that clung about his jaw and cheeks. "And his name? Did you find out about that?" Amron had been curious upon meeting the ranger as to why they called him Whitebeard. As Robert Borrington had said, he wasn't so old as the name suggested, and some years younger than Amron was, he supposed. *About forty,* had been his guess on meeting the man, who stood tall and thewy, robust and tough as teak. His hair was unwashed and unkempt, hanging in shades of black and grey and when Amron shook his hand, he could feel his long experience of the wilds in the calluses and pits and scars that marked his rough tight skin.

"The men say it's on account of the beard of frost he wears," had been Walter's answer, as they'd trotted along through the foothills on their stout shaggy garrons. "From all the time he spends in the mountains and the like." Walter had risen early on their day of departure to learn what he could of the man, breaking his fast with a few of the soldiers finishing the night watch. "He rarely spends more than a few days back here, they say. Returns only to give report to Lord Borrington, before heading back out. Can't stand the company of the men and they don't much like him either by the sounds of it. I'll see what I can do to get through that thick frosty hide of his, though. Who knows, maybe I'll have more luck?"

Well, it seemed that even Walter Selleck's luck had its limits, because he'd failed on that account and quite spectacularly so. His attempts to unearth anything personal about Rogen Whitebeard had been futile, and met with snorts and withering stares, typically followed by a good view of the man's black-cloaked back as he prowled away through the snow. Again and again he'd tried and again and again he'd failed. "He's a vexing sort, truly," he'd said some days later, as they made camp in a cave Whitebeard had led them to. "I've met his like before, but none so surly as this. But I'm not to be defeated. I'll break him down eventually."

Amron didn't much care either way, and had no time for all these wild conjectures. Many of the rangers were Bladeborn, and some were even from the greathouses, though never heirs or anyone of particular importance. There was some nobility in joining the Rangers of Northwatch, however, and thus third or fourth or fifth sons might be sent to train with them when young. Keen senses were valued, as was a particular intent to explore, and willingness to spend much time alone away from the comforts of the world. A lot of them will have been squires to Varin Knights, only to fail in their attempts to rise through the order, and be sent to Northwatch instead. To Amron's mind, Rogen Whitebeard was one such man. And so long as he continued to guide them as he'd been doing so far, nothing else mattered.

"Did you know?" he asked Walter as they continued to wait for the ranger's return. "That Whitebeard would join us?" He remembered Walter's playful little comment when he'd told him the news. *His best ranger to guide us, you say? Well...aren't we lucky.* "Were you just being impish, or did you know we'd have help?"

"Well I hoped for help, to be sure," Walter said, giving the rabbit another look. "I can hardly lay claim to knowing, though. More expecting, I suppose. I didn't imagine Lord Borrington would allow us to head out without a guide, after all."

No, but I did, Amron thought, feeling a little foolish for that. "And if he wasn't here?" He'd come to realise that Walter might not know these mountains as well as he'd made out, and Whitebeard had led them from danger twice already, helping them avoid a perilous rockslide at one point and away from a nest of snow-snakes at another. "How many times would you have gotten us lost by now?"

"Lost?" Walter scoffed to the suggestion, giving the coney another turn. "Might be that we'd be further on. I'll not pretend I've got a map in my head like Whitebeard does, but I don't exactly need one. I'd have chosen a path and it would've led us through. Vandar lights the way, my lord, and will see us safe to his tomb."

Before Walter could slide into another sermon, the subject of their discussion returned, emerging from around the corner of the rift. His cloak was frosted white as his beard and his hood hung low over his narrow amber eyes. "What news, Whitebeard?" asked Walter, standing. "Is the pass open?"

Rogen Whitebeard didn't answer him. He kept toward the fire and removed his black leather gloves, rubbing his hands over the heat. "The flesh is blackening," he identified, looking at the rabbit on the spit. "You should eat."

"We were waiting for you," Walter said. He took no insult from the man's truculence, smiling in his merry, crooked way. "We thought you deserved the first bite, seeing as..."

"I'll not eat. The coney is for you." He looked to Amron. "You must keep up your strength. We are hardly beyond the foothills, and already you struggle."

Amron wasn't used to being spoken to like that, but he could scarce deny it. His leg was usable when on level flat ground and he could hike stairs and towers well enough, but this was different. The uneven terrain made his limp ever more evident and the ache in his right thigh was growing more troublesome by the day.

"You must stay warm," Rogen Whitebeard went on, pulling the rabbit from the gentle licking flames. "How long have you been sitting in my absence?"

"For the duration of your absence," Walter said. "What else are we to do? You told us to remain here."

"Move. Get on your feet and move to stay warm."

"Isn't that the fire's job?"

Whitebeard ignored him. "Lord Daecar, your leg will stiffen if you stay idle." He handed him the rabbit. "Eat. You need muscle and meat. And a lot of it at your size. Eat."

"We have cured meat in our bags, Rogen," Amron offered in cordial protest. "Venison and beef and salted pork..."

"To be rationed with care," Whitebeard cut in, standing over him in his billowing black cloak. He looked to grow more grumpy by the second when they conversed this long, as though words were a sickness to him. "The game I catch will make us less reliant on our provisions. Now eat. And none for him." He gave Walter a wilting glare.

"I'll not deny Walter his share, Rogen. We must all keep up our strength. Not just me."

Rogen Whitebeard looked at Walter like he was dead-weight dragging them down, then flung his eyes back to Amron. "You are my charge, Lord Daecar, not this man," he said in a curt voice. "I would have you heed my words if you wish to make it to the mountain and back alive."

He holds no reverence for me, Amron saw. *Not for my name nor title nor what I've accomplished.* It was such a rare reaction to be treated like this. *Though perhaps it's what I need?* He might have been peerless when clad in steel, but here in the mountains and the wilds he was but a novice, unused to the clamour and the cold, the winds and ridges, and he could see all that in Whitebeard's face when he set his eyes upon him. Yet so much as it stung him to be talked down to like this, he accepted it. *I deserve to be humbled,* he thought. *Out here, Rogen Whitebeard is lord, not me.*

"The pass is open," the ranger went on, turning away down the fissure. "Beyond this cleft we will be exposed. The snows are thicker. The going will be slow. There is a scarp on the south face of Mount Mornay where we may shelter the night. It is some five hours from here, and will be arduous." He turned to look at Amron again. "You'll need the strength, Lord Daecar. So eat. We leave in five minutes."

The route was as Rogen Whitebeard said, a high pass atop the central ranges of the Weeping Heights, heaped with heavy snows and exposed to the gale-force winds. For hours they battled on, unable to speak but for shouting into one another's ears, which happened once or twice as Whitebeard spotted trouble and called orders to take a slight diversion. The demands placed on Amron's right leg were more than he could bear at times, though there was nowhere to stop or rest so he had no choice but to press on. And all the while there was little to see but the swirling snow-squalls that ripped around them, and the shadowed peaks that loomed up high to the east and west as they went.

It was dark when the soaring form of Mount Mornay began to shape itself ahead, its south face of sheer rock climbing beyond sight into the skies. Its peak was one of the highest in all the Weeping Heights, Amron knew, and perhaps its most challenging. Only Mornay the Fearless was confirmed to have made the summit without succumbing to some tragedy along the way. He'd been an adventurer of unyielding courage and the finest mountaineer of his age, conquering the mountain some six hundred years prior without the use of godsteel. He wasn't Bladeborn at all, in fact, but a simple commoner from northwest Vandar, sired by a blacksmith and scullery maid, which made his feats all the more remarkable.

They found a shaded stretch of open rock beneath the looming south face of the mountain, and Rogen Whitebeard set about erecting the shelter. There were no trees nearby, nothing but rock and snow and towering peaks, but they'd made sure to lash some firewood atop their canvas packs that they'd gathered in the foothills. As Walter and Amron set about starting the fire, the winds decided to settle, and above them the clouds saw fit to scatter. Stars blinked awake in shades of white and gold and a stillness took hold, such as they'd not known for some days.

"He must be an inspiration for you, Walter," Amron said, as they laid the firewood. He turned his eyes upward, yet even as the clouds cleared the summit of Mount Mornay eluded them. "Addison Mornay. He was a man of Lakeside as you are, if I'm not mistaken."

Walter Selleck's head bobbed up and down, strands of lanky hair frosted against his forehead. "Aye, he was. A man after my own heart, to be sure. But Mornay was an adventurer born whereas I've been made, so to speak. There are others who'd better claim to have been inspired by the man. I have a friend who revers him, in fact. Ranulf Shackton. You know the name?"

"I've heard of it, yes, though not had the pleasure of a meeting."

"And a pleasure it is. There's no man more cordial in all the north."

Amron gave a smile as they stacked and fixed the wood. He knew of a few famed adventurers still living, Master Shackton among them, though the great age of exploration had long since come and gone. There wasn't much left to discover, really, but for what lay beyond the known world, out to the west of the Tidelands and east beyond the Stormy Sea. Explorers and scholars had often debated whether there was more to the world than they knew, and many subscribed to the theory that there were other landmasses beyond their current reach. What expeditions had gone out, however, had never returned. It was thought that any exploration to the east was near impossible due to the violent storms there. And west the currents and winds were wild and unpredictable, confounding sailing ships and bringing them home before they could drive their way through the curious patterns of weather. It had even been postulated that the gods had never perished at all, but simply moved on, forging and reshaping other lands and worlds to start afresh, as a painter with a blank white canvass or a sculptor with a rough hunk of rock. Amron believed in no such notion. The world was what it was, as far as he saw it, and what lay beyond was merely a product of man's imaginings and no more.

Still, he always liked to hear another man's opinion on things so posed the question to Walter as they worked. "Do you imagine the world we know is the sum of it, Walter? Or does something more lie beyond?"

Walter was working his knife along the flint, trying to catch a spark. He raised one of his smiles at the question. "What lies beyond, my lord, is not east or west or north or south, but above and below. The Long Abyss and the Eternal Halls. And those can only be explored when we die."

Rogen Whitebeard stepped over with a face as grim as death. Without a word he snatched the knife and flint from Walter's stubby-fingered hands and ran the blade's edge along the stone. A spark flew and caught light on the lint and in moments the fire was breathing bright, drawing shadows upon his face. "Why are you here?" he then growled, staring at him. "If you cannot even cut a spark what use are you? You are no navigator, nor warrior, nor huntsman that is clear. Are you a priest? Is he your private parson, Lord Daecar? Because I would say his sermons are wasted here."

He didn't care to hear Walter's answer and with the shelter set up, grunted something neither man could hear and headed off into the darkness. Walter seemed only bemused by the man's intrusion. "Well at least he's speaking," he said. "I would call that progress, even if he continues to be entirely mean-spirited."

Amron expressed a weary sigh as he watched Rogen Whitebeard fade into the pall of night. "All rangers hate excess, Walter. They travel lean and light where they can, and your presence will seem unnecessary to him."

"Well it mightn't if he'd be good enough to hear my story." Walter had tried on several occasions to explain to Whitebeard who he was, but the man had shown no interest in listening to him. All he saw was a shabby little man who sucked up rations and rarely stopped blabbering. "Does he think it was his doing alone that helped us avoid that avalanche? Or that nest of snakes? Or the sundry other hazards that might have caused us trouble? Much of our fortune thus far is down to my light, Lord Amron. It shields us all in subtle ways, whether we know of it or not."

Amron wasn't so sure about that. Whitebeard spent his life up here and was quite capable of avoiding such perils without Walter's ambiguous assistance. "You cannot claim every near-miss as your own, Walter," he reprimanded. "It seems these miraculous powers of yours grow stronger by the day."

"Perhaps they do, as I near the place of my blessing." Walter shrugged as they settled onto a pair of rough rocks beneath the endless escarpment, finding a smooth enough landing for his backside. "But I see what you mean. I'd not want to suggest Whitebeard isn't qualified to lead us...on the contrary he has shown a mastery of his trade thus far...but that mightn't be enough when we come down the other side of these mountains, my lord. It would behoove him to listen to me then, rather than dismiss me as an anchor and a pest. Only I know the way. Only I shine the light."

The flames took well to the wood, aided by the shelter of the south face and calming winds. Amron sat and listened to them as they whirled about him, less a gale and more a whispering breeze, flowing up through the valleys and between the peaks from east to west. Within them he could hear the strange song these mountains were known for. It was said that the wind itself was a lament for the dead, the product of all those who'd come up here to weep for those they'd lost. For centuries people had climbed here in grief, to take to the high passes and call out to the winds and the wilds in the hope of hearing their loved ones' voices in return. And so Amron perched by the fire, in that strange eerie place, and listened to the winds as they whistled past his ear.

"Might you call out for your son, my lord?" Walter asked him. "See if he might reply?"

"Aleron?" Amron looked into the darkness, shaking his head. "No, I...I don't think so, Walter. I do not imagine I'd hear his voice." He tried to smile. "He will be feasting with Varin. I'd not want to disturb him."

Walter Selleck's poorly arranged teeth appeared behind his smile. "You don't believe it, do you? That the dead will hear you up here?"

"You read me well," Amron said. He'd never believed it, in truth, else he might have come here when Kessia died to call to her. *Might I try now? Call out to her and see what she thinks of this foolish quest?* The idea held little appeal. *She'd only admonish me for leaving Lillia behind,* he thought with an affectionate smile. *And might that just turn me around?* He couldn't think about that, and the thought of hearing Aleron's voice again was equally distressing. *What will he think of me, for what I did? For not telling him the truth of who Ludlum was. For letting him die as he did...for all of Varinar to see...*

He swallowed hard against the thought as the winds brushed past him, whispering as they went. "And you?" he forced himself to ask, needing the distraction. "When you made for Vandar's Tomb, was it in part to cross these mountains? To weep into the heights?"

"I'm supposing it was," Walter nodded. "I can scarce remember those days now, beyond the depression and the anger and the grief. But whether it was my intent or not, I stopped here a night, likely not far from where we are now." He looked around, though the landscape was vast and featureless beyond the tall peaks and great snow-mantled slopes cloaked beneath the veil of night. "It might have been right here, such as I remember. Many of these peaks look much the same to me."

"And you called to them? Your wife and children?"

Walter gave a slow nod. "I called to them," he whispered, as they sat listening to the wailing winds, the aching laments of the living and the lost. "What I said I've long since forgotten. 'I love you. I love you all.'" He smiled. "Perhaps that's all it was. Or perhaps I just sunk to my knees and sobbed, I don't know. I was too lost to my grief to remember."

A grief well earned, and like no other, Amron thought, looking sorrowfully at the man. Walter Selleck had lost more than Amron had, more than many a man would ever be able to bear. A wife. Three children, the oldest but eight and the youngest a newborn babe. And his father and mother besides. All perished in a fire that blazed through his home, a property that had doubled as his working premises too. He'd been a carpenter and woodworker, a humble furniture maker in Lakeside where he lived, well regarded by the local community for the care and attention he gave his creations. Walter had told Amron that it was a business rival who'd set his home afire. "A man by name of Podrick Percival," he'd confided in him over an ale one night. "We'd been rivals for years before that day, mostly petty stuff till things turned ugly. I got a contract he'd been coveting and that turned him to malice. I've no thought that he intended to hurt my family, just destroy my workshop, but the man he hired for the job had other ideas. A miscommunication I'm supposing it was."

And a deadly one, as far as he went on to explain. It had been summertime, when the residents of Lakeside came together to celebrate the solstice. The festivities were the best in all of North-west Vandar, as crowds came from far and wide to watch the boating races on the water, and browse the fine colourful market-places that so swelled that time of year. Walter's family were thought to be absent from the house, but his wife and two of his children had come down with a case of summer flu, so the rest of the family remained to tend them. Walter had gone to the water-front to put ink to parchment on his latest contract. "I stopped after to fetch my wife some flowers, and pick up a pricey bottle of spiced wine to celebrate, and some gifts for the kids," he'd said. "Twas one of the happiest days of my life, truth be told, but when I heard tell of the fire, so it soured to the worst." His life after fell to blackness. To the bottom of the bottle. To promises of vengeance. Amron knew such vices intimately, and he knew grief too, though where he'd suffered a heavy loss so Walter had been subjected to an altogether more unspeakable tragedy.

"Did you ever find him?" he asked now, as they sat quiet before the flames. "You never told me. Did you get justice for what Podrick Percival did to your family, Walter?"

Walter drew a wry smile. "Justice? No, my Lord Amron, twas no justice could be done after what he did to me, lest I murder his family too and take away all he had." He spoke as a man who'd passed through a thousand bitter nights in agony, and come out the other side wise and fair. "But I'd never be able to do that, nor would I ever wish to. Did I seek to hurt the man himself, kill him for what he did? For a time, yes, but that time has long since passed. I have escaped that darkness, my lord. I live only now in Vandar's light."

Amron kept his eyes on him for a time. "And if you saw him again? If I helped you find him?"

"I'd not wish you to," he said, as though he didn't even want to consider it. "It would only stir matters I have long since left behind. What happened to my family was a horror that no man should ever endure, yet I have not once believed it was Podrick's desire to harm them. Nor could I count myself innocent in the tragedy. I played my part in our rivalry and did much myself to provoke him. Had I been a better man they might still be living, and I'd never have gone north in my grief, nor would I be here with you now." He turned his eyes beyond the fire, to the glowing white plains, gleaming beneath the light of the pale silver moon. "What happened had to happen," he said, in a voice that refused to believe otherwise. "The death of my family. The loss of my business. All I've been through brought me to this moment, as it has with you. Your maiming. The death of your son. Such horrors can force a man to do extraordinary things. And in our grief, my lord, we have been driven toward something greater."

Amron gave no answer. He'd sooner have retained his strength and his son and never have come here in the first place. This quest might be extraordinary, but he'd rather it wasn't necessary. *And him?* he wondered, giving Walter a glance. *Does he truly believe his own words? Would he not rather his family were living than to possess these powers? What good is such a blessing, if you need be so cursed to receive it?*

"I am here to guide you," Walter went on, sensing his lord master's doubts. "To help you restore your strength, so you might fight for Vandar in the Last Renewal. That is why I'm here, my lord. I am but a humble conduit. But you...it is you who will wield the blade. It is you who will make the difference."

Amron reached forward, gently massaging at his right thigh. There had been many global wars, many renewals of the War Eternal, but not once had it ended for good. "Last Renewal?" he asked. "You believe that the last great war approaches?"

Walter's face took on a framing of great purpose, and for a moment his teeth seemed straighter, hair washed and combed, eyes gleaming bright with that curious inner light of his. "The gods gather their followers," he said in a deeply fervent voice. "All across the world they are bestirring, my lord, and you are one of Vandar's greatest, one of his champions." He gave him a single staunch nod. "I know now why I was given this light. It was not to seek adventure, nor save lives, but to lead you into this darkness. When I first received Lady Amara's letter, I knew it in my soul.

And thus did I come to you...to lead you and serve you and die for you if I must. As Vandar wills it, so it shall be done."

Amron lifted his eyes to the heavens. The stars were so thick in places they seemed as clouds, coloured in mixed tones of purple and blue against the tall black peaks that sought to reach them. Every time the world fell to war, people proclaimed the Last Renewal, yet not once had they been right. Some had been celebrated prognosticators, known for calling correctly their predictions and prophesies, yet even they'd been wrong. Amron took Walter Selleck to be one of them. *He cannot know what is to follow,* he thought. *There is not a man living who can.*

"I might take to the shelter," Walter said, breaking the long silence between them. "It has been a long day, my lord, and my poor short legs are weary. I sense you wish to be alone."

Amron placed a genial paw onto his shoulder, gripping through the furs. "Thank you, Walter, and get some rest. I might wait up a little while longer, to make sure Whitebeard returns."

Walter stood from the rock he'd been perching on. "Of course," he said, turning to look out over the great white tundra. "The man grieves, I imagine, as we do." He looked to Amron with a final word. "If you listen closely, perhaps you'll hear him."

As Walter stepped away, Amron reached into his cloak and took ahold of his godsteel dagger, set opposite the sleek longsword he'd elected to take too. His eyes sharpened as he gazed upon the slopes and craggy peaks, layered into the distance beyond the scope of his sight. There, far off in the blackness, the shape of a man appeared, staring out from the top of a precipice. His eyes were to the west, away over the Heights, his long black cloak rippling in the restless breeze.

Amron inclined his head and listened, through the wailing and the weeping on the wind, the soft lament of a thousand voices. He filtered through it all and narrowed his attentions on Rogen Whitebeard alone. And there, out in the distant darkness, he heard him.

Whispering to the winds.

Weeping for the dead.

35

Saska

Saska sat in Elyon's desk, reading by firelight within the safe confines of his tent. Before her on the table were at least two dozen books, heaped in haphazard piles and arranged in no particular order. She'd had time enough now to read through several of them, and discard several others that didn't take her fancy. Right now, she was reading a tome dedicated to the War Eternal, a great meaty thing of twelve hundred word-packed pages that described, in sometimes excruciating detail, the score of Renewals that had brought the world to war over the past three thousand years.

"When will we ever learn?" she muttered to herself, sitting back, closing the book tight. She'd had enough of that one. She reached out and took up her cup of wine, spinning the stem between her fingers. The tome was entitled 'The War Eternal: A Full History'; an apt, if rather dull name for the contents therein. Saska had hoped for some more insight into when or if it might end, but hadn't learned much on that account. There had been common mentions of 'The Last Renewal' throughout, though only in the context that it was brought up every time the world fell to war. *More a hope than expectation,* she thought, as she pushed the book aside. She took a sip of her wine and sat back, lazily looking over the other books she'd not yet had a chance to flip through. Her days here had been long and in large part spent alone, with Elyon's attentions often required elsewhere. Only at night did they get some time together, sharing stories and sharing wine, though not once had they shared a bed since that first fateful night. *It's for the best,* she thought, as she stood and walked to the brazier. She picked up a poker and gave the coals a prod. *It would only complicate things, as he said.* Though it all felt complicated enough.

Outside, the distant blur of battle continued to beat away at the bitter night air. Saska stepped over and searched through the flaps, though could see little beyond the collection of grand Vandarian pavilions arrayed in this part of the camp. It was somewhere past midnight now, she figured, and the battle had been raging loud and fierce for some hours already. Through the night skies she could see the thin trails of fire and smoke as the trebuchets and catapults launched and swung, sending barrels of pitch and tar at the walls, battlements and beyond. *Do they hope to burn those walls down, to undo stone with fire and flame?* It didn't make sense to her. She'd seen those walls and climbed those towers and knew that no keg of burning pitch was going to do anything to the fort defences. There were some wooden buildings inside, stables and stalls and the like, though they were mostly kept to the northern side and out of reach from these attacks.

She drew away, gave the brazier coals another poke, and dropped back into Elyon's chair. Late though it was she felt restless, alert and alive and part of that was for concern for Elyon. The siege had been escalating for some days now and despite Prince Rylian's desire to limit loss of life, men were starting to fall. *He's in his armour, his full godsteel plate,* she thought. *He'll be fine.* But that wasn't strictly true. Elyon would be better protected than most, yes, but also a beacon for the Rasals to aim at. Many of their bowmen had Bladeborn blood and used godsteel-tipped arrows and quarrels. When shot by great sturdy longbows they were quite capable of piercing godsteel armour, and they weren't even the worst of it. There were some twenty swivel-mounted scorpions upon the battlements too, and each had a generous consignment of godsteel-capped bolts stacked alongside them ready to be loaded. Saska remembered how Marian had pointed them out when they'd stopped at Harrowmoor some weeks ago, telling her how effective they were against godsteel-clad soldiers. *And now Elyon's out there, probably being stupid and heroic,* she thought. *And if he should be stretchered back to camp with a bolt through his belly, then what?* The notion made it feel like she'd taken a bolt to the gut herself, and she didn't much like that either. *I care about him too much,* she realised, taking a sharp sip of wine. *I came here to cut Kastor's neck, and instead I've fallen for some boy...*

She cast the thought aside. It wasn't fair, nor true. *I haven't fallen for him,* she told herself. *I just like him a bit, that's all.* He'd shown her a rare kindness and seemed just as mentally muddled as she was, and their nights together had been a rare light in the darkness of these long wretched weeks. At night, Elyon would typically sit at his desk and ask her what she'd read, and she'd ask him about the goings on in camp, the siege, and any other news he'd heard. A couple of times he'd been called away to the long-house for a feast, but each time he tried to return early. And each time she waited up, eager to see him before he slept and rose and left her again to see to his daily duties.

They were the moments that gave her solace as she awaited her departure from this camp. A departure that would bring with it a mixed blur of feelings. Guilt at failing in her duty. Anger at knowing Kastor yet lived. Shame to return to Marian with nothing to report but the loss of her chastity. And sadness...yes, she'd feel that too, at having to leave behind the man who so tenderly took it.

Another sip of wine went down her neck to settle her thoughts, and her eyes scanned over the books before her. Most were of little interest. A yellow leather-bound book about the Suncoats and their fighting styles looked intriguing at first glance but made joyless in presentation. *Surely such a book should have diagrams and pictures?* she thought, passing it up again. It didn't, just long endless passages describing a truly staggering array of attack and defensive manoeuvres and sequences. Elyon had spent time poring over it at night but to Saska it was truly soporific. Others were similarly so. A tome on the history of the Rasal houses was similar to one she'd already read at the university in Thalan, but a great deal more boring. Another went into great depth about the sundry swords, spears, shields and other weapons and armour commonly used in various parts of Vandar. There was a book about the Steelforge that Elyon seemed to cherish, but Saska had found overwrought and poorly written. The young Daecar even had a book about poetry with him, though not once had he opened that up, and a pocketbook that he wrote in occasionally, scribbling notes at night.

She looked at that one now, set a little to the side, and drew it toward her. He'd made no mention of it, so she didn't consider it too personal or off-limits, so opened it up and flipped through. Inside she found lists of names, titles, and short descriptions of the men and women they belonged to. It looked to be a method he used to better remember people, and was perhaps one of the reasons he was so well liked. Most people had no great memory for names but this would help correct that, especially for a man so familiar with the social scene. Recalling an old acquaintance's name without prompting would ingratiate him to them, after all. *A simple trick,* she thought, *but an effective one.*

She flipped to the most recent listings, curious as to whom he might have met these last days and weeks. Most were knights and lords among the Tukoran ranks, scribbled in with their names, ranks, houses, and rough descriptions of their appearance and the occasional character trait. Most took up no more than a couple of lines, but there was one, a couple of pages back, which caught her eye for the depth it went into.

'Don Mears,' Elyon had written. 'Regular foot soldier under House Caldlow. From Broadway. Late thirties. Wife and three girls. Sullen and gaunt, but seemed a good, honest man. Was on watch at the camp perimeter, seeing to the boys labouring there. Bit sour at first but soon warmed up. Joked that the boys would be fodder for the bowmen but took it back. But...might they? When the siege comes, who knows. Kastor's building dummy siege weapons to draw fire, so why not dummy soldiers too? Even Bladeborn. Find some of the older boys, dress them up in something mimicking godsteel, and send them in to draw enemy fire. Hope it doesn't come to that. But...who knows.'

Saska felt a slow creeping dread as she read the rambling note. Elyon had told her nothing of this. He was willing to help her get out of here, and had even tried to contact Marian, without result thus far...but he wasn't about to betray any secrets of the siege, should she slip away to Harrowmoor and pass them on to its commanders. *Him and his damn honour,* she thought. *He'll not let me try to kill Kastor and he'll not speak to me of anything much that matters.* And did this? Did this matter? She wasn't sure, but already her mind was turning to dear sweet Del, who'd drifted from her thoughts these last weeks. But might he be here, in camp with her? Might he be under threat of being used as fodder for quarrels and bolts? He'd been taken from Lord Quintan's lands under Kastor's rule, and would have been swept up into the sprawling northern army, not the south. *If he's still alive, then he'll most likely be here. He might have been mere metres from me all along without me ever knowing it...*

She was on her feet in an instant, pacing, thinking. Elyon had been quite explicit about her staying in the tent, but mostly to stop her from trying to kill Kastor. She wasn't going to break that particular promise, but she could bend his rules a bit. She was back at the desk, taking a final short sip of wine to give her courage. *I'm going,* she then thought. *I have to try to find out if he's here, at least.* She made a snap decision. Time was short and the night's bombardment likely wouldn't last much longer. If she was going to try to find Del, there'd be no better time than now.

Rushing over to one of the central support poles, she fetched her cloak from its hook, throwing it about her shoulders, shoving Elyon's notebook into her pocket. The coat was dark and heavy and the hood would help conceal her. Outside, the world was full of the rush and thud of the siege. She surged over to the flaps and peeked out. The Vandarian camp was ghostly quiet, and the rest would be much the same, she hoped.

Turning, she sped to the drinks counter, shoved the table aside, pulled up the loose plank beneath the table leg, and fetched the godsteel dagger she'd safely stowed there. Slipping it into her inner coat pocket, she returned the table to its proper position, and darted out into the night.

36

Elyon

The trebuchet swung with a great groaning whoosh, the counterweights plunging low and the throwing arm rising high. As it hit the cushioned crossbar, the sling let loose its charge, sending a huge barrel of pitch toward the flaming fort in the distance.

Elyon watched its arc, surging away into the murky blackness and up over the walls. A moment later the burning barrel was gone, leaving only a trail of shaky smoke in its wake as it smashed and burst, exploding out of sight. Down the line, another call bellowed out, "Fire!" and a second trebuchet swung on its mechanism, casting a blazing barrel into the outer bastions. The snows gleamed beneath it as it passed, sparkling momentarily before being sucked back into the darkness, as the cask cracked into the wall, causing a small troop of bowmen to scatter.

Elyon couldn't tell if any of them were hit or set alight this time, though he'd seen a fair few burning that night. Some had even leaped through the crenels in their mad agony to escape the licking flames, seeking salvation in the muddy waters of the moat below. Others had staggered the other way in their madness, toppling off the wall walk into the yard beyond. But they were few and from what Elyon could tell, their own forces were faring a lot worse.

Further up the slope, a half dozen siege weapons were burning, catapults and ballistas battered by defensive fire. There were two siege towers among them, several scaling ladders, and perhaps two of three hundred men who'd been caught in the onslaught. Elsewhere, another trebuchet had fallen to a mechanical failure, the counterweights sticking fast as the barrel of pitch burst alight in the sling. Several men had been caught as the shower of tar came down upon them, rushing off in a flaming frenzy onto the frozen moors. Other dummy siege weapons had been deployed and destroyed during Lord Kastor's mad bid to take the fortress himself. The onslaught up the slope had been his idea. "If I can get just two dozen men over the walls and into the gatehouse we'll have the fort by night's end," he'd said during the war council that day. Prince Rylian had eventually allowed him the attempt, though never seemed too happy about it, and this was the result. *Desperation*, Elyon thought. *Before too long we'll be mounting a full scale siege, with every tower and ladder and man we've got...*

But that wouldn't be tonight. Tonight was intended as another test, one of half a hundred they'd done. Elyon marched over to Lord Kanabar as the trebuchets under his charge were loaded and unleashed. More tongues of flaming fury went fizzing through the air, leaving ragged red trails in the night. "My lord, how long will this go on for?" he asked. "We are doing nothing to their walls nor spirit so far as I can tell. Isn't it time to call it a night?"

"I'll relent once Rylian gives the order," the Lord of the Riverlands responded, his breath frosting beyond his red bearded lips. "These siege weapons are his, not ours, Elyon."

"But not the barrels of pitch. We brought half of those ourselves and we're doing nothing but wasting good supplies."

"We have plenty." Lord Kanabar looked out at the fortress, wrapped tight and warm in a huge fur coat. He had a large host of his Riverlanders in formation about him, as did Lords Shorton and Fullerton with the Lakelanders, assembled nearby. The Tukorans were doing the same, with some ten thousand men arrayed neatly in units across the length of the southern and eastern slopes encircling Harrowmoor. Tall siege towers loomed among them as the trebuchets and catapults whooshed and swung, though it was all nothing but a show of strength. Rylian had spoken of it earlier. "We march out in force tonight," he'd told the commanders. "We show the Rasals what awaits them if they continue to refuse to yield."

Well they were refusing to yield and no spread of soldiers and siege weaponry, no matter how vast, was going to unman them. Should Kastor's misbegotten plan have worked then the army would at least have been ready to swarm the fort, but that had never seemed likely.

Elyon could see Lord Kastor now, some way off in his fine godsteel armour, marching impatiently up and down his lines. He'd survived the onslaught, but only just, almost taking a ballista bolt to the neck, though several knights of his house had succumbed. His contemptible nephew, Sir Griffin, wasn't one of them. The sneering knight was marching alongside him now, holding a note to hand, prevailing upon his lord uncle some favour, it looked. A moment later, Sir Griffin was turning and moving back toward the siege camp a few hundred yards away, calling upon one of his men to go with him.

Elyon watched him go with a piercing glare before the arrival of Vesryn drew his eyes. He turned back as his eminent uncle strode over in his full godsteel plate, looking every bit the First Blade, despite what his detractors said. "Our underminers have been buried," he announced. "And there's been a sally at our eastern flank." The blood sprayed across his breastplate suggested he'd been involved. "I arrived to drive them off but we lost several dozen in the attack. I feel this night has yielded no reward but to fortify Rasal resolve. Elyon, accompany me as I report to the prince."

Elyon took to his uncle's side as they marched westward along the siege lines, out of the reach of the Rasal defences. Though that meant they were perfectly safe, it also meant that their own bombardment was never going to reach any further than the outer walls, or just within them, where they'd inflict little to no damage at all.

"Kastor's plan was folly," Vesryn said as they went, looking to the Greenbelts assembled on the snowy slopes nearby. "He has only weakened our ability to effectively siege this fortress, though in this case I do not blame him. The plans he laid out to us when we first arrived were exhaustive and well thought out. Had we followed them through originally we might not have wasted time."

"Only men," Elyon said. "Kastor's plan will see us lose thousands, Uncle."

"We have lost hundreds this evening with nothing to show for it. I'd say losing thousands to win the fort is a small price to pay."

There was a sharpening edge to Vesryn that Elyon was beginning to see, a ruthlessness he'd not noticed before. *He grows fierce and furious in the face of his doubters,* he thought. *And paranoid too.* He gave the Sword of Varinar a glance, clutched in his metal grasp and gleaming radiant in the gloomy night air. "Does it not grow heavy, Uncle, wielding it so long?"

"It feels no heavier than a regular godsteel blade to me now." Vesryn marched on, imperious, as others watched him go. Wreathed in silver armour and bearing a golden blade he looked magnificent. *And he's starting to know it too.*

They were soon nearing the prince's van, as Rylian stood stoic and solemn with a host of Emerald Guards at his back with their godsteel spears and shields. Banners fluttered around him, bearing the crossed hammer and blade of Tukor, as men in brown and green spread out upon the plains. A number of short sorties had been ordered to determine Rasal response patterns, but Rylian had remained largely risk-averse thus far. He turned as Vesryn approached. "My lord, how goes the assault on the eastern flank?"

"Poorly, Your Highness." Vesryn thrust the Sword of Varinar into the churned earth at his feet. "Our efforts to undermine the fortress walls have failed. The Rasals got wind of it and countermined our tunnels, burning them out and collapsing them. The men defending the attempt were caught in a sally and slaughtered. I arrived to drive them back before they could cause any further chaos among our ranks." He engaged Rylian with a firm stare. "It is time for an all-out assault, not just a show of one. We can ill-afford to lose hundreds of men in these futile exchanges."

Rylian kept his eyes on Vesryn's for a time, then turned back to look at the towering fortress walls. The barbican was a brute, flanking the thick stone gatehouse, and beyond the bailey rose up high and tall into the moody black skies. "These exchanges haven't been futile, Vesryn. Had your undermining efforts succeeded we might have brought down part of the wall. The same can be said of Lord Kastor's assault. A risky venture but a worthwhile one. I would sooner lose hundreds to open the door than thousands."

"You lost thousands when passing the Links," Vesryn retorted, his temper shortening by the day. "I have heard the reports, Rylian. The border assault was costly, but worth it. The same is true here."

"I find it curious to hear you speak like this." Rylian turned on him, a shred of patience lost, clad in slim rich godsteel armour of silver and green. "You have spoken frequently of sparing as much blood as we can during this siege, just as Lord Kanabar has. My strategy has been intentionally conservative to satisfy that end, yet now you stand before me, willing to sacrifice thousands. Pray tell of the change."

Vesryn took a moment to himself, letting out a sharp foggy breath. His blood seemed up from the battle and that would only foster reckless words. Inadvisable words. "I am not challenging you, Rylian," he said after a time, keen to avoid a quarrel. "And you're right. I have spoken openly in support of your strategy and would not like to claim otherwise. But now things have changed. The Rasals are dug in and will not relent without a full scale assault. If we wish to take this fortress, we can no longer afford to dally. I see no other way at this point, other than to stand down and surrender the attempt."

"Which we cannot do," said Rylian. "Neither my king nor yours would accept such a failure." He turned his eyes over the slopes, scattered with the ruins of trebuchets and towers, catapults and corpses. The fort looked grand and imposing upon the hill, lit all over by burning pitch and tar. At a glance it seemed ablaze, but it was all no more than superficial. "You may be right, Vesryn," the prince went on, staring out at the towering walls. "I will write my father and seek his counsel. He expressed his support for my strategy and has been keen for us to stage a slow siege thus far. Curious, yes," he said, seeing the raised eyes on both Vesryn and

Elyon's faces, "but true. His letters have shown a desire to unlock Harrowmoor without excessive bloodshed, but it would seem now that such a thing isn't possible. I will enquire as to his thoughts, and advise you do the same with Ellis. We lead these armies, yes, but it would be better to keep our kings' feathers unruffled."

"I agree," said Vesryn. He was always keen to keep King Ellis informed of matters going on in camp, though largely now as a courtesy.

Rylian turned to his side, to address the collection of commanding knights and officers at his flank. His sons, Robbert and Raynald, were among them, always tailing their father to better understand how to lead. And Elyon could see Sir Mallister not far off too, accoutred in breastplate and emerald cloak, tall silver spear and shield in his grasp. He'd been put in charge of leading a large portion of the shield-bearing soldiers, a promotion so far as Elyon could tell. *His fortunes rise as his father's do,* Elyon thought. *And his sister?* Elyon had heard nothing further of her coming to the camp and was happy for whatever delay was holding her up. With Saska still safely tucked away into his tent, having Melany return was a complication he'd rather avoid.

Rylian gave orders for his commanders to call the retreat, before requesting Vesryn do the same. It didn't take long after that for the trebuchets to relent in their bombardment, for the skies to settle into a deep gloom, for the walls of Harrowmoor to fade once more into the murky night as the fires were put out. Off in the distance, Elyon could hear the sound of cheering within the fortress, thousands of voices spreading across the battlements and wall walks, up in the towers, within the gatehouse and brutish barbican. They did that each and every time they held them off, a great jubilant cheer that did nothing for the attacking army's morale.

Well earned, Elyon thought, as he joined his uncle and started on the short walk back to camp. He found himself rather liking the Rasal resolve, despite the losses they inflicted to his own men. *Because they're our men too,* he thought. *We're all one and the same.*

Already the wagons and wains were rolling out to collect the dead, rattling past the palisade wall of the camp. "Are we to feast tonight?" Elyon asked, though it didn't look like anyone would want to. It was late and they were tired and there was hardly much cause for celebration.

"Sir Bradbury fell at the eastern wall during the sally," Vesryn said, stone-faced. "It was by Sir Wallis Paramor's hand, I'm told. Some vengeance for the loss of his younger brother."

"Then it should have been me he sought out," Elyon said.

"I killed Sir Brendan, not you." Vesryn's mirth had fled him now, and every word came fierce and rough. "Any Varin Knight who wishes to toast Sir Bradbury can do so in the longhouse with me. I do not expect Rylian will wish to feast at this hour, but the Kastors may toast their own fallen too."

Elyon nodded. He didn't know Sir Bradbury well, but any Varin Knight lost was a tragedy. They could hardly afford to spare them, leastways not to these equivocal assaults. "I'll get out of my armour then join you there," he said, thinking of Saska, who'd been so good as to help him into and out of his armour, in lieu of the squire he no longer had. "I shall try not to be too long."

He moved off at those words, eager to see how his tent-mate was getting on.

37

Saska

Saska slipped inside the barracks, turning her eyes over the sleeping occupants. A fierce stink of fetid air assaulted her, that of half a hundred pubescent boys sleeping in their rows, each wrapped up within a poorly padded sleeping bag. They were squashed in, hardly able to turn over without rolling onto the boy next door, coughing and shivering and murmuring in their sleep. Saska took one look around and realised Del wasn't there. All these boys were too young and too small.

She slipped back out, her cloak working well to conceal her thus far, but on this occasion found herself bumping right into a big bellied soldier. "Oi, what're you doin' out this late. Need a piss, do you boy?"

Saska kept her eyes down. "Sorry, sir. Yes sir," she whispered.

"Well get to it." He gave her a shove as she stumbled off to the side, then continued on her way. She spun down the side of the tent out of sight, emerging on the other. Another small billet marquee came into view, one of several dozen packed tight into this warren. She darted her eyes left and right and then pushed through the flaps. Snoring, murmuring, muttering reached her ears. A couple of the boys were sobbing. Slipping her hand into her pocket she took ahold of her godsteel dagger and the interior came into clarity. These boys were young too, some barely into their teens to look at their cherubic faces, their wretched eyes curled tight in misery and fear. She hissed a breath and moved back into the night, trying to recall which tents she'd seen and which she hadn't. They all looked largely the same and there was no great method to their placement.

Out there, in the southern fringes of the camp, there were few fires and few guards and little care given to the rear defences. At the northern side of the encampment, facing Harrowmoor, a crude stretch of wooden wall had been erected, but not here. *The boys are the wall,* she thought, because that looked to be how their tents were vaguely arrayed. Any Rasal attack here would have them slaughtering untrained boys and not soldiers. *Spare parts,* Saska thought. *Expendables.* An anger flared in her at that, and whether these boys were to be used as arrow-fodder or not, the conditions they were being kept in were dreadful. She saw a few guards sitting around a rare fire nearby and marched over. "Anyone know Don Mears?" It was the name in Elyon's notebook. A good man, apparently, and honest. *Maybe he'll have answers, or know where Del is?* And he was from Broadway too, under House Caldlow. Saska had worked in Lord Caldlow's kitchens when she was a girl. *Perhaps he'll speak to me? Perhaps he'll help?*

It was a fanciful idea, and not fully thought through as she stood there before the haggard huddle of men, warming their hands at the fire. Most didn't even look at her, but a couple did. One said, "What's it to you? Get back to the whorehouse or the scullery, or wherever else you came from. You ain't meant to be out here."

"I'm here under the orders of Lord Vesryn Daecar." She plucked the name from thin air, thinking it would be lofty enough for them to take notice. She didn't judge that they could see her properly in her cloak either, and had given up entirely on her Aramatian accent by now.

"The *Fake* First Blade? Oh he sent you did he? Sure." The man turned back to the fire and reached for the grog as it moved around the group, swilling.

Another was looking at her, a dark shabby beard sprouting out of his cowl. "What'd he send you for?" he grunted in an accusing voice. "We've had enough of those Vandarians sticking their pointy noses into our business. You go back and tell him that. Ain't nothing to fear in the Daecar name now that the Crippler's lame, and the Echo's dead."

There is, Saska wanted to say. *Elyon will make a great lord one day, and you'll eat your filthy words.* But she said no such thing. "Don Mears," she merely repeated. "He's a guard around here. Where is he?"

The men ignored her, returning to their insolent chatter. Saska took a sharp pace forward. "*Your* names, then," she said. "I'll bring them to Lord Daecar and let him decide what to do with you. I'm sure he can spare time from the siege to teach men like you some respect."

"He can try," grunted one of them. Saska was having a hard time determining who was speaking; they all sounded much alike. "Send him down if you wish. I'd be glad to put a shiv in his neck."

The men grumbled in agreement. One laughed loudly, drunken. "You're talking about the First Blade of Vandar." She was finding herself appalled by their impudence, if not surprised. "He'd have every one of you butchered on a breath."

"Would he now? His brother, maybe, but not him. You tell him that, girl. Tell him he ain't feared, not around here."

Saska determined to leave them at that, seeing no profit in furthering the exchange. She spun and marched away, as they cackled in her wake. "Back to master," called one. "Go tend his flaccid ego, wench. See if you can get it to rise."

That led to more coughing laughter, though soon enough Saska was out of sight and earshot too, stepping a little further into camp. As the men's voices died down, a short silence took its place. *Odd*, she thought. It hadn't been so quiet all night, not with the siege going on up the slopes. She hurried through camp to get a look at Harrowmoor, and saw that the siege lines were beginning to break up. *Shit.* It wouldn't be long before Elyon returned and she'd not want him to find her gone.

Standing in a small yard between the tents, she took a final look around. *Are you here, Del?* she wondered, wanting to call for him, to scream his name. *And then what?* She hadn't much thought about that. Was she going to take his hand and flee into the night, make him a deserter and a fugitive too? If caught he'd be hanged for that and there was no result more likely. *I can slink and run and hide, but him?* Del was always clumsy, always awkward, even when they went hunting in the woods outside Willow's Rise. More times than she could count he'd frightened off a deer or rabbit by making too much noise, or speaking at the wrong time. He was a decent tracker, that was true, and could spot game well enough, but half the time he scared them off before Saska could even nock and draw.

She turned, realising there was a better way. *Elyon*, she thought, as she began hurrying back through the camp. *Maybe he'll help. Maybe he'll be able to find out if Del's here, if he's safe and alive. Maybe even help get him out?* That last one was unlikely, but the others he could do. A word from his lips would be plenty to find out if there was a lanky farmhand called Del among the army. It was enough to satisfy her, as she sped from shadow to shadow, darting away from peering eyes, hurrying up toward the heart of the encampment. She caught a glimpse up the slope and saw the rear-guard forces now on their way back, the rest about to follow. Some carts and wagons were trundling out through the perimeter wall to gather the dead. But how many had fallen? There was a lot of wreckage out there, peppering the expanses south of the fortress. It looked to have been a costly night.

She gave it no further thought as the Vandarian encampment came into view. Each was distinct and clearly marked by their colours and banners and the livery of the soldiers on guard. Saska ducked down low and sidestepped between a tight pair of pavilions, avoiding a patrol in silver and blue, and then sped straight across the yard and into Elyon's tent. She turned, began fastening the straps, and then heard the voice behind her.

"Take her, Borgin."

She spun to find a great ugly brute of a man leaping from the shadows, wrapped in boiled leathers and mail. Before she could reach to her godsteel knife he had her arms twisted up behind her back, hauling her around to face the man ahead. She blinked through the suddenness of it and took in the callous slant of Sir Griffin Kastor's smirk. "Now where have you been sneaking off to, Tilda? We were told we'd find you here."

Saska thrashed in Borgin's arms, as his horrid breath panted behind her. He gave a short rough laugh in her ear. "Remember me, girl? I rode you all the way from that shithole we found you in. Said I'd see you again soon, didn't I?"

A shudder went up her spine at his words. And up went Sir Griffin's lips. "You didn't think I'd forget about you, did you? Forget what you did."

"I didn't do any..." Her voice was strangled as Borgin's rutted hairy hand reached around to throttle her.

"Thank you, Borgin," said Sir Griffin. "There really is nothing for you to say here, Tilda. You don't have Lady Cecilia's protection anymore, and my men...well, they are starved of their spoils, now that all the girls have gone." He stepped in and smiled, cold like a stone, then with a sudden rush reached out and grabbed her cloak, spinning her around, dragging it off her body. He threw it aside onto the bed as Borgin's grip on her mouth eased, and through her lips a few tight words squeaked.

"Elyon...will be back...any moment." Then she tried to scream, but her voice was cut off as Borgin's hand slapped back over her mouth, and a second later Griffin was pulling a piece of cloth between her lips, tying it around her head.

"On the bed, Borgin," he rasped, breathless. "Teach her some manners before we take her."

She felt herself shoved forward, as hot rageful tears erupted from her eyes. Her head was a blur of fiery panic, blazing, as the man's huge weight came down atop her. He held one arm back, but she managed to get the other free, forcing an elbow up into his nose. She felt a crack and burst of blood. Then a grunt and a fist, driving hard into her skull. "BITCH!" Her head blurred as Borgin began ripping at her clothes, tearing them off her.

Sir Griffin was standing aside, laughing. "The Vandarians

think they can do anything. Steal our plunder. Send away our women. And the Daecars...oh they're the worst of all. But Elyon will see what happens when he crosses us. Oh, he'll see..."

Blood was raining down from Borgin's twisted nose, staining the covers, dripping hot into Saska's short black hair. She wriggled in his grip, reaching for her cloak. Sir Griffin was still talking but she heard nothing of what he said. Just the wild panting of the reeking oaf above her, the grunting as he wrestled with her flailing arms. He got a grip of her and pulled her back upright, turned her, then slapped her hard across the cheek. The impact had her tumbling sideward, her sight blurring, skin stinging. She landed on the bed and his stink followed, and his hands kept grabbing, groping, ripping. But hers were reaching. Reaching for her cloak, reaching to her pocket, reaching for her blade...

Her fingers touched godsteel. The blur in her head was gone. Lying flat on her stomach, with the brute's weight over her, she twisted with a sudden surge and plunged the knife right through his eye. The man gave out a shuddering groan as she pressed it deep and deeper still, right through the back of his skull. Blood flooded from the socket, down the steel, soaking her hand. She pushed him off her with a strong thrust, and his loose-limbed body went tumbling with a thump to the floor. To the side Sir Griffin was drawing his blade, staring slack-jawed at what she'd done. The shock of it made him fumble, and as he staggered back, Saska pounced.

Her knife slashed, cutting an inch through his cheek as he backed away. Blood rained red from the wound, as he let out a girlish shriek, hauling his sword from its sheath. He swung without control in a panic, and she went under and up, driving her knife deep into his groin, cutting through his leathers and the light links of mail. He tried to scream out but his voice seemed paralysed, caught in his throat. Thick sheets of blood and gore emptied from between his legs and he stumbled and slipped in the mess. Saska loomed over him.

"Please..." he whimpered. "Please, don't..."

She went down to her knees. "For Mattius," she said, driving her knife into his throat. She might have mentioned the woman he'd beheaded in Baymoor, or Albert Westham, or the legions of others he'd made suffer, but she didn't. Just Mattius, the boy he'd strung up for the practice of his bowmen. *Just a boy,* Father Pennifor had said. *Just a boy.*

She stood and watched the blood bubble from his throat.

She stood and watched him die.

38

Elyon

The longhouse was already filling when Elyon passed it by, the knights and lords gathering to toast the lost. "Sir Elyon, are you coming for a drink?" called Sir Lancel, standing outside with Sir Barnibus and a selection of other Varin Knights. "We're going to lift a cup to Sir Bradbury. I've a fine anecdote about him that you'll not want to miss."

"I'll be over shortly, Sir Lancel," Elyon told him, not slowing in his stride. "I'd prefer to escape my armour first."

"We'll see you soon, then."

Elyon gave an affirming nod as he hurried past, moving briskly beyond the longhouse and toward the Vandarian camp. Sir Dalton was stepping out of the infirmary as he passed, as several men were being stretched inside. Elyon felt obliged to say something, though would rather not engage with the man. "Visiting your nephew, Sir Dalton?" he asked him. "How does he fare?"

"Why don't you ask him yourself?" Dalton was never far from grim but that was particularly short. He wiped some flecks of mud and blood from his face, sighing. "That was discourteous," he recognised. "Excuse me. Several men under my charge died tonight, and others are close to following. The Rasals raided our lines from a sally port. I should have seen it coming."

Elyon stepped toward him. He wasn't aware that Sir Dalton had been there. "My uncle told me about the attack. He never mentioned you, Sir Dalton."

The narrow-faced knight took that as an offence. "And you, Sir Elyon?" He looked him up and down. "Sparkly clean as always, I see. Did you even set foot beyond the siege lines?"

"There was no need. I was stationed with Lord Kanabar."

Dalton gave out a bitter laugh. "Of course. Ever does your uncle try to keep you safe."

Elyon wasn't having this. "You think me a coward, sir? That my uncle gives me preferential treatment?"

"Both have crossed my mind, yes. They are quite natural conclusions to draw."

"And you are welcome to draw them. Now if you'll excuse me..."

"Your uncle concerns me, Sir Elyon." The comment took Elyon off guard as he took a pace away. He stopped and turned, as Sir Dalton stood thin and grim in his lithe silver plate. "You must have seen how he struggles. The Sword of Varinar is too great a burden for him."

"He bears it well," Elyon returned. "He drove the men off who assaulted you, Sir Dalton, and you might want to thank him for that."

"Oh yes. What a hero." He stared with those narrow stern eyes, unsmiling. "That blade makes a man unstoppable. Your father was such before he bore it, but not your uncle. There are others who would better wield it and others who better deserve it."

"I will not hear of this," Elyon cut in. "Vesryn is First Blade by royal decree and it's time you accepted that, Sir Dalton."

Dalton stared at him for a long moment, his mouth narrowing and jaw tightening all the while. "He is succumbing to its lure," he then said. "You know he is, Elyon. A First Blade who is unsure of his claim grows paranoid. And paranoia makes one unpredictable. That cannot do. It will not do."

"It will have to bloody do." Elyon had reached the end of his patience. "But for treason there's nothing that can be done,

Dalton. If you might just support Vesryn rather than undermine him..."

"I have my pride and principles. I'll never support that man." With that, Sir Dalton Taynar marched away, his slim armour grinding, clanking, misting as he faded away into the shadows.

Elyon spat out a breath, then continued on his way. Vesryn's decision to send Rikkard and Killian away no longer seemed like wisdom, but folly. He'd not put it past the likes of Sir Dalton Taynar to stage a coup. The man and his allies had been driving Vesryn to despair, subverting his rule, ignoring his orders, laughing behind his back and even openly before him. *If Vesryn grows cold and callous it's Dalton's fault, not my uncle's,* Elyon thought angrily, as he pressed on through the camp. He'd told Vesryn that he'd stay with him, to support him and back him up, and nothing in that had changed. He might have gone south to Dragon's Bane with Rikkard and Killian but he didn't. *I stayed for him,* he thought. *And he needs me more than ever now.*

All such matters were heavy on his mind when he crossed the yard and smelled the blood.

The iron taste of it was hot on his tongue and warm in his nose as he approached his tent, and a fear blew through him, swift and sudden. *Saska,* he thought, rushing forward, all other matters cast aside. He reached the flaps and tore his way inside and in an instant, his eyes took in the horror. "My gods...Saska..."

She stood before a body on the floor, staring down in silence. A bloodied blade was fixed to her grip, dripping red tears. Another body was beside the bed, lying in an awkward heap. Pools of blood drenched the wooden deck. More of it was spread across the covers, the curtains, the desk and chairs. It was everywhere. The sight and stink of it. Everywhere.

Elyon spun and fastened the flaps. He sped over to her, but his touch had her flinching. "Saska. It's OK..." He gently drew the knife from her grip, wiped it down, and set it aside. "What happened?" Only then did he realise she was staring down at the body of Sir Griffin Kastor, blood soaked through the deck beneath him, spattered across his breastplate and mail. "I saw him leave the siege a while ago," he said on a whisper. "He came for you?" He glanced to the other man. "They attacked you?"

She nodded coldly. "They were here when I got back."

"Back?" He didn't understand. "You left?"

"I went looking for a friend. I wasn't gone long. When I got back they were here. They attacked me. Now they're dead." Her words came cold and distant, as she stared down at the body.

"Saska." He spoke in a soft voice, gently turning her toward him. "Are you OK?" He glanced down at her. Her clothes were torn and tattered, her right leg almost entirely exposed. There were abrasions at her neck, her collarbone, a stinging red mark on her cheek. "You were defending yourself," he saw. That was obvious enough, but she needed to hear him say it. "This is not your fault."

Her eyes had a frozen quality to them. She managed a short nod, then said, "It's happening again. It's the same...as with Quintan. And Master Orryn. Llana. Del..." Her voice became a whisper and she turned off to one side. "I still don't know what's happened to them. I...I told you about that. About Lord Quintan..."

She had. The Lord of Twinbrook had tried to rape her and she'd killed the man in her old master's bedchamber. There was a horrid echo to all this. He pulled her into his arms. "This is different," he assured her. "I can cover this, Saska."

She pushed away, took a step back. A frown swept over her eyes. "No, I'll not let you. I'll not let you ruin your life for me."

Elyon was trying to think through it. Trying to ignore the stink of iron and shit. The deep red blood, lit by the firelight. The bodies cut up about him. A few times his mind flashed back to his father, but he pushed the thought away and steadied himself. "I have history with Sir Griffin," he finally said. "No one will be surprised to hear that we've quarrelled." He nodded to himself, coming to some plan. "These affrays can get ugly, especially after a battle. Our blood was up." He looked down at the dead Kastor knight. "Our blood was up from the siege and I found him here in my tent. He taunted me, and we drew knives. It ended worse for him."

Saska was shaking her head. "No...it won't work. You've just got back..."

"And you've just killed him." He could tell that clear enough. The boy's blood was still draining and he hadn't yet gone cold. "I gave him that scar on his neck, Saska," he explained. "It'll go a long way to explaining things. Griffin never much liked me after I cut through his armour in that tourney, and nearly took his head clean off." He thought a moment more, then added, "It's a believable story. People won't have reason to doubt it."

"But...what if they do? I did this, Elyon. I should take the blame..."

"No. They'll string you up for it, but not me." He was thinking again, thinking of how better to present the illusion. "Cut me," he then said. He turned to her and drew his knife. "Take my blade and cut me."

Her brows fell. "What? No..."

"It'll make it more convincing."

"It's convincing enough. He's only in a breastplate and you're fully armoured. There's no way he'd have cut you."

She was right, he realised, and that gave Elyon pause. *They'll call me out for dishonour,* he knew. *For knife fighting a man when I held such an advantage.* He turned his eyes over Sir Griffin once again. He had a deep gash on his cheek, and his throat had been punctured, but there was more, a great gory puddle at his groin. Hardly a noble death, to have his manhood slashed through. *And they'll call me out for that too.* But what other choice did he have? If they knew Saska was here, or in any way involved, they'd string her up and flay her living. *I can't allow that,* he thought. *Better my honour be stripped than her skin.*

He turned his eyes around the room, looking to the man beside the bed. He was a nasty looking brute, his nose cracked, face rutted with scars. Elyon thought he recognised him from back at the Kastor warcamp though couldn't be sure. "And him?"

"One of Griffin's men," she said. "I rode with him when they captured me in Baymoor. He always looked at me funny. This..." She gestured to her torn clothes. "This was all him. Griffin just stood by, laughing. He liked to do that. Like his uncle..."

"Satisfy yourself that you killed one of them," Elyon said. "He isn't Cedrik but he's the next best thing. Many will thank you for it." *Or me,* he thought, *when I take the blame.* He looked again at the other corpse, the man he'd seen Sir Griffin summon from the siege. "A common soldier," he identified. "But a capable one by the look of him. I'll say Sir Griffin came with backup, that they ambushed me here, but I fought them off."

He went over it a few more times in his head. *It works,* he thought. *Yes, it works.*

"It was Cecilia," Saska broke in. Her skin was turning ghostly pale now. "It must have been. It's her revenge." She shook her head, once, twice, thrice, and blinked away a brewing tear. "I've ruined everything for you. I'm so sorry, Elyon. I never wanted..."

She trailed off as he took her into his arms, surrounded by bodies, surrounded by blood. But he didn't care. *I'll get her out,* he told himself. *I'll not let her fall for this. I'll not.* "Don't mention it. Maybe you can repay the debt one day?"

She pulled back and looked up into his eyes. "I hope so. I'd not want to part...not like this."

They didn't have much choice in that now. Elyon's attempts to find out if Saska'a mentor was in Harrowmoor had thus far failed, and he'd not yet figured out what to do with her. Sending her north was an option, but might only lead her back into the clutches of Tukor should they take the capital. In truth he'd figured only one solution that would see her safe from these lands for good. One that gave him pause for its permanence, because the simple reality was...he didn't want her to leave. "You need to go south," he made himself say. "You need to leave the north for good."

She was already shaking her head. "I can't. I'm an agent of the Rasalanian crown. I can't leave."

"Then what?" He knew she'd say something like that, though had hoped she'd be less stubborn with a pair of murdered men in his room. "Where else can you go?"

"I don't know. East. I can head east to the Stormwall Hills. Marian's uncle will take me in."

"Lord Payne? Does he know of you?"

She shook her head. "Unlikely. But he'll shelter me, until Marian can catch up. It won't take long for her to learn that I'm there..."

She didn't look certain of any of that. "And if the Tukorans get there first? How do you know that his lands haven't already been razed?" He didn't let her answer. "No, Saska. I'm not going to send you off somewhere unless I know it's safe."

"And south is safe?"

"Safer than here."

"You don't know that."

"I do." He took her arms firmly, so firm she flinched and tried to draw back, but this time he wasn't letting go. "Marian should never have sent you here, Saska. You told me your friend Ranulf went south, and the girl you trained with, Leshie? Go to them. Go to Solapia. Or Aram, if you'd prefer. Anywhere but here. Anywhere..."

"I can't." She pulled away. "I was cast out of Aram once, Elyon. They don't want me. I won't be safe there either."

"Why?" She'd not made mention of this before, though it looked important by that reaction. "What do you mean cast out?"

"It doesn't matter."

"It does. By the Steel Father it does!" His voice was rising and that wouldn't do. He took a sharp look at the exit and tightened his tone. "I've told you my secrets, Saska, every last one of them. I thought you'd done the same. Tell me who you are."

"I'm nobody, Elyon. An outcast. A maid. A spy. I'm Tukoran and Rasal and Aramatian all at once. I'm nobody."

"I don't believe you." He turned and walked away from her, peering out through the tent. The longhouse was like a flame attracting moths, though the camp would be filling now as the soldiers and siege weapons returned. "We can't waste time like this. They'll expect me at the feast and someone will soon come to check on me." He turned. "You need to be gone by then."

There was a strain in her eyes. "I can leave through the south of camp," she said. "I went down there earlier. It's quiet and undefended. I can sneak through, no trouble. Work around through the moors, and into the fort. Marian will be in there, I know it. She said she'd be close. She told me she would be."

"And what else did she tell you?" Elyon took a stride forward. "I'm not going to let you enter that fortress. I'm not going to let you die."

"I won't die."

"You will. You'll be caught and cornered and killed, Saska. And if you find Marian inside, she'll suffer the very same fate." He took a step toward her. "The fortress will be under an all-out assault in days. Women will be raped and children will be slaughtered and every man who offers challenge will be slain. I'll not have you join them. I won't, Saska."

"And I'm not letting you ship me off on some boat."

"Even after all this?" He was getting aggravated now, angered by her wilfulness. "Even if I cover for you. After I save your life? I made a godsteel promise that I'd keep you safe, and I will..."

"You made that promise to Cecilia. It means nothing," she cut in.

"It means something to me." He took another stride. "I made that oath on my honour, and by Varin I'm going to see it through."

Time was running short, he knew, and there was nothing for it now. The girl was maddeningly mulish and he wasn't getting through to her. *I'm sorry, Saska, but there's no other way,* he thought. *If we delay any longer it'll get you killed. This is for your own good.*

It all happened quickly after that. Within moments he'd spun around her back, taken her into a chokehold, and throttled her unconscious. She wriggled for a moment or two, but had no power to stop him. "I'm sorry," he said as she struggled in his grip. "You'll thank me later, I promise." That struggling didn't last long. Her legs soon went limp and arms flopped down to her side, and with all that, it was done.

At least, a part of it was. A small, tiny part. He drew her into a chair and sat her down, then gave the tent another scan. He'd need to report the bloody affray with Sir Griffin and his cutthroat immediately, but Saska couldn't be here when he did. But where to put her while he arranged her passage to the coast? Who among his allies could he trust?

There seemed only one possible answer.

He stepped through the flap, out into the cold, and right across the yard to his uncle's tent.

39

Ranulf

Ranulf Shackton stood aside in the library as the Book of Thala was inspected.

"Is everything in order, gentlemen?" asked Vincent Rose, accoutred in a golden vest with crimson lining and deep purple satin trousers. There was a slight edge to his voice as he looked at the king's agents, his lips forced into a rictus smile. "I do hope King Janilah understands why I kept it these last weeks. My hand was forced, I hope he knows. I put all this in my letter."

The lead agent was Bladeborn, his belt fastened with a pair of broad silver blades with horned, bull-head pommels. He'd introduced himself as Sir Kevyn Bolt, one of Janilah's sworn swords. "We have no orders to kill you, if that's what you're worried about, merchant," grunted the knight. "The king is wise and forgiving, and may have need of you yet."

Vincent Rose loosened a little at that. "Very good, sir. But I hate that you've had to come all this way on my account. Please, do have some refreshments." He gestured to the servants he'd summoned, all standing to the side with trays of seafood and fruit and sweet breads and wines.

"We have no time for indulgences." Sir Kevyn was a large man with a spherical, shaven head, fierce brown eyes, and broad shoulders, and looked much like the bull the Bolts had for their sigil. He turned back to the scholars as they carefully picked through the pages, one by one. They were about two thirds of the way through now and Ranulf didn't want them to go much further. *Or else they might discover what I did,* he thought, trying to remain quite calm. But by some luck or blessing, Sir Kevyn Bolt cut matters short. "That will do," he grunted. "I want to be back on the ship by noon." The wise old scholars he had with him turned and nodded. "Pack it up," he ordered . There were several other soldiers in their party too, and a host more down on their great galleon in the docks. It seemed Janilah had sent a small army to retrieve the tome. *But he'll not find what he's looking for,* Ranulf thought. *King Godrin has made quite sure of that.*

"Are you sure you won't have any refreshment?" Rose asked, as the men set to work, neatly closing the book and placing it into a purpose-built trunk. "I could have it delivered to your ship, if you'd like."

"If it pleases you," said Sir Kevyn. Then his face took on a shade more interest. "You're a wine merchant, I hear?"

"Among others things, yes. I have vineyards across Solapia. Would you like some? I could have several crates brought to the docks, Sir Kevyn. How many would you like?" Vincent Rose knew just how to get a man on his side and hadn't taken long to find Sir Kevyn's vice. The journey back to Ilithor would take him many weeks and it would go a lot quicker with half a hundred bottles of wine for company.

"We're a force of some sixty in all," Sir Kevyn Bolt said. "Half a bottle per person per day would suit us." The Tukoran knight didn't look interested in doing the calculations.

Nor does he look capable, Ranulf thought, as Rose merely smiled and said, "That won't be a problem, sir. I'll make sure you have more than you could possibly drink."

"We're Tukoran. We can drink a lot."

"Of course, and famously so." Vincent smiled graciously. "Would you like to sample our recent vintages and select your favourites? I have a tasting room downstairs. Please, do come with me."

Sir Kevyn looked enticed by the prospect. "Much obliged," he said, then bellowed orders to his men to transport the book safely to the wagon outside.

Rose drew him off after that, as Ranulf watched the Book of Thala removed from the library and ferried off down the corridor. It was bittersweet watching it go. There were a great many secrets he'd been unable to unearth and many passages had been left entirely untranslated. *But I got what I needed,* he thought, with a deep bracing breath. *I got it, and I burned it, just as King Godrin instructed.* An instruction written many years ago, and that thought still made him lightheaded. But he was part of something bigger now. Something that would shape the fates of all. *I will keep the secret, my king. Until the time is right, I'll keep it...*

"You've got that far off look again," said Leshie, sliding over in her red leather armour. "What are you thinking about?"

"Nothing much," Ranulf lied. They walked to the gallery above the split staircase, observing from the railing as the Book of Thala was carried down. "I suppose I'm just disappointed not to have more time with it."

"You've had time enough," Leshie told him sourly. She wrinkled her nose as she watched the old scholars work down the steps and into the capacious marble hall. "Personally I'm happy to see the back of it. It's been dull dull dull watching you labour over that boring old book all day long. I miss the old you. I miss your stories."

Well I've got a story to tell, he thought, though of course he didn't say it. He'd been selective with what he unveiled to little Leshie and would keep these latest revelations under lock and key. He smiled at her and tried to be cheerful. "I'll be back to my old ways soon, I promise. Though full disclosure, Leshie...I don't plan to stay here long."

"Nor does Vinny," she said unexpectedly.

"Oh?"

She shrugged. "He's planning a trip to the mainland. Overheard him speaking to some of his crew down at the docks, when we were there to meet Janilah's men. Told them to make the ship ready for departure tomorrow morning. I'm sure he'll tell you about it later."

He did, though not until dusk, once Sir Kevyn and his cohort had left, and he'd spent time seeing to matters of business in town. Only when he'd returned from all that did Vincent fetch Ranulf for a privy chat, leading him onto one of his prettier verandahs to sip winter wine as the sun came down. "Fetching colours," he said, as the skies burned red and rusty, with radiant streaks of brilliant vermillion cutting through the clustered clouds. "It's why I've made my home here, above all other places, these sunsets. I have a lust for them that can never be sated. I suppose you've seen some spectacular ones in your time?"

"We'd be here all night if I were to enumerate them, Vincent."

"Quite so." They clinked glasses and took a sip. Then Vincent Rose said, "I'm leaving for Sutrek in the morning, and would like it if you came with me. There is a man by name of Pal Palek I have business dealings with. An interesting man, certainly, and one I imagine you'll like to meet. He'll most assuredly like to meet you, my friend." He grinned and supped his wine. "After that, you'll be free of my service. I know these weeks have been quite strained, but I do want to remain friends, Ranulf."

"I hope for the same, Vincent."

"Good. That is good. All great friendships face these sorts of tests every once in a while, don't they?"

Ranulf looked to the dusky skies, and away from that look on Vincent's face. There was still something there that concerned him. A little twitch of the mouth. A little comment out of place. It was perhaps just another tool in the man's arsenal. He could allure with his wealth and threaten with a look. *A dangerous man,* Ranulf thought. *And though no one would think it to look at him, a cold and cruel one too.* "Just so long as our friendship doesn't face any more such hardships," he said eventually. "Not for the time being, at least."

"No, of course, of course." Rose's eyes moved away. "So, where will your next adventure take you, my friend, once you finally break from my fetters?" He continued looking out, smiling at that little comment, before his lips disappeared behind the rim of his cup and returned flat and cold.

"I have had an itch to visit Aram," Ranulf said. "I wonder if you might help me find a ship that will take me from Sutrek, once your dealings are done with this Pal Palek."

"Oh that shouldn't be a problem. Will you need some money too." He looked over.

"I have money, thank you. Leastways enough to get me by for a time."

"Get by? Please, Ranulf, have you not grown accustomed to the high life in my company? No no, I'll hear nothing of it. You'll have money and plenty of it when we part. You deserve it, for all the good work you've done."

"You're satisfied then?" Ranulf dare not look into his eyes. "With what I unearthed for you...from Godrin's passages?" He'd given him a few tidbits now to cloak his true discoveries, though they were hardly what the merchant would have had in mind when he first took possession of the tome.

"Hmmmm...*satisfied*," Rose said, considering it long and hard. "A tricky old word, I've always thought. I'd say you know me well enough to understand that I'm never quite satisfied, my friend." He laughed, the sonorous sound ringing out across the colourful gardens. "Didn't I tell you, I always want more."

It wasn't quite an answer, but would have to do, and Ranulf wasn't about to ask again. "Well, I hope that will change one day, Vincent. Perhaps you might consider joining me on one of my next expeditions? Turn your mind from power and profit for a time, and give in to a more soulful experience."

"I give in to a soulful experience each night when I take the twins to bed." An idea came upon his face. "How about this...you let the twins tend you tonight and I'll agree to come along on one of these jolly adventures of yours. What do you say?"

"You know what I'll say."

"Golly man, you are a strange one." Vincent Rose huffed and drew back, furling his left leg over his right. "I could send a boy instead, if that's what you'd prefer? No one here will offer judgement. It's quite common, you know."

"I prefer to sleep alone, thank you."

"As do I, but we're not talking about sleep. We're discussing what comes before."

"Yes, I understand that."

Vincent grinned like a wolf watching a lamb. "It makes you so awfully uncomfortable, doesn't it? I'll stop." He relaxed deeper into his fine cushioned chair. "For what it's worth I rather respect your discipline, Ranulf. And you've needed it these weeks, dealing with me. I know I'm not always easy, and your work? All those long nights spent alone in that fusty old library."

"I wouldn't call it fusty. It's quite a sweet-smelling place."

"Helped no doubt by young Leshie's presence, hmmmm? She smells terribly sweet, that girl. And she tastes sweet too. All over, she does."

"Vincent, if you're to persist in talking like this, I'll leave you." He shifted forward and made to stand. "Leshie is but seventeen. You're old enough to be her father. Please, do not speak of her like that. It is quite unbecoming."

"Seventeen, is she? I thought she was younger."

Ranulf stood. "I'll leave you, then."

Vincent's laughter began ringing out again. "Oh calm yourself, calm, I am only jesting dear friend. I know just how old Leshie is, and much else besides. Why so prickly? Can you not take a joke?"

"When it involves her, and such topics as these, no. In truth some of what you say makes my skin crawl."

"Oh it does?"

"Yes, it does." He found a great deal running through his head, though knew better than to give voice to it. Still, he did say, "You lack in grace and scruples, Vincent. That is something money cannot buy."

"And you lack in good humour, fun, and all the things you once possessed." Vincent Rose swapped his legs, shaking his head. "I find myself looking forward to our parting in these moments, Ranulf. What is it that weighs so heavy on you? That sucks the colour from your skin, the meat from your bones. You'll be a gaunt man soon if you're not careful. Haggard and bitter and old."

That stung more than he expected. Because he had been a

gaunt man not long ago, and haggard too, though never bitter. Even in his long incarceration in the dungeons of Ilithor and Lallymoor he'd never lost his spirit, but here he had. "You're right," he said eventually. "I've grown more grim than I once was, but can you blame me? It's wartime, Vincent. I don't feel like playing the raconteur right now."

"Well you should, because there's no better time for it. Wars make for wonderful stories and songs, and they're bloody important too. We have to keep our spirits up, not sink into a sulk. I never thought that in you. Or have I worked you too hard?"

"There's that," nodded Ranulf, slumping back into his chair. "You know I haven't much liked what you've asked of me. It goes against my principles. Surely you can understand that?"

"Of course...of course I understand," he said, though it felt a lie to Ranulf. "But it's over now, and we've both seen the last of that book. Good riddance, I say." He flung out his hand and sent his cup of wine with it, as it clattered and crashed down the cobblestone path. "I should have done that to the book, seeing what it's done to you, my friend. I'd sooner have that wretched tome shredded than watch you wither away."

"That's kind of you to say." *Though utter rubbish,* he thought.

"I'm not kind enough, clearly. I can't be, can I, to put all this pressure on you." Rose blasted out a breath as a server boy came with a fresh chalice of wine. "But...*is* there anything you're hiding from me, Ranulf?" he asked. "Now I'm not accusing, just...enquiring. Gods man, there must be something you're not telling me to lay you so low. So? Is there? Anything at all?" He leaned over.

"Nothing, Vincent," Ranulf said wearily, staring over the gardens. "I have told you that a hundred times, and you wonder what sets me on edge? I do so wish you'd trust me."

"I do trust you," he assured him, but they were words. Just words. "Of course I trust you, my dear, dear friend." They sat in silence for a time, looking to the great nebulous glow around them as the skies bled into darker shades of purple and pink and red. Eventually, a gong sounded in the house, and Vincent took to his feet. "Dinner," he said, rubbing his hands. "I'm told the chefs have prepared something quite delicious for our last night here. I asked that they send us on our way in style. Shall we?"

It was a fine dinner, all told, but Ranulf didn't have much of an appetite. He nibbled and supped and chatted and the tension was set aside. But all the while he thought of little but Godrin. Of the Wise King's words, written two decades ago. A direct message through time, for Ranulf only to read. And when he took to his chambers, he made straight for his desk, drew quill and parchment and started scribbling. He'd done this each night since he'd translated the passage, since he'd translated it, memorised it, and burned it by Godrin's order. And the original text... he'd burned that too, tearing the page from the Book of Thala and setting it to the flame. *Thank the gods they didn't check,* he thought, as he wrote out the passage once more. *But they'll find out what I did eventually. And then they'll come for me,* he knew. *They will never stop coming for me then...*

He completed the passage - it wasn't particularly long - then read it through once more. It was his method of memorising it, of searing it into his mind, and part of the passage was a method too. *The most important part,* he thought, and the part he most needed to recall. So he read it through twice more, to be absolutely certain, and then set the corner of the paper to the flame. The blaze spread, the sheet blackened, and the ash curled and fell to the desk.

And with that, the secret was struck from existence once more. To live in the minds of Ranulf and Godrin only. *And soon it shall only be me,* he thought, with a deep mournful throb to his heart. *Soon our great king will be gone.*

40

Elyon

Elyon stood in the longhouse, the cold pale morning light flooding in through the open doors. Before him the members of the war council were gathering, the Tukoran and Vandarian lords and knights who'd consider and deliver his sentence. It was an unofficial trial, and wasn't expected to last long. "You'll have the backing of every Vandarian present," Vesryn had told him, "and Prince Rylian too. Don't worry, son. Stick to your story and it'll all blow over soon."

He'd said that some hours ago, before the night had turned to day, though already the falsified story of Elyon's encounter with Sir Griffin had spread through half the camp. Only Vesryn knew the truth of it; there had been no helping that. "She was one of Lady Cecilia's breeders," he'd explained to his uncle of Saska, though chose not to reveal the entirety of it. "I took her under my protection a week ago, but she always feared a reprisal from Sir Griffin. He took his chance while I was away, and she had no choice but to kill him. But I'll not let her suffer for it, Uncle. I need you to help me get her out."

Vesryn hadn't been especially happy with all that, though he wasn't happy about much these days. "Let me see her," he'd said, and Elyon had led him over to his tent, unveiling the bloodbath within. He took one look around, then turned his eyes over Saska, unconscious on a soft-padded chair. "I recognise this girl. She was in Kastor's tent the day we arrived at his camp."

Elyon had half forgotten that in the rush of it, but it worked in his favour. "She was. They abused her, defiled her," he lied. "I had to protect her, Uncle. And I'll not let her die."

They'd worked out a plan together after that, secretly moving Saska to Vesryn's tent, before Elyon rushed off to report the fatal affray with Sir Griffin. *And now she's gone,* he thought, as he stood before the knights and lords in the longhouse, the braziers burning slow and sombre around them. Vesryn hadn't been keen to keep Saska in his custody for long, and had helped make arrangements to send her south without delay. She'd been carted off in secret only an hour or so ago, and would be some miles from the camp by now. The thought gave Elyon some comfort as he stood awaiting his own fate. The doors were closed, shutting off the light, and a brooding gloom settled upon the cavernous room. Rylian was first to speak.

"Last night an old rivalry turned bloody," he said sombrely, wreathed in a warm umber cloak. All were as such, in leather and furs, standing dark and sullen before hm. "Let us start by hearing Sir Elyon's side of it." He held out a hand. "Elyon, please."

His account hadn't changed much since he'd first thought it up, and he'd repeated it several times by now to get it all straight. He cleared his throat and set his eyes with a weary regret. "My lords. Good sirs. I stand before you shamed by what I have done, but know that I had no choice. Sir Griffin and I have long been rivals, as His Highness has said, and he held against me a deep resentment for a wound I once inflicted upon his neck. That resentment has festered during our time in camp and last night it reached its climax." He drew a breath and looked around, though the men before him seemed but shadows and shapes, hidden within the deepening gloom. "I returned from the siege lines to find Sir Griffin and the soldier named Borgin in my tent. A short exchange of heated words were shared, before both men came at me with their blades. I pressed my dagger through the eye of Borgin, and slashed at Sir Griffin's face. What happened next I can't rightly remember. A flurry of attacks, I recall, that ended with my knife through Sir Griffin's neck." He looked around again. "That is the sum of it. I took a few moments to recover my shock and then came right here to the longhouse to report it, as you know. Many of you were here when I did so..."

"Many of us were," came a voice. "And thus many of us have now twice heard your lies." Elyon found the face of Lord Kastor in the gloom, shadowed and grim and vengeful within his hood. "If my nephew was in your tent, Sir Elyon, it was not for the purpose you speak. Lies," he said in a voice as cold as frost. "You perjure yourself in the sight of gods and men, and for that alone you deserve death."

The shapes and shadows gave their opinion on that, a rumble of noise fogging through the room. "What evidence do you have of this?" questioned Lord Kanabar loudly. "Why was Sir Griffin in Elyon's private quarters if not to goad and taunt him, as you Kastors so like to do."

"Do not speak ill of the dead, my lord," hissed Cedrik Kastor. "I know for a fact that my nephew went to the accused's tent in search of something quite different."

"What?" asked Prince Rylian. "Do not draw this out, Cedrik. We have not time for it, not today. Speak of your nephew's purpose."

"He was your nephew too, Rylian, if not by blood," Cedrik bit. "I would hope to remind you of that."

That was true, though Rylian didn't look eager for their connection to be pointed out. Griffin had been son to Caleb Kastor, Cedrik's younger brother, and both were younger siblings to Rylian's shrewish wife, Clarris. *A loveless marriage,* Elyon knew, thinking of what Rylian had told him of his consort. Clarris Kastor had been hand-picked by Janilah in a bid to merge the two houses and secure the kingdom, and a wise union it had turned out to be. *A wise but unhappy one,* he thought, though Amilia, Robbert and Raynald had come of it, so Rylian had to be satisfied with that, at least.

"I am aware of who Sir Griffin was to me," Rylian said after a short pause. "But let us not bring nepotism or sentimentality into this. It is the truth that matters, so speak of it, Cedrik. What was Sir Griffin's true purpose in entering Elyon's privy space without leave?"

"To root out a possible spy," the Lord of Ethior said, with a bitter twist to his lips. "Griffin received word that the accused was harbouring in his pavilion an agent of the Rasal crown. He went to seek her out, and that is when Elyon returned. I have no doubt that the quarrel involved this girl, not any alleged rivalry the two shared. My nephew challenged the accused and Elyon Daecar took it upon himself to silence him. A noble purpose was thus met with a shameful act of murder." He turned his eyes about and his voice reached higher and further. "Murder, I say. The only sentence can be death."

More murmuring swelled in the air, though Prince Rylian was swift to settle things. "Evidence, Cedrik. I have no time for spurious and circumstantial claims." He looked at Kastor straight. "Do you have any?"

"A note. My nephew held a note on his person, telling of this spy."

Rylian shook his head. "No note was found when Sir Griffin's body was searched."

Elyon gave Vesryn a swift and grateful glance at that. His uncle had told him to search the boy's body, just in case, and he'd uncovered the very note in question, hidden among his small-clothes. At least, he supposed it was the note Kastor was referring to. The paper was soaked in blood and Elyon had been quick to see it destroyed. But a spy? Who had known of that but him? He stood in quiet thought as an argument broke out, several of the other lords joining in the debate. *Did Cecilia find out about Saska's true identity,* he wondered. *Or was it just guesswork on her part, no more than a cruel conjecture that turned out, by chance, to be true?* Either could be the case, though the latter seemed more likely. She'd hardly be like to keep Saska around if she knew she was a spy, after all, nor send her into Elyon's arms. *Unless she's playing some trick, some grander game I'm not aware of?* Cecilia had proven herself her father's daughter in that regard, and he wouldn't put it past her. *But either way, it doesn't matter. Saska's gone now, and they'll not track her down. I've done my part,* he hoped, he prayed. *I've kept to my godsteel oath.*

The squabbling continued for a short time longer, until Rylian's voice sliced through it, cutting like a sword. "Silence!" he demanded. "If there is no tangible evidence against Sir Elyon, then I see little to do here but let him go. I am sorry for your loss, Cedrik, but Elyon is heir to House Daecar and it is incumbent on us to take him at his word, in the absence of any other."

"Hear hear," called out Lord Kanabar, and Lords Shorton and Fullerton were calling too, and several others were stamping their feet. "Your nephew was a cur, Kastor, and got what was coming to him. Don't pretend you cared for the boy. We all saw how you treated him."

If Lord Kastor had his blade he'd have drawn it at that point, but godsteel wasn't permitted at these privy trials. "You call my nephew a cur? Even as his blood stains the decks of this man's tent," he seethed, pointing at Elyon, "you call him out for contempt?"

"I call it as I see it. As we all see it..."

"*See* it?" Kastor broke in. A sour smile snapped onto his lips and he turned to Sir Dalton, the crest of House Taynar - an armoured knight, planting his blade into the iron earth at his feet - embossed onto his leather jerkin. "Sir Dalton revealed to me last night that he saw something too, my lord. Please, Sir Dalton, unfetter your tongue so we may hear it."

Sir Dalton Taynar took a short step forward, emerging from the shadows at the rear. His thin voice crawled out from his cowl. "I spoke with Sir Elyon moments before he returned to his tent and this unpleasant affray took place," he said. "As the last person to see him, my testimony might add weight to proceedings."

"And what testimony is that?" demanded Prince Rylian.

"One relating to his state of mind, Your Highness. That being one of frustration, resentment, and anger. The Daecars are known for their tempers and Elyon is no different. He was febrile and agitated from the night's siege and spoke in a manner to suggest he'd do something rash." He stopped and let that settle, then added, "It seems to me that Elyon may well have been the aggressor in the confrontation, and not Sir Griffin as he claims..."

"You treacherous bloody snake, Taynar," rumbled Lord Kanabar, turning on the man. "You'd speak out against one of you own?"

"I speak only of what I saw." Dalton gave Elyon a cold hard look.

"This is but another attack on House Daecar," claimed Lord Shorton in his nasally voice.

Lord Fullerton bobbed his froggy face. "I call for Sir Dalton's slanderous testimony to be struck out," he said. "We have all seen how he seeks to undermine Lord Vesryn and this is naught but another subversion."

"Bloody right it is," bellowed Wallis Kanabar.

"He's a good man, Father," came the sincere lively voice of young Prince Robbert. "Sir Elyon wouldn't have killed Sir Griffin without cause. I know he wouldn't."

His twin Raynard stood by his side, nodding in agreement, and Elyon gave them both a thankful smile. Then came a rough voice in retort. "This isn't about liking, noble prince, nor popularity. It is about truth and justice." That was said by Lord Gershan, the mean old Master of the Moorlands, sworn bannerman to House Kastor.

Then another of Kastor's men, Sir Gavin Trent said, "We should search for this girl, this spy. She may hold the key to this." He'd been a high ranking Emerald Guard once, but was now a senior commander in Kastor's northern army, and had the blustery voice to match.

"No such girl has been sighted," Prince Rylian put in to that. "And there's nothing to suggest she was a spy at all, Sir Gavin. If only we had this missing note." He gave Cedrik Kastor a doubtful look.

"And if she should escape to Harrowmoor?" Sir Gavin went on. "She may feed them whatever secrets Sir Elyon let slip."

"Or told her willingly," suggested Kastor, sticking the knife a little deeper. "Let us not pretend that Elyon Daecar has been supportive of this siege. He stands aside in every meeting of the war council, brooding and scowling, and taking no active part. It might just be that he's smuggled secrets to Harrowmoor himself. Would that not explain our failures thus far?"

"Enough," said Vesryn. He took two sharp paces from the group and turned on them, his back to Elyon, protective. "There is no evidence of any of this, none at all, and this malignant defamation of my nephew will stop right here and now." The room stilled to his voice. "You speak of a note, Lord Kastor. Where is it? We hear of this girl, this so-called spy. Where is she? Elyon was active in helping to free the captive Rasal girls from this camp, many of whom were taken against their will by Sir Griffin's own hand. That is what stirred this confrontation. Griffin's toys were taken away and he held Elyon responsible. He invaded the privacy of my nephew's pavilion with the express purpose of ambushing him, and took one of his best killers along to help. Those are the irrefutable facts. What transpired thereafter we will never know for sure. We either believe Elyon or we do not. Unfortunately Sir Griffin isn't here to give his own account."

Cedrik Kastor was about to speak again before Rylian cut him off. "Don't speak, Cedrik. I think we've all heard enough and we have more important things to be doing." He looked around. "There's no evidence to consider the gibbet and for my part I'm grateful for that. We can ill-afford to lose a man of Elyon's standing and skill at this time." He paused a moment. "I lean toward letting him go without reprisal, but will not make the decision unilaterally. We must be united. What say you?"

The hands went up immediately, and the voices came shouting forth. "Let him go," called out Robbert and Raynald together.

"Free him," said Lord Shorton.

"This is a farce," complained Lord Fullerton.

"A bloody great farce," agreed Wallis Kanabar.

Vesryn said it all with his eyes, and Sir Dalton stayed deathly silent. But then came the others, the Kastor men. "He cannot be allowed to escape without penalty," said Sir Gavin Trent resolutely. "Whether in self defence or not he killed a highborn knight. That can't pass unpunished, just because of his name."

"The pillory," said Lord Gershan in his mean old gravelly

voice. And he fit it too, with that stooped back and hooked nose and the glower that never left his face. "Lock him in the public stocks until we've won the fort. We all saw what he did to poor Griffin, mutilating the man between his legs. There was dishonour in that, dishonour I say...so let's see him shamed in penance."

"No," said Rylian firmly, staring at the bitter old man. "The stocks are for common criminals, my lord. I'll not condemn Elyon to that humiliation."

"The lash, then," came the smooth clipped voice of Lord Cedrik Kastor. He turned and looked Elyon straight in the eye, and smiled. "It is the least he deserves."

"The lash," repeated Prince Rylian in a quiet voice. He gave Elyon a quick glance but no more. He wasn't to have any say in this. "Would that satisfy you?" Rylian's eyes moved over the others. Over the Vandarian lords and knights. "Ten lashes?"

"Twenty," said Kastor.

"Ten." Prince Rylian set his eyes on him. "Ten is plenty, Lord Kastor. Be content with that."

"Content? Ten lashes in exchange for the murder of my brother's son?"

Rylian turned away and ignored the comment. "My lords? Can you accept?"

They shared a few glances, then Lord Kanabar spoke for them. "I suppose we have little choice."

The privy trial ended abruptly there, as Elyon stood where he'd been standing all the while, watching as the doors were pulled open and the light flooded back in, chasing the shadows and gloom away. It seemed his punishment was to be carried out immediately. Kastor was already marching out with his allies in tow, calling orders for the camp scourger to be summoned. Two guards came forward to take Elyon out, though Rylian quickly waved them off. "You need not escort him. He'll go without a fuss."

I will, Elyon thought, trying to control the hammering in his heart. He'd suffered the occasional injury in his time, when sparring or fighting in tournaments, but nothing quite like a flogging. He drew a breath and tried to calm himself as he fell into step beside the prince. "You did well, Elyon," Rylian told him as they filed back out into the brisk morning air. "Many others would have spoken up with such slander spoken against them, but you stayed silent and stoic. Well done."

"Well done indeed, though none of this has been necessary," grunted Lord Kanabar. "Is it wise to incapacitate one of our finest knights at this time, good prince? You know how dangerous the lash can be."

Elyon knew too. Men commonly died from serious floggings, though typically when they were lashed across the chest, not the back. Loss of blood or organ damage or infection could kill them, and those perils were all well known. "I'll make sure the cuts are shallow," Rylian assured Lord Kanabar. "And we have the finest medicines here, my lord. He'll be well tended after."

Outside the longhouse a long wide flogging pole was being brought out and hammered into the ground. Word was spreading of the public punishment, and already men were flocking. There were few common soldiers here, mainly knights and officers and highborn lords, but in a fashion that made it all the worse. *Be strong,* he told himself, as the preparations were made. A hum spread through the air. Everyone was looking at him. *Be strong. Stay quiet. Don't call or cry out in pain.*

Vesryn said something similar, as he took to his nephew's side. "It will all be over quickly, son. Stare forward, focus on something. Me." He drew his eye. "I'll stand ahead of you. Look at me, right into my eyes. OK? You'll do that?"

"Yes, Uncle."

"Every man needs a few scars," Lord Kanabar said, trying to be bullish. "You're far too pretty, Elyon. A few licks on your back will suit you."

"Of course, my lord."

Men came forward to unclothe him, though Vesryn snarled at them until they backed away. "He can do it himself. Elyon, bare you back."

He did so, unfastening his jerkin and removing his shirt. His pale skin shone bright under the winter sun, his chest shadowed by curls of black hair. A coldness wrapped about him, the bitter wind causing him too shiver. *That isn't fear,* he wanted to tell the crowds. *It is the cold, that is all. I'm not afraid. I'm not.* He drew away from his allies and toward the whipping post, and his hands were tied about it. The crowd thickened and curdled, encircling him as a grim-faced man stepped forward, wreathed in a sleeveless black vest and breeches and bearing a long thin curled up whip. Prince Rylian was calling out Elyon's crimes and punishments. *Ten lashes,* was all Elyon heard. *Ten lashes. Ten lashes...*

Then all of a sudden there was a strange eerie silence. He could hear the scourger behind him unfurling the whip, pulling it through his palm with the slide of leather on skin. His feet crunched over the frosted ground, judging the distance, moving into position. Elyon held his eyes forward on Vesryn, who stood clear amid the blend of bodies and shapes. The faint murmur fled into a deeper silence, the air frigid and deathly still. A breath filled Elyon's lungs. Another. He waited, staring, trying not to blink, trying not to think...and then came the crack and the slash.

Pain flared through his upper back, a searing sting like nothing he'd ever felt. He bit down hard and pressed forward against the cold hard post, as a second slash cracked and ripped at him. His left knee half buckled but he pushed up and stayed standing, planting his footing...and just as he did the third lash kissed him. The fourth came a second later, and now his head was swimming and spinning and blurring. The fifth slackened his jaw enough for a short grunt of pain to slip through his cold blue lips. He clamped them shut before the sixth came cracking. *I'll not cry out, I'll not.* He looked forward through the crowd, and found the shape of Vesryn there, urging him on. *I'll not. I'll not.*

CRACK. The sixth was lower, at the bottom of his spine, licking like a flaming tongue. His hips thrust forward from the singeing pain as his skin peeled open and a shudder spread through the crowd. There was a hot wetness running down his back, rich red tears weeping from the welts. *Four more. Just four...*he thought, setting his jaw, firming his footing. He took himself to another place as the whip bit at him for a seventh time, then an eighth. *I'll not cry out, I'll not.* He stared forward at his uncle. *I'll not.*

The last two were the worst. The last two cut the deepest. He could feel the scourger putting everything he had into them. He could hear him grunting as he swung with all he had, hurling his arm, snapping his wrist, following through harder and harder still. They were the worst...but they were the best. *The last,* he thought, as the echoing snap of the tenth lash rang out across the yard. He could breathe again, properly breath, but still he didn't make a sound. He just stood there, trembling, as the blood rained down his back, and the crowd began to break up, cracking and separating like floes of ice.

And through all that, Vesryn came forward. Quickly he came, until he was right before him, tearing off the rope from Elyon's wrists, a worry in his eyes. "Help me get him to the infirmary," he called, looking to the side. It was Sir Mallister who came to help, throwing Elyon's arm over his shoulders to prop him up. Elyon looked at him and saw in his face his sister. *Melany*, he thought. "Will she come?" he managed to ask, though his voice was strangely muddled.

Sir Mallister looked at him with that kind handsome face. "Who's that, Sir Elyon?"

"Your sister."

The Emerald Guard smiled. "I wait in hope," he said. "I will write again and tell her you need nursing, sir. It may hasten her arrival."

Elyon managed a weak smile as they began helping him across the yard, though as he tried to think of Melany, another girl took her place. *Saska*, he thought, and for a second he thought he saw her, hiding around the side of a tent ahead. Then he blinked and she was gone. *Saska...who are you?* She'd been so evasive, but why? He thought again of the dream he'd had, when she'd faded to silver and blue. *Who is she?* he wondered, as they drew him through the camp. *Will I ever get to ask her again? Will I ever get to find out?*

They turned down a lane between tents, as others trailed behind them. He could sense some concern among them, but why? *They're only cuts,* he wanted to say. *Shallow cuts, that's all.* But someone behind him was saying different. "Some of these are deep, Your Highness," the man said in a hurried voice. "These two in particular. These last two. I don't like these..."

He heard a grunt in response. "I'll have that scourger flayed," growled Rylian. "I told him not to go so hard."

"Your brother-in-law put him up to it." That was Lord Kanabar, with that great stormy voice of his. "The scourger was Cedrik's man."

More words were shared, more voices joining in, but it was all becoming a blur now, muddled and confused. Someone called out that he was losing a lot of blood, and he could feel cloth being pressed against his wounds as they hurried on. But there wasn't much else he remembered. Just the rush of it, the worry, the blear of bodies about him. There was a vague feeling of entering a marquee and being set down on a bed, the sting of salves and balms, the prick and tug of a needle. Noise surrounded him, and movement. But soon even that was gone.

And then only silence remained. Silence and a lightless dark.

41

Janilah

"It seems my new First Blade wishes to lay Harrowmoor to a full siege, Janilah," snivelled King Ellis Reynar as he ran his eyes over the note. "Have they not been doing that already?" He laughed awkwardly. "I'm a little confused."

"I believe my father has been trying to win the fort with the scalpel not the hammer, good king," said Amilia, sitting beside him at the feast table, as the lords and ladies and noble knights of Ilithor hummed and bustled about them. "We don't want to kill them all, do we? They will be our soldiers soon, once we take Rasalan under our charge."

"Yes, I suppose they will." Ellis spooned a measure of steaming soup into his mouth, flinched and drew back. It was too hot for the poor weak man. "I...I think I'll let it settle," he chuckled, dabbing his mouth with a cloth. "I've never had much tolerance for hot food."

"Or cold rooms," said Janilah.

Ellis's pencil neck twisted in his direction. "My king?"

"I just find it curious, Ellis. You seem unable to handle extremes of any kind."

Ellis chuckled again, expressing a weaselly smile. "I admit I like to stay in the middle ground where I can." He looked left and right. Everyone else at the table was happily ladling soup into their mouths without issue. "I think you're built quite hardy up here," he noted. "The cold braces you for such things."

"What else does Vesryn say?"

"Oh..." Ellis shuffled about in his excessive layering of silver-blue robes and took up the note again. He had to peer close to read, shortsighted as he was. "Seems they've tried everything and are losing men, without notable yield. He says he believes they can take the fortress with losses of between three and four thousand." He set the note aside and smiled. "I'd say it's worth it, wouldn't you?" He looked at Janilah. "Or...or not? My king? What do you think?"

"I am still pondering." Janilah turned, having heard all this from Rylian's crow already. "But will of course be sure to tell you when I have made my decision."

Did I say that too loud? he wondered, as several lords and ladies offered him a discomfited glance. *Should I be so obvious?* He'd been as tactful as he could reasonably manage when dealing with Ellis in public settings thus far, but today he found he didn't care. What did it matter, after all? *The primped cloying masses will bow and scrape no matter what I say or do.* He could probably stand up right now and take Ellis's head off, and see no reprisal at all. The thought made him smile, so hard he almost laughed.

"Might I enquire into the joke?" asked the woman seated beside him, mantled in blue over silver and with a sparkling little tiara atop her head. It was Ellis's wife, the rather sow-faced Queen Elitha. *Not a particularly handsome woman,* he thought. *but not completely unlikeable either.* She was stronger than her husband...but then so was a blade of grass, so it wasn't really saying much...and came from good old stock. One of the Oloran clan, and a relation of Nathaniel, Ellis's new Greycloak Commander.

"I don't much care for jokes, Elitha," he told her, banishing his smile as swift as a hare hurrying from a hunting dog. "I was just imagining the death of good King Godrin. It always delivers a smile to my face."

"That is morbid, Janilah. And not something to joke about."

I'll joke about whatever I bloody like in my city, he thought. But said, "Of course. Most unseemly of me."

"He can't be long for this world, surely," said Amilia down the table. "Father says he looks like a crumpled piece of parchment," she tinkled. "And that son of his, Hadrin. A grotesque little man, and bitter as a cold wind. They say he's gone into hiding, craven that he is. Some think he may have even left Rasalan and sailed south. He is Seaborn, after all, and much better on waves than wall walks."

"Do not give mind to specious rumours, Amilia. I'm sure he'll reappear soon."

"You know this?" asked Ellis. "We will need to see him to the pyre as well as his grim old father, Janilah. If we're to take the kingdom we cannot be merciful. We must be ruthless, so their lords fall in line."

"Yes, Husband," smiled Elitha, though she didn't look much better when showing her teeth. "You see you have something Cousin Amron lacked. He would never have dared be so bold."

Daring and boldness were in fact two qualities Amron Daecar had in abundance, though Janilah saw no profit in saying it. Ellis liked that, though, lifting his receding chin and curling his lips into a smug indecorous smile. It seemed his wife's job was to rub his ego, though she didn't seem to do so with much relish. *A dutiful woman,* Janiliah thought. *She has that going for her at least.*

"Did you hear about Elyon and Cousin Griffin?" Amilia then asked in a more sombre voice. "Melany had word from her brother, just this morning. He wrote of some altercation between them. A fatal one. He's dead, apparently...Griffin." She shook her head. "A horrible thing. Mother is distraught."

Your mother is always bloody distraught, Janilah almost bellowed. He could not stand the woman. Clarris Kastor had done her duty and delivered Rylian a fine trio of children, but beyond all that she'd been a cold cheerless presence about this palace for far too long. Even now she couldn't summon herself to come to dinner, preferring the quiet solitude of her chambers where she wallowed in her unending grief. *And for what? Her ignoble father, who slipped in his piss and cracked his own head open on the hearth?* The sour old fool had died a death befitting of a drunken dullard, not a great lord, but that was over three years ago now and it was high time she moved on. *But this won't help,* he thought. Clarris was feeble as a fawn in the jaws of a lion and this latest tragedy would only add to her woe.

"A great shame," Janilah put in. "But I'm told it has all been resolved."

"How so?" asked Ellis. He had an eager look on his face. "Is Elyon's head to be put on the chopper's block?"

Janilah was beginning to despise this man and his pathetic attempts to be ruthless and regal. "His punishment has already been carried out. He got ten lashes and ten gashes for his trouble."

"A flogging? Is that all?" Ellis gave out a huff, and tried his soup once more. But of course it was still too hot. *This man is no king,* Janilah thought, looking down at him through his narrow deepest eyes. *No king at all.*

"Don't sound so disappointed, Husband," said Queen Elitha, always on hand to offer a gentle scold. "I'm sure justice has been served, and Elyon was always a very pleasant young man. I'd not believe he would murder Sir Griffin without cause."

Ellis had an ugly little look on his face, a spiteful look. "I'm not so sure, Elitha. Elyon is as his father born, volatile and quick-tempered. He thinks himself untouchable."

"Now come, Ellis. You're being unfair. Elyon is heir to a greathouse now, and you'll need his support in the years to come. There's no sense in being antagonistic."

"He isn't here, Elitha. I'd not say this to his face, of course."

"Nor should you say it behind his back. Do not let your resentment for Amron trickle down to Elyon. Judge him on his own worth. He is young and may yet thrive. Now..." The queen turned her eyes to Amilia, sitting to the right of her husband. "You said Sir Griffin was a cousin of yours, Amilia? My condolences for your loss."

Amilia gave her a grateful look. "Thank you, Elitha," she answered with courtesy. "The only son of my Uncle Caleb. But in truth I'll not grieve for him, nor will many others I fear. Sir Griffin was always a troubled boy, and prone to cruelty and unkindness.

He would torture animals as a child, I recall, and more than once I saw his father lay a hand on him for it. He took me to the woods once, when we were little, and showed me a rabbit he'd caught in a snare. It's leg was broken but he didn't finish it off, as a good huntsman should. He poked and prodded at it and laughed all the while as it screamed, and it was still alive when he started to skin it. I ran and told my father, and it caused no end of trouble. I didn't much like him after that."

"That's horrible," whispered the spider-quiet voice of Princess Lyriss, sitting beside her mother. "How could he do such a thing?"

"Boys can be cruel like that, darling." Her mother patted her frizzy head. "But I'm sure he grew out of such habits as he matured."

Lyriss had big cow-like eyes, though wasn't much to look at. She was only thirteen or fourteen so far as Janilah knew, but judging by her parents would never flourish into much of a beauty. "I hope so," she sniffed, looking close to tears. "Who could torture an innocent rabbit? It's evil."

Her mother ran a hand over the girl's freckly cheek. "There's a lot of evil in this world, sweety, but much goodness too. The gods see to the balance, and chose Elyon to survive the affray. I think that says a lot, don't you?"

Lyriss thought about that a moment, then nodded. "I do hope Elyon is OK. Was he injured in the fight?"

Amilia gave answer to that. "I do not believe so. Just the cuts to his back, from the whip."

"I expect it was a gentle flogging," Queen Elitha said without hesitation, keen to assuage her soft little daughter's fears. "Or did you truly mean what you said, Janilah?" She lowered her voice, turning to him. "Ten gashes from those lashes?"

"It was a turn of phrase, Elitha. I don't know for certain how the boy fares."

"He'll be quite all right, I'm sure." The queen turned back to her toothy daughter. They looked the pair. One piggish, the other horsy, and Ellis had a great deal of the ferret about him. *Quite the farmyard family,* Janilah thought, allowing himself the petty jest.

"Do you like him, Lyriss?" asked Amilia. She could always be relied on to probe. "Elyon? He's a very dashing young man, wouldn't you say? Perhaps you might marry him one day?"

The girl shook her head. "He wouldn't want to. I look like a donkey, people say...and anyway, I don't want to either." She looked nervous all of a sudden. "I'm in love with someone else."

"Love," teased her mother. "Now how can that be, darling? You're far too young to know what that means."

"I *do* know what it means." the princess insisted. "I love him."

"Who?"

"Wendel," she mumbled. Then louder, "Wendel Taynar. I love him. I do. I want to marry him."

King Ellis gave out a scoff. "That boy is no match for you, Lyriss. As a princess, you'll marry a prince. Or a great lord at the very least. But I'd favour a prince, of course, not least your grandsons, Janilah." He shuffled nervously in his seat. "I've been meaning to corner you about it, actually. A match between Prince Robbert and Lyriss would favour us both, I feel, and do much to secure our alliance. I know that is what you had in mind for Amilia, when you betrothed her to Aleron Daecar, but a merger of royal blood would be even more profitable."

"But I love Wendel. I don't want to marry..."

"Quiet, Lyriss. The kings are talking."

The girl hushed at that, and looked like she wanted to cry. Janilah set his cold dark eyes on his fellow monarch. "We'll see," is all he said. "Let us get through this war first, before making any promises we may be unable to keep."

"Of course, of course..." Ellis turned to the side, then raised a hand. "But, if I may..."

"Apologies, good king, but I've been summoned." Janilah stood and paced from the table toward the guard standing nearby. He'd spotted him arriving a few moments ago, and was waiting for an appropriate time to leave. That seemed about perfect, interrupting the sniffly king like that. He joined the member of his royal guard at the side of the feast hall, as the merriment continued. "Yes, Sir Fredrick?"

Sir Fredrick Ruxmond was one of his sworn swords; the best of the knights who served in the palace. He had a half dozen of them, each draped in a great mantle of striped white, green, and brown, with dual godsteel swords at their belts. "My lord." The man bowed. "Lady Cecilia Blakewood has arrived. She awaits you in the throne room."

"Very good. Thank you, Sir Fredrick."

He asked the knight to relay a message of his departure to his table, and stepped from the hall. When he arrived at his throne room, another of his swords, Sir Owen Armdall, stood waiting. "Make sure no one enters, Sir Owen." The tall handsome knight nodded and opened the huge bronze doors, closing them once Janilah had passed. Ahead, his daughter awaited in a generous bearskin cloak, standing at the bottom of the dais with her hands clasped neatly at her waist. "Cecilia. You made good time." He stepped toward her, voice echoing around the spacious white stone chamber, and gave her a single peck on the cheek. "How was the road?"

"Well travelled," she said with a smile. "The Vandarians had carved an easy path for us to follow to the Links. After that, the ride across Tukor was swift and uneventful."

They turned together and moved up the steps to the dais, past Janilah's simple but stately stone throne, and out toward the high balcony. She had sent him notice of her return, though their correspondence had been scant of late. "You mentioned that Rylian ordered you to leave the camp," he said, as they reached the iron railing, curved into the shape of a half moon as the terrace jutted out from the palace. "I suppose I shouldn't be completely surprised. He has never much approved of what you do."

"He grows insubordinate, Father," she said with a note of bitterness. "I do believe he is beginning to covet your throne."

Janilah let out a rough laugh. "He's a prince and an heir. Of course he covets my throne. It would be unusual if he didn't. Now tell me, how many girls did you bring?"

"Five," she said. "None are special. The only one that was got away."

"Yes, you suggested as such in your letter. This girl you sent to bed the Daecar boy. I'm supposing you played a hand in this affray I've heard so much about?"

"You know me so well, Father. It was of course by my design, though the result wasn't as I'd hoped. Still, Sir Griffin's death is some solace. I always despised that boy."

"Many did, I'm learning. And your intention?"

"Principally...to punish the girl for crossing me. I rather enjoyed her, you know, even if there was something in her that never quite added up. Still, she disappointed me, and needed to be disciplined. So I compiled a note with a few scurrilous details and had it anonymously sent to Sir Griffin. I suspected he'd salivate most over the prospect of maltreating the girl, but should have known he'd make a mess of it. They say Elyon killed him but I rather suspect it was her. Trust a Daecar to be chivalrous and take the blame."

Janilah had always enjoyed his bastard daughter's dry sense of humour. "And this girl. Who is she?"

"Well that's what I can't work out," Cecilia said, expressing a perplexed frown. "A liar, certainly, and not a friend. I wrote in the note to Sir Griffin that she was a spy, though that was pure conjecture on my part..."

"We have caught and killed a number of Rasal spies in the past months, smoked out from their burrows," he informed her. "They train young girls to infiltrate and deceive; hardly an honourable practice, but one that has no doubt proven effective. Perhaps she was there for Rylian? To await a chance to kill him."

"Or Cedrik," Cecilia offered. "We know how the Kastors feel about southerners. I did sense some animosity in her toward them. It could have been nothing but a personal vendetta."

"At least then it would have meaning," Janilah said. "Otherwise the killing of Cedrik Kastor would have little true merit. Lords are like weeds. Pull one and another sprouts up in his place. Killing Rylian would be more impactful, but even then Robbert would become my heir and we have a replica of him in Raynald too, so..." He shook his head, staring out over his city. "Most men leave no footprint, Cecilia. They walk their lives on solid stone and you'd never know of their passing. Some walk in mud and leave an impression, but soon the rain washes by and the prints fill in. But then there are a rare few who stride upon wet mortar, and their prints fix and last a lifetime. Kill one of those men and you change things. There aren't many of them around."

"There are some," she suggested, though there was a note of care in her tone. "The Daecar boy, Elyon...I've come to believe that he knows, Father, that you're behind the undoing of his house. That is perhaps no risk in itself, but if he should tell Amron..."

Janilah cut her off. "He won't. Not without evidence. And his house has seen no such undoing, don't be dramatic. They have lost an heir, that is all, and have a ready replacement to hand. It is hardly the calamity people are making out."

"Tell that to Amron. One-legged and one-armed he may be, but..."

"But nothing. He's a cripple, and I'll soon be a god. And his son is a striped man now, with ten reasons to rest a while. Their suspicions are of no concern. It is the *other* Daecar boy who worries me. Your son, Cecilia. He is the only Daecar that matters right now." He turned to her, his shoulders widened by the thick pine-green cloak he wore. A wind rustled through it, dusting him with flakes of snow, and for a good long while she said nothing. "How do you feel when I say that?" he asked her eventually. "When I call him your son."

"I feel nothing." She forced a smile to her lips. "I may have birthed him, Father, but he was never my son. That is what I teach my girls. They carry children, but are not mothers. I practice what I preach. The boy was born to service." She turned away. "He is not my son."

He watched her for a time, and had never been quite sure of all that. Janilah was calculating and even callous at times, but he certainly wasn't witness. He understood that there was a bond between mother and child that could never be entirely eradicated. *Only controlled and contained,* he thought, and that comprised the essence of Cecilia's work. She was best suited to selecting and guiding the right subjects through her breeding programme because she had been through it all herself. *But still, it has wounded her,* he saw. *A wound that will never fully heal.*

"I will try to make sure he isn't killed when the Nightblade is retrieved," he told her. It was the best he could offer, and a lie. He saw no other way but to slay the boy now, such was his attachment to the blade. *And an attachment I understand.*

"I care not whether he lives or dies, Father. It matters only that the Nightblade is recovered." She stared out as she spoke, looking to the expanse before them. The throne room was high up in the loftier parts of the palace and the palace was high up in the loftier parts of the city. Either side of the balcony, towers and walkways and paths broke into the mountains, and ahead, the city sloped down in increments through the valley, all the way off to the plains beyond. "You will find him soon, I'm sure."

"I was sure once myself, but my faith has been sorely tested." He couldn't hide the frustration in his voice. The Nightblade was missing, the Frostblade unfound, the Book of Thala still to reach him. He had despatched Sir Kevyn Bolt to fetch it some weeks ago, but whether or not it was in his possession yet he wasn't sure. *Is it on the way back to me?* he wondered. He still considered it the key. To the location of the Frostblade, and more...

"He has picked up a few names, I hear," Cecelia put in, though she spoke with little energy when discussing the boy. "The Ghost of the Shadowfort is a particularly frightening title. Hadrin's Horror isn't much better."

"Silly names and no more," Janilah dismissed. "If the boy was smart he'd run and hide but it seems he's quite happy with his newfound notoriety. There are rumours he felled a kraken just east of the Tidelands, you know. A fanciful tale, I'm sure, but it seems some of the crew he sailed with have taken a liking to him, and entered into his service."

Cecilia looked surprised by that. "Truly? I would imagine him a more solitary creature."

"They are trained to be," nodded Janilah, "but it would appear he's raging against all he's been taught. I've had word from Gerrin. He has recently entered into conference with Lady Greyskin of Greywater."

His daughter gave a brisk nod. "Lady Shark. A most ghastly woman, I've heard."

"I assume you're referring to her particular methods of instilling fear in the local population? To that I would say she's highly effective, though in this case had little idea who she was dealing with. According to Gerrin, there was some skirmish on a beach over in the east of Passway Key. The boy Jonik and his crew had run aground after a storm and spent several days repairing their ship. On departure, some half dozen of Lady Greyskin's Bladeborn cutthroats came seeking duties for their passing, only to be slaughtered. Several others got away and reported that one Emeric Manfrey fought alongside the boy."

Cecilia's face swelled with surprise. "Emeric Manfrey? The exiled lord?"

"The very one. Word is he sails with the boy and this rag-tag crew he's enlisted. They head south, I'm told."

"Any idea where?"

"Manfrey has an estate outside Solas. The exile will return there, I would say. As for the boy? I cannot be sure. Gerrin has asked for patience in his hunt. I am finding mine acutely tested."

"Some consider patience a virtue, Father."

"Then I am bloody virtuous," he grunted, staring bitterly out over his city. "At times I think my plans are unravelling, Cecilia. Soon I will have the north, but I need more than that to win this war. I need those blades, and I need that book. If I cannot get those, then all my efforts will have been for nothing."

"Time, Father. You need only time."

It was trite counsel, but there was wisdom in it too. But time wasn't a currency he was rich in anymore. Robust though he still was, he was starting to feel the advanced years of his age. All this plotting and scheming had sapped his energy, and not everything he was doing sat well with him. *Necessary evils,* he thought, but evils nonetheless. *And how many more will I commit? How many acts of dishonour...to secure the north, to win the war, and earn my own Table besides?* He had no answer except one.

As many as it takes, he thought. And in the days to come, the world would know of them.

42

Saska

Saska sat on the back of the wagon as it bounced down the rutted road, her wrists and ankles bound. About her there was a great deal of rattling, a constant chorus of clanking bottles and crates, and one she'd been listening to for some three days since leaving the siege camp at Harrowmoor. It had near driven her mad, but what could she do? *Just sit and accept your fate,* she thought. "I'm exactly where I'm meant to be..."

"Oh here she goes again," came an amused voice ahead. "You hear that, Lance. 'I'm exactly where I'm meant to be'." The man turned back to look at her. "Why do you repeat that so often, girl? Is it a personal mantra of yours?"

She glanced over at him, smiling down at her from the driver's seat. He was one of a pair of chaperones in whose company she'd awoken three days past, riding her south on this rattling wagon of theirs. Both Varin Knights apparently, and trusted friends to Elyon. Sir Lancel and Sir Barnibus, one sleek and handsome, the other wide and not. Both were agreeable, though, even if they had fettered her like a common criminal. But she could hardly blame them for that. She had tried to escape once, after all...

"I like to remind myself that I'm on the right path, even if I don't understand it," she told Barnibus, as he looked at her with that cordial grin on his ruddy face. "Helps me rationalise things."

"Couldn't you have remembered that before you tried to dash off a couple of nights ago? That wasn't how I wanted to spend my evening, running about through the moors looking for you."

That was an exaggeration. She'd only made it about a hundred yards from their camp before they snared her, which given they carried godsteel and she didn't, wasn't too bad an effort. They wore no Varin cloaks, though, or other such vestments, and were travelling under the pretence of common merchants delivering a consignment of whiskey and wine to the southern forces in Shellcrest, a gift from the Vandarians. When she'd run off it had been through confusion and desperation, though where she was planning to go, she had no idea. The last thing she could remember was arguing with Elyon in his tent, before he darted in all of a sudden and strangled her out. When she woke it was dusk the following day and there were two cloaked men sitting at a fire in an abandoned village on the moors. She was up on her feet in an instant, and making for the hills, before they caught her and brought her up to speed.

"We're taking you to Shellcrest, girl, to fetch a boat down south," the young man she later learned was called Barnibus told her. "Direct orders from the First Blade. Now sit and don't make a fuss, or we'll have to tie you up."

She'd made a fuss, so they'd tied her up, and hadn't seen fit to unfetter her yet. She thought that her regular repetitions of her so-called mantra would help them trust her - and help give herself some succour - but its effects had been limited. But still she kept to it. "I'm exactly where I'm meant to be," she whispered again, just for herself this time. They were Godrin's words, and she had to trust them. Trust that her failure would be worth it, in time. That her abandonment of her duty would serve a greater purpose. "I'm exactly where I'm meant to be..."

"Looks like we've got company on our tail," called out Lancel, turning to look over his shoulder as he guided the horses up a rise in the road. Saska looked back too and saw a blur of brown-coated soldiers cantering up the snow-bordered track behind them, a glitter of mail and studded leather tunics beneath their cloaks. "You'd best get hidden, girl." he told her. "Quickly now, or they'll see."

In an instant she was on her feet and rolling sideways into an empty crate, assigned for this very purpose should anyone draw near. She landed with a thump in a graceless sprawl, finding the exercise particularly difficult with her limbs all bound up tight. With Lancel at the reins, it was on Barnibus to complete the deceit, leaping into the rear of the wagon and fixing the lid, then hauling another crate atop her to further her concealment. A noisy rattle sounded as he manoeuvred the casks, her vision reduced to a few thin slits of light filtering through the slats. Within moments she was safely tucked into the rear of the wagon by the driver's seat, hidden within the heaped barrels, boxes, and caskets loaded heavily upon the wain.

"Looks like a full dozen," she heard Barnibus say outside. "Tukorans certainly. From Harrowmoor most likely."

"Any Bladeborn among them?" asked Lancel. She could hear the shift in their tone, the tension.

"Leader looks a knight," confirmed Barnibus. "Got a mountain on his hauberk, with tumbling rocks either side. That's the crest of House Marsh from Rockfall. They're bannermen of the Kastors. Keep your steel hidden, Lance, but near to hand, just in case. And you don't make a peep in there, girl. Not a sniff nor a sound, understand? I don't want to have to kill anyone on your account."

The mounted troop was soon upon them, the thudding gait of the horses growing louder as a man called out. "Well met, friends, well met. My name is Sir Cleon Marsh of Rockfall. We're conducting checks on the roads south of Harrowmoor. Pray tell of your quarry and haul."

"Well met, Sir Cleon," said Barnibus, roughing up the edges of his nicely cultured voice. "Our quarry is the standing force in Shellcrest, and our haul is for their pleasure; wine and whiskey and plenty of it. We have heard sorry tales of poisoned barrels down at the coast and good Lord Kanabar has seen fit to provide a bounty. We'll not have any more proud Tukorans clawing at their necks and turning purple, not on account of these dirty Rasals and their tricks."

"You come from Harrowmoor?" Sir Cleon asked, as the troop clattered about alongside them, the horses snorting and stamping noisily. Lancel brought the wagon to a slow rattling stop.

"Aye, sir," said Barnibus. "We came up with the army from the Lakelands. We're merchants by trade, and I won't lie - Lord Kanabar is offering us fair reward for this delivery. Seems the men in Shellcrest are starved of safe liquor. With all these poisonings, they live in fear that their next drink will be their last."

"It's a sick world we live in when a man cannot drink in peace," added Lancel, putting on a growl. "A sick, sick world."

"True enough," agreed Sir Cleon. "Might I take a look? We're on the trail of a fugitive from the camp, a girl of some eighteen summers, short black hair, southern skin tone. Pull back that tarp, if you don't mind."

"No southerners here, unless you're counting the wine," said Barnibus with a chuckle, as he clambered about onto the rear of the wagon and drew away the sheepskin tarp. "Lord Kanabar brought most of it from his own stocks. Generous man, he is. Who do you serve, if you'll permit the query?"

"I'm under the charge of Lord Huffort of Rockfall, who serves within the northern army of Lord Kastor." Saska could hear the man dismounting and moving to the rear of the wagon. There were enough crates and casks and barrels to make the prospect of checking each of them a labour most men would prefer to avoid. "I'll ask that you open some of these up, Vandarian. Just routine. I'm sure there's nothing untoward here."

"Nothing at all, sir," Barnibus said cheerfully, as he picked out a couple of crates. Saska could tell he was making an effort of it, taking his sweet time prising each casket open. With a few huffs and puffs, he'd unveiled their contents. "Satisfied?"

There was a short delay as Sir Cleon did his inspection. Then he answered, "Partly, but I'm charged with being suspicious too. How long have you been on the road?"

"Oh I don't know exactly. Been a jolly slow slog so far, in this weather. What do you think, Ben?"

He'd used that name for Lancel several times so far. "Hmmm, a good week I think," the lissom, light-haired Varin Knight fibbed. "Spent at least two days stuck in the mire, I should say."

"You're carrying too much weight," identified Sir Cleon. "You've enough here to spread over at least two carts. Clearly you're not used to these conditions, or these roads."

"Aye, I'll confess we don't tend to trade in these parts this time of year, nor deal with stocks this cumbersome either. Perhaps we've misjudged the cart's capabilities." Barnibus gave a laugh. "That in mind, perhaps you might want to help us, good sir? Take a crate or two off our hands to lessen our burden? I'm sure the men of Shellcrest can spare a few bottles."

"You'd risk your register like that? Surely your liaison in Shellcrest will be expecting a particular number of crates in the consignment?"

"Oh I have no doubt, sir...but sometimes things fall off wagons, especially in conditions like these. Like a crate of whiskey, for example. I can tell them we lost a cask or two to the bogs and they'll not quibble."

"They'll be too drunk to care," laughed Lancel. "Go ahead, help yourself."

There was a short silence as Sir Cleon considered it. Then, "We can take a bottle or so in each of our saddlebags, I suppose. So long as you're sure, gentlemen?"

"Of course, of course," said Barnibus. "You'd be doing us a favour. Go on. Take what you wish, and we'll be on our way."

There was a lot of snorting and stomping after that as the men swung from their steeds and gathered at the back of the wain. Then came the clinking and clanking as the bottles were eagerly pilfered, the shuffling as they were stowed in saddlebags, and the grateful grunts of the soldiers who would be getting terribly drunk tonight. When they were set to leave, however, one of the other men asked. "Don't I know you?"

Saska couldn't tell who he was referring to, squashed up in the dark as she was. At least until Lancel answered, "Me, sir? I wouldn't imagine so, lest I've sold you a pelt before. It's what I trade in mostly. I work with hunters and trappers out of Mistvale and..."

"No, not bought fur from you, no..." The man was clearly thinking hard about who Lancel might be. *And if he works it out?* Saska didn't want to dare think about that. "Arg, it ain't coming to me. But I'll think it up sooner or later, I always do."

"He always does," agreed another man in a deep lumbering voice. "Renford's got a way with faces, he does. Never forgets 'em. Never."

"Until today, clearly," came the voice of Sir Cleon. "We'll not hold you up any longer, gentlemen. Much obliged for the whiskey. If we should spot you stuck in a quag, we will of course come to help dig you out."

"Might be that you do," chuckled Barnibus. "Are you heading for Shellcrest as well?"

"We're watching the roads in the region, such as we can, in search of this girl. So no, not Shellcrest exactly but we believe she may be headed there or thereabouts, in search of passage off these shores. Lord Kastor is quite intent on catching her, given her alleged part in the murder of his nephew." He paused, then asked, "I suppose you haven't heard about that, if you left the camp before the tragedy occurred?"

"Can't say we have, no," said Barnibus. "A murder, you say?"

"A most unpleasant one, yes, by the Crippler's son. He's been duly punished, of course, but it feels like justice took a day off when they gathered for their privy trial."

"Ten lashes," came a grunting voice. "For murder! How can that be fair?"

The dozen or so men in the company began grumbling about bias and corruption and the fact that the privy council comprised too many Vandarians who'd never dare condemn a man like Elyon Daecar. And all the while Saska sat there in the musty darkness unsure of how to feel. Relief, in part, to hear that he'd suffered no worse a fate than a flogging, and yet distress and regret, and a hot burning guilt that she'd put him through it all in the first place.

"Anyway, if you should hear anything of this girl, do make

sure to report it," Sir Cleon was saying. "And beware of this route, if you're to stay on it to the coast. There have been reports of massacres in these parts, men hacked up and brutalised on the road. You ought to be OK; it appears soldiers are being targeted, not merchants, but do be forewarned, gentlemen."

"Forewarning 'em won't much help, sir," said one of the men in a quivering voice. "Ain't none who can stop that monster, lest your name's Amron or Rylian or some such. And even then I ain't so sure."

"Monster?" queried Barnibus. "What type of monster?"

"A giant," said the same man. "That's what they say. A giant clad in steel."

"It's the King's Wall," came another voice. "They say that old Godrin's sent him out to bludgeon every Tukoran he finds. He's been set free of his service, they say. That his only order is to kill as many of us as possible, to put the fear in us till we flee..."

"I've heard he massacred ten full trained men-at-arms," burst in an excitable man. "Cracked half their heads open with his fists, he did, and left them right there on the road with their brains leaking out like yolk..."

"He can cleave a man in full godsteel plate clean in two, they say," squeaked another. "My cousin Peet saw him up close once. Was so tall, he said, that he could straddle a horse without his feet ever leaving the ground."

"A little pony, perhaps," offered Sir Cleon.

"No, twas a destrier, and a big one, Peet told me. And he's as wide as he is tall too. Got shoulders like a broadback, he does. And hands as big as trenchers."

"Some say he never takes off his armour," one of the other men said, though Saska was starting to lose track of them now. "Not to wash nor sleep nor nothin'..."

"Well then he mustn't smell particularly pleasant," Sir Cleon said in a straight voice. "But trust simple men to believe everything they hear." He gave a chuckle. "Now come, let's not give breath to these silly rumours. We don't want to overly frighten our new friends here, do we? As I say, gentlemen, this is all just soldier hearsay, and I'm sure you're under no threat. Now I'll thank you kindly for your generosity, and bid you good day."

"And you, Sir Cleon," said Barnibus. "Be safe out there."

Saska listened as the troop of soldiers saddled up and set off, charging off up the road in a great fog of noise. Neither Barnibus nor Lancel spoke for a good while until the sound of hooves had long since fled southward. Only then did she hear the creak of movement as one of them climbed onto the back of the wagon and rearranged the crates and barrels. Then with a groan of wood the lid came off her casket and a great rectangle of light blurred her vision, fading to unveil the smiling, round-cheeked face of Sir Barnibus looking down at her. "Well then, crisis averted," he said, his clipped cultured voice resuming its service. "Is that true what he said? You were there when Elyon killed Sir Griffin?"

Saska pushed herself up on her shackled legs, wincing as she unfurled her knees and stood. She turned her eyes to the bleak grey skies as a light sleet began to swirl and fall. "Didn't Elyon tell you what happened?"

"He didn't have much time, to be honest." Barnibus reached out and helped her from the crate. "Elyon was already being taken into custody to await trial. It was Lord Vesryn who gave us the order, though it is of course unofficial. We're all taking a risk for you, girl. I do hope you're worth it." He smiled and gave her ankles a quick look. "Might be better if I unbind you, so you can climb in and out more easily," he said. Then he leaned in, his checks beet red from the biting winds, flaps of hazel hair hanging out of his hood. "You promise you won't try to run again? Would be folly out here with Sir Cleon and his men around."

Saska offered him a quiet, thankful nod. "I promise."

"Any objections Lance?"

The towheaded knight shrugged. "Fine by me. But best we tie her up at night while we're sleeping."

"Oh, we're not going to be sleeping, not anymore. We'll each take a watch, two hours on, two hours off. I'm taking no chances with these soldiers about. And the Wall? I imagine that's all just rumour, but I'd not want a man like that stumbling into us on a cold dark night."

Barnibus finished unbinding her and clambered back over onto the driver's seat next to Lancel, asking that she stay low for a while until they found somewhere to stop for the night. The skies were beginning to darken and all about them a wet sleety snow was falling and swirling on the breeze. Saska dropped down among the barrels, pulling her cloak tight around her shoulders. The snows were patchy further south of Harrowmoor, and where they'd gathered and then melted upon the road long tracts of muddy slush had formed. It had slowed them somewhat, though not the two days Lancel had suggested. The combined power of the horses and the knights was plenty enough to haul them free if ever they got stuck.

She watched the two men as they bumped along, listened as they chatted and bickered as brothers, though if they were they hardly looked alike. Both were of an age, though, somewhere in their early twenties, she thought, dutiful and noble, and took to their task without complaint. Saska had come to believe that Vesryn must have ordered them not to speak to her much, so rarely did they do so, nor did they probe for answers as to who she was. So she sat, for the most part, in solemn silent thought, wondering what she might do when they parted with her in Shellcrest, whether she might try to find Marian again, or head for Lord Payne's estates, or sail north, not south, and all the way back to Thalan. To see Astrid again, perhaps, and maybe serve with her in the palace. *Because isn't that all I'm good for? I'm no spy, clearly, nor am I much of an assassin. I'm just a beacon for evil men to assault and abuse,* she thought, bitter and cold as the leaden sleety skies. It had happened too many times now, and she'd been forced to kill too many men off the back of it. *But no more,* she promised herself there on the back of that cart. *I'll never let it happen again...*

The world was falling to dusk when they rolled off down a side-track and came upon the husk of an old village, a shadowy place full of old stone structures and wooden shacks that had been abandoned and burned during the invasion. Outside the rectory a pit had been dug and filled with charred corpses, half covered in snow. Old burnt bones poked out, black on white, and there was livestock in there with them, Saska saw. The head of a horse. The hind legs of a cow emerging from the tumble of death and decay. She stayed on the wagon as Lancel guided it into an old stables, its roof partially caved in, before the two men saw to unhitching and tending the horses.

"You know how to make a fire?" Barnibus asked her, as he found a pail of water for the horses to take a drink. Saska nodded to that and he added, "See about fetching some firewood, and no games, missy. Try to run and I'll bind you again, make no mistake. But none of us want that."

He had a kind way about him, they both did, and Saska had no intention of undermining their orders. She didn't need to go far to gather kindling and timber; half the ramshackle buildings provided plenty. Once done Barnibus pointed to an old bell tower north of the village, up a sharp incline. "Get it lit in there. The stone will conceal us." He handed her flint and a simple steel blade. "That's not for keeping, just for the fire, understand? We'll join you in a moment."

The tower was damp and cold and grey, its interior a winding staircase giving access to the belfry. The last of the light was spilling in from the upper windows at the top, though at the base all was dark and gloomy. She set the kindling and cut a spark from the flint, breathed into the flame, and had the fire going in no time. When the others joined her it was already crackling well and warming the stout stone interior. "Good job," said Barnibus, giving the place a quick inspection. "We can share watch from up in the belfry, Lance. Looks like it'll provide a good view. "He went to shut the heavy oak door. It had been knocked off its hinges some time ago, it looked, but with a bit of an effort, he was able to shift it into place. "That'll keep the light out and warmth in. Girl, you tend the flames, and don't let it burn too bright. We don't want to make this tower a beacon now do we?"

"No, sir," she managed, and that got a smile from them.

"I suppose it'd be nice to get a name from you too," Lancel suggested, peeling back his frosted hood. "It seems so rude to be calling you 'girl' all the time. Any would do, really, even if you just made one up."

They both looked at her expectantly. She mightn't want to unveil the truth of who she was but giving her name should be fine. "Saska," she told them. "I should have told you earlier, I'm sorry."

"We've been sworn not to ask, Saska." Lancel smiled and then removed his cloak, setting it to dry near the fire. Beneath he wore traveller garb of dark leathers and wool, wreathed around his willowy figure. "And don't worry, we're sworn not to tell either."

They ate hunks of bread and cheese that night, and the darkness swelled into a deep uninviting thing. Saska found herself a pleasant enough nook among the tumbled stones, watching the shadows dance and twist on the walls, listening to the wind as it whistled its haunting tune. It made a ghostly ghoulish sound when it blew down through the tower, and crept through the gaps left in the broken oak door, and the fire made shapes to match it. They stretched and warped and reached toward her as she drifted off to sleep, and in her dreams they changed again, growing and looming larger, cackling louder, bearing in.

Then all of a sudden she was in a woodland, thick and tangled and close. She saw a figure emerging through the branches ahead, a great shadowy shape, faceless and formless but for the vague structure of a man. The shadow pressed forward and she pressed back, tripping on a root, falling into the filth. And when she looked up the shroud was upon her, and its face was coming into view, clearing and changing from one man to the next. Modrik then Quintan then Borgin and Griffin, and Cedrik too, and others who'd looked and leered at her over the years. She scrambled back but the shadow kept coming, and a cackling laughter came with it, the eerie overlapping sound of a dozen different voices. "Stay away," she warned. "Do not come any closer," but the laughing only grew louder, and the thing only grew bigger. "I warn you, stay back. Stay back or I will kill you."

The shape and shadow engulfed her vision, and suddenly the trees were gone, and the forest was no more, and she stood in a chamber and a bedroom and a tent all at once. They changed as quick as the faces, the voices. Modrik. Quintan. Griffin. All closed in, and still she backed away, until suddenly she felt something cold and hard and deadly between her fingers. She raised the knife, a gleaming misting blade, and a great wash of vigour and might came upon her. "You'll not touch me again!" she roared, slashing at the shadow, which writhed and whirled and screeched. "Never again! Never!"

She fought the shade away, pointing her blade forward in triumph as it fled back into the shadows. Yet it didn't go away, not completely. It lingered there instead, softly pulsing at the edge of her sight, before reforming into something deeper, something darker and more ancient. "What are you?" she called out, her voice echoing now in a great chamber. "Who are you!" The shadow gave no answer, as it took form into a cloaked figure. A primal terror moved through her, until something else fortified her spirit. The knife in her hand was no longer a knife, she saw, but a great glowing blade, so bright she could barely look upon it. She held it forward to the horror ahead. "Go back!" she warned. "Do not come any closer! Go back to the shadows! You are not welcome here!"

The cloaked shadow made no move. It made no sound. It just stood and watched and waited...waited, until suddenly bursting into a great spirit of shadow and flame. The light was blinding, tearing at her eyes, and all around her the world turned ablaze. She turned left and there were hills and forests and towns burning. And right there were cities and forts and castles on fire. Above her dragons surged and screeched, a dozen of them, a hundred. Thousands of screaming voices filled the air. Men and women ran about her ablaze. Horses galloped, trailing licking red flames. And still that creature of fire and shadow watched. It watched...and it waited...

She woke from the nightmare in a cold sweat, a heavy racing in her chest. The fire had burned down to a gentle glow of embers and she heard a light snoring nearby. She peered through the gloom and saw Barnibus lying across from her, wrapped in his cloak. There was an ache in her back from the stones she'd been lying against. Rubbing her muscles she stood and stretched, then began working up the spiral staircase to the belfry. She found Lancel up there on watch, sitting up against the wall, though at a glance it looked like he'd fallen asleep. "Lancel," she whispered, but that didn't wake him. She crept forward and went to one of the large stone windows looking out over the moors. A sense of dread still burned inside her.

"It was just a dream," she whispered to herself, needing to hear her own voice. All else was deathly silent, the wind gone, the air still. "Just a dream, that's all."

She looked over the moors, to the shapes and shadows out there. The skies were thick and heavy, a sleety rain still falling, and she could hardly see much without godsteel. Only the forms of trees and old tumbledown buildings, and...

She stopped and squinted, staring. There was something out there, something moving. A large shadow, as the creature in her dreams, gently shambling over the hills. She dropped down so she was just peeking over the lip of the window, as the shadow passed by. But as she looked out it stopped and stared at her, looking right toward the tower. She ducked out of sight, her feet scraping on the stone, a thick heavy throb punching hard at her chest. For a few long heartbeats she dare not look up. A dozen passed, then two, before she drew the nerve to guide her eyes back over the sill.

And when she did, the shadow was gone.

43

Jonik

Jonik marvelled at the great orb built at the heart of the harbour.

"It's made of cedar wood from the foothills of the Scales," Emeric told him, as they stood side-by-side at the prow of the ship, "but gilded in a light plating of gold. The panelling is dented to give an undulating effect, in mimic of the sun." He smiled broadly, taking a bracing breath of air. "I've always thought the structure and metalwork to be quite magnificent. Unlike anything you get in the north."

Solas was known as the 'City of the Sun' and this gigantic orb was its most famous monument, a great guiding light for all ships to follow as they cut a course down the Lumaran coast. Further to the east, the capital city of Lumara, Lumos, had a similar orb depicting the moon, and elsewhere stars and other celestial bodies were favoured and worshiped down here.

"Has it ever broken free of its platform, Lord Manfrey?" called Devin as he pulled down the foresail with Braxton. He gestured toward the orb, known in the common tongue as the Sun of Solas, which was built upon a thin stone platform that looked precariously lithe for the size of the spherical monument atop it. "One good swipe with your sword and it'd come tumbling down upon the ships in port, wouldn't it?"

"Fear not, young Devin," Manfrey told him, "the platform isn't so frail and flimsy as it looks. Nor is the Sun of Solas so weighty as it seems. It may be large, but it's hollow inside and not heavy enough to do serious damage. Just appreciate its beauty, if you will. There are few structures quite so magnificent, not in all the world."

"I can think of a few," grunted Brown Mouth Braxton in return, as he pulled at the lines. "The statues at Tukor's Pass for one. I'd say they're more spectacular than this here orb, Lord Manfrey, and by quite some distance too."

Jonik thought the same. This shimmering sphere was quite beguiling but Jonik had never seen anything to quite match the grandeur and sheer magnitude of the twin monoliths that marked the Tukor-Vandar border. They were some three hundred metres tall, built by Ilith of solid stone and etched in staggering detail in the likeness of the gods the two kingdoms were named for. They faced in opposite directions too, standing some two hundred yards apart. Looking south was Tukor, marking the entrance into his kingdom, bearing in one hand his hammer and the other his blade, with a broad kite-shaped shield on his back. Looking north was Vandar, with a single great broadsword plunged into the earth at his feet, and a huge rippling cloak that trailed the earth behind him. Across the centuries, Fireborn riders had attempted to destroy the monuments a hundred times before, but could do little more than blacken the stone with dragonfire. And still they stood, ever restored and resplendent, standing vigil upon the north.

"Those statues are one of a kind, it's true," Manfrey conceded. "I suppose you've seen the statue of Drulgar at Dragonfall too? A ruggedly wondrous thing."

"Not had the fortune, no," said Braxton. "There are a great many wonders in this world I long to see. I suppose I can tick this one off the list now."

The Sun of Solas grew brighter and more blinding as Invincible Iris cut her path into the harbour, ending the second week of their journey from the Golden Isles that had, after the dragon sighting some eight days past, gone without incident. There had been a couple of concerning moments when they saw red-sailed

Agarathi galleons off the coast, but had been swift and agile enough to outrun them and avoid any altercation. Beyond that, the weather had behaved, the winds had been right, and no more colossal creatures had seen fit to unsettle them.

The crew continued to pull down the sails as the ship edged over the calm, gentle waters. Within the harbour a great bustle of activity was taking place, as ships came into dock, and others jostled their way out into deeper waters. Many of the larger vessels were anchored some way out, though others were being rowed in as the men took to the oars. A couple of the smaller cogs and caravels were being warped in, men pulling on fixed ropes and drawing the ships right alongside the wharfs for easy disembarkation. A couple of others were being towed by little tugs, and by the manner of it all there seemed to be a schedule of sorts being observed.

"We'd best drop anchor here for the moment, Captain," Emeric called out. "While we await further orders."

They did just that, awaiting their turn, and not long after a skiff came rowing out to greet them under the blazing early afternoon sun. Inside the little rowboat sat a glum-faced dockworker on the oars and a rather more official looking man bearing a square of parchment clipped to a board. He held a writing instrument of some kind between his fingers, his skin some shades darker than those they'd met in the Golden Isles. "Happy afternoon," he said, speaking in a rich exotic voice common among the native Lumarans. "I hope your journey here to the City of the Sun has not been arduous." He looked up with a perfunctory smile. "What is your purpose here, please?"

"I own an estate to the northeast, a little further up the coast," Emeric said. "I expect you will know of me. Emeric Manfrey. I have lived in these parts for many years, and passed through this harbour too many times to count."

The man dipped his head. "You are known to me, Master Manfrey," he confirmed. "Is this the sum of your crew?"

The rest of the men were gathered on the main deck now, but for Captain Turner who, as ever, was clinging like a lover to the wheel. "Yes," he said. "We're a rather paltry number for a vessel of this size. I suspect you're wondering why?"

"You have been reading my mind," the official said, getting the phrase a little wrong.

Emeric smiled down from the gunwale. "We happened upon a baneful storm in the Tidelands," he began. "My own charter ship went down to Daarl's Domain, but by some fine fortune, I came into the acquaintance of Captain Turner there at the wheel." Turner raised a hand and waved. "This is his ship," Emeric said. "It too was caught in the same storm that plagued me, and he lost two thirds of his crew to the waves and winds, and something a great deal more foul. These here men are those who survived. They have kindly provided me passage here, along with some dozen horses I purchased, and will be helping me bring them to my estates."

"I see." The official wrote a couple of quick notes. "Then you will need some help in getting the ship docked. I shall have a pair of tugs brought out to row you closer to shore, at which point men will assemble to warp you. Does that sound satisfactory?"

"Most satisfactory, thank you."

"Good. We have a busy schedule as you can see. Many ships coming to Solas at this time. The wait may take a while..." The man stopped and smiled, looking up at Emeric, who seemed to know how things worked here, as he reached into his pocket and tossed the man a generous measure of coin. "Thank you, Master Manfrey," the official went on, after checking the contents of the pouch. "You will be next in line for mooring."

The man gave an order in Lumaran for the oarsman to leave and off went the skiff, cutting its way back toward the jetties. A minute or so later, the tugs came out; small but sturdy little boats with lines and ropes and strong men at the oars. Braxton and Devin saw to tying the ropes as the tugs began guiding them into the wharf.

"Expensive business docking here," Jack o' the Marsh jested as they slid upon the sparkly waters. "How much did you give him?"

"Enough to get to the front of the queue," Emeric said, "and pay for the dockworkers' time. Don't worry, this one's on me. I'm eager to return home, truth be told, and don't want to languish in a line of ships for half a day."

That seemed fair, and soon enough Invincible Iris was being brought into the wharf and fastened at the mooring posts. A full score of men saw to warping her in, labouring hard and bare-chested under the beating sun, sweat glimmering on their dark skin as they pulled at the ropes. Once the ship was secure the gangplanks were set and the horses led off, several looking a bit shaky after several long stuffy weeks at sea.

"You OK?" Jonik asked Shade as he walked alongside the noble black steed. The thoroughbred had been a little frosty over the last week, refusing to be brushed and groomed and otherwise ignoring Jonik's attempts to apologise for the length of the journey. "Oh don't be grumpy," he said, as Shade lifted his chin and refused to acknowledge him. "We got here as quickly as we could. But that's it. Enough boats. I promise."

Shade offered a snort in reply to that, then trotted off to join the other horses on the docks.

"He knows you're lying," Jack o' the Marsh put in. "Unless you've decided we're all staying on solid ground from now on..." He raised his reddish brows. "So, have you?"

"I don't know, Jack. I told you already. We're seeing Emeric safely home and then...well, we'll see."

"Righto." Jack slapped a meaty hand on his back and stepped on, joining the rest as they worked to corral the horses. A little way off, Emeric was now in discussion with a separate official wearing a floppy tunic of light yellow linen, embroidered on the chest with a circular golden disc and thin metal rays shining off it. It was a heraldic pattern for Solas, Jonik imagined. He stood by a moment, watching as the two men progressed through a strained discussion. Emeric was doing a lot of nodding and frowning and the small slender official was doing a lot of talking and gesticulating. Then it ended with a cordial shoulder-clasp, as Emeric reached with his right hand and took the man's left shoulder, and his companion did the same. It was a common gesture of greeting and parting here in Lumara. Then Emeric stepped over.

"Trouble?" Jonik asked, watching as the official moved away to deal with another issue further down the docks. "Was he the harbourmaster?"

"A version of it, though that's not what they're called here," said Emeric with a disquieted etch to his eyes. "His name's Upo Utappa, a good man and one I've known a long while. Nothing much happens in these docks that he doesn't know about, nor the city proper." He turned his eyes inland, to where the city walls of Solas loomed, fluttering with yellow banners bearing that same sun-disk sigil as Upo had worn. "He says there's been unrest in the city ever since King Dulian was murdered. It rather confirms what Dax'or Zin told me in Lizard's Laze. The jingoists are crawling from the woodwork and many more than I first supposed. King Tavash's warmongering rhetoric gives them confidence, Upo says. He advises we wait for nightfall before passing through, lest we find ourselves set upon by a mob."

"It's become that bad? Northmen getting openly attacked in the street?"

"There have been incidents of that nature, yes. Only yesterday a pair of Rasal merchants were beaten to death a few streets within the walls. The local city guards are trying to restore order, but it's a great deal worse than I feared. There have been multiple clashes between the loyalists of Empress Valura's pacifistic regime and the empire's militarist factions, and this is just the start." He looked to the others concernedly, standing nearby with the horses. "This is no great time to visit for a northerner, my friend. You might want to consider getting right back on Iris and leaving."

"I can't. Shade would kill me." Jonik managed an unlikely smile. "Is there no way we can bypass the city?"

"We could rent a smaller boat and sail a little down the coast," Emeric said, thinking. "There are some points along the Sunshine Bay where we might disembark, not large harbours like this one, but smaller towns with jetties large enough to dock a galley. Though we'd need one big enough to ferry the mounts, and that mightn't be so easy at short notice."

"Sell them," suggested Jonik. "I always felt you only ever bought them to curry favour with us in the first place, and secure passage. So sell them. Not all, no...we can keep a few to ride, and

Shade of course, but the rest you could part with." He looked around. "I'm sure there would be willing buyers here."

"It's possible Upo could track one down for me, yes." Emeric scratched his groomed black beard. "But we'd still need eight, lest we ride double. And I don't imagine the men will like that."

Jonik could imagine the pairings. Soft Sid and Grim Pete on one. Turner and Braxton on another. Jack and Devin riding a third. *Would that leave me riding with Emeric?* He didn't imagine Shade could bear them both when carrying godsteel, and the horse would be sure to disown him if he asked. It didn't seem feasible, in truth, and what of the other godsteel blades they'd scavenged from Lady Shark's men? Were they to just be left on the ship, unprotected? He shook his head, not wanting to think about that now. *You're not a merchant, Jonik,* he told himself. *Those blades are irrelevant to you. Forget about them.*

"We'll need a mount each," he decided. "Though maybe Grim could ride with someone, small as he is, so we could probably get it down to seven. Do you think we could find a boat that could take us?"

"I'd have to ask Upo. But so long as it's only a few miles, it shouldn't be a problem."

"And how far did you say it was to your estate?"

"A day's ride northeast, though if there's trouble on the road it'll slow us."

"So we'll not be there today?"

Emeric shook his head. "No. If we hire a boat and sail down the coast, we'd be best camping out somewhere quiet and secluded, and riding from dawn. We'd be there for afternoon if so. The alternative..." He looked at the others. "Well I doubt they'd like it. It'd mean passing through the city in secret after dark and then riding overnight, and that brings dangers too for the horses, given the terrain. Each comes with risk, neither with much reward."

"Then let's go with the least awful option," Jonik suggested.

Emeric nodded. "I'll see if Upo can help."

As the exiled lord saw to that, Jonik saw to the others, telling them of the plan. "Seems we've come south at the wrong time, lord," Turner then said, looking over at the high pale walls. The city beyond was all yellow and gold and bronze, peppered with round-topped gleaming towers. "I've had a few funny looks already, so I have. Is there need to hire this boat? Can't we be taking Iris down the coast and laying anchor off shore?"

"You tell me, Captain. Would you be happy leaving her in some unprotected bay at the mercy of thieves and bandits?"

"Hmmm, I suppose not." He tugged at a few strands of his salty brown beard, which had grown increasingly wild over the last month. "It's the same down in Lumos, is it? This riotin'? And further east?"

"Emeric didn't say. But I would imagine so, yes. It seems all the south is on the brink of civil war." Some of the men were looking a bit cowed by that thought. Grim Pete's eyes were wide and staring and more hollow than normal, Devin's usual confidence had been subdued, and Brown Mouth was rubbing nervously at his jutting jaw. "You think it's too dangerous, being here?" Jonik had to ask them. "I'm happy to release you from my service, if you'd prefer to sail back to the Tidelands. I can continue with Emeric on my own..."

"Not a chance," said Jack without hesitation, his fiery hair catching the sun. "We're not cowards, are we Gill?"

"Dumb question, Jack. Course we're not. The only craven among us is Grim, and that's fine...every crew needs a mascot, after all."

"I'm no coward," Grim protested. "I'm just smart. Only stupid people fear nothing."

"And smart people fear everything, I suppose?" Turner gave out a rough laugh. "Then you must be a genius, Grim, and wasted out here at sea."

Jonik raised a hand. "Emeric is seeing to selling the horses we don't need, and booking passage down the coast. If there's anyone who'd rather not come, they can stay right here on Iris." He rather hoped a few might agree to that. There was no sense in all of them going, and it'd be useful to have someone guarding the ship. "Grim, perhaps you should stay?" he offered, giving the cadaverous man a way out. "I'd prefer to have someone watching the ship. Sid can stay with you. Light the lanterns at night and people will know the ship is occupied. Can you do that?"

Grim Pete nodded dutifully. "If that's what you wish, milord." Then that quiver of fear moved through him, as he looked toward the city. "It's contained, is it? The rioting? It won't spill out onto the docks?"

"The docks are well protected," Jonik said. "You'll be fine until we return."

"And when will that be?" asked Braxton. "We're to ride these horses to Lord Manfrey's estate and then come right back here?" He looked around. "Excusing the question, my lord, but you've not told us much about what you wish to do after."

"And for that I apologise, Brown. I had hoped to see how things were here before coming to any decision. We'll escort Emeric home first, as agreed, then consider our next move."

He could see their doubts, but no one said anything to that. *One step at a time,* he told himself. He rather hoped that Emeric would remain in their company, but the exile wasn't likely to come to a decision himself until he returned home. *And thus my decision will follow his,* he thought, as Emeric Manfrey marched back toward them, dressed in a studded green brigandine over his white cotton shirt. "Have you explained to them our plan?" he asked Jonik, who nodded. "Good. Upo says there's a trade cog docked down the harbour that will give us passage east. Its crew have been summoned to take the oars, and will row us right up to shore in a cove of our choosing. It'll allow us to land on the beach and not worry ourselves with a jetty. The horses can disembark down the gangplanks."

It was fair news, and would make things a great deal easier. "Sid and Grim are going to stay on the ship," Jonik told him, "so we'll need only five mounts and Shade. The rest can be sold. Did you find a buyer?"

"Upo is working on it. He asked to give him an hour, then we can be on our way."

That hour went quickly, as Emeric moved off once more, Grim and Sid returned to the ship, and the rest walked toward the heart of the harbour to take a closer look at the Sun of Solas.

"Much bigger up close, isn't it," said Devin, as they stood within the huge warped shadow beneath it, cast half way across the docks. "Must be some fifty yards high."

"And wide. They like their orbs here, don't they," said Jack. There were many of them, all over. The tops of the towers were perfectly spherical and half the merlons atop the ramparts were spheres too. So were many of the crests and banners and flags, and half the Lumarans in the harbour had shaved heads and faces, with gold buttons on their clothes and necklaces of gilded pearls around their necks. "They worship the natural world here," Jack went on. "Animals. Plants. Celestial bodies." He gestured to the huge orb above them. "Sola was Master of the Sun, brother to Lumo, Mistress of the Moon. Both were followers of the goddess Lumara during the War Eternal, the balance to her two sides. Lumo was peaceful. Sola was vengeful. It seems nothing much has changed. Even after thousands of years they still fight for the soul of who she was."

"But Lumo was the senior," said Jonik. "When the Five Followers came together after the gods fell, it was she who joined Varin and Thala and Ilith and Eldur, not Sola."

"True," nodded Jack o' the Marsh. "It's why Lumos is the capital city here, and named after Lumo. And why most have traditionally seen the southern nations as peace-loving. Lumara was thought to be the benevolent goddess, the one who tried to prise Agarath and Vandar apart, but not all conform to that belief. It's where the Patriots of Lumara derive their strength and support. They started here in Solas, Emeric told me, under the patronage of the former City Master, Helio Zon. People think they rose up in opposition to the formation of the Empire after the war two decades ago, but that isn't true. They have been around for over a hundred years, spreading their tendrils through the south, and people say they were instructive in uniting the southern nations to join Agarath in war the last time."

"And that's their plan now?" Devin asked, eagerly soaking up Jack's knowledge. "To do the same again?"

"Yes, but it's a little more difficult this time. Before the War of the Continents the southern nations were separate...allied yes, but not united in the same way they are now. Lumara was always the most powerful, and as soon as they joined Agarath to fight the north, Pisek and Aramatia and Solapia all followed, one after another." Jack turned his eyes over the harbour, filled with sailors and merchants and dockhands from all those nations. "The war was so bloody that the nations south of the Scales lost all their taste for battle. Their rulers came together to contemplate and consider all that had happened, and decided to forge themselves into a united empire under the rule of Queen Falua of Lumara. Thus she was installed as the first Empress of the Lumaran Empire, and ever since there's been a steady peace. Now her daughter Valura rules, though she is young and untested and will look a lamb to a lion with the Patriots rising up. They will be growling from here to Aramatia and stirring the people into war, inciting revolution. Soon enough, Empress Valura and the other national rulers may have no choice but to submit."

"Or else she'll be overthrown," put in Braxton, who stood nearby with Captain Turner, gazing upon the colossal orb. Braxton took a step toward them. "But the longer they squabble about all that down here, the better it'll be for our brothers up north. No way the Agarathi can defeat the northern kingdoms alone...no way. They'll need allies, they will, and so long as they're bickering down here, the north'll have time to unite, and put this sorry business between Tukor and Rasalan behind them."

Jack was smiling and nodding. The men didn't tend to go deep into war and politics, but the young Marshlander seemed to rather enjoy it. "I agree entirely, Brax," he said. "But either way, another Renewal's coming, and I don't think there's much stopping that now. People will be claiming it's the last one, as they always do. Who knows, maybe they'll be right this time?"

The Last Renewal, Jonik thought. The Nightblade had called him a champion. *You're to be a champion in this Last Renewal,* it had whispered. But was it right? How much did it know? Was it Vandar's voice truly whispering to him, or just a fragment of the Fallen God? A darker piece, a more...malevolent piece. Gerrin had warned him not to fall to the Nightblade's lure, but he had, he knew that now. *We are one,* he thought, holding the hilt. *Only death can part us now...*

"Seems Manfrey's concluded his business," came the voice of Gill Turner, pulling Jonik from his thoughts. He saw Jack looking at him with that curious slant to his eyes, and quickly drew his hand from the handle. "I'd say we'd best leave sharpish, lads. Never been looked at so filthy in all my life." Turner pointed out onto the water. "And those red sails in the harbour trouble me too. There be Agarathi men about."

They all looked out at the grand galleon docked off shore. The sails were furled, deep red and black. Agarathi for certain "Agents meeting with the City Master?" Jack suggested.

"Aye," nodded Turner. "And best if we don't run into 'em. We have enough to worry about as it is."

They all agreed on that point. A run in with the Agarathi was the last thing they needed, and now they had the Patriots to deal with too, and the mob, and that wasn't to mention the Shadow Order and sundry cutthroats on their tail. Jonik's lack of discretion had stirred rather more trouble than he'd anticipated, though the happenings down here were hardly of his doing. He led the others back along the harbour front, beyond the waterside city walls, to find Emeric once more in conference with Upo Utappa. The port master had come through for them, it seemed, as several of the horses were being led away. Shade looked none too happy about that, though he wasn't going to be happy about the next thing either.

Jonik sidled up to him, and laid a conciliatory hand on his muscular black flank. "I suppose you know we're going back on the water, then?" The horse side-eyed him, then peevishly flicked his mane. Jonik smiled. "It's only a few miles up the coast. Don't be such a baby."

"Foal," said Jack, taking the bridle of another horse. "A baby horse is a foal." He gave Shade a smile. "Don't be such a foal, Shade."

Shade snorted his disdain for that comment, just as a distant blur of noise began spreading through the city. Jonik turned to Emeric, who turned to Upo, whose round brown eyes were looking toward the city walls. "Another riot," the small Lumaran official said. "You had better be on your way, Emeric."

The two once more performed the shoulder-clasp gesture of parting. "Thank you, my friend. I will see you again soon, I hope."

They wasted no time in leaving after that, hurrying the horses down the waterfront and onto the cog, as the bare-chested oarsmen pulled them out into the harbour, stroke after powerful stroke. Clutching the hilt of the Nightblade, Jonik could hear the frenzy unfolding in the city. It sounded like there were hundreds of them, thousands, clashing and fighting and brawling. He'd told Grim Pete the violence would be contained beyond the waterside walls, but hearing that, he wasn't so sure. And hearing it, Emeric was looking more troubled than ever.

Jonik didn't need to ask why. He was a well known Bladeborn exile with a famous name and a large estate just a day's ride away, *A target for the militarists,* Jonik knew. *The very sort of man they want to purge.*

44

Godrin

The wise old king of Rasalan sat quiet at the desk in his solar, tucked far back into the rear of the Palace of Thalan. His wizened fingers held a pipe to hand, a final indulgence, and all about him the smoke swirled and wafted, warm and pungent and tinged with sweet spice.

His desk was a journey, laden with chapters of his life. *A life well led,* he hoped, though even now his memory was fading with the heaping of years on years. It had been an incremental slide, his mind sometimes sharp, sometimes dull, a slow dwindle many years in the making that had begun to quicken of late. *But not today,* he thought, and what a blessing that was. He smiled, old and nostalgic, as he looked over the letters, the drawings, the maps and notes and scrolls of parchment spread out before him. They told the story of his years, in a fashion, fetched from a chest he kept stored beneath his desk, some etched by his own hand, others by his children or grandchildren or others whom he'd cherished and loved.

"Have I lived well?" he wondered out loud, though there was no one to hear him. "Have I done enough?"

He'd done his part, that was all he could say, but the rest was out of his hands now. His fingers crept through the papers, pulling one out that he valued most of all. It was a translation from the Book of Thala, written by the goddess herself thousands of years ago. A passage that had remained untranslated for millennia, before Godrin had become king, working day and night for years to unearth and uncover her secrets.

What he'd found within had startled him; a message from Thala herself, meant for his eyes alone. A message that was part prophesy, part instruction, and part riddle. A message that had been broken down, split among a select few, becoming pieces of a puzzle that, one day soon, would come to form a whole.

"Good luck, Ranulf," he whispered now, thinking of one of those few. "I do hope you're playing your role." The words brought a short chuckle from his lips. He'd coded a message for the unassuming adventurer just as Queen Thala had him, giving him a piece of the most prized puzzle of all. "Use it wisely, old friend, because my part in this is done." He allowed himself a smile. "I will join Thala now in the Halls of Rasalan, and take my seat to observe."

He reached forward, then, his aching old fingers taking up a candle, set in a holder on his desk. He lifted the sheet in his hand to the flame, which took its edge, burning through the parchment, devouring the words that, now, would remain with Ranulf alone. He watched as the paper blackened and curled, and even as he did so, he could hear the footsteps outside. Laying down the charred paper, he looked up. The door opened.

"Father." His son walked in, dressed in his whale-hide armour, black and grey and pitted like stone. Dark circles hung under his eyes, lank strands of greying hair slicked across the sides of his head. "Where is Sir Ralston?"

"Gone," croaked the fading voice of the king.

Prince Hadrin stared at him, a shadow upon his ageing face. He was past fifty now, though looked older, grim and gaunt. "Gone?" He looked around, as though it was a trick. "He is the King's Wall. Where is he?"

"He is gone, my son. Do not worry. He will not stop you."

Hadrin stared at him. Godrin could hear others outside the door, though none entered. He knew that Sir Munroe, the

Commander of his King's Guard, would be there. *He has turned, and been bought,* he thought. *As has my son.* "You know, then?" Hadrin asked, looking through his sallow eyes. "You have seen it?"

"I have seen the darkness." Godrin smiled from his little cushioned seat, too frail to stand. "I would get up, but I have not the legs for it." He looked at his son without hate. "You will do it yourself?"

"I must."

Godrin continued to watch him. "I have denied you too long," he said. "Do not curse yourself for this, Hadrin. You will have all you ever wanted. You will have all you deserve."

A doubt hung heavy upon Hadrin's dour face. He stood a little beyond the door, a mist of pipe smoke floating about him in the dim-lit rustic room. "You have forced me into this, Father. I have long hated you for what you did."

Godrin dipped his eyes to the desk of rich walnut, scattered with his papers and letters and maps. "You loved her, I know, but she could never have been yours. Her union with Amron Daecar was beyond my control, Hadrin."

"You were weak." The prince drew his black-steel dagger, its handle of pure white whalebone. "You made no stand for me, for your own son. You let the Vandarians take her. She was meant for me, Father. I loved her, and you let her go."

"I had no choice..."

"Choice." Hadrin made a hissing sound. "Your choices have led us to war and ruin, but I will not stand for it any longer. You hoard your throne, as you hoard the Eye, even as your sight fails you. I cannot let it go on. I must have the Eye, Father. Only I can use it..."

"You'll never master it, Hadrin. You have never been patient, nor wise..."

"You speak to me in this way!" Hadrin stamped two paces across the room, the smoke swirling around him. He pointed the knife. "You, who sits and festers here, who gets laughed at by his own court! I will master the Eye of Rasalan. It will show me what must be done."

"You won't," Godrin whispered. "I think you know that really."

He inched back in his chair, waiting, as his son came forward. The black knife came to his neck, pressing. "I have to do this," Hadrin said. There was a shudder to his voice, a doubt. Godrin looked up into his welling hateful eyes. "I have to, Father. I must be king. I must..."

Godrin reached up and set his wrinkled fingers over his son's hand. "I know. I know, son." He urged him forward, feeling the cold kiss of the knife on his neck. Its edge cut easily through his skin. The blood began to trickle, warm down his throat. "It takes but one firm swipe, my boy," he said, as Hadrin hesitated. "Be strong." He pressed at his hand. "Be strong. It's OK."

Hadrin's hand was shaking now, and in his eyes the king could see it all, the jealousy and envy and hate, the misery and malice, the jibes and jests of a thousand lords and ladies and knights who'd mocked him through the years. Hadrin had never been a wise man. He was spiteful and petty, resentful and weak, yet Godrin loved him all the same. So he looked up into his weeping eyes and smiled, and gently urged his son on as he cut the black blade through his neck. The blood flowed stronger, warmer, flooding down his tunic, and all the while he held that smile, and held his son's hand in his.

I love you, my boy, was his final thought.

And then the world went dark.

45

Ranulf

They rode out from the city of Sutrek upon the great golden camels common to these lands. Each had a dual hump between which a quilted leather saddle had been set, and to a man of middling height like Ranulf Shackton, the drop to the ground looked alarmingly long.

"You looked nervous, Ranulf," laughed Vincent Rose, who was dressed in a flowing golden kaftan that rather matched his giant humpy steed. "One would think you've never ridden a Piseki camel before."

"Truth be told I haven't," Ranulf admitted, as the camel paced freely along the sand on its padded two-toed feet. "I have always favoured desert horses and ponies whenever travelling south of the Scales. And even then I've never been much of an equestrian. I far prefer to keep my feet on the ground, or on the deck of a ship."

"A great shame. You're rather well built for riding, I would say. They have races all over these parts, camels and horses both, and many of the best jockeys are of a similar build to you."

"Small and light," Ranulf said. "Yes, thank you Vincent. I am no Amron Daecar, I know."

"Oh, I don't know. I suspect his lame leg and arm will wither away, now that they're of no use to him." He gave a cruel laugh. "Which was it, again? The right leg and left arm? He will look awfully strange, once those limbs begin to atrophy. He'll be all lopsided and deformed."

"An inelegant joke, Vincent," Ranulf scolded. "You're better than that."

"I'm glad you think so. But doesn't it just go to show how little you truly know me?"

There was more truth in that than Ranulf cared to admit. He didn't imagine that anyone had ever truly known Vincent Rose, with all these layers he wrapped around him.

"They're so much bigger than I thought," called out Leshie, looking more diminutive than usual between those two mountainous humps. "I feel like I'm twelve feet off the ground."

"You are," said Ranulf. "The south is full of superfauna, Leshie. Most camels aren't this large, but of course we can trust Vincent to hire the very best of the best."

"I'm glad you appreciate my continued generosity, Ranulf."

They were riding at the front of the column, with some two dozen others trailing behind, split between soldiers and servers and satisfiers of Vincent Rose's particular needs. Leshie performed a dual purpose, guarding Vincent by day and tending him between the sheets by night, though of course the Lumaran twins, Nephys and Tephys, were also there for that. Most were dressed in garb suitable for the climes, and Ranulf was no exception. His body was covered in a cream cotton kaftan, fastened at his narrow waist with a burgundy sash. He wore a light-weaved scarf around his neck, to be drawn up over his mouth and face should the winds pick up. The others were similarly accoutred, some wearing headcloths, others supple leather armour and silk. And then there was Leshie, who'd foregone all that and continued to dress in the lobstered red leather armour Rose had given her, with her gleaming godsteel dagger and sheath bouncing along at her hip.

"You must be hot in that, Leshie," Ranulf called over to her. "Does it not grow unbearable under this sun?"

"I'm OK," she said chirpily. "So long as we're moving and there's a bit of wind, I'm fine."

"A scarf at least," Ranulf offered. "To help block the sun." Leshie was very fair-skinned, with that strawberry blonde hair and those patches of freckles on her nose and cheeks. "You don't want to burn."

"Oh stop fussing over her, Ranulf," complained Vincent. "You sound like some overbearing father. She knows what she's doing."

"I have a scarf in my saddlebag," Leshie kindly assured him. "I'll get it out the next time we stop."

"We won't be stopping until we reach Pal Palek's estate," Vincent told them. "He's only a couple of hours into the desert, not far. I'm rather excited, you know. He's a terribly interesting fellow. Has all sorts of animals within his menagerie, all very well treated of course. He likes to collect things you see. The animals he gathers are typically sick or lame or motherless, and at the mercy of the wilds, so he takes them in and brings them back to health."

"Sounds like a caring man," Leshie offered, as they moved among the wide sloping dunes.

"Oh he is. Very caring." Vincent looked over at Ranulf. "Very caring indeed."

A set of cold fingers gripped at Ranulf's heart at that look in Vincent's eye. The man continued to unnerve him with those odd glances and comments, and they'd come often during their trip from Solapia. It had taken some seven days for them to reach these lands, starting with a five day voyage down the Coast of Plenty, and then continuing with a short two night stay in Sutrek, a city of sun and sand, silk and spice and no end of bustle. There was no place more lively, no place more colourful. A man could find himself lost among the bazaars and markets and winding mud brick streets for weeks and come out having had the greatest time of his life. There was talk that Lumos, and Solas in particular were falling to rioting and unrest but if there was any such trouble in Sutrek, Ranulf hadn't seen it.

But fine as those two days were, he was never far from making for the docks and chartering passage down the coast. He had an urgent design to travel to the city of Aram, some three hundred miles east along the coast, and the trip would be markedly shortened by travelling under sail and oar. *But if I must, I'll hire a horse and take the Capital Road,* he thought. It was paved with wide flat sandstone cobbles in the better sections, and between much of the route between Sutrek and Aram was a dream for travellers, with many little settlements and tented taverns lining the route. *Still, I'd far rather sail.* He'd travelled the full length of the Capital Road once from Eagle's Perch all the way to Solas and beyond, and what an adventure that had been, but times were different then, and northerners a great deal safer. *The road won't be so safe, not anymore,* he knew. And going by ship would take but four or five days, rather than the two to three weeks he'd have to endure on horseback.

He turned to Vincent Rose as they padded along the sand. "How long do you intend to stay with Pal Palek, Vincent?" He'd hinted it would be a short stopover, though what business he was to conduct with the man, he'd refused to say. "One night? Two?"

"Are you eager to part company with us, Ranulf?" Vincent's ample cheeks had caught a tan, bunching now as he smiled.

"You know I am keen to take a trip to Aram, before the whole of the south falls to chaos..."

"I do, though you've not yet told me why."

"Am I obliged to?" Ranulf asked. "You've said nothing of what we're doing out here."

"Oh, have I not? I quite remember telling you I had business with Pal Palek."

"With you that hardly narrows it down. There is not a man alive who has his fingers in so many pies."

Vincent Rose untethered a loud guffaw. "I'll miss the weave of your tongue, old friend. You do complement me so."

Ranulf wasn't certain what he meant. "Are you trying to say I flatter you, or make a good sidekick?"

"Both." He laughed again, picking up the pace a little and drawing a metre or two away.

Ranulf urged his camel on, catching up. "And?" he pressed. "How long are we to stay?"

"Oh I don't know. That rather depends on you, my friend."

"How so?"

Vincent Rose didn't answer, not at first. He let the silence curdle for just enough time to make Ranulf uncomfortable, then said, "All in good time, Ranulf. Now come, let's not dawdle. Pal will be eagerly awaiting us."

They rode on for another hour, as the morning turned to afternoon, and the air grew stuffy and close. The camels were pacing in their idiosyncratic way, their left legs and right legs chopping back and forward in a two-beat languid gait, and the wind blew hot and sandy, gusting and swirling about the dunes. This southern extreme of the Pisek Desert wasn't entirely barren nor entirely made of sand, however. There were some rocky outcroppings here and there, and copses of cacti and acacia among them. Even some flowering plants, Ranulf saw, though those were rare, and for the most part it was brown and yellow and red in a hundred shifting shades.

Eventually, Rose pointed forward with a rattle of bangles and bracelets. "The compound is just over yonder, up over that rise. You can see some of his soldiers there, you see." He gestured a little eastward. "Up there among the rocks. And there." He pointed further west. "Can you not see them?"

Ranulf had to squint, but could just about make out the framing of huts and squat looking towers camouflaged among the outcroppings. "Does Pal have many soldiers, Vincent?" He could see a couple at each watching post, some half dozen of them, and imagined there would be many more beyond his sight.

"Oh yes, he's rather well stocked with fighting men."

Ranulf wasn't liking this. There was something about the whole affair that was beginning to prickle his skin. "Is he militant?"

"Militant?"

"Yes, militant." Ranulf looked out as a large sandstone compound came into view among the dunes and outcroppings, emerging through the shimmering haze of heat. There were towers, walls, dozens of armed men with no particular consistency to their garb or the weapons they bore. Blades, blunts, maces, flails and all sorts were hitched on belts and backs. "These men are members of the Patriots of Lumara," he said. "Why have you brought me here, Vincent?"

"Because you're such wonderful company, Ranulf. Why else?"

Why else? Why else...He had no answer, because Rose had that devious look in his eye again. Something called for him to twist his lumbering camel about and have it make straight for Sutrek, but that option had long gone...nay, it had never existed. He was two hours from civilisation and at Rose's mercy. "If you have something in mind for me here, Vincent, just tell me." He glanced at Leshie, who had a measure of concern in her big blue eyes. "Is this your way of tying up loose ends? For your theft of the book?" Leshie had warned of that, but he'd not heeded it. "We'll not speak of it, you know that. You needn't do anything rash..."

"Oh Ranulf, Ranulf..." Vincent Rose laughed, "you fret like a maiden on the eve of her wedding. I have no plans to tie up loose ends, if that truly concerns you. You imagine I would have you killed? Goodness no. And Leshie as well? I rather think she'd put up a good fight, don't you?"

Leshie's expression said she would, but her tongue unleashed no words to support it. Men were coming forward now from the cluster of thick stone buildings, dressed in black rawhide armour with ugly metal studs. Their camels slowed and bleated, some rumbling loudly as they drew into a yellow stone courtyard within the sandstone walls. Other noises filled the air, all manner of creatures shrieking and growling and bellowing and hissing. Beyond the courtyard stretched large gardens with enclosures of generous size. Colours bloomed all over. He could see all sorts of exotic species lazing about on rocks or by watering holes, or swinging through the branches of the trees cultivated here. A loud bellowing roar indicated the presence of a Piseki lion, a huge desert dwelling cat that liked to dig and sleep beneath the sand at night for warmth. Elsewhere, a pair of sunwolves were being saddled in the stables. They were as big as horses and terrifying when in formation, and used as cavalry during war.

When they dismounted, climbing carefully down from their colossal camels, Ranulf found Leshie staring about with eyes like moons, big and bright. This would be her first exposure to such exotic beasts as these and it appeared Pal Palek's menagerie was as exhaustive as Rose had said. "Those men are Sunriders," the girl whispered, staring at the pair of soldiers saddling the sunwolves. The great golden beasts sat calmly on their haunches as the straps and buckles were fastened, their long pink tongues lolling as they panted to stay cool beneath the blazing sun. "I've heard so many stories about them, from the war. And the Starriders and Moonriders too. They say they bond to them, like the Fireborn do with the dragons. Is that true, Ranulf?"

Ranulf bobbed his head. "It's similar, certainly, if not exactly the same. The bond between Fireborn rider and dragon is an entwining of souls, a process only made possible by the power of the Bondstone. I suppose you've heard it called Agarath's Soul before? It is the magic of that divine soul that connects dragon and man. The Starriders, Sunriders, and Moonriders use no such device or artefact, but have in their veins a magic that calms the beasts, enabling a bond to form. It is akin to how a Bladeborn bonds to godsteel. Only those with the blood of Varin can wield Ilithian Steel, and only Lightborn with the blood of Lumo and Sola can tame the great beasts in the south."

Leshie was still staring across the yard at the great golden wolves. "I've heard it's dangerous to try to bond with them. And the starcats too. But mostly the moonbears. I read that they're as big as mammoths. That they can kill dragons sure as the other way around."

"They have been known to, yes. Moonbears are solitary, rare, highly territorial and extremely aggressive. Most Lightborn who dare trek to Moonbear Mountain to try to tame one never make it back, and only the greatest ever bond to them. The larger the beast, the more perilous the task. It takes a certain character, courageous and stout of heart, to ever attempt such a thing..."

"Pal Palek would be most happy to hear you say so," interrupted Vincent Rose, stepping over in his silk gold kaftan, tied loosely at his thickening waist by a chequered sash of blue and crimson weave. "He is himself a Lightborn of high birth, and has a quite magnificent sunwolf of his own."

Ranulf frowned. He knew many of the Lumosi and Solasi houses in the south, though wasn't familiar with the Paleks. "He's of a Solasi house, I suppose?"

"Because of the fine company he keeps?" Vincent grinned. "It's not quite so black and white as that, Ranulf. You really are funny. Do you suppose that every Lumosi Lightborn is peace loving and every Solasi Lightborn yearns for war? You'll be surprised to hear, then, that Pal Palek is indeed descended of Lumo. I'm sorry to shatter your neat interpretation of the world, old friend, but it would seem your beliefs are quite dated."

"This is not about belief, but knowledge. It is well known that those descended of Sola are more inclined to war than those descended of Lumo. Not always, of course, but commonly, yes."

Vincent Rose let out a laugh. "You live in the past, Ranulf. It hardly matters these days which Lightborn line you derive from. I've met countless Lumosi Lightborn who would see all the north burned if they could, and just as many Solasi Lightborn who'd be quite happy to extend the hand of friendship and see war end once and for all. If the Lumosi were as peaceful as you claim, then Lumara would never go to war, nor drag Pisek and Aramatia and Solapia in with them. But they do. They've been active in almost every Renewal and have fallen to civil conflict more times than I can count. To say that the Lumosi Lightborn are somehow peaceable is, and always has been, utter nonsense..."

A clapping echoed across the courtyard, drawing their eyes toward the wide stone entrance to the sandstone fortification. A man of middle years and middle height stood there, enrobed in a coiling pattern of red, brown, and golden silks, a dull smile painted across his dusky face. He had above his lips a thin black moustache, and from the very bottom of his chin fell a twin beard, striking down like a fork into a pair of sharp, spiralling points. "Well said, Vincent," Pal Palek called out in a rich Piseki accent. "It is rare to find a northern man of such wisdom. Come, join me inside where the air is cool, yes. I know you do not take well to the heat. My people will see your host housed."

As the rest of the party were taken off, Vincent, Ranulf, and Leshie followed the man into his fortress, passing through the entrance and into a high-ceilinged hall. To the left and right, staircases gave access to the upper and lower levels, and across the hall sunlight streamed through a door that led to an inner courtyard and garden. At the heart of the hall a sculpture of Lumara towered, showing the goddess in swirling robes upon a great rearing bear, holding aloft a gleaming staff with one half painted gold, and the other silver.

"A common depiction of Lumara," Ranulf whispered to Leshie, as a host of scale-mail soldiers followed them in, shutting the doors. "The staff represents her two sides. The moon and the sun, for her followers Lumo and Sola..."

"This one likes to talk." Pal Palek turned sharply, cutting him off. There was a coldness to that look on his face that brought a chill to Ranulf's skin. "I take it you are Ranulf Shackton, the scholar and explorer, yes?"

Ranulf tried to smile, dipping his head to a bow. "The very one, sir."

The Lumosi Lightborn turned his eyes upon him, up and down. Then his eyes went to Leshie, to the blade at her hip. "This one is Bladeborn. One of your guards, Vincent?"

"She performs many duties, Pal," the merchant said. "Not all of them to my liking."

Leshie didn't know what to make of that. "Vinny? What do you mean?"

"You know what it means."

Leshie shook her head. "I don't. What are you talking about?"

Pal Palek's eyes moved over to the far door, where a huge sunwolf came loping through from the sun-drenched courtyard outside, its coat a golden-grey and shoulders rippling with streaks and striations of muscle. The beast passed the statue, and approached Pal Palek's side, the top of the man's head hardly reaching to its back. Leshie shifted backward a step as the wolf came in at its master's flank, wrapping her fingers around the hilt of her godsteel dagger. "You do not want to do that," Palek said, reaching to run his fingers through the beast's golden fur. "Argis does not like godsteel. If you pull out that blade he will kill you, yes."

There was a scar slashed across the beast's lower jaw, exposing its vicious teeth. *A wound from the war,* Ranulf imagined. "What is happening here?" he demanded, refusing to move back a step. "What exactly are you trying to get at, Vincent?"

"I wonder, Ranulf," said Rose, as several soldiers began closing in around them. "Perhaps I have been vexed by your continuous lies? Perhaps I have come to believe that you have been hiding something from me. Something rather important."

"I have told you to the contrary a hundred times."

"And not once have I believed you."

"So this is a set up? You have deceived us into coming here, so you can enact some vengeance for my betrayal?" Ranulf glanced at Leshie, standing stiff beside him. "If so leave her out of it. She knows nothing..."

"Then you admit there is something to know?"

The comment had been folly. "That is not what I meant," Ranulf said, trying to backtrack. "You told us just minutes ago that you had no intention of killing us..."

"I don't. How would I get the information you have kept from me if you were dead?"

"Then what? Torture? You can strip the flesh from my bones and I'll say nothing, Vincent, because damn it I've got nothing to say."

"You're lying. I've known it all along."

"He's not," breathed Leshie, her hand gripping hard to the hilt of her blade. The great beast Argis loomed ahead, watching her with its dark amber eyes, ready to strike should she make a move. She'd have no chance against such a foe, none at all.

But Vincent wasn't giving them much choice, and he seemed to identify that. "Oh Leshie, calm down my sweet," he said to her, taking a short step forward. "I mean you no harm. Truly. After all the time we've spent together? Do you really think I could hurt you?" He smiled to pacify her. "Just take your hand off the dagger, sweet girl. Please, for me..."

"He's done nothing wrong," Leshie went on, hardly seeming to hear him. "Neither of us have."

"I know. I know that really." Rose was walking toward her,

smiling, his hands gently outstretched. "Just...let go of the blade, Leshie. No one needs to get hurt here. You know that's not what I want."

"He's right, Leshie," Ranulf said. "Let go. There's no sense in drawing godsteel here. It will lead only to bloodshed."

Leshie hesitated a moment longer but seemed to see that her cause was hopeless. She gradually unfastened her fingers from the hilt, drawing her hand away, and no sooner had she done so than a pair of men surged in from behind her. Before she could react they were wrenching back her arms and grappling her into restraints, fettering her wrists in chains, unbuckling her belt as sheath and blade fell heavy to the ground. And all the while Leshie was scrambling, struggling, and screaming out at the top of her lungs. "I'll kill you for this, Vincent! I'll kill you! I'll kill you..." Her words were soon cut off as a hand slapped over her mouth, muffling her voice as she was dragged off without ceremony.

Ranulf watched on, utterly impotent to act. "It'll all be OK, Leshie," he tried to assure her, calling over the commotion. "Nothing will happen to you. It will all be OK." A part of him actually thought that might be the case. *This is a bluff, a trick, that is all,* came a burning hope. *He means to use her to force my hand, but I cannot yield. For our late great king, I cannot...*

"Now, Ranulf," purred Rose's self-satisfied voice, watching without a care as the girl was taken away. "Might this serve to untether your tongue?"

Ranulf spun back on him. "You are a coward, Vincent," he said sharply. "To bring her into your devious schemes? She is innocent in all this..."

"Is she now? A spy is innocent? Oh don't think I didn't know all along where her allegiances lay. I have never trusted Marian Payne's pets, old friend, and rarely keep them long in my company. I had hoped Leshie would betray you, but it seems she's quite willing to go down with the ship. For that I commend her, but now her fate lies with you. So tell me, Ranulf, and tell me now. What are you hiding?"

"Nothing." The word barked through Ranulf's lips without hesitation. "I have nothing to tell you that I haven't already said. It doesn't matter what you do to me, or to her, that fact will never change."

"More lies. Lies stacked on lies stacked on lies. If they were bricks you could build a great fortress with them. But alas you are here, within Pal Palek's, and you'll be staying here until you decide to speak." Vincent Rose gave a smile, as though they were chatting over the weather. "It truly is a fine menagerie that Pal has here, you know, but you've only seen one side of it. He has a rather different collection downstairs. Would you like to take a look?"

Ranulf was forced into the gloom beneath the fort, trailing down a set of stone steps at the tip of sword and spear. It didn't take long for the sounds to reach him. The wailing and sobbing and shrieking, the manic laughter of desperate men. Into a wide stone cavern they went, dug with pits topped with iron grates. Pal Palek guided them down a central walkway, lit every twenty yards by low-burning torches on poles. Either side, buried in the gloom were men kept solitary in their cells. Some were pacing and muttering, or sitting and sobbing, or raging and screaming and scratching at the bare-rock walls, tearing off skin and nail. A putrid stench poured up from several cells where the privy shoots had become blocked and clogged. From a couple came the nauseating reek of rotting flesh as the dead were left to decay.

But despite the horror, Pal Palek walked with a grotesque look of satisfaction on his face, as he passed by the cells and pointed, and spoke of his fine collection. "This one was a Varin Knight," he said of an old hunched figure, sleeping in his once-blue cloak. "I have had him here since the war. And this," he pointed to another, "was an Emerald Guard, a distant relation to the Warrior King, yes..." He marched on, pointing, gloating. "I have many Bladeborn here. And some Seaborn too, yes, I have those. And even a pair of Forgeborn of Ilith. I have them making weapons for me. They are the lucky ones, I say. They have some purpose, yes."

On he went, describing this man and that man, and every one of them was northern by birth and blood. "What you lack is a famed adventurer," said Vincent, his puffy face bunched to an ugly grin, warped by the firelight. "Best you start speaking quickly,

Ranulf, or else you'll become a permanent resident here. Not the sort of adventure you had in mind, I wouldn't say. A slow descent into madness." He laughed again.

Soon they were arriving into the distant recesses of the cavern, where the darkness thickened to a pall of stinking black, and the mutterings and madness of the encaged men grew louder and more deranged still. One was screaming incessantly at the top of his lungs, stopping only to splutter and draw breath, before screaming anew. Another was repeating the same name over and over and over again. There was a woman back here too, laughing and cackling hysterically, and someone making a strange clucking sound like a chicken.

"This one thinks he is a rooster," said Pal Palek, with a cold cruelty etched in his eyes. "He was a lord once...now I have made him into fowl. He is one of my favourites, one of my best, yes."

"He crows every morning," added Vincent with a chuckle. "It'll help you tell the time, Ranulf. Maybe that'll stave off madness for a while, hmmmm?"

"Me going mad will not help you, Vincent."

"Oh I beg to differ. Once you break - and believe me, that won't take long - you'll be much more pliant."

They came to a stop near the far wall, amid all that cackling and shrieking and clucking, and Pal Palek reached out with his torch, letting the firelight reveal the small dank space within. "This is yours," he said. "The last man here died some months ago. There. He will keep you company, yes."

His bones were not yet fully revealed, his sunken body layered in papery skin, shrivelled and grey, and the tattered old rags he'd worn. "Well wasn't that thoughtful," said Vincent. "Come on Ranulf, say thank you, don't be discourteous. Not many people get to have a cellmate. And I'm sure this one's better than Lord Cluck, wouldn't you say?"

Ranulf didn't react. He could still hear the clucking lord about thirty yards away, but only just through the rest of the clamour. He stared down into the small filthy cell as a guard went to the far wall, disappearing into the darkness before returning with a short ladder. The other unlocked a section of the iron grate for it to be set inside. "It doesn't have to be like this, Ranulf," Vincent whispered in his ear as the cell was prepared. "You are my friend and this is not what I want. Believe me. Pal Palek is a cruel man and will make your life a living hell, and poor little Leshie's too. He abhors northmen, and only tolerates me for the dealings I do with the Patriots." He grabbed his arm, drawing his eye. "You don't want any of that, I know you don't. Think of Leshie, Ranulf, think of the girl. She's like to suffer worse than you here, but you can change all that, right now. Just tell me what you found in the book. Tell me, and we can leave, right now, all of us together."

Ranulf stared into the shadowed, pleading eyes of Vincent Rose, and saw something more than greed in them. He saw fear. *Fear that I've found something Janilah will want. And that they will come for him next, lest he finds out what it is...*

But still...what could he say? Lie again, and build that wall a little higher? He couldn't think, not with all the shrieking and crowing and cackling about him. Not with the suffocating stink and darkness and the purply-black eyes of Pal Palek watching, ever watching.

"I can see you need some time to consider," Vincent said, drawing back in displeasure. "I'll return soon, and by then, will hope you have something to tell me." He smiled, or tried to. "I will do what I can to keep Leshie safe until then, but...no promises, Ranulf. I have very little authority here."

The hands were on him with that, the hard firm hands of militant men. They dragged him fiercely across to his cell, where Pal Palek waited. "In," he commanded, and Ranulf had no option but to obey. So down he went, down that ladder and past the spiked iron grate. Down into the stink, and down into the darkness. The darkness of his cell. The darkness of his thoughts.

46

Janilah

Janilah sat in his shield-backed white stone throne, as his granddaughter stepped before him. She wore a long green satin gown beneath an ermine cloak, and to her flank and two paces back came Lady Melany Monsort in demure raiment of blue and white robes. Behind them, Sir Owen Armdall and Sir Fredrick Ruxmond manned the double bronze doors in their striped mantles of white, brown and green over their godsteel mail hauberks. Cecilia filled the complement, watching like a vixen from the side as Amilia approached the foot of the steps and dropped her head into a bow. "You summoned me, Grandfather."

Janilah nodded. "King Godrin is dead." His voice rang out through the grand white chamber, curling around pillars and filling every corner, every crevice. Janilah held his smile as his words echoed and returned to him. *King Godrin is dead....King Godrin is dead...*"He fell yesterday evening at his palace in Thalan. I received word but an hour ago, and wished for you to be the first to know."

Cecilia tittered to the side. "He fell of natural causes, I take it?" But she knew otherwise, he could see.

"So it will be claimed, yes, but the truth will soon get out." He looked around. "The Wise King's death was at Hadrin's hand. His son bore the knife that cut his father's neck." There was a visible recoil from all the women. It was becoming of them to react as such. A senile old wretch Godrin may have been, but he remained a king, and deserved that at least. "Hadrin has been crowned king in a small private coronation, and will correct the course his father set." Janilah met the eyes of his granddaughter and unveiled the reason for her summons. "You will wed him and birth an heir of Lukar blood, Amilia. It is your duty to unite our kingdoms."

Her face turned to horror. "No," she blurted out. "No...I'll not. I'll not, Grandfather. Please don't make me..."

"You'll do your duty to this house and this kingdom. You'll do your duty to the north."

"Please, no." She pressed forward to the steps. "You cannot make me. He is vile, and old and..." She was close to weeping, holding her hands at him in prayer. "I cannot be with that man, not after Aleron. I cannot do that, Grandfather, I can't..."

Janilah lurched to his feet, his royal pine-green cloak hanging from the silver clasps at his shoulders. "You will do as I say!" he bellowed. "Hadrin is a king, and you will be his queen. Aleron Daecar has nothing to do with this."

"He does! I loved him!"

"You loved an echo and an idea, nothing more." He stared at her in displeasure. "You disappoint me, Amilia. I hand you a kingdom and you cry over a ghost. Lukars marry for position and profit, not love. You have always known this. Spare me your tears."

She didn't take that advice. Those tears were coming hot and free, and she'd lost all semblance of dignity now. "I won't do it," she repeated, and then twice more. She stared at the ground, her head rushing left and right, hair flailing about her. "If it wasn't for you, Aleron would be alive." She looked up, heedless of her tongue. "It was you, I know it. It can only have been you..."

Her words sank into the depths of that hall and left in their wake a cold deep silence. Janilah stared at her until her wilfulness withered and her eyes fled away to the side. "The princess is weary, Melany. Take her from my sight until she calms."

"Very good, my lord." Melany moved in and curled an arm

around Amilia's dainty waist. "Come along, Amilia. I'll take you to your chambers."

Amilia shoved her away, quite unlike her. "I don't want to go to my chambers."

"It's best you do, Princess, just for now." Melany urged her on, as Cecilia observed matters with an inquisitive smile. The king's bastard turned to look up at him with a frown, as though to wonder why he'd not informed her of all this.

"You know..." she then said. "I think you're rather lucky, Amilia."

Amilia pulled from Melany's coaxing, and looked over at her. "And why's that?" she spat, she sobbed. "Because I get to be a queen? *His* queen?"

"Well yes, and how fortunate that is, when the king in question will be such a weak one." Cecilia grinned. "Are you not a Lukar, Amilia? Is there no ambition in you to further yourself? I would not imagine a union with Aleron Daecar would have achieved that. It would have elevated he, not you, but now..." She gave Janilah a short glance, and saw in his eyes a permit to continue. "Well, I rather think being Queen of Rasalan will suit you, and kings do seem to be falling of late."

Her smile was sly and her meaning was clear, and true enough, kings were seeing their lives cut short right now. *Some are falling and others are rising,* Janilah thought, and on that account, not all his work today was done. The crow he'd received the previous night had been the watershed moment he was waiting for, and today he'd take the north as his. That thought brought to him a dull thrill, yet it was only one part of his plan. He held in his hand a coin, one side polished to a shine and the other still requiring of a good hard scrub. Political control of the northern kingdoms would not be enough, he knew, not to fulfil Galin's promise, nor win the War Eternal. For that many elements remained unresolved, but today was a good day. A day that would only get better.

Amilia was still thinking. Thinking and calming with each passing beat of her heart. "A child will be no fighter, Grandfather," she then said, wiping her eyes, smearing her makeup.

"Hadrin is Seaborn. He is weak." She sniffed, looking queasy at the thought of bedding him and Janilah could quite understand that. "Aleron and I were to sire a great warrior. Our son was to be as Varin reborn. Is that not what you wanted?"

Janilah took his seat. "A kingdom is more valuable. There are many warriors in Rasalan that will now be mine to command. I have done this to save lives. Do you not see? Godrin would never have submitted, and would have dragged us into a long bloody war, and all the while our enemies grow stronger. That I could not allow. By the tip of my quill, I have won you a kingdom. Now go and make it a queendom."

Amilia had no choice but to move past her disgust at the proposition, and focus instead on its appeals. Hadrin was a repellent little creature, true, but he was confident his granddaughter could tame him. In truth he rather expected this reaction, but could see now she would move past it. *Go cold, child,* he thought. *Go cold and do your duty, and do not think your life unfair.*

"The wedding," she whispered, as Melany handed her a silk handkerchief to dab at her eyes. "Where will it be?" She gulped down a breath, almost gagging on the thought. "When?"

"To be decided. We have an opportunity to bring the north together and put past slights behind us. There are too many shadows and ghosts between us, too many. Let us cast them aside in a public show of unity." He watched her all the while as he spoke and could sense no further dissent in her. "Now return to your chambers. Drink some wine. Dry your eyes. When next I see you, you'll be smiling ear to ear. You will sparkle like the Jewel of Tukor. Now go."

He turned his eyes from her, as Melany led her from the hall. Once they were gone Cecilia asked, "I suppose you've had this plan in mind for some time, have you? By the tip of your quill, you said. That is some fine penmanship, Father."

Janilah watched as Sir Owen and Sir Fredrick shut the huge bronze doors, patterned with panels depicting the great Siege of Ilithor three centuries ago. Outside, the Hunt brothers were stationed; Sir Maxwell and Sir Rees, two more of his sworn swords. The final pair were absent. Sir Kevyn Bolt would be sailing from Solapia by now with the Book of Thala, and Sir Edwyn Huffort, third son of the Lord of Rockfall, was on guard at the foot of the steps, beneath Tyrith's forge. All were sworn to kill for him and die for him by unbreakable oath, and were some of the finest swordsmen in all the kingdom. Gerrin had once been a part of their number, but Janilah didn't want to think about that. It would only stir thoughts of the boy and today...*no, today is a good day. There is no sense in souring it...*

"Are you unhappy that I did not tell you?" He looked into his daughter's green eyes, flecked with thin dashes of blue.

"I might have offered counsel if you did," she said. "But it would appear to me the ink had dried some time ago on this deal. I suppose you were waiting for news of Godrin's passing before you felt sure enough it would happen? I understand why you didn't tell me prematurely."

"There is always the risk of a late change of heart, though I felt confident Hadrin would follow through. He gets a kingdom and a beautiful princess, as he has always wanted. That it is two decades late makes no matter. So long as he submits to my command, there is no reason why it cannot yield a profit for us all."

"And the Rasal lords? Will they submit to him?"

"They have no choice, lest they join their late king. Once they stop and think a moment they will realise it is for the best. Godrin's mind had turned to folly, and he'd grown belligerent in his advanced age. I claim no pride in these underhand tricks, but they serve a valuable purpose."

"No pride at all, Father?" Cecilia's full lips twisted at the corners. "This is quite a coup for you, I would say. You deserve to toast this triumph."

He gave a nod, and permitted that she gather two cups of wine from the serving table left of the dais. "I will toast the result," he said, once she'd handed him a cup, "if not the method. My honour compels that of me."

"Honour can be so restrictive," Cecilia said, as they raised the golden goblets. "If you must go beyond its suffocating boundaries every once in a while, to serve such an important end as this, then I would consider that quite worthwhile."

"Your silver tongue is in good order, I see." He managed a quarter smile, his lips parting for a mere moment behind his thick grey-brown beard. "Have you had it polished of late?"

"Oh Father, you do jest." They drank, a long deep sip. Then she said, "You do seem in giddy spirit, I must say. A well earned jubilation."

"You exaggerate. Not once in my life have I felt giddy or jubilant."

"Your own version of it, then." She grinned, rather giddy herself it would seem, and then lifted her cup again. "So, our toast...let us put words to it." She thought a second, then smiled victoriously. "To the north," she said. "*Your* north, Father."

Outside, he could hear footsteps, a patter of leather approaching down the royal corridor and through the antechamber to the throne room. "Not yet," he said, passing her back the wine. "Take this away, and observe. I will ask you after if I should feel prideful, Cecilia."

Her forehead wrinkled to a frown, but she said not a word as she deposited the goblets back on the table. Janilah straightened his cloak and then sat up, stiff and straight in his throne, his rough hands resting upon the cold stone arms. He even felt a distant ripple of nerves and that was quite something. *I must do this delicately,* he knew. It was another plan long in the making, though not one he'd agreed to with such relish. *But necessary,* he thought, *if I'm to gather the Blades.* The Windblade was locked in the Steelforge vaults under Lord Godrik Taynar's keeping, and the ambitious old lord was refusing to give it up for love nor money. *But a crown?* And then there was Vesryn Daecar to deal with. He'd been informed of some alarming things about the new First Blade of late, that if unattended might lead to further trouble. It seemed the man's tenuous hold on the Sword of Varinar was making him rather prone to temper and recklessness and that wouldn't do. *No, I need a steadier hand wielding it,* he thought, *to be passed to me at the right time.* Vesryn was no longer that man, he'd come to see. It was time for a new house to rise.

The doors opened.

A great groaning gave out and there was the splendid King Ellis Reynar, as regal and grand as a king could be. Janilah quietly scoffed at the thought, and stood. "Good king Ellis, have you heard the news?"

"I have, Janilah, oh I have..." He bustled forward, trailing what seemed like a hundred robes of silver and blue. "We must have sailed under a lucky star in this great white ship of yours." The man was beaming. The poor stupid man. "Do we celebrate tonight? Do we feast? Or is that in poor taste? Regicide isn't typically reason to raise a glass, and patricide as well...I can hardly believe it." He was approaching the steps now, as Janilah sat quite still. "Is it true what they say? Hadrin cut his own father's throat?" He shuddered visibly. "He was always an unseemly sort, but this?"

"King Hadrin is to marry my granddaughter, Ellis. I thought you should probably know."

"Oh...oh well, that...that changes things then. I'm sure he'll make a fine husband…“ He smiled awkwardly as his small host followed behind. There was Sir Nathaniel Oloran, Commander of the Greycloaks, and a pair of others of meagre skill, dressed in gleaming breastplates, leather gloves, and silky silver capes. One was Sir Gerald Strand, and the other was Sir Alyn Porter, both men of the Ironmoors and sworn to House Taynar. That was not by chance; Janilah had engineered their being here. He'd also made quite sure that Ellis's wife, Elitha, and toothy little daughter, Lyriss were absent, for this was a show they'd best miss.

"Fear not for the slip of the tongue, Ellis." Janilah stood and gestured for the Vandarian king to join him by his throne. "And do not be concerned about poor taste. I'm sure a rich Solapian vintage will wash it down." He turned to the side. "Cecilia, if you don't mind." She began duties as serving maid, bringing them their cups of wine. "Have you met my natural daughter, Ellis? She's a Blakewood, daughter of Lady Jeyne."

"I've not had the pleasure." Ellis took her hand, as they gathered at the top of the dais by the throne. "Well met, Lady Blakewood. I have heard tales of your mother's beauty. It seems you took after her, not your father."

He must be mad or drunk to make such a quip, Janilah thought, but let it pass. "Oh I quite agree, Your Majesty," Cecilia tinkled. "It was that beauty that turned my father's eye. How do you like the wine?"

Ellis drew on his chalice, then made a series of smacking sounds, before running his tongue around his puckered mouth and little ferrety teeth. "It's quite lovely. Notes of cherry and pomegranate, and just a little hint of smoke. From the vineyards west of Arore, I take it?"

"Very good, my lord," said Cecilia. "You have a strong palate."

It's about the only strong thing about him, Janilah thought, as he turned to the hall. "Sir Nathaniel, do join us," he called, looking to the Greycloaks. "Sir Gerald, Sir Alyn, don't stand on ceremony. Cecilia fetch the flagon. Wine for everyone, I say. And you...of course, Sir Owen, Sir Fredrick, share a drink. I know you're on duty, but I'll allow it just this once. The brothers Hunt still man the door, fear not. We're quite safe in here, I'm sure."

He began laughing, and King Ellis was quick to follow, then the rest of the knights of Tukor and Vandar joined in. "I do not believe I've ever seen you so mirthful, Janilah," Ellis noted, as Cecilia handed out the wine. "Bravo, I say, bravo." He raised his cup; the wine was strong and would see a little man like Ellis Reynar sotted within no time. "To our triumph," he said. "To a united north." Janilah lifted his cup and slowly drew a small sip, as Ellis enjoyed a full gulp. "Pray tell how you learned of this, Janilah? Did Hadrin write you himself?"

"It was by the hand of Sir Munroe Moore."

Ellis gave out a splutter. "The commander of Godrin's guard?" Janilah understood the reaction. Any such man would be expected to fall on his own sword sooner than betray his king, but Sir Munroe had long since grown vexed by his liege lord's unusual behaviours. "I hope you'd never betray me as such, Nathaniel." Ellis chuckled in his uniquely insecure way.

Sir Nathaniel could hardly look at him. "Of course not, my king."

"Well I'd hope not." Ellis threw back another gulp of wine. "And what of the Wall? I might believe that Sir Munroe could turn, but Sir Ralston? I take it he was killed during the affray, defending his king?"

"There was no affray, Ellis," Janilah said. He took another small sip of wine, knowing Ellis would mimic him. "I'm told King Godrin sat alone in his private solar when his son entered. The Wall was nowhere to be seen."

"He abandoned his liege? Goodness, I had never taken him for a coward."

"There have been rumours that he roams the Lowplains, my lord," said Sir Owen Armdall. He was a fine specimen of chivalry, tall and lean with locks of rich brown hair. As with all of Janilah's sworn swords, he had dual godsteel blades, their hilts and pommels shaped into the likeness of oak trees. It was the Oak of Armdall, their crest. All his sworn swords had their blades designed as such, in lieu of bearing their coat of arms on their livery. "Some have posited that the King's Wall is there by the late king's order. There have been several ambushes that bear his prints."

Ellis stroked his narrow receding chin. "I do wonder...perhaps Godrin saw of his own fall? He may have sensed this treachery and sent Sir Ralston to enact some vengeance? I would not wish to be Hadrin right now, to be sure." Another nervous little titter escaped him, and he drew on his wine.

"A brute Sir Ralston may be, but he is just one man," put in Cecilia. "I do not suppose that he offers much threat. And men at war do love a story. I'm sure these rumours have been greatly exaggerated."

"I agree," nodded Janilah. "One embittered knight is of no concern, no matter how large he is. Now Ellis, do have more wine. I see your cup is dry. Cecilia, would you?"

Cecilia continued in her duty, pouring the king's cup nice and full and glancing all the while at Janilah with a curious, and rather amused, glint in her eye. *She does love her games,* he thought, and here she had joined the greatest one of all. *I wonder if she has figured it out yet?* He knew of course that she had. Cecilia wasn't short of wit or cunning and there was an energy in the room, an unspoken tension, that was quite unmistakable. It was in Nathaniel's dour expression, for his honour was soon to be sullied. It was in the silent darting looks of Sir Gerald and Sir Alyn who knew what would happen next. Ellis's chalice was near to overflowing when Cecilia drew away the flask. "You do spoil me, Lady Blakewood," he said, "but perhaps I ought to slow down?"

"Nonsense." She gave his arm a gentle stroke, as she passed him, filling Janilah's cup next. "Are we not here to celebrate?"

"Well yes, but..." He tottered a little upon the stage, almost reaching to the throne to steady himself. "This wine is rather strong, and it's early yet. It might be better that I pace myself."

"No, I don't think so." Cecilia smiled. "I'd say it's better that you relax, handsome king, and enjoy this day of triumph. Or are you worried that Queen Elitha will scold you for drinking yourself to a state so early?"

"The thought had come to me," Ellis admitted, giving out a tipsy laugh. "She has had words with me once or twice during my time here. I have taken too fondly to the wine, I feel. A most welcoming host you have been, Janilah."

"And you a congenial guest." Janilah almost choked on the lie, turning his eyes over the knights. They stood aside, unspeaking. The Greycloaks were looking out in different directions, their thoughts their own. "A breath of air will steady you, Ellis," Janilah continued. "You have asked many times to take in the view from my private balcony here." He gestured behind his throne. "Let me grant you that wish, to freshen your lungs and treat your eyes. The wind does wonders for a cloudy mind."

"Oh it does," nodded Cecilia. "Wrap up tight now, good king. It is breezy today."

Janilah opened his arm out and led Ellis over to the semi-circular balcony, jutting from the rear of the throne room. The others stayed behind, silent. Ellis was pulling his layers of robes about himself in preparation, still clinging to his chalice. They worked through the arched doorway and onto the wide balcony, and the iron railing that encircled it. It was flat enough at the top for them to set down their drinks, built to hip height. Janilah raised a hand to his city. "So, what is the verdict, Ellis? Does the view make the wait worthwhile?"

"Oh goodness yes..." Ellis's small head bobbed up and down on his quill-thin neck, poking out from the heaps of silver-blue robes. "Miraculous, Janilah. I do declare it the finest view I've ever set eyes on. The finest view in all the world."

"So they say." Janilah swung his arm to the right, where a great tower surged high among the mountains south of the city. "The great watchtower of Hammerhigh," he said. "Tallest point in the southern peaks of the Hammersong Range. From the summit you can see over a hundred miles in all directions." Then he turned Ellis's attention northeast, where the surging summits of the Three Peaks broke into the heavens, shrouded in cloud and fog. "There are no taller peaks in the world," he said. "Only the lonely mountain of Vandar's Tomb matches them." He pointed out other landmarks, all bursting from the low mists that swirled about the stone walkways and arched bridges, the white court-yards and pointed spires. And then, finally, his hand pointed directly north, to the towering edifice of the northern heights that rose up beside the palace, blending into the silvery fog. "But up there is the greatest treasure in this city, Ellis," he said, in a quiet voice. "If you listen carefully, perhaps you might hear him?"

Ellis looked confused. "Hear who, Janilah?"

"The heir of Ilith, up in his forge." He smiled at the look on the Craven King's face. "Oh yes, the line of Ilith lives. And the demigod's forge has been found." He lifted a thick-knuckled finger to his bearded lips. "But do keep it secret, good king. There are so few who know. Can I trust you not to tell anyone?"

Ellis Reynar's beady little eyes were earnest. "Of course I will," he said, trying not to slur. "Of...of course I will, Janilah."

Janilah stared at him, and knew it was time. "Yes," he said, "I know."

With that, he reached out, grabbed a bundle of robes on the king's narrow back, and threw him over the balcony rail.

And now the north is mine.

47

Elyon

Elyon lay in the infirmary tent as the nurse rubbed roseweed oil into his back. "The wounds are healing well, sir," she told him. She ran her index finger down several, though her touch was gentle and there wasn't much pain. "These will scar worse than the others. But you will have lines on your back for all ten, I'm afraid."

Her name was Aliss he remembered. "Don't worry, nurse Aliss," he said, "I can't see my back when I look in the mirror. And all fighting men should have a few scars, they say."

But these weren't the scars they wanted. The licking white lines of a whip tended to call out criminals and malefactors, not the noble warrior Elyon wanted to be. *Yet there was nobility in what I did...to protect her,* he told himself. Not many would ever know that, but he would, and that was good enough. "You will need to stay here for another day or so until I feel happy to remove the sutures," nurse Aliss went on. "After that I will be able to discharge you, so you can return to the comfort of your private tent. I will come by daily to apply the salve to speed your healing, and change your bandages."

Elyon nodded, as she continued to apply the balm, rubbing it around his lacerations, while being careful not to disturb the stitches. "How long before I can clad godsteel again and swing a blade?"

"Not for a fortnight at least, if you're to be careful. Straining yourself too soon may only open up the cuts, and delay your recovery. I will continue to monitor you, sir, and offer counsel on when you might resume your training."

"Much obliged, Aliss." She was a large woman with a stern disposition and homely face, not much to look at, but diligent in her work. Elyon had no intention of circumventing her guidance. He'd been unconscious during the first go round, when his wounds had been treated, and didn't want to suffer the same when awake. They'd shorn the skin to a clean edge, he'd been told, rubbed salt, wine, and vinegar, and sewn him up before he lost too much blood. Apparently it had been touch and go at one point. The cuts were deep, to his lower back in particular, and his heart had slowed worryingly as they worked to stem the flow. Thankfully, they'd managed that without cauterising the wounds and thus avoiding even uglier scarring. "You were lucky," Vesryn told him, when he woke two days later. "I thought I lost you there for a time, my boy."

It had been dark and late, Elyon remembered, though in truth his memory of waking was weak. He'd fallen back to sleep again a short time later, and slept right through to the following afternoon, but during the short time he'd woken, he'd asked his uncle of Saska. "Have you heard of her?" he had whispered, as men coughed and snored around him, and the night nurses tended their ails. "Did they get out OK?"

"I've heard nothing, and that can only be a good thing. Sir Lancel and Sir Barnibus will see this thing done. And you will owe them, Elyon. You will owe them for taking this risk."

He knew that full well. "And you, Uncle. I owe you as much..."

"You need not repay me," Vesryn had said, in a dour thoughtful voice. "I have done you ill, Elyon. It is I who owe you, not the reverse."

Elyon wasn't certain what to make of that, and his uncle had left before he could question him on it. Vesryn had helped him get Saska out. He'd killed Sir Brendan Paramor when the knight was set to slay him. *Two lives saved. Mine and hers. And yet he says that he is in my debt?*

Nurse Aliss completed her latest application of ointment and set about applying fresh bandages, wrapping them around him as Elyon shifted to his feet and stood up. In a bed nearby, the figure of Sir Rodmond Taynar was stirring, emerging from another of his long salubrious sleeps. He'd been here some weeks now after taking a bolt to the belly, though was fast on the mend and would be back on his feet in no time. He rubbed his eyes, yawned, and looked over at Elyon with a smile. The two were of the same age and friendly enough, and Rodmond was a far cry from his grim gloomy uncle. "You're still here," he noted. "I always imagine I'll wake to find you gone."

"Then I'm sorry to disappoint you again, Rodmond." Elyon smiled at him. "I'll be leaving in a day or two, nurse Aliss says."

"Good. I'll be glad to be free of your snoring. A man your size does make a noise." Rodmond's narrow face drew into a smirk and he turned his eyes to the tent flaps, some twenty yards away. It was a large marquee, though hardly packed tight with beds and bodies. No, this infirmary was reserved for the lords and knights and highborn men of Vandar. The others down in camp would be near to overflowing but not this one. "It's awfully quiet out there. Are they not sieging tonight? I thought the full assault was to go ahead?"

That had been the rumour, though for some reason, it had never materialised. "I suppose they're waiting for us to recover, Rodmond," Elyon jested.

"Quite." Rodmond continued to look out. "There is something, though." He turned his head. "Cheering. Do you not hear it?"

Elyon hadn't been paying much attention, but yes, there was something. A distant clamour down toward the edge of camp, on the northern side facing Harrowmoor. It was growing louder too, spreading. Soon enough there came a murmuring of voices outside. He could hear soldiers clanking and rushing through the mud and snow, heading north. The cheering came closer, and closer still, until it seemed right on top of them. And then suddenly a man burst inside the tent, a great beaming smile on his face. He wasn't a man Elyon recognised, a soldier in Kanabar livery, with a huge, blade-antlered elk on his surcoat. "They've surrendered," he exclaimed, looking around. His face erupted into a huge broad grin. "The white flags have gone up. Harrowmoor...it's ours!"

"What? Why?" asked Elyon, taking a step toward him. "They've held out for weeks. Why would they suddenly surrender?"

The soldier was already half way back out into the cold night air. "Some say the king is dead, Sir Elyon. King Godrin. His son has brought an end to the war."

He was gone a second later, and Elyon was on the move. "Sir Elyon, I'd advise you not to go anywhere just yet," scolded nurse Aliss as Elyon went to a dresser and grabbed a cloak, pulling it over his shoulders. "I'm sure you'll learn what has happened in good time." Rodmond was climbing to his feet as well. Aliss grunted. "Not you too! Sir Rodmond, please sit back down. You're in no condition..."

"Stop fussing, Aliss," Rodmond said, snatching up a cloak of his own. He joined Elyon at the door where they pressed their feet into boots, and together the two infirm young men went trudging out into the cold. Outside, the camp was a whirl of movement as men sped to get a look at the fortress up the hill. Among the dull black battlements, the white flags were flickering and flapping on the wind. Some were raised, others being drawn up. The sloping hills were still scattered with the carcasses of siege weapons half hidden in heaps of snow. They'd not attacked the fortress in three days, and the snows had fallen thick in that time, covering over the tracks and swathes of land churned up by the movement of men and wagons and wheels. The hillside looked pristine, yet beyond, outside the siege camp, dozens of trebuchets and catapults and scorpions, breaching towers and tall strong ladders had gathered in preparation for the full scale siege that had never come. Some thousand score of men bustled about them, their formations broken down as the white flags went up. They were cheering loudly now, and so were all the reserves in camp. And away at Harrowmoor, the gates were opening.

"I wonder if they didn't see all this and hoist their flags in surrender," said Sir Rodmond over the blustery wind, pulling his cloak tight.

"They've not quelled to our strength as yet. I believe what the Riverlander said."

"That Godrin is dead?"

Elyon nodded. "That the war is over."

Out of the gates of Harrowmoor, a small host was riding now, a blur of shapes in the distance. Above them, the white banners of peace were held high upon their poles, and from the great gathered host at the edge of camp, riders went out to greet them. The two sides came together upon the snows midway between the camp and fort in a short exchange, their standard-bearers riding before them. All went silent as they observed the custom of surrender, a single white flag folded and presented. Elyon imagined it would be Lord Donal Paramor presenting to Prince Rylian, though couldn't be sure from this distance. Even the banners were hard to make out, though he was sure he saw Paramor's merman and Rylian's blade and hammer, and the elk of Kanabar, the bear of Kastor, and a small clutch of others. A few further words were exchanged, only a minute or two passing before the two parties separated and returned to whence they'd come. It was a short formality, an overture for surrender and peace. But peace...Elyon could hardly believe it. *The war is over,* he thought. It was what everyone had wished for, a cessation of hostilities, but something wasn't sitting right. Off in the longhouse, he could hear drums starting to play. They were beating out, deep and loud and joined by skirling skins. All through camp, others joined them, the beating and the wailing, as a great fog of noise began to fill the air. "They'll feast tonight like never before," Sir Rodmond said grumpily. "I'll be damned if I'm to miss out."

"You look like you could use a good meal, Rodmond."

The man wasn't much like his uncle in disposition, but was rather similar to him in design. Not especially handsome, nor large, but skilled with blade and bow. Rodmond had eyes that were a little too close together, a long hairless chin, and hollow cheeks. His hair was dark, short and scruffy, his frame slim and wiry. He gave a laugh. "I need an ale. Every man in camp will be getting sotted tonight and we'll be with them, Elyon."

"What will your uncle say?" Elyon teased. "I'm not so sure he'll approve, Rodmond."

"There's no lie in that," Rodmond admitted glumly. He always went into his shell whenever Sir Dalton came to visit, losing his smile and chirp. The idea of his loyal nephew befriending a Daecar would make a man like Sir Dalton Taynar feeble in the gut. "I do wish he would move past his animosity, in truth. I have tried to tell him so, but..."

"But you've been unable to?"

Rodmond inclined his head. "I'm rather weak when it comes to him, I'm not too shy to say. I'm his heir, you know, until he has a son of his own, but I've never much wanted that, even if I'm just a temporary stand in. That was never to be my path. You have to be born into that, I think."

"I wasn't," Elyon put forward, looking over at him. The cold was invigorating him, filling his lungs after a week in that tent. It felt good to be on his feet again.

"No, but you were always second in line of direct descent. Not me. It's different when you're born of the second son of a lord. You're not groomed for it in the same way."

Elyon could hardly deny that, though in truth he'd never expected to become Lord Daecar either, and still hoped that was some way off. "Well for what it's worth, I'd say you'd make a better lord than your uncle. Then perhaps we might help heal the rift between our houses?"

"My grandfather would first need to fall, then my uncle, but one can hope." He gave a devious smile. "But anyway, I'm going to get some clothes on. Perhaps we might share a drink in the longhouse before my uncle arrives?"

Elyon had to laugh. He hated all these silly rivalries. "I'd say we should be sharing a cup when he enters, Rodmond. Show your uncle and mine how it's done. But first we'll have to outwit nurse

Aliss. She'll be trying to shackle us back to our beds, you can be sure of that."

"She can try all she likes. This is one feast I'm not bloody missing."

Elyon didn't disagree, nor did he waste time in returning to his pavilion to dress. He pulled on a white shirt, brown leather tunic, woollen breeches and boots, then wrapped himself up in a fur-collared cloak, and all the while he tried to keep his eyes away from the reddy black bloodstains on the deck. Once garbed he went to his chest, unlocked it, and drew out his godsteel dagger, attaching it to his swordbelt. The touch of godsteel firmed him as he poured himself a cup of wine and took his first good look over the room. At the bed where Saska had slept. At the desk where she spent her days. At the spot where she'd put her knife through Borgin's eye, and slashed Sir Griffin's manhood clean in two. The girl had wriggled her way into his head and never been far from his thoughts, and more than once she'd appeared in his dreams as well. It wasn't love, no, it was something different. A deeper attachment, almost. *Secrets,* he thought. *And destiny.* There was something of that about her, something profound and important that he couldn't quite figure out.

He sighed, stepping to the counter, filling a cup of wine. *I probably never will,* he thought, taking a sip. His back felt strange wrapped in bandages, pinched by a thousand stitches, and numbed from the roseweed, he couldn't quite be sure if he wasn't doing himself any damage. *Just take it slow,* he thought, sipping the wine. Out through the camp the drums were still going, and the heavy rustle of men was filling the air as they returned to their fire pits and tents. He moved over to the exit, and looked out, just in time to see his uncle march across the yard in his gleaming interlinking plate, the Sword of Varinar sheathed at his hip. Elyon pressed eagerly out. "Uncle. Uncle, I heard what happened."

Vesryn glanced over. "Inside, Elyon."

They entered the First Blade's tent, warmly lit by twin braziers, escaping the shuddering cold. It was the first time Elyon had been here since sneaking Saska across to hide. He looked to the spot where they'd placed her, though she hadn't remained there long before being secreted away by Lancel and Barnibus. He'd be unlikely to hear anything of them until they returned to camp, and that wouldn't be for another week or so. And if the war here was truly over? They'd be sure to head south soon, to fortify the coast. *To Dragon's Bane. To Killian and Rikkard.* The thought of seeing them again gave him great succour, for Vesryn was not the man he was. He watched his uncle now as he laid the Sword of Varinar on his thick oaken desk, the wood creaking beneath the blade's great weight. Then he said, "I hear Godrin's dead."

The First Blade nodded, a cold grim look on his ashen face. "They're saying he died of heart failure," he said. "Hadrin has been crowned king and ordered all his lords, knights, and subjects to lay down arms." He pulled off his gauntlets, setting them aside, then said, "Princess Amilia is to wed him, Rylian says. A marriage to unite the kingdoms."

Elyon felt his skin crawl at the notion, a swarm of fiery ants running all over him. *Aleron to Hadrin. There could hardly be two men more different.* "What does Rylian make of it? I have seen him grow weary of his father's commands. This one must rankle."

Vesryn shook his head. "It's a perfect political match." He glanced to his armoured forearms. "Help me with these."

Elyon stepped over and began unfastening the delicate links and chains and straps that secured his uncle's armour, starting with his vambraces. "So Hadrin's absence? He must have been travelling north, to overthrow his father."

"To kill his father," Vesryn said, as Elyon slid off his left vambrace, placing it aside. "Hadrin has long coveted his father's throne. As he coveted your mother. Now he has a kingdom and a beauty of his own." He looked at Elyon. "Godrin's death was no accident, Elyon. He was murdered in a coup, no matter what they say."

Elyon stopped in his work and stared into his uncle's dull blue eyes. Vesryn had committed to the belief that Hadrin had been behind the ruin of their family, but that had been a cover, Elyon knew. *A cover for his guilt?* "He acted by Janilah's command," Elyon said. "Patricide and regicide in exchange for a kingdom and a queen." He watched his uncle carefully, then cut right to the core of it. "Janilah had Aleron killed," and with that he saw his uncle's mouth twitch and tighten. "It was never Hadrin behind the ruin of our family...and you've always known that, haven't you?" There was a challenge in his voice now, a challenge for the truth. "You always knew it was Janilah."

Vesryn let out a long slow sigh, shutting his eyes for a moment. He looked weary. Weary of the lies, and half-truths. Of the weight of his guilt. He gave a slow nod. "I knew," he said in a deep breathy voice, staring dully at the desk. "I can't lie to you anymore, Elyon." He filled his lungs, stood a little taller, and turned to face him. "I knew who Fitzroy Ludlum was all along. I knew...and did nothing. I did nothing to save him. Aleron..." His eyes fell, and his face crumpled like paper, coiling in shame and regret and grief. "Aleron is dead because of me."

And there it was. The confession Elyon had always wondered might come. The explanation for his words when Elyon woke six nights past. *I have done you ill, Elyon. It is I who owe you, not the reverse...*Elyon drew away from his uncle and turned, thinking. And from behind him came Vesryn's voice. "Are you going to kill me? I'd not blame you if you did, Elyon. But I would pray you first hear the truth."

"I'll hear it." Elyon turned. He flexed his sword hand, though there was no great rage in him, no great hate, not yet. He just wanted to understand. He was done with the lies and deceits. "Did you know Aleron was going to be killed?"

"No." Vesryn said it quickly, and with honesty enough that Elyon believed him. "The Shadowknight was only meant to defeat him in the final of the Song of the First Blade, and then leave the city. I would never have let it happen if I knew Aleron was to be killed. Never. I promise it."

Elyon said nothing, not for a long cold moment. He'd worked that out already. It would have been enough for the assassin to beat Aleron and then disappear, leaving Ellis to name Vesryn his new First Blade by royal decree. The order to kill Aleron had come later. *To free Amilia from the bonds of her betrothal,* he now knew. *So she could wed Prince Hadrin instead...*"Did Ellis know?" he asked.

"No. This was of Janilah's design. He wants the Blades of

Vandar, Elyon. All of them. He feels they will help him win the war."

Elyon took that in and saw no lie there either. "He expects you to hand the Sword of Varinar over?" It was a ludicrous notion. The Sword of Varinar would never be held by a Tukoran. *Never.*

"Expects..." Vesryn whispered. "But I'll not." His eyes were dark and greedy all of a sudden, fixed to the golden blade on the table. "Never." That final word came a soft hiss from his lips. He stared at the steel for a long moment, then blinked and drew back, as if coming out of a dream, looking older and more worn than ever. The patches beneath his eyes were thickening, wrinkling, his hair frosting grey. "I will not walk to his drum, not anymore. I have a mind to go there myself. I have a mind to kill him."

Elyon took that on. He gripped it tight and looked his uncle deep in the eye. "Would you? Would you do it for vengeance, Uncle? Or for penitence?"

"I would do it for Aleron. For you. For Lillia, and your father. I would do it for Amara." A fresh grimace spread across his face. "I have learned to love her, but it was not always so." He looked up. "It was your mother I once cherished. Your mother I once loved..."

Elyon drew his dagger. "Do not speak of her." He took a sharp pace forward, but Vesryn just stood, waiting, accepting whatever he might do. He even lifted his neck, exposing his throat above his gorget.

"Do it, if you will," he said. "I'll raise no hand to stop you."

Elyon grunted and drew away, thrusting his dagger back into his scabbard. A ripple of pain ran through his lower back, and he feared the sutures had come loose. "Did she love you back?" He turned back to face his uncle, keeping some five paces away, should he do something rash. "Are you trying to tell me something? Tell me that you're my father?"

"I wish I was, Elyon. I have wished for a son all your life. But your mother never loved me, not as I did her. We grew close when she first came to Varinar to wed your father. A brother she took me as, but I saw her as something more. She had a way...half the men she met fell for her, Elyon, and more so those who were young and stupid like me. I am shamed by what I did. I have carried that shame all my life."

"What did you do?"

Vesryn sighed, but there was nothing for it now. The truth had to come, he knew it. "I helped Janilah steal a son from your father," he explained. "I hoped I might use the secret to destroy his honour, make Kessia doubt him, so she might fall in love with me. But I never spoke of it, not once. Janilah gave me his cousin instead, and so Amara became my wife. It was my treachery that made us barren, I know it. The gods cursed us to bear no children, for the wickedness I did."

Elyon turned away. He needed to think on all that. The noise was loud outside now. The drums. The skins and pipes and strings. The merriment was spreading all through camp. The drinking and dancing. The brawling and bedding. But those drums were loudest, banging an incessant beat, thud thud thud in his skull. And then it came like a hot poker to his brain. "Cecilia," he said, spinning back. "It was she who bedded Father, who stole his seed during the war. The assassin...my half brother, he's....he's Janilah's grandson."

Vesryn's voice was weary, a withered stricken thing. "Jonik is born of Daecar and Lukar blood. Son to Amron. Grandson to Janilah. He was born and raised a weapon, a weapon now turned against its master." He looked up, some feeble pleading look in his eyes. "I knew who he was, but not of his intention. Not that he'd kill Aleron. I promise it," he said again. "I promise it, Elyon."

"And Father?" Elyon cut in, because that had been forgotten thus far. He stared at his uncle, and saw his face change, sinking, souring, turning away, and he knew. "You knew he was going to try to kill him?" *He must have, to set all this in motion. Aleron no, but Father?*

Vesryn gave no answer, but just stood there in silence, and that was all Elyon needed to know. He drew his blade and still Vesryn said nothing. And for a full minute, they just stood there as the camp roistered about them, a glut of dread and doom at the heart of all that revelry. Elyon considered it all long and hard and then pressed his dagger back into its sheath. "You're not worth it." He drew back a pace, moving for the flaps. He'd heard enough, enough to condemn him. "You would have let him die to keep your dirty secret. To protect yourself, you'd have let your own brother die." And still Vesryn said nothing. Still he just stood, his eyes slowly drawn back to the only thing that gave him comfort, the only thing that gave him solace. "You don't deserve that blade," Elyon spat, but even that got no reaction. *He is lost, truly lost.* "You are no uncle of mine."

Elyon punched through the tent flaps with those words, into the maelstrom of noise. He had to be away from him, had to give himself time. Time to understand? Time to forgive? He wasn't sure on either, but he needed time regardless. The yard beyond the longhouse was busy with bodies, soldiers in green and brown and blue all gathered about, swigging from clay bottles and iron tankards. Inside it was quieter, just the highborn lords and knights permitted entry. He spotted Sir Rodmond to one side, gesturing him over as the drums thumped and the bags wailed, and the musicians fiddled and blew. "You look ashen, Elyon," he called over the noise. "Have your sutures broken? Are you losing blood?" *I just might be,* he thought, but forced his face to a smile and took up the goblet Rodmond offered. "My uncle isn't yet here. So let us drink freely."

How pathetic it was that they had to worry. Elyon downed his drink. "Another?" He waved over a servant and he filled their cups, and along came Lord Kanabar too. "My lord." Elyon inclined his head. "How did it go at the parley? Better than the last I'll bet." He tried to focus, but could think only of Vesryn. *I should kill him for what he did...I should go back and slit his throat.*

"That would depend on who you're asking," said the red-bearded lord, wrapped in a handsome silver and green tunic, printed with his elk. "I feel the Rasals aren't so happy. It is an ill enough day to lose a much-loved king, but another to have to surrender your nation to a foreign ruler. We have testing times ahead, Elyon, but whatever treachery Hadrin might have committed, at least this futile war is done. I hope you'll use your tongue wisely, my boy." He gave him a smile. "We'll need men like you to bridge the gap between our peoples, just as your father once did."

"You give me too much credit, my lord." Elyon was trying to calm, trying so damn hard, but every word was coming short and sharp from his lips. "I'm not my father."

"And you don't give yourself enough." Lord Kanabar turned his eyes over the pair. "I'm surprised to see you two here. Have you fully recovered, Sir Rodmond?"

"Near enough, my lord. Neither Elyon nor I wished to miss out on the festivities this evening. We shall stay for but a few."

"I'm sure." Lord Kanabar turned. "I saw your uncle making for the rookery, Rodmond. Is he expecting some news? He seemed in deep thought, and I mean that as no compliment. I have a mind to say he's up to something."

"If he is I'm not aware of it," Sir Rodmond said, and Elyon imagined that was quite true. Rodmond was too open and generous to be included in his uncle's inner circle of schemers.

The drums were beating loudly, thudding hard into Elyon's ears. He turned his eyes around. More men were filling the long-house, bustling about the tables. Lord Shorton and Lord Fullerton arrived, joining them. Drinks were handed out. The men drank long and deep. Elyon spotted Rylian arriving with his sons, and there was Cedrik Kastor too, in the company of Lord Gershan and Sir Gavin Trent, who'd condemned Elyon to the lash. He stared across at them and they right back. Lord Gershan broke free and shambled over in a grey doublet, his back bent double by age. On his chest was his standard; a brown serpent coiling around a heathery hill. The Master of the Moorlands looked up along the uneven ridge of his hooked nose at Elyon. "You've some nerve being here tonight," he accused, pointing up at him with an old shaking finger. "After what you did. Do you have no shame?"

"Clear off, Gershan," said Lord Kanabar. "We want no quarrel tonight."

"Should be he who clears off, not I. I was told he'd be heading to Dragon's Bane once his cuts knitted together. Return to the heel of his Uncle Rikkard. Man like you will only cause upset and discord." He pointed again. "Half the Greenbelts want your head."

Elyon was in no mood for this. "Then line them up and let

them try to take it, my lord. I will fight any man who calls me out for dishonour. Any man."

"Oh you will?" Gershan licked his rumpled lips. "Lord Kastor will be happy to hear it. Are you saying you'd accept should he challenge you, sir?"

"In a heartbeat, my lord." He glared over at Cedrik Kastor, who was sneering across the hall. "Just tell me where and when..."

"That isn't going to happen." Lord Kanabar placed a hand on Elyon's shoulder, drawing him back. "We'll not sacrifice good men to petty feuds."

"Petty feuds you say?" Gershan snickered, his mouth twisted like a rope. He stared straight up into Wallis Kanabar's great rusted forest of a beard. "This man murdered Lord Kastor's beloved nephew. There was no justice in his sentence, and here he stands, as evidence of that. One week, and he drinks and laughs as though nothing ever happened." He turned back to Elyon. "Shame, sir, and I say it again...shame!" He pointed, near enough to pick Elyon's nose, and the young Daecar couldn't help himself, swiping the man's hand away. The Master of the Moorlands let out a little shriek as his arm went sideways. "Cur! My finger...you broke my finger!" He turned and staggered away holding his hand as though it was severed at the elbow, to a light chorus of laughing from the River and Lakelanders nearby.

"That was unseemly of me," Elyon said, over the drums and wailing skins. He watched Lord Gershan stagger off and bleed back into the crowd. "I shouldn't have done that."

"He earned it," said Sir Rodmond. "Slippery old snake had it coming."

"A Taynar defending a Daecar," chuckled Lord Fullerton, his many chins wobbling. "Something I never thought I'd see."

"You came to some accord in the infirmary, I suppose?" asked Lord Shorton, peering down that oversized snout of his.

"I'd not say that, my lord. Elyon and I have always been on friendly terms. It's just this business with my uncle and his..."

"A most troublesome business," intoned Lord Kanabar. His weary old eyes crumpled beneath a frown, and he shook his ruddy cheeks. "And not one I see a simple solution to. That blasted blade does more harm than good when good men start to bicker over it. We might just send it back to Varinar and store it in the vaults alongside the Windblade. Or better yet, toss it to sea and let the krakens fight over it instead."

Lord Shorton looked aghast. "You don't mean that, Wallis."

"I just may, you know. Any weapon that causes this much discord is no weapon of ours...it becomes nothing but a weapon of our enemy."

A blast of cold air ripped through the longhouse, sending tendrils of flame from the braziers and lamps reaching out to the side. Elyon looked to the door, as Sir Dalton arrived, trailed by the mountainous Sir Taegon Cargill and elegant Sir Brontus Oloran. All wore their full godsteel plate, sending a ripple of worry up Elyon's spine. Men looked over as Sir Taegon stamped forward and cleared a path, bellowing for quiet at the top of his lungs. "News!" he called out. "News from the west....Quiet! QUIET!"

The drums and skins and pipes began to fade off as a heavy murmur rang out through the hall. As the music quietened so Prince Rylian called out. "What is this, Sir Dalton? Do tell why you interrupt our merrymaking."

Sir Dalton raised a letter. "I have just received word from Ilithor of a most distressing nature. Be quiet, please, to hear me! Quiet!" It wasn't like Sir Dalton to shout as such, and that suggested something serious. The rest of the musicians stopped in their plucking and blowing and banging, as every man present turned to the heart of the hall. Once he had their attention, Sir Dalton went on, waving that scroll above his head. "I have word from Ilithor, from Sir Nathaniel Oloran, Commander of the Greycloaks." He paused and Elyon's heart hammered and then he called out, "Our good king is dead! Ellis Reynar has had a fatal accident in the palace." The murmuring grew louder again, and Sir Dalton had to raise his voice yet further. "He fell...he fell," he called. "From a balcony in the palace, a calamity for the north! He is dead, my lords, good sirs. Our noble king is dead!"

A hundred voices filled the air, calling a hundred questions. A short burst of anarchy broke out as Sir Taegon bellowed for calm and quiet. "QUIET! QUIET! LET HIM SPEAK!"

Sir Dalton stood still and calm. The tumult died down. "My father, Lord Godrik, will continue to sit the throne in Varinar," he called, and there was something different in his voice, something awkward. "Our late king fell without a son, without an heir. My father will..."

"Amron Daecar is king!" called one of the Lakeland knights in interruption, bearing House Shorton's flock of black birds against a silvery lake. "He is Ellis's cousin, his closest male kin! All hail King Amron! Long live King Amron Daecar!"

Sir Dalton looked enraged by that as a chorus of voices sang out among the Vandarians. Men were looking over at Elyon. "You're a prince, Sir Elyon. Prince of Vandar!" called one over the cacophonous din. "You must lead us in your father's stead," said another. Lord Kanabar turned his eyes over to him. "I would support you, Elyon. You would have my fealty, always."

Elyon didn't know what to say, where to look. He found that Sir Rodmond had fled back into the crowd at the coming of his uncle. But in his place was Sir Mallister Monsort, sweeping in with a broad smile. "My goodness, two kings dead in a day," he said as the din swelled and men shouted and Sir Taegon bellowed for calm. It went on for a time until the giant threw his fist into a long oaken table, shattering the thing to splinters. "Silence! SILENCE!" he roared. "Let the Prince of Vandar speak!"

No one knew what to make of that. Many looked over at Elyon as though expecting him to make a speech, but he was struck dumb by the whole affair, and feeling a warm sensation on his back. *I'm bleeding,* he realised, but that was that. His mind was back on the drama. *My father...king?* He'd always known that Amron was closest male kin to Ellis, but never thought it would come to this. Ellis had no sons, no brothers, no father or uncles. *And now he was gone. Dead. Fallen from a balcony. Or pushed?*

"Amron Daecar will not be king!" called the thin cutting voice of Sir Dalton Taynar, splitting the air. Sir Taegon dragged a table over to him with an earsplitting scrape and Taynar leaped atop it with a clunk of steel on wood, holding his scroll aloft. "King Ellis wrote a decree making my father his heir at his death. Amron

Daecar will not be king! He will not! The king is Godrik! King Godrik of House Taynar!"

The uproar among the River and Lakelanders was loud enough to blast the walls off the hall. Men began shouting, throwing fists to the air and worse. Through the crazed throng Elyon could see Cedrik Kastor shouting orders to his lords and captains. A moment later his Greenbelts were bellowing in support of Sir Dalton's claim. The two sides faced off amid the hall, some falling to brawling. Wine and ale and mead flew everywhere. Trenchers were upturned as the servers went running for the sides, squashing into corners. The next thing would be swords, daggers, spears, and slaughter. Rylian saw that, leaping up onto a table. "My lords! MY LORDS! Men of Vandar, of Tukor, be silent! Calm. CALM!...stay your hands." He looked to Elyon, and urged him to stand high too, and a second later the men around him were pressing him forward, up onto a bench, a table.

"Speak," urged Lord Kanabar. "Speak to calm them, Elyon."

Elyon cleared his throat. Two hundred faces were on him. "Calm," he said. It was all he could think of. *Rylian had said it, so why not I.* "Calm, gentlemen! Let us hear what Sir Dalton has to say. There is more to this story we haven't yet heard."

The hall followed the lead of the men on the tables, and a sense of order was soon restored, returning to a heavy murmuring. There was ale and wine and food everywhere, but no blood, not yet, and it'd be best to keep it that way. "My thanks, Sir Elyon," said Sir Dalton in as generous a voice as he could muster. "And I hear you." He turned to the Riverlanders and Lakelanders. "I hear you, my friends. Long have you revered...have we all revered Amron Daecar, but his day is done. King Ellis wrote by his royal hand that my father, Lord Godrik Taynar, lead us forward at his death. None expected it, but it *has* happened. It has. There can be no dispute. None can question the divine hand of the king..."

"How did he die?" called a knight of House Fullerton. "You say he fell? How can that be?"

"He slipped and fell, yes," answered Dalton. "King Ellis had been drinking to the end of the war, and in some quantity, I'm told. He leaned over a balcony edge and lost his footing on the stone at his feet, and was unable to cling onto the railing..."

"Which balcony? Where was he?" came another question, from somewhere in the back.

"He was in the palace, the throne room." Sir Dalton waved the scroll. "There were several witnesses that say he fell of his own doing. Sir Nathaniel Oloran, his own Greycloak commander, is among them."

Sir Dalton turned to look down at Sir Brontus, who called out, "My cousin Nathaniel would never lie, nor betray his king. He speaks the truth."

"There were others," Dalton added. "Sir Gerald Strand and Sir Alyn Porter. Both Greycloaks. Both present."

"Both Taynar men!" roared a broad-faced Lakelander in Shorton livery. "I smell treachery!"

"Cast that man out!" spat Sir Dalton. "I cast out any man who calls treachery against men of the Ironmoors! I cast out any man who questions their honour!"

A good deal of bustling followed, though not much else, and the threat was soon forgotten. Then another brazen man made a more daring suggestion. "Two dead kings in a day and the Warrior King claims the north! It stinks of treachery. I'll say it. I don't care." He pointed from the midst of the throng toward Prince Rylian. "You know it, good prince. Your father has done this. Can you claim otherwise?"

Rylian remained quite calm as the air swelled with noise. He raised his hands to call for quiet. "We have heard Sir Dalton's testimony. Three sworn Greycloaks of King Ellis witnessed his fall and have confirmed it an accident. There is no recourse to debate that here. Unless you were there, sir, and flew here on a dragon?" Laughter spread, and that was some relief. Rylian's hands went back up. "Friends, my kin, it is beholden on us to unite. King Godrin was north of ninety years old and King Ellis was lost to a cruel twist of fate. That they died a day apart speaks of coincidence, nothing more. And you say my father claims the north? I do not see how. King Hadrin now rules these lands, and it would seem Godrik Taynar claims the crown in Vandar. Three kings, my friends, and three kingdoms, as it has always been. But united, now, in a common goal."

On it went. More men called out their concerns, and more answers were given. The claim of Lord Taynar was questioned a hundred times in a hundred ways, and Sir Dalton found a hundred answers, each a deviation on a theme. Elyon was thinking. If Ellis had indeed written a decree to cut Amron from his line of succession, that would be that. It was law now, and done. No matter how much the East Vandarians bleated and whined, there would be no way to change it lest they enter into civil war, and they wouldn't. They couldn't. The war was south not west, and they should be thankful that this one in the east was done. And so Elyon stood there, up on that table, silently applauding the Warrior King. No matter what Rylian said, this was all him. The prince knew it. Elyon knew it. Every bloody man here knew it. But there was nothing they could do. And they all knew that too.

When all the crowd were spent of their questions, Sir Dalton drew their attention. "I do not see Sir Vesryn here...for Sir Vesryn he will be again, and no lord." He lifted the scroll once more, and Elyon saw the deep pleasure curling on his lips. "With Ellis's death his claim to the Sword of Varinar has been lost. He will step down forthwith from his post and resume his service as Varin Knight, and nothing more." He scanned again. "Where is he?"

"In his pavilion," Lord Kanabar called over. "Pray tell who will claim the title of First Blade?"

He needn't ask. "I shall take it, as was my right all along," Dalton told them. "I name Sir Brontus my second and captain, as defeated semi finalist in The Song of the First Blade. I would ask for witnesses to follow me to Sir Vesryn's pavilion. I had hoped to corner him here, but...he may not go down easily."

Go down? Now it made sense why they were so clad in godsteel, though it wouldn't much help against the Sword of Varinar. Elyon's heart rushed into a heavy beat as he bounded down from the table and pushed through the crowd to the doors. *Do you still wear you armour, Uncle? Do not fight,* he thought. *Do not...*

His anger was gone in that instant, and it told him well enough that he cared for the man still. A worry thickened in his blood and he felt suddenly lightheaded. Men clogged through the doors like a slow-moving river choked with debris, eager to follow Sir Dalton...*Prince* Dalton...as he marched in gleaming plate through the camp. Outside the festivities were still going on. The drums beat, the skins skirled, the strings thrummed. Men were singing, hooting, crooning as they gathered at flaming pits, their tendrils tickling the black belly of the sky. Elyon pushed on, rushing now as a warmth spread down his back. He could feel a sticky wetness there beneath his tunic and shirt, but on he went, ignoring the blur in his head. "Sir Dalton, wait, hear me," he called, but the man was too far off. "Sir Dalton, he is not in his right mind. My uncle will not hand you the blade, he'll not! Do not do this now. Not now!"

They worked through the lanes between tents, breaking into the yard around which the highborn men of Vandar were housed. Dalton was already there, standing outside Vesryn's tent, Sir Taegon and Sir Brontus to his flanks. A mist of divine dust rose above them, silver and blue and glittery gold. Other Varin Knights stood here, stood there, blocking any exit, any way out. Sir Quinn Sharp, Sir Marcus Flint, Sir Ramsey Stone, and others, many others. All knights of houses under Taynar and Oloran and Cargill lands. All dissenters of Vesryn's claim. Some held bows, godsteel-tipped arrows nocked. The rest bore their misting blades, surrounding the tent. Even in full armour Vesryn would succumb should he fight. Not even the Sword of Varinar could save him from this.

"Sir Dalton..." Elyon pressed forward through the bodies, panting, and came in behind them. "Let me...let me speak to him. He'll listen to me." He could feel blood draining down his back now, warm against the frigid air.

Dalton Taynar gave a glance, but ignored him. "Vesryn Daecar, you are hereby commanded to lay down the Sword of Varinar and step out of your tent, by the royal order of King Godrik Taynar of Vandar," he called. "Submit and you will be allowed to serve in a capacity as Varin Knight, all slights forgotten. Fail to do so and you will die here this day." He stopped. "Do you hear me, Vesryn? I give you to the count of ten, before I fill your tent with bolts and arrows."

The threat had no effect. The ten count came and went, but no arrows were loosed. Dalton grunted and turned to Elyon, his bluff failing. "Go," he hissed. "Bring him out. *Unarmed*, Sir Elyon. I'm counting on you."

Elyon did as the man bid him, crossing the yard, reaching the flaps. Two hundred pairs of eyes watched him. Two hundred lips were sealed. Not a sound stirred the air. Not a sound outside the tent. And not a sound within...

He knew it before he even pulled the canvas door aside and looked into the space beyond.

Vesryn Daecar was gone. And he'd taken the Sword of Varinar with him.

48

Jonik

The cog had pulled in at an empty beach some five miles up the coast. They stepped out onto the silk soft sand, paid the ship captain his dues, disembarked the horses and walked them up inland through the rocks.

It was a rugged hike, and the sun beat down in powerful waves, but before too long they'd reached the coastal road. It was well tended, wide and oft travelled, according to Emeric, and the main overland route between Solas and Lumos several hundred miles to the east. "They call it the Capital Road," he told them. "It stretches all the way to Sutrek and Aram and up the east coast of Aramatia to Eagle's Perch. It's some two thousand miles long, all told. There's no longer road in the world."

They weren't to travel it, however. For one it wasn't safe and for two it wasn't going the right way. West would bring them right back to Solas and east would keep them along the coast to Lumos, and the dozens of settlements in between. Emeric's estate was north of their position, and though there were roads that would take them, he opted to ride cross-country.

It was country Jonik wasn't used to, nor any of the others in the party. Beyond the coast sparse grasslands spread into undulating hills, patched with clusters of palms and expanses of rugged rock formations in shades of red and rust and brown. Much of it was arid, hot and unwelcoming, yet there were lush swathes of verdancy too, some naturally formed around oases and waterholes and others by the design of settlers and farmers and the estates of the rich and wealthy.

"Are there many northerners living out here?" Jack asked Emeric, the daylight fading into a deep red dusk as they worked over a section of rocky windswept hills. "I've heard many came to live here after the war. Merchants and businessmen mainly who prefer the warmer climes."

"The quality of life is often considered better," Emeric said, riding a sorrel courser that could handle the weight of his blades, so long as they kept to a canter. "There's a class system, of course, and large parts of these lands are owned by the landed aristocracy, but they're not so strict and fussy about their neighbours as their counterparts in the north. The likes you talk about are predominantly welcomed, no matter where they're from. Merchants, traders, businessmen, artisans...all such sorts have settled here, and elsewhere across the empire. But now..." He paused a moment. "Well now who knows? If things go on like this they're like to be driven out. The empire has prided itself on these new values of cooperation and community between the continents for two decades, but soon enough it'll become as narrow-minded as the north once more. Let me ask you this, Jack...have you ever seen a rich southerner settle in the north? You're from the Marshlands. Are there such men in East Vandar that you've seen?"

"I'm ashamed to say no, Lord Manfrey," Jack said. "Though I do know that southerners settle in Rasalan. They have always been a more welcoming people."

"That they have, and it's one of the reasons why Janilah is so intent on destroying them." He shook his head as they trotted beneath the darkening dusky skies. "It's such a shame to see the same thing happening here. Southerners will be fleeing from the north, and northerners from the south, and the dividing lines will be raised, as clear and stark as ever. It takes but a few powerful zealots to beat the drums...Janilah and Tavash and the Patriots down here, and all the world rushes right back to war."

It was a sad indictment, though in that war Jonik would have his part to play. *And Emeric? He sounds like he'd sooner go to war with the north than the south.* The Lord of House Manfrey, who fell in love with a southerner and was exiled as a price. Jonik could quite understand his resentment, but who was it truly against? Lord Modrik Kastor who cast him out? King Janilah who did nothing to stop it? If he wanted vengeance, he'd have to look elsewhere. Modrik was dead and Janilah untouchable, but then there were others who could pay by proxy. *Might that satisfy him?* he wondered. *If I should help him seek justice, might he help me seek it too?*

He trotted along in thought, until Emeric called for them to come to a stop in the shadow of a rocky outcropping. It loomed some ten metres above them, giving shelter from the wind, and concealing them from anyone passing upon the hilltop road a little to the north. "It'll stay warm enough tonight, so you'll not need a fire," Emeric said. "Jonik, I'd ask that we split watch. Let me fetch a couple of hours sleep, and then I'll take over. I don't expect I'll find rest easy." He turned to the others. "We ride on at dawn."

Jonik didn't sleep well, his mind full of shadows and forts and storms and mountains, of poor broken gelded men and the service they endured. He woke a half dozen times and drifted off the same, until finally opening his eyes to a soft pink blur in the east. Emeric was already standing up at the top of the ridge, his silhouette cast noble and pensive against the pale morning light. Jonik stretched and hurried to join him. "A red dawn," Emeric merely said, staring sombre to the hills. "I fear the worst, Jonik. I fear death has come upon these lands this night."

He said little that morning as they continued north, riding hard as their mounts could manage upon the rocky terrain. When they neared a well-worn road, Braxton suggested they take the risk, until the sight of distant riders forced them to retreat. They rode off to a nearby copse of palms and watched as the host galloped by, wild and raving, swinging scimitars and flails and spiked maces above their heads. Jonik was certain he saw bloodstains on those blunts and blades, and their rawhide mail armour looked blackened by soot. Some had shields too, round and bronze with gilding around the edges, fastened to their backs or the flanks of their mounts. Their cloaks were assorted colours, and so was their skin, shaded from a deep dark brown to a light golden tan.

"They ride for Solas," Jack said, a worry in his voice. "You don't think..."

He didn't say it, but they all knew it. They were militant, murderers, Patriots of Lumara. And they were coming from the north...

"We ride on," Emeric said, his voice punching urgently through his lips. He pulled the reins and charged his courser up and onto the road, the dust still clouding from the passing of the host. "We ride hard for the north. No stopping now! On me!"

He didn't care to keep off the road after that, close as they were now, and Jonik sensed they all knew what had happened before they even arrived. With the reassuring touch of his godsteel dagger in his palm, he sniffed the air and smelled it. The burning. The fire. The crisp and crackle of corpses.

"On! On!" Manfrey was kicking his spurs hard now, hard and harder still, but his horse wasn't bred to bear godsteel this long. It tired soon enough, his front legs starting to buckle, and Emeric leaped right off it and continued on foot. The rest came in behind, barely catching him up for the speed he was travelling, the eagle-blade of House Manfrey already clutched in his hand, gleaming. And there ahead, over the lip of a rise, came the sight of smoke, billowing and clouding and blowing on the breeze.

"No..." Jonik heard Emeric call. The exile charged on up the hill, kicking up dust from his heels, before coming to a swift sharp stop on the hilltop. Jonik galloped in with Shade, springing from the saddle to join him. "No..." Emeric was saying. "No...NO!"

That last one came a bellow, brutal from his lungs. He set off down into the valley, as Jonik trailed behind, and the others came thundering behind on the mounts. Ahead, in a wide open basin between the hills, the once-picturesque estate of Lord Emeric Manfrey was a ruin of fire and smoke and death. The central white-stone villa was black and burning, heavy puffs of thick fiery smoke pouring from the doors and windows. The outbuildings too had been put to the torch, some still belching black fumes, others smouldering, all utterly destroyed. Bodies lay everywhere. It looked like some of the staff had been locked in one outbuilding or another, and burnt alive. Others lay beyond the main house, unburnt but slaughtered as they fled, pools of rich red blood stark against the pure white of their linen and cotton clothes. Nothing had been spared. No one. The peaceful gardens that encircled the house were razed, the olive fields and groves and lawns all blackened, shrivelled and scorched. Even the statues had been torn down, the fountains demolished, bodies thrown into the pools and ponds to blacken and bloody the water.

Jonik followed Emeric down the hill, drawing the Nightblade for the good it would do. There was no one here, no one to slay or save. It seemed certain that the score of men that had passed were the culprits. *They ride for Solas,* Jack had said. *Was he right?* Ahead, Emeric was making for the main house, some fifty yards away. Before Jonik could catch up and stop him he was pressing right through the arched front entrance, past the pillars, and into the belching fumes. "Emeric, stop!" he called, but too late.

The man faded into the darkness, calling out names as he went. "Brewilla! Kestan! Puli! Is anyone here! Brewilla!"

His voice ripped out, desperate, as the others caught up, pulling the reins and jumping from the saddles. "Check the dead!" Jonik ordered them. "See if anyone lives!" Then he turned and followed Emeric right through the doors, plunging into the smoke and flame with a sleeve over his nose and mouth. "Emeric!" he coughed. "Emeric, where are you?"

The smoke swirled about him, stinging his eyes, blinding him. He could make out the space of a large open hall, furniture flaming about him. Emeric was still calling, somewhere upstairs. "Brewilla! Brewilla, where are you? Puli! Kestan. Brewilla! BREWILLA!"

Jonik followed the voice, pulling upon the power of the Nightblade as his body faded and blended, joining the smoke. He moved through the house as one with the billowing fumes, the flames licking around him in great tongues of swirling red light. He weaved through them, up the stairs, down the corridor, searching. But the voice was gone. "Emeric!" he called out, pulling his sleeve from his mouth. "Emeric, can you hear me?"

He stopped and focused, listening. And that's when he heard the whisper, coming from a room down the hall. "Brewilla…" He sped along the landing and inside, to find Emeric crouched over the lifeless body of a woman. He was stroking her hair. "Brewilla..."

"We have to go, Emeric!" The man stayed where he was, stroking the woman's long black locks. "Emeric, the house is coming down. We have to go!" He marched in and grabbed his arm, but the exile shoved him away. He stared up with eyes shot red, stained and strained with grief. "Emeric...please, the floor may collapse any moment. Let me carry her outside. Will you let me do that?"

"I will do it." The exile whispered the words, but still made no move to take her. His ancestral blade lay to one side, misting. "Carry my blade for me, Jonik," he whispered. "Follow behind, should I fall."

Jonik did as he was bidden, picking up the eagle-blade as Emeric lifted Brewilla gently to his arms. They worked down through the house as quickly as they could, as it cracked and roared about them, threatening to come down any second. Not a moment after they'd passed down the stairs, a great crashing sounded and they collapsed upon themselves, as the pillars crumbled, and the upper floors followed, the entire hall caving in just as they pressed back out into the light.

The others were checking the bodies nearby. All rushed over as soon as Emeric and Jonik appeared, the exile laying the woman down. She was dressed in a scorched white gown, her skin dark, face beautiful. Lifeless, Jonik saw, as Emeric held his palm to her cheek. He had told him in Lizard's Laze that Brewilla was his head housekeeper, but he knew now that wasn't true. "She was more to you than a maid, wasn't she?" he asked, as tender as he could, as Emeric stared down at the woman's face, young and peaceful.

"I loved her," he whispered. "For many years...I loved her."

Jonik said nothing, giving Emeric time as he stared down at

her smooth round face, stroking at her hair and cheek. A half minute passed, then another, until he finally shut his eyes, dipped his head, and stood with a face of cold stone. "The Patriots did this," he said. "It can only have been them."

Jonik stared at him, at the heartbreak etched into his eyes. "What do you want to do?"

Emeric turned his eyes down to his beloved. "We will bury her," he said. "Then we will bury the rest." The others were watching in anguish from the side. "And once that's done, we'll rest a while. We'll rest and think, Jonik. Think long, and think hard, about how we're going to kill them."

Jonik remained silent, unsure of what to say. But from the others came a voice. "They were riding for Solas," said Jack, looking just as stricken as the rest. "We might want to start there."

"We might," murmured Emeric, as the world crackled and burned around them. He knelt down and picked up Brewilla once more, as her long black hair tumbled in a smoky shower over his arms. He stared into her face. "I will bury her alone, in the place she cherished most. Please gather the others, if you can. Be gentle with them, my friends. All were kind. All were good. Not one deserved this fate."

The afternoon passed, slow and wretched, as the bodies were gathered and lined up beyond the villa. It was grisly work. Some had lost limbs. Others were charred to the bone. Every one of them was drenched bloody and black by the end, but not a single complaint was uttered. Two hours later, Emeric returned. "She loved to walk in the olive groves at the edge of my lands. I am sorry I took so long."

"You need never apologise, Lord Manfrey," croaked Turner. "I lost a wife myself once. I understand how you feel."

Emeric gave him a soft smile. "She wasn't my wife, Captain, but I loved her all the same." He looked over at the line of bodies, placed within an open courtyard. "You have gathered them, thank you. But if I may ask...would you help me dig the grave?"

"We'll work all night if we have to," said Devin, teary-eyed and earnest. "All day and all night, milord. As long as it takes to see them to their rest."

Emeric looked at the boy with a fatherly affection. "That is kind, Devin. But they may come back, so we cannot stay long. I should not have gone so far." He shook his head, self-scolding. "There is weak soil over here."

He led them to a place to dig, and using blades and spades and whatever tools they could find, dug a great big pit. The dead had numbered two shy of twenty, and each needed their space. It was long hot dirty work, and still, not a grumble or complaint was uttered.

It was dark when they were done, when the men and women had been put to the earth, and the soil covered atop them. Emeric said a prayer for each, most in Lumaran, several in Piseki, and a couple in the tuneful Aramatian tongue. He stood by the grave, somehow knowing where each was, looking to a certain part of the pit as he spoke. And there was a magic to the man, to his shift of tongue, the delicate manner in which he spoke. When he was done he turned. "They have passed," he said, "with the prayers of their gods. We will see them now in the sun and the moon, in the stars that light the night skies. Brewilla will shine bright, I know it. Her soul was always full of starlight."

They moved from the grave and back to the horses; Shade had gathered them nearby to keep them calm. "We must leave now," Emeric said. He looked them over. "Can anyone recall features of the men who passed us? It will give us a lead to follow."

Devin's head went up and down. "There was one missing an ear," he said. Burnt or cut or torn off, I don't know, but it left an ugly pit and scarred flesh around it."

"Another was tall and broad, much bigger than most folk," said Braxton. "You could tell by the way he sat the saddle, and the horse beneath him. Must have been seven feet high, and had a wild mane of black hair too. Not many men like that about."

"One had a hook for a hand," Jonik added. "His right hand. He should be easy to track."

Emeric nodded, and spoke in a listless voice. "That is a good start. We will make camp and return to Solas tomorrow, so Jonik and I can make inquiries. I would advise that you all return to the ship and leave these lands, but I can see that none of you will. In truth, there are few places that one can call safe now. But do think on it. Think long and hard. If you wish to go, no one will think the less of you for it."

They left with those words, riding back into the empty hills, as each man turned to the quiet solitude of his thoughts. That night, when the world was sleeping, and a deep thick darkness had fallen upon the lands, Jonik drew the Nightblade and faded into black. He blew off as a fog to the highest point he could see, searching the distance for the gleaming Sun City of Solas, far away at the coast. And staring out over the hills, he asked, "Is this my path now, great lord? Is it the Patriots of Lumara on whom I'm to wage war?"

He looked at the Nightblade as it rippled and fogged before him. *Your path is not a straight one, Jonik,* it whispered. *It winds as a river does, left and right, and this is but another turn. Trust it, child, and let the water take you downriver. The journey will make you a champion. The destination will win us our war.*

As ever he did, Jonik accepted that. He set the Nightblade back to its sheath, and spent the night alone, watching over his friends from that quiet lonely hilltop.

49

Amron

Out over the western edge of the world the last light of the day was fading, the clouds lit in radiant shades of red and purple, the horizon below burning soft and warm in long thin sheets of flaming amber. Away in the distance, the mountains of the Weeping Heights shallowed into foothills, the towering peaks of the central range behind them now. Beyond was a vast white desolation, pockmarked with patches of black woodland, frozen lakes, rifts and ridges and chasms so deep it was said they never ended.

The Icewilds, Amron thought as he stared out, wrapped in leather and wool and fur. But still he shivered. There was a chill in his bones that would be there forever now, he felt. A chill so deep it would never unthaw.

"Take a good long look," said Walter Selleck, his bedraggled beard dangling with little shimmering icicles, as they caught the last glow of the sun. "Out there the sun doesn't rise this time of year, not deep in the north where we're going. We'll have another week of it, maybe, an hour or two per day. But then it'll be gone, out like a wick." He tried to clip his fingers through his thick padded gloves. "Best get used to the darkness, Lord Amron. We'll be seeing a lot of it soon."

Amron stared out as the light ebbed away to deeper shades of crimson and violet. The days had been growing shorter, the nights longer and darker and colder. At first they'd been stopping when dusk fell, making camp to stay warm and rest, but for the last week they'd not been able to. If they only moved in daylight they'd never get anywhere, and Walter was right, they had to get used to it. "I doubt even my godsteel will let me see clearly out there," he said. "I still marvel at how you managed it, Walter. Truly."

Walter bobbed his head, though perhaps he was just shivering. "So do I, thinking back," he said, teeth chattering as the last of the warmth receded, and the winds cruelly began to pick up. "My memory of it is so fragmented. It's all moments, bits and pieces of a whole. But when I stand back and think of it..." He shook his head. "I should have died a hundred times on the way. How I reached that mountain unscathed...that I will never know."

Rogen Whitebeard stepped over toward them, the dark grey tangles of hair on his face twisted with frost and dressed all in white. "Blind luck," he said in that low growly voice of his. "Is that not what you claim, Selleck? To be the luckiest man in the world?"

"That claim came later, Whitebeard. Before I reached Vandar's Tomb I wasn't so lucky. I'm not sure anyone would call the death of their entire family to a fire an act of fortune."

Whitebeard made a grunting sound. "A tragedy," he said, and that was the closest he came to sympathy for the man. "But the fact remains...you were lucky to cross these mountains without facing your end, let alone the Icewilds." He reached out with a long rangy arm, wreathed in black, and pointed. "The perils we have faced will multiply from here. The foothills stretch some thirty miles before reaching the Silver Scar. Beyond is another two hundred miles of desolation and darkness." His sinewy neck twisted left, and his upturned amber eyes narrowed. "We would do well to stay away from the Deadwood. Not even the tribes go there lest they must. And we must be wary of them too. Most stay in the foothills, but some rove beyond, stalking the chasms and the caves. Be on your guard, always. For man and beast both."

Amron had come to appreciate Rogen Whitebeard more and more. He'd not gone all the way to Vandar's Tomb, not like Walter had, but he'd ranged these lands more than any man living and understood them better too. *But how far will his knowledge take us?* Walter continued to claim that his light was guiding their way, protecting them in some vague, nebulous way, but Amron had to admit he'd seen little of it so far. There had been no miraculous escapes, no close brushes with death. Beyond the avalanche they'd avoided, and the nest of snow-snakes they'd crept past, little else had troubled them. Just the winds, and the cold, and the endless ache of their march. All enough to sap and drain a man, but not enough to kill him so long as he was prepared. They had ample rations. They had ample furs and pelts and warm winter clothing to protect them from the gelid air and brutal bitter winds. And they had Whitebeard. A man of few words but clear and expressive action. He checked every pass for dangers. He led the way on every march. He was careful, meticulous, and dedicated to his task. Without him they'd be lost.

"We should continue," the tall surly ranger said now, turning his eyes down the pass. To their right, the last great peak of the Weeping Heights climbed into the gathering darkness, its slopes clothed in tall thin pines and shorter spruce, their needles and branches clothed in glittery hoar frost. Left, the mountains were shorter, tumbling away into the plains below where the sun's glow was withering away with a last final kiss of red light.

"Should we not wait?" Walter suggested. His eyes were on the route down. "I presume you'll want to make for those woods, and work down through the trees?"

"It is the best way," Whitebeard said brusquely.

"In this light?" They had moved in darkness a few times thus far, but not when navigating steep declines, with rutting roots and rocks hidden beneath the snow. "I propose we make camp and wait until morning." He pointed east. "There are some rocks there for shelter. And the winds are picking up..."

"The mountain will give us cover as we descend," Whitebeard said. "It is an east wind. Do not worry yourself, Selleck. I will go first. You need but tread in my prints and no harm will come of you."

The man was not for convincing, nor for debate. He set off without further consideration, crunching deep tracks in the snow.

Walter threw Amron a troubled look but had no option but to continue. "You might want to put your foot down with him once in a while, my lord," he grumbled over the wind, as they hurried after the ranger. "You let him run rings around you."

"Don't be sore, Walter. You'll have your day soon."

His accusation was hardly fair either. Amron was naught but a babe in swaddling out here, and Rogen Whitebeard the wise old master. *A scholar to a lackwit,* he might have said, but then again, he did rather agree with Walter on this one. The dying dusk was fast in retreat now and deep shadows were creeping dark and gloomy over the slopes. When they hit the first trees it only got darker. "You stay near to him, Walter," Amron said. "I have my godsteel to steady me. Stay between us."

The trees weren't tightly packed, but they were tall and eerie and their branches were waving and rustling a strange ghostly tune. Pine thickened in the air, a rich damp smell, and somewhere far off, far far off, he thought he heard the distant call of a wolf, howling on the wind. If Whitebeard heard it too he gave it no mind, pacing on into the shadows and gloom. For all the man's virtues out here he had a tendency to set a quick pace that the others struggled to keep up with at times. Walter was not built for this, short and stubby and paunchy as he was, and Amron's right leg was still stiff and achy, a pain he'd learned to ignore and endure. The mornings were the worst, when he woke after his stunted sleep, breaking from dreams of which he cared not to speak. Often Whitebeard would be up and ready and ordering them on, but it always took some time for Amron's thigh to thaw and warm. By day's end, he was often too weary to talk, too cold and tired and broken, but on he went. On and on, as the days shortened and the skies darkened and the perils began to close in.

He'd had a sense of that too. That they were being watched. For some days he'd thought it just his imagination, a trick of the light and the whispering wind, but later Whitebeard had confirmed it. "There is always something watching out here. Or someone," he'd said, and those words had been enough to unsettle even the Crippler of Kings. Now he was always looking, always listening, and seeing nothing. "Most of the tribal people here are skittish and timid and not likely to go near us," the ranger explained. "Those are the ones you'd never know were there. If they want you to see them, you'll know it. They will show themselves if they feel threatened...or if you have something they want."

"Ours furs and clothes?" Walter had offered to that.

"They have fur, plenty of fur. You live long enough out here and don't want for something like that." He shook his head. "No, it is food that can grow scarce in winter. Some may look at you, Master Selleck, and see a week's worth of meat."

Amron didn't want to know how much sustenance he might provide. Walter had a belly on him, true, but his arms were quite weedy and he was shorter than Amron by almost a foot. "There are cannibals here?" is all he'd asked.

"Don't sound so appalled, Lord Daecar," growled Whitebeard. "When you have nothing to eat, you have no choice. These are not good lands for farming, as you can tell, so they must go where the food is. Some rove into the Banewood, or so far south as the coastal ranges, north of the Tidelands. Others venture into the Icewilds. There is game to be had there, though it is scarce. As are the people here now. They have withered for centuries. Not many remain."

"They might want to consider going south," Walter said pithily.

"They do, and they die." Whitebeard set his jaw and marched off.

And now he was marching again, striding away into the moody woodland, as the snowy slopes fell at a steep angle beneath them. The snows leaned out as they went, the trees forming some buffer above them, and soon Amron was feeling the press of hard rock and roots beneath his leather boots. It was a welcome feeling after spending the last few days knee deep in white, plugging and pulling his legs from the thick sucking snows as they'd crossed over the high passes. Here it was light, no higher than his ankles, though that came with its own dangers. Beneath his soles he could feel the slippery scree, the patches of ice, the thick strong roots poking from the soil.

"Slow down, Whitebeard," he heard Walter calling over the winds, sensing the same. "Have a care, it's almost sheer. One wrong foot and you'll go tumbling."

His words were prophetic, and in part a cause of what came next. Turning, Whitebeard barked something back at him, and taking his eyes off the earth at his feet, caught his foot on a hidden jut of rock. The ranger was usually as sure-footed as a mountain goat, but as he twisted and tried to retain his balance, so a fierce buffeting wind swished violently across him, sweeping down through the trees. The press of the squall was enough to have him tripping, upending into the snow. He landed with a thump and a grunt and Walter was first to react, launching forward. Amron hardly saw what happened next, but the next thing he knew, Walter was in the snow with Whitebeard, holding his leg like a limpet, and the two were rolling and barreling down the slopes in an uncontrolled spin. A second later, both men had disappeared into the gloom, leaving a trail of churned snow in their wake.

Amron gave careful chase, pulling his walking stick from his pack for extra purchase. Three-legged, he crabbed down the steep slope between the trees in a crouch, following the trail. The gusts at his back were coming with more persistence now, pushing him on, deafening him to the calls of his companions in the distance. The descent was steep and growing steeper still. Hitting a tree at pace could snap a neck or back, and even a twisted ankle would be a problem out here. *Minor injuries are not so minor in the wild,* he remembered his father telling him once, when he was just a boy with a head full of adventures. *A broken wrist can make a bow unusable for hunting. A sprained ankle can make you vulnerable to predators. A small cut, untreated, can become infected. Everything is compounded when you're far from home, son.* All that was more true than Amron had ever appreciated. And if Walter or Whitebeard should be hurt? If they should require attention, what then?

Poking at the frozen ground with his walking stick, he shambled on as quick as he dared...but when he saw the track end, and the world plunge to darkness below, Amron knew they were both dead. Careful as he could he approached the edge of the precipice. To the left and right, the slopes continued down into the basin, but here an escarpment climbed out of the earth to form a cliff. They'd gone right over it. *So much for Walter's luck*, was the first thought that came to mind. An ugly thought. A bitter thought. And then he heard the laughing.

"Walter! Rogen!" he bellowed, peering over the edge. His voice echoed into the night. Below was a drop of some twenty yards, leading to the tops of a cluster of pines. Amron searched through the wintry gloom and saw that the snows atop the trees had been disturbed where they'd fallen through. "Walter! Rogen!" he called again. "Are you all right!" and this time he heard a call back.

"My lord, do be careful on the descent," shouted the luckiest man in the world. "It really is rather steep!"

He found them some twenty minutes later, having navigated a path down a gentler slope, and cutting back into the foot of the cliff. It was sheltered by the wall of rock and the copse of pines and it seemed his friends had taken it as a good place to set camp. A fire was already burning, smoke swirling up into the black branches of the trees, and Whitebeard was finishing the shelter. Amron stepped in, bewildered to find both of them in such rude health, with nary a scratch upon them. "What happened?"

There was something triumphant about the smile on Walter Selleck's face. He looked up past the trees they'd tumbled through, and to the top of the cliff some sixty yards above them. "I thought we'd take a shortcut, my lord. The going was so perilously slow."

Amron considered the fall. It was enough to shatter any man into a dozen pieces. "The branches broke your fall?" It was the only explanation, but even then...

Walter pointed to a large bank of snow that had accumulated at the bottom of the cliff. There were two suspiciously human-shaped depressions in the drift. And then it all made sense. "You lucky bastard." Amron had to laugh, a barking guffaw loud enough to stir all the beasts of the Icewilds. He looked over as Whitebeard diligently erected the shelter. "Well, Rogen? Are you convinced yet?"

The ranger stood upright, his black-cloaked back to them, frosted white. For a moment he was perfectly still, before he turned with a begrudging look on his narrow wolfish face. "Now I am starting to understand why he's here."

It was all he said, though when Amron had heard laughing from the top of the cliff, he was quite sure it had been from them both. He stepped over to Walter. "You couldn't have planned that any better," he whispered, glancing at Whitebeard. "What a way to get him onside, my friend. Are you sure you didn't trip him?"

Walter gave a devious look, then said, "I'm just happy to share my light."

They shared more than light that evening, as by way of celebration, and thanks, Rogen Whitebeard unearthed a small clay bottle of brandy from his pack. "I like to keep alcohol for medicinal use," he told them with a shift to his orange eyes, as they gathered around the fire in that secluded little glade. "But today I feel we have turned a corner." He handed the bottle to Walter. "I am sorry I doubted you, Master Selleck. And you, Lord Daecar. I do not take well to company out here, but I believe now what you say." He even managed to smile. "Lucky indeed, Walter. But we'll have more to face than a tumble out there."

Those worries were for another day, and they saw no sense in saving any of the brandy that night. It wasn't a large bottle, not shared between three, but after some weeks of abstinence it was plenty enough. A warmth spread down Amron's throat from the first sip, sending fiery fingers reaching through his chest, and he let out a long shuddering sigh. "I suppose this is the last time I'll feel warm in a while," he said. "Will it be safe to start fires out there, Rogen?"

"Safe? No...nothing will be safe." Rogen Whitebeard took the clay bottle and swigged. "Fire can be a beacon, yes, but it can frighten some beasts away too. It will depend which we face. Some are drawn to it, others not. We will judge it as we go."

"We can always cuddle for warmth," offered Walter, smirking. "I rather enjoyed snuggling your leg earlier, Whitebeard. Maybe we should take our relationship to the next level, and spoon at night. What do you say?"

"I say you must be drunk. Give me this." He took the brandy back, and had a swig. Then he looked at Walter again, said nothing for a moment, then asked, "What is it like?" Walter pursed his lips, waiting for elaboration. "The mountain...Vandar's Tomb? I have seen it, but only from afar. But you..."

"So you believe me now?" Walter was rubbing it in a bit; Whitebeard had already admitted as such. At risk of being churlish, he gave a proper answer. "It is magnificent," he said, smiling distantly as though seeing it right before them. He even lifted his eyes, looking through the tall black trees. "I have seen mountains all over the world, but nothing like Vandar's Tomb. It stands alone. No range. No foothills. A volcano, really. And you can feel it. The warmth, the fires inside, right deep down beneath the earth. There were forges there once, and great mines, and storerooms and chambers where the miners and hewers and soldiers would sleep. Now all that's just rust and ruin, forgotten and abandoned."

"Did you see much of that?" Amron found himself leaning forward before the flickering flames. They'd spoken of this before, but he always found new questions. New things he wanted to know. "Did you take time to explore before you climbed down into the depths?"

"A little, on my way out." Walter bobbed his head. "But I was eager to get back home. To restart my life. There is godsteel still there, you know." He lifted his brows. "Not all of it was mined."

"The accounts at the Steelforge document all that," Amron told them. "They had more than they ever thought they'd need, so shut the mines and closed the forges. It's sat dormant now for centuries, but for a few intrepid visitors." He gave Walter a genial nod.

"I have always wanted to know of the shape," Whitebeard said in a soft low growl. "From the distance it looks like any mountain, but I have read that from some angles, it takes the vague form of a man. The shoulders and the head, with a cloak and hood, and even a face with a beard. They say this is Vandar himself, the form he took at his death. That he gave his body as a parting gift to be mined into godsteel by his people. That Varin cut the heart from him, to be split into the Blades of Vandar." His eyes turned to Amron. "What was it like, to bear a fragment of him? You held the Sword of Varinar for twenty years, Lord Daecar. Did you grow attached to it, as they say."

Amron had never heard Whitebeard talk so much, but there was a deep interest in his eyes, something almost childlike in the curiosity on that grisly hollow face. "I was fond of it," he admitted, though that wasn't the half of it. He could see they wanted more, deserved more than that. "At times, it became something of an obsession, I'll confess, but they were few. It was a crutch, during times of stress and grief. But to get too attached would be folly, my father always taught me..."

"Did it whisper? His voice...did you hear it?"

That was from Walter, and Amron was starting to feel a familiar discomfort. He'd never liked fielding questions like these. People had learned not to pose them. "The whispers would come and go," he told them. His voice was a little short. "Kings and First Blades learned not to listen to them, nor trust them."

Whitebeard frowned at that. "But is it not the voice of Vandar? Who is a king or lord to ignore the voice of a god?"

"It is an echo," Amron told him. "An echo of Vandar's spirit only. The blades are said to have taken on their own personalities, that they can force themselves upon the unprepared and vulnerable, and bend them to their will. Vandar was a god of war, Rogen, indomitable and all powerful. And what is a blade forged for if not to kill, to take life? In the hands of a man untrained to deal with such a responsibility, a great deal of damage can be done. A man's will must be his own, whether he holds a Blade of Vandar or not. For otherwise he may fall to chaos, and to madness. Otherwise, he might become a great peril to himself...and to others."

Rogen Whitebeard was nodding pensively, staring into the flames as he listened. He blinked a couple of times and then looked away, as Walter said, "Those blades were forged by Ilith to be held by a demigod. Is it any surprise that humble men might fall to their will? Even kings and great lords of powerful bloodlines can become thralls to their power. The Blades of Vandar seek war, and always have. They seek champions to fight in the War Eternal. Like you, Amron. They seek men like you."

"Then they abandon men like me too." Those words came as a grunt. "I no longer hold the Sword of Varinar, lest you forget."

"For now," said Walter. "You may yet hold it again."

Amron didn't want to delve any deeper into that. He took up the clay bottle and enjoyed another swig to warm his insides. Then he looked at Whitebeard. "Who have you lost?" he asked him. "When we passed Mount Mornay, I heard you in lament, weeping to the heights. Walter is of the belief that we have been brought together through tragedy. That it is our grief that drives us." He peered at the ranger. "You were facing west, not east. There was someone out here that meant something to you, wasn't there? That is why you range here alone, and for so long. You come to these heights to remember them."

Rogen Whitebeard didn't say anything for a long moment. Once or twice Amron thought he had crossed a line, that the ranger might stand and show him his back and stride away into the blackness, as he'd done before when probed of his past. But this time he didn't. They had turned a corner, he'd admitted. So he nodded and said, "I knew a girl. A sweet girl, and kind. She had white hair, though she was young. That is common among some of the tribes here, and one in particular. Their hair is all white like snow, and some have skin like milk...pale and glassy." He turned his eyes into the woods. "We call them Snowskins, one of many peoples here. I was injured once, and they took me in." He reached out and pulled up the leg of this quilted breeches, unveiling the great scar down the front of his right shin. "I broke my leg on a fall, and they found me, nursed me to health. This girl was my carer. She was generous to me, and gentle. She was...beautiful." He turned away. "I visited her again, each time I returned. I developed a love for her, something I have never spoken of until now." His eyes were gleaming now in the firelight, his voice no more than a soft rasping whisper. "One day, I came back and found that she had been killed in a dispute. A man had tried to claim her, but she wouldn't go with him, to be taken for a wife, or bear his brood." He smiled a sad rueful smile. "She loved me, and refused to go with him. Elurra. That was her name.

Elurra who saved me, and changed me. Elurra who died for me." He turned his eyes down, and said no more.

A long silence crept upon them, and in the winds the whispers were heard. The laments of those they'd loved and lost. Amron looked at Whitebeard and understood him now. Understood why he spoke so seldom, and sought solitude out here for so long. "You were young when you met her?" he asked in a delicate voice.

Whitebeard nodded. "Yes. Young and...different, then. I have forgotten what it is to care for someone, someone living, at least. Only Elurra. She is the only person I have ever cared about. So I come here for her, always."

Another long hush clasped at them, choking the air. After a long sombre moment Walter murmured, "Grief binds us, and drives us. It brought me into Vandar's light. It has crafted you into the ranger you have become. It now draws Amron here, to seek salvation." His words became more fervent. "We three together will reach that mountain. It is *our* task, Rogen, to guide him. That is why we have suffered. It has all been for a higher purpose."

"A higher purpose..." Rogen Whitebeard stared into the fire, then stood. An anger flared in his eyes. "Keep your higher purpose," he said. "I will help guide Lord Daecar for Lord Borrington commanded it of me. That is why I am here, Walter. I do not care for your war."

With that, he did what he had done so many times before. They only saw the back of him, as he marched away into the gloom.

The next day, little was said. They broke their fast with salted pork, teak-tough bread and old cheese. Whitebeard spent the early part of the morning hunting in the dim dawn glow, but returned without spoils. That did nothing to improve his mood. "We should go. The light will not linger so long anymore."

They continued down through the western foothills, the short levity of the last night forgotten. Whitebeard had escaped to his thoughts, and set a hard pace. "It seems he's gone back around that corner he turned," Walter noted, as they worked through a vast vale between the forested slopes. There was more shrubbery on this side than Amron had expected. Thistles and bracken and sedge spouted among the tall pines and sentinels, and there were a few scattered ash and elms about, lost of their summer coats.

"Just a blip, I hope," Amron said. "You heard him last night, Walter. He'd never spoken of the girl before, and that brandy had loosened his tongue. He's regretting he said anything. And you can be too pious."

"Mayhaps that's true," the luckiest man in the world admitted. "I thought the timing was right, but got it wrong. Still, he knows now. He knows why he's really here."

To guide me back to health? Amron thought. *To make me into a champion?* He was more inclined to side with Whitebeard on this one. Amron had followed Varin's scriptures as any good lord and knight should, but he'd never been especially devout. There was war coming with the south, that was all he knew. A war he needed to fight in, one way or another, as he had the one before. But this talk of it being the Last Renewal? Of the gods gathering their champions? That he wasn't so sure on. So he just nodded, and walked on.

The darkness came a fraction earlier that day. They'd made it another ten miles north, Whitebeard estimated, making decent time through the low foothills and steep valleys, passing foreboding woods and glassy frozen lakes. But in the days and weeks to come, their grant of daily daylight would recede more sharply. *Curse our fortune to travel these lands this time of year,* he thought. Even when the mountain was mined, operations would be curtailed when the deep winter darkness fell, and opened up again when the light bloomed and stretched and chased all the shadows away. In summertime, the distant north wasn't so encumbered. It stayed brighter for longer and was warmer too. *But here we are, so don't think about it,* he told himself. *You don't have the choice to wait.*

They camped in a rift, and woke the next day to a heavy snowfall that near buried their shelter. "Did an avalanche come down on us overnight?" Walter asked. It was only half a jest.

Whitebeard fought his way through the snow with his godsteel dagger, and set off into the pre-dawn gloom to hunt again. His blood-bond gave him excellent senses, essential for any true ranger, though not once had the man spoken of the house that sired him. "It doesn't matter," he had said when Amron asked him. "I am a ranger now, sworn to watch over these lands. This is where I belong. My past has no bearing."

He'd said that a week ago and it made a good deal more sense now that Amron knew about Elurra. The rangers gave up all prospects, lands and titles when settling at Northwatch, and were commonly third and fourth sons of lesser lines. *Men that don't matter to their fathers,* Amron thought. Most great lords cared only for their heirs, and whatever pretty eligible daughters they might bandy for a good match. Sons lower down the pecking order were of less value, and if unsuited to life as a chivalrous knight or awkward at court, were sent out here. There was honour in the posting, true, but it was one few young Bladeborn truly wanted. Rogen Whitebeard seemed uniquely adapted to the life, but was he as such before he met her? Before Elurra? Amron would never likely know.

It was another long day, and in the afternoon the air thickened with snow again. It slowed them down, and forced them to stop prematurely as the night closed in, a little earlier still than the day before. The same thing happened the next day, and the next, until eventually the foothills edged down into the low hilly plains and the vast desolation of the Icewilds spread out before them, a hundred thousand square miles of dread and darkness and doom.

They lined up, looking out, from their final camp in the mountains. A cold hand curled around Amron's heart, squeezing. Every breath filled his lungs with ice. *Ice.* It was everywhere. Ice and snow and silver and white, as far as the eye could see, scarred with patches of black and dark grey. The distant shadow of a forest. The great frozen river of the Silver Scar, cutting its way down from the mountains and through the barren lands beyond. There were great fingers of rock, poking up from the ground, curled and twisted as though trying to grip at the bleak grey skies. Rifts and chasms ripped across the world, as though those same fingers had gouged them out. *This is a place of giants and monsters, of demons and devilry,* Amron thought, staring out. Not much quelled him, but that sight did. He looked at his companions with a renewed respect. *What sort of courage did it take to step beyond these borders? The Weeping Heights were one thing, but this...*

"We leave before dawn," Rogen Whitebeard said. Walter nodded. Both their faces were set. "We will have light for a time, but must get used to walking in darkness. Soon the sun will be gone...and it shall not return."

Amron Daecar, the Hero of the North, hardly slept a wink that night. He lay and thought of his dead wife, his dead son, the baby he'd never seen grow. He thought of Elyon, of Lillia, of Amara, Vesryn, his friends, his men, his people, the north. He thought of every man, woman and child who would soon fall beneath the great shadow of war. *A shadow more dark and deadly than what we'll face out here,* he thought. It was enough to firm and fortify his spirt as he rose, warmed his leg, wrapped his furs, and broke his fast.

Once all that was done, they turned and faced the darkness. And into its haunting embrace, they went.

50

Saska

Saska sat at the window seat of her room in the inn, looking out over the harbour. It was a fine day, a bit blustery by the flapping of the flags and sails, but bright and sunny and not too cold. She took up a piece of bread from the wooden plate next to her and sawed off a bite with her teeth, chewing. "When will the captain be ready to leave?" she asked, mouth full, glancing over at Lancel and Barnibus, who sat in discussion at a table across the room.

"Midday, he told us," answered Barnibus, supping at a well-earned wine. After ten days on the road he deserved it. Who cared that it was still morning? "He's got a private cabin for you. Not a big one, but it'll be yours."

"We'll pass your thanks onto Elyon," Lancel added, with a grin. "Your fare's coming right out of his pocket, though I imagine he can afford it."

"His pockets are deep as the Long Abyss," jested Barnibus. "Any message you want us to pass onto him, Saska?"

She could think of more than one. *Thank him for saving my life, for protecting me, for taking those lashes to the back. Thank him for being so gentle, so kind, so understanding. Thank him for having such good friends as you*...She looked at the two knights, loyal to a fault. "Nothing I can ably express," she said. "Nor to you. For helping me get here."

"Ah, it hasn't been so arduous, really," said Lancel, reclining on his wooden chair, one leg folded over the other. "It's been rather fun, actually. The siege was growing dull, waiting around for the full assault. Nice to be on the road again."

"Do you think it's happened by now?" Saska asked them. "The siege?"

She was thinking of Marian and the men, though didn't know if they were there or not. She'd half hoped that they'd appear on the road, that they'd been tracking her all along, but they hadn't. And now here she was, waiting to sail south. A few wings of anticipation fluttered through her at that, as she looked into the harbour. The ship was a little way down the coast, being loaded by the deckhands, a simple two-masted caravel with blue and black sails bearing merchant markings. That had been the true purpose of all that whiskey and wine they'd carted here. It was a bribe and a gift for the captain to look the other way. A few dozen crates in exchange for carrying a random southern girl back home? Why not? There weren't many shipmen who'd turn that down.

Saska was still looking out at the ship when Barnibus answered, "Probably. Word the night we left was that the full assault would go ahead within days. It's been ten. So yeah, probably."

"Then I'm sorry." Saska turned back to them. "I know you Varin Knights live for this stuff. I feel I've denied you a chance to claim a noble kill, or win a great victory."

Lancel's handsome face was in a fond smile. "Not to worry, Saska. We'll have plenty of opportunities to win glory. I'm not sure sieging Harrowmoor was where we'd find it."

No, you'll find it out there, Saska thought, looking back over the bay. There were a couple of massive Tukoran war galleons lumbering across the water, cruising a protective patrol of the coast, but for the most part the fighting here was done. Some hundred ships had been lost, Lancel had told her last night when they'd arrived. "The fighting was fierce out in the bay at the start, but didn't last too long. Most of the Rasal navy sailed back up the east coast toward the Windwake Isles and Stormhold. They knew a lost cause when they saw it."

Now much of the coast was settled and calm, they'd heard. Shellcrest had been won some time ago, and so had Calmwater, and Doublebay Harbour would be next. Prince Rylian's southern forces were marching there now, apparently, leaving garrisons at each city they'd won. She'd seen that when they'd arrived here, the three of them dodging a couple of Tukoran patrols before they got to this creaky little inn where they'd spent the night. It wasn't big. Just one small bed, that they'd given Saska as the two knights split the watch. She might have argued if she'd had the strength, but after kipping in keeps and ruins and woods for over a week, she couldn't deny the pull of the wool blankets, the feather mattress, the stuffed pillows. *Another thing I need to thank them for,* she thought, as the two men continued their discussion. She hated being in so many peoples' debt, but her life had forced her into that. Orryn. Marian. Ranulf. Elyon. Vesryn Daecar had helped too, and now she had to add Lancel and Barnibus to that list. *One day I'll repay them all. One day,* she thought, taking another bite. *One day I'll clear all my debts...*

But...there was one more thing she did want to ask. One thing she never got to request of Elyon before he choked her out, and she woke up in those woods. She hated to do it, but... "Could you do something for me, when you get back to camp?" The men drew from their discussion. It was about the best route back, so far as Saska could hear. She had their ear. "There's a boy I knew, taken from my village. He's called Del. He'll be sixteen, tall, dark messy hair. Skinny. Kind. Shy." She smiled as she spoke of him, feeling nostalgic, and this was about as much as she'd told them of herself, or anyone she knew. She looked up. "I think he's in with Kastor's forces, one of the boys in the labour camps. I was just wondering if you might...I don't know, see that he's safe, I suppose." She hated to ask. Hated to. "Maybe...maybe Elyon could take him on as a squire, or something?"

"Is he Bladeborn?" asked Barnibus.

"No, he's just...just a boy."

"Then he couldn't be a squire, not to a Varin Knight."

Barnibus thought a moment. "But he could serve his house, do duties in camp." He seemed a bit confused. "He's Rasalanian?"

"Tukoran," Saska said. She'd told them nothing, really, of where she was from. "Elyon will know. I told him about Del...a bit, anyway. Do you think he'd mind? There was a man..." She tried to remember the name. "Don Mears, I think. A soldier written in Elyon's notebook. He might know." She was spitballing now. "I just want to know he's safe."

They seemed to catch on. Whether Elyon found Del and took him in or not, Saska wouldn't know it, not from where she was going. She just needed reassurance, that was all, and Lancel gave it. "We'll pass on the message, Saska. But if he's just a labour boy, I'm sure he'll be OK."

She thought of what Elyon had written in that little notebook. He'd wondered about the boys being used to draw fire. 'Fodder for the bowmen,' he'd written. She hoped that wasn't true. Not with Prince Rylian in charge. Not with the Vandarians there. Just a wicked tactic that Cedrik Kastor might deploy. *But not the rest. No, not the rest.*

She smiled at them. "Thanks. I would give you an address to write me, but...well I'm not sure where I'll be."

"The ship will dock in Aram," Barnibus told her, as he had already. "But it might be able to stop somewhere along the way, if you'd prefer? I could speak with the captain. A few more coins might convince him."

"You've been too kind to me already. I could never ask that." Saska glanced out of the window. There looked to be a bit of a commotion out there, someone gathering a crowd, calling out. She paid it no mind. *Just a town crier, calling news.* "And Aram works for me." She had to try, didn't she? Try to see if she could find out the truth of her mother? *And maybe Ranulf's gone there?* He'd said that he would, after going with Vincent Rose to Solapia. That gave her hope. She was still loathe to abandon her duty, but it was something at least.

The noise was getting a bit louder outside, drawing Barnibus over to join her at the window. He looked through the dirty glass, frowning.

"Soldiers?" asked Lancel across the room.

"No, just commoners. Seems a town crier's gathered the people at the docks." They were a little south of the city proper here, in something of a secondary port, a little down the coast from the main one. The dock wasn't nearly as busy, she'd been told. The main harbour was home to a hundred ships, but here there were less than a dozen on the water.

"Anything interesting?" Lancel said, as he relaxed in his chair, yawning. He shrugged. "Maybe the siege at Harrowmoor is over?"

It seemed plausible. The gesticulating of the man looked to suggest important news. "Wait here," said Barnibus. "I'm going to go down and check."

Saska watched from the window as Barnibus emerged from the stout timber frame tavern and paced out across the dusty docks, dressed in a weathered woollen cloak. Neither Barnibus nor Lancel had enhanced hearing from their blood-bond, she'd come to see. It had surprised her. She'd asked them about it a few nights back when they stopped for the night, finding a cluster of willows and rocks by a river in which to make camp. Hidden in that natural little fort, she'd said, "I thought all Varin Knights had enhanced senses from godsteel?"

When they told her that wasn't true, and that such gifts were rare, she realised just how little she knew. Marian had always told her that, of course, but hearing it from these trained knights felt different. "My eyesight gets a bit sharper," Lancel had told her, "and Barny can hear a bit better, but it's not that noticeable."

"And what about Elyon?"

"Elyon," Lancel laughed. "Well Elyon has the lot, but he's a Daecar, so he should. His brother did too. Aleron." His face soured. "The world feels less without him."

She saw a flicker of pain in his face. "You were friends?" she asked softly.

Both men nodded. "We knew him from hip high," said Barnibus. "We were best friends, the three of us. We were meant to win battles together, win forts and castles and wars." He smiled a reminiscing smile, then it slipped away and he poked at the fire and whispered, "The gods were cruel to take him so soon."

The gods were generous with their cruelty, Saska had thought to that. *As callous as they were kind.* People always said that the gods made a game of war, and if that was the case, they seemed to still be playing it...

It didn't take long for Barnibus to return, hurrying back across the docks below and into the inn. A moment later he was pressing through the door and stepping inside with a twist of bemusement to his face. "What...what is it?" asked Lancel.

Barnibus let out a short laugh. "The war's over," he said. Then he laughed again, a brisk huffing sound. "Here, at least. That's what they're saying. The Rasals have surrendered. The war's over, Lance."

Lancel shifted up in his seat, a grin broadening on his slim high-cheekboned face. "Not just at Harrowmoor?"

"The whole kingdom." Barnibus smiled back at him. "Seems King Godrin died of a heart attack and Hadrin's been crowned. They say he never wanted war, so has called for his people to lay down their arms." He looked over to the window. "Good for you, Saska. You'll not have to worry about warships in the bay."

Saska wasn't thinking about that. "Godrin's dead?" was all she asked, hearing little else. She'd only met him once, but that meeting had been important to her. *You're exactly where you're meant to be.* She'd let those words warm her on cold nights, brace her when she felt lost and alone, but now? They felt smaller, somehow, with him gone, quieter in her head. She turned her eyes out of the window. Some people were weeping, embracing. Others were celebrating, cheering. A beloved king had been lost, but a war was over. And she didn't know what to think. *Do I still have to leave? If we have peace here, should I not stay?* She turned her eyes back to Barnibus. "Are you sure? He's...truly gone?"

"Truly," he said. "But we'd best not linger here too long. I'm sure the captain is eager to set off. Have you got your things?"

Saska didn't have any things. "What things?"

"Right. Um...." He looked around. "Here, take this. I'll not have you boarding that ship with nothing to your name." He handed her a small pouch of coins. Then he set about emptying his pack onto the bed, clearing out his own possessions, and filling the empty satchel with whatever food they could spare. "And take this too. Ship food can be grim."

Lancel was rummaging through his own things too. He gave her a thick grey woollen scarf for the chill nights, and a few rolls of parchment, quill, and ink pot. "I don't know if you're much of a writer or artist, but take these anyway. They'll keep you busy in your cabin. And the quill doubles as a pricking knife. If someone tries something with you...some deckhand or sailor or whatnot...you take that quill and stab him in the eye, you understand?"

She smiled, though hoped she'd never have to. "Thank you, Lancel. And you, Barnibus. I don't deserve all this."

Barnibus waved a hand. "Think nothing of it. They're trinkets, that's all." He went to the window and looked out. There were more people in the harbour now, and that wasn't ideal. "Best get you safe aboard the ship. Come on, we'll take you down."

She wrapped up in her cloak, threw the satchel over her shoulders, and pulled up her cowl. The air outside was brisk and colder than she'd realised, a chill wind whipping in from the sea. It looked rough out there though nothing too bad, all blue and churned white waves. She walked between the two men, both a good head taller than her, flanking her as they moved through the docks.

The news was spreading everywhere to a strange mixed song of sobs and celebration. Some were disconsolate, on their knees, hands clasped to the pale blue skies. Saska saw a group gathered at the foot of a small stone temple, standing in a circle and holding hands, heads raised, humming the Mourning Prayer. Others weren't so stricken, smiling and laughing and talking in excited tones. The end of the war meant more to them than the death of a white-haired old king they'd never met and never would. Hadrin would replace him now, a paper king on a paper throne, because Janilah was the real ruler here. Did they know that? Did they care? Vincent Rose had said that once, when she and Leshie first met him in Thalan. He'd said that it made no difference to most people who governed them, and Saska was seeing that now. And so on they went, moving down the docks as the town crier gathered another crowd ahead. He was up on a stack of crates, ringing a bell, calling out loud for all to hear, "King Godrin is dead. Hadrin has been crowned king. The war is over," and that led to more shock, more wailing, more misery and merriment. More noise. So much noise. So much noise that none of them noticed the troop of soldiers approaching behind them...

"Turn around, sir," came an order. It was close, just a metre or so back. All three turned at once and came face-to-face with a broad-shouldered knight dressed in a brown surcoat over mail. His crest was a mountain with rocks tumbling down either side. And now Saska remembered the voice. *Sir Cleon Marsh,* she thought, looking to the dozen well-armed men beside and behind him. She tried to dip her eyes and turn away, but the damage was done. He'd seen her. "Renford remembered who you were," the knight said, looking at Lancel. Saska could sense both he and Barnibus reaching into their cloaks. "Never forget a face, do you Renford?"

A man behind him shook his head. "No, sir, never. They always come to me eventually."

Sir Cleon smiled. "What are you doing down here, Sir Lancel?" he asked, looking to the tall, towheaded knight. "And pretending to be merchants? Curious. Most curious."

Several of the soldiers were shifting to the sides now, to get into position around them. The crowd continued to move here and there, unaware of what was happening, sobbing and smiling and singing. Saska managed to glance over to her boat. The final loads were going on, and the ropes were being untied. When Lancel spoke, his voice was dangerous. "Turn around, Sir Cleon, and pretend you never saw us. You don't want to make this ugly."

"I'd rather not, no," Sir Cleon admitted. "But that will be up to you." His eyes went to Saska. "I take it this is the girl we've been looking for. Hand her over and we'll go without a fuss. We'll say no more of it."

Saska took a short step forward before either Lancel or Barnibus could speak. "I'll go with you," she said, looking up at Sir Cleon. "I'll not have anyone else get hurt on my account."

"Smart girl. And brave." Sir Cleon turned his eyes over the others. "Let her go easy and I'll say none of this to Lord Kastor. I'll tell him we found her hiding in a ditch somewhere. You needn't sully your names. This is on Elyon Daecar. This is his mess."

Barnibus stepped forward, to join Saska's side, then Lancel followed. "You misunderstand, sir," Barnibus said. "This girl is not who you say. She will not be going with you."

"You would die for her?"

"*You* would." Barnibus drew his sword with a ring of steel, and no sooner had the misting metal caught the light, as Lancel drew his, and Sir Cleon drew his, and every man in his company pulled steel from sheaths. The crowd saw and screamed and began scattering, and in that chaos, the giant appeared.

He came from nowhere, emerging from the throng, throwing off a heavy fur cloak. Beneath was steel. *A steel giant,* Saska thought, staring up at his eight foot frame, and as he came so every man turned to him. His armour was marked and scratched and stained, a huge flat-topped great-helm on his head. Beneath the thin black eye-slits were a hundred little holes for ventilation, and through those holes the giant's breath fogged.

"Mercy," said the soldier standing nearest to him. He raised a hand and backed off. "Mercy...please mercy..."

He said no more. From dual sheaths at his hips the Wall pulled his huge swords, their cross guards curved like fins, their pommels the heads of whales. With an easy swipe he took off the man's head, a crimson geyser shooting from his neck. Several others roared and rushed in, their blades banging feebly off his thick godsteel plate. The giant swung, left and right at once. One man was split at the hip and another at the shoulders. Bodies slipped apart, innards tumbling out onto the cobbles, steaming. Several more of the soldiers screamed in horror and tried to rush away, but Lancel and Barnibus sprung, cutting them down. Sir Cleon moved to blockform, facing off with the beast as he swung and hacked and butchered them. "Monster!" he roared. "I'll not quiver to you!'

He didn't quiver, but he did die, and it didn't take long either. Saska watched as Sir Cleon launched himself forward, swinging fast and swinging furious with his misting godsteel blade. One strike was parried with a great shattering clang. Another Sir

Ralston let scratch right across his breastplate, leaving a thin white scar. A third attack missed entirely as the giant surged in past it, gripping Sir Cleon's neck in his huge gauntlet, lifting him off the floor, twisting. The crack was sickening. Bones burst through Sir Cleon's neck, spraying blood, and his eyes rolled backward, body spasming. The King's Wall tossed him to the side and looked Saska right in the eye. "Your ship is leaving."

Saska spun. The gangplanks were being drawn in and the caravel was being pushed off the wharf by poles. There were men at the oars, ready to pull. She turned to find Sir Lancel and Sir Barnibus giving chase after the final two soldiers. They had to kill them to preserve their identities. *If one gets away...*

She couldn't think about that right now. Her eyes flashed about the dead men scattered across the waterfront. *So much red,* was all she could think. She'd never seen such a massacre, and half of the Wall's armour was splashed with gouts of blood and brains and gore. People were still running from the scene, screaming. Others were watching from windows. Saska pulled her cowl lower, and found the giant putting his cloak back on, his blades sheathed. He stepped forward. "Go. Quick."

Saska went. Quickly. She turned and ran for the ship, feeling the ground tremble beneath her feet. Some of the deckhands noticed and started calling out in alarm. The captain turned from the wheel and began bellowing orders. *Too slow,* Saska thought. The ship was drifting further from the jetty, a metre, two, three, more than she could jump without godsteel. She didn't need to. Her legs suddenly left the ground as Sir Ralston scooped her up into his left arm. The salt wind whipped her face, blowing hard as the giant charged and puffed and leaped, soaring high and far and landing on the main deck with a great crunch of cracking timber.

Some of the deckhands went immediately running off up the ship in a panic. Others just stared in shock. There was a lot of calling and shouting, and over all that, a loud voice broke out from the quarterdeck. "What is the meaning of this!" The captain rushed down, younger than Saska had imagined, no more than thirty. "Who are you?"

Saska slipped from Sir Ralston's arms and pulled back her

cowl, landing lightly on the deck. "I'm what you get in exchange for all that whiskey and wine below decks." How she spoke so calmly she didn't know. "But you get him too." She nodded her head up at the Wall, standing like a statue at her side, and folded her arms.

The captain looked utterly bewildered. "You're the Wall," he recognised. Sir Ralston was wearing his cloak, but couldn't hide his size, nor the helm beneath his hood.

"He means no harm." Saska took a chance on that. He'd just slaughtered those men for a reason. Got her on the ship for a reason. And he didn't seem to be leaving either.

"I mean no harm," he confirmed, in a voice so deep it felt divine.

The ship was still drifting off the wharf, but the men weren't pulling the oars. That would take the captain's say so. "Why aren't you at the king's side?" the man asked. He had a pleasant countenance, friendly even with a frown. Long brown hair was tied in a tail at the back of his head, his chin and cheeks dusted with fine gritty stubble. "You're his wall..."

"I *was* his wall."

The giant still didn't move. He just stood there, like he was made of rock. Saska had to say something, lest this man call the guards. "He can take my cabin. I'll sleep on deck. I'll scrub and clean and do anything you need." *Not anything,* she thought, as a couple of the deckhands eyed her amorously. But somehow the Wall seemed to know. He moved for the first time, turning suddenly, and the sailors scampered off into the shadows in retreat.

The captain laughed. "Never seen a man of your size before." He said it like it was a reason to keep him around, something to amuse him. "Bet you've got some stories, hey?"

The Wall inclined his head, though didn't look like much of a raconteur.

"Saw you killing some men back there. Why was that?" The ship was still drifting, a bit of wind caught in the few hoisted sails, moving slowly out toward the harbour wall.

"They were Tukoran," Saska blurted out. She knew well

enough that this captain was Rasal. "Rapists. murderers. The Wall was protecting me."

"The war's over, you know, or did I mishear?" The captain shrugged, but seemed to be enjoying himself. "We're not meant to be taking chunks out of each other anymore." He looked up at the steel giant. "But I suppose you know about that better than I do, sir. Forgive me, if I'm being impertinent. Who am I to question a highborn knight like you."

The Wall said nothing.

"Oars, men!" called the captain suddenly, turning. "Pull us off this rock, aye! And someone tell Lanky Larry to clear his cabin. We've got a superstar aboard who's going to be needing it."

They cut the waves quickly after that, two banks of blades pulling at the water either side of the boat. Saska shot a look back to shore but saw that Lancel and Barnibus were already gone. The docks were all but deserted still, though a few brave souls were creeping back out to check what was going on, probing at bloody cleaved bodies, seeing if there was anything to thieve. "That's what I love about this job," the captain said, leading them up onto the quarterdeck. "Never a dull day." He laughed, displaying that typical Rasal spirit. "Name's Rikki Bowen, and this here was my father's ship. The Steel Sister, we like to call her, though don't ask me why." He smiled at Saska as the waves began to churn beneath them, past the harbour wall. "And you are?"

"Saska," she said, quite done with using fake names.

"Saska, nice to meet you." He reached out a hand. "And you, Sir Ralston." His head went almost vertically up to meet him. "You going to be keeping that helm on the entire trip?"

The Wall gave no answer.

"Well then," Captain Rikki Bowen rubbed his hands. "To Aram we go." He grinned stupidly and drew a huge breath of salty air. "Feel free to get comfortable. My men will show you to your cabins."

Saska's cabin was small, but more cosy than she'd have thought. She had a little bunk, a little desk, and a bit of space to store her things. There was no window, though, but she hadn't expected that. She unpacked the meagre possessions the knights had kindly given her and then sat on the bed, and tried not to think too deep on what had happened. Then the door opened and the Wall arrived. He had to go sideways to enter, and stoop low, and couldn't stand up straight when he got inside.

Instead he went down on one knee. "I have a message from King Godrin."

Saska would have stumbled back if she had any space to do so. "What? You came to bring me a message?" He inclined his head, and was no longer wearing his helm, though was otherwise armoured heel to neck. His face was rutted and scarred and grim, his head bald and bumpy, and he looked older than she remembered from the one time she'd seen him. "What is it?"

"Me," he rumbled, and looked her right in the eye. "I am to protect you. No one will lay a hand on you again." He pulled a sword from his sheath and laid it at her feet. "I am your Wall now."

51

Lythian

The crowd were roaring and the drums were beating. Dragons swirled and screeched as they whipped across the blazing cobalt skies. Lythian stared forward at the man dressed in paper armour and holding a pitted iron blade. He'd been dressed in a mocking mimicry of godsteel plate, just as Tomos had when he'd died. *And me,* Lythian thought, looking at Borrus. *They clad us all the same for our deaths.*

The hordes within the stands were demanding they fight, an ugly raucous din in the air. They were a blur of colour and noise and hate, filling the dragon-scale tiers within the Pits of Kharthar, and growing more restless by the moment. "The one who lives will live!" the new Lord of the Nest, Vargo Ven had announced when they'd been dragged from their cell, wrapped in this painted pasteboard armour and thrown out onto the sand. "His Lofty Magnificence, King Tavash, proclaims the victor worthy of his mercy. If one should kill the other, he will live! To take a life will be to save his! Now let us see them fight!"

It was a final humiliation, a last effort to debase them before they were slaughtered by claw and fang and flame. To kill a fellow Varin Knight would not be favoured by the Steel Father, that is what they thought. They weren't wrong, not in most circumstances, but these were rather exceptional and Varin surely knew that. *Didn't he?* Lythian stared at Borrus, his big belly shrunken to that of a regular paunch, his dark grey dinted shortsword hanging limp by his side. The man looked like he might keel over and die before he could even take a good swing. "So what do you think, Borrus? Should one of us take the deal?"

Borrus reached up with his spare hand and tore off his paper helm, the visor ripping half off as he threw it to the ground. The crowd gave a cheer as though they thought he was about to attack. Sir Borrus Kanabar laughed, though there had never been a weaker sound. "Once more, they prove just how doltish they are. Do they really expect us to fight?" He turned to look at Vargo Ven who prowled about beneath the king's royal terrace, draped in his scaly black armour and glittery gold cloak. There was a cruel twisted smile on his dusky face. He knew full well they'd never agree to any bargain. "Why not fight me yourself, Ven?" Borrus tried to shout, but his voice was too rusty and weak to battle above the din. He cleared his throat and tried again. "Coward! I call you coward! Give me godsteel and make it a real fight. You're craven as your king." He looked out to the crowds. "Every one of you! A coward and cur to the last man."

Only Lythian heard all that, though Borrus's gesticulations were easy enough for the people to translate. They began booing loudly, the din turning darker. It was pantomime, just one big show. And they'd been on this stage for far too long.

"Lay down your sword, Borrus," Lythian said. He removed his own helm and let it slip through his fingers, then did the same with his blunt iron blade. It landed with a clunk and puff of dust. Then he got to work on the rest of his armour, pulling off the paperboard plates around his shoulders, his arms, his chest and legs. "Enough games. Let's show them we're not for playing with."

Borrus began doing the same, throwing his sword to the ground with as much force as he could summon. Where Lythian shed the insult of his armour with dignity and diligence, however, Borrus tore them off like a man possessed, giving them the treatment they deserved. Paper pauldrons and vambraces, gorgets and gauntlets and greaves went flying. The mob bellowed out their shock and appal but Borrus was just laughing, a scratchy sound scraping up his throat and through his lips. *We have nothing to prove,* Lythian thought, turning to face Vargo Ven, and the form of King Tavash Taan, sitting cross-legged in his black-wood throne beneath a crimson canopy. If those little malformed drakes came running, perhaps they'd take up their blades again and fight back. But against each other? No. And he said that with his eyes.

King Tavash raised a hand and called for hush. The quiet waved through the crowd, and above the dragons settled in their screeching, some gliding and wheeling silently overhead, others perched at the summit of the scaly black back of the great dragon arena. Suddenly Borrus's wild panting could be heard, loud as a bellows, and Lythian could feel the steady weak run of his heart, pulsing in his neck. The drums settled, quiet and slow, ba-dum...ba-dum, and somewhere off behind him, outside the arena, he could hear the crowds who couldn't get in, teeming in their tens of thousands along the red pavestone paths.

All waited for Tavash to speak, but his voice had become too pure now for these pits. Vargo Ven was his fist and his voice, the dagger in his hand, the dragon beneath his saddle. "The king's mercy has been forsaken and denied," called the Lord of the Nest, his clear cold voice ringing out through the stands. "These men have proven themselves cowards in the eyes of gods and kings and men." He spoke in the common tongue for their benefit. Most invited within the pits would speak it and speak it well, the puffy primped dragon-less Fireborn and fatuous ranks below them. "They are broken men, we can all see. Too weak to hold their swords. Too frightened to take up arms." He stopped in his haughty pacing and turned to them, pointing. "Their presence here is an insult now. They bring a reek to this great city, and need fester here no more. It is time for them to end. *I* will see it done."

Vargo Ven raised an arm, piercing the azure skies and above came a great echoing roar. Lythian looked up. Borrus looked up. Every man in the crowd looked up, but Vargo Ven just smiled. For here came his bonded dragon, here came Malathar the Mighty, the great brutish short-snouted beast plunging through the skies in a blur of black and gold. The masses gave chant to him, calling his name, and so came the drums again to join them in their beat, *Malathar, ba-dum, ba-dum...Malathar, ba-dum, ba-dum...*

He landed at Vargo Ven's side in a thumping cloud of billowing bronze dust, a hulking mound of black armour and scales, spat with flecks of glimmering gold. Lythian and Borrus drew side-by-side to face the creature, as the Lord of the Nest climbed up its wing and slid into his saddle. The dragon's short neck reared up, his massive maw layered with rings of teeth, white on black. From the sides and top of his spade-shaped head flared a thousand spikes and horns, shorter at the front and growing longer as they went back, and atop his dome were the largest of all, two thick gilded horns curving backward like a ram, veined with a patten of branching black lines. They framed the figure of Vargo Ven, seated behind them with his hands on the leather reins, as Malathar swished his thick muscular tail, barbed with a hundred killing blades.

"Do you think we have a chance?" Borrus had a smile on his face. "Just imagine, Lyth. We'd sit right next to Varin for the rest of time." He glanced down at the pathetic iron blades at their feet. "Let's say we have a go?"

"Not with a thousand of those swords, and a thousand men could we put a dent in his hide." Lythian knew Borrus was joking, but said it anyway. "Gods, Borrus, doesn't this bring you back?"

"It should," Borrus said. "I fought them once." He was still smiling, the wonderful defiant man, turning his eyes over a couple of the wide pale scars that sliced through Malathar's black hide. "See that one on his neck, down his chin. That was one of mine. Almost got the bastard until he jerked back and drew away. Was the closest I ever came to killing a dragon."

Well that was closer than most, and Malathar would have been some prize. There weren't many men living who'd bested a drake in a duel. Amron, famously, and Prince Rylian too. Janilah had also slain one when he was a younger man, and so had the King's Wall, who'd taken the entire head off a smaller beast in a single chop, it was said. There had been a few others. Sir Patrik Taynar, younger brother to Lord Godrik, though he'd turned old and senile, Lythian had heard. The Old Bull, Lord Petyr Bolt was another. His son Kevyn was one of Janilah's sworn swords now. Others had killed dragons in battles, though usually they'd been hit by a scorpion bolt and wounded, or weakened by godsteel-tipped arrows and quarrels, or set upon by multiple knights at once. A one-on-one duel was different. There was a purity to that particular brand of dragon-killing, and a rarity too.

"I remember that fight," Lythian finally said, as Malathar loomed, stamping toward them on the baked sandy earth, gouging great rifts with its claws, snarling spouts of smoke and fire. "You were brilliant that day, Borrus. I'll look forward to hearing you tell that tale at Varin's Table. I might even recount it myself."

"You'll have to. It's all a bit of a blur to me now." Borrus shifted a half step closer, until their shoulders were nearly touching. His once-ruddy face was pale, cheeks sunken, the skin beneath his eyes weary and black. "It's my honour to ascend beside you, Lythian. I couldn't have chosen anyone better."

"And I you, Borrus. It has been a great pleasure serving beside you all these years. Now let us sit beside one another at the eternal feast. I would say we've earned that much."

The dragon was near now, near enough to smell its breath. The hot reek washed over them, and the crowd were lost to a hushed anticipation, and the drums were beating, ba-dum, ba-dum. Above them the sun was coming and going as the dragons went back and forth, around and around. *They look so small up there,* Lythian thought, *with Malathar so close.* He squinted against the glare above as the shadows crossed the sun. But there was one that was larger...larger and getting larger still. He peered through the dusty yellow light and found that it was coming nearer. Coming from far off. Larger it got. And larger...And then the people were noticing. Noticing and pointing and turning their eyes up. Even Malathar sensed something. The brutish black beast's dark yellow eyes narrowed suddenly, its thick nostrils flaring, its muscular neck turning, twisting, looking up.

And in that instant Lythian knew. He knew the shape of the beast. He knew the size. And every man, woman, and child knew it too. "Garlath," someone shouted, then someone screamed it,

"GARLATH!"...then a dozen did the same, then a hundred, then a thousand. Borrus's eyes had widened. "Garlath," he whispered, and Lythian's lips were twisting into a smile. A smile of wonder. A smile of hope. The dragon caught the sunlight, lighting up its scales in shades of grey and blue. A roar gave out. A roar to match Malathar, nay better him. A roar that shook through to Lythian's very bones, that sent the pebbles and stones chattering at his feet.

Some people in the crowd were leaving, fleeing in the face of the coming of the beast. Lythian's eyes fled to the floor and in an instant he was reaching for the blunt iron blades at his feet. He scooped them and thrust one into Borrus's hand. "Back," he shouted. "Back..."

They'd made it only a few paces before Malathar swung his thick neck and noticed them. It didn't matter. Too late. Another bone shaking screech rattled the world and down came Garlath the Grand, opening out his huge blue wings to slow his plunging descent, reaching forward with his curving talons to snatch Vargo Ven from his perch. The Lord of the Nest screamed something and Malathar hunkered down low to his haunches, and pressed off across the arena, kicking up huge rocky clods of earth with his claws. Garlath landed in his wake with a shuddering tremble, taller, wider, longer, bigger. His massive chest swelled in a pattern of slate and silver and blue, his wings seeming to reach from one side of the pits to the other. In the stands people were emptying now into the corridors and exits, screaming, rushing, pushing and shoving. The skies were swirling and wild, the dragons falling to chaos. Lythian peered up there and saw a sleek grey bolt shooting through their midsts toward them.

"He will take you, Lythian," came the booming voice of Ulrik Marak. The former Lord of the Nest sat astride Garlath in the Body of Karagar, the greatest suit of armour in Agarath. At his hip rested a black scabbard that seemed to glow from within with a deep orange light. Steam was rising off it, like the divine mists of godsteel. But the Fireblade wasn't godsteel. The Fireblade was something else. "Borrus, you must come with me," commanded Marak, as Garlath sunk down on one side, angling his huge leathery wing for Borrus to climb. "Use the horns. Quickly! Quickly!"

Across the arena, Malathar was spinning and facing them. Lythian could see the red light glowing in his chest, his neck, brighter and brighter, spreading up and up his throat. Suddenly Garlath swung about and unfurled his wings as the spout of red flame and smoke came pouring from Malathar's maw. The fire crashed like a wave against the beast as the two knights threw themselves to the dusty sand floor.

A hundred things seemed to happened next. Garlath and Marak were surging across the sand in attack, scratching and biting and flapping at Malathar and Vargo Ven, as they swirled skyward in a flaming maelstrom. From the top of the pits, that grey bolt came cutting and opening its wings and landing. The multi-coloured glitter beneath Neyruu's sparkling underside flashed a thousand shades of red and orange, blue and green, and above her Kin'rar Kroll was calling out something in his flapping silver cape. Behind them, a host of red-caped dragonknights were rushing with their tall black spears, speeding through the mouth of the arena. A heavy clunk sounded at Lythian's feet and he turned his eyes down to find a misting longsword with a gentle v-shaped hilt lying upon the sand. Now Kin'rar's voice cleared. "Your blade, Lythian! Your sword!" he called, as the Knight of the Vale looked up. In her right talon Neyruu had a second, broader blade, which she threw with an acute deftness toward Borrus. "And yours, Borrus! Take them up! Take up your blades and fight!"

When Lythian flung his pitted iron shortsword aside, and took up his own godsteel blade, he felt at once one and whole again. The long cruel weeks of starvation and humiliation and incarceration were blown aside, and so came in their place a steeling surge of light and warmth and strength. Turning, he looked into the face of Borrus Kanabar, and the great burly man stood tall and full and grand once more. He looked a decade younger, a decade slimmer, a shimmering glow seeming to fizz the air about him. They looked at one another, and smiled. "At least if we go down," called Borrus, "we'll go down with bloody godsteel to hand!"

The dragonknights were still surging in, black spears forward, a full score strong. Up on the southern stands now, Garlath and Malathar were crashing through the tiers, setting fire to half the stadium. People were screaming and fleeing. Soldiers were emerging from the lower levels and the subterranean training grounds, and up in the royal balcony, the preening lords and ladies were clogging the corridors in retreat. Lythian had a mind to make chase and go after King Tavash but set that quickly aside. Godsteel would give him a boost but it wouldn't last long; in his condition, he'd soon tire.

"On me, Lythian! On me!" Borrus was bellowing as he marauded for the host of dragonknights. For a moment Lythian was two decades in the past, watching Borrus charge the field and lay siege to the Agarathi lines. But these were no common soldiers, and Borrus had no armour.

"Hold, Borrus," Lythian roared through his parched lips. "Hold!"

But Borrus was already there, doing what he did best. Some men came alive in war and Borrus Kanabar was one of them. Before Lythian could join him, two dragonknights were dead, cleaved of limb and lance. A third had lost an arm at the elbow and was backing off, trailing blood, as Borrus swung in a wild fury. But there were over twenty more, thrusting and jabbing and trying to get around him with their spears. Borrus ducked, he weaved, folding back the years, tall and mighty and fearless. But the red-caped knights were moving around him, and those thin long spears were prodding, poking. One caught Borrus in the upper left arm, slicing a deep laceration, and the Knight of Varin bellowed and took his life as payment. Lythian rushed to his side, slicing spears and swatting swords as he went. "Back to back, Borrus! With me! Back to back!"

They formed up, sweaty and stained, dressed only now in bloodied rags. Lythian's presence stilled Borrus's bloodlust, and they fell into a worn routine. In war when outnumbered this was the form. Back to back, with a full view of all enemies. When they saw a weak point, an opening, they'd surge through it together, making space. They did that now as the dragonknights shuffled and sidestepped and tried to close them in. Above them, Kin'rar and Neyruu had shot back skyward, chased by a pair of drakes. The huge colossal forms of Malathar and Garlath were still crashing around the tiers, wreathed in flame. Other soldiers were still coming for them, but...Lythian frowned. Through the ring of dragonknights he could see fighting. All across the sand, men in common clothing were drawing hidden blades from their belts and cloaks and attacking the city soldiers and guards. There must have been fifty of them, a hundred, emerging from the crowds, causing chaos.

Lythian wasn't sure what was happening. A revolt? An uprising against Tavash? Were these men in league with Marak and Kin'rar? It seemed planned, organised, but he had no further time to consider it as the dragonknights continued to close in, pressing the pair to the far side of the arena, near the exit, near the mouth. Lythian shot a look through and outside could see the teeming masses flocking and fleeing. A spear surged for his flank and he chopped right; another came for his chest and he slashed left. Borrus prowled, a large target true, but slick as a snake when striking. He lashed out at the nearest knight, catching the man on the chin with an upswing, splitting his jaw. Two others came Lythian's way, pulling striated black and red blades from their scabbards, forged of dragonfire. There was no better steel in Agarath. Two swings came at him and Lythian parried left and right. Another spear was prodding from the side. He sidestepped, swung through it, and lurched forward at dizzying speed, cutting the man through. Borrus followed, and they were back to back again, but panting, tiring, and the circling knights could see it.

Then suddenly Neyruu was shifting their way through the skies and pitching down in a sharp descent. The dragons chasing her weren't so agile, banking hard as the arena stands came up before them, climbing back into the blazing skies, choked with flame and smoke. The sleek grey drake landed with a great tremble and let out an ear piercing shriek, causing half the dragonknights to flee. The rest wasted no time in flinging any remaining lances her way, to which Neyruu took umbrage with a sweeping swish of her tail, scattering them across the sands. "We must go," Skymaster Kin'rar Kroll cried out over all that. His eyes swung upward, as Garlath broke away from his bout with Malathar. "Marak is coming. One of you will fly with him. My saddle will not take you both."

"We can hold onto the..." started Borrus, but Kin'rar cut him off.

"You must be saddled and hold tight. Dragon-flight is perilous; you will fall lest you are secure."

Lythian began pushing Borrus forward. "Go, I'll wait."

"I'll not leave you..."

"He's coming, Borrus." Garlath was crashing through the tiers, reaching the sand, lumbering their way. There was a great gouging tear at his left flank, a suggestion of damage to the flap of his right wing, and a dozen other rips and wounds. Blood was leaking freely to the sand as he came, though beyond, Malathar looked in worse shape. "I will ride with Marak. Go, now!"

The command was enough. Borrus relented, rushing for Neyruu, scrambling awkwardly up the side of her shimmering flank. Kin'rar shifted forward in his saddle, perching on the pommel as Borrus dropped in behind, shackling himself as best he could with the straps and buckles. It was all Lythian could do not to stare in disbelief. A Varin Knight riding a dragon? Such a thing hadn't happened in an age, or ever. "I will see you in the skies, Captain," called out Kin'rar. "We did not forget about you. I am sorry it took so long..."

So am I, thought Lythian, *or else Tomos might still be alive.* But he said nothing as the dragon flapped and beat the air, and the dust billowed about him, and Borrus clung like a leech to the Skymaster's waist looking as out of place as a man could be. And as they rose, Garlath was still thundering his way, looming, soaring, appearing before him. Snorts of swirling smoke poured from his nostrils as those great orange eyes stared down. Lythian felt a moment of primal fear. This was the beast that had slain King Storris and Gideon Daecar. The dragon that had rained terror during the war with the Lord of the Nest atop it. *And now here he stands before me. And now I am to soar the skies astride him...*

"Lythian." Hearing his name snapped him out of it. He

looked up at Marak, the Fireblade smouldering at his hip. *The blade that had killed a thousand Bladeborn...* "Climb up, now! Garlath tires. We must go."

The horns were rough and sharp around the dragon's rippling neck, some so wide he could scarce get his fingers around them. He climbed up and up and up, five metres from the ground, ten. There, Ulrik Marak awaited, clad in the red-black dragon-plate Body of Karagar from heel to neck. His short salty-black hair was slick with sweat, his jaw set to a clench. He said nothing as he shifted forward and grunted for Lythian to climb behind him into the saddle, looking tiny upon the hulking dragon's broad scaly back. It felt like the summit of a mountain, rough and rocky, black and grey, though beneath his feet Lythian could feel the deep thrumming of the dragon's breath, feel the heat spreading from his fiery core.

He looked out as he fumbled with the straps, though Marak seemed less concerned about that as Kin'rar had been. "Hold on," he merely said, in a bass grunt thick with the accents of Agarath. "We fly far, Lythian. Deep into the Scales."

The rough armour pinched and bit at his rag-clad chest as Lythian reached forward, holding to Marak's waist. The Skylord growled something in Agarathi and Garlath swung, facing toward the maw that gave exit from the pits. Then all of a sudden, the beast was running, charging for the gap, crouching low as he burst out through the high yawning archway. His upper scales ripped through the teeth of the dragon's jaws as they broke out beyond the arena, and Lythian looked around and saw the chaos outside. People were still fleeing. Some had been caught in the crush and trampled. Soldiers lay dead in deep red pools of blood, and some in common clothing too, cloaks and tunics and skins. But it was just a glimpse, a flash, for a moment later his eyes were blurring, and the wind was rushing, and Garlath was running, rising, flapping, flying.

I'm flying. All other thoughts were banished. The streets fell away, the stadium, the city. Within moments they were wheeling right, Marak gently leaning the same way as Lythian's stomach lurched and twisted. He almost brought up the gruel they'd served him that morning, but gulped it down, blinking out in wonder. And in a giddy stupid moment he smiled, and laughed, as the great sandstone city of Eldurath became a blur of gold and red and amber beneath him. And beyond were greens and blues of the delta, and the gleaming Askar River cutting east to the Scales. The Great Grasslands went endless to the south and west out there, somewhere out there, was the coast and Crystal Bay, and all the world beyond.

But north, he thought...and then he finally heard Marak's words. *We fly far, Lythian. Deep into the Scales...* "You must turn, Marak," he shouted suddenly. "To Vandar...you must fly me to Vandar..."

Marak didn't answer. *Can he even hear me?* The wind roared so loud he could barely hear himself. He looked around through the silver-blue skies as they went up and into the thin low clouds. A wetness rained against his face, though he dare not reach a hand to wipe it away should he slip and fall to the abyss. His blade had been shoved into the side of the saddle and he yearned to reach out to take it. *To still me, and brace me,* he thought. *To feed me its power so I might see.* But what he'd see up here he didn't know, for before long they were rising into thicker clouds, darker clouds, wetter clouds. The world grew bleak, the bright light of the sun became a faded blur behind them, and for a long while there was nothing but the roar of the wind and the occasional deep thump as Garlath flapped his mighty wings.

How long that went on for Lythian couldn't tell. *An hour? Two?* At one point, Marak twisted his neck in his gorget and shouted, "Storm has come down from the Scales. We are lucky. It hides our retreat." But he said nothing else until the thunder started to crack and echo and the skies were scratched by jagged fingers of lightning, silver and blue. "We descend," he then shouted. "It is not safe so high."

That time Lythian did bring something up, spluttering out a mouthful of vomit as Garlath arched his shoulders, swung his spiked tail, and plunged down through the clouds in a skin-peeling dive. The spew went right over his shoulder, thankfully, as he clung so tight to Marak's armour that he shredded the skin of his arms. But he didn't care about that. His time as Tavash's prisoner had give him a lifetime's worth of new scars and these ones, these cuts...*I'll take them*, he thought, squinting through the rush of air, the wind, the rain. *I'd lose an arm to be free of that place.*

They worked down low and lower still, until finally they burst out of the sopping grey canopy and the lands came into view below. Down there the world was rough and ragged as the dragon's back, with ridges and scarps and juts of high black rock surging from the earth. He looked forward, over and beyond Garlath's horned head as they flattened out, flying beneath the clouds, and out there saw the horizon climb higher, the rough lands becoming foothills, the foothills becoming mountains. "Where are we?" he called, as another clap of thunder rumbled through the skies. "They're the Scales ahead..."

"The Western Neck," Marak answered, as the thunder trailed off. Garlath entered a more languorous glide and as they slowed the winds grew quieter. "The Scales are shaped as a dragon, its head facing west, tail in the east. Some say the spirit of Agarath lives in the mountains, as with your Vandar and his tomb."

"How far have we gone from Eldurath?" Lythian called. He'd heard the mountains were several hundred miles away. *Can we have travelled that far?* It seemed impossible. On horseback that would take them a week or two, even more depending on the terrain. But by his judgment they can only have been flying for hours.

"These westernmost ranges are almost two hundred and fifty miles from the capital." Marak pulled a hand off the reins and pointed south. "The great city of Loriath is out there, two dozen miles. If the weather were clearer you'd see it."

Lythian peered in that direction, but could see so little through the blustery mists and rains. Loriath had been founded by Eldur's eldest son, Lori, who was seen throughout the north as a figure of deceit and treachery, along with his wicked younger brother Dor. After Eldur's death, it was said they murdered Varin in vengeance, ambushing him during the signing of the peace treaty at Death's Passage. It was one of the reasons the parley was considered so sacred, to avoid such perfidy again, though exactly what happened that fateful day was hard to know for sure. Needless to say, the

Agarathi told a different story, revering Lori and Dor as heroic figures who knew that Varin had to die to secure a lasting peace. That with the Fire Father joining Agarath, the Steel Father needed to join Vandar to keep the balance. Which telling was true, the world would never know for sure.

Soon they were rising again in line with the foothills, as the thundering clouds grew thinner and quieter, and the setting sun cut shards of pale wan light through the pall. The storm was behind them, lumbering westward over the Great Grasslands. Lythian searched the lands below but could see little sign of life beyond the clustered trees, black and thin against the growing dusk. "The Nest," he called out. "Is the Nest not to the north of here?"

Marak flicked his wide chin to the distant peaks to the north-east, a set of black fangs rising higher than the rest. "The fortress is there, among those mountains."

The home of the Bondstone. The source of their power...Lythian stared out, but those peaks were dozens of miles away, fading with the fall of the sun. "Vargo Ven commands now?"

"I should have killed him," Marak grunted. "Dragons fighting dragons, Lythian..." His voice was thick with regret. "This should not be the way. Tavash...Ven...they have driven us to this."

"Us? You and Kin'rar? Are there others, Marak?" Garlath was beating his wings again, rising higher, flying faster. Lythian had to bellow against the roar of the wind to be heard. "Have other Fire-born joined you? Is it to be civil war?"

He couldn't hide the hope from his voice. Civil war in Agarath would distract them from war with the north, hold their advance across the Red Sea. It would give the northern kingdoms time to come to peace, to prepare, to unite...but Marak was quick to douse those flames. "We are but a few," he told him. "Some you saw today. But they are not my men, Lythian. We all answer to a higher power."

Lythian's probes were drowned by the howls of the wind, the beat of Garlath's great wings, the squalls of soaking rain. He found himself trembling violently now as the sun sunk lower and the world grew darker and they went higher and higher into the hills. Eventually, after more time had passed, Garlath began to slow, bending his back into a gliding descent, shifting and turning his colossal wings as they worked left and right around valleys and peaks. It seemed wild below, the craggy sharp scarps tangled and coiled with dark green bushes and trees. He could see no paths, no tracks or routes. They couldn't be too far from Lumara now, the great saltflats and sunlands beyond these ranges. *Is that where we're headed? He'd said deep into the Scales, but the southern side of the mountains edged into Lumaran territory...*

And then, all of a sudden, Garlath opened out his wings into huge vertical flaps, swung his legs down, and came to a shuddering halt atop a rugged hill. About them, the valleys were thickly dressed in conifers, and away east the peaks rose a great deal higher. They'd landed in a lower depression, well hidden and concealed by the forests and pikes, and there, down among the trees, Lythian could see the faint swirl of smoke coiling through the branches. "Come, Lythian. We will get you warm."

The Knight of the Vale could scarce move he was so cold. His arms felt locked to Marak's back, frozen and bloodied, and he needed help to get down, weak as he'd become, as Garlath folded his shoulder to the rock and Marak supported his short descent. The touch of his blade helped, though, as he pulled it from the side of the saddle. "I have heard it called Starslayer," Marak said, looking down the length of the misting steel, glowing with the faintest of yellow lights. "It is the ancestral blade of your house, is it not?"

Lythian nodded as they began down the side of the hill, edging into the gloom of the woods. "It was my father's and his father's before him, going back a dozen generations. House Lindar is not a major house, but we have a proud history. In the Twenty First Renewal, my ancestor Sir Willem Lindar used this blade to defend his men against an onslaught of Starriders. He killed a half dozen that day, it is said. The sword took the name Starslayer in turn." He turned back as they went, to find Garlath still standing upon the hill. "He will stay there to rest?"

"He will remain close, yes, and find somewhere to hide so he might tend his wounds. He will be quiet now, for a time. The dragons are proud, Lythian. It has not been easy for him, to fight Malathar as he did today. Nor bear a Varin Knight and godsteel blade atop his back."

"I understand," Lythian said. "A break in brotherhood is a scar on the soul. I am sorry it has come to this."

"And I am sorry for Sir Tomos. I wish we had come sooner."

They continued in silence, moving into the trees, as the gentle light of fires softened the gloom. A rustle in the thicket spoke of a man on guard, and there were others through the trees, Lythian sensed, keeping watch for coming peril. On they went, until the shape of ruins appeared, choked by weeds and sprouts of sedge. The curtain wall was barely knee high, but there was a little more to the gatehouse, and part of an old roundtower was still standing some five or six metres from the ground. Beyond, the yard was thick with fir and larch, the ground heavy underfoot with cones and needles and mud. More soldiers appeared, sitting around fires, a score or two in a cobble of leathers and cloaks detailed in their crests. Lythian saw a dozen different dragon-sigils from a dozen different houses. Some looked to be dragonknights, others common men and soldiers in roughspun tunics and patchwork armour.

"This way." Marak led him on through the inner wall, up a rise, to the ruins upon the bailey. There the hillside rose to give a view of the surrounding valleys, breaking out through the trees. Beyond the tumbled stones of the main keep Lythian found Kin'rar and Borrus. The latter was wrapped up in a thick black robe, looking weary beyond reckoning. Lythian went and took him into an embrace.

"You're here," he said, clinging hard to his friend, as a man came forward and put a cloak around his shoulders. Lythian drew back and wrapped himself tight in the sheepskin, then placed Starslayer next to Borrus's blade, propped up against a block of pitted stone, bright against the gloom. "When did you arrive?"

"Some twenty minutes ago, I would say," Borrus said. "I think I weighed poor Neyruu down, elsewise we'd have been here a lot sooner."

"You were still quicker than us."

"Garlath is not the fleetest dragon," Marak intoned, stepping in. He turned to Kin'rar. "Has Borrus seen him yet?"

"Not yet. We were waiting for you, my lord."

Marak looked through the final set of ruins, and the clutch of trees that clad the hilltop. "Come, I will take you."

He led them out toward a plateau, giving a view over the hills and mountains beyond. There stood a man in a regal crimson cloak, emblazoned on the back with a fiery motif; eight rings of swirling flame enclosing the head of a dragon. He looked out over the lands, a cascade of rich black hair tumbling over his neck and shoulders, staring southwest. "Your Highness, I have brought them to you," said Marak, and the man turned.

Lythian blinked through the half light. *Dulian?* was his first thought. *But how...the king is dead.* And then it came to him. Then he knew. "Prince Tethian," he said, bending his neck into a bow. Borrus glanced over in confusion, then inclined his head too.

The Prince of Agarath smiled. His face was so much like his father's, only as Dulian had been during the war. Young, noble, handsome. His eyes were rusty red, skin a soft gold, hair a deep inky black. "I am surprised you recognise me, Captain Lythian. I do not believe we have ever met."

They hadn't. Of course they hadn't. Tethian had been but a small child when his father Dulian went to war, the only child he'd sired before Amron Daecar took away his ability to bear more children. Kin'rar and Marak had told them that Prince Tethian had gone missing, that he was thought dead. All that was writ across his face as he stared at the man. "I...forgive me, Your Highness. I am...I am surprised to see you alive, is all."

"You have endured a lot of surprises today, Captain." Tethian's voice was smooth and subtle in the warm tones of his people. "Not many know I am living, it is true."

Lythian's head was a blur of questions, one fighting another to be spoken. But Borrus got to the crux of it. "Where have you been?" he asked, his eyes tumbling beneath a heavy frown. "You have let your cousin take the throne. The rule of Agarath is rightfully yours, Prince Tethian."

"Mine?" Tethian let out a short chuckle. There was something in those red eyes. Something Lythian couldn't place. "No, Sir Borrus. The rule of this kingdom is not mine, nor is it Tavash's. Nor was it my father's before him, nor my grandfather King Tellion who led us through the war. Let my cousin sit the throne. Let him play at war. He has not the sight to see what comes." He smiled openly, and then said, "His war is not mine, Sons of Varin. It is the War Eternal that I fight in, the only war that matters. And there is but one man who can end it. One man who is not a man at all."

End it? Not a man at all? Was Tethian driven by the same dementia that ailed his father? Lythian stared at him, unsettled, as Marak stood tall and stoic to the side, and Borrus struggled to stay standing, so weak and weary as they were. But in that moment Lythian's mind was suddenly clear. And that emblem on Tethian's back...that ancient crest...he knew it. "You bear the crest of Eldur," he whispered, staring at the pattern, embroidered into his black leather tunic as well as his cloak.

Tethian only smiled. "I do," he said. "For it is the Fire Father whom I follow. He is the only one who can bring the balance, Lythian, the only one who can command the Bondstone." A shimmer of red light caught in his eyes as he glanced at Lord Marak. "Agarath's Soul burns bright and the dragons fly wild from the Wings. It is just the beginning, the beginning of the calamity to come. If we do not act, Sons of Varin, all these lands will fall to flame and ash and death. All the north. All the south. We must unite now to stop it."

"Then take the throne from your cousin," said Borrus, looking at the man through a tired set of eyes. "Take the crown and call for peace, as is your divine right."

"The crown holds no power to end the War Eternal. No crown does, Sir Borrus."

Borrus released a sigh. He looked confused and cold and in no mood for the man's company. "We were promised we'd be sent home," he said. "You promised us that, Marak. You and Kin'rar. I would have you fulfil that oath. We have our own war to fight, and will play no part in yours."

"We are all playing a part, big and small, whether we know it or not. My cousin wishes to win the north, as your King Janilah wishes to win the south. These men see but a part of the picture...but they are blinkered to the full truth."

"And what truth is that?" asked Lythian.

"That the gods *are* war, Captain," said Prince Tethian. "That they will quarrel for eternity should we not stop them. Through his broken Heart, Vandar whispers, does he not? His body has armed your people, and brought war after war after war. And Agarath too is guilty. His Soul calls the dragons, bonds them to the Blood of Eldur. We seek war as you do, that I will not deny. But how long can it go on? The War of the Continents was one of the bloodiest Renewals of all. They get worse each time. They bring more dread and death and destruction. And now we stand at the edge of the abyss, as the Last Renewal spreads its darkness." He lifted his chin. "It will bring a chaos upon all the world should we not act to stop it."

Borrus gave a weak huff to that. "Your father was said to be mad, good prince. One might say the same of you..."

Marak turned sharply to look at him. "Hold your tongue, Sir Borrus. You speak to a prince of Agarath."

"I speak to a man who claims Eldur is alive," Borrus returned. He looked back at Tethian. "Does he whisper to you as he did your father?"

Tethian's smile remained. "I do not believe Eldur ever whispered to my father," he said. "That was a cruel device of Cousin Tavash to take control of the crown. My father's delirium was true, my friends. But Eldur's whisper? No, I do not believe so."

"But you believe he lives?" asked Lythian. He needed to hear it from him. "You say Eldur will bring the balance. That only he can stop this war."

Tethian gave a nod, then turned his eyes southwest. "Eldur never died after he fought Varin at the Ashmount. Varin showed him mercy, as you know, and let him return to Eldurath to die among his family and people. Many believe he did, but not all." He looked at Lythian. "You are a learned man, I hear. I am sure you have heard the myths? That he bore a cloak and staff and disappeared following the battle?"

"Some say he went to the mountains, to die with the Bondstone," Lythian remembered. "Others believe he journeyed to the Wings, so he might die with his dragons in peace."

"It makes no matter where he died," said Borrus impatiently. "He's dead, that's what's important."

But there was something on Tethian's face that said different. "It can be hard to find the border between myth and truth," he said. "Time distorts all, would you not say? And that which you know to be true in the north, we know quite different in the south. Myth and truth, my friends. They can be one and the same, when seen from a different view. And my view has grown clear these last years." He looked at them straight. "By Varin's mercy, Eldur lived. This very night, he rests beneath the Wings."

Borrus gave out a great spluttery snort. "You believe this, Marak?" He turned on the Skylord. "You tell me to hold my tongue...to *this*?" He shook his head. "I will not hear it. I'll not! I demand you meet your oath and take us home. I demand it on your honour, Marak."

Marak said nothing. For a long moment he stayed silent as stone.

"Then I'll go myself. I'll not listen to this...he's as mad as his bloody father." Borrus marched off to the ruins, though Lythian just watched and let him go. He was well acquainted with the bluffs of Borrus Kanabar and there was no way he'd go stalking off beyond the safety of these outlaws in his condition. "I am sorry about him, my lords," he said. "We have suffered a long ordeal, and only want to return home. He will be more agreeable by morning, once he's rested."

"You need not explain," said Tethian, his smile relenting for the first time. "I quite understand how you've suffered, and can only express my sorrow that we did not help you sooner. You will be well tended here. Perhaps it would be best for you to rest. I should have waited until morning before so burdening you."

"My thanks." Lythian dipped his head. He too was struggling to stand now, and felt entirely underdressed standing before someone so eminent. "I will be better armed to understand what you're saying come the morrow, Your Highness."

"I'm sure you will, and would hope you come to the right decision."

Lythian had to ask, though a part of him didn't want to. "Decision, good prince?"

"Yes, the most important decision you will ever make, Captain. Tomorrow you will decide whether you're to help us or not. You will come to me, and tell me true, whether you will help us end the War Eternal."

End, or win? Lythian thought. For there was a deep distinction there. He looked at Tethian with a growing strain of disquiet. "You wish me to help you raise Eldur from the dead?" He found his head shaking as he spoke the words. "I do not believe he lives, Your Highness. And if he does..." He could barely bring himself to consider it. "Eldur is the great enemy of my people. You cannot expect..."

"Eldur is the key," the Prince of Agarath cut in. "He will rise, no matter what you do, and the heir of Varin will rise to join him. They will bring the balance, and set the world to order. Without them, all will be darkness and dread, fire and flame. There can be no hiding from that now."

Lythian didn't question him any further, nor did he have the strength to hear more. He was fast forgetting some of the detail already, his mind a sieve through which Tethian's words poured through. *But that last? The heir of Varin?* King Lorin was the last of the Varin line and fell without an heir. It seemed another part of Tethian's delusions, for that was all this could be.

So he left him there, and returned to the ruins to rest, settling in beside Borrus in his thick woollen cloak. And as he slept, so he soared high into the skies again. High above the mountains and forests and rivers, the cities of the south and north, east and west, and all the people in them. He soared so high he could see all the world, up and up and up he flew. A great burst of joy sprang upon his face, for he was free, free of his cell, free of Eldurath, free of Tavash and Ven. *I can go home*, he thought, *home to Vandar. To Amron and Elyon and all the others...*His smile grew broader and his lips spilled with laughter, and higher and higher and higher he flew…

And then out he looked once more. Out upon the world. And

his laughter was gone. And his joy was ash. And the lands were thick with black and red. Black for smoke. Red for fire.

For all the world was burning.

THE END

The Bladeborn Saga will continue in Book Three - ***An Echo of Titans***

ALSO BY T. C. EDGE

THE ENHANCED SERIES (MAIN SERIES):

The Enhanced (Book One)

Hybrid (Book Two)

Nameless (Book Three)

Assassin (Book Four)

Captive (Book Five)

Renegade (Book Six)

Invader (Book Seven)

Avenger (Book Eight)

Defender (Book Nine)

Nemesis (Book Ten)

Sequel (to main Enhanced series, and Warrior Race series):

The Enhanced: Awakening

The Enhanced: Conquest

The Enhanced: Fractured

The Enhanced: Invasion

THE WARRIOR RACE SERIES (ENHANCED UNIVERSE):

The Warrior Race (Book One)

The Red Warrior (Book Two)

Angel of War (Book Three)

CHILDREN OF THE PRIME SERIES (ENHANCED UNIVERSE):

The Chosen (Book One)

Trial of the Chosen (Book 2)

Blood of the Chosen (Book 3)

March of the Chosen (Book 4)

War of the Chosen (Book 5)

Fall of the Chosen (Book 6)

Rise of the Chosen (Book 7)

Fate of the Chosen (Book 8)

VARIANT SERIES (ENHANCED UNIVERSE)

Variant (Book One)

Initiate (Book Two)

Survivor (Book Three)

Pathfinder (Book Four)

Legend (Book Five)

Prodigy (Book Six)

Worldkiller (Book Seven)

OTHER BOOKS BY THE AUTHOR:

THE WATCHERS SERIES:

The Watchers Trilogy:

The Watchers of Eden (Book One)

City of Stone (Book Two)

War at the Wall (Book Three)

The Watchers Trilogy Box Set

The Seekers Trilogy

The Watcher Wars (Book One)

The Seekers of Knight (Book Two)

The Endless Knight

The Seekers Trilogy Box Set

THE PHANTOM CHRONICLES:

The Last Phantom (Book 1)

Phantom Hunter (Book 2)

Phantom Legacy (Book 3)

Phantom Unleashed (Book 4)

www.ingramcontent.com/pod-product-compliance
Lightning Source LLC
Chambersburg PA
CBHW020719310726
48979CB00004B/982

* 9 7 8 1 0 6 8 5 1 8 2 1 8 *